THE BIG BOOK OF
WESTERN ACTION STORIES

The Big Book of Western Action Stories

EDITED WITH AN
INTRODUCTION AND
HEADNOTES BY

JON TUSKA

BARRICADE BOOKS
New York

Published by Barricade Books Inc.
150 Fifth Avenue
New York, NY 10011

Copyright © 1995 by Golden West Literary Agency

Printed in the United States of America.

Library of Congress Cataloging-in-Publication Data

The big book of western action stories / edited by Jon Tuska.
        p.   cm.
     ISBN 1-56980-048-0 (cloth)
        1. West (U.S.)—Social life and customs—Fiction. 2. Adventure
stories, American. 3. Western stories. I. Tuska, Jon.
PS648.W4B54 1995
813'.087408—dc20   95-21902
                                                    CIP

First printing

Acknowledgments

"The Code" by Ernest Haycox was first published in *The Frontier* (6/26). Copyright © 1926 by Doubleday, Page & Company. Copyright © renewed 1954 by Jill Marie Haycox. Reprinted by arrangement with Golden West Literary Agency. All rights reserved.

"The Strange Ride of Perry Woodstock" was first published in a greatly abridged version under the title "Death Rides Behind" by Max Brand in *Dime Western* (3/33). Copyright © 1933 by Popular Publications, Inc. Copyright © renewed 1961 by Jane Faust Easton, John Frederick Faust, and Judith Faust. Copyright © 1995 for restored material by Jane Faust Easton and Adriana Faust Bianchi. The name Max Brand™ is registered as a trademark with the U. S. Patent Office and cannot be used without express written permission. Reprinted by arrangement with Golden West Literary Agency. All rights reserved.

"Lost Dutchman O'Riley's Luck" was first published under the title "To Save A Girl: or Lost Dutchman O'Riley's Gold" by Alan LeMay in *Collier's* (9/27/30). Copyright © 1930 by P. F. Collier & Son Company. Copyright © renewed 1958 by Alan LeMay. Reprinted by arrangement with Golden West Literary Agency. All rights reserved.

"Land Without Mercy" by Wayne D. Overholser was first published in *Big-Book Western* (8/42). Copyright © 1942 by Popular Publications, Inc. Copyright © renewed 1970 by Wayne D. Overholser. Reprinted by arrangement with Golden West Literary Agency. All rights reserved.

Table of Contents

Introduction

The title of this book is in part homage to the pulp magazine, Big-Book Western. For readers who may have been too young to recall its halcyon days on the newsstands of this country or for those whose memories of it have grown dim, let me say that it had an interesting history.

In 1930 Henry Steeger had worked for Dell Publications for almost three years. One day he invited Harold Goldsmith to join him for lunch. Goldsmith was the business manager for the Ace Publishing Company owned by A. A. and Rose Wyn. It was Steeger's idea that the two should join forces in a new pulp magazine publishing venture. Steeger would handle the editorial side of the business and Goldsmith would be in charge of the business side.

Steeger borrowed $5,000 from his step-father and Goldsmith borrowed and invested a like amount. The long years of the Great Depression had begun. It was not an auspicious time to start a new business. Yet, with this initial capitalization, the new firm, called Popular Publications, Inc., was able to negotiate about $125,000 worth of credit. The one-room office was located in the Daily News Building at 210 East 42nd Street. Four pulp magazines were launched, all bearing the date October, 1930. They were *Battle Aces*, *Detective Action Stories*, *Gang World*, and *Western Rangers*.

Press runs for the first issues were set at 100,000 copies. *Battle Aces* sold the best, at 80% market penetration, the others between 40% and 60%. This may not have been an especially promising return, but sufficient income was generated to keep the company afloat. The first big success came with the launching of *Dime De-*

11

tective, the premier issue dated October, 1931, followed by *Dime Western*, the premier issue dated December, 1932. Steeger had hired free-lance pulp writer Rogers Terrill to edit *Dime Detective*. *Dime Western* was added to Terrill's group in due course. T. T. Flynn, a regular contributor to *Dime Detective*, was recruited by Terrill to try his hand at a Western story for the first issue of *Dime Western*. Also among the contributors to that first issue were Western writers with whom Terrill had become familiar when he was writing for *Action Stories* and *Lariat Story Magazine* published by Fiction House: Walt Coburn and Eugene Cunningham. Cliff Farrell, a regular contributor to Clayton Publications' *Ace-High Magazine*, was also asked to contribute a story.

Dime Western was an astonishing success, giving Street & Smith's *Western Story Magazine* the most serious newsstand competition it had experienced since *Lariat Story Magazine* hit the stands with the issue dated August, 1925. *Dime Western* had the same number of pages as *Western Story Magazine*, but it was a nickel cheaper. There were no serials, as there were in *Western Story Magazine*, so buying an issue of *Dime Western* did not obligate a reader to buy more issues. Beyond these economic and marketing factors, however, *Dime Western* also introduced a new dimension in the Western story. The Western protagonists in the stories in this magazine were increasingly shown as men surrounded by armed camps of opposing factions and are seemingly threatened from all sides. This is essentially the structure of "The Last of the Black Tantralls" by T. T. Flynn in the first issue and Rogers Terrill regarded this story as a paradigm for what he wanted to see in the magazine.

Western Rangers had been retired by Popular Publications with the issue dated April, 1932. *Dime Western*'s phenomenal success on newsstands prompted Steeger to believe that its format was obviously the right one for the reading public. It was while at the dinner table with a friend who was talking to Steeger about a summer he had spent at a ranch out West that the notion for a new Western fiction magazine was born. While it would have the same kinds of stories as *Dime Western*, it would be bigger—160 pages instead of 130—and it would cost 15¢. It was called *Star Western*.

Little in mass merchandise publishing ever happens in a vacuum. Probably one additional incentive for Popular Publications to launch *Star Western* featuring longer stories at a greater cover price was *Big-*

Book Western which hit the stands with the issue dated Fall, 1933. It was published by Two Books Magazines, Inc., with an office located at 80 Lafayette Street in New York City. The premise behind this magazine was simple. It would offer to the reading public two new Western novels which in their hardcover editions would each be listed at $2.00 and one or two short stories—all for 15¢. The two novels in the first issue were "Rocky Rhodes of Roaring Gap" by W. C. Tuttle and "Outlaw Blood" by Tom Roan. These were not really book-length novels—which at the time averaged between 70,000 and 80,000 words—but condensed novels of about 40,000 words each. Tuttle's novel would be published in book form only in the British market as ROCKY RHODES (Collins, 1936). Tom Roan's novel featured hero Dave Steel who was known as the Rio Kid. It would later appear in hardcovers from a lending library publisher under the title RIO KID (Godwin, 1935). It should be noted that Roan's Rio Kid is *not* related in any way to the character later created by Davis Dresser under the byline Don Davis in a series of four novels published by William Morrow and Company in 1940 and 1941 nor the magazine character, the Rio Kid, created by author Tom Curry who began appearing in *Rio Kid Western* from Standard Magazines in 1939.

Roy de S. Horn was the editor of *Big-Book Western* as long as it was published by Two Books. It became a bi-monthly with its second issue dated January-February, 1934 and it remained bi-monthly until the issue dated July, 1934, when it became a monthly. No matter what the frequency of issuance, the format remained the same. In the issue dated August, 1934, the two featured novels were "'Peaceful Brady,' Trail Boss" by Frank C. Robertson and "Outlaw Guns" by Wes Fargo. The Robertson "novel" was later expanded and appeared in a hardcover edition only in the British market as TRAIL BOSS (Collins, 1935). Wes Fargo was a pseudonym for author E(dward) B(everly) Mann and appeared in an expanded edition later that year titled GAMBLIN' MAN (Morrow, 1934) under the byline E. B. Mann. It is a Billy the Kid story and was obviously offered to Two Books by the hardcover publisher for magazine serialization. The E. B. Mann byline was reserved exclusively by Mann for his appearances in Popular Publications pulps like *Dime Western* and *Star Western* and for his book publications. Wes Fargo was the byline he used for Two Books and Les Rivers was the byline for his appearances in

Western pulps published by Ace like *Western Trails* and *Western Aces*. Once Two Books launched *New Western* with the issue dated November, 1934, Mann had a short novel titled "The Bronco-Buster" by Wes Fargo in the second issue, dated January, 1935.

Two Books' marketing strategy was to extend the successful formula of *Big-Book Western* over two magazines. The last monthly issue of *Big-Book* was dated December, 1935. The next issue of *Big-Book Western* was dated March, 1936, and now it was again a bi-monthly. *New Western*'s second issue appeared in January, 1936, and the third issue was dated March, 1936. Tuttle, Robertson, Roan, and Wes Fargo were usually the authors with long stories appearing in both of these magazines.

William Colt MacDonald joined the Two Books roster with the short novel, "Three-Notch Cardigan," in the first issue of *New Western*. MacDonald would not expand this story for nearly two decades when it finally appeared as THREE-NOTCH CAMERON (Doubleday, 1952). MacDonald's most popular series characters were the Three Mesquiteers. He introduced two of them, Tucson Smith and Stony Brooke, in "Restless Guns," serialized in Clayton Publications' *Ace-High Magazine* in late 1928 and early 1929. The serial was published in book form by Street & Smith as RESTLESS GUNS (Chelsea House, 1929). Lullaby Joslin joined these two to complete the trio with LAW OF THE FORTY-FIVES (Covici, Friede, 1933). Both this latter novel and "The Gun Branders," also featuring the Three Mesquiteers, were serialized in pulp magazines published by Harold Hersey in the early 1930s. The third Three Mesquiteer novel and the first one to be filmed—by RKO in 1935— was POWDERSMOKE RANGE (Covici, Friede, 1934). It was serialized in one condensed reprint installment following book publication in *Big-Book Western* under the title "Winchester Welcome" in the issue dated March, 1935. I have included in this collection MacDonald's short novel, "Gun Fog," which first appeared in the penultimate issue of *Big-Book* as published by Two Books and dated November, 1935. It has never been otherwise reprinted.

In 1935, *Big-Book Western* introduced its "True Western Department" with features in the form of memoirs by Emmet Dalton, the most literate member of the notorious Dalton gang, and Major Gordon Lillie who had earlier made his reputation as "Pawnee Bill" with a Wild West Show. The articles by Emmet Dalton were actu-

ally taken from his book with Jack Jungmeyer, WHEN THE DAL-
TONS RODE (Doubleday, Doran, 1931). In addition to his memoirs, Dalton also wrote screenplays for Hollywood Western films and
occasionally even acted before the camera in bit parts.

Because of the success of *Dime Western* and *Star Western* which,
during the bottom of the Depression, often sold as many as two million copies of an issue, Popular Publications launched *10 Story
Western* with the issue dated January, 1936, and bought both *Big-
Book Western* and *New Western* from Two Books. *New Western* under
the Popular Publications banner lasted all of nine issues before it
ceased publication. It would, however, be successfully reintroduced
by Popular in 1940 and this time it lasted until 1954.

The acquisition of these additional magazines and the expansion by Popular Publications in its own offerings in the total number
of monthly magazines it published placed an acute burden on managing editor, Rogers Terrill. He began to delegate his editorial duties and hired Western writer, Mike Tilden, to whom he entrusted
the job of editing *Dime Western*. David Manners came to Popular
Publications to edit *10 Story Western* and was also made the editor
of *Big-Book Western* and of *Star Western* through 1938. The first issue
of *Big-Book Western* under the banner of Popular Publications was
dated April-May, 1936, and carried an unsigned column written by
Rogers Terrill titled "We Buy A Magazine!" It stated in part:

With this issue *Big-Book Western Magazine,* for many years under the
aegis of Mr. Roy Horn, joins Popular Publications' string of westerns. And we, the editors, think that we should tell you why.

Popular Publications broke into the western field several years
ago with *Dime Western Magazine,* a magazine that at the time was a
radical departure in its line. Up to then most westerns were straight
blood-and-thunder stuff, action for action's sake, and if the story
wasn't much good but was exciting it was all that mattered. But apparently the readers were getting fed up on that kind of thing so we
thought up a new magazine and took our chances that it would fill
the bill. *Dime Western* had all the action that anyone could want; but
more important than that, the action was woven into a story of
people who could actually have lived—a story of characters who were
true to life, true to the West. *Dime Western* made a big hit; so big, in

fact, that we knew we had something that would go over for more than only one book. *Star Western* came next, a bigger book than *Dime*, with more stories in it and two novel-length tales instead of only one. Then we brought out *Rangeland Romances*, in which our authors tell the love stories of young men and women in the West. Following that came *10 Story Western*, with more stories, though slightly shorter in some cases, than you'll find in the other three books.

But now and then we'd get a letter from some reader. Maybe he'd write to *Dime Western* or maybe *Star Western*; maybe he'd like all our stories or maybe he wouldn't. But many of these readers said that they liked the longer stories best; in the novels, they said, they really got to know the characters while, in the shorter stories, the authors didn't have time enough to build up their hero and heroine to full-sized folks. There were quite a few of these letters and after the stack grew high enough it set us to thinking. There must be two kinds of readers, we decided, those who read a tale for the story, and those who read for the characters in the story. Or maybe all people like a change in fare now and then and would sometimes rather read long stories instead of short ones. So why not start a magazine for those folks who like all long stories?

But about then we happened to look at a newsstand and it occurred to us that there were a lot of magazines already and that one more wouldn't make much of a splash. We found *Big-Book Western* down there on the newsstand and liked it. We knew Roy Horn, the editor, so we looked him up. Yes, he said, *Big-Book Western* was doing pretty good business. Mr. Horn liked his magazine very much but, after some persuasion, was argued into making a dicker with us. Now *Big-Book Western* is an established member of the Popular Publications cavvy.

Some of this, of course, was merely self-congratulatory hyperbole. Street & Smith's *Western Story Magazine*, the first of the Western pulp magazines, ran many fine, character-driven stories and serials by Max Brand, Cherry Wilson, Robert J. Horton, Robert Ormond Case, Jackson Gregory, and Walt Coburn—to name some of their most popular authors. Fiction House's *Lariat Story Magazine* and, after 1929, *Frontier Stories*, Doubleday, Doran's *West*, and one of the most successful and ultimately the longest survivor of all Western pulp magazines, *Ranch Romances*, first from Clayton Publications and later from Warner Publications, featured excellent, character-driven Western stories. Yet, there is also no denying the fact that beginning with *Dime Western*, Popular Publications gradually became the leading publisher of Western pulp magazines where all stories, however long, were complete in each issue, and this predominance lasted from 1934 well into the 1950s.

In the Popular Publications string, *Big-Book Western* was ranked fourth, following *Dime*, *Star*, and *10 Story Western*. Although there were exceptions such as Walt Coburn who received 3¢ a word no matter in which of these magazines one of his stories appeared, *Dime* generally paid contributors 2¢ a word, *Star* and *10 Story* 1¢ a word, and *Big-Book* 2/3¢ a word. David Manners continued to edit *10 Story Western* and *Big-Book Western* under Rogers Terrill's guidance through 1939 when he left Popular Publications to join the staff at Standard Magazines under managing editor, Leo Margulies. Mike Tilden became editor of *Big-Book Western* in 1940 and he retained this position until the final issue.

Big-Book Western at Popular Publications remained a bi-monthly from the April-May, 1936 issue until the December, 1938 issue when it became a monthly for that one issue. There was no January, 1939 issue, however, and the magazine returned to bi-monthly status with the February-March, 1939 issue. When with the issue dated November, 1939, *Big-Book Western* again became a monthly, it finally made the grade and it remained a monthly until the issue dated April, 1949, after which it was again a bi-monthly. *Big-Book* was combined with *Walt Coburn's Western Magazine* with the issue dated March, 1952, and ceased publication altogether with the issue dated September, 1954. Over the duration of its publication Two Books published sixteen issues of *Big-Book Western* and Popular published 124, for a total of 140 issues. The cover price of 15¢ was retained by Popular until 1944 when, briefly, the price was lowered to 10¢. In 1945 the price was again increased to 15¢ and this was its cover price until the issue dated November, 1946, when the price was raised to a quarter and it remained there until the end.

The first issue published by Popular offered readers "Two Full Book Length Novels!" In the case of that first issue these novels were actually 35,000 words in length and consisted of "Owlhoot Lawman" by Cliff Farrell and "Guns For A Gambler" by Jack Drummond. Occasionally, an actual book-length novel was still featured in condensed form in *Big-Book Western*—L. P. Holmes's BLOODY SADDLES (Greenberg, 1937), for example, ran in one installment in the March-April, 1937 issue under the title "Outcast's Doom Patrol"—but this was really an exception rather than the rule. The lengths of the "book-length" novels that were featured continued to drop in terms of the number of words. "Turncoat Gunman" by Peter Dawson in the issue dated June, 1940 is under 35,000 words. "Gun Song At Funeral River" by Tom Roan in the issue dated February, 1942 is closer to 25,000 words. "Troopers Of Hell's Outpost" by William Heuman in the issue dated January, 1946 is 20,000 words.

When the price was increased to a quarter and more pages were added, the blurbs on the cover and the table of contents were changed to read "Four Complete Book-Length Novels" but, by that time, the actual length for the supposed "book-length" novels was about 12,000 words while the standard book-length among trade publishers of hardcover Westerns was around 60,000 words. David Manners supplied the story guidelines at *Big-Book Western* for the "Writer's Market" in the August, 1939 issue of *Writer's Digest* and they really did not change very much over the next fifteen years:

We use short stories from 3000 to 6000 words; novelettes from 9000 to 10,000 words; novels from 18,000 to 25,000 words. We use completely fictionized stories of historical Western characters and incidents—2000 words. No poetry. Reports are prompt. Payment is 2/3¢, up, on acceptance.

Through 1950 below the title of the magazine on the table of contents page on the left-hand side it was noted in block letters—"All Stories New"—and on the right-hand side "No Serials." Presently this was changed on the left-hand side to "All Stories Complete." This change was made necessary because now, along with new stories by such Western writers as John Jakes, Gordon D. Shirreffs, and Will Cook, there were reprints of stories by notable authors whose stories had *never* appeared in *Big-Book Western*, and were originally published in other Popular Publications Western magazines.

Street & Smith announced in *The New York Times* in 1950 that the pulp era was over. It hadn't happened suddenly. Already by 1944 even Street & Smith's *Western Story* had become a monthly. Notwithstanding all the talk about paper shortages and increased production costs, the greatest threat to pulp-magazine circulation was posed by paperback reprints of hardcover novels from Pocket Books, Bantam Books, and Dell Books, among others, all priced at a quarter. When the War Department declared a paper shortage in 1943, this did not in any way interfere with the underwriting of Armed Services paperback editions of hardcover books and for these paper was available in quantity and the per unit cost for producing a paperback for domestic consumption was significantly decreased while the title's overall profitability for the paperback publisher was increased. The hardcover publishers often lowered their royalty participation on these Armed Services editions or provided the texts free of charge to the paperback publishers. An entire generation of service men and women became accustomed to reading books in this format and in this size.

An even more serious inroad came with publication of D. B. Newton's novel, RANGE BOSS (Pocket Books, 1949). It was an expansion of "Gunhawk's Kid" in *Western Novel and Short Stories* (12/47). The magazine version came about because Newton's agent, August Lenniger, had had a rush order for a 35,000-word story from this magazine's editor and Newton obliged by abridging the novel he was at work on between stories. Then, no longer faced by a magazine deadline, Newton went back at his leisure and wrote the novel the way he had intended to write it. When he sent this expansion to Lenniger, he fully expected it to be offered to Phoenix Press, a lending-library publisher that was paying him a flat $150, no royalties. However, Pocket Books recently had done well with its reprint of a lending-library Western novel, L. P. Holmes's FLAME OF SUNSET (Samuel Curl, 1947). The quality of Holmes's novel was definitely atypical and it should never have been sold to such a market in the first place. However, Lenniger did not make that mistake with Newton's new novel. He sent it to Pocket Books directly where it was accepted. It appeared as the first *original* Western novel ever to be published by Pocket Books and was so successful it sold over 450,000 copies, in contrast to a Phoenix Press book which seldom topped 3,000, the usual press run, and which was never reprinted by the firm but only offered for paperback reprint. Understandably, hardcover publishers were not enthusiastic about a paperback reprint company entering the field of publishing original Western fiction and they forced Pocket Books to retreat, at least for a time, by threatening to withhold reprint rights on titles Pocket Books wished to acquire.

Such strong-arm methods couldn't be expected to work for very long. In 1950 Fawcett Publications which had started in pulp magazine publishing in the 1920s and had expanded into comic books after the war founded its Gold Medal imprint. These books were all original novels, not reprints; and, since Fawcett did not depend at all on reprints, threats from hardcover publishers of holding back titles were meaningless. Several prognostications at the time even had it that this move spelled the demise of hardcover publishing in the United States. After all, who would pay $2.00 for a book by a given author, if one by him could be purchased for a quarter? However, there was another way hardcover publishers could fight to protect their turf. Les Savage, Jr., provided the incentive.

Savage expanded a short novel, "Lure of the Boothill Siren" in *Lariat Story Magazine* (5/49), into a book-length he titled WILD HORSE EMPIRE. It was the first Savage novel August Lenniger sold to Fawcett Gold Medal. Bill Lengel, the editor at Gold Medal, changed the title to THE WILD HORSE. The theme of the novel— a horse that cannot be tamed and a woman who can never be satisfied settling down with one man—Lengel demanded be rewritten to allow the protagonist and the woman to marry at the end and the horse to be tamed. Savage fought him about the horse and won that point. It was published under the Les Savage, Jr., byline. Whereupon Doubleday took umbrage, claiming to Lenniger that Les Savage, Jr. was a Double D author—his second book for the firm, THE HIDE RUSTLERS (Doubleday, 1950), had just been published—and therefore Doubleday claimed exclusive rights to the Savage name as a byline. Lenniger grew so unnerved by this contretemps that, henceforth, not only would the seven subsequent Gold Medal novels Savage wrote appear under pseudonyms but he also insisted that with every client a switch in publishers automatically meant the adoption of a new byline. Clifton Adams quit the agency over the practice. D. B. Newton stayed on and ended up with six bylines, to the detriment of his public visibility. By 1954 Savage had won back the right to use his own name even on original paperbacks, but Lenniger kept the practice of name changes a hard rule until he sold out his agency to John K. Payne in 1978.

For all of his interference with Savage's plots, Bill Lengel was also a financial advantage to him. Doubleday paid Savage an advance of $500 for a Double D, no more than $1,000 for the long historical novels he would write published by Hanover House, a Doubleday subsidiary. Lengel started Savage at a $1,000 advance for THE WILD HORSE (Fawcett Gold Medal, 1950) and kept increasing the advances over the years until RAILS WEST (Fawcett Gold Medal, 1954)—developed from "Six-Gun Sinner" in *Western Novels and Short Stories* (5/50)—commanded a $3,000 advance. Before long, Dell Publishing began issuing its First Edition paperback Westerns by such authors as Luke Short, T. T. Flynn, and Peter Dawson.

American News Company which since the Civil War had been distributing most magazines and some tabloids to the nation's newsstands also distributed paperback books to the racks. An issue of *Big-Book Western* was on the stands for two months and then it was replaced by the next issue. RANGE BOSS or THE WILD HORSE were racked again and again, month after month. All the paperback publisher had to do was reprint these titles from the same plates.

However, there is an unpleasant epilogue to this phenomenon. American News Company collapsed in 1957 due to mismanagement. The paperback publishers opted to develop the independent distributors in the various regions and markets of this country rather than to create their own distribution networks. These independent distributors gained so much power that by the beginning of the 1990s they alone decided what title would appear on what rack, where on that rack, and for how long. Mass merchandise paperback novels came to be treated the same as quarterly magazines so that the maximum longevity for a new paperback novel in 1994 was three months before their covers were ripped off and sent back to the publishers and the rest pulped, just as had been the practice decades before with back numbers of pulp magazines! What all this has meant, among other things, for readers of Western stories is that large economy collections such as this one and trade paperback Westerns will increasingly replace the pulp paperback books just as the pulp paperback books replaced the pulp magazines.

In assembling this collection of Western stories I have tried to remain consistent with *Big-Book Western*'s promise of four "novels" in each issue—as these were defined by the editor of the magazine in the 1940s—and sixteen shorter stories of varying lengths. I should also mention that some of the Western authors with stories in THE BIG-BOOK OF WESTERN ACTION STORIES never appeared in *Big-Book Western*. Ernest Haycox and Alan LeMay in the 1930s were published mostly in *Collier's*, a slick weekly magazine where the pay was much better. However, both of these authors began their careers writing for pulp magazines. Haycox, in particular, has had to be included because it was his stories in *Collier's* that greatly influenced the kinds of stories authors like Luke Short, Peter Dawson, Frank Bonham, Wayne D. Overholser, and Will Cook, among others, wrote for pulp magazines and many of these authors came eventually to publish their own stories in *Collier's* and *The Saturday Evening Post*. Alan LeMay never appeared in *Big-Book Western*, but he did have stories published in *Dime Western* under a byline fashioned as an anagram to his real name: Alan M. Emley. In the years 1933 and 1934 Max Brand appeared in *Dime Western* and *Star Western*. In fact, the story by this author which I have chosen is taken from the author's own typescript for his first Western story for Popular Publications which appeared in the fourth issue of *Dime Western*. In 1949 Popular Publications launched a new magazine titled *Max Brand's Western Magazine* and it enjoyed a successful run. Four of the authors with stories in this collection—W. Ryerson Johnson, Les Savage, Jr., Frank Bonham, and Edward Gorman—have had single-author Western story compilations appear from Barricade Books in the Classic Western Tales series of trade paperbacks and others among these authors will eventually have single-author collections included in this series.

In making my selections for this book, I have chosen several stories which deal with similar themes, but whose resolutions are as different as are their authors. It is for the reader to determine those stories whose values seem closest to the mark and those that seem aberrant, those that are enlightening about the human condition and bring a new awareness of the dimensions of the human spirit, those that may seem too narrow, and those that truly encompass nobility of soul.

There are those who scoff today at the obligatory ranch romance conclusion to many Western stories and numerous writers have striven to devise ingenious alternatives to ending a story either with a death or a romance. Many of the stories I have assembled here do not avoid romance. I suspect the desire to avoid it may be ultimately a reflection of the state of our society as we near the last years of the 20th Century, with our high divorce rate, the prevailing view that marriage is at best a temporary condition, and the fact that fewer couples are choosing to have children. Yet, ironically, it has been my experience over the past fifty years that longevity is often the result of having had at the center of one's life a sustaining love affair. Without it (and without children) the prospect of old age may well constitute the most forbidding of life's intimidating specters.

I have restored, where I felt it necessary, the authors' original versions of their stories. The reader will ultimately be the richer for it. Let me provide one example. When Rogers Terrill bought Max Brand's "The Strange Ride of Perry Woodstock," he retitled it "Death Rides Behind" for its appearance in *Dime Western*. It is interesting to contrast how Terrill was able, by editorial intercession, to diminish this author's poetic imagery and sterling prose into something almost mediocre. Here is how Max Brand opened the story:

An owl, skimming close to the ground, hooted at the very door of the bunkhouse. That door was wide, because the day had been hot and the night was hot, also, and windless. Therefore, Perry Woodstock jumped from his bunk, grabbed his hat in one hand and his boots in the other, and still seemed to hear the voice of the bird in the room, a melancholy and sonorous echo.

The owl hooted again, not in a dream but in fact, farther down the hollow, and Woodstock realized that he had not been wakened by the voice of the cook calling to the 'punchers to "come and get it," neither was it a cold autumn morning at an open camp, neither was there frost in his hair nor icy dew upon his forehead, and his body was not creaking at all the joints....

And here is how Terrill altered that opening scene:

The door of the bunkhouse was wide, because the day had been hot and the night was hot, also, and windless. Perry Woodstock jumped from his bunk, grabbed his hat in one hand and his boots in the other. Something had awakened him. Some sound had come to that door. He stood tense for a moment.

His nerves were on edge, his heart pounding with the effect of some strange alarm....

Frederick Faust, who wrote as Max Brand, was invariably a master of understatement and eschewed the obvious. His knowledge of human character was too subtle for this to be otherwise. There was no subtlety when Terrill completed his revision. Here is the way Faust ended his story:

"Rosemary!" he broke out at her, "I've got to say something to you."

"Don't," she said, "because words are silly things between us, now!"

And the way Rogers Terrill recast that ending:

"Rosemary!" he broke out at her. "I've got to say something to you!"

"Don't," she said, "because words are silly things between us, now. When two people are in love they have no need for them..."

And together, riding stirrup to stirrup, they left the mountain top where love and death had waged grim battle for the pair of them...

<hr />

Authors are certainly not infallible but, where editorial intervention altered the intent and meaning if not the poetry of a story, for the reappearance of those stories here I have extended the courtesy to their authors of publishing them as they were written. Such restorations of titles or texts, or both, are accordingly noted in the Acknowledgments. This impulse has been inspired by my belief that the development of the Western story is the single most important literary movement in the history of the United States and that it comprises the only unique body of literature which this country has contributed to the wealth of world culture. The Western story is unique to this country because of where it is set: in the American West. There was no place in all history quite like it before and there is no place quite like it now.

The Western story at base is a story of renewal and that is what has made it so very different from any other form of literary enterprise. It is refreshing, even revitalizing, in these days of a medically over-educated culture obsessed with health and terrified of old age and dying to behold once again generations of Americans to which such obsessions and terrors meant nothing. It is spiritually encouraging in these days of political correctness, timidity, and herd-notions such as one-settlement culture that wants everyone to believe in a lock-step approach to life to contemplate those generations where individual, cultural, and ethnic differences were abundant, where not one culture but many co-existed even if warfare between them was unceasing. We have benefited from that time. There is no one idea and no one cause that can possibly ever win endorsement from everybody. We still live now with that reality of the frontier as part of our social existence.

Above all, the greatest lesson the pioneers learned from the Indians is with us still: that it is each man's and each woman's *inalienable* right to find his own path in life, to follow his own vision, to achieve his own destiny—even should one fail in the process. There is no principle so singularly revolutionary as this one in the entire intellectual history of the Occident and the Orient before the American frontier experience, and it grew from the very soil of this land and the peoples who came to live on it. It is this principle which has always been the very cornerstone of the Western story. Perhaps for this reason critics have been wont to dismiss it as subversive and inconsequential because this principle reduces their voices to only a few among many. Surely it is why the Western story has been consistently banned by totalitarian governments. Such a principle undermines the very foundations of totalitarianism and collectivism because it cannot be accommodated by the political correctness of those who would seek to exert power over others and replace all options with a single, all-encompassing, monolithic pattern for living.

There is no other kind of American literary endeavor that has so repeatedly posed the eternal questions—how do I wish to live?, in what do I believe?, what do I want from life?, what have I to give to life?—as has the Western story. There is no other kind of literary enterprise since Greek drama which has so invariably posed ethical and moral questions about life as a fundamental of its narrative structure, that has taken a stand and said: this is wrong; this is right.

Individual authors, as individual filmmakers, may present us with notions with which we do not agree, but in so doing they have made us think again about things which the herd has always been only too anxious to view as settled and outside the realm of questioning.

The West of the Western story is a region where generations of people from every continent on earth and for ages immeasurable have sought a second chance for a better life. The people forged by the clash of cultures in the American West produced a kind of human being very different from any the world had ever known before. How else could it be for a nation emerging from so many nations? And so stories set in the American West have never lost that sense of hope. It wasn't the graves at Shiloh, the white crosses at Verdun, the vacant beaches at Normandy, or the lines on the faces of their great men and women that made the Americans a great people. It was something more intangible than that. It was their great willingness of the heart.

What alone brings you back to a piece of music, a song, a painting, a poem, or a story is the mood that it creates in you when you have experienced it. The mood you experience in reading a Western story is that a better life *is* possible if we have the grit to endure the ordeal of attaining it; that it requires courage to hope, the very greatest courage any human being can ever have. And it is hope that distinguishes the Western story from every other kind of fiction. Only when courage and hope are gone will the Western story cease to be relevant to all of us.

THE BIG BOOK OF
WESTERN ACTION STORIES

Ernest Haycox during his lifetime was considered the dean among authors of Western fiction. When the Western Writers of America was first organized in 1953, what became the Golden Spur Award for outstanding achievement in writing Western fiction was first going to be called the "Erny" in homage to Haycox. He was born in Portland, Oregon. While still an undergraduate at the University of Oregon in Eugene, he sold his first short story to *Sea Stories*. His name, however, soon became established in all the leading Western pulp magazines of the day, including Street & Smith's *Western Story Magazine* and Doubleday's *West*. His first novel was FREE GRASS (Doubleday, Doran, 1929). In 1931 he broke into the pages of *Collier's* and from that time on was regularly featured in this magazine, either with a short story or a serial that was later published as a novel. In the 1940s his serials began appearing in *The Saturday Evening Post* and it was there that modern classics such as BUGLES IN THE AFTERNOON (Little, Brown, 1944) and CANYON PASSAGE (Little, Brown, 1945) were first published. Both of these novels were also made into major motion pictures although, perhaps, the film most loved and remembered is STAGECOACH (United Artists, 1939) directed by John Ford and starring John Wayne, based on Haycox's short story, "Stage to Lordsburg." No history of the Western story in the 20th Century would be possible without reference to Haycox's fiction. He almost always has an involving story to tell and one in which there is something not so readily definable that raises it above its time, an image possibly, a turn of phrase, or even a sensation, the smell of dust after rain or the solitude of an Arizona night. Harry E. Maule, who edited *The Frontier* for Doubleday, Page & Company, first published "The Code" in the June, 1926 issue. He later reprinted the story under the title "Trail Town" in *West* (9/14/32), another Doubleday magazine. This marks the first time it has appeared in book form.

The Code

As he sat beside the door of the Last Chance, huddled over on an upended barrel, he looked truly like a figure of the West's remote and stirring past. There was but little light left in the street; the day waned swiftly before the long shadows stealing across the turbid Arkansas. But still he was visible to the passersby, if they cared to look. The buckskins he wore were of an incredibly ancient pattern and grimed and greased with long, long usage. The moccasins on his feet were rubbed through. No cap covered his head, nor could any cap conceal the iron-gray hair that rolled down upon his gaunt shoulders. It was clearly evident that he had once been a towering man; even now in the shriveling period he was taller than most of those who circled by him and pushed open the saloon door.

But he was as thin as the hitching rail in front of him, and his face bore a stamp of mortality long deferred and overdue. The loose skin of his face was a grayish, burned color; his eyes had retreated far back into his head and when he raised a hand it was in a slow, energy-conserving manner.

Yes, he was visible to the passers-by, if they cared to look. But he was a land-mark, a fixture in that town—a town which measured its nativity by months—and it was no novelty to stop and look. Moreover, it was at that hour when men hurried to the bar for the ceremonial drink which initiated the night's boisterousness. For this was Dodge, the youngest, wickedest, and most westerly town on the far-flung Kansas plains. Hither men were drawn from the remote corners of the wilderness to slack the thirst of long solitude. Good men and bad men and none overly endowed with sympathy.

The night fell like a blanket and a light prairie wind sprang up. Travelers, saloonward bound, found the old-timer's feet stretching out in their path, a trap to the unwary. Most of them muttered a word about the "damned old nuisance," and circled around. But there came one who made no detour. Striding forward, he met the sprawling legs and, like a drunkard, reeled against the hitching rack.

"Gabe, you leather-faced stinker, why in hell do you pick this hyar p'ticklar place to sleep?" he yelled, in a harsh voice. "Git outen my way or I'll jest natcherally kick that bar'l from anunder yore carcass."

"War a time," muttered the old man, slowly, "when I'da skelped you fer that. Cuss me fer a Digger ef thar waren't."

"So? Wal, that time ain't now. Yo're a blot on the civic pride o' this hyar town. Ain't done nothin' but sit on that bar'l, right smack in front o' my drink emporium, fer six weeks. Likewise I near t'busted my laig on yore fool shins. I reckon I'll move you outen hyar now. Git to the middle o' the street."

A more humane man would never have said that. But this was the West, and this was Dodge, where the cherished gifts were strength and speed of arm, where the greatest virtue was courage. Human life was cheap. Youth ruled with high hand and age sat silently in the shadows.

"Go on, git out thar!" growled the injured party.

"I give ye warnin', Elvy Smeed," said the old-timer with a raising voice, "you been pesterin' me too damn' long. Mind yore own business an' thar'll be more people to trust ye."

"You a-callin' the turn on *me?*" shouted the irate Smeed, looming up in the shadows.

"It's an old man's privilege to speak the truth," retorted Gabe and raised an arm in self-defense.

"Y'old panhandler, I'll make them eye teeth o' yourn click!"

Smeed laid hold of Gabe. The barrel splintered and the old man stumbled in a painful fashion across to the hitching rail while a knot of railroad section hands, in for a night's drinking, guffawed. Smeed pursued his objective with a swiftly rising anger. "Go on, git outen hyar. Ain't goin' to have you roostin' like the angel o' poverty in front o' my place." His hand secured itself in the shabby folds of the buckskin suit; Gabe clung obstinately to the rail, spouting his resentment.

"Laws gimme strength!" he panted. "I'm an Injun if I wouldn't skelp yore ornery haid! You drap them dirty hands offen my duds!"

One skinny arm swooped and fell aimlessly on the tormentor. It was like the settling of a feather; the crowd whooped in glee. The next minute the amusement died and all were milling to and fro in confusion. A new actor arrived on the scene with a spreading of two abnormally long arms and a booming voice.

"Mister, hold yore hawss. Mebbe I can furnish you with a little more exercise than the old-timer."

Smeed swung and faced a Herculean figure. It may have been that the deceptive shadows added something to his bulk, but undeniably he was a head taller than any man in the circle and it seemed as if his chest would have fitted two ordinary humans. His gangling arms swung suggestively at his sides; when he spoke again, it was in the manner of a lazy-humored character roused to mild sarcasm.

"Isn't anybody willing to give you a tussle? Well, here I be if it's a wrasslin' pardner you want."

"Friend," retorted Smeed, "it ain't proper eti-ket to horn in war you wasn't specially asked. Jest retire to yore own manger and feed a while."

"Oh, I'm not bashful," the newcomer chuckled softly. "I'm a prairie flower and it sure hurts my feelings to see the old gent handled that way. Not to mention any names, but its my opinion there's somebody hereabouts who's plumb skunk."

"Honin' in to get an ear bit off, ain't ye?" sneered the saloon-keeper.

"Well, if you'd bite me, I'd sure get hydrophobia."

Smeed made an unfortunate move with his arm and was the next moment locked in a stifling embrace.

"You're a no-account fellow." The newcomer's voice took on the edge of malice. "I'd lief bust your ribs as not just to show you how it feels to be bullied. Supposing *you* get out of here and try the middle of the street?"

The advice was accompanied by a prodigious heave. Smeed rose into the air and described a short arc, falling with a sharp explosion of breath. It was the opening move of a possible gun-play and the bystanders broke ranks and vanished into the darkness leaving only the newcomer staring at the bent figure of old Gabe.

"Pardner, you'll sure overlook my horning in, but I saw you didn't have a gun on your person, so it made things a little different," he explained.

That was a pleasant fiction, an easy way to salve a man's pride. He spoke to the old-timer as an equal, to whom all courtesies were due. It was like giving water to a dusty plant. Gabe straightened his shoulders and peered upward.

"I'm obleeged, stranger," he said. "The cussed critter needs breakin', that's a fact."

Smeed, rolling in the dirt, groaned with as long accent of pain. The newcomer strode forward and reached down.

"No foolishness, *hombre*," he warned. "Me, I'll just toss your gun out of reach."

The weapon clattered against the side of a house somewhere in the darkness. Gabe approved with a vigorous tirade against Smeed's general character.

"He ain't got no respectable friends, nohow," he concluded.

"Well, just to prove you haven't any hard feelings against me for butting in, supposing we mosey in for a drink of hogwash."

Old Gabe assented with an eagerness that was only too evident. The big man swore under his breath, said, "Sure, sure," and took his new-found companion by the arm. Together they walked through the saloon door and into the smoke and clamor of half a hundred men engaged in fevered pursuit of the goddess luck. Gabe made his path to the counter. "Gimme some o' that pizen you sells honest men!" he called loudly.

The bartender grinned and tapped the counter.

"Money in sight, Gabe," he reminded.

"The refreshments," corroborated the newcomer, "are on me. Don't ask no questions and don't delay the gent's thirst."

He seemed no smaller under the scrutiny of light, this towering stranger, than by cover of darkness. The bartender spent one swift glance up and down the man and shook his head.

"Cowboy, what garden did they raise you in?" he asked, in awe.

There was no doubt of the big fellow's trade. The fancy boots with the high heels and jingling spurs, the chaps and the broad-brimmed hat proclaimed the fact. And, had these bits of apparel been lacking, certain physical characteristics would have betrayed him as a man of the plains. The pale blue eyes were set in an unwavering gaze as if accustomed to far sweeps of ground and brilliant rays of sun. The face, marked by a heavy jaw and a bold, hawk-like nose, was lean and whipped by the elements. A mustache of golden yellow drooped on either side of a thin, compressed mouth. A shock of similarly colored hair fell below the rim of the hat.

A certain distinction, a certain gaiety marked the man as he stood beside old Gabe and gravely saluted with his glass. Dozens of diverse characters roamed the broad saloon hall—the soldier, the buffalo hunter, the section hand, the trapper—but even in such a crowd of types he was unmistakably different. A beaming humor was on his face and when he put the glass down he expanded his chest and struck it with a fist.

"Old-timer, I sure feel festive tonight," he exclaimed. "I've come a long ways for a frolic. Now where's the excitement in this here wickiup?"

But old Gabe had found a sympathetic companion and was in no mood to lose him. He poured himself another glass of whiskey and threw it down. The deep-set eyes took on a brighter shine. He swept out his own long arm and pointed to the twisted and lumpy fingers.

"Y'see that arm? Y'see them scars and them knots? Wal, *compadre*, that comes o' settin' beaver traps in ice-cold water. I guess old Gabe Pilcher's fetched more beaver pelts down the Missoura than nary a man now alive."

"So that was your business, huh?" interpolated the cowboy genially. His eyes roved throughout the crowded hall, strayed to the gaming tables and rested momentarily on the vision of a girl, done up in spangled clothes and with her hair combed up in a jet-black knot, sulking by the far wall. The whiskey gurgled down old Gabe's throat and the rheumatic arm plucked at the cowboy's shoulder.

"I begin's to feel suthin' like myself," Gabe informed him. "Y'see this aggregation of mortals? Bah, they don't know nothin'! Nor they ain't seen nothin' like old Gabe's seen."

"She was purty tough in the old days," encouraged the cowboy.

A passing trio stared at the old man and grinned derisively at the listener. He shoved back his hat a little and fastened his steady, inscrutable gaze upon them. The amusement died and they lost themselves in the crowd.

"Tough? Wal, say, I'd like t'have that ornery son-of-a-gun, Elvy Smeed, up whar I useter pitch my lodge." The eyes seemed to retreat the farther and a reminiscent gaze fell over old Gabe's face. His fist hung tightly to the cowboy's shoulder. "No, sir, they ain't the men now that thar war forty year back. Why, say, I c'n remember mighty clear...old Bill Williams with the hatchet face who got rubbed out up in the South Park, Jim Bridger, La Bonte the wild 'un from Kentucky, and the Portygee, whose name nobody never did rightly know. That cussed Portygee ran off with my squaw, but she waren't a good provider, nohow, so it wa'n't a loss. I crossed the Bitterroots an' got me a Nez Percy. They make the cleanest housekeepers."

"Have a drink," urged the cowboy.

His eyes were returning to a certain poker table in the center of the place. The smoke and the clamor rose heavily to the ceiling. An accordion and a guitar strove to make an uncertain duet while the girl with the knot of jet-black hair danced with the self-same pout on her face.

"Hah!" cried the cowboy, with the zest of life in his blue eyes. His big chest rose. "Old-timer, this is sure a comfortable place for a lonely prairie child to be. Have another drink."

The old-timer flung out his gnarled fist at the crowd.

"They ain't got no innards!" he spoke angrily. "Nowadays, a big party goes out to kill a couple Pawnee bucks an' figgers they done right well. In my day I traveled a thousand mile plumb through Blackfoot country alone...and a bigger devil nor the Blackfoot never drawed breath. There war a time...."

He was embarked on a fragment of his odyssey, telling it with all the circumlocution and all the gusto of the inveterate gossip. He lost the air of feebleness; the hump in his back disappeared. Likewise he appeared to gain dignity and importance as the story of his physical prowess was carried back to his own ears. One by one the names of the mighty rolled from his slow tongue: of Sublette and Smith and Jackson and of the others who first penetrated the dark and unknown territory of the Missouri headwaters. The cowboy drooped his head and listened with a beaming face; one of his big paws went across the older man's shoulders and thus he stood while the long yarn wound to its close.

"Sure now?" he asked in amazement when old Gabe had finished. "Palmy days, huh? You're a ring-tailed snorter, *compadre mio*. Have another drink."

His face swept the room. The music came faintly to him and the girl swung lazily in her dance. The cowboy gripped his whiskey glass and waited until a turn of her white shoulders brought their eyes together. The swaying of those white shoulders stopped momentarily; a flash of teeth erased the pout. Her chin rose a trifle and she dipped to the rhythm of the guitar, keeping his gaze as she glided away.

"Happy days!" said the cowboy, and drained his glass. He reached into the woolen jeans and brought forth a long pigskin wallet whence emerged the chinking of silver. It was a rather fat wallet and it smote the bar heavily. The cowboy dragged out four or five pieces and shoved them forward to the bartender.

"Treat yourself," he commanded, "all the drinks are free to the old-timer all evening."

The old-timer, standing by still flushed with the heat of his story, caught the changing expression of the bartender's face as he observed the wallet slide back into the cowboy's pocket. The ancient face closed down in shrewd suspicion. The gnarled hand fumbled for a cob pipe.

"Gimme some matches," demanded old Gabe, reaching over the counter. He tamped down the tobacco and glanced across the pipe bowl to the cowboy. "These," he remarked sententiously, "are shore onscrupulous diggings."

The cowboy seemed to hear it only vaguely. His attention was fixed upon the nearest poker table.

"See you later, old-timer," he said, and cruised away.

Old Gabe deserted the bar and retreated to a spot along the wall where he might command a view of the door and the poker table at the same time.

"He didn't noways git the meanin' o' that remark," he soliloquized through the tobacco smoke. "And thar he goes, plumb into crooked hands. Ef they don't bust him before an hour my name ain't Gabe Pilcher."

The cowboy shouldered aside a ring of spectators and, finding a vacant seat at the table, let himself cautiously into it and reached for his money again.

"Just pass me a stack, banker," he requested. "Here's another guest to feed the kitty."

While the first hand was dealt him, he inspected his neighbors with a bland and fleeting glance. It was the customary table of six men, one of whom was dressed in the black suit and starched shirt of the professional gambler. The others seemed of varied types. He was aware of an answering glance from the gambler, but without appearing to notice it he picked up the cards and became engrossed in the game.

It became evident, after the first dozen hands, that luck was perched on his shoulder. He seemed to bet without reason, threw away good hands and held mediocre ones, yet the stack in front of him grew. The professional gambler called for a fresh deck loudly and lit a new cigar. The cowboy beamed and rattled his chips.

"Oh, lady, isn't this a cheerful home for a lonely prairie child!" he exulted.

The girl with the knot of jet-black deserted the music and crept over to the table, putting a hand on the cowboy's shoulder. Regretfully he lowered his cards to the green baize and turned.

"Honey, I sure am gratified to have you hanging around, but it makes me nervous if anybody else gazes upon the spots of these pasteboards," he said.

"No!" said the girl sharply. "I see nothing...I tell nothing! Go on."

"Up ten," called the professional gambler impatiently. "Play cards, mister."

The cowboy stared thoughtfully at the girl's provocative face. A faint odor of perfume assailed his nostrils. He shook his head.

"It's been some little time since I smelled anything like that," he observed. "All right, honey, I reckon you're honest." He palmed the cards and, with the infinite care of the zealous poker player, proceeded to peep into the minute slits created between each. "No," he announced, "I'm not anxious to participate. Pass."

The dealer looked up for a fraction of a moment; the professional gambler twitched his nose and transferred the cigar to the other corner of his mouth. The girl's fingers closed on the cowboy's shoulders with great pressure. Old Gabe, looking at the scene with disillusioned eyes, shook his head.

"'Pears as if they had him baited, but he slipped the hook," he meditated. "Wal, he'll go fer a killin' yet. Ain't but two honest men sittin' thar an' they don't count."

His interest had changed immediately to another part of the room. The door opened and Elvy Smeed, nursing an arm, limped through. Old Gabe slid farther along the wall, better to screen himself. But the saloonkeeper went straight toward the counter and the old-timer saw the bartender lean across the boards and speak swiftly to his chief. Smeed raised his head quickly and after a space sidled around to stare at the poker table graced by the cowboy. The bartender's hand was hovering above a whisky glass as if measuring off something. Smeed nodded and reached for a bottle. Old Gabe saw him beckon quietly.

In a moment two men stood at his side, studiously indifferent, fairly small men with white, feminine hands and solemn faces. They drank. Smeed appeared to be speaking to the ceiling but other ears heard his words for not long after the small men turned in a careless manner and their eyes, too, fell upon the cowboy. Smeed nodded and went behind the bar.

Old Gabe's rheumatic arms trembled and the cob pipe emitted furious spirals of smoke. "Them's Smeed's hired killers!" he muttered silently. "Cuss me ef the rat don't mean to have a leetle private murderin' done. Waugh! That's how the stick floats! Ef this coon was jest twenty years younger, he'd take a hand. Cuss me ef I wouldn't now."

A rift in the ranks of the bystanders allowed old Gabe to see the cowboy's cheerful face more clearly and to make out the arm of the dancing girl as it rested on the big shoulder.

"Wal, now!" exclaimed the veteran in a kind of pitying despair. "Foolin' with Smeed's woman, too. Oh, thar'll be lead flyin', er my name ain't Gabe Pilcher."

He lost himself in meditation, the pipe smoke eddying around the long whiskers. A problem in personal morals confronted the old man and, although he was versed and trained in the Western code, he found himself sorely perplexed. A gathering cloud of trouble descended about the unsuspecting cowboy's head. Murder in some dark lane of the town was almost certainly his fate unless he were warned. But when old Gabe tried to persuade himself that it was his duty to deliver that warning, he shook his head and bit into the pipe. There was no stronger dictum in all the sweep and breadth of the plains than that which forbade interference with another man's affairs.

The cowboy had been quick to apologize for his intrusion into Gabe's quarrel with Smeed even when Gabe was without a gun and almost a public charge. There could be no doubt, then, that the big man would bitterly resent transgression into his own dealings. It was a move unpardonable, and old Gabe, with an instant liking for his new-found friend, wanted to commit no error that would lower him in the other's estimation. So he puffed furiously and watched the poker table with sad eyes and a wrinkling of his forehead.

Affairs at the table took a swift, sudden turn. The cowboy, barricaded behind a comfortable pile of chips, riffled his cards and peered cautiously at them. The dancing woman, standing as still as a statue, cleared her throat and hummed a measure of song. The professional gambler had passed and the man to his left opened the pot with a rattling of chips. Once again the woman exerted the pressure of her hand and when the cowboy studied his cards with an impassive face, as if debating, she leaned forward.

"Come drink with me, big man," she invited. "This waiting is stupid."

The gambler looked up with a twitching of his nose. A thin, meticulously kept hand struck the table. "Fannie," he said, "it isn't polite to interrupt a gent's playing."

The cowboy laughed genially, threw his cards down, and shoved his stacks of chips toward the center of the table.

"Cash in, dealer," he demanded.

"Quittin'?" asked the gambler with a singsong voice.

"The lady," exclaimed the cowboy, "asks my company for a drink and it'd be sure unhandsome to refuse."

"Mebbe the game ain't blooded enough to suit you," suggested the gambler. "Mebbe you'd like to give us a run for yore money."

The cowboy laughed again and scooped his winnings into his wallet. "Why, no," said the cowboy rising, "it isn't that. Your style of play just makes me tired. It isn't crooked enough to be interesting. I learned all your parlor tricks when I was a kid."

"Crooked?" sang the gambler. The ivory face wrinkled and the shoulders drooped in unison with the well-kept hands. The dancing woman screamed and the bystanders leaped away. The big man took hold of the table's edge and flung it directly into the gambler's face, weaving aside like a fencer. A gun roared; the table splintered and the chips cascaded down. In a moment the cowboy had the gambler's arm pinioned, the weapon skittering along the floor.

"Happy days!" said the cowboy cheerfully. "I'm obliged for the entertaining session. Now don't be foolish, mister. Don't you reckon I might get mad? Where's the lady who wants to drink with me? Honey, lead me to the bar."

"Cuss me," breathed old Gabe in admiration and fear, "if he ain't spry fer such a big 'un. Oh, thar'll be hell to pay afore long."

It seemed as if it were a true prophecy. The cowboy and the woman whom old Gabe had described as belonging to Smeed walked up to the bar. There, looking on with a bleak, disfavoring eye, stood the saloonkeeper, one hand tugging at a massive watchchain, the other gripping a whiskey bottle.

"Your joint?" asked the cowboy. "Well, isn't that interesting. Sure hope you don't object to my presence here at the festive counter."

"Reckon yore money's as good as any's," growled Smeed.

The dancing girl stared at Smeed and turned sulky. With a deliberate hitching of her arms she caught the cowboy around the neck and drew his big head down.

"Man," she whispered, "you clear out of here, *pronto*. They'll lay for you and trim you."

Then, as if to complete some provocative remark, she kissed him. Smeed's face turned thunder black and his hand gripped the whiskey glass until the knuckles were white. But he kept his peace while the assembled and expectant multitude looked on.

"Happy days!" bellowed the cowboy and beckoned with his arm. "Barkeep, water the house. It's on me. Step up and render a prairie child's farewell to Dodge in a liquid one!"

The dancing girl touched her glass and smiled in the saloonkeeper's face. "So long, big man."

Old Gabe limped around the edge of the crowd and waited for the cowboy to work his way through, bound for the door. He heard the big man's genial, noisy farewell, "Happy days!" and he clucked his tongue.

"Oh, he's a spry 'un, but thar'll be hell to pay," he muttered again. The crowd parted and Gabe thrust out his arm. "Young feller, I reckon you got a portion o' excitement, cuss me if you didn't."

The cowboy clapped the old-timer on the back. "Well, see you in the sweet by-and-by. Me, I'm heading south to meet the pie-faced cows. So long!" he called.

Gabe looked around. Nowhere did he see the two smallish men with the delicate hands. No doubt they were outside in the dark, waiting to stalk their quarry. He clung to the big man.

"If you ain't p'tic'lar, I'll walk along to the next saloon," he suggested.

"Sure!" The cowboy took him under the arm, and together they disappeared through the swinging doors, left the smoke and the noise behind them, and groped a path down the dark street to where the beacon lights of another saloon beckoned. Old Gabe cleared his throat.

"It's a hard town, young feller," he said. "Take an old man's word that thar's a lot o' wickedness roamin' atween hyar and the river." He paused, waiting for some kind of encouraging reply. None came and it seemed as if the cowboy had refused his confidence. But old Gabe ventured upon the privilege of old age and added, significantly, "If I was a young cuss, I'd shore keep my gun loose an' my tracks covered. It's easy to settle grudges atween night an' mornin'."

"Yeah," said the cowboy.

Old Gabe sensed a certain dryness in the answer and shook his head. He had gone as far as the code would permit him. His warning found no response. This strapping, genial man—who reminded old Gabe so strongly of his own stirring youth—walked gaily into a death trap.

They came to the door of the second saloon. The cowboy disengaged his arm. "So long, old-timer," he said. "I'm heading for my horse and blankets."

Old Gabe stood a moment while the footsteps of the cowboy crunched on a broken board and then vanished. The veteran's mind worked swiftly. Nearly all the cowpunchers who drifted into Dodge tethered their horses and rolled their blankets beyond the tracks in a grove of cottonwood hard by the river. Doubtless this would be the big fellow's lodging place for the night and thence would the Smeed gunmen go, posting themselves for an outline of the man's body or a telltale wisp of campfire.

Old Gabe looked up to the black heavens where the stars pricked so remotely. He swore and moved his rheumatic arms. "Cuss me, Gabe Pilcher, it ain't nowise right," he confided to himself.

He forgot the infirmities of his body and went quickly inside the saloon to the bar.

"Tim," he muttered, "jest lend me yore gun a minute. I shore got a chore to do. Bring it right back."

The bartender grinned.

"Hell, I don't want my wee-pon hocked fer whiskey," he protested. "I'll *give* ya a drink."

"It ain't that," persisted old Gabe. "Jest pass it over fer ten minutes."

"Git outen the way, y'old bum, an' let the cash customers in."

Gabe turned around with a despairing click of his tongue. The deep-sunk eyes darted here and there but saw no single person who would lend him so necessary a thing as a gun.

"Ne'mind," he muttered. "I got to warn that durn fool summow."

He stumbled out and began a cautious progress toward the river, the same direction whence the cowboy had gone. His feet struck the rails of the Atchison switch track and presently he stood somewhere near the grove wherein he believed his friend to be. But he could advance no farther, nor could he call out. He was isolated and helpless.

At first he appeared to be completely alone, but as he stood undecided he began to distinguish various murmurs and uneasiness in the night. The lapping of the river along the sandy bank bore up among the soft rustling of the trees. A hard object thudded against the rails behind and left him tense. A night bird hooted in answer to another, and close upon the heels of its call arrived the soft whinney of a horse among the trees. That, decided old Gabe, was the cowboy's horse, signaling the approach of its master. Immediately, other ears in the night took note of the fact; old Gabe heard the cautious grating of feet, swinging around his right.

It left him with a sudden cold resolve. He fumbled in his pocket and reached for the matches which the bartender has passed him earlier in the evening. He tore one from the packet and sighed like a man very weary.

"I got to let him know he's bein' follered," he resolved. "He's a spry 'un, Gabe Pilcher. Jest like you war."

The match burst into a small, lonely ball of flame, shielded outward from his face by the gnarled fingers, a fitful compass point in a black world. The repercussion of guns broke the sibilant peace and woke a hundred echoes. Old Gabe, standing none too surely on his feet, saw the orange mushroom of flame come from two separate points, not more than three feet apart. The light dropped out of his fingers and made a dismal arc. He sighed again, a long gusty emission of breath, and sagged down; but before he fell he saw another point of the flame spurt out from the direction of the trees and heard the blasting answer of a gun. He struck the ground with his rheumatic arms and groped for the bullet hole in his chest. He seemed unable to find it as the energy flowed swiftly from his ancient body. He turned half over, and raised partly up on an elbow.

"Wal, he heard them lily-fingered gun-toters," he muttered. "Cuss me ef he didn't. Gabe, yo're a gone coon."

And then his throat formed one last defiant phrase, a phrase that bridged forty years and put him back in the high Rockies with his comrades. "Green River, waugh!"

He went to the last rendezvous as he had gone to many another, with hope.

Frederick Faust was born in Seattle, Washington. He wrote over 500 average-length books (300 of them Westerns) under nineteen different pseudonyms, but Max Brand™—"the Jewish cowboy," as he once dubbed it—has become the most familiar and is now his trademark. In 1917 Faust met Robert H. Davis, an editor at The Frank A. Munsey Company, and began contributing stories and serials to *All-Story Weekly* and *The Argosy*. In 1920 Faust expanded the market for his fiction to include Street & Smith's *Western Story Magazine* and his popularity helped increase its circulation from a half million copies an issue to over two million. It was not unusual for him to have two serial installments and a short novel in a single issue under three different names. Popular Publications agreed to buy 200,000 words by Max Brand in 1934 and a good part of this fiction consisted of the seven short novels featured that year in *Star Western*. It was hoped Max Brand's popularity would do for *Star Western* what it had done for *Western Story Magazine* a decade earlier. It worked so well that in the bad times of the late 1940s Popular Publications started a new pulp called *Max Brand's Western Magazine*. It lasted as long as *Big-Book Western* did.

Some of Faust's Western stories recently published for the first time in book form include SIXTEEN IN NOME (Five Star Westerns, 1995), "LUCK" (Circle (Westerns, 1996), and three collections of short novels and stories published by the University of Nebraska Press. These days a work by him is either newly published or reprinted every week of every year in one or another format somewhere in the world.

The Strange Ride of Perry Woodstock

An owl skimming close to the ground, hooted at the very door of the bunkhouse. That door was wide, because the day had been hot and the night was hot, also, and windless. Therefore, Perry Woodstock jumped from his bunk, grabbed his hat in one hand and his boots in the other, and still seemed to hear the voice of the bird in the room, a melancholy and sonorous echo.

The owl hooted again, not in a dream but in fact, farther down the hollow, and Woodstock realized that he had not been wakened by the voice of the cook calling to the 'punchers to "come and get it," neither was it a cold autumn morning at an open camp, neither was there frost in his hair nor icy dew upon his forehead, and his body was not creaking at all the joints. No, he could remember now that he had come down to work on this ranch in the desert unappalled by the fear of heat, for he felt that he could have worked in a furnace the rest of his days and never found the temperature too great.

His nerves were still on edge, however, and his heart pounding with the effect of that strange alarm. He went to the door of the bunkhouse—he was the only person in it—and stood there making a cigarette and watching the silver flowing of the hills towards the horizon, for it was full moon. He lighted his smoke, blew out the first lungful with appreciation, and then distinctly saw that a man was wrangling the horse herd down in the mesquite tangle in the hollow.

Other than himself and the "old man," nobody in the world had a right to work up those horses. Since the "old man" was snoring with a deep, thundering vibration in the ranch house nearby, it stood to reason that the fellow down there below was either a thief or something perilously close to it. Perry Woodstock did not hesitate. By the time he called the rancher for whom he worked, the mischief might be done and the fellow fleetly away, beyond pursuit. Besides, Woodstock was not the man to ask for help.

He simply stepped into his boots, then into his trousers, buckled a gun belt around his hips, and went hatless down the slope. As he went, he saw the horses spread out in a flashing semicircle, galloping hard from the mesquite. The soft sandy soil muffled the beat of their hoofs. They gleamed under the moonlight. But the gray mare was not tossing her bright mane in the lead, as usual. No, for the very good reason that she was the one that the stranger had on the end of his rope now. Perry Woodstock nodded in agreement; she was certainly the best of the lot!

A man who could pick horses so well might be able to pick guns even better. Woodstock rubbed the palm of his hand hard against his hip and flexed his fingers once or twice, as a man might do to supple his hand before dealing a pack of cards. In the meantime, he saw that a second horse stood in the biggest patch of the mesquite, its dropped head hardly rising above the tops of the brush. It was tired, very tired. The desert dust had been washed from its body by the rivers of its sweat. It was burnished and shone under the moon, but it was dead on its feet.

Yonder fellow who now cinched the saddle on the gray mare and then worked the bridle over her head had been riding hard and long. There was no doubt of that. And that made Woodstock feel all the more nervous about the prospect of the fight. For a man who simply exchanges mounts can hardly be called a thief. All he wins is a little boot perhaps and, if he changes horses often enough, even that works out in the long run. Furthermore, a man who rides through the night in that manner is not apt to be easily stopped.

The progress of Woodstock became slower and slower as he drew nearer the other. He came to a depression that practically covered him from sight. Now he walked with his Colt in his hand; he stalked with long and stealthy strides. He was in pointblank range when he saw the stranger swing into the saddle. Would the gray mare put on her show? She would!

It had cost Woodstock a dozen hard falls to learn her repertoire of tricks, though he well knew how to tie to a horse. Now the brim of that rider's sombrero began to flop violently up and down. The gray had her head and kept it low. She beat the ground as though it were a drum. In mid-air she snaked herself into complicated knots. She never landed on the same foot. Her rider was tall and his length of leg helped him to get a knee hold, but after half a dozen jumps he was pulling leather, and a moment later the mare whirled, executed a neat reverse, and slammed the stranger full length on the ground.

The reins were hanging under her nose. Therefore the gray did not run off but stood with ears pricked to watch the enemy rise. He was badly shocked. He got up in sections, as it were, first propped on his hands, then struggling to his knees, then to his feet with a final effort. At that point he saw Woodstock and Woodstock's gun.

"Touch the sky, brother," said Perry Woodstock.

The hands of the stranger rose shoulder high, struggled for a moment there, then went up above his head, encouraged by the careless surety of the manner in which Woodstock held his gun. At the hip he kept it, with a half-bent arm. His forefinger was not on the trigger for the good reason that no trigger was there. Instead, the ball of his thumb was hooked over the hammer. Of these points, the stranger made himself quickly aware before he hoisted his arms on high. His short mustache bristled a little as his lips pressed together.

"Who are you, brother?" asked Woodstock.

"Name of Joe Scanlon."

"Joe, show me your back for a minute and keep those hands up a little closer to the moon."

Scanlon turned his back. In spite of his slender body, he was strong. Now that his arms were raised, his shoulder muscles bulged in hard knots that Woodstock assessed with a competent eye. He slipped a hand under the left armpit of Scanlon and felt the gun that hung there, beneath the loosely-fitted coat.

"I thought you were one of those spring-holster boys," observed Woodstock. "Just drop that gun in the sand, will you? And drop it slow, Scanlon."

He put the muzzle of his own gun against the small of Scanlon's back while the revolver was accordingly produced and dropped on the ground. With a few dexterous movements, Woodstock fanned his prisoner and found no other weapons.

"All right," he said, "now step back."

Scanlon faced him, but his glance went beyond Woodstock, to watch the silver outlines of the hills in the distance.

"You want money or trouble?" asked Scanlon.

"You got plenty of both?"

"I'll tell you what…I'm in a hurry."

"House on fire, eh?"

"I've got a wife and three kids over in the mountains, yonder." He jerked a thumb over his shoulder at the delicate outlines of moon-haze and snow which represented Los Diablos mountains. "The wife writes to me that Bert has diphtheria and I hit the road. That bronco yonder is a tough bird. It's a roan all the way to the bone. But it played out. I aimed to help myself to a horse right here, when I seen them in the field. If there was any boot to pay, I could fix that up on the back trail."

"Where you from?" asked Woodstock.

"Down on the Fielding ranch. You know? The Fielding Brothers."

"How do they feed down there, now?"

"Nothing but beans."

"Brother," said Woodstock, "it's not so much what's in a lie as the way it's told that counts. The Fielding outfit is down yonder. You wouldn't ride through here coming from the Fielding place. Not by five points on the compass, if you're headed for Los Diablos range. And Jerry Fielding hates beans so bad that he won't have 'em on the place, boiled or baked or nothing."

Joe Scanlon shrugged his shoulders. "You're one of these particular *hombres*," he said. "But that's all right. If one lie won't suit you, I could try another. But wouldn't it cut things short if I paid my way on this division of yours…and paid high?"

Woodstock bumped the iron weight of his knuckles one by one against his broad chin. He cocked his head a little so that the moon-light illumined from a different angle the furrows which labor and pain had worked in his young face.

"I broke that gray mare, brother," he said gently. Even when he spoke so quietly, there was apt to be a soft boom and vibration about his speech. "She's four, and nobody had given her a ride. I rode her. Ever see a kid hammer a doll on the ground? That's the way the mare hammered me. Some of the sawdust and stuffing ran out of me, now and then, but finally she agreed to be friends. Come here, Molly."

The mare came up to him, shaking her head at the tall Scanlon, switching her tail nervously.

"If you'd stolen this mare, I would have followed your trail till my eyes rubbed out, but the trail would have been a blank, pretty soon. I'll tell you what, Scanlon. I'm what they call broadminded. I can take my whiskey neat, and I can use a beer chaser, too. But I hate a horse thief more than a Mexican hates his mother-in-law. You want to buy her, but your money's no good." He looked askance at the dark muzzle and the white brow of the mare. "Not a damn bit of good," he added.

"I saw she was the best, but I didn't read her mind," said Scanlon. "I'll make a deal for the next best in the lot."

"I'm a hired hand, and I don't make bargains."

Scanlon's entire body twitched nervously. "D'you aim to hold me?" he asked.

"I aim to do that," declared Woodstock, "until the sheriff hands you on to the jail." He waved towards the tired mustang. "Get your outfit back on that roan," he commanded.

Scanlon obeyed. As he cinched the saddle in place, the tired roan groaned under the pressure and swayed.

"You won't hold me that long, though," observed Scanlon.

"Won't I, brother?"

"Not alive," said Scanlon. "The boys that are riding on my trail now will see to that!"

II

Woodstock had lifted Scanlon's revolver from the ground by this time. Like his own gun, it was triggerless, and the sights had been filed away so that they might not catch in leather or cloth in a time of urgent speed. This examination of the Colt made Woodstock squint a little as he stared at Scanlon.

"Who are you, brother?" he asked.

"I've tried one yarn on you. What's the use of trying another?"

"Who's riding your trail? A sheriff and his mob?"

"Put reverse English on that, and you have the idea." Still, anxiously, Scanlon watched the hills that gleamed against the sky. Then he burst through every barrier, exclaiming: "Partner, the law don't want me. Not now. It's wanted me in the past…and it's had me, too, had me plenty. Will you give me a break? I've got money on me. I'll pay you five hundred bucks for the worst mustang in that lot, but I've got to get on my way. I'm not a horse thief. The job I'm riding on is so big that things like that don't matter."

"Who are you, Scanlon?" asked Woodstock, frowning.

Into his words came a soft beating of many hoofs. Scanlon whirled towards the sound. It came not over the hills but up the center of the shallow valley, and now they saw five riders coming fast, with the dust of their gallop streaming up into a long cloud that hung motionless in the air like the funnel of smoke that stretches behind a speeding locomotive on a windless day. Over the ground beside them rocked the black shadows of horses and men.

"Look!" shouted Scanlon, throwing up his long arms. "There's what I am…a dead man! They've got me!"

He drew from his pocket a used shotgun shell which had been refilled with a paper wadding, as it seemed. This he dropped in the hand of Woodstock. The whites of his eyes showed to the pink. His lips gaped wildly over his words, as he cried: "You've held me for them, damn you. Now, if you're a white man, find Harry Scanlon on the shoulder of Grizzly Peak. Tell him I'm dead. Give him this!"

He got to the roan as he spoke the last words, went into the saddle like a mountain lion leaping for a kill, and roused the tired mustang with the terrible rowels of his Spanish spurs. "Take this!" cried Woodstock, and threw him the revolver.

Whatever life was in the roan responded. He broke away in a gallop that fanned out the tail of Scanlon's coat, and for a minute the bewildered Woodstock thought that there was actually a chance for the fugitive.

Scanlon and the five went out of sight in the draw beyond the mesquite tangle. On the farther side, Scanlon appeared, still in the lead, but even in the distance it was possible to see that the roan had ended its race. It moved with a laboring gallop, like a rocking horse, and behind it the five riders swept up the slope on racing horses.

Steel winked in their hands. Scanlon turned with a poised revolver. And Woodstock suddenly bent his head, closed his eyes. The reports of the guns made him look again, in time to see Scanlon falling. His foot caught in a stirrup. He was dragged a little distance, his body flopping, a dust cloud whipping up behind it. Then the roan fell under a fresh volley, and the five closed on their prey. Every man dismounted. They huddled over Scanlon like eager wolves over a dead companion.

"I held him," said Woodstock, aloud. "I held him till they could catch up."

He began to beat his right fist into the palm of his left hand. It was a dream. The moonlight separated the thing from daylight happenings. There was the stillness of a nightmare over it all. And the hoot of an owl had begun it.

The five scattered away from the dead man. It was almost a surprise to Woodstock to see that a body remained. They were on their horses, sweeping off to the left, and again at a full gallop they disappeared among the bright hummocks of sand.

Woodstock, still lost in that dream, hesitated. Perhaps it would be best to rouse Jud Harvey, his boss; perhaps it was wiser to go straight towards the place where the body of Scanlon lay, with the roan fallen beside him, small in the distance. He had not quite made up his mind, thoughtfully rubbing his hand over the withers of the gray mare, when he heard again the sound of the hoofbeats. Then, looking up the slope, he saw the five riders coming between him and the house. It was like an Indian charge. Their heads were down. The manes of their horses flew up, glittering in the moonshine. It was all Indian, except the silence, and that silence froze the blood more than the yelling of fiends.

That trance which had held Woodstock snapped. There was no bridle, no saddle on Molly. Never before had he tried to ride her bareback, and the chances were great that she would snap him off her back and go frolicking on while he sprawled on his back, and the gunmen swept over him. It was that old used shotgun shell and the paper in it. That was what they wanted. They had failed to find it on Scanlon. If he held it between thumb and forefinger—if he showed it so, and made a gesture of surrender, perhaps they would not shoot him down.

Then before the eyes of Woodstock appeared the contorted face of Scanlon, like a ghost, the whites of the eyes showing to the pink, the lips gaping and gibbering about the words. Woodstock flung himself on the back of the mare and called to her. Her response nearly jerked him off her back. It was sudden as the flight of an arrow from a bowstring, but an arrow does not gather speed through the air, and every bound of the mare was longer. One hand wound into her mane was all that kept Woodstock in place. He slewed sidewise. The working of her supple body threatened to slide him off. Only by degrees he managed to pull himself into position until his knees had their grip. He had to forget saddles and remember the days of his boyhood.

Still she was gathering speed. The shoulder muscles came back in hard ripples under his knees. He felt the strength of her back pulsing. It was a dizzy thing to look down to the whipping strokes of her hoofs. A bullet kissed the air above Woodstock's head; the sound of the explosion followed on its heels. He risked a glance over his shoulder.

No wonder they had started shooting! Oh, the beauty of speed, and how she pulled away from them. From the tip of her nose to the tip of her tail she stretched in a straight line, quivering with effort. He looked back again. Two of them had dismounted, lay flat on the ground, and steadied their rifles for the distant shot. The other three, still riding hard, fanned out to either side to give the marksmen a fair chance. Woodstock, with a pressure of his hand on the neck of the mare, turned her down an easy slope to the left.

Wasp sounds bored through the air about him. He reached the bottom of the hollow and swung the mare to the right. The shooting had stopped. All the pursuit was for the moment ended. And framed within the walls of the draw, he saw far before him Los Diablos Range. Grizzly Peak was somewhere among them, one of the lesser brothers in that collection of giants. *On a shoulder of Grizzly Peak, find Harry Scanlon if you're a white man, and give him this!* What was it? One man had died for it this night. How many had died for it in the past? How many would die hereafter—for a bit of paper wadding in a used shotgun shell?

They came over the bank of the draw behind him now, three riding to the front, two far, far to the rear. A foot in a gopher hole, a stumble over one of the rocks would end the race, still. But it was as easy to think of a hawk stumbling in the sky as to think of the gray mare faltering on her home ground. Farther behind, farther behind fell the five. Then, suddenly, they began to drop from the picture, and he knew what that meant. Rather than burn up the strength of their horses, they would cut down their gait to a lope and so try to run their trail into the ground.

There was still plenty of running in the mare, but he called her back to a hand gallop. He patted her shining neck, and she turned her head a little, and pricked her ears for him. Suddenly he felt that he was cut loose from all familiar shores and, like a mariner of ancient days, bound for coasts of unknown adventure in unknown seas.

To keep to beaten trails would be to invite the pursuers on the way he selected. Instead, he chose a line and held to it over rough and smooth. A good many times he had to dismount and make his own way over the rocks, turning to watch the mare follow him like a struggling cat, her armed hoofs clanging and slipping on the stones. As they advanced into the wilderness, she seemed to draw closer and closer to him. She came to his voice; she came to his gesture.

What would Jud Harvey think when, in the morning, he found his hired man gone, and the gray mare gone also, and that dead body stretched on the hillside opposite the ranch house? Suppose they attributed the killing to Perry Woodstock, now missing? Suppose they loaded him with the name of horse thief, as well?

He could give them, in return, a precious tale about the hoot of an owl and an old used shotgun shell! But he seemed to have turned his back to such actualities. As he climbed into the mountains, he climbed into a new sphere of life.

The desert foothills were marked with Spanish Bayonet, gaunt figures. He found a valley with a trickle of water running through it, drunk it before it ever reached the sands. There were big cottonwoods here. He mounted over rocky slopes spotted with scrub oak. Then he came to the first scatterings of pines. He breathed of them before they met his eyes. He roused some valley quail and heard their three bold notes, without the soft ending of the call of the desert quail. The sound pleased him. On the whir of their wings his spirit was raised, also. It seemed easy enough to find Harry Scanlon, deliver the shell—and then? Drop back to the quiet old days and ways again?

The pines grew taller, thickened. They dimmed the moonlight which presently went out altogether as he entered a dense fog. It was one of those clouds which he had looked up to many a time from the heat of the ranch in the desert, seeing them laid along the side of the mountain or over its shoulders like a white feather boa around the neck of a woman.

Rain fell. In the darkness the mare almost grazed the trees, time and again. He had to trust her, often blindly holding out his hands to either side, but so they climbed with the forest until they came to a more scattering growth above, found the moon a dead thing, setting on the edge of a sea of clouds, and the dawn beginning over the upper peaks.

At the top of a great divide, Perry Woodstock made his first long halt. He sat on a rock so long that the mare began to graze, sniffing tentatively at the strange mountain grasses before she cropped them. The light grew. Yonder in a cañon a waterfall whose song he had heard came arching into view, carrying the daylight swiftly down into an abyss. Rose entered the eastern sky, moving around the horizon. Off a crag above him, a fish hawk slid into the still bosom of the air, balanced over a hollow where night still lay, and then began to sink into the depth with easy circlings.

At last, all in a moment, the day was there, though the sun had not risen, and from his height Woodstock saw a lake stretched blue as paint between the dark of a pine forest and the golden brown face of a cliff. Up from that lake rose the hawk with something flashing at its feet. It flew so close that Woodstock could see the fish clearly, held by the back and pointed head forward so that it could be steered more easily through the air.

Woodstock stood up. Every mountain had a different face; every one had a different name. He wished with all his heart that he knew them all. When he turned, the clouds were thinning. As through doors, he looked down through openings at the desert. It was just beneath him! He seemed to have climbed a sheer wall from the height of which he looked, as it were, into the flat back yard of the world, swept monotonously clean and bare.

He found a way down to the lake with Molly following behind him like a dancer, studying the places where he stepped before she ventured on the perilous slope. Never once did she slip, though she set some rocks tumbling. One of them was a good-sized boulder that leaped far out, smote the blue face of the lake, and sent upwards lightning splashes of water. The noise of the impact smacked the ears of Woodstock a long moment later, repeated and repeated by echoes loud or small.

When they got to the verge of the water, he stripped, plunged as if into liquid ice, then stood on a rock at the margin, laughing at the blue gooseflesh that puckered his body while he whipped away the wet with the edge of his hand. For he had a feeling that he was washing himself clean of the dust of a commonplace existence. A dead man had passed him the key to a new world, and he was determined to try the lock of whatever door he found.

For breakfast, he pulled up his belt, smoked a cigarette, watched Molly at work in a rich pasture, and then started again on his journey. He circled the edge of the lake, weaving back and forth among the aspens which fringed the water, and by whose presence he judged that he was a full seven thousand feet above sea level. Douglas spruce covered the northward facing slope down which he had just come. Yellow pine grew on the opposite wall of the great hollow; but very few of either of these giant races drew near to the water. They confronted each other like huge armies and the bright yellow-green of the aspens was pleasant about the blue of the lake.

Woodstock looked twice at the fisherman before he really saw the man standing at the edge of an indentation of the lake. His boots were as dark as the roots that projected into the water. His trousers were the color of the soil, his flannel shirt a rusted brown like the trunks of trees, and his hat was exactly the color of his gray beard. His body was long and thin and he had a long, thin, brown face. Out from his hand extended a light pole from the end of which a fishing line dropped to the water, seemed bent sharply to the side, then disappeared far down in the glassy lake. He was watching his rod, not the stranger or the stranger's horse, when Woodstock spoke to him. Then he turned his head and a pair of blue, calm eyes. So an animal, when it is both well-fed and fearless, may slowly move its head and look towards a noise.

"Hello, stranger," said Woodstock. "What's the good word up here?"

"The fishhawks have the fun around these here parts," said the old man. "That one that went shoulderin' by you, a while back, yonder on the edge of the mountain, he come down and socked his hooks into the only trout that's worth catchin' in this water. All I've got is small fry. But the smaller they are the sweeter, I guess, and I'm old enough to have patience now. Come back yonder where I got a frying pan, and I'll give you a breakfast."

So he left off fishing, picked up a line with a shining, shivering huddle of fish at the end of it, and walked ahead to show the way. He had a fine carriage and a noble stride—only his step was slow and his knees had not the supple spring of a young mountaineer.

Very nearby an old gray mule with legs crooked inward at the knees and a scrawny neck was working without much interest at the grass in a clearing. It was not so much a clearing as a lane that had been beaten and broken into the woods by the fall of an immense yellow pine, a good hundred and fifty feet, perhaps, from its uptorn roots to its head. When at last after a long life some hurricane took it by the top and slowly pried it loose from its deep moorings, it had smashed down many lesser trees of its kind, so that there was a wreckage under and all about its huge body, and in the interstices grew excellent grass, mixed with the sprouts of young trees—not yellow pines, but the lodgepole pines whose seeds fall instantly on every scarred place in the woods.

At a point where the trunk had snapped in two in the fall, leaving a huge face of yellow splinters higher than Woodstock's head, the old fisherman had camped. The mule was hobbled. A light cotton tent was stretched on pegs, and Woodstock saw the black spot of last night's supper. He asked no questions, but set to work gathering firewood. Among green shrubbery, he found one pale ghost, so he broke up these dead, brittle twigs and brought them back to the fire that had been kindled already by the fisherman. Two pairs of skillful hands make the work go forward with a magic speed. In a trice they were eating hardtack, fish fried brown, and drinking black coffee.

"They're good and fat," said the fisherman. "You take a fish that ain't got no fat on it, and his meat sort of fills up your belly but don't feed you none. Lean fish is like straw for horses. Puffs you up, but keeps you hungry! But you can make a march on food like this, and spare your horse all the way."

He hooked his thumb towards the gray mare. She and the hobbled mule, leaning far forward, stretching out their necks, were cautiously touching noses. When that was done, the mare squealed with a sudden indignation, hitched herself half way around, and jerked up her heels a time or two as though prepared to batter in the ribs of the mule. The old mule, flattening his ears, lifted his head till his neck was like the throat of a camel, and turned slowly away in disgusted dignity.

"That girl, there, she don't like my Alec," said the old man. "She says he's a worthless nigger. She says that he's poor white trash, is what she says. But that don't matter to you. You like her pretty face, son."

"She saved my life," said Perry Woodstock, dreamily. "Come here, Molly."

She came to his hand, and sniffed it. He laid his palm between her eyes.

"I'm Dave Hixon," said the man of the forest. "Who are you? Not that you need to answer. A gent that has to leave without a saddle or a bridle ain't likely to take a name along with him, neither."

"I'm Perry Woodstock." The mare moved away. Woodstock followed her with his eyes, while he asked: "Why did you camp here, Dave, when you could have got closer to the water, and had everything handy?"

The old man pointed to the broken trunk of the tree. "I used to prospect for gold. Now I hunt for the sort of yarns that the mountains can tell you. See where I've chipped into that tree and split it with wedges, here and there? I've only got part of its story. It's eleven hundred years old. Just about exactly. I've counted the rings. I know its starvation years, where the rings are close together. Seven of 'em in a row, when it was a youngster about three hundred years old. That drought must of near killed it. When it was a baby about fifteen years old, the snow bent it over like a bow, and it was that way a coupla or three years. Then it begun to straighten again. God wants trees and men to grow straight.

"I found a place where the ants and the borers begun to wind into it. They meant slow death and sure death unless the doctor come along. But he come. He was Doctor Texas Woodpecker. He laid his ear to the heart of the tree and he heard enough. So he done an operation with the chisel edge of his beak and took out the trouble, and swallered it for a fee. Life went on for the yellow pine. It wrote its story on him. You read the rings and see. The wounds are filled up with resin, but they're there. It was about five hundred years old when the snow piled up so high on a branch that the branch broke off and took a chunk out of its side. Along about fourteen ninety-one, an Indian shot an arrow into that tree. I found the flint head, soldered all around with dead resin. Come along about fifteen hundred and fifty or so, somebody tried the edge of an axe on the instep of this tree. Spaniards. They're the only ones that would of had steel in this part of the world. But the Americans come, and forest fires with 'em. Three times that pine got scorched bad, and all within the last eighty years. We're a pretty mean people, son, and we work with steel and fire. When the lightning struck the head of that tree, I don't know, but there's a lot of us that begin to die in the head while the body's still sound."

"That's what you hunt for?" asked Perry Woodstock. "Yarns like that?"

"Yep. They ain't wrote in words, but they're all in the flesh of the stone or the trees or the earth."

Perry Woodstock wondered at him quietly. And the old man endured the gaze like a face of stone, unmoved. "You're telling me that the things we do don't amount to much," said Woodstock. "The trees, even, see a lot more than we do, though they stand still. I guess you're right, but everything that's young is foolish; and I'm still young. I want to find a man in these mountains. I don't mean him any harm. I'm just bringing him a message. His name is Harry Scanlon. Know him?"

Dave Hixon stirred in a way that showed his mind was moved as well as his body. "There's a Harry Scanlon living half way up the side of Grizzly Peak. He's got a blind wife, Theodora, uncommon fast with her knitting. And he's got a daughter, Rosemary. What would you want with him, son?"

"No harm," said Perry Woodstock. He stood up. "Where's Grizzly Peak?"

"They've changed a lot of the names of these here mountains," answered Dave Hixon, "but Grizzly is a name that don't change none too easy. There…you can see it through the gap. It ain't more than ten miles, but every one of them miles is worth ten."

"Then I better start. I'm thanking you, Dave."

He held out his hand, and the bony fingers of the old man closed over it, retained it for a moment, while he said: "You're young enough to keep hoping for tomorrow. But it'll be just like today. The trouble is that we always want to hurry things up. We put in the spurs, and we get the blood on our heels. But no matter how hard you ride, all you can get to in the end of your life is a kind of stillness, dead or living, and all the blood you'll have to wash away in the silence, one of these days."

He released Perry Woodstock, and the boy turned instantly away. He called over his shoulder. The gray mare followed him, was seized by a fit of hilarity, and ran joyously before him under the somber trees. But there was no flight of spirits in Woodstock. He trudged straight on for three hours, until a hill raised him above the trees, and he had the rugged height of Grizzly Peak all before him. He stared at it a moment, then took out the shotgun shell, pulled from it the paper slip, and read on this, in ink which time had turned brown: Walsh and Porcupine on line and Oliver and Gray at the flow find a big stack work one-third down.

IV

Perry Woodstock labored on until late in the afternoon before he heard, far ahead, the clinking of a hammer on iron. He trusted that meant he was close to the habitation of Harry Scanlon. So he paused a moment to straighten his back and shoulders and draw a few deep breaths. The magpie which had been accompanying him for the last half mile, darting in and out among the trees and brush, or gleaming suddenly far overhead, now sat on the tip of a branch and was cradled by the resiliency of the little bough. A shining, tailor-made bit of black satin and murder was that magpie. When Woodstock whistled, it talked back querulously. It kept examining him with an eager eye, as though it expected Woodstock to turn into edible stuff before long.

He went on. The big yellow pines on that southern slope of Grizzly Peak gathered together in dense ranks, as evenly spaced as trees that men have planted. There was no undergrowth. There was no grass, but only the brown, slippery padding of pine needles over the ground. The gray mare grew nervous, and pressed up to the very shoulder of Woodstock. She was at his side when he came to the clearing, and stopped. For in a step he had changed worlds.

Passing through that fence of great yellow pines, he stepped from the wilderness into a tiny farm. For the mountain here put out a shoulder of several acres as level as a floor checked into fields with log fences. The yellow-green of wheat covered one patch; another was newly ploughed and the sods were still shining while birds worked among them for roots and worms and insects. Two cows moved slowly at their grazing in a bit of pasture and, near the snug cabin that was backed against the upper slope of the mountain, a girl was spading in a vegetable garden. Beyond her, at the door of the cabin, sat a woman knitting. The needles flashed with the speed of her work.

The girl was nearest. Perry Woodstock made for her with the mare still just behind him, snuffing down the various fragrances of the pasture and stepping with dainty exactness along the narrow path between the beds of vegetables. Woodstock raised his hand to his forehead before he remembered that he had no hat. And the bare-headed girl returned that salute, instantly.

She leaned on her spade, holding it with a gloved hand. She wore a dress of blue gingham faded to a dirty gray. There was a big patch at her knees, but over her shoulders lay a white collar as clean as snow and it made the frame for her face. The gentle quiet and beauty of the place seemed to have given birth to her, and her eyes were both soft and fearless, like the eyes of wild creatures before they have heard the hounds baying and the guns of the hunters.

She smiled at Woodstock as he paused, and for pure joy he smiled back at her. But he was sorry that his skin was swarthy and that his wind-entangled hair was black. If he had been blond, he would have been closer kin to her. Now that he was so near, he saw that she was not tall. It was her way of standing and the lift of her head that gave her the appearance of height.

"You're Rosemary Scanlon," he said, "and my name is Perry Woodstock. I've brought your father a message."

From the mountain-side behind the cabin the hammer strokes chimed again on iron. She pulled the glove from her right hand and held it out to him, warm and strong to his touch but small. That was how she was—all of her small, but strong and warm with life. She kept on smiling her approval, yet it was only as though she were approving of a fine, strong tree, or a cloud in the sky. There was not a line about her eyes. There was not a line in her face, except what the smiling made. Perry Woodstock began to lose himself in her presence as a convalescent loses himself in the peace and sweetness of the open air.

"I'll take you to father," said the girl. "He's drilling in the new shaft. What's the name of the mare?"

"Molly," said Perry Woodstock.

"She's beautiful," said the girl. "She's the most lovely thing!"

She stretched out her hand. Woodstock stepped aside and watched the mare lean forward until her knees were trembling. Molly sniffed at that brown hand, and then tried to gather it in with a furtive, thievish upper lip. The girl laughed. Molly tossed her head. And then the three of them went on, with Rosemary Scanlon in the lead. She walked first because the path was so narrow, but she kept turning a little so that he could watch her smile, that assured him she was glad he had come. In her profile he could see more clearly that ethereal beauty of the very young and about her mouth that delicacy of those who drink freely of life and find all of it sweet.

As they came nearer, the woman at the cabin door stopped the rapid work of her needles and dropped her hands on the soft pile of knitting in her lap. Her hair was white, yet it only served to make her face seem younger. Her dark eyes were as bright as those of a girl, but her head was not turned exactly towards them, and Perry Woodstock could have known that she was blind without any further telling.

"Rosemary, what's the trouble?" she asked.

"There's no trouble," answered the girl. "Only a man called Perry Woodstock is here with a message for father. He's shorter than father, but his shoulders are heavier. He's about twenty-five and he has dark hair and dark eyes. He has no hat, and his gray mare follows him without a saddle or a bridle. She's the most beautiful thing. She's nibbling at my hand now."

"No saddle and no bridle…that means trouble," said the mother. "What *is* the trouble, Mister Woodstock?"

Her head turned a little from side to side, anxiously hunting for him. He came closer. He bowed a little and spoke distinctly, as though to a child.

"There's no trouble. I wouldn't bring trouble. Only a message to Harry Scanlon."

As he spoke, her eyes found him and he felt the shock of the meeting. Something was missing from the center of the pupils, and something from the spirit took its place.

"You've come without a hat. There's no saddle and no bridle on your horse," she said quietly. "What drove you here, then? And what can be following?"

Her conviction made him glance hastily over his shoulder; but he only saw the blue, smiling eyes of the girl. "There's nothing following, I hope," said Woodstock. "And I have to see your husband. It's important for me to see him."

The blind woman stood up with the knitting between her clasped hands. "There's trouble," she murmured. "I knew there was trouble!"

"I'll take him to father," said the girl.

Woodstock was glad to escape from before that questioning face. If she was blind, her touch was all the more sure and she had found him at once as a messenger of evil.

"Little things will worry my mother," the girl was explaining. "She didn't wish to make you unhappy, but shadows we can't see are always crossing her mind. You're not angry, are you?"

"I'm not angry." He looked suddenly at her. "How could I be angry...with your mother?" he asked.

Girls are very quick to seize upon compliments. They have a singular perception, a delicacy of apprehension that finds them in the darkest moments, and then they are apt to flush, to turn away suddenly, to brighten all over with agreement and with delighted shame, but Rosemary met that piercing glance of his with an untroubled eye.

"I knew you were kind and gentle the first moment I saw you," she said. "I could tell by the way the mare followed you. And there is something secret and darkened about the eyes of men who are...well, unhappy...and...."

Words entirely failed her. She was still thinking the unspoken thing as they went up the slope behind the house towards the clanking sound of iron on iron. So they came to the mouth of a shaft with a windlass set over it and a dump sprawling down the side of the mountain. It was a dump that had been worked for many years. The upper part was loose, but the lower sections of debris had been soldered together by the rains and the snows of many seasons. A new shaft was being sunk beside the old one. A man was on his knees in the shallow hole whanging a drill-head with a single jack, dealing out powerful blows.

He got up to meet them. He looked like Joe Scanlon. He was the same height. He had the same sort of a head and face. He even wore a short mustache. But all of him was made larger and more roughly. The mustache was a shaggy gray brush, and his eyes were buried under the frown of the laborer. He looked a stern and a bitter man who was quite divorced from the peace that covered this mountain farm but, when Woodstock gazed more closely, he thought he could see, as if through a heavy mist and far away, a resemblance to Rosemary, a fatherhood. There would have been a gulf between them, but this resemblance bridged it.

"This is Perry Woodstock, Father. He's come to give you a message."

The big man strode from the hole and shook hands. His fingers were leathery with calluses. But Woodstock, after greeting him, turned a little towards the girl. She accepted the hint at once.

"I'll go back to the house and cook something. You look hungry, Mister Woodstock."

She was gone at once. Woodstock dragged his eyes away from her and faced the father, squarely.

"I've got some bad news to start with, and some other news afterwards that I can't make out," he said.

"Let's get farther back in the woods," answered Scanlon. "My wife has ears that can hear thoughts as they move in your brain. We'll get farther away."

He stepped off quickly through the pines until the green twilight of the woods covered them. One long, golden finger of sunshine slanted through an opening and poured itself on the pine needles until they seemed to smoke and burn. There Scanlon paused and began to stoke his pipe.

"Now let's have it," he said.

"You've got a brother called Joe," began Woodstock.

Harry Scanlon tamped in the charge of cut plug with unnecessary force. "What's Joe been doing now?" he asked. "Are you a friend of his?" He did not lift his head until he came to the last part of his question.

"I never saw him until last night. Something got me out of bed...I was working on a ranch yonder in the desert...and from the door of the bunkhouse I saw a man rounding up the cavvyard in the moonlight. He picked out this mare here. She threw him. I got down there in time to see him fall. I made him take the saddle and bridle off the mare and put them on his own horse, which was spent. I think I meant to turn him over to the sheriff. I hate horse thieves. But then a gang of five riders came up the hollow. Your brother, Joe, said they were after him. He hopped on his horse and ran for it. They caught him and killed him…and the horse, too. Then they came back and cut in between me and the ranch house. I was standing like a fool. I was sort of sick. I had to jump the mare without a saddle or a bridle, and she took me away from 'em."

"Joe's dead, is he?" said Harry Scanlon. "Well, he never did much good."

His voice was not as his words. There was such emotion in it that Woodstock decently made a pause in which all his attention went to the making of a cigarette. After he had lighted it and carefully put out the match, he went on: "Before Joe Scanlon hopped his horse, he gave me this, and told me to take it to you, on the shoulder of Grizzly Peak. That's why I'm here."

He handed over the shotgun shell, watched the thick fingers of Harry Scanlon worry the paper out, saw the sheet unfolded, and a blankness come over the face of the big man.

"That's why they were chasing your brother. To get that, I guess. It seemed to mean as much as his life to him."

"I've got to get over the mountain and down to the place where they murdered poor Joe," said Scanlon. "This paper…did you look at it?"

"Yes."

"Make anything out of it?"

"No. Not a thing."

"Walsh and Porcupine on line," read Scanlon aloud, putting in punctuation of his own. "And Oliver and Gray at the flow. Find a big stack. Work one-third down." He shook his head. "It stops me," he said. "I make nothing out of it. It's gibberish."

"It's gibberish a man was ready to die for and other men were willing to kill him for it," said Woodstock.

"Five men?"

"Yes, five."

"That would be Waley and some of his gang. God knows I told Joe what would come of herding with the brutes, but…well, he's ended." The fierceness went out of his blue eyes and there was only trouble in them. "He was only twenty-eight. He was only a kid," said Scanlon softly. In the pause, the gray mare turned her head from one man to the other.

"You mean Black Jim Waley?" asked Woodstock.

"That's who I mean." Scanlon crumpled the paper and thrust it into his pocket.

But the name he had heard jumped through the brain of Perry Woodstock like a freezing wind. "Black Jim!" he repeated. "Look here, Scanlon. Whatever you do about this is your own business. I've done what your brother asked me to do, and now I'm going to get out of here. Will you lend me a saddle and bridle?"

Scanlon began to nod his big head, answering: "You're scared, eh?"

"You bet I'm scared," said Woodstock. "I've seen Black Jim. I've seen the Mexican, too, the fellow whose face is all one scar. Who is he?"

"That's Vicente."

"I saw 'em once, and that's enough. If you've got an old saddle and a bridle, I'll hop on the gray mare and get out of here. How they feel about me now, I don't know, but if that's the crowd that wanted my scalp yesterday I'm taking it for granted that they want it today."

"I don't blame you," agreed Scanlon. "We'll go down to the house. I can fit you out with a saddle and bridle."

They left the woods and saw that the sun was nearing the top of a western mountain. Rosemary Scanlon was at work with her spade again, moving the handle from side to side as she jammed the blade deep enough in the sod. Her mother sat in the doorway with her idle hands still folded on top of her knitting and her blind eyes fixed upon some future darkness. Scanlon paused, stared at her an instant, and then went on with Woodstock to a shed which was built against the side of the house. A rusty blacksmith shop was fitted up in one end of it. All sorts of harness hung from pegs in the other end of the room, and a saddle and bridle were produced from the trappings.

Woodstock fitted them on the mare, arranged the stirrups at the right length, and led the mare around to the front of the house to say his adieus. The sun was rolling like a great wheel of red gold down the side of that western mountain. With its light it enriched the forest and the green farm and laid a glow upon the face of Mrs. Scanlon.

"What's the trouble, Harry?" she asked, as she heard his step.

"Wait a minute," he said. "And Woodstock, you wait too, will you? I want a little advice before you go. Rosemary, come here!"

The girl came, hurrying. She wore boots, there were clumsy gauntlets on her gloves, and she swung both hand and foot in walking like a true mountaineer, yet nothing could cloud her grace. And still, at a little distance, she looked much taller than the fact.

"Come inside," said Scanlon.

The women passed into the house. Scanlon waited for Woodstock, who squinted into the semi-darkness of the place with an unpleasant sense of entering a trap. However, he could not shy at a shadow. He passed inside the waiting gesture of Scanlon and went into the room.

V

Theodora Scanlon went back into the deeper gloom at the end of this dining room-kitchen, and stood by a table with her knitting gathered up under one arm. "We ought to stay outside to talk, particularly if there's trouble," she said. "The sunlight is beautiful now."

She touched her face, on which it had been falling. It seemed to Woodstock that some of the gold remained glowing upon her. Rosemary had gone to the stove, where she stirred a big iron soup pot that was forward over the fire. The smell of cookery had soaked through the air.

"It's this way," said Scanlon, after waiting a moment to gather his thoughts. The girl turned from the stove and faced him. She was directly facing the light that streamed through the doorway, so that it poured over her rough horsehide boots and cast a deep reflection from the floor over her entire body. "It's this way. Yesterday…last night Woodstock saw your Uncle Joe, Rosemary. He gave Woodstock a bit of paper in a shotgun shell just before five riders came up and murdered him. They chased Woodstock when they didn't find what they wanted on Joe. Woodstock brought the written message to us in spite of the way they hunted him."

Here Scanlon paused. Neither of the women said a word. The girl grew a little taller, that was all.

"We've always talked things over," went on Scanlon, "so we have to talk this over. The message is gibberish, as far as I can make out. It says this: 'Walsh and Porcupine on line and Oliver and Gray at the flow find a big stack work one-third down.'" He refolded the paper, more carefully, because his thoughts were on other things, and added: "The five men who killed Joe were probably Jim Waley and some of his gang. Suppose they had some right to this bit of scribbling…or thought that they had. Suppose that Joe stole it away from them. Suppose they killed him because of that. We know that they hunted Woodstock afterwards, and it must have been for that reason. Well, what Waley starts for, he generally finds. He's probably feeling his way through the mountains on the trail that Woodstock left behind him. Now, then, there's two things that we can do. We can try to fight Waley…if he's the murderer…or else we can admit that he's stronger than we are and give up what he's hunting for. That would save our scalps, and it would save Perry Woodstock here, who doesn't deserve to have any trouble out of it. That's the problem. I want you two to think it over before Woodstock goes."

He laid the folded bit of paper on the edge of the table. A silence began and marched deeper and deeper into the mind of Woodstock. He turned his head nervously and looked from the shadows towards the west, where the sun was out of sight and color was beginning.

Then the girl said: "Uncle Joe died trying to bring that string of words to you, Father. It may not seem to mean anything, but it *must* mean something. It means a good deal, or Jim Waley would not murder one of his best men on account of it. And if Joe died to give it to us, we're cowards and worthless if we don't try to take advantage of the first and only thing he ever did for us. He always said that one day he'd try to make a return to you, Father, for all you've done for him and all your disappointment in him. He's trying to make that return now. He's trying to wash his hands clean, and we've got to help him do it!"

There was not a word of sorrow about the death of her uncle. Her voice remained so perfectly steady that Woodstock began to peer hard at her. He could scarcely believe it when he saw bright drops issuing from her eyes, and running down her face.

"Where does he lie, Harry?" asked the wife and mother.

"He lies in the sheriff's hands, now, most likely," said Scanlon. "What's your word on it, Theo?"

"Rosemary has said all I could say," she answered.

"I might have known that my women would see it that way," muttered Scanlon. "Now, Woodstock, you tell us what it means to you, and how we can help you, the way you've tried to help us? And if you have any advice, I'm a man that's always glad to hear it!"

Said Woodstock: "I advise you to stop talking this way. You're wondering what you can do to finish out the thing that Joe Scanlon began. But before you've gone ten steps in that direction, Jim Waley, if he's the man behind, will eat up the lot of you. I know some of the things that Black Jim has done!"

"So do I," nodded Harry Scanlon. "I tried to get my brother out of Waley's gang, and I know all about what Waley can do. Rosemary…Theo…you've heard what Woodstock says? And he's a brave man, at that. He'd give up, if he were in our boots."

The answer of the girl came instantly, indignantly. "He wouldn't if he were in our boots. He's only trying to keep us out of bad trouble. That's all!"

"Trouble," said the quiet voice of Theodora Scanlon. "I knew he brought it with him!"

"Stick up your hands, all of you," said a man at the doorway. "All of you…!"

Swift as a bird pecks a fallen grain, so Rosemary Scanlon leaned and snatched the little fold of paper from the table, and thrust it at the big iron soup pot on the stove. From the corner of his eye, Woodstock saw this, and the flicker of fire shadows that danced on the ceiling above the uncovered flames in the stove. In the meantime he, like Harry Scanlon, was lifting his arms and turning towards the doorway.

Black Jim Waley was there. Two faces like that could not be, so long, so yellow, so filled with timeless evil that the man seemed neither young nor old. The black hat was on his head and the black scarf wound about his throat, seeming to cut his head off at the chin. He carried a double-barreled shotgun, sawed off short. The big muzzles covered both the men in the cabin.

It was still easier to see the man at Waley's side, for his face glistened as though it were wet. It was a shapeless white blur with a pair of black eyes dropped into the mask. That was Vicente, of course. At the sight of the pair, Woodstock grinned like a dead man. He was reaching well for the ceiling. So was Harry Scanlon.

The voice of Theodora Scanlon said quietly: "Now it's come! What is it, Harry?"

"It's Black Jim Waley, ma'am," said the man with the yellow face. "At your service! You, there…bring me that paper. Don't think that I'm a whit easier on the women. I'd as soon drill you as your pa. Bring that thing here to me and, when I talk, you jump to it!"

"It's right here over the fire in the stove, Black Jim," said the girl. "If you shoot me, the bullet won't keep me from dropping it into the flame. And there's enough heat to eat it and swallow it whole before you could snatch it out. Do you see the shine of the fire on my hand?"

"Scanlon," said Waley, "tell the rattle-headed fool to bring that to me! You know that I mean what I say."

The calm, deep voice of Scanlon answered: "Rosemary, do what you think best. I never think fast enough when a pinch comes."

At that, out of the straining throat of Woodstock burst a cry. "For God's sake, give him what he wants!"

His voice shook; his whole body was shaking. The yellow face and the white were double forms of death itself that stared at him.

"The kid talks sense," said the horrible face of Vicente. Only when he spoke could one see where his mouth was in that mass of scar-tissue.

"You!" thundered Black Jim. "Bring it here to me. Western chivalry…is that what you're banking on, you fool?"

"You're more afraid of the fire eating the paper," said the girl, "than I'm afraid of you. You won't shoot. You're shaking in your boots now, and I know it!"

Black Jim put a long leg into the room. He wore boots of beautiful, shining red leather, with his trousers stuffed into the tops of them. Men said that it was because he wanted the world to know that he walked in blood.

"Tell the damned brat to bring it here, Scanlon, or I'll mop the head off your shoulders. Speak to her," he commanded.

"Speak to her!" said the shaking voice of Perry Woodstock.

The calm tones of Harry Scanlon answered: "Rosemary, dear, I guess you know what's best to do."

There was a muttering snarl. It was exactly like the whining voice of a bull terrier. It came from the shapeless face of Vicente, the Mexican.

Black Jim seemed speechless, and it was Mrs. Scanlon who said: "Harry, are you helpless?"

"Ay, Theo," he answered. "It looks that way. They've got the guns on us."

"Then, if we have any hold on them, in turn we must bargain, Harry."

"Bargains be damned!" yelled Black Jim. "If you think...."

Here something stopped him. It must have been something about the girl, for his glance was going straight past Woodstock towards the place where she stood.

"Look out," said Vicente, in a half secret aside.

"Hold on...you there!" exclaimed Black Jim. "You're singeing the edge of the paper now, you half-wit."

He withdrew the foot that had entered the cabin. The gray mare, as though attracted by these brawling voices, came within the range of Woodstock's view, pricking her ears, stomping with one forefoot raised, like a dog pointing.

"You can give us time," said the girl. She had the calm of her father. To Woodstock there was something terrible in her voice. It was that of one who puts no value on life compared with the brightness of a clean soul. A fantastic simplicity breathed from her, and Perry Woodstock for the first time guessed what martyrs may be made of.

"Time for what?" demanded Black Jim. "You can see that we've got you. D'you think that I'll back down now?"

"I don't know what you'll do. We'll still be in your power if you're not standing there in the doorway with your guns. You could fire the grass and burn us out, if you wanted to. But we have to have time to talk this over. We can't make up our minds all in an instant."

"Rosemary," broke in the voice of the mother, "are you sure that you have a right to what you hold? Are you sure that it doesn't belong to...him?" She made a slight pause before the last word, laid a slight emphasis on it.

"It was stole from me," declared Black Jim. "And the man that stole it is...well, it's mine. And I'll have it."

"If it's yours, you know what it means?" asked the girl.

"Of course, I know what it means."

"If it's yours, you know what it means, and you can remember the words on it. There aren't many of them. If it ever belonged to you, you know all about it."

"I'm no long hand at remembering," said Black Jim. "Matter of fact...."

Her voice cut straight through his and stopped him. "I don't believe you. I think you lie. If ever you'd had it, it would be printed in your brain now, every word of it."

"There's a way of stopping your tongue," said Black Jim. "There's a way of taking tongues out through the throat!"

"We want half an hour...alone," said the girl. "Shall we have it?"

"No!" shouted Waley, and his face went insane.

Woodstock groaned. His hip was against the table, and he had to support himself there. He could see the quivering of the trigger finger of Waley, wrapped over the triggers of the heavy gun.

"Get away from the house," said the unmoved voice of the girl. "I'll count to ten, and then you'll be away from that door or else this bit of paper will burn. We ask for half an hour. It isn't much. At the end of that time, we'll let you know whether we fight it out or else surrender."

Waley looked at Scanlon hard. He looked a brief time, with more satisfaction, at the frozen face of Woodstock. Then he said: "Well, I don't know that it matters. Half an hour later will serve as well, for us. All I know is that it's a conundrum that none of you can ever work out. You can have your half hour. Use it to try to figure out what the paper says. You haven't the key, and I have. ¡*Adios, amigos*!"

He turned and walked from the door; Vicente silently followed him.

VI

Woodstock reached for a chair, slumped into it, and covered his face with his hands. He was still shaking. Through his fingers he was aware of the blood-red sunset that filled the doorway. All of his own blood and strength had gone into it, it seemed. Then there was a trickle of shame that began to fall into the cavern that had been his heart. The cold of it rose in him, and rose. It was more icy than the fear.

"Now, Rosemary," said the voice of the mother, "we have only a half hour. Your wits are better than ours. You will have to tell us what to do, my dear."

"Ay, Rosemary," said the father. "The way you lead us will be the best way. It always is. I thought we were all dead just now, but you've given us a moment for breathing at the least."

A hand touched the shoulder of Perry Woodstock. He looked suddenly up into the face of the girl. There was neither disgust nor pity in it, but only an open friendliness.

"I was a yellow dog. I howled!" groaned Woodstock.

"I've heard a doctor say," answered the girl, "that a lot of people who are afraid before the operation are the bravest when they're under the knife. Besides, Vicente and Black Jim are like things that come out of a grave. They're too horrible to be real. It was like a nightmare, and you weren't prepared for it."

There suddenly was no world whose opinion could shame him, for the only audience that mattered was Rosemary Scanlon.

"Why should the young man have to stay in the trap with us?" asked Mrs. Scanlon.

Woodstock got suddenly to his feet. "I've been sick," he said, "but now I can try to be a man again. I brought the trouble to you, and now I'll try to help you through it."

Big Harry Scanlon pointed a hand at him. "You're not shamed, boy," he said. "And you're not beaten. Anybody can have the shakes. Let's put our heads together."

All four of them drew close. The sunset glowed faintly through the door and showed their faces and their gestures. All the rest of the room was darkness, and the stove gave out a humming sound behind them.

"Joe died to bring us this," said the girl, holding out the torn fragment of paper. "That's the beginning. And Perry Woodstock went through the danger of dying to get it to us. This is a fight, and it's wrong to give up a fight before we're beaten."

"We're beat now," answered the father. "There's five of them. We're in their hands. They could burn us out. They could do anything they want with us."

The blind wife and mother had come out of the darkness with her hands stretched before her to feel the way, but it was a though she were bringing gifts. She said: "After trouble comes, Harry, it has to be met and, wherever we owe a duty, it has to be paid."

"Well, we can all die like pigs in a pen, if that's what you call duty," answered Harry Scanlon, half angrily. "Rosemary...she can die with us!"

He turned to her and would have put an arm around her, but she stopped his hand. "I'm not a girl or something that's to be pitied. I'm just one more person in the trap that holds all of us."

A shadow fell over them from the door. It was the gray mare who now stood there, looking into the darkness to find her master. Perry Woodstock stared back at her.

"I've got an idea," he said.

"Go on, boy," urged the deep, gentle voice of Scanlon, the laborer.

"He ought to be free from us. This is not his fight," said Theodora Scanlon.

But the girl said: "He's one of us, because he wants to be."

That gave Woodstock strength to say: "There's the gray mare, waiting. Suppose she could be used?"

"Shall we ask her advice, too?" suggested Scanlon harshly.

"Hush, my dear," said the blind woman, and with a sure touch she found his hand.

Woodstock leaned forward until they could see his face clearly, the pallor and the strain of it. He looked like a man charging in a lost cause and as a last hope. "Suppose that one of us jumped on the horse and raced for the trees," he said, barely whispering the words.

"He'd be shot down," snapped Scanlon. "Those fellows are marksmen, and Black Jim doesn't know how to miss."

"Suppose," insisted Woodstock, "that they *did* miss. It's the worst light in the world. It's twilight and sunset and moonlight all mixed together. Suppose that they missed and one of us got free…wouldn't they feel sure that that one was carrying away the thing that they want? Wouldn't they follow? Would they dare to let one person go? No, they'd all follow."

He stood up straight, having spoken, and gripped his hands hard together behind his back, as though he hoped to crush the trembling out of his body, the uncertainty out of his brain. This idea of his was taking hold on their minds.

Scanlon suddenly said: "Maybe it could be done. Maybe it's the only way. We've got to fight, somehow, and I don't see anything else to do. Because suppose that we give them that bit of paper, they know just the same that we've learned what's written on it, and they couldn't give us freedom till they've collected whatever is to be gained. But if one of us shook loose, they'd all feel that their information was about to be scattered over the world. They'd have to chase!" He added: "I'll take the chance. It's my duty to take it."

"You're too heavy," said his daughter. "But I can ride well. And I'm a lot the lightest. I'll take her! I'll ride to get help...."

"Wait a minute," breathed Woodstock. He pumped out the words, one by one. That was what he had known from the first, that if his idea was accepted, he was the only one who could perform the task. "None of you could ride the mare. She bucks like a fiend unless you know her. I'll take her. I'll take the paper along with me, too."

"We can't let him go," said the blind woman. "It's only duty that makes him do it, and what duty does he owe to us?"

"I brought you trouble," answered Woodstock. "Now I'll try to take it away. That's right enough."

"You can't go, boy. I wouldn't let you!" exclaimed Harry Scanlon. "I know my job when I see it...."

"He's going to go," Rosemary said. "You can't stop him. He wants to go through the fire. *I* know how he feels."

Woodstock swallowed hard. He pushed one hand through his tousled hair. He felt for his gun and gripped it hard. The feel of it was reassuring. Then he managed to say: "So long, everybody." He went on, inanely: "I'm glad I met all of you."

"Stop him, Harry! You can't let him go!" cried the wife.

"No, he can't go for us. I won't let him go!" The heavy step of Scanlon came up behind Woodstock, as the latter stood at the door. Scanlon paused. He was saying: "Don't stop me, Rosemary. He'll be gone in an instant if I don't stop him."

"You can't stop a man from being himself," said the girl. "If I were he, I'd want to do the same thing, if there were enough heart in me!"

That was what Woodstock heard as he gathered the reins on the withers of the mare and stared about the clearing of the farm. It had seemed a very small place, when he came to it, but it seemed dangerous miles to the secure shadows of the trees. Five men were not enough to scatter about over such a distance and yet, every time he picked a goal and a harborage, he was certain that the point would be guarded by a rifleman. It seemed as though Black Jim Waley— who could not miss—would certainly be at each of those spots. Where would they be? Well, they would be in the trees on either side, as close as possible to the house. Suppose, then, that he rushed the

mare straight down the length of the farm instead of galloping for
the nearest cover?

"Let him be, Father."

"Now, Rosemary…out of my way."

Woodstock heard that behind him, and then made one step outside the door, flinging himself into the saddle. The suddenness of
the move made the mare whirl. The drive of his heels into her flanks
sent her wildly scampering. But she had her head, and as she ran
she bucked, pitching here and there as a boat might pitch in a chopping cross current. She was not three strides from the cabin door
before voices yelled out of the trees. Rifles exploded. The noises hammered at his very ears. He thought that he could hear men breathing
close by, running out at him from the tree-shadows, moving faster
than the mare, overtaking her.

One red cloud hung in the west like a flag that has flapped itself to sere rags at the edge. The tree tops glistened. There was a
soft glow on the pasture—the wheat field was a dull yellow mist. And
still the mare bucked, while he cursed her, prayed to her, gasping,
biting off his words. Still she jerked him here and there, head down,
bounding like a cat at play.

The bullets were all about him. Each sang one note of a song,
a brief note. But not one of those fierce voices struck into his body.
Then he realized that the wild plunging of the mare was making
those sure riflemen miss Molly, all unawares, was playing his hand
for him!

His throat opened; his heart opened; he yelled like an Indian,
and the cry suddenly straightened out the mare in a blinding streak
of speed. Back there they would be watching from the dark doorway
of the house. Hope would be in them, also. Before him, the trees
rose higher, the wind of the gallop pulled at his hair, and whispered
at his ear. Then the darkness of the woods received him as water re-
ceives a diver from a height.

They were slipping, sliding down a steep slope that was sheathed
in thick coatings of pine needles. They made only a rushing sound
over which he heard voices shouting, and the snorting of horses, and
after that the rapid beating of hoofs.

A sort of cold triumph of fear came over him. He pulled up the
mare to a walk and moved to the left at right angles to his first course.
The noise of the pursuit seemed to rush straight at him.

VII

To flee headlong through the sunset gloom of the woods was dangerous. Also the noise he made would lead them after him, as though he carried a light. Yet the mare in walking made no sound whatever and, though the river of shouting and hoofbeats seemed to flow straight at him, he would not hurry her. He merely turned in the saddle with his revolver poised. That was how he heard the charge pass behind him, scattering through the woods. He saw only one rider dimly flickering for an instant, among the crowding trunks. That was all.

He let the mare come to a dancing trot, for she was full of excitement. The forest began to move more rapidly about him as he took the same way that he had come up the side of Grizzly Peak. Slipping a hand into his pocket, he touched the crisp bit of paper on which the conundrum was written. How far would they follow him? Or would they turn back to resume their siege of the cottage?

The moon, standing higher, showed him the way clearly enough. The short summer night passed rapidly as he wound through that rough gorge and came at last to the lake set among the aspens. He had intended to ride straight on over the trail that he had taken when coming into the mountains and, descending to the desert beyond, he could find fighting men in the town of San Lorenz and guide them back to Grizzly Peak to disperse whatever danger hung over the cabin of Harry Scanlon. But now that he was at the lake among the aspens, he remembered old Dave Hixon and went straight to the former camp of the mountaineer.

Hixon had not moved. The same rag of canvas was giving him shelter in the same place beside the great column of the fallen pine tree. The hobbled mule stood up and cocked its ears towards the intruders. Then it stretched forth its starved neck, opened its mouth, closed its eyes against the moonlight, and made the hollow roar with its bray. Old Dave Hixon came out from under his little tent and stood erect, at once wide awake and unafraid.

"Sorry to disturb you up like this," said Perry Woodstock. "I didn't think that the mule would make such a racket."

"It didn't scare me," answered Hixon. "Old men are like skunks. Nothin' wants to bother us. We walk through the woods and everybody gives us room, because an old gent like me is likely to ask for a hand-out, and a skunk has things about it that are just as mean. How are things with you, son?"

"Well enough," answered Woodstock. "How does it go with you?"

Hixon pointed towards the fallen tree. "Along about sixteen twenty," he said, "there was a whale of a fire that chewed at one side of the tree, pretty bad and must of nigh killed it. But it lived through and put on bigger rings than ever afterwards. And around sixteen eighty-five, another tree nearby must have fallen, and it rammed the stubs of a coupla broken arms into my friend, yonder, but the old pine, it just throwed a bed of resin around the chunks of woods that had been whanged into it, and it went on growing just the same! You hit the back trail out of these mountains pretty fast, son, didn't you? Ain't the lay of the land to your liking? Wait till I stew some coffee for you. You look kind of fagged."

He gathered some dead embers, lighted some shreds of barks, and presently had a small fire burning. Woodstock looked rather anxiously among the trees, for such men as hunted him now would notice the smallest sign.

Then he said: "I was stopped by a conundrum."

"What's that?" asked the other.

"Sort of a puzzle in words. A riddle. It goes like this. 'Walsh and Porcupine on line and Oliver and Gray at the flow....' Just nonsense, eh?"

"Walsh and Porcupine on line, eh? And Oliver and Gray?" said the man of the mountains, pausing as he measured out coffee from a bag. "Walsh and Porcupine...those would be Hurdle and Thompson."

A door of hope opened in the mind of Perry Woodstock. He stared at that old face, lighted above by the white of the moonshine and from below by the yellow sheen of the fire. "Hurdle and Thompson?" he echoed. "Hurdle and Thompson? What does that mean?"

"They've changed the names of mountains a whole lot, lately," pursued the old man. "Hurdle Mountain, that used to be called Mount Walsh, from a gent called Walsh that worked a streak of pay dirt on the side of it in the old days, thirty, forty years ago. And

Thompson Peak was called the Porcupine, about the same time. I dunno why. Porcupine ain't a very good name for a mountain, unless it bristles a good deal."

"Hurdle Mountain and Thompson Peak, then! Where are they?"

"Well, wait a minute. Lemme get my bearings. Look yonder. There's old Hurdle. That one with the white top and the two heads, and the summit strung in between the two points like a clothes line hitched up kind of loose. That's Hurdle Mountain. You can't see Thompson from here, but it ain't that far. What's them other names?"

"Oliver and Gray," said Woodstock, beginning to breathe quickly. "Oliver and Gray...."

"That would be Mount Promise and Eagle Mountain, or Eagle Peak some call it, and a fine name for a mountain that is, too! Promise ain't a bad name for a mountain, neither. There's sense in names like that. But old Tom Oliver that got a mountain named after him was a doggone trader that got furs for whiskey. God rot him, he was a mean man, I'm here to tell you!"

Woodstock got out the bit of paper and, with a stub of a pencil, made the necessary substitutions of names. The script then read: "Hurdle and Thompson on line and Promise and Eagle." Sense came instantly from nonsense. If they were mountains, one was to find the point where Hurdle and Thompson mountains were on a line— a point at which Mount Promise and Eagle Peak were also on a line. After reaching that point, there was a flow, and a stack that was to be worked one-third down. Whatever these words might mean, there was now a beginning for him to work on.

He fell into a wide-eyed dream in which he saw five men riding on his trail, and in the distance the shoulder of Grizzly Peak, and the cottage of Harry Scanlon. He took a cup of coffee from Hixon and was regardless of the heat that scalded his throat. For his mind was on fire. He felt that he had placed his foot on the first rung of an important ladder. He could hardly wait to swallow the coffee. Fatigue was no longer in him. He rose to go.

"I've got to hurry on," he said. "You chart those mountains on the back of this scrap of paper, will you?"

It was easily done by Dave Hixon. He marked down Hurdle Mountain and spotted in the others one by one, with short, sharp descriptions that held them in the mental eye of Woodstock. Then they parted. It was already the gray of the early dawn when Perry Woodstock turned the mare westward up the steep side of the hollow where the Douglas spruce met the yellow pines that covered the northern slope, and in the pink of the dawn he had come to a pass that pointed as straight as a leveled gun barrel towards the double top of Hurdle Mountain. There he stopped, at a place where he found the black, round scar of a newly-built campfire, with a heap of pine boughs still fresh and green beside it. Where another man had slept in comfort, he could sleep in turn, and no matter how exposed the position, no matter who might be following him, he determined to have rest. For, after all, the five had ridden long and hard after Joe Scanlon before they took up his own trail. He had against them at least the advantage of half a night's sleep, and perhaps they had paused long before to rest.

He had hardly stretched himself on that fragrant bed before oblivion washed over him in a black wave. It was noon when he wakened with a cloud over his brain, dry thirst in his throat, and above all a ravenous hunger that soon made him forget his other troubles. He had picked up the saddle to put it again on the back of the gray mare when, shuffling through the grass towards her, his foot turned over a rusted axe-head with half its hickory haft remaining lodged in the steel. It seemed to him luck, a stroke of distinct good fortune that placed in his hands a tool without which few men care to travel through a wooded country. When Molly was saddled and bridled, he lashed the axe behind the cantle, half smiling at his folly in doing so.

He rode on now with hunger making him as keen as a wolf's tooth, and found the pass opening out onto a high plateau from which he could spot down every one of the four mountains that Hixon had named and described for him. Porcupine Mountain could have been called "The Pig" as well, for the summit of it was like a pig's head thrusting up at the sky, with fat jowls half clothed in a bristling forest. He rode, now, to get the desired points in line— "Walsh and Porcupine on line...."

That ride took him back on the plateau to a region of mingled darkness and shine that turned out to be the broad, black sweep of a lava flow. He was already well inside the borders of it, sometimes with black cinder dust under hoof, and sometimes the polished gleam of basalt or glass, sometimes things that looked like half melted boulders, and sometimes huge heaps of clinkers, as it were, when he remembered the last words of the conundrum.

"*At the flow find a big stack, work one-third down.*" At the lava flow, find a big stack, such as one of these clinker-like heaps of melted stone refuse, and work it one-third down in order to find whatever the secret might be. The thought struck home in his mind as clearly as ever a bell-hammer struck home on bell-metal. He forgot the mere hunger for food.

In the meantime he was drawing Hurdle Mountain and Thompson Mountain to a line. When he had established that, Mount Promise and Eagle Peak were still far from lining up. He had to ride on another full mile. The gray mare was beginning to cough from the effect of the whirling wreaths of lava dust before, riding with his head turned back, he was able to check the mare. Now the two lines, cutting across the four mountains, met at a point. He had only to find the big stack. Facing to the front, he saw it rising before him—a gloomy bristling mass at least fifty feet high, looking as though it had been freshly cast out from the fire room of some enormous steamer.

VIII

Beyond any question this was the "big stack" and at first glance the thing seemed an enormous heap of cinders which, in a day or so, one could heave right and left and actually "work one-third down." He had hardly begun to climb, however, when he saw that the entire mass was really welded together. It was a sort of tufa, or stone that had been blown into a porous state when the volcanic eruptions had occurred how many hundreds of thousands of years before? Big knobs and lumps as large as a man could surround with his joined arms projected from the mass. Sometimes he felt the friable stuff crumbling a little under his feet. Once or twice he actually disengaged small fragments that went rattling down to the ground, one of them bounding under the very nose of the mare. She danced away, whinnying anxiously to her master. She even put her forehoofs on the steep slope as though she wanted to climb after him; and he felt that the black desolation around her was enough to make her yearn for any companionship.

Now that he stood on the top he could scan a great part of the blackness of the flow. Everywhere it was the same, night-dark dust and cinders, or else shining patches of melted rock as brilliant as glass and glaring the sun's reflected light back at him. It was a relief to glance from the lava flow to the dark green of the forests that covered the mountains around the plateau. He wondered what one of them had once been a crater, or what side of a peak had opened to let out the gush of lava, but there was nothing that appeared truncated towards the top except the wide crest of Hurdle Mountain, and that seemed too far away.

The eruption had occurred so long ago that some of the lava had rotted away with time and now there were various small growths that had taken a rooting on the rock, most of them shrubs that would have been at home on the desert, mere puffs and tawny dust clouds of foliage that could defy long drought. Chiefly, from that low summit, he scanned the pass through which he had ridden towards Hurdle Mountain, half expecting to see five horsemen riding over the lip of it, small as ants with the distance. But he saw nothing, not a living thing.

So he descended, as nearly as he could judge, a third of the way from the top and made the circle of the heap. It was a hard task, for there were a thousand crevices. Some were shallow. In some, the length of his arm and the revolver added to it could not find bottom. In any one of these might be the thing he sought, for which one man already had died, and for which others were ready to imperil their lives. He himself, as he searched, felt that guns must be trained upon him, and that he was no more than the fishhawk which catches the prey and renders it again to the frigate bird that sails in the higher air with a sharper beak and more cruel talons. It was very hot, but he began to sweat with anxious fear as much as with the warmth.

He completed his first circle of the mound and found nothing. He began to guess that he would have to search out one of the shrubs which he had seen and use a branch of it as a probing tool among the small-mouthed caverns. But he started again around the steep wall of the "stack," prying with eye and hand. A crisp, dry rattling with a certain deadly resonance about it that was familiar to him made him start back from one hole. He had probed it, and the muzzle of his revolver had touched something soft, yielding. Now, out of the entrance to the hole glided a five foot diamondback. It coiled, almost in striking distance, its terrible flat head couched with the supple curves of the neck ready behind it. Like green jewels were the eyes. Woodstock fired at them, and the twisting, bleeding thing fell in tangle after tangle down the side of the lava to the level below. There it still writhed as Woodstock, when his shuddering ended, thrust the gun cautiously into the hole again.

Where one snake has found a shelter, there may be others of its kind. Scaly horrors wriggled over his back and neck when the gun's muzzle touched again on something soft, yielding. He leaped away, staggered, almost fell in his turn from the slope. But this time nothing issued from the hole. Perhaps the second snake was waiting there. Perhaps it had coiled and even now the head was ready to strike. But a rattler cannot feel alarm without giving out its natural signal of danger and there had been no sound from the hole after the issuance of the first snake. There are tales that owls will sometimes live with snakes....

He lighted a match, stretched in his hand a little way, and peered. What he saw was something that looked like cloth. He poked it with the gun again. It was a sort of rough canvas or tarpaulin, so far as he could make out. He reached in, touched the thing with his fingers and half in horror, as when one grasps an unclean monstrosity, he jerked it forth from the hole.

It was a mere tarpaulin wrapping, worn and battered, but still securely tied. He cut the wrapping open. Within was a second covering of canvas and, within this, three or four sheets of oiled silk, perfectly sound and strong. As he slashed that open, his mouth was working, and his nostrils. His face was like that of a man resolved on a murder. It might have been a throat that he was cutting, when he pulled the silken wrapping wide and looked down at some flat, small bundles wrapped in paper.

He took one out. The size and shape of it were slightly suggestive. He tore open the end of the wrappings, and found under his eyes a thickly compacted sheaf of greenbacks! He flicked a corner of them. They were all fifties! How many? Twenty—forty—two hundred of them in that one sheaf, and there were other packages of the same size.

No wonder that Joe Scanlon had been willing to die for this thing. No wonder that Black Jim Waley was so hungry on the trail. He would do more murders than one for such a prize. Even the girl yonder in the cabin, even Rosemary, that blue and golden beauty, that brave and gentle soul, might have the life crushed from her, if Waley thought the killing would bring him any closer to the goal. And at the same instant that hysterical joy opened the heart of Woodstock, fear closed his throat and froze his tongue against the roof of his mouth.

He turned with cold sweat running on his face and scanned the surroundings. Even the mountains seemed to be spies that watched his actions, that read the denominations of the bills. But there were no men in sight; there were no leveled rifles shining at him.

He snatched the remaining nine bundles from the silken lining of the tarpaulin, and then dropped the lot as though they burned his hands, for underneath them, unwrapped, was a little pool of light, yellow, green, red, and stainlessly bright crystal. He scooped them up in both hands as if he were about to drink. He began to laugh, soundlessly. Joy made his eyes wander from side to side. Topaz, emerald, pearl, ruby, diamond, they burned without heat; they shone with lights that danced as fast as the tremor of his hands. Even huddled in a heap, they were so large that they could be picked out, one by one. Any one of them seemed of more worth than all the greenbacks in all the paper packages.

He had not taken all the contents in the hollow of the wrappings. When he looked down again, he saw many more gems, and also the grim long body of a revolver. He took out his wallet, poured the jewels into it, stuffed the packages of greenbacks into his pockets, and then lifted the gun. It seemed to say, with a grave and somber voice: "All of this is mine!" It was the dragon on watch over the hoard, but the life was frozen out of it.

It was an old-fashioned gun, but it was still capable of business, that was plain. It was an old single-action Colt. Perry Woodstock noted at once that the sights were filed away and the trigger was gone. Perhaps that gun had belonged to the man who wrote on the paper, in ink now time-faded: Walsh and Porcupine on line and Oliver and Gray at the flow find a big stack work one-third down.

After one knew the key to the riddle, the thing was all too palpable. It seemed a madness that the man had ever written such words. Surely not to imprint the scene on his own memory. Woodstock, in one glance around, burned the picture forever deeply in his own mind. How had the money been gathered together? What dead hands had once counted it with a fondly lingering touch? What dead fingers and what lifeless throats had worn the jewels? Dead, it seemed, they certainly must be. The revolver said that in clear words.

He who had used it, long ago, had known how to fan a revolver, how to turn the small weapon into an automatic from which a stream of death might spring. Perry Woodstock himself had learned that art in his boyhood and practiced it ever since. He had never used it on a human being. He hardly expected that he ever would be called upon to use it, but there was a fascination in working a gun as the great masters of the old time had worked them, as this old Colt had been used surely. He turned it curiously in his hand and on the butt, filed small and close together, he found eleven little notches worked into the steel. Eleven notches! Eleven dead men!

The money stuffed into Woodstock's pockets, those jewels that made the great, hard lump just over his heart so that he was aware of its beating, had been paid for with eleven lives, at least. And in that count, there was no reckoning made of Joe Scanlon. There was no reckoning made of what might happen in the future, for there was no cloud of darkness gathered as yet over the eyes of Black Jim Waley.

He wadded the tarpaulin together, twisted it hard, and thrust it back into the hole from which it had come. Then, with guilty, hurrying steps, he retreated down the side of the "stack." He felt now a wild desire to get rapidly away from this place and from these watching mountains, away to some great city where money has more meaning, and the law is nearer at hand for a shelter. But then he remembered the girl as he swung into the saddle. If this treasure were the key that opened the door of the future, two people must pass through it, and not one.

IX

From the high plateau Woodstock could see clearly the outline of Grizzly Peak, looking wonderfully near. Towards it, above timberline and between two lower mountains, opened a pass, and Woodstock made straight for this. In not many hours, he promised himself, he would again be at the cabin of Harry Scanlon, and he would sweep all the family away with him on an avalanche of prosperity. There was enough for all. If he had brought them trouble, he now would bring them an immense reward. There was danger in making that return because, of course, Black Jim Waley might keep lookouts on the ground, but he felt it far more highly probable that Waley would now be feeling his way through the mountains, trying to get on the trail of Woodstock, letting the Scanlons go.

That was why Perry Woodstock laughed and sang so often as he journeyed up the slope through the pines and towards the pass that pointed on towards Grizzly Peak. When he reached timberline, the blue lake of the sky was without a single ripple of wind, only dark edgings of cloud were massed along the northwestern horizon high enough to furnish a perfect foil for the white of the snow summits. From this part of timberline, however, snow had melted away and left the trees and shrubs as the storms had tormented them into wild shapes. Those which managed to stand up a good height had branched only towards the southeast. They looked very like the feather headdresses of the Indians. But most of the trees never had managed to raise their heads. Time went by them slowly. There were little limber pines of fifty years growth but not more than a foot in height. He saw an Englemann spruce drawn back along the ground by the torturing hands of the wind and turned into a snaky monstrosity full of twists and writhings. Trees hundreds of years old were here on their knees, as it were, or lying prone to endure the force of the storms, and they made Woodstock think of hard-fighting outposts that never can conquer but that will never give up. Among them he managed to recognize some Arctic willows, and there was the alpine fir, the black birch, the quaking aspen.

A ptarmigan in its brown summer suit flew out from a thicket, decided that there was nothing to fear, and lighted on the top of a rock twenty yards away. Woodstock rolled it over with a bullet and toasted and ate the bird at a spot a little farther on, where there was fine pasture for the gray mare. There, as he ate, Woodstock ran his eyes along the timberline as it extended for miles until it was lost in blue haze. It was drawn level as a watermark, as though the lower and duskier air had a weight and color and left its stain upon the mountainsides. Through those lower strata of atmosphere he could look into profound valleys and see distant plains and rolling lands.

He sat on a throne not unlike a king but like a tiny pigmy looking out over a vastness.

He finished the ptarmigan. It was a big bird, and a fat one. Without salt, the ravenous fire of his appetite had consumed it half raw with infinite relish, and could have enjoyed another feast of the same size. But now he stretched himself with his back against a boulder, and made and smoked a cigarette. Distances he no longer regarded, but considered instead the ebbing and flowing tide of sound about him, for the bees had come up here on the heights, climbing on strong wings, and afterwards they would blow down the wind, heavy with pollen as they labored towards their hives. For though above timberline where trees could not grow, there were flowers in streaks, in patches, brilliant bands that encircled melting heaps of snow, dapplings of color on the backs of boulders, even, and then here and there whole happy meadows of bloom. He knew a great many of their names, such as the paint brushes and the white-blooming wild buckwheat, the daisy, the purple monkshood, asters and goldenrod. He saw gentians, pinks, forget-me-nots, and the blue eyes of columbine. But there were many flowers that he could not name. He never saw them, except up here where the winter was king most of the year and in the brief summer every plant was forced to bloom suddenly and with all its might before the next wind was iced and the frost came biting at the roots.

The world seemed nothing but a varied beauty to Perry Woodstock when the gray mare came suddenly close to him, snorting, lifting her head. He knew that danger signal well enough to sit up. And over the slope, mounting like ships over the curve of the sea, he saw the heads and shoulders of three men, and then the nodding heads of their horses, and two more riders behind! They were not two hundred yards away when he gained the saddle on Molly and rode for his life.

They were coming like five devils, when he glanced back. Their horses seemed fresh in spite of the climbing they must have done and the gray mare, unused to this altitude, would not last longer that one burning sprint. He thought of the foolish ptarmigan that had sunned itself in the brightness and warmth of this happy world just before a bullet struck out its life, but he himself was a greater fool than that poor bird, for he had known that five men like five wolves were after him.

He dared not ride straight up the pass, as he had intended. It was open, easy ground, to be sure, but it was far too clear. If he began to gain in the race, those five rifles would come into play and this time they would not miss. He chose instead to drive the mare towards the northwest through a field of boulders. Looking back, he could see heads and shoulders bobbing behind him, sometimes glimpses of a whole horse and man, and he knew that the good gray mare was at least holding her own. Looking ahead, he saw that the dark clouds were blown over half the sky, blotting out the upper mountains and drowning the lower slopes in trailing shadows of rain or of snow. Golden veins of lightning showed on the forehead of that storm and thunder began to speak among the mountains. His heart began to fail him. Twice he had escaped them, but the third time would surely be fatal! There is law to chance. One number cannot always be winning.

He was sure of that when, a moment later, the storm reached him, first with some shrewd cuffs of the wind, then with a driving rain that pricked his skin like points of ice. He looked back and, through the gray pencil strokes of that downpour, he saw that they were nearer—not all five of them, but two in the lead, one a tall rider, and one a shorter, wide-shouldered man. They would be Black Jim Waley himself and that ghoulish lieutenant of his, Vicente, the 'breed.

Already the mare was beginning to labor. The wind beat straight against her. The thin mountain air was burning out her lungs. He knew that by the flare of her nostrils. Though her heart was gallant, she would have to lose. Then came a thick mist of snow. He was glad of that simply because it shortened the chances of those five marksmen behind him. But they gained still. They drew nearer. Once again he could mark their silhouettes distinctly through the smother of the storm. Five minutes more of that rate of progress would bring them up to him.

On the right he saw a gully opening, its floor slanting up at such an angle that a horse could hardly make headway there. He turned the mare towards it, and asked for the last of her strength. She gave him that with all her brave heart, but a hundred yards of that uphill running stopped her to a stagger. He flung himself to the ground. Running on, he saw through the thickening storm that the men behind him also had dismounted. They were no more than gray shadows that flickered and went out and appeared again. So he knew that he had gained a little vital distance by his last maneuver—not much, and no safe obscurity, for the eyes of hawks were behind him, straining and red with eagerness.

He thought of snatching out the treasure and dropping it, but he knew that that would never stop them. They wanted the money, but they wanted his life now almost more than the cache which he had found. He stumbled into a snowbank. It seemed to him a fatal trap. The snow clung about his legs. He floundered through it and dashed on, blind with fear.

Something thundered before him. He saw a pale thing gleaming and then lightning that jerked from the clouds to the earth revealing the face of the waterfall that filled the end of the ravine up which he had been toiling. On each side the water, in other ages, had carved out cliffs that were hand-polished, as it were. Not even a mountain sheep could have climbed them. But beside the waterfall, wet and obscured by its spray, there was a jumble of boulders that climbed up. He could not see the top. The driving clouds obscured it, but he rushed at that clumsy ladder with his last hope between his teeth.

He was drenched with freezing water in the first ten seconds. A moment later his left hand slipped from a precarious hold and he swung on one hand, looking down through coils and swirls of storm clouds at shapes that clambered beneath him, seen in one glimpse and then blanketed away from his eyes again. He swung himself up. A frenzy flowed through him. A dozen times he hung by a fingernail on the edge of his death. He was near the top when the wind struck him like a torrent of water and pushed him to the side over the wet, smooth surface of a rock, until his legs extended under the beat of the waterfall.

One hand by fortune found a crevice that enabled him to haul himself out of that danger. As he rose and stood, out of the white steam of the cloud, he saw a man climbing, lifting head and shoulders high to gain the very rock on which he stood! The lower part of that body was drowned from sight, as though in milk, but Woodstock could see that face clearly, brown as an Indian's, and now contorted with effort and savagery. One arm was bare to the elbow, with a big blue and red design tattooed on it.

Woodstock saw these things while he braced himself against an upper rock with his hands and then kicked the climber full in the face. The weight of the blow knocked the fellow backwards. His hands gripped wildly at nothing. Then the dense cloud swallowed him. His scream sprang up against the ear of Woodstock, but a stroke of thunder overwhelmed all other sound. Woodstock climbed on.

He reached the top of the waterfall, found there a rapidly rising ground, and staggered on up it. Above him the cloud turned brilliant white. It opened in spots to let him see the glorious blue sky above. He was slipping on ice and snow when he came at last out of the arms of the storm and stood in the dazzle and blaze of the upper sky.

X

He went on, always up, stamping his feet to make them bite into the ice and the crusted snow on which he was climbing. Beneath him, now, the storm had moved from horizon to horizon. Here and there tall islands of clouds rose above the lower masses, but these islands dissolved and were licked away by the billows of mist that ceaselessly beat against them. Out of this whole sea of smoke that rushed endlessly towards the southeast stood the shining tops of the mountains, all encased in gleaming ice. And above and behind all this was the dark blue of the mountain sky, now trembling with the force of the wind.

Perry Woodstock saw all of this without joy. There was in him nothing but the frantic labor of escape, for out of that sea of clouds monsters were about to emerge and fling themselves on him. He glanced ahead, squinting till his eyes were almost shut, in order not to be blinded by the glare of the ice. He saw that the slope above him became broken, here and there, where the rocks arose in sheer cliffs. In the crevices ice was still lodged, but from the southern smooth faces of the cliffs the sun had eaten away the winter casing. Up a massive tower like a chimney that was about to fall in ruins, Woodstock climbed. The first move was the hardest one. He had to take a run and hurl himself up to grasp with hands the upper edge of the first course of that titanic masonry. After that the going was easier, yet he was giddy when he gained the top, and his body shook. As he lay flat on his face, looking over the edge of this upper platform, all his muscles twitched, and the breath that had left him would never come back. There was not air enough among all these windy summits to furnish him with a single life-giving breath. And still the others had not come!

There were only four of them, now—but what a four! Thunder exploded beneath him. The rocks on which he lay quivered, the echoes pealing along the valley below, and now they came, Vicente first, Black Jim Waley behind him, and finally two more, rising from the cloudy sea. Yet Woodstock could not rise to flee again. He could not even gain his hands and knees to crawl on. He could only lie there like a trembling mass without bone of verve in it, while the four followed his sign up the slope.

Once Black Jim Waley paused, shielding his eyes with a hand, and looked straight up at the top of the rock chimney where Woodstock lay. Yet Perry Woodstock could not move enough to withdraw his head from view. If Black Jim saw his quarry, at least he gave no token of the discovery but went on again with small steps, gradually edging up the trail.

They came out onto the rocky shoulder from which the chimney sprang into height. Black Jim leaped twice to reach the top of the first block, and twice he failed. When Vicente offered to heave him up by the legs, Waley shook his head. He pointed at the height of the rock, still shaking his head to deny the possibility that any man could have climbed up this way. That instant Woodstock was able to breathe freely, to the bottom of his lungs, and the strength that had left him poured back through his body.

Still he watched them as they turned their attention to the possible ways in which the fugitive might have traveled. They examined the snow for sign; they examined the rocks that stretched nakedly down, in one place, to the solid sheeting of clouds. They looked at a stretch of ice where footprints of a man would probably make no impression. Then they conferred. Vicente alone went off over the ice, picking his way with infinite care over the slippery steep of it, but Black Jim and the other two climbed down the rocks, and once more the sea of clouds swallowed them.

Vicente was gone from sight around the shoulder of a cliff, and Woodstock sat up with a deep groan of relief. It was the third time, the narrowest call of all, but again luck had favored him. He could think now of that broken body which must be lying, smashed out of recognition, at the bottom of the waterfall. So he would be lying himself, if one of twenty chances had gone against him in that climb. He stood up, found his knees fairly strong beneath him, and scanned the world again.

He could make out nothing at first. Those peaks which he had learned to recognize by their entire outline were indistinguishable now that nothing of them appeared except the white summits, clad in ice and burnished by the sun. He remained there, resting, until the storm broke up as suddenly as it had washed across the sky. From the northwest out of which it had come, it broke into irregular masses—in half an hour the entire sea of white had withdrawn, except for certain irregular piles that dwindled in the southeast. The brown uplands appeared again. He saw the flashing arch of the very waterfall beside which he had climbed through the mist. The voice of it he thought he heard among the other sounds that trumpeted faintly to his ear through the thin mountain air. He saw timberline, the darkness of forests beneath it, the green of the lowlands beyond. He could recognize several of the mountains now, but he climbed towards the nearest high shoulder of the peak he was on in order to map out the lay of the land more exactly.

It was a steep bit of going in which he had to zigzag back and forth, carefully watching the planting of each foot. If he fell, he might roll a thousand feet, and then drop a thousand more. He was near the top of the slope when he heard a crunching footfall coming over the snow towards him. A mountain sheep, perhaps? Nothing else was apt to be moving at this altitude among the snows. But as he stepped up the last of the incline, he saw before him, looking gigantic against the sky, the wide shoulders and the scar-white face of Vicente.

In the same instant they saw one another. In the same moment their hands leaped for their guns, yet there was time for Woodstock to see the grin of joy begin on the face of Vicente, and to hear the commencement of his animal whine of content. Their guns came out in one flash, but Woodstock's foot slipped and dropped him to one knee. That, he always knew, was why the bullet of Vicente parted his tousled hair instead of splitting open his skull. His own shot struck home on metal. Vicente's gun was flung back against his face, knocking him flat and, as he sat up, stretching his hand vainly towards the Colt, he saw Perry Woodstock covering him with deliberation.

Vicente began to nod. Blood was running down his face from a cut in the forehead. "That was a good trick, *señor*," he said. "If this were not my last day, I would practice that same trick and use it in the next time I had to fight. But all good things come to an end, even Vicente." He began to laugh, which made his face more horrible than ever. He broke off to say: "Hai! Look, *señor*! I part your hair for you. I made a good crease. You won't need a comb, the next time. Only a brush will do."

"Lie on you face," said Woodstock.

"I'll take your lead in the front," answered Vicente. "Make a good steady aim. That is all that I ask. And why should I ask that of a man who is such a master with a revolver? It was a pretty trick, *señor*. By the good God, even Black Jim Waley has no better trick in his whole parcel!"

"I'm not going to shoot you, Vicente," said Woodstock.

"No?"

"No, I'm not going to murder you."

"Murder?" queried Vicente, beginning to gape. "Would you call it that? Shooting Vicente…would you call that murder?" At this, he began to laugh once more, more loudly than ever. He held his aching sides as he considered this idea—that the shooting of Vicente might be termed murder.

"Lie on your face a moment, while I fan you for more guns," said Woodstock. "I tell you again…I won't shoot you, Vicente, unless you force me to."

"Well," answered Vicente, "not even a sheriff with his oath sworn on a Bible would take Vicente alive if he had a chance to take Vicente dead. However, you are young, and young men can't help being fools."

He stretched himself face down, as he spoke, and extended his arms above his head.

"I only had the one gun with me, *señor*," he said, his voice muffled by his position. "But there is a little knife in front of my right hip, in a scabbard that fits inside the trouser leg. You are welcome to that *amigo*."

Woodstock found it. "You can stand up, Vicente," he said.

The half-breed rose. He began to grin again, his mouth twisting to the side.

"If I tie your hands," said Woodstock, "you won't be able to climb down from here. If I don't tie your hands, you'll take the first chance to shove me off a cliff, and you're likely to have chances like that on the way down."

"Ha?" grunted the 'breed. Then he added, suddenly: "Look, *señor*. If you are really such a fool, then Vicente will be a fool too, for once, and give his promise to be a prisoner and never lift a hand against you."

"I don't want your promises," answered Woodstock. "I wish to God that my bullet had split your wishbone for you. Then you wouldn't be on my hands."

"I understand that, *señor*," agreed Vicente.

"But now that you're here without a gun, I can't very well polish you off in cold blood."

"You are young," repeated Vicente, "and young men are mostly fools. Not Vicente, though. At your age, my hand was well in."

"All I can do," went on Woodstock, "is to promise you that I'm going to watch you as well as I can all the way to the bottom of the mountain. And if I see any move that looks suspicious, I'm going to drive a slug into you, Vicente. Is that fair?"

"*Señor*, if you were a judge in heaven, you could not be more fair and just," said Vicente, with another twisted grin.

"We go back this way," said Woodstock, pointing.

"You are doubling back, eh?" exclaimed Vicente.

"For the horses," said Woodstock. "We'll take a longer way around, but I think that's the safest direction. I've an idea that Waley will keep up his hunt for me a long time before he goes back to the ravine where the horses are."

"*Señor*, have I called you a fool!" exclaimed Vicente. "I was wrong. I bow to you."

And he took off his hat and bowed to the snow.

XI

It was the purpose of Perry Woodstock to take a roundabout, and therefore an easier, way about the side of the mountain in order to get back to the narrow valley in which the horses had been left, and so to climb down the floor of the ravine by an easier stairway than the Giants' Ladder that ran down beside the waterfall. He merely

asked Vicente if the wound in his forehead was painful and should
be dressed, but the half-breed pointed out that the bleeding had
stopped. So they started on the way.

"Vicente," said Woodstock, "will you talk to me?"

"Shall I tell you stories, *señor*?" asked the half-breed. His eyes
narrowed. It was impossible to tell whether he were amused or ma-
licious. The horrible slab of his face was incapable of any subtleties
of expression.

"Tell me the story of the money in my pockets, and the jewels
in the wallet."

Vicente sighed. He appeared to be thinking for a moment, before he answered: "The money and the jewels are worth more than
the story that goes with them. If you've got one half, you might as
well have the other. How do you pay me for the story, *señor*?"

"How should I?" asked Woodstock.

"Freedom is a beautiful thing."

"Should I set you free if you tell me the story?"

"You should not," said Vicente, making himself a cigarette as he
walked along. "Not unless you want robbery and murder to succeed
in the world. But although you are brave and wise, *señor*, I think you
are not so clever as you are kind."

"Why do you think that?"

"Because you were riding to come again to the cabin of Harry
Scanlon, just now. That is true?"

"Yes."

"Instead of taking what you found and using it for yourself,
you paid for it with your own danger. They have no claim on it.
And I, for one, said that you would be taking the out trail, but Black
Jim knew better. He had seen your face. He said that there was
too much kindness and honesty in the fool. You would go back to
the Harry Scanlon family to divide with them. And he was right!
That was how we happened to overtake you on the way from the
lava flow."

"Tell me something, Vicente."

"As much as I can."

"How long have you been in this business?"

"Of stealing and killing?"

"Yes."

"Since I was eighteen. I was a beautiful young man, *señor*. When a girl looked at me once, she looked again to make sure that her eyes had not lied to her and, when she gave me the second glance, I took her heart in my hand and kept it as long as I pleased. I found the prettiest Mexican girl in the mountains, one whose father had two thousand sheep and two houses, and thousands of pesos. Everything could be divided in two for the present...half for him and half for Vicente. Afterwards, it would all come to Vicente. So I decided to take her. She accepted me, this only daughter of a rich man. On the wedding day, I took my bride as far as the door of the church, and there a cursed wild cat of a she-Indian threw acid in my face. I only had time to throw my left arm in front of my eyes, and after that I was put to bed for a few weeks. They could not help the flesh burning away, but a great doctor turned the scars white instead of red."

Here Vicente laughed, without any apparent malice in his voice. He ran the flat of his hand over the flat slab of his face, and in this way wiped away the laughter.

"After that," said Vicente, "the daughter of the rich man screamed when she saw me. But if I could not have her, I thought that at least I should have her father's money, and so I took it. That was how I began, and everything followed in time until I met at last my master, the devil, whom you have seen."

"And then this business of the money? And the note that Joe Scanlon was carrying?"

"Some of us were together in a saloon, *señor*, not long ago, and into the saloon came a man who walked like a cat when a dog is in the room, and he talked from the corner of his mouth. 'Prison!' said Black Jim at once, and therefore bought drinks for this man who said that his name was Mason and that he had been thirty years in prison. Thirty years, *señor*! A life...a life!"

"Yes," agreed Woodstock. "A life, I suppose."

"Black Jim asked him what he would do with himself. Mason was a little drunk, then. He began to be excited. He threw an arm above his head and shouted: 'With three words I bring into my hands the key to a treasure. Though the key itself is a conundrum.' Joe Scanlon was there and asked him what the three words were. And he shouted back, 'Three Scott forty-eight,' and fell to laughing.

Then he had another drink and, when we looked around, Joe Scanlon was gone.

"Our oldest man came up and said to Black Jim: 'That is Mason of Partridge and Mason, the bank robbers.' I happened to hear this. And it meant something to me. Does it mean something to you, *señor*?"

"I think I've heard of them," said the boy. "They robbed a bank in St. Louis. They took a quarter of a million in bank notes from the Farmers' and Merchants' Bank, the way I remember it."

"And now that money is making your pockets fat, *señor*!" sighed the half-breed, glancing aside at Woodstock. "But after Black Jim heard the name of Mason again, and who he was, his brain began to work, and it worked very fast and sure, as it always does. He knew of Partridge. He knew that Partridge was wounded in the same gun fight during which Mason was captured. It was said that Partridge, after being hurt, took all the loot that belonged to him and Mason and cached it away, and swore that he would never touch a penny of it until his friend was free to spend it with him. He didn't live long to prove that he would be as good as his word. For the wound he had grew worse, and he died of blood-poisoning in the house of his father, who was a rancher. This was the story, and I had heard it, and so had Black Jim, but my mind did not work as fast as the chief's.

"He took us out and made us saddle our horses. There were four of us with him. And he rode hard across country with us for eight miles, until we came to the old Partridge house. Black Jim Waley and I stole into it. It was the middle of night. We found the library. We found a set of books that all looked alike, and the name of Scott was on the back of every volume. The third volume was not on the shelf with the rest. It's place was vacant, and we found the book lying on the table. Black Jim Waley opened it and, between pages forty-seven and eight, on both pages, we found a little impression made, as though a fold of paper had made it.

"Black Jim said to me, in a whisper, 'Do you see? The third volume of Scott, and page forty-eight. There was a paper here and in the paper were the directions for finding the treasure that Partridge cached away. The fool of a Mason talked on his way to the place. And Joe Scanlon, the dog, has out-thought and out-run us all! Does he think that he can hunt for himself away from the whole pack of us?'

"With that, he left the house, and I with him, and we struck out after the thief until, far ahead of us, in the moonlight, we saw a horseman jogging. When he saw us, he ran for his life. That was Joe Scanlon, *señor*, and you saw what happened on the rest of that night. That is all the story. It is simple, and the moral is in your pockets and your wallet!"

He gave one of his hearty laughs again. One would have said that he enjoyed the oddity of the tale as much as he would have enjoyed the possession of the money.

"I understand," said Woodstock. "Did you manage to trail me all the way to Harry Scanlon's house?"

"No. As soon as you took to the mountains, and we lined out in your general direction, Black Jim guessed that you were riding to Harry Scanlon's place. We all knew where that was."

"When I broke away, you all guessed that I was carrying the paper with me? That was why you followed?"

"The paper, or a copy of it. What would the difference be? We knew that we had to stop you. We tried our best. Then we found your trail and followed it. We knew the sign of the hoofs of the gray mare by that time. Yes, I think they are printed in my mind to endure forever! They are printed in my mind as though in rock. In the lava flow it was hard work. We cut ahead for sign, and found the dead snake...you had shot it?"

"Yes."

"Then we could see where you had climbed the side of it and, in a little while, we reached the place where you had left the tarpaulin. Black Jim shook out the rags of the oiled silk. And two little sparks of light dropped out of it. One was a green streak and one was red. An emerald and ruby, *señor*, that you had left behind you in your hurry, and yet up to that moment you would have been glad to work three years for the price of either stone! After that we started on your back trail and suddenly Black Jim shouts out and began to laugh, and he swore by his own sacred devil that you were riding back with the loot to reach the house of Harry Scanlon. There, *señor*, I have told you the story. You are to judge what it is worth?"

They had come across the ridge and were passing down a steep descent where the snow had been sheltered from the sweep of the wind and lay deep. It was crusted over, but the crust had worn thin, and there crumbled under their steps. Beneath them, this valley head opened on a wide prospect of river and hills and woodland far below. Just to the right was the divide they would follow, when they were a little lower, and come out at the side of the ravine up which the chase had run through the storm not long before.

"The story's interesting," said Woodstock. "I don't wish you harm, exactly...but I think you're right...I'd be a fool if I turned you lose in the world again!"

There was a rushing sound, very much like wind in leaves, but seeming to come out of the very snow over which they walked and, as Woodstock finished, Vicente broke in upon him with a yell of fear, pointing back. The snow was piled loosely enough, but perhaps it was their passage that had unsettled some of it. At any rate, straight above them and shooting fast down the slope, already throwing up a tail of snow dust high in the air, a snow slide was driving down on a widening front that threatened to engulf them.

XII

There seemed only one haven from the sweep of that danger and this was a group of rocks that thrust their heads up above the surface of the snow on the left, and the two men made for it. Down the slope, Perry Woodstock felt and heard the onrush of the avalanche. He dared not look aside at it while he fled at the heels of Vicente They were already near the rocks when a white arm shot out, picked up Vicente, and threw him into the air like a ball. Then a flying cloud overwhelmed Perry Woodstock. It turned him over, whirled him, beat him, shook him with ten thousand furious and brutal hands.

Up to the surface he shot at the end of that half second of immersion. He saw that Vicente had grappled with both arms the point of a rock, but he had not yet dragged from the sweep of the snow the lower half of his body. Looking back at Woodstock, as at a swimmer in a flood, the half-breed suddenly lunged out with both legs as far as he could kick.

The utmost reach of Woodstock fastened his grip on one heel. But on that straw he climbed. A comber of snow loomed over them, swelled high, burst and broke. If there had been any solid part to it, both Woodstock and Vicente would have been swept away, but it was merely the light froth of newly fallen snow. There was a stifling moment, and then the two men found themselves lying face downwards on the red, raw, wet clay of the mountain side.

They got to their feet, Woodstock planting himself firmly against the treacherous inclination of the mountainside, and Vicente staggering a pace or two while they watched the progress of the slide. Widening its front, gaining mass and momentum every instant, it came to a small ridge a quarter of a mile below where, it seemed likely, the sweep of it might be checked. But the head of the slide rushed over that embankment in a single step, sprang out in a mighty arch, dropped from sight, and smote the slope beneath.

The thunder of that impact boomed in the ears of the watchers before they saw the front of the avalanche shoot into view off the lower level. It was transformed now. It ploughed the snow away, cut down to the rock, gathered thousands of tons of loose earth, picked up boulders, hurled them on high, and then used them with terrible hands to beat away whole ledges and add burden to the slide. The landslip—it was a snow slide no longer—reached timberline, still widening its triangle. It swept on through the forest of the valley below. Woodstock could see trees in full plumage, and naked masts, flung into the air like black ashes that dance above a fire. A continual departing roar poured back upon his ears until the landslide reached the river at the far bend of the valley. That mass of water it dashed into a white cloud that hung long in the air, while the accumulated mass of the avalanche dammed the waterway from side to side.

A long while afterwards the distant roar of those final impacts came hurling back to the ears of the watchers. Then the echoes took up a long, diminishing tale. Still there was a ringing in the mind of Woodstock when Vicente turned to him and said, with his horrible grin: "That's like being God, *señor*. How would it be to go around the world flaying a valley here, and scalping the hair of a mountain there? Suppose there had been a little town down there in the valley...what would it be now except splinters and a little red paste mixed into the heap yonder?" He began to chuckle, slowly rubbing one shoulder, kneading the muscles.

"When I caught hold of your heel, did I almost pull your arms out of their sockets?" asked Woodstock, curious.

"Almost," nodded the half-breed.

"What made you save me?" asked Woodstock. "You could have let me go. Nothing could have helped me."

"I would have been sorry to see one man take so much good money to hell with him," said Vicente.

Woodstock grinned. "But if I'd gone with the money, you would have been free. You would not have hanged, Vicente."

"Well," said the other, "when it comes to bargaining, I know how to make a price, but I wouldn't value Vicente at a quarter of a million in hard cash and another half million or more in jewels."

"March ahead of me," said Woodstock, shortly. "Keep to the right, and go out along the divide."

So they came out over the narrow ravine at the head of which the waterfall was shaking out its flag of white silk. In the floor of the valley they could see the horses, their heads down as they grazed, but no sign of a man on guard over the small figures.

They found an easy way to the bottom of the ravine. The gray mare came like a dog, frolicking at the sight of Woodstock who put the other five horses on two long leads, fastened the ends of the rope to his borrowed saddle, and mounted. Vicente, meanwhile, sat on a rock and calmly smoked. Woodstock turned last of all to his captive.

"What am I to do now, Vicente?" he asked.

"Put Vicente quickly out of pain. That would be the best thing," said the half-breed. "Or else bring me to the next sheriff. But you will do neither of these things, because you're what Black Jim called you. You remember that I gave you a way out of the snow slide, and that is all you can think about."

"Well," said Woodstock, "I suppose you are right. But tell me one thing."

"A thousand, *señor*. If I can keep you here talking long enough, Black Jim may return. Half his mind must be troubled about these horses all the time that he's away hunting for you. He may come back at any time."

"Tell me only this: if we meet again, are we enemies?"

"Why not?" asked Vicente.

"Well, we have done little services for each other, and things like that make most men friendly."

"What have we done?" answered Vicente. "You have given me my life two times, but my life twice over is not worth the money that I kept from going to waste in the slide."

Woodstock sighed a little as he looked at that inhuman face. "Vicente, you have a clear brain. You read the mind. Now tell me what I intend to do next?"

"That is clear and simple, *señor*. You will ride hard, now that you have left me and Black Jim floundering on foot. You will go to the house of Harry Scanlon, quickly put him and his wife and daughter in the saddle, and off you will run, the four of you, to get to some big town where money can be turned into land that cannot burn and houses that cannot be stolen. Then you will marry the girl and give the world more honest fools like yourself. She is too good to be amusing, but such men as you, *señor*, had rather be right than be happy. The newspapers will then publish your picture. You will work hard to become richer and richer…and in the end some free man, some happy man like Black Jim or Vicente, will find a way to inherit all of your money."

"Good bye, Vicente," said Woodstock. "I hope your neck is stretched at the end of a rope before long."

"*Adios, señor*," said Vicente. "I could not wish for you a sadder life that you wish for yourself!"

When Perry Woodstock came again out of the darkness of the forest and into the little green farm of Harry Scanlon, he was still a good distance from the house as the girl ran out of it and came towards him, calling out his name. He jumped to the ground to meet her. The gray mare followed slowly behind him, with five fine horses trailing her on the lead—a downheaded lot from weariness were all the six in that group.

Out of the doorway, also, came big Harry Scanlon with his arm about his wife, pointing out to her blind face the direction from which Woodstock was coming. They were laughing with happy excitement, the father and mother, but the girl was weeping. She was trying to laugh, too, but only the tears were real, Woodstock thought. She caught his hand and walked on with him, hurrying a little ahead so that she could partially turn, and so scan him from head to foot.

"We thought that they must have shot you to bits, and that you'd ridden off to die in the woods, and that they'd followed and found you, and gone on with that murdering bit of paper. We've been hunting every minute, since trying to find…your body! And here you come back to us safe and sound!"

"I whistled at the bullets, and they let me alone," said Perry Woodstock.

The tears kept running out of her eyes, but she dwelt on his face, scanning it like a book. She seemed eager for the good news, but incredulous of it. She was laughing breathlessly, too.

They were close to the house, now, and Harry Scanlon's big voice was saying: "Stop crying over him, Rosemary. Don't make a big baby out of yourself. Give me your hand, Perry." He crushed the very bones of Woodstock with his grip. There was a fierce happiness in the face of Scanlon. His eyes, like those of the girl, seemed to be finding something in Woodstock's soul, and taking possession of it.

"I want one of his hands, too," said the blind woman, feeling her way forward.

Woodstock took both of her reaching hands in his. He put his other arm around her and led her back towards the house. Her raised face was close to his shoulder, and she was saying: "When I heard the rifles crashing, and the horse still galloping, I kept asking if you'd fallen yet. And they said that you were still in the saddle. Then I knew that bullets could not strike anything so brave."

"My God," said Perry Woodstock, "how happy I am to be here with you, as if you were all of my own blood. Come into the house. I've something to show you!"

They gathered around the table in the main room of the cabin. By this light, Woodstock could see more clearly the big rag rug on the floor and the burnished pots and pans that hung on the wall behind the stove. He thrust his hands into his pockets, fumbling.

"Stop crying, Rosemary!" commanded her father. "You didn't cry when we thought the poor lad was dead. Why should you cry because he's alive?"

"Because I'm too happy," she answered. "Because I feel as though all the happiness in the world had poured into this room, and that we can find some way of keeping it."

Woodstock heaped the packages of money on the table. He opened the mouth of his wallet and poured out the pyramid of jewels. Through the showering exclamations he told all the story as he knew it and as he had learned it from Vicente.

"It's half and half," said Woodstock. "Half to you and half to me."

The big hand of Scanlon dropped on his shoulder. The two women were silent, with puzzled faces.

"If there's a quarter of a million here stolen from the bank in St. Louis," said Scanlon, "I guess that money goes back to them, Perry, eh? And as for the rest, none of it belongs to us. It's all yours, if you can't find the owners of the jewels. And after thirty years that would be a hard job, I suppose."

Woodstock stared at him, blankly. "I would have kept the money, too," he confessed. "But you're a cut above me, all of you. Well, let the cash go back to the bank. But the other stuff we split half and half. I never would have had a look at any of it, except that Joe Scanlon gave me the message to take to you. It's half and half, man! No other way but that. You're going to get into the saddle now, all of you. You're getting out of this place and coming along with me to some town big enough to make us safe; because Jim Waley and Vicente and the rest...bar one...are all alive and ready to hunt us. They may be coming near to us now."

"We can't go," said Harry Scanlon. "I wouldn't leave the place. None of that stuff is mine...."

"Rosemary, make him get into a saddle," urged Woodstock.

He hardly heard her words. He only knew that somehow she managed to get her father out of the house. And he was standing alone with the mother.

"I've got half a minute to say something to you, Missus Scanlon," he said.

"It's Rosemary that you want to talk of," said she. "But you needn't. I've never had eyes to see my dear girl, but I know all that you could want to say."

"I love her," said Perry Woodstock.

"Of course you do," said the mother. "What a foolish boy you'd be if you didn't!"

"When I came back," said Woodstock, "she seemed pretty glad to see me. She seemed so glad that I began to have a crazy hope that she might care a little about me too!"

"Dear lad," said Mrs. Scanlon, "do you think there are many men in the world as young and as gentle and as brave as you are?"

"I'm no more than a cowhand. I'm a farm hand and a cow-puncher. That's all I am," said Perry Woodstock.

"Tell her that," said the mother. "And see if it keeps her from giving you her heart as freely as a song."

"We must go," said Woodstock. "We have to start. Come with me."

He guided her carefully.

"You mustn't tremble, my lad," she told him. "It will all be right, the instant that you speak. She's never been taught the lying ways of most girls, never speaking what their hearts desire."

He helped her into the saddle on the smallest and gentlest of the horses. Carefully he fitted her feet into the stirrups. After looking at her with a strange tenderness, he turned to the gray mare, and found the eyes of Rosemary on him. She was laughing a little, but not in a way that made him blush, not in a way that mocked him, merely as though she understood and were happy in her understanding.

"Ride first with me, Harry," said the mother. "You know the way best, and they want to talk together."

"Ay," sighed Harry Scanlon, "I suppose they do. But keep close, Perry."

"Ay, ay," said Perry Woodstock.

And he fell in beside the girl. She had not so much as a look for him, but her glance was away among the trees, or up at the blue patches of the sky.

"Rosemary!" he broke out at her, "I've got to say something to you."

"Don't," said she, "because words are silly things between us, now!"

Alan (Brown) LeMay

was born in Indianapolis, Indiana, and attended Stetson University in DeLand, Florida, in 1916. Following his military service, he completed his education at the University of Chicago. His short story, "Hullabaloo," appeared the month of his graduation in *Adventure* (6/30/22). He was a prolific contributor to the magazine markets in the mid 1920s. In 1929, two years before Ernest Haycox, LeMay with the story, "Loan of a Gun," broke into the pages of *Collier's* (2/23/29). During the next decade LeMay wanted nothing more than to be a gentleman rancher and his income from writing helped support his enthusiasms which included tearing out the peach-tree orchard so he could build a polo field on his ranch outside Santee, California. In the late 1930s he was plunged into debt because of a divorce and turned next to screenwriting, early attaching himself to Cecil B. DeMille's unit at Paramount Pictures. LeMay continued to write original screenplays through the 1940s, and on one occasion even directed the film based on his screenplay.

THE SEARCHERS (Harper, 1954) is regarded by many as LeMay's masterpiece. It possesses a graphic sense of place; it etches deeply the feats of human endurance which LeMay tended to admire in the American spirit; and it has that characteristic suggestiveness of tremendous depths and untold stories developed in his long apprenticeship writing short stories. A subtext often rides on a snatch of dialogue or flashes in a laconic observation. The following narrative, which has not been previously collected, is one of the short stories LeMay wrote for Collier's.

Lost Dutchman O'Riley's Luck

Just as a man is getting things going so that the future looks pretty good, Steve Hunter reflected, something always happens to take him down a peg. He had thought some pretty harsh things about himself from time to time; but he had never expected to be picked out as a come-on for one of the most frazzled, worn-out skingames known to the West. Yet there sat the man who called himself O'Riley, costumed as an old-time prospector down to the last whisker—down to the last ore sample, Hunter had no doubt, in the pocket of O'Riley's pants.

"You must have heard your pa speak of Dennis O'Riley," the old reprobate was pleading.

"Never heard of him," Steve Hunter professed, making his face look blank.

It was true that the name of Dennis O'Riley had sometimes entered the thousand tall stories that had featured the declining years of Wild Bill Hunter, Steve's father. But finding the name of someone once known to Wild Bill—someone long since disappeared—would have been easy to any impostor; about as easy as looking up Wild Bill himself, as easy as finding a white granite mountain there in the high Sierras, where Steve Hunter was now running his pack outfit.

"I can't understand it," said the old man. "Wild Bill never mentioned Dennis O'Riley? Why, me and him...me and him...well, at least," the old man tried again, "you know about Lost Dutchman's gold!"

"Never heard of it," Steve declared.

The man who called himself Dennis O'Riley sat back, flabbergasted. "Never heard of...well, I'll be...." He pulled himself together. "Back in the 'Eighties," he proceeded sententiously, "a feller wandered into Buck Springs with his pockets full of the richest ore samples these here mountains ever seen. He had mountain fever...pretty near died. But when he pulled through he knew that he was rich." O'Riley leaned forward. "He started back to his discovery. But Buck Springs picked up as one man and followed along, burro, pick, and pan, hundreds of 'em; and he took to twisting and turning in the hills, to shake 'em off. And in the end he did lose 'em, too. And then...." O'Riley hitched forward to tap Steve's collar bone with a gnarled forefinger "and then, what do you suppose?"

"He got mountain fever again."

"Eh?" said O'Riley. "No, sir! He found that *he* was lost, too!"

"You don't mean to tell me," said Steve, who had heard the story ninety times.

"Wait till you hear the next," said the old man. He drew himself up for his great effect. "I, Dennis O'Riley, am the Lost Dutchman himself!"

A shocked silence fell between them. Steve turned to his shaving mirror, a broken triangle tacked to the log wall. The face that looked back at him was cleanly shaved, lean and brown; from above high cheek bones comprehending blue eyes stared soberly. "So this," he thought, "is what a born come-on is supposed to look like...." He asked his visitor, "Are you of the Dublin Dutch, or one of the Amsterdam O'Rileys?"

"I admit," said the infamous wowser testily, "it's a little peculiar that the original Lost Dutchman turns out to be of honest County Kerry blood. But what does a bunch of Westerners know about different nationalities, anyway? The sun had prob'ly bleached out my hair the color of winter hay, I expect is the root of the matter."

"That explains it," Hunter accepted. "And now where is your sample of most astounding rich ore?"

"Right here," said O'Riley, bringing it out with a flourish. "It was considerable larger in size but it wore down by time."

"And where," Steve pursued, "is your picture of your penniless niece?"

"Granddaughter," O'Riley corrected him. "How did you know I got her picture here?"

"Isn't that the usual play in a case like this?"

"If you keep on having these damn' fool fits of giggling," said O'Riley with annoyance, "opportunity is going to pass you by!"

"Heaven forbid," said Steve. "Get on with the description of your penniless granddaughter."

"Well," the old man said grumpily, "she has a sort of kind face, so she has."

"This part of your spiel isn't nearly as well worked up as the other," Hunter criticized him. "You ought to get hold of a more powerful description. Well…trot the chromo out."

From a pocket of his brush jacket O'Riley dug a snapshot print, showing a girl on a horse. "She's staying down here at the Two Pine boarding house," O'Riley explained.

At first Hunter thought the girl was one he had known before, for a swift, odd sense of recognition touched him as he perceived the clean, alert lift of her head, and the slim, relaxed grace with which she sat in the stock saddle. Her face, in the shadow of a big hat, was less clearly shown; but he could see that, from the camera's angle at least, this girl was lovely, too lovely to be connected in any way with the crooked old wowser who was trying to sell a mythical mine. A gust of anger stirred him.

"I don't know where you got this picture, nor who it's of," he growled at the old man, "but this I'll tell you flat: this girl hasn't any connection with any blue-sky mine, nor with any Dutchman named O'Riley, either, and I've a mind to see you jailed!"

"Gimme that back!" shouted O'Riley.

"All right. But I'm going to drive down to Two Pine. I'm going to find out if this girl is there. And if your story doesn't tally, this country isn't going to hold you, you hear?"

"I won't ride with you," snorted O'Riley. "I'll go back by hand, the way I come!"

"Suit yourself."

O'Riley wilted. "My story's too good," he almost whimpered. "It's so good nobody will believe it. I've got to have help, and have it soon! But if old Wild Bill's boy won't believe me, who will? I've tried a hundred fellers and they're as bad or worse than you. God knows," he told Steve, "I'd like to haul off and bust you one. But you come very close to being the last shot in my gun." Suddenly his voice turned shrill, intense, and he shook his clawed hands before Steve Hunter's eyes.

"It's there," he shouted. "I know it's there! I know right where it is. A fortune, an everlasting fortune, lost in the hills...and I can't get to it! I tell you, I *know!*"

He jerked from a pocket a United States survey quadrangle, folded in innumerable accordion pleats. "It's these new maps showed me the light," he declared, shaking it out. "I can stand here and put my finger on millions...millions boy, you hear me?...right here on this map. But if I don't set my finger down, your chance is gone, and maybe mine, and maybe hers too, and the fault is yours!"

Steve Hunter blew smoke through his nose and studied the old man. It was incredible to him that anybody could lie so well. "Well, I still figure to drive to Two Pine," he said.

"That's more like Wild Bill's boy!" said O'Riley with emotion. He led the way to Steve's battered mountain car at a shambling run.

———⟫●⟪———

Down in front of the Two Pine boarding house a long blue roadster stood, its chromium fittings a bright dazzle in the sun.

"That rig," said O'Riley, standing up to point, "belongs to the swivel-eared jackass that wants to stake me, and horn in on my mine. Only I won't let him. Trying to trim me! That's him at the wheel, and the other one is my granddaughter. Hey, June!"

Steve Hunter angled in beside the blue roadster—and found himself looking directly into the eyes of the girl whom he had pronounced a myth. It was the girl of the snapshot all right. Only this time there was no intervening shadow and no hat to hide her face. It was a thin face, tanned and lively. The soft, fine hair that framed it was the color of sunlight through autumn leaves, and her eyes—Steve could not have said whether they were green or brown or blue, or sometimes all three, in changing lights; but they were gentle, humorous, and awake.

"You're Steve Hunter, aren't you?" said the myth. "This is Wally Parker."

Steve shook hands with the smooth-haired young man at the wheel without noticing him much. He was absorbed with the baffling contrast between the old wowser, with his weather-reddened nose and historic whiskers, and the slender, smiling girl in the other car. If this truly was O'Riley's granddaughter, all that preposterous story about Lost Dutchman's gold needed a different explanation than that which he had so readily supplied.

Wally Parker broke in. "Aren't you the Hunter who runs the Three Bar pack outfit? Can I speak to you a minute?"

"Sure." Hunter, stepping to the boardwalk, found himself drawn along the walk by the stranger, out of earshot of the girl.

"I suppose," Parker began, "you've heard O'Riley's story by this time. I'm the boy that drove him up to your place this morning. You didn't see me. I let him out a little way down the road."

"Where do you come in?" Steve asked.

"I," said Wally Parker, "am the boy who takes a special and particular interest in June O'Riley."

"Oh, you do?" said Steve.

"O'Riley," said Parker, "is obviously the victim of self-hypnosis. He's told the story of Lost Dutchman's gold so often that he believes it himself...so much so that he has even convinced his granddaughter to some extent. I'm telling you this," he explained, "so that you will not think I'm an idiot."

"Thanks. I'm glad to have it cleared up."

"The O'Rileys," Parker went on, "are...bankrupt. They can't seem to understand that when June and I are married there will be no cause to worry about that. Meanwhile, this gold scare is a persistent nuisance. I can't chase the O'Rileys all over the West forever, you know."

"No?" said Steve.

"No," said Parker, "and I'm not at all sure that I like your tone of voice. However, you happen to fit my plans, so we'll overlook that. The trouble is, the old lunatic won't let me finance the final search and, since nobody else is idiot enough, there the matter rests."

"Not a bad place for it."

"I don't agree with you. Didn't I mention that my plans are held up until the O'Rileys abandon this outlandish notion? Now, I want you to pack O'Riley to wherever the old fool thinks he has lost his mine. I'll pay all expenses, with a substantial bonus if June is convinced that Lost Dutchman's gold is nonexistent."

"That is to say," said Steve Hunter, "you want me to pretend to take up his proposition myself?"

"Exactly."

Steve Hunter looked Parker over slowly. He couldn't make out exactly why the man in front of him roused him to instant resentment with his every word. Wally Parker was tall, slim, blond, and clean-looking. He had too small an eye, perhaps, too long a nose, and too smooth a way; but none of these things accounted for the pleasure with which Steve considered eliminating Parker with one long wallop of his right hand. He rolled a cigarette.

"Not at any price," he said at last. "I wouldn't touch it with a ten-foot pole."

Parker shrugged. "Oh, very well. I'll get somebody else."

"You think you will?" said Hunter.

He did not understand, then, what made him do what he did next. Certainly he had no belief in Lost Dutchman's gold. He could only tell himself, afterward, that it had seemed a good idea at the time. He walked to the blue car, where June was talking eagerly to old Dennis O'Riley.

"Don't you fret, Miss O'Riley," he heard himself saying, "I'll help you find your darned old mine!"

"Oh, good boy!" said June O'Riley.

———————— >►●◄ ————————

Long Thunder Mountain turned out to be old Dennis O'Riley's objective—a sufficiently inaccessible place in which to lose his gold. Not until the eleventh day did it loom over them, gaunt, black, and austere.

"This is it," Dennis O'Riley exulted, "this is it! It all comes back to me plain. I'd know that hill from the floor of hell!"

For an hour they pressed upward across the deeply carved face of Long Thunder. And there, incredibly, half an hour before dusk, they came upon O'Riley's ancient stope. One thing, at least, was decided for Steve Hunter in that moment. If he had any further doubt as to the sincerity of either the girl or the old man in their quest for Lost Dutchman's gold, it vanished here. No one could doubt the reality of the tears which the old man tried to hide as they trickled into his beard, nor the overwhelming emotion of June O'Riley as she hugged her grandfather close in her arms.

The old man snatched a pick-pointed hammer from a pack and rushed into the dark mouth of the stope. For ten minutes, while

Hunter unsaddled his pack animals and made camp, he could hear the ring of steel on stone. Then finally O'Riley came running toward Hunter, both hands filled with fragments of rock. He pressed ragged chunks into Steve's hands. "Look at that! Look at that!"

Steve looked, turning the fragments over, holding them close to his eyes in the failing light. He saw a dark volcanic-looking rock, which he could not immediately name, marked with innumerable small irregular inclusions of a steely gray, something like the wings of a Plymouth Rock hen, and his spirit dropped heavily.

Now, Steve was no geologist. He didn't know a lot of things that there were to be known about the vast sheers of rock among which he lived. Yet he had spent his life in these hills and he knew gold when he saw it: and this was not it.

"O'Riley," he said, "this isn't the rock you got your sample from."

For just a moment Lost Dutchman O'Riley let his embarrassment check his enthusiasm. He coughed twice and shifted his feet. "Now that we've actually found it and you can see that it's rich," he said, "I suppose I may as well admit that the sample I showed you didn't come from here. I know as well as anybody," he said, "that there's nothing quite so exciting as plain, free gold, so I just run in that other sample to make my story more interesting." O'Riley's enthusiasm surged up again magnificently. "You know what that is?" he shouted. "You know what that is?" He extended the gray and black rock fragments to Steve once more in hands that shook with excitement. "That's *graphite delirium*. Graphite delirium, man!"

"Graphite, what?" said Steve. A curious anger was upon him, an anger that somehow made him want to laugh, yet left him without energy for laughter or anything else.

"Graphite delirium," cheered O'Riley again. "Rich in gold, rich in silver, and there's a million tons of it under the hill. We're rich, man, rich!"

"I see," said Steve. He didn't know all the geology there was to know; but he was not impressed by graphite and he knew that delirium was a state of mind. The painful thing was that June's hopes would now be riding high upon the old man's mad imagining. He turned his back upon O'Riley and the worthless stope.

Next morning, putting on as cheerful a face as he was able, Steve Hunter set to work. That day he spent in digging and chipping little pot holes in the rock, systematically, in lines radiating from the abandoned stope. He sketched a rough map of the location with his pot holes marked upon it, and from each digging he took a sample which he carefully put away in a little bag marked with its map location. Yet all day long he saw not one trace of the yellow color for which he hoped against hope. He was only going through the motions that he would make if the discovery was real; and he knew that he was stalling, unable to make up his mind what he was going to say to June.

"People think what they want to think," he told himself. "She'll never believe me against the old man. We'll take back the rock samples and get them assayed. She'll have to believe the assay. There's nothing I can do here."

The next day they started back.

Steve Hunter kept to himself quite a bit during those two weeks of the return. When spoken to directly concerning the Lost Dutchman's mine, he always grinned, but answered briefly, without committing himself. Sometimes June reproached him for his apparent indifference. Once, when they sat in front of a campfire, while O'Riley slept, she turned to him.

"Don't you realize what's happened, Steve?" she said. "Why, we're rich, Steve! All three of us. Don't you realize this is the mine that Granddad had been hunting almost all his life?"

"I don't exactly rate a share," he said soberly. "All I've done is lend you some mules, June, and come along for the fishing. I was glad to do that, June. That you should know."

"Of course, you own a share!" she insisted. "A half share, just as Granddad said to begin with. Nothing else will do!"

He whispered to himself, "'Graphite delirium.' Oh, good Lord!" He wanted to caution her not to believe too strongly, to prepare her for what he knew must come. But when his eyes met the dancing firelight reflected in hers, he could not.

"I've made a thousand plans," she persisted. "I suppose there'll be some delay while the mine is organized and all that; but after that…first of all, I'm going to have tons of pretty things to wear, like Mother and I used to have before Dad's business went smash. Oh, wait until Wally Parker hears about this! You know he never believed in Granddad at all."

"Well," Steve commented, "that was mutual."

"Granddad doesn't understand Wally, and that's a shame, too. Wally Parker is a peach in every way."

"Are you going to marry Parker?"

He had surprised himself by asking that. But somehow in the high, thin air of the pine forest, with its close stars, they seemed very near together.

"Marry him? I don't know," she answered. "If Dad's business hadn't crashed, I suppose I would be married to him now."

Steve Hunter said nothing.

"I suppose I'm foolish," she went on presently, "but you see Wally's family have so much money I couldn't possibly think of marrying anybody like that when we had nothing at all."

"Must a million marry a million?" Steve asked.

"I don't mean that. But, Steve, you don't realize how completely, utterly broke I was before we found the Lost Dutchman mine. When Dad died, he left nothing at all. Even the insurance had lapsed. I put every last dollar...literally...into coming out here with Granddad to take just one more look for his lost mine. It was a wild, crazy thing to do, I know. Do you know how broke we were when I first saw you in Two Pine? We had just enough to pay our board bill for two more days. As close to the edge as that!

"So...you see...it wasn't a question of millions at all. If I had married Wally any time after Dad's crash, some day he would have got to thinking I had married him only as a rescue, not because I loved him at all. If I had had anything at all...enough to carry on with and hold my head up for a little way...it would have been different, but I didn't, and I couldn't marry him even when I wanted to. Do you see?"

"And now?"

"It's all different now," she said and her voice seemed to sing in his ears. "I feel as if I had escaped from some terrible trap! "Steve," she said, her voice very low, "do you realize that we owe everything in the world to you? If I hadn't come out here, if we hadn't found you...."

"Shush, child," said Steve. He didn't dare look at her; he kept his eyes deeply on the dying embers.

"You're nice," she said unexpectedly, and for a moment laid her hand upon his. And still he sat motionless with his eyes on the coals.

"Good night, Steve. Excuse my talking so much."

"Good night."

By the time he had delivered the O'Rileys at the Two Pine boarding house, he had made up his mind what he was going to do. He went first to Harry Weir, the local assayer, and dumped his bags of rock rubbish on Weir's floor.

"You've got to do something for me, Harry?" he said.

"When the best trout guide in the country says that, there's only one answer, Steve."

Steve thanked his stars he had friends. "All right. Assay this worthless rip-rap first. Then you're going to buy the O'Rileys' right in the mountain this junk came from."

"With whose money?" said Harry Weir skeptically.

"Mine," said Hunter. "Only, my name is going to be kept out of the deal."

"Sounds like a shenanigan," said Weir.

"Call it what you like. You ought to know me well enough by this time to take a chance." There was a short wordy struggle, and an explanation or two. But in the end Weir, indebted to Steve for more than one free pack to his favorite streams, agreed to all Steve asked.

Next he went to Abe Cramp—a slouching, unshaved figure always to be found at Cramp's Two Pine corral. Just as Steve Hunter made a business of supplying transportation upon the mountain trails, Abe Cramp made a nice thing of horse trading with the trail men, who owe their whole existence to horses and mules.

"Abe," said Steve, "if you still know where you can sell the Three Bar, you can have her now…lock, stock and barrel, name and brand, and I guarantee not to set up another pack outfit within a hundred miles in the next five years."

"How much?" said Cramp.

"Six thousand cash, today."

Abe Cramp studied him. "I won't horse-trade you, Steve," he said at last. He masticated his straw, devouring it slowly. "I could easy beat you down, but I won't. I'll offer six if you want."

There was a silence. Then, "Sold," said Hunter. The word came hard, but he had decided what he was going to do.

The straw dropped from Abe Cramp's mouth. "You mean I've bought the Three Bar for six thousand?"

"You heard me, Abe."

Cramp took off his two-gallon hat and slammed it on the ground. "Then you're a fool!" he shouted. "You're a fool, you hear?"

"Maybe I am," said Steve.

"You've built you up the best pack outfit in the best stand this side of the backbone of the Rockies. You've got the best stock and the best equipment of any packer I ever saw, and I've seen them all. You get the cream of the fishermen, the cream of the deer hunters…they know your name and they come to you, more of them every year A few years more and you'll own this country, Steve! Don't you do it, don't you sell!"

"I'm set on it, Abe."

Abe stared. "You'll cuss hell out of yourself for this, Steve, some day." He led the way to the house.

It took all day to get that deal straightened out, but there was a certified check for six thousand dollars in Steve Hunter's pocket when he pulled up in front of the Two Pine boarding house again. It was dusk, and in the unpainted board houses that line Two Pine's hundred-foot-wide-street, warm yellow lights were beginning to show. But no light showed in Steve Hunter's future as he sought out June O'Riley. When at last she sat beside him in his parked car, he knew that he had reached the moment he had dreaded, that he could no longer put off telling her the truth, as he knew it, about the Lost Dutchman's gold.

"Look here," he said, "look here…I've got to tell you something. I've got bad news."

"Steve, what's the matter?"

"The mine," he said, "the mine…it isn't as good as you've been thinking, June, you and your grandfather."

"Are the assays finished?" she asked, almost inaudibly.

He rushed over that, anxious to be finished with what he was trying to do. "You remember," he said, "we staked three claims on the Lost Dutchman ledge, one in your name, one in mine, and one in the name of Dennis O'Riley?"

"But the understanding was," she said, "that we were to pool all three claims."

"I know," he said, "but I'm pulling out of that agreement."

"You mean you're selling out separately?"

"Yes." He made his face expressionless and hard lest it give him away, for at this point he had to leave the narrow path of facts as he saw them, and launch into the fiction for which he had sold his packs. "Now, as to the claim that is in your name: Harry Weir represents Catlin Mines, Incorporated. He's going to offer you six thousand for your rights."

"Six...but I thought...." June pressed the back of her hand against her mouth and stared at him wide-eyed.

Never in his life had six thousand seemed so small, so foolishly inadequate. "I'm sorry, June," he said. "God knows, I'm sorry, but listen, June. Do you believe that I shoot square, and that I know these hills?"

"Of course, Steve," she said in a small voice.

"Then sell," he told her. "The six thousand seems like nothing, I know, but it's every cent your claim is worth, and more. And if you can bring yourself to think that it's anything at all...," unconsciously he slipped into her own remembered words, "anything at all, enough so that you can carry on for a little way...then maybe, after all, it wasn't a wasted trip."

They sat in silence while a great sense of vacant weariness overwhelmed Hunter.

"One thing more," said Steve. "Forget this million-marry-a-million stuff. It's all wrong. I'm sorry we didn't find a mine that would put us all on the same money level as Wally Parker. I don't know how many millions he has, and I don't care, but get this: if he owns all there is, he still isn't good enough to saddle your horse. If you want him, take him, and never let the thought come into your head again that where you're concerned money counts."

Once more they sat silently. Steve, his hands on the wheel, was looking straight ahead. "I've got to take some fishermen into the upper basin after steelhead," he said. "I've got to go now, I guess, and if I don't see you any more, God knows I'm sorry this thing came out like this. That's all I can say."

Somehow he could not bring himself to look at her. After a moment she left him, without a word; and still he did not look after her, but only sat there, staring at the dusk. Presently he smashed into gear and drove down to the assayer's office where Harry Weir was working in a crowded little room full of bits of rock, retorts, and acidulated smells.

"I've been looking for you all day," said Harry Weir.

"Listen," said Hunter, "this morning you promised to help me. Now I'm ready to tell you what you have to do."

"But first...," began Weir.

"Listen to me," Steve snarled at him. "I have here a certified check for six thousand dollars. You're to take that check. You're going to buy the girl's claim from her in the name of an imaginary company...Catlin Mines, Incorporated. Get that? I've already talked to her. You...."

"If you'll let me get in a word edgewise...," begged Harry Weir.

"Listen! Above all, she's not to know I'm back of this. I'm out. I've...."

"I'm trying to tell you...," said Weir, raising his voice.

"Will you listen?" shouted Steve.

"No," yelled Harry Weir, "you big jug-head! These samples of yours are rotten with sylvanium!"

"And what the devil is sylvanium?" said Steve.

"Gold, sliver, telluride, you big ignoramus. Those little gray marks are twenty-four per cent gold and thirteen per cent silver!"

The breath went out of Steve Hunter as if by the kick of a mule. Harry Weir, enjoying himself hugely, rolled a cigarette in acid-stained fingers and sat back to watch his news soak in. If this was true, Steve Hunter was thinking, then June O'Riley and her old wowser of an ancestor had found Lost Dutchman's gold in truth.

"Some call that type of deposit 'graphic tellurium,'" Weir was saying. "Ever hear of it?"

Hunter had no trust in his luck. It was incredible that the senile old wowser had by a weird freak of chance—*or was it?* What if it was no freak of chance at all? Certain of Weir's words had a strangely familiar ring. Could it be that old O'Riley...?

"You mean...you mean to say...?"

"I mean to say you've stumbled into something. Of course, if it's only a small intrusion...."

There's a big long ledge of it," said Hunter faintly. "If there isn't ten thousand tons...."

"You're overestimating," said Weir.

"I was there, wasn't I? I know what...," he broke off abruptly. "Good Lord," he whispered under his breath.

For the first time he saw exactly what he had done. June O'Riley was in possession of invaluable holdings and he, through the name of an imaginary company, had tried to buy her rights for six thousand dollars. He stood silently while the blood drained from his head and a slow, cold sweat appeared upon his forehead.

"Don't take it so hard," said Weir. "You should have seen how coolly O'Riley took it, just as if he'd been sure all along."

"He was here?"

"He left just before you came in."

So, then, they knew all about it already—his trivial offer, and the true value of the Lost Dutchman's deceptive gold. He knew what June must be thinking of him now; and he wondered if Wally Parker was at her side.

"If it's an extensive ledge," he heard Weir saying, "I guess you've hooked into your millions, all right."

"Oh, he has, has he?" said a voice from the door. In the whirl of the moment they had not noticed Wally Parker's long blue car slide to a stop in front of the assayer's office. "So you've made your millions," Parker repeated. "Now, isn't that odd! That explains the rumor that you sold your outfit for six thousand dollars, Hunter; and it explains," he added deliberately, "why you offered Miss O'Riley six thousand dollars for her rights."

O'Riley pushed in past Parker's elbow. His voice was shrill and enraged. "Trying to trim me!" he shouted. "Trying to trim me! Why, you damned...!" Words failed him and he shook furious fists under Hunter's nose. "Graphite Delirium!" he got out at last. "Graphite delirium! And you made out you didn't know what it was!"

"So," said Steve, "that was what you meant. Graphic tellurium! Well, I'll be...."

It was worse than he thought. The discovery was not even the accidental coincidence he had supposed. Old Dennis O'Riley, however he had garbled his scientific terms, had yet known what he was about; and Steve Hunter had been the only one of them all who had been dead wrong, a fool who had made himself look like a crook.

"I suppose," raged Dennis O'Riley, "that there's the check for six thousand that you was going to buy me and June out with?" Hunter had forgotten that the check was in his hand. He stared at it stupidly. "Oh, you big horse thief!" yelped O'Riley. "Oh, you big...!"

Steve Hunter rolled the check into a little ball and shoved it down into his pants pocket. "Out of the picture," he mumbled to himself. "Out of the picture, once and for all." Dazedly, without a word to the others, he turned to the door. Wally Parker still stood in the doorway, however, and made no move to get out of his way.

"Stand aside," said Steve, his voice very thick and low.

Parker did not obey. "I've had my eye on you," said Parker slowly. "The first time I saw you I recognized you for what you are…an ignorant, shifty, hill-billy crook."

Hunter stared at him. Perhaps he was still dazed by the overpowering significance of the assayer's report; perhaps he had not comprehended that Wally Parker was there at all.

"And yellow, too," said Parker. "I'd knock a man down who said that to me."

Steve Hunter said, "For once you're right." Parker suddenly started back, throwing his arms in front of his face; but all Steve's unexpressed bitterness against the turn of the luck was in the right hand that he brought crashing through. Parker's feet flew from under him, so that he seemed to pivot in mid-air with the shock of the blow; and he lay where he fell, in the doorway, a stertorously breathing heap. Hunter hardly glanced at the fallen man as he stepped over him and out into the night.

Ordinarily it was not in this man to evade his fate, but it may be that he would have avoided June O'Riley then if he had seen her in time. He did not. A breathless figure came racing along the boardwalk to collide with Hunter with such force that she would have fallen if he had not caught her in his arms. For a moment or two June O'Riley clung to him, out of wind.

"Steve, what's happened?" June gasped.

Hunter cast a despairing glance at the door of the assayer's office. Too many explanations of what had happened were already waiting for her there—versions he was not going to be able to dispose of, he was sure. But Weir and old Dennis O'Riley had carried Wally Parker inside, and for the brief present June and Steve were alone on the Two Pine boardwalk.

"It isn't so," he said inanely. "June, it isn't so."

June O'Riley disengaged herself. "Steve, Granddad said he talked to the assayer, and that you were wrong: that Lost Dutchman's gold is real!"

"June, that's true."

"Then…you were wrong all the time!"

"Yes, I was wrong."

"What makes me mad," said June, "is that Harry Weir tried to buy us out for next to nothing, when he must have known…."

"No," said Steve; "that wasn't Harry Weir. I just used his name."

"Steve! Are you trying to tell me that you were buying my share yourself? It's true you sold the Three Bar so that you could offer me six thousand for my claim?"

"Yes," he said.

"And what," she asked queerly, "have you got to say for yourself?"

He hesitated, then looked her in the eyes.

"Nothing," he said. "Not one word!"

There was a silence in the Two Pine street.

"I think," she said slowly, "that you are the most generous man in the world."

Steve Hunter was struck dumb. For a long moment they stood looking at each other through the starlit dark. "You didn't think, then…," he got out at last, "you didn't believe…?"

Suddenly he saw that she was laughing at him, and he paused. And now it occurred to him for the first time that he might have misread the light he had been seeing in her eyes, that his greatest error might have been in supposing that she would ever disbelieve in him at all. Inspiration swept him, overriding his insistent distrust of his luck.

"You come here a minute!" he said, and caught her in his arms.

Dennis O'Riley came stamping out of the assayer's office. "Graphite delirium!" he was yelling. "Tried to trim me! Tried to trim me!" He checked abruptly and, as he spoke again, his voice was as if the unbelievable had seized him by the beard. "Well, I'll be…! Well, of all the…!"

"Oh, shut up," said June O'Riley.

Wayne D(aniel) Overholser won four Golden Spur awards from the Western Writers of America and has a long list of fine Western titles to his credit. He was born in Pomeroy, Washington, and attended the University of Montana, University of Oregon, and the University of Southern California before becoming a public school teacher and principal in various Oregon communities. He began writing for Western pulp magazines in 1936 and within a couple of years was a regular contributor to Street & Smith's *Western Story Magazine* and Fiction House's *Lariat Story Magazine*. BUCKAROO'S CODE (Macmillan, 1948) was his first Western novel and remains one of his best. In the 1950s and 1960s, having retired from academic work to concentrate on writing, he would publish as many as four books a year under his own name or a pseudonym, most prominently as Joseph Wayne and Lee Leighton. THE VIOLENT LAND (Macmillan, 1954), THE LONE DEPUTY (Macmillan, 1957), and THE BITTER NIGHT (Macmillan, 1961) and are among the finest Overholser titles. Many of his novels are first person narratives, a technique that tends to bring an added dimension of vividness to the frontier experiences of his narrators and frequently, as in CAST A LONG SHADOW (Macmillan, 1955), the female characters one encounters are among the most memorable. Almost invariably, his stories weave a spell of their own with their scenes and images of social and economic forces often in conflict and the diverse ways of life and personalities that made the frontier so unique a time and place in human history.

Land Without Mercy

A numbness was in Jett Cater when he rode down the ridge to his little Three Leaf Clover ranch house, and it wasn't from the fight talk he'd made at the Rod Munger place. The numbness came from what he saw, or rather what he didn't see. The corral was empty. The bay that Lena rode and little Hap's pinto were gone. It had finally come. Lena had left and she'd taken Hap with her.

Jett dismounted back of the house. There was no use going in. He knew what he'd find—an emptiness like that in his heart. He'd known it was coming. Known it all spring, but that knowledge hadn't really prepared him for it. This wasn't any life for a woman born and raised in a city. There was no neighbor within five miles but the Munger boys on Crazy Creek, and they weren't what a man could rightly call neighbors. No, it wasn't a life for a woman, but that wasn't why she had left. He had failed to make her see that he needed her. He stared blindly at the house, and let the bitterness of that thought pour through him.

Slowly Jett walked around the woodpile, through the dog kennel, and past the barrel where Hap used to hide. There was a game Jett played with the boy. Hap would reach out and grab his leg. Jett would yell, "An Injun's got me," and fall to the ground. Screaming, Hap would pretend to scalp him.

They'd never play that game again. Lena would take Hap to Portland, where he could go to school. Maybe it was just as well. Maybe this wasn't any place for a boy either, out here in the sagebrush of the high Oregon desert. He'd grow up and be just like his dad, Jett thought bitterly, trying to make a go of a two-bit spread, and failing at that just as he'd failed at making his wife happy.

The back door squeaked as Jett opened it and went into the kitchen. He'd aimed to fix that door, but never had. He knew it had made Lena nervous, but still he'd never fixed it. He stood staring at the geranium on the window sill. Lena had pinned red tissue paper around the coffee can. Every day she'd watered it, and it never had bloomed. He wondered, as he had so many times, what color its blossom would be.

Then Jett saw the note on the table. Lena had left it under the sugar bowl. He lifted the sugar bowl and opened the folded paper.

> Dear Jett:
>
> I can't stand it any longer, Jett. I'm taking Hap with me back to Portland. Sell the ranch for what you can. You're not happy. You've never forgotten when you were free. You are now, Jett, free as the wild land you love. Hap and I will be all right. I'll stay with the folks. Mother can take care of him when I go to work. I'm afraid you will want him, but after you think about it a while, I know you'll see that would be the wrong thing. I want you to come to see him if you're ever in Portland, but don't try to take him, Jett. Let him have his chance.
>
> Lena.

Funny how still the house was. As he folded the paper, the crackling sound seemed to echo. Hap was always running from the kitchen to the front room, laughing and yelling, and wanting to go with Jett if there was any riding to be done. The boy had gone a lot of times, and left Lena at home alone.

It had been a mistake, their marriage. He'd tried to make it go, Jett told himself; tried harder than he'd ever tried anything, but it hadn't been in the cards. He'd ridden for a dozen outfits in the Harney Valley, around Winnemucca, over in Idaho, but he'd been ready to settle down when he'd married Lena. She was wrong when she said he wasn't happy, but he had never been able to make her understand about that. Words had never come easy to Jett Cater, words that he should have said to her so long ago. Now she was gone, and she'd taken Hap.

Jett thought of his trouble with the Munger boys. They'd homesteaded on Crazy Creek a year ago. They'd cut his wood, killed his beef when they were hungry. He'd put up with it as long as he could. He'd ridden over to tell them that this morning. None of the boys was there. Just Rod Munger's wife. She'd heard what he had to say, a hard-eyed, shrewish woman, and then she'd cussed him off the place. Only powder smoke and lead could settle it now. Rod's wife would tell them that when they came in.

Jett stared at Lena's letter. He wondered what she would have done if she had known where he had gone. She wouldn't have understood that, any more than she understood so many of the strange ways of this wild land, or the stubborn pride that was so much a part of Jett Cater. His gaze strayed around the room, stopped on the geranium, and the thought came to him that it might have been different if it had bloomed. She had brought it back with her last time she'd gone to Portland, and planted it in soil she'd brought in from the garden.

Lena and Hap would be in Two Moons by now, but there wasn't a train out till morning. She'd have to stay in the hotel overnight. And he had the right to say good bye to Hap. She couldn't take that from him. There were so many things she didn't see right. He wasn't free. A man was never free. There were always some bonds of pride. Someday the Three Leaf Clover would be a paying spread. Maybe next year. There was this business with the Mungers. It had to be settled.

Jett went out of the house, swung into the saddle, and turned his horse's head toward Two Moons. He'd have his last game with Hap. It would be a memory for him and the boy.

It was four o'clock when Jett jogged his horse down Two Moons' dusty street. Anybody could have seen him coming for the last two miles. He wondered idly if Lena had looked out of her hotel window, and what she was thinking if she had seen him. Maybe she wouldn't want him to tell Hap good bye.

Horses were racked in front of the hotel, Layden's store, the Gem Saloon, but nobody was on the street. That puzzled Jett. He thought no more of it until he turned into the stable, and Whitey Adams, the hostler, reached for the reins.

"You know they're here, don't you, Jett?" Whitey asked. His words came together, fast and scared.

"Who?"

"The Mungers. The whole damned tribe. Rod, Kip, and Solo. They're waiting."

Jett saw it then. Word had gone around. That was why no one was on the street.

"How did they know I was coming to town?" Jett asked curiously. He lifted his gun from leather, gave the cylinder a whirl, and dropped it back. He wished this could wait till tomorrow, but there was no dodging it now.

"Seems like you were over to Rod's place," Whitey said, still talking fast. "Rod came just after you left, followed you, saw you head for town, came on ahead. Kip and Solo were already here. They've done a pile of talking."

"Thanks." Jett turned, wondering if he should leave some message for Whitey to tell Lena and the boy.

The odds were heavy against him. The Mungers were not of the nester breed. They were bad.

"Better not go through the door," Whitey said hoarsely. "They're watching it. Don't let 'em know I told you, but they're figuring on letting you have it when you come out of here."

"Where are they?"

"Rod's over in Layden's store. Kip's in the Gem. I don't know where Solo is."

"Thanks," Jett said again.

He strode the long length of the barn, past Hap's pinto and Lena's bay, and into the alley behind the barn. In the lot across the alley was a corral and a hay stack. Beside the stack was a pile of boxes and barrels. Solo Munger might be hiding around there somewhere. Jett thought of that, but it was a chance he had to take. He had Rod and Kip pegged, so he'd take care of them first.

Another alley lay between the livery stable and Ma Jenkins's restaurant. Jett hugged the stable wall so that his shadow wouldn't fall into the street ahead of him. He glimpsed Rod Munger's whiskery face behind the window of Layden's store, his eyes on the front door of the livery barn.

Rod never knew what hit him. Jett's right hand arched back to the Colt at his hip and he came into the street, the gun blazing. His first slug blasted the window pane, parted Rod's whiskers, and smashed him back into a pile of potato sacks.

"Come into the open, you yellow Mungers!" Jett roared.

Kip Munger batted through the flap doors of the Gem, two guns in his hands, both beating out a steady rhythm of leaden death. A bullet went *thwack* into the stable wall behind Jett, but his surprise appearance from the alley must have unnerved Kip. Jett didn't give Kip time to steady down. He put two slugs into Kip's long body. The last one knocked the killer off his feet. He kicked spasmodically, flopped over, and fell off the saloon porch into the street.

Jett was past the stable's hitch rail when he saw Layden in the store door. He was waving Jett back and yelling something about Solo's being above him. Jett didn't get it for a second, not until another gun roared. Solo was above him somewhere, probably in a hotel room on the second floor. The hotel was next to Ma Jenkins's restaurant. There was a chance Jett could get into the hotel from the back and trap Solo in his room.

Jett didn't wait to shove new loads into his gun. He raced the length of the alley, came into the open space back of the stable, and turned toward the hotel. Then he stopped in mid-stride and whipped his body around. Somebody was hiding in the maze of boxes and barrels!

For just an instant he paused, his gun lifted. He'd heard the scuff of a shoe, but he couldn't tell which barrel it came from. The boxes were too small to hide a man, but a barrel could. He heard it again. The end barrel. A damn fool thing for a man like Solo Munger to do. Maybe it was that thought that stopped the squeeze of Jett's trigger.

"Jett!" It was Lena's voice, fear crazed. She was running toward him from the hotel.

"Lena, get back!" Jett yelled, and started for her.

Solo's gun spoke then from somewhere above Jett.

The bullet cut through the wide brim of his Stetson and lifted a geyser of dirt. Jett raised his eyes, saw Solo bellied down on the roof above him, and pressed trigger. Solo had fired a second time. Jett felt the bullet slice through his Stetson again, felt the sting of it as it lay open a gash along his forehead, but that was all the shooting for Solo Munger. He rolled down the stable roof.

"Jett." Lena was in Jett's arms, holding to him and sobbing. "That was Hap in the barrel."

A cold sweat came to Jett's forehead as he visioned what he had almost done. "He wanted to surprise you," Lena was saying between the sobs. "He saw you before you rode into town. He said you'd bring your horse out to the corral, and he'd surprise you like he does at home. I didn't know. I didn't know. I thought you'd like that."

Jett held the boy close to him.

"You're bleeding, Daddy," Hap said, and touched Jett's forehead.

"I've got a little cut, all right," Jett agreed, "but it ain't much. Here now,"—he shoved Hap through the hotel door—"you get back up to your room."

Jett Cater's chore was done. All three Mungers were dead. The townsmen gathered around Jett, slapping him on the back and saying it was the best piece of gun work they'd ever seen in Two Moons. They wanted to set up the drinks, but Jett said that would have to wait. He needed a sawbones. It wasn't much of a cut, the medico said as he put on a bandage.

There was hope in Jett's heart when he crossed the street to the hotel, hope that hadn't been there a few minutes ago when he'd ridden into town. Lena had come into his arms back there behind the livery stable. Maybe she'd…. He shook his head. No, he couldn't expect her to come back. No use to bank on it, but he could try.

They were waiting for him, Hap and Lena, his son and his wife who wasn't his wife now.

"I was mighty scared." Hap was grinning. "I'd just got into that barrel when I heard it. I didn't know what to do, so I just stayed there."

"You did right, Button, only after this you'd better wait till we get home to play that game."

"Can I ride with you tomorrow, Daddy?"

Jett looked at Lena, but she didn't meet his eyes. She hadn't told the boy. "How about going over to the store and getting us some peppermints?" Jett asked, and tossed the boy a dime from his jeans.

"Sure," Hap cried joyously, and scooted out of the door.

"Looks like you didn't break the news," Jett said.

"No, I…I couldn't." Lena was looking at Jett now, with a hunger in her eyes.

Jett twisted his Stetson in his hand. "'Tain't much, our Three Leaf Clover, but I reckon it'll be a heap better now, with the Mungers gone. I'll sort of keep it going, and maybe someday Hap'll have a decent spread when he gets big enough to run it."

"I'm not going," Lena said. "I thought I was until I…until what happened just now."

Jett held out his arms. "Let's forget that, honey. I never knew what it would be like without you till I got home and…."

Lena's lips stopped his words. She was still in his arms when Hap came in again with a sack of peppermints held tightly in his hand.

"Whatta you kissing Mamma for?"

Jett winked at the boy. "Your mamma needs kissing, son. I kinda got behind in my kissing, but I'm gonna catch up."

"You think that geranium of ours will ever bloom?" Lena asked, smiling a little.

"I reckon it will, honey," Jett answered. "When you love something enough, and keep taking care of it, it's just got to bloom. The trouble is we didn't take care of things enough. Hey, there, Button, don't eat all them peppermints. Doggone it, don't you think anybody else wants some?"

(Allan) William Colt MacDonald was born in Detroit, Michigan.

His formal education concluded after his first three months of high school. His first commercial writing consisted of advertising copy and articles for trade publications. While working in the advertising industry, MacDonald began contributing stories of varying lengths to pulp magazines and his first serial, a Western story titled "The Red Raider," was published in *The Lariat Story Magazine* in four parts (8/25 - 11/25). MacDonald was, it seems, uncomfortable with the short story form and actually wrote very few of them in the course of his career. He began contributing short novels to *Ace-High Magazine* when it was owned by Clayton Publications. Harold Hersey, who edited the magazine, was an enthusiastic mentor. "Don Gringo of the Rio Grande" was serialized in *Ace-High Magazine* (6/9/27 - 8/18/27), but it was not published in book form until three years later when it appeared as DON GRINGO (Chelsea House, 1930). The serial version was followed by a short novel in one installment, "The Outlaw Buster" in *Ace-High Magazine* (9/3/27), which quite recently was published in book form for the first time in the British market as SNAKE HUNT (Hale, 1994). "Gun Country" was serialized in *Ace-High Magazine* in six installments (4/8/28 - 6/17/28) and was published in book form the next year as GUN COUNTRY (Chelsea House, 1929). MacDonald later commented that when this book appeared, "I quit my job cold." From the time of that decision on, MacDonald's career became a long string of successes in pulp magazines, hardcover books, films, and eventually original and reprint paperback editions. Wallace MacDonald, Allan's son, recalled how much fun his father had writing Western stories. It is an apt observation since countless readers have enjoyed them now for nearly three quarters of a century. "Gun Fog" originally appeared in *Big-Book Western* in the issue dated November, 1935.

Gun Fog

Tobacco smoke hung thick in a haze near the low ceiling of the Topango Saloon. Through the open windows of a side wall a faint dawn breeze filtered through, lifting the smoke in gentle swirls and making a trifle brighter the illumination spread by the shaded hanging lamp above the poker table. The low-burning wick, competing palely with the faint gray light entering the windows, showed five men seated around a table, their hands moving restlessly with cards or piled stacks of chips. Now and then, one of the players spoke in a monosyllable or grunted disgustedly, as the case might be. Few words were spoken. Play went on.

Beyond the circle of light, snoring placidly on a stool behind the bar, slouched Hippodrome Casey, better known as Hippo, proprietor of the saloon. The barkeeper and the poker players were the only occupants of the Topango Bar. Both front and rear doors had been closed and bolted hours before.

Gray dawn spread swiftly along the silent, deserted streets of Topango Wells. Along the eastern horizon there came a softness of rose-pink which blended with the mauve of early morning. Somewhere down the street, a block away from the Topango Bar, a window-shutter made a sharp sound in the silence and fell to the earth, banging a man's shins in the descent. The man swore loudly and with sudden intensity. The shutter was picked up. Silence fell again.

One of the poker players in the Topango Bar spoke abruptly: "It's mornin'."

"But Knight's play," another put in, chuckling at the feeble joke.

"All-night play," another amended, then: "Well, what you doin', Knight?"

"Not so well," Jerry Knight smiled whimsically. He studied the cards in his bronzed fingers, a lean, red-haired individual still well under thirty. His smoky-gray eyes contemplated the pasteboards dubiously before he pushed his remaining two chips to the center of the table. "And raise it a mite," he advised.

"You're licked right now, cowboy," Kelt Flecker laughed. It wasn't a nice laugh. In fact, there weren't many people who liked anything about Kelt Flecker. But Flecker was a sort of boss in the Topango country and foreman of the Circle-F outfit on top of that. His features were brutal, his eyes small and shrewd. He met Knight's raise and upped the pot another chip.

The other three players, Tim Beadle, George Corwin, and Herb Jacklin were Circle-F punchers, dressed like their boss in range togs—woolen shirts, sombreros, faded overalls, and high-heeled boots. Holstered six-shooters completed the costumes.

Play went around the table and returned to Jerry Knight. The other four waited for Knight to act. Jerry's good-natured features crinkled to a rueful smile. "That's all, there isn't any more," he drawled.

Kelt Flecker said, "You plumb cleaned?"

Knight smiled whimsically, "Two hundred dollars, horse, rig. I arrived yesterday evenin' a stranger in a strange land, and I been took in."

Tim Beadle frowned, "You claimin' our game ain't straight?"

"Now, I wouldn't go to say that," Knight replied gently. "The luck just ain't been runnin' my way. Usual, an all-night session like this one will bring a change of luck two or three times, but I been on the skids ever since the first hand was dealt."

Kelt Flecker mused, "Two hundred dollars is a heap of money to lose, cowboy. A savin' of several months' wages, I suppose." He watched Knight narrowly while speaking.

Jerry nodded, meeting the glance even-eyed. "Yeah...wages." There was just the barest pause between the uttering of the two words.

Flecker repeated, "Wages," and laughed again, pure skepticism tinging the tones. The three Circle-F hands smiled.

"And so," Knight yawned carelessly, "you *hombres* can finish the hand without me. I'm forced to drop out."

"Wait a minute," said Flecker. "Knight, you're a stranger in Topango Wells. We like to give you all the chance possible to win back what you've lost, just to show you we're square shooters. You ain't done yet."

"How you figurin'?" Knight took a new interest in the proceedings. "I got a bandanna and a sack of makin's left...that's all."

"Wrong," Flecker said promptly. "You got your guns yet."

Knight's brow wrinkled. "I sort of hate to part with my irons."

"You may not have to," said George Corwin.

"Good guns are security for chips with me any time," Flecker said smoothly.

"How much security?" Knight wanted to know.

"Enough to stay and raise...if you're game."

Knight smiled, drew his guns from holsters, placed them on the table before Kelt Flecker. "I always was a sucker for a gamble."

Kelt Flecker shoved some blue chips across the table. Jerry looked surprised, shrugged his shoulders, and accepted them. Play went on. Five minutes later, Knight said philosophically, "Easy come, easy go. Now I *am* finished, cleaned, done. Next thing I know, if I stick with you sharks, I'll be rollin' back to my home range in a barrel."

Flecker smiled genially. "You sure do have the breaks against you, Knight. Just where is your home range? You ain't said."

Jerry evaded that with, "I ain't intendin' to neither. You *hombres* would be takin' that away, too, I reckon."

"We could try, leastwise," Flecker grinned widely. "What you aimin' to do now, Knight?"

"I been wonderin' about that myself," the red-haired cowboy chuckled. "Money, guns, horse, and rig gone. Well, I still got my ambition. Gents, you're lookin' at a cowboy for sale."

Herb Jacklin said, "Kelt, we're short a hand."

Flecker nodded thoughtfully, "But I don't think my bosses would let me take on another."

"I'm lookin' for a job," Jerry said, "though yesterday at this time I didn't think the cards would tell me to go to work again."

"Look here," Flecker said suddenly, "I'd like to help you out, Knight, but my bosses been after me to cut expenses. We do need another man, but I can't see the wages to pay one. At the same time, I hate to see the work get behind. Havin' the best interests in the

Randall Land and Cattle Company at heart...which same is my boss...I aim to try and stake 'em to the help needed...."

"What's the point you're headin' for?" Knight wanted to know.

Flecker explained, "I'll stake you to eighty dollars' worth of chips. In return, Knight, you sign a paper consenting to work for me for two months. If you lose, I get a cowhand free of wages. If you win, you can buy the paper back."

Knight grinned broadly, "You can't tie that for big-heartedness, Flecker. Gimme them chips."

"As soon as you've signed said paper," Flecker returned. "I'll make it out...."

"Hey, wait a minute," Jerry interposed, "instead of takin' all chips, I would like my guns back."

"Forget it." Flecker waved one careless hand. "I'll give you the chips, like I said, and throw in the guns...and also yore horse and rig. How's that for a proposition?"

"Not to mention the shirt off'n your back, eh, if I ask for it?" Jerry chuckled. "You're sure too generous for your own good, Flecker."

"Kelt always was soft-hearted," George Corwin commented.

Flecker smiled good-naturedly, drew a small notebook from an inner vest pocket, tore off one sheet, and scribbled with a stub pencil for a few moments. Tossing the sheet and pencil across to Knight, he said, "Write your moniker, cowboy...and here's the chips. Now, with a new start, mebbe your luck will change."

"I'll bet you it will," Knight nodded.

But it didn't. Twenty minutes later when the first rays of the morning sun threw a broad bar of light across the table, Jerry tossed his cards on the board, face up. "You win, Flecker. Three kings can top jacks and tens any time. When do I go to work?"

Flecker laughed. "I won't rush you, Knight. Anyway, you get grub and a bunk for two months. Here's your guns. And here"—in a sudden burst of generosity—"here's five dollars. I don't want to make it too tough."

"You've found one square rod, Knight," Jacklin said.

"Looks thataway," Jerry agreed. "But I don't want to sit in no more poker games with you *hombres*. You'd won my good reputation next."

For just a second Flecker's face hardened. "I reckon we got that already, Knight."

The eyes of the two men locked in a brief challenge. Jerry said easily after a moment, "Well, you had to get one some place, I suppose."

Flecker's face flushed. "Meanin' what?"

Jerry laughed suddenly, lounged back in his chair, stretching his arms, and yawning. "We were talkin' about my rep as a poker player, wa'n't we?"

"Oh," Flecker said and relaxed, though it wasn't yet clear in his mind what Knight had meant. Before he had time for further thought on the subject, Jerry suddenly straightened in his chair, gathered up the scattered cards, and decked them. Rising from his seat he walked to the bar.

Flecker stiffened suddenly, "Where you goin' with them cards?"

Knight turned back, looked surprised, "Just givin' 'em back to the barkeep," he explained, tossing the deck down on the long counter. "They're his cards, ain't they?" Before Flecker or the others had an opportunity to reply, Jerry went on, "Hey, Hippo, wake up. We're through and cravin' an eye-opener. C'mon, Flecker, I'll buy a drink. Step up fellers. We'll drink success to the Circle-F. I sure aim to do my share of the work."

The other four men strode to the bar. Hippodrome Casey slid his comfortably proportioned form off his stool, yawned widely.

"You gents through at last? My gosh, what a session. You got to be a hound for draw to stick it that long. Who's the heavy winner?"

"Kelt is," Knight grinned. "He got a top hand to help put the Circle-F on a high-payin' basis. 'Course, I'm plumb cleaned out of money an' such material things, but I sure feel like I got a chance to get ahead in my new job."

"Cleaned out, eh?" mused Hippodrome. He shoved Jerry's money back across the bar. "That bein' the case, you'll need that money, cowboy. This one'll be on the house. Drink hearty, gents."

The liquor was downed, glasses clattered back to the bar. Corwin said, "If we get ridin', we can reach the ranch before breakfast is over."

"I'm ready to take on food," Herb Jacklin nodded.

"I ain't figurin' to make no hard ride on an empty stomach," Kelt Flecker grunted. "We'll eat at the Chinaman's where we had supper last night. Reckon our horses is still at the rack down there, anyway. We'd have to go get 'em. Anybody that craves to ride home before he eats is welcome to do it, but I'm payin' for the chow."

"Feelin' good this mornin', eh, Kelt," Tim Beadle said.

"Some," Flecker agreed. "C'mon, Knight."

Saying good bye to Hippodrome, the five men sauntered toward the door, unbolted it, and stepped outside.

II

JERRY FINDS A FRIEND

On the street, Jerry hesitated. "You fellers go ahead down to the restaurant," he suggested. "I'll be with you in a minute."

Flecker frowned suspiciously. "What you aimin' to do?"

"Get my horse," the new hand said promptly. "If you'll remember back to last night, I didn't leave my bronc standin' in front of the Chinaman's place. He's around back of the saloon, under that horse shelter. I'll be right along as soon as I get him."

"Oh." Flecker's face cleared. "All right, Knight. We'll be looking for you."

Flecker and his three hands drifted off down the street, past various buildings with high, false fronts, the high heels on booted feet clumping loudly along the plank walks in the early morning silence. A few pedestrians had put in an appearance by this time.

Jerry rounded the corner of the saloon, passed between it and the neighboring buildings. At the rear of the Topango Bar he found and filled a water bucket, then proceeded on to the horse shelter where a wiry, black gelding whinnied at his approach. Watering the beast and filling a feed trough with food took only a few minutes. Leaving the horse, Jerry approached the rear door of the saloon which by now had been unbolted. Opening the door, he passed through into the bar.

Hippodrome Casey was yawning sleepily and polishing glasses when Knight entered. A look of surprise crossed his face. "Cripes! You back a'ready? Thought you was eatin' breakfast."

Jerry smiled, though an icy gleam brightened his smoky gray eyes. "Figured you and I might as well get acquainted, Hippo. I won't keep you but a second."

Hippodrome looked uneasy. "What's on your mind?"

"I'm more interested in what's out of my pocket," Jerry smiled. "Hippo, Kelt Flecker is a right good poker player, ain't he?"

Hippodrome replied warily, "We-ell, I never knew him to lose with any regularity. He knows the cards...."

"In more ways than one," Jerry laughed. "Let me see that pack we were usin'."

"Oh, shucks, there ain't nothin' wrong with them cards," the barkeep protested. "Hell, I saw you break the seal on that deck yourself before you started play. They're fairly expensive cards, too, made by a reliable company. Nothing wrong with them."

"Let me see 'em." Knight's voice was smooth.

Hippodrome hesitated, then reached to his backbar and tossed the cards in their cardboard case on the bar. Jerry examined the broken seal, then laughed shortly.

The barkeep said, "What's up? Ain't them cards all right?"

"I ain't looked at the cards yet. Yeah, Hippo, you're right about these cards bein' made by a reliable company. *But* whoever steamed this seal off the cover, didn't replace it exactly as it was in the beginnin'...."

"Huh! What you talking about?" The barkeep's surprise was genuine, Jerry decided, after looking steadily into Hippo's wide open eyes.

"All right, Slim, mebbe you ain't in on it," Jerry conceded. "We'll see what else we can learn." Sliding the cards out of their case he scrutinized the backs of the pasteboards closely for several minutes.

Hippo said, "What you lookin' for?"

"Marked cards. And I've found 'em. Nice little example of blockout work, Hippo...."

"Block what....?" The barkeep looked puzzled. "Hey, what you talkin' about?"

"Blockout work it's called. Look here. You see, the backs of these cards have got pictures of a little dog at either end. See? That dog's wearin' a collar. The cards are printed in red on the backs. Now, take a look at the dog collar on this ace of diamonds. Look close. See how someone has taken some red ink and filled in that white collar on the pup. It's right small. You'll have to look close. But if you know what to look for, you wouldn't have any trouble findin' it. Now take this king of clubs. Note how the dog's right forefoot has been blocked in with red. Now, here's a queen of spades...."

"The dirty low-lifed scut!" Hippo exploded suddenly. He gazed unbelievingly at the cards. "Any more?"

"Sure," Jerry laughed, "look 'em over. Here and here. Here's another...."

Hippo swore long and with considerable intensity. By now Jerry Knight was thoroughly convinced that the plump bartender had no part in the deception. "Where'd these cards come from?"

"Kelt Flecker," Hippo exclaimed angrily. "He put one over on me."

"How come?"

"Couple of years back," Hippo explained, "Kelt started kicking about the cards I kept here. They were cheap makes, I admit that, but good enough. Kelt goes in for these all night poker sessions now and then, and he complained that my cards didn't stand up under long handling. Well, inasmuch as I furnish cards free to anybody that wants to play, I wa'n't goin' to buy expensive decks."

"And so," Jerry put in shrewdly, "Kelt offered to furnish his own cards if you'd keep them here for him."

Hippo looked startled, "Now how in hell did you know that?"

"It's an old game, my fat one. It's been worked right often. Flecker simply bought new decks, steamed off the seals, changed the back-markin's so he could recognize 'em, put 'em back in the case, and resealed...."

"My God! Was anybody ever so dumb as me? Say-y-y, I'll bet I tell that big crook a thing or two...."

"No, you won't. Listen, Hippo, you aren't to mention a thing about this. You just keep you eyes and ears open."

"Say," Hippodrome Casey had a new thought, "did you know these cards were marked when you were playin' last night?"

"I suspected it. The only time I was allowed to win was on the small pots. When the kitty was plumb full, I lost."

"Why in time didn't you say somethin'?"

Jerry laughed softly. "And me a stranger on a strange range? Playin' against a foreman and three of his hands. Hippo, I put some value on my life."

"Guess you were wise at that," Hippo conceded. "It wouldn't do to buck the Randall Land and Cattle Company."

"I don't get you?"

"That's the big company that is runnin' things around Topango Wells. Swallowin' up everythin' in sight...land and cattle. Owned by some old crook back East. Kelt Flecker rods the Circle-F which is one of the company's largest properties. Feller named Bristol Capron lives here in town, calls hisself the resident manager. Between Capron and Flecker this range hereabouts is pretty well made to toe the mark. Me, I don't talk back so much my own self, but I'm damned if I'm going to let Kelt pull a slimy trick like this card deal in my barroom. I always run a pretty straight place. Live and let live is my motto, but...."

"I'm askin' you, Hippo, to keep your mouth shut...for a spell leastwise."

"But what you aimin' to do, Knight?" Hippo asked curiously.

"I ain't sure yet. I got a job with Flecker. Let's see what he aims to do first. For some reason he was plumb anxious that I take a job with him. His big-hearted talk didn't fool me none...."

A voice from outside intruded on the conversation. "Hey, Knight, what you doin'?" It was Tim Beadle's voice.

Like a flash, Jerry swept the cards off the bar to the floor back of the long counter. "You ain't seen me," he whispered swiftly. "And keep your mouth shut. I'll be in again one of these days."

Whirling, he moved quickly and silently through the rear entrance. The door closed softly on his exit. A moment later Tim Beadle strode into the saloon to find Hippo industriously sweeping the floor back of the bar.

"Hey, you fat slob," Beadle growled, "where'd Knight go?"

"Huh!" Hippo's mouth dropped open in apparent dumb amazement. "How in hell do I know? He left to get breakfast with you *hombres*. If you think I'm ridin' herd on all the strangers that come into this town, you got another guess comin'. What'd he do, run out on that agreement he made with Kelt?"

"That's what I'm wonderin'. He left us to get his horse which is supposed to be out back. Ain't turned up since. I figured he'd come in here again."

"Ain't seen him." Hippo resumed his sweeping. Muttering an oath Beadle strode through the rear exit and found Jerry under the horse shelter just pulling tight his saddle cinch.

Beadle growled, "What in hell you been doin'?"

Jerry glanced back over his shoulder. "Oh, hello, Tim. Sorry if I kept you waiting. My pony was actin' like he had the heaves when I come out. Fooled around with him some, and he 'pears all right now."

"Oh, we was wonderin'." Beadle appeared placated. "Probably a lot of chaff and dust in that feed bin. I've seen horses act that way before. It comes, and then goes just as fast. Hurry up. Your nag will be all right."

"I reckon. You fellers through eatin'?"

"All but Kelt. He eats enough for two ordinary men. But he don't like to have his orders disobeyed. He expected you to come along at once."

"I didn't know I was under orders."

"You better find it out right *pronto*, Knight. Kelt is good natured up to a certain point. After that, well, he'd just as soon lift your scalp as not."

"Is that so?" Jerry laughed shortly. "He won't be liftin' no scalp of mine."

"Don't get proddy, Knight. He'll lift it and make you like it, any time the idea hits him. Kelt is plumb bad medicine to cross, and in your position you better build your loops just as he tells you to."

Jerry swung up to the saddle. "What do you mean...in my position?"

Beadle laughed sarcastically. "All right, don't admit nothin' you don't have to. It ain't my business. But cowpoke, if you don't play the game Kelt's way, it'll be played in a way not to your liking, *sabe?*"

"Dam'd if I do."

Beadle laughed shortly. "All right, I won't say no more, cowpoke. But you won't be able to run no bluff on Kelt."

In front of the Topango Bar, Beadle mounted his pony and the two men jogged down the street. Arriving at the restaurant, they found Herb Jacklin and George Corwin rolling cigarettes in the shade of the wooden awning that extended above the narrow sidewalk.

Beadle said, "Kelt still eatin'?"

Corwin shook his head, nodded toward a building on the opposite side of the street. "He's gone across to see Capron."

Jerry glanced across at the two-story brick building with its huge letters RANDALL LAND & CATTLE COMPANY painted across the front. Three windows were placed across the second floor which, no doubt, comprised the living quarters of Bristol Capron, the resident manager of the company. Below, on the ground floor was the entrance flanked on each side by a large window on which was also painted, but in smaller letters, the name of the company.

"What kept you so long, Knight?" Jacklin asked.

"Horse bothered me a mite," Jerry explained easily. He added certain details to the story.

Jacklin nodded and said, "You better go grab your breakfast. Kelt will be ready to ride in a little while."

Jerry went in, ordered food and coffee, ate it hurriedly. He had just emerged from the restaurant when a shout from across the street greeted his ears: "Hey Knight, come over here."

Kelt Flecker was standing in the doorway of the building. As Jerry crossed over, Flecker advanced to meet him. Flecker growled, "What kept you so long? I was commencin' to think you'd gone back on your agreement."

Again, Jerry explained glibly that he'd been bothered about his pony which had shown tendencies toward the heaves. Flecker's brow cleared as he cut short the explanations with, "Come on in and sign the payroll. Capron is sort of peeved at me gettin' him out of bed so early, so you better not say anythin'. Just leave things to me. No need to say anythin' about our agreement you signed. What Capron don't know won't hurt him."

Jerry nodded and followed Flecker into the office of the Randall Land and Cattle Company. The lower floor was a large room with not a great deal of furniture. A few chairs were ranged along one wall. In a corner stood a huge iron safe.

Near the window, seated at a desk, was a scowling-visaged individual with thin, sandy hair and grayish-appearing skin. His eyes were cruel and set deeply in sockets, his nose long and pointed. He was only partially dressed in dark trousers and a colorless shirt. His features still bore the marks of sleep.

"This is Knight," Flecker said, propelling the cowboy before him. "Where's your payroll list, Capron?"

"Dammit, Kelt," Bristol Capron snapped, "I don't like this. I told you not to sign on another man."

"Oh, hell," Flecker said wearily, "his wages won't break the company." It was evident the argument had been in progress before Jerry arrived. "After we got more time to talk, I think you'll see the wisdom of hirin' Knight."

Capron shrugged dubiously, reached to a desk drawer, and produced a small ledger, which he opened, and growled at Jerry, "Put your name down here."

He paid scarcely any attention to the cowboy while Jerry signed the book. When Jerry had straightened up from the desk, Flecker said, "Bris, I'll be in, in a day or so, to talk this over with you."

Bristol Capron nodded curtly. "Your talk better be damn' convincing," he snapped.

Flecker laughed. "C'mon, Knight," he said. "We'll be gettin' on." Taking Jerry's arm, as though in a hurry to leave, Flecker urged the cowboy through the doorway. Half way across the street, Flecker chuckled, "No use givin' Capron time to ask questions. You've signed the payroll. I'll collect your money for you."

"And keep it, eh?" the cowpoke cut in.

"You ain't no kick comin'," Flecker protested. "I staked you. You lost. If I get my money back, that's all you need to care."

"I reckon," Jerry nodded.

They joined Corwin, Jacklin, and Beadle in front of the restaurant. The three men looked rather curiously at Knight but didn't say anything. Horses were mounted and the five riders swept out of town, heading west along the trail that led to the Circle-F.

III

WANTED FOR MURDER

A trifle over an hour later, Jerry and the rest arrived at the Circle-F Ranch. The buildings were large and in good condition, the huge rambling ranch house being at present boarded up and not in use. Kelt Flecker lived with his crew in a long bunkhouse, one end of which was fitted up as an office. Besides Kelt and the hands whom Jerry had met in Topango Wells, the crew contained a cook and three other 'punchers who were at present engaged in various tasks about the barns and corrals.

Flecker led Knight into the bunkhouse, pointed out several vacant bunks. "Take your choice," he said.

Jerry threw his blanket roll over a lower bunk, then asked, "When do I go to work?"

"Tomorrow mornin'," Flecker replied. "We been up all night. I aim to take it easy today. You'll find I ain't hard on my men, Knight…providin' they always do as I tell 'em."

There was something ominous in the last words, but Knight paid no attention to the foreman's manner. He nodded shortly, "I always been able to take instructions any place else I worked, Flecker."

"That's fine. Keep on doin' that and you and me won't have no trouble."

The day dragged along. Jerry talked to the other 'punchers whose names were Steve Hackett, Shorty Wing, and Frank Reed. These three were men of his own age and lacked the hard-bitten look of Flecker and the hands with whom Jerry had played poker. They talked but little, although in the course of many careless conversations Jerry discovered that Hackett, Wing, and Reed knew very little of affairs concerning the Circle-F. The three drew their pay and apparently did but little work for it—though that was, it appeared, Kelt Flecker's fault.

"Softest job I ever had," Shorty Wing told Jerry. "I ain't had to get into a saddle for nigh onto two weeks now. Kelt keeps us three at tinkerin' jobs, mendin' harness or fixin' corral posts and such. Him and the rest do what ridin's done. For all the cow work us three do, we might just as well be some of them damn' hoe men south of the river."

"What hoe men?" Jerry asked.

He and Wing were seated on a bench just outside a big hay barn door. Flecker and the other poker players were stretched, snoring, in the bunkhouse. Reed and Hackett were a short distance away, engaged in cutting circular strips from a cowhide with which to manufacture a rawhide rope. It was plain the two were just killing time.

Wing was explaining, "I mean them hoe men located south of Aliso Creek."

"I'm strange to this range," Jerry hinted.

"Sure enough, y'are." Shorty Wing showed a freckled grin. "I'd forgot that. Well, you see, the Randall Land and Cattle Company have a lot of small farms staked out to sell to suckers over that way. These pore benighted hoe men come out here from the Midwest to become dirt farmers. Cripes, they can't even raise enough to keep themselves from starvin'. When the creek's up, there's pretty good irrigation, but come hot weather the water peters out and the crops is ruined. Payments on the land can't be made, so the Randall Company takes back the farm and the following spring catches a new sucker with it."

"That," Jerry mused aloud, "is dirty."

"You think so too, eh?" Wing looked pleased. "That's the way it looks to Reed and Hackett also. We mentioned the fact to Kelt once, but Kelt got sore. Told us to keep our mouths shut about what wasn't our business."

"Whose business is it?"

"Flecker says that's Bristol Capron's end of the game. Shucks! Knight, just as soon as I gather me a coupla months' more wages I'm quittin'."

"Gettin' sick of your job?"

"Me and Reed and Hackett are plumb sick of loafin'. We ain't got enough to do. There's somethin' funny goin' on. I can't see what you was hired for...." Wing stopped abruptly, looked away. "It ain't none of my business," he said, half apologetically, "just forget I said anythin'. Shore, Knight, we like out jobs fine. Let's drop the subject."

Jerry smiled, "I don't talk much and I never did have a habit of repeatin' what I hear."

"I kind of sized you up thataway at first," Wing smiled sheepishly, "and blurted out a lot of palaver."

"I'm interested and I don't talk," Jerry said. "What did you mean by somethin' funny goin' on?"

"You tell me and I'll tell you," Wing frowned. "You see, this Randall that owns all the land hereabouts...or most of it...lives in the East...Kansas City, I think. He leaves everything to Capron. I just wonder, sometimes, if Capron might not like to run the company in a hole."

"And then what?"

Wing shrugged his broad shoulders. "I ain't thought that far. On the other hand, it sometimes looks like the Randall Company was out to hog the whole country. The company holds notes on all the ranches hereabouts, and said ranches is losin' cattle...more cattle than they can afford to lose."

"What other ranches are there?"

"The Rafter-K is about fifteen miles due north from Topango Wells. The Coffee-Pot's the same distance to the northeast. South of the Circle-F is the 2-M...Mart Monroe's outfit. Then there's several small outfits scattered about. They seem to change hands pretty regularly."

"Does the Circle-F make money on its beef?"

"It sure should. I don't know what prices it got, but there was a mighty big shipment went East last fall."

"Just one shipment?"

Wing shook his head. "There was several."

"Any Circle-F shortage on stock?"

Wing shrugged his shoulders. "You got me. I don't get into the saddle enough to know just what's what. You'll have to ask Kelt Flecker, or one of his older hands. Hackett and Reed wouldn't know, either. Why you askin'?"

"Put it down to bein' curious," Jerry smiled. "With cattle disappearin' thataway, it's a wonder some of the ranches haven't called on the Cattlemen's Association to investigate."

"Mebbe they did." Wing frowned, then went on. "There was a *hombre* named Wolcott come here about three months back...."

"Range detective?"

"I don't know for sure. He roamed around the country until it happened."

"Until what happened?"

Wing took a deep breath. "Nobody rightly knows. Wolcott was found dead...shot to death...a few miles to the west of here. A cowhand that worked for the Circle-F...Ridge Conway...was found dead, near him. The two had shot it out. Conway was a right mean cuss."

"Does that pin anything on the Circle-F?"

"That ain't for me to say. The sheriff in Topango Wells is still investigating. It was known that Conway and Flecker was right close, though Flecker claims that him and Conway had a fallin' out two days before the bodies was found. Also, that Conway had quit his job directly after said fallin' out. And here' somethin' else: Wolcott had been shot in the back as well as from in front."

Jerry nodded slowly. "Provin' that Ridge Conway had somebody with him and that between them, they got Wolcott...even if Wolcott did get Conway first."

"Somethin' like that. Sheriff Drake is still lookin' for that third man."

Knight looked, musingly, off across the range where the San Lucia peaks etched rugged lines against the western sky. The sun was on its downgrade stretch now. Neither man spoke for some time. Finally, Knight said quietly, "I thought a heap of Dennis Wolcott."

Wing stiffened, looked puzzled. "You knew him?" he frowned.

Knight nodded. "Knew him well."

"But...say, look here...you asked me a few minutes back if he was a range detective...just like you'd never heard of him."

Jerry smiled thinly. "That was just a feeler. I wanted to see if you knew anything, or what they thought of Wolcott around here."

"Oh," Wing added after a minute. "Well, was he a Cattlemen's Association man?"

"I don't think so."

"Are you?"

"Am I what?"

"Dang it," Wing grinned, "you know what I mean. Are you working for the Cattlemen's Association?"

Jerry laughed, looked Wing straight in the eyes. "Far from it, Shorty."

"Well, what...?" the other commenced, then paused. "Oh, shucks, it ain't my business. Let it go. But, say, in case you need a pard, keep me in mind."

"Thanks, Shorty. I'll remember that."

Steve Hackett and Frank Reed approached the two. The conversation shifted to other subjects. The sun had dropped below the San Lucia range by this time. There came a sudden banging on a dishpan and the cook's loud call to supper. The cowboys rose and sauntered across the ranch yard to the cook shack.

After supper, Kelt Flecker tried to inveigle Jerry into another poker game, but Jerry refused to rise to the bait: "Nothin' doin'," he grinned ruefully. "I'm aimin' to get some shuteye. I expect you'll be findin' a job for me tomorrow." A short time later the men turned into bunks.

The following morning after breakfast, Jerry cut a horse out of the saddler's corral, saddled, then found Flecker to get instructions regarding the day's work. Herb Jacklin had already saddled and loped out of sight over the nearest swell of range. The other men were scattered about the buildings. His horse waiting nearby, Jerry stood to receive instructions from Flecker.

"You bein' a stranger to this part of the country," Flecker commenced, "I've drawed you a rough map of the range hereabouts so's you won't get lost. Here, take a look at this." Flecker produced a small black leather wallet, which he opened, taking out a sheet of white paper on which was crudely drawn, in lead pencil, a rough map of the surrounding country. "Now, you see," Flecker went on, "here's the San Lucia mountains to the west. Here we are"—pointing to a dot on the map—"right here. This is the Circle-F. Now, heading toward the southwest you'll cross Aliso Creek which runs a south-east course after headin' in the mountains. The creek is the boundary line between our outfit and Mart Monroe's 2-M spread."

"You aren't going to tell me you're having trouble over bound-aries with the 2-M," Jerry put in.

"Hell, no. Nothin' of that kind. We're right friendly with the Monroe outfit."

"That's good. I'd hate to get mixed into any range wars."

"Cripes!" Flecker growled. "Do you think I'd send an innocent stranger into a mess of that kind?" Without waiting for a reply he went on. "Now, here's what you do: cross Aliso Creek, then ride for the point where the creek corners into the foothills of the San Lu-cias. There's always a bunch of 2-M cows hangin' around there. They're prime stock...and they never have no riders near 'em. You commencin' to get my point?"

Jerry's eyes narrowed. "Thought you said you were on friendly terms with Monroe."

"Hell's bells! We are." Flecker chuckled. "But if he's fool enough to leave his cattle unguarded, we'd be bigger fools not to take care of 'em for him. All you got to do is cut out about twenty-five or thirty 2-M critters and drive 'em over to our range. Then you head for Camino Cañon...see, on this map. It's about eight miles to the north-east of here. Nice wide cañon, lots of grass. You'll find some of the boys there to take the stock off'n your hands. That's all you got to do."

Knight was seething with anger. "Looks pretty rotten to me," he stated flatly. "Rustlin' a friend's cows...."

Flecker burst into sudden laughter that shook his bulky shoulders. "Sho', now, Knight, you didn't think we aimed to steal them cattle, did you? Shucks, boy, that's a right unkind thought. We just aim to take care of 'em for a spell."

"Yeah," Jerry snapped, "until you can run 'em over the state line and sell 'em...said state line, accordin' to this map, bein' just be-yond the exit from Camino Cañon. And I suppose you got forged bills-of-sale ready too. Flecker, you're a lousy cow thief!"

Flecker's face clouded up like a thunderstorm, one hand dropped to holstered gun. The next instant he jerked the hand away as though it had touched something hot. Knight's six-shooter had appeared as though by magic and held a steady bead on Flecker's middle.

"Go on, jerk it!" Jerry invited angrily.

Flecker slowly shook his head. "Not me," he refused. "I sort of lost my temper for a minute, but there's other ways of convincin' you that you're wrong. Put that gun away. We got to be friends, Knight."

"I'm not convinced of that either," Jerry said quietly. He put the gun away, half expecting Flecker to make a sudden grab for his own weapon. But Flecker's hands still hung loosely at his sides.

"You refusin' to do what I tell you?" Flecker half snarled.

"I'm refusin' to turn cattle rustler!"

"Oh, like that, eh?" Flecker sneered. "You forgot you signed an agreement to work for me, take my orders? You breakin' that agreement?"

"I'm willin' to do the work, honest work," Jerry said slowly, "but no honest man would expect me to live up to an agreement as long as you give crooked orders."

"You're a hell of a *hombre* to talk about bein' honest. Mebbe you'd like to go back to the penitentiary, Knight?"

"Huh!" Jerry stiffened. "What you talkin' about?"

Flecker's loose lips widened in a nasty grin. "Don't try to bluff me, Knight. You ain't a good enough poker player for that. I suppose you're goin' to try and tell me you aren't out on parole right now? And that you've already broke that parole by steppin' out of the state that paroled you, that you'd only served three years of a ten-year stretch. I suppose that's news to you, eh?"

Knight was silent. After a moment he swallowed heavily and said, "Right interestin' information, Flecker."

"Dammit! I told you not to try a bluff on me. I remembered hearin' your name when we met you yesterday. There was an article about you in the *El Paso Gazette* when you were paroled six months ago. Last night I looked up that old paper. Want to see it?"

Without waiting for a reply, Flecker produced a newspaper clipping and held it before Knight's eyes. He said mockingly, "Knight …better known as Jerry. Fast man with a gun, eh? You was too fast once, wa'n't you?"

"There was mitigating circumstances," Jerry said slowly. "It tells about that, right here."

"Mitigatin' circumstances don't bring a dead man to life," Flecker chuckled evilly. "You done your three years then, because somebody offered you a job, the state authorities paroled you. But what's happened to that job? Another condition of the parole was that you wa'n't to leave the state. Knight, you're a hell of a long way from Texas and between here and there there's been a stage hold-up fairly recent, by a feller that answered your description. I happen to know that. And you blow into Topango Wells yesterday with talk about havin' wages in your pocket. All right, make up your mind. I'm losin' patience. Do you want to go back to the pen, or are you ready to obey my orders?"

Knight looked glum, downcast. Finally he sighed, started to climb into his saddle. "Reckon I've got no choice in the matter," he spoke heavily. "Guess I'll have to obey orders."

Flecker guffawed triumphantly. "I figured you'd listen to reason, cowpoke. You be a good *hombre* and we'll all make money. Cross me, and you'll find yourself starin' a series of steel bars in the face. And don't figure to drift out of the country when you leave here. One word to the authorities, and I'll have a manhunt on your trail. Oh, yes, Knight, be sure and pick nice, plump cows."

Jerry gulped, started to swing the pony around. Flecker said, "Here, take this map with you." He replaced the map in the wallet and handed it up to Knight.

"I won't need that leather case, Flecker."

"Go on. Take it. I don't want it. It's been kickin' around for the past year or so. You'll need that map a lot before we get through. It'll keep better if you got a case to carry it in. I don't aim to be drawin' maps for dumb cowpokes all the time. Get goin', Knight. I'll see you at supper."

Jerry yanked his hatbrim over his eyes, turned the pony, and started off. Flecker snickered, "Don't go away mad. Ain't you goin' to say good bye?"

But Jerry kept going without another word.

Flecker laughed and turned back toward the bunkhouse. Tim Beadle and George Corwin were sitting on a bench just outside the door.

Beadle said, "Did the sucker take the bait?"

Flecker laughed triumphantly. "Cripes! He didn't have no choice in the matter when he seed what we knew about him."

"Bet he was surprised," Corwin commented.

"He was downright flabbergasted," Flecker grunted. "All right, you two, you better get your hawsses and ride for Camino Cañon. You know, just in case he does get there with some cows. It might not happen today, but it will, one of these days, damn' soon. Jerry Knight, eh? Hell's bells! It ain't goin' to be long before he gets lost in a fog…a fog made by powder smoke. And he won't *ever* find himself again neither…not if old Mart Monroe draws a bead with that .30-30 of his'n. Men, the scheme is airtight!"

IV

JERK 'EM HIGH, COWPOKE!

Heading toward the southwest, Knight pushed his pony along at a sharp gait until he was well out of sight of the Circle-F ranch buildings. Only then did he slow his pace, his course bringing him nearer to the San Lucia range. It was good grazing country hereabouts, rolling land with here and there clumps of sage, of prickly pear. As ten miles drifted to his rear, the terrain commenced to lift toward the San Lucia foothills and now and then he had to turn the horse aside to avoid tall upthrusts of reddish-brown granite.

Half an hour later Jerry neared the line of low cottonwoods, dotted with small alder trees, that lined either side of Aliso Creek. He pushed on and drew his pony to a splashing stop in the center of the broad, shallow stream of clear water which didn't reach quite to his stirrups. While the pony was drinking long droughts of the cooling creek, Jerry drew out the map Flecker had furnished and studied it intently.

As he was about to replace the folded map back in the black leather case, a tiny gold fleck in the leather caught his eye. Jerry frowned and studied the case carefully. At some time a name, in gold lettering, had been stamped into the leather. Someone had gone to great pains to scratch out the gold in an effort to obliterate the name, but the marks of the letter-stamp were still visible under close scrutiny. An *e* showed up quite plainly, as did a *c* and a *t*. Further study brought out a capital *D* and a capital *W*.

He grunted with satisfaction, reined the pony out on the opposite bank, and rolled a Durham cigarette. Inhaling deeply of the tobacco smoke, he checked the pony's tendency to move on, and again gave his undivided attention to the letters on the black case. One by one the letters revealed themselves to his eyes, until they spelled out the name: Dennis Wolcott. It was all clear to anyone who cared to devote a little study to the partially obliterated letters.

Jerry's eyes narrowed as he gazed in deep thought across the range. In a fight with Ridge Conway, whom Wolcott had killed, a third man had slain Dennis Wolcott by shooting him in the back. According to Shorty Wing, Conway and Kelt Flecker had been friends. It was Flecker who had given Knight the black leather case. Was it Flecker who had shot Wolcott in the back?

"That," Knight muttered grimly, "is somethin' I aim to find out before I leave this range. The way things are shaping up I may be forced to leave a lot sooner than I expect...mebbe on the fast end of a lead slug."

He put the map and leather case away and touched spurs to his pony's ribs, clearing the trees that bordered the creek, but following its winding course deeper into the foothills. Here the grass grew luxuriantly, though jumbled heaps of large rocks barred his way from time to time. Then, quite suddenly, Jerry dipped down into a wide grassy hollow across which were grazing about three hundred white-faced cattle bearing on the right ribs a 2-M brand. Jerry glanced quickly and cautiously around. Excepting himself there wasn't a rider of any kind in sight. He moved toward the cattle.

"Flecker said to cut out twenty-five or thirty nice plump cows," Jerry growled resentfully, "but he's one damn' fool if he figures I'm goin' to waste any time choosin'. I'll cut out a bunch from those nearest me and then fan my tail out of this territory just as fast as I can drive cow critters. I don't reckon it would be very healthy to be caught stealing another man's beef in this section."

He uncoiled his rope and, using it to startle the cows into motion, started toward the nearest animals. For ten minutes he worked strenuously cutting out some twenty cattle from the herd. Then quite suddenly it happened.

Jerry was just reining his pony around a tall upthrust of rock in pursuit of an obstreperous cow when a leaden slug flattened itself against the granite with a sort of silvery splash. At the same instant the report of a rifle shot reached his ears. With one quick motion Knight jerked his pony to a halt, whirled in the saddle as he spun the pony around to face the unseen rifleman. There was nobody to be seen. In front of Knight were scattered only boulders and waving grass. He crouched low in the saddle, one fist clenching the butt of his six-shooter, eyes peering rapidly about but seeing no motion anywhere. Jerry raised his voice: "Show yourself, *hombre*, if you want another chance. That shot was right close, but if you want another you got to put in an appearance."

This was largely bluff and he knew it was bluff, but he hoped to frighten the hidden assailant into coming into the open. But the bluff didn't work. The answer when it came surprised Knight. It consisted of a single scornful laugh from a point much nearer than Jerry had dreamed. He moved his head slightly to view the high, wide granite boulder—it was nearly the size of a small house—from behind which the laugh had come. And now Jerry saw the end of a rifle barrel pointing his way and the rider behind the gun.

The rider spoke contemptuously: "Jerk 'em high, cowpoke. I've got a bead on you. Take your hand away from that gun. Put 'em up! Quick!"

There was nothing else, under the circumstances, for Jerry Knight to do. Slowly, he raised his hands high above his head, then lowered them, clasped, across the crown of his sombrero.

"Now will you come into sight?" he challenged coolly. "Or are you afraid to?"

Again that scornful laugh, as the rider pushed into full view, walking her horse slowly toward Jerry, the rifle still "at ready" and cuddled against her side.

Jerry said, "Thought it was a girl's voice. Nobody but a woman would miss a shot at that short a distance."

"It wouldn't occur to a dumb man that I might have missed on purpose, would it?" the girl snapped angrily. "Cow thief, I could have bored you plumb center."

"I'm wonderin' why you didn't?" he asked mildly.

"Probably because I'm a fool," the girl said bitterly. "It's a good thing for you it wasn't Dad or one of the boys. Nope, I'll just take you prisoner and let them decide what's to be done. Loosen your gun belts, drop 'em to the ground. Hurry up, now, or I'll forget that I'm soft-hearted. Quick!"

Looking into the girl's flashing black eyes, Jerry saw that she meant every word. At the same moment, even while he was dropping his guns to the earth, he couldn't suppress the involuntary exclamation that left his lips. The girl was really pretty with great masses of blue-black hair coiled beneath her old slouch-brimmed sombrero. Her nose was straight, her red lips and chin determined. A man's blue denim shirt, rolled to the elbows, exposed well-tanned, rounded arms. She was in man's overalls and on her feet were a well-worn pair of high-heeled riding boots. The horse she sat was a wiry little chestnut.

The girl said again, contemptuously, "Dirty cow thief!"

"Sort of harsh words, ma'am," Jerry said reprovingly.

"Well, aren't you? I've been watching you, saw you cutting out 2-M cattle. I saw you were a stranger and I hesitated to shoot on that account, but we've lost enough cattle the past year. Well, answer me, aren't you a cow thief?"

"It sure looks thataway, ma'am," he grinned.

The girl frowned at the cowboy, failing to understand such levity under the circumstances. "You mean, you aren't? That you have a plausible reason for...."

"Yes, ma'am." Jerry's grin widened. "You see, I was only following the boss' orders."

"And he told you to steal our cows?"

"Yes'm. Told me just where to find 'em."

"Well, my grief! What sort of...say, cowboy, are you crazy?"

"Just a mite batty, I expect," he said humbly. "Maybe it's the view."

"The view?"

Jerry explained. "Uh-huh. And a sudden idea. You know, the scenery. It *is* beautiful. I don't know where I've seen such a pretty sight. And then I got my idea: I thought, gosh, it'd be great to be married to such scenery. And the whole idea sort of made my head swim...."

"Stop it!" The girl's cheeks flushed red. "You *are* insane, I reckon."

"Yes'm, I don't ever expect to be the same again. My name's Knight. My friends call me Jerry, but I reckon we'll have to put down the whole she-bang on the license."

"What are you talking about?"

"The wedding license. You and me. Say, I bet you ten bucks your name is Monroe."

"A cow thief would bet on a sure thing," the girl sneered.

"I'd put my money on you, any time," Jerry said lazily. "The first name is Marie, Violet, Abigail, or I'm a liar."

"You are," the girl said shortly. "It's Alice."

"Right pretty name. But I had to find out somehow. Yep, you and me will get along fine, once we come to an understanding."

"You're going to come to your understanding a heap quicker than you expect. Turn that horse, mister, and ride slow in front of me."

Jerry made no move to obey. He said, instead "I can't Alice. I got to do what my boss told me to do. I don't think he'd like it if I came back without some of your cows."

"Who is your boss?"

"Kelt Flecker."

The girl's lip curled up disdainfully, "That snake!"

"Ain't you sort of hard on the whole snake family, miss?"

The girl's dark eyes narrowed. She hardly knew what to make of her captive. "I reckon I am, at that," she conceded coldly. "But snakes are cunning...at least."

"Don't you think that same applies to Flecker?"

Alice Monroe shook her had. "If he had brains, he wouldn't send anybody quite as thick-headed as you to rustle our cows." Jerry flushed as the girl continued. "I can't see how he came to hire you. I'll bet you're just something the cat dragged home."

"No'm," Jerry said humbly, "Flecker won me in a poker game."

"My grief! In a poker game?"

"Uh-huh. Flecker was demonstratin' something I already know...that three of a kind beats two pair." From that point on, Jerry went ahead and told the girl just how he had happened to go to work for the Circle-F.

The girl listened to the tale with growing amazement, believing Knight in spite of herself—and finding herself liking the cowboy at the same time. She relented a trifle and some of the acid went out of her voice. "Well, that beats me!" she exclaimed.

"It beat me, too," Jerry grinned.

"I've never heard anything like it. And just because you signed that paper to follow orders, you think you have to turn cow thief! Even after you discovered you were playing with marked cards. Cowboy, you are a bigger fool than I thought."

"It sure looks thataway," Jerry admitted whimsically. "Right now, I'm plumb kicking myself for not looking into this neck of the range a long time ago."

"You find it interesting?"

"She sure is."

The girl's cheeks flushed under Jerry's admiring stare. "We'll talk about the business at hand," she reminded, trying to keep her voice chilly, but not succeeding very well. "I've decided to let you go."

"Supposing I like bein' a captive? Supposing I don't want to be let go. Y'know, you really ought to consider my feelin's in the matter," he chuckled.

The girl had already lowered the rifle muzzle. Now she threw up one hand in a hopeless gesture. "It's no use trying to talk sensibly to you," she stated emphatically. "Here I'm trying to get our talk on a common-sense basis, and you...."

"All right," Jerry broke in, "I'll behave. Now, what do you want to do?"

"I want you to pick up your guns and ride back to the Circle-F as fast as your horse will carry you. What you do then is no concern of mine."

"We won't argue that right now," Jerry said dryly. "What are you intending to do?"

"I'm going to get back to the ranch and tell Dad about you, repeat the things you've told me about Flecker sending you here to rustle our cattle and so on. It's the proof we've been needing. We never have liked Flecker. We've suspected him, but couldn't get proof. And then we'll get Sheriff Buck Drake on the job and...."

"I wouldn't, were I you," Jerry advised, shaking his head. "You wouldn't get any place. Flecker would only deny that he had sent me over here. I'm a stranger in the country. It would be Flecker's word against a stranger's...and Flecker would win. You'd have tipped your hand, given your plans away. No, we better let it ride and not say anything about you letting me go. And I'll just consider myself lucky."

"You certainly can," the girl stated flatly. "If Dad or one of our 2-M hands had been watching these cows today, you wouldn't have received a warning. They'd have shot on sight."

"I reckon so...," Jerry broke off suddenly to ask: "Does your dad always keep somebody on guard over these cattle?"

The girl nodded. "Every day. For the past three months. We had to do something, the stock was disappearing so fast. But Dad sent out a warning, notifying he'd shoot on sight anybody he found rustling his cows. Everybody in the San Lucia country knows that, and we haven't, so far as we know, lost a cow since."

"Do you reckon Kelt Flecker knows it?"

The girl laughed shortly. "Better than anyone else. Dad told Flecker, directly to his face."

Jerry frowned, then speaking as though to himself, "Dennis Wolcott was killed by an unknown...."

"Yes, he was," Alice Monroe took up the thought. "You know about that, eh? I'll tell you something else. It's suspected that Kelt Flecker is the unknown, but Sheriff Drake has never been able to prove it. Flecker claims he broke with Ridge Conway a couple of days before the killing of Conway and Wolcott. Sheriff Drake is still looking for that third man."

Jerry laughed softly, "And if you'd shot and killed me...you or somebody else...and something of Dennis Wolcott's was found on me that would sure make it look like I was the third man in the case, wouldn't it?"

"It certainly would. Have you anything of Wolcott's?"

Jerry nodded. "Flecker gave me a black leather wallet that once belonged to Wolcott. By looking close you can make out Wolcott's name, stamped in the leather."

"It certainly looks," the girl's dark eyes narrowed, "as though Mister Kelt Flecker was trying to get some evidence shot off."

"A nice piece of framing," he agreed.

"That settles it," the girl said decisively, "now we've simply got to go to Topango Wells and tell the sheriff what we know."

"Not yet," Jerry contradicted. "Before we spill any beans, I want to know a few more things about this range."

Alice Monroe eyed Jerry speculatively. "You aren't a range detective, are you?" she said seriously.

Jerry grinned and shook his head. "Not none. Matter of fact, if I told you who I really am, you'd laugh at me. You wouldn't even believe me, mebbe."

The girl was puzzled, but didn't press the question that rose to her lips. Finally she said, "All right, I *think* you've spoken the truth. I won't say anything for a time…to the sheriff. But I am going to tell Dad. Now, you better pick up your guns and ride."

"Tell your dad I'm askin' him to keep his lip buttoned for a spell."

Alice Monroe looked dubious. "I'll do what I can, but he'll have to suit himself."

Jerry nodded, and swung down from the saddle to retrieve his six-shooters. At that instant there came a sharp whining noise as a leaden slug passed dangerously close to his head. From the hillside at the backs of the two came the flat report of a Winchester.

V

GUNSMOKE FOG

The next instant, Jerry had whirled to the girl's side and had swept her out of the saddle, keeping the horse between the girl and the assailant on the hillside.

"Down, keep down!" Jerry said sharply.

"I'm down." Alice Monroe's voice was cool. "It's you he's trying to hit. Not me. If you hadn't chosen to get your guns at that very instant, he'd have hit you."

"Who is it?"

"If I knew, I'd tell you."

Cautiously, peering above the pony's neck, Jerry scanned the hillside which was covered with trees and brush. There wasn't a soul to be seen.

"See him?" the girl asked.

Jerry shook his head. "Not a sign…." He broke off suddenly, catching sight of a horse darting through the trees, but the rider was too far away to be recognizable in the leafy shadows.

"I think," Jerry said swiftly, "we've got him cornered. He figured when he finished me, you'd turn your horse and clear out as soon as possible. He'll have one tough time coming down out of that brush without being seen by us. You stay here."

"What are you going to do?"

"Try and catch me a skunk," the cowboy laughed grimly. "Keep behind rocks. I'll be...."

"But Jerry...!" There was a note of fright in the girl's tone.

"Yes, Alice," Jerry grinned. "Gosh, we're sure gettin' acquainted...first names in use already. Wait here for me."

His guns were already buckled on as he vaulted to the saddle and wheeled the pony. Then he started at a direct run toward the hillside. The girl gazed after him with wide, anxious eyes. Jerry was nearing the line of brush and trees that grew halfway up the slope. Then yards farther, a puff of black smoke burst from the brush. The report of the gun reached her ears. But Jerry's pony was still climbing, it's speed undiminished. An instant later, he reined the little beast into the shadowed depths.

Ten minutes passed. Fifteen. Silence on the hillside now. The sun beat down warmly on the anxious figure of the girl, waiting for some sign of Jerry or the unknown gunman. Once she examined her rifle. Abruptly, a shot sounded through the silence. Five minutes later there came a second shot. Then two more in quick succession. Alice choked back the cry that rose to her lips, her eyes wide on the motionless hillside.

Meanwhile, Jerry had pushed through the trees and was peering sharply about. Cottonwoods and alders and scrub oak barred his path. Jack pine appeared frequently. There wasn't a soul to be seen. Low hanging cottonwoods forced Jerry to dismount and lead the pony through a veritable jungle of range growth. Suddenly, from Jerry's left, a shot roared. This time a six-shooter. Though the shot flew wide of its mark, Jerry gave a sharp cry and dropped to the earth. Rolling over and over he quickly screened himself behind a mass of tall brush and waited.

Silence. Overhead, spots of sunlight pierced the thicket. Insects droned unceasingly in the quiet. A minute passed and reached to five. Stealthy footsteps sounded on dry leaves. A branch snapped loudly. Then, peering to right and left, six-shooter in hand, came Herb Jacklin, his mind intent on finding and finishing the job he had commenced. Seeing Jerry's riderless horse he stopped suddenly, tensed to shoot. He was facing partly away from Jerry's position. Now Jerry rose to his full height.

"You lookin' for somethin', Jacklin?" he said clearly.

Jacklin's gunhand swung up in a swift arc and, as he whirled to face Jerry's voice, a vile oath left his lips. His gun roared as Jerry jerked sidewise, his own guns snapping into view. Jerry's right hand thumbed one swift shot. Almost on top of the explosion came the sound of the left gun. Jacklin stiffened, started a scornful laugh that turned to a cough. Then his body jack-knifed and he pitched forward on his face. He was quite dead before Knight reached him, turned him over.

Gunsmoke fog drifted lazily through the sun-spotted shadows. A breeze lifted, swept away the last remnants of the swirling gray haze. Knight straightened himself from the body, looked around. His face was hard and grim.

"That's one, Dennis," he half whispered. "It was probably Flecker that got you, but this scut was in on it all right."

He stood looking down at the motionless form a moment, considering while rolling a cigarette. A match was lifted to his lips with steady fingers. Then he reloaded his guns and strode to his horse. A short distance away he found Jacklin's pony, slapped it on the rump, and started it off through the brush. Then he mounted and loped quickly down the slope where Alice Monroe awaited him.

He forced a smile as he dismounted at the girl's side. She was white-faced, tremulous. Finally her lips parted in a half whisper: "Well?"

Jerry said easily, "Lots of skunks in those hills."

"Skunks don't use guns."

Jerry smiled down into her eyes, giving her confidence, steadying her shaken nerves. "This one did," he said quietly.

"Who was it?" the girl insisted.

Jerry evaded that. "You tell your dad about this," he said. "Better have him come out and look things over. You better get on your pony and drift now. But first I'd like the lay of the land around here. Who's Bristol Capron?"

"Manager of the Randall Land and Cattle Company. A slimier reptile never lived, in my opinion. I don't trust him."

"The company put him in the job."

"He's a fit man for such a company."

"What've you got against the Randall outfit as a whole?"

"They're thieves…land hogs, cattle hogs. They're trying to gobble up every bit of wealth in sight. I tell you, Ira Randall wouldn't dare come to this part of the country." Her voice was bitter. "He'd be lynched on sight. This country hates him worse than poison. He's wise to stay in the East."

"Mebbe you're wronging Ira Randall," Jerry said quietly.

"If so, you'll have to show me where," the girl flamed. "His company has issued mortgages to poor farmers who couldn't possibly pay them off. It's foreclosed on ranches. I tell you, the Randall Company is nothing but a greedy, merciless bloodsucker. What do you think Flecker was stealing our cattle for?"

"I'm waitin' to hear."

"So Dad would go broke and have to give up the 2-M. Capron has already made several offers, but they're so small, cheap, that Dad refuses."

"The company holds a mortgage on the 2-M?"

"No, thank God for that...but it would like to. Capron is trying his best to ruin us, so the company can get the 2-M."

"Any particular reason for the company to be so eager to get your outfit?"

"Plenty," Alice Monroe snapped. "Palo Verde Pass."

Jerry looked puzzled. "You'll have to explain that."

"Palo Verde Pass cuts through the San Lucias about six miles southeast of our ranch house. It's part of our holdings. The T. N. & A. S. Railroad would like the pass through which to extend its line which, as you probably know, terminates at Topango Wells at present."

"Seems to me," Jerry said, "your dad would be wise to give the railroad the right of way. He could make some money and...."

"You wouldn't understand," the girl interrupted. "You see, right at the mouth of the pass there's a nice stretch of tableland that overlooks this whole valley. Before Mother died, she and Dad had always planned to build a house at that point." The girl's eyes grew wistful, slightly moist. "Some day I want to build a house there myself. This is pretty country. It's a pretty pass. I don't want it ruined by coal smoke and cinders and steel rails. We don't want a lot of money. Only enough to get along comfortably. If the company would only leave us alone...I mean, the Randall Company...."

Jerry said gently, "I see your point, girl. But people the other side of the San Lucias need a railroad."

"There's Camino Cañon, then," the girl flared. "It's more on a line with the rails already laid. The T. N. & A. S. would sooner have it. By using Camino, it would have a shorter, more direct route."

"Why doesn't the railroad use Camino Cañon then?" Jerry asked. Remembering the map Flecker had furnished, he continued, "Camino Cañon is just about eight or nine miles due west of the Circle-F, isn't it?"

"Nearer eight," the girl nodded. "The railroad can't get it because Camino Cañon is on Circle-F holdings and the Randall Company won't sell…that is, it will sell, but at a terribly prohibitive price. The railroad refuses to be held up that way. I don't blame it."

"Oh, I see." Jerry was quiet for a spell, then he changed the subject. "You better be getting along now. Tell your dad what's happened. Also, tell him not to count his cows tonight or he'll find himself twenty or thirty head shy."

The girl started to mount. Now she swung up to the saddle and snapped at him, "What?"

He nodded, repeating, "Twenty or thirty head shy."

"Now, look here, cowboy…," Alice bridled.

"Shucks, I got to carry out the boss' orders. Now, now, wait a minute, don't you go to flyin' off'n the handle thataway. I know what I'm doing."

"I wonder if you do." The girl looked puzzled.

"Yeah, you can bet on it. And you may lose a few cows, but you stand to win in the long run. Take my word for that."

"We-ell," the girl hesitated, "it sounds crazy, but…but…."

"But you'll let me leave with the cows and not shoot at me any more? Fine! We're gettin' along right well, Alice. But you haven't seen anything yet. I've got plans…."

"What kind of plans?"

"'Member what I said about a license?"

The girl's face crimsoned as she touched spurs to her pony and moved rapidly away.

"I've got other plans, too," Jerry called after her. "Leastwise, I'll have 'em drawn. Plans for a house…a house on that pretty table-land you were telling me about."

The girl kept going. Jerry raised his voice again, "Hey, I'll be back tomorrow after more cows. You'll be here, won't you?"

The girl turned in the saddle, "You couldn't stop me, now, cowboy," she laughed back, "but I'll have the whole 2-M crew with me. ¡*Adios!*"

Her horse broke into a swift lope and a moment later she had dropped behind a rise of land.

Jerry mounted, again set to work cutting out 2-M cows. In a short time he had gathered twenty-five head and turned them toward Camino Cañon. It was about three in the afternoon when he arrived at the cañon, driving the cows before him. Tim Beadle and George Corwin were awaiting his arrival, though they seemed somewhat surprised at seeing him.

Beadle said, "Got here all right, eh?"

"Sure, didn't you think I would?" Jerry said gravely.

"Didn't have no trouble, or nothin'?" Corwin persisted.

"None at all."

"Wa'n't nobody ridin' herd on the cows?" Beadle appeared puzzled.

"Flecker told me they left the cows unguarded," Jerry stated. "Didn't you know that?"

Beadle and Corwin exchanged glances, but didn't bother to answer Knight. Beadle said to his pardner, "I reckon they must have give up watchin'...."

"Who?" Jerry cut in.

"Never mind," Corwin replied. "Come on, we'll throw these cows in with the others."

The three men got behind the small bunch of Herefords and drove them into the cañon whose sloping walls were covered with grass and scrub oak. Rounding a bend in the cañon, Jerry saw about fifty more 2-M cows, penned up in a crude corral built of loose rock. The trail through the cañon was little frequented and the rock corral was screened, to a large extent, by tall brush and cottonwoods. So there was little likelihood of the rustled cows being discovered by anyone unless he were led to the spot.

Jerry said, "Huh! More cows, eh? Were you fellers over on 2-M range today?"

Beadle shook his head. "No, these is just strays we've picked up from time to time. We been holdin' 'em here for a spell. In case any of the 2-M hands did discover this beef stock, we could always say they'd strayed over here, and we was just holdin' 'em until we had a chance to turn 'em back."

"Strays, eh?" Jerry said thoughtfully. "I shouldn't think them cows would be likely to stray away from good grazin' and cross Aliso Creek to come over here."

Beadle winked at Corwin. "Knight," he said humorously, "you'd be surprised where 2-M critters stray sometimes."

Corwin laughed and nodded, then said, "You can go back to the ranch now, Knight. Tell Kelt you delivered the cows okay and that we was here waitin'."

"You two comin' in?" Jerry asked.

Beadle shook his head. "Nope, we got some drivin' to do tonight."

Jerry reined his horse around, waved one hand in farewell, and headed for the Circle-F.

VI

THE 2-M OUTFIT

The ranch cook was just beating the dishpan to announce supper when Jerry rode in, turned his horse into the corral, and carried his rig to the bunkhouse. Kelt Flecker and the three Circle-F hands were already seated at the table in the cook shack, delving into spuds, bacon, and beans. Flecker looked up in some surprise when Jerry entered and greeted the rest.

"You carry out my orders?" he demanded.

Jerry reached for a platter of bacon as he nodded. "Sure, delivered those 2-M critters to Corwin and Beadle."

"Never mind that," Flecker said hastily. He looked quickly at Wing, Hackett, and Reed who were gazing questioningly at Knight. Flecker went on, "We'll talk it over later, Knight. And you mean Circle-F critters...not 2-M, don't you?"

"Reckon I do," Jerry nodded.

"Didn't lose that map, did you?" Flecker said after a time.

Jerry shook his head. "It helped a heap."

"Sure," Flecker said heartily. "You hang onto that map and the case you carry it in. It'll come in handy."

Supper was finished in silence. Afterward, Flecker drew Knight outside and asked for details regarding the 2-M cows. Jerry supplied the story, adding, "Corwin and Beadle had another bunch of cows waiting in Camino Cañon. Said they were 2-M strays."

"We've had them a long time," Flecker boasted brazenly, "just waitin' to add a few more before runnin' 'em over the state line. Say, you didn't see nobody over on the 2-M range today, did you?"

"You mean 2-M hands?"

Flecker nodded. Jerry shook his head. "Nary a hand," he said smoothly.

The two were standing near the corral. Darkness had descended, only the squares of light from the cook shack and bunkhouse punctuating the dense gloom. Overhead only a few stars showed through.

Flecker said after a time, "Herb Jacklin wasn't with George and Tim was he?"

"I didn't see him in the cañon," Jerry replied truthfully.

"I wonder why in the hell he ain't back?" Flecker sounded irritable.

"Where'd he go?"

"I sent him on a job," Flecker returned vaguely.

A sudden movement several yards away took the attention of the two men. A dark shape moved in the gloom. Flecker reached for his gun, then halted and went cautiously forward. A moment later he scratched a match, then a violent oath left his lips.

Jerry hurried forward. "What's wrong?"

Flecker swore again. "Here's Herb's horse. Now where in hell's Herb?"

Jacklin's horse had finally wandered home. Jerry scratched matches while Flecker removed Jacklin's rifle from the saddle boot and examined it.

"Looks like two shots had been fired," Flecker announced after a time. "That's providin' Herb started out with a full magazine, and I reckon he did. But where in hell is Herb? Hope nothin's happened to him."

Jerry said, "Mebbe his horse bucked him off, and he's walking."

Flecker shook his head. "That horse can't be made to buck. I 'member the day Herb took all the buckin' out of him. The horse pitched Herb off...just once. Then Herb took to beatin' it over the head with a loaded quirt every time it moved sudden. Nope, that horse was sure broke of buckin'...say, Knight, you didn't hear any shootin' today, did you?"

"Come to think of it, I did," Knight admitted.

"Huh! What? Why didn't you say so before?"

"Reckon it slipped my mind."

"When was this? Where?"

"It was just before I pulled out with the 2-M cows," Knight replied truthfully enough. "Up on the hillside, among the trees and brush. There were several shots fired."

Flecker swore violently. "Why didn't you see what was goin' on?"

Knight laughed scornfully, "Listen, boss, would you have stayed, under the circumstances? Here I was on a strange range, picking up another man's cows. Hell's bells! You're lucky I delivered the cows at the cañon!"

"But you might have...."

"How did I know that Jacklin was over there? What did you do, send him to spy on me? That's a lousy trick...."

"Take it easy now, Knight. I didn't say Jacklin was over there." Flecker's voice was placating. "As a matter of fact, that shootin' didn't mean anythin'. Pro'bly somebody shootin' at targets or out to get a few birds for supper."

"That's probably it," Jerry agreed, grinning in the darkness.

Flecker appeared worried. He and Jerry walked slowly toward the bunkhouse. Finally Flecker announced, "Look here, Knight. You know where that corral is in the cañon now. Tomorrow, you go over to the 2-M range, get some more cows, and bring them to that corral. I'm ridin' tonight."

"Where're you going?"

"I'm worried about what's happened to Herb," Flecker snapped. "Can't tell what's shapin' up, with him not returnin'. I'm goin' to saddle up and join Corwin and Beadle. We got to get them cows out of the cañon, in case there'd be any sort of investigation on the way. You stay here and carry out the job like I've told you. We'll probably be back in three days."

"Take that long to get those cows over the state line?"

Flecker nodded. "Two days to go and find a buyer and so on. Me'n George and Tim can return in a day. But, hell, I'm losin' time, foolin' around here."

Muttering to himself, Flecker dashed to get his saddle, returned to the corral, and saddled up. Five minutes later, he was riding, fast, out of the ranch yard. Suddenly he pulled up short in a scattering of sand and gravel, and yelled, "Hey, Knight."

"Yeah, what you want?"

"You take charge until I return. Carry out the job I give you, but give them other hands enough work around the ranch to keep 'em busy until I get back."

"I'll take care of it," Jerry called in reply.

Again came the rush of hoofs as Flecker departed rapidly. Jerry chuckled, "Kelt Flecker is sure disturbed. Jacklin's not showing up has got him worried."

He made his way toward the bunkhouse and found Shorty Wing standing in the doorway.

Shorty said, "I heard Kelt givin' you orders. So you're roddin' the outfit until he returns, eh?"

"Looks thataway," Jerry smiled.

From inside the bunkhouse, Steve Hackett asked, "What job you got picked for us tomorrow?"

Jerry stepped into the bunkhouse, nodded to Frank Reed who was also there, then said, "You *hombres* are due for some riding early tomorrow. Kelt has about seventy-five 2-M cows that he figures to sell over the state line. We four are going to cut out a hundred Circle-F critters and return 'em to the Monroe outfit. We've got to keep the account balanced, pay a debt with interest, if you want to put it that way."

"What!" The three cowboys spoke as one.

"You heard me," Jerry chuckled. "Game to do it?"

"Cripes, yes!" Again a blending of three voices. Shorty Wing added, "Say, what sort of game you pullin'?"

Jerry said, "Kelt's worrying because Jacklin hasn't showed up."

"But where is he?" Reed asked.

"I killed him," Knight said tersely. "Flecker sent me rustling 2-M cows in hopes I'd get shot while doing it. He sent Jacklin to spy on me. I met a girl there...."

"Alice Monroe?" Hackett said.

Jerry nodded. "We got acquainted. I reckon Jacklin, watching me, figured I might tell what I knew, so he took a shot at me. I climbed the hillside after him. We shot it out."

"Well, may I be damned!" Wing said in amazement.

"Mebbe we'll all get shot," Jerry speculated, "when Kelt learns I'm bucking him."

"Ain't that the truth!" Reed exclaimed fervently. "There'll be plenty lead thrown. Looks to me like the air was due to get fogged up with gun smoke."

"Say, Jerry," Wing queried, "why should Kelt send you over there to get you killed?"

"He'd like it to look like I was the third man in the Dennis Wolcott killing."

Wing interrupted to say, "I told Steve and Frank about you knowin' Wolcott. They both think you're a range detective."

"I'm far from it." Jerry smiled a bit grimly. He added details about the map and the leather case with the obliterated name.

The four cowboys talked for another hour before turning in for the night. The following morning they were in the saddle by sun-up, paying no attention to the questions of the inquisitive ranch cook who was curious to know where they were going.

It was about an hour past mid-morning when Jerry, accompanied by Wing, Hackett, and Reed, pushed about a hundred head of Circle-F cattle across Aliso Creek and onto 2-M range. Clearing the trees that bordered the course of the stream, Knight saw Alice Monroe and a spare elderly man, seated on horses, watching the approaching cattle with puzzled eyes. Jerry rode forward to meet the girl. Alice put her pony into motion as did the man beside her.

"Hi-yuh, Alice," he greeted cheerfully. "I'll bet this is your dad."

"You guess right," the girl smiled. "I've already told him you were crazy, but after seeing these cattle, I guess he knows it."

Jerry reined his pony around, put out his right hand. Mart Monroe accepted it rather dubiously. He looked suspiciously at Jerry and then toward the approaching cows and cowpunchers.

"Look here, young man," he said crisply, "I don't understand this at all."

"I bet you don't either," Jerry grinned and changed the subject. "Find any skunks up on that hill yesterday?"

Mart Monroe said grimly, "One...name of Jacklin. We buried him, right there." His piercing blue eyes drilled into Knight's. "That's one thing that leads me to trust you but...but I don't understand these Circle-F cows. Why did you bring them here?"

Jerry explained, "There's about seventy-five 2-M Herefords on their way into the next state right now. I'm just paying you back, Mister Monroe. I'd hate to see you lose any stock."

Monroe gasped. "But...but..., look here, I can't take these cows. We'll have to do this legally. Do you think I want Flecker accusing me of rustling?"

"We're doing it legally," Jerry grinned. He drew a sheet of paper from his pocket, handed it to Monroe. "Here's a bill-of-sale for one hundred head."

Monroe accepted the paper, read it. He looked about ready to explode. "Now, look here," he stammered, "we can't do this. Your name is signed on this paper. You haven't any right to sell Circle-F cows...."

"That paper clears you, see?" Jerry said earnestly. "If trouble comes from this, it descends on my head. You're in the clear. Now, don't ask questions. I know what I'm doing."

"Are you a....?"

"No, I'm no range detective working for the Cattlemen's Association," Jerry said calmly.

Monroe's eyes opened widely. "How did you know I was going to ask you that?"

"Nearly everybody else has," he grinned. "Nope, Mister Monroe you'd be surprised if you knew what I am."

"Well, what are you?"

Jerry didn't reply to that. By this time the cows and cowpunchers were much nearer and he turned his pony to rejoin them. He shouted to Shorty Wing: "Keep 'em moving, Shorty."

Again he wheeled his pony and drew to a stop near Alice Monroe and her father.

"I don't know as I like this," Monroe was saying, shaking his head. "This might make trouble."

"Sure, I expect that," Jerry said calmly, "but trouble for Kelt Flecker. You know you've lost cows...far more than this hundred head."

Monroe started to swear, glanced at Alice, checked himself, and nodded vigorously. "A heap more. By the great shorn spoon!"

"You'll get back every head," Jerry promised, "or at least the same number of head, if you'll leave things to me. Of course, I'll have to steal a few of your cows now and then to make Flecker believe I'm on the job. If you'll just warn your hands not to throw any lead my way, I'll be much obliged. I might get hurt if that continued."

Alice smiled, said, "You almost did, cowboy."

Monroe was still protesting. "But why can't we just tell the sheriff what we know? That will settle Flecker's hash."

"Sure, but will it return property that folks around here have lost?" Jerry asked.

"Well," Monroe conceded, "mebbe not. You figure to right the wrongs the Randall Company is guilty of?"

"I'd sure like to try."

"You're carvin' out a big job for yourself, son." Monroe's blue eyes held a sympathetic light. "And you're running big risks."

"Mister Monroe," Jerry asked, "can you get me a list of the folks that have lost money through the Randall Company? You should be pretty well acquainted in Topango Wells."

Monroe shook his head dubiously. "I can get you the names that are still in this part of the country, but a good many families, discouraged, have left for other parts."

Knight nodded. "Do what you can, anyway. I reckon I'll have to get most of the information from Bristol Capron."

Monroe laughed scornfully. "Capron wouldn't tell you a thing."

"Mebbe I could persuade him," Jerry said grimly. He looked up, saw the Circle-F cowboys approaching, and said, "Well, we'll run off some more of your cows and get going. Better separate those Circle-F animals, so you can keep count."

Monroe still looked puzzled, but he nodded consent. "I'll head back now, and send out a couple of men."

"I'll see you tomorrow," Jerry said.

Monroe turned his pony and dashed away. Alice waited a few minutes. Jerry said, "Does the clerk in this county issue a pretty engraved license, or is it just one of those plain ones?"

Alice crimsoned. "Jerry...!"

"And about that house we're going to build on that tableland," he interrupted, grinning, "how many rooms do you plan to have? Mebbe you ought to draw up some sketches."

"They're all drawn...," the girl started, then stopped.

"I'll be over some night to look at 'em," Jerry stated.

"Cowboy, stop this foolishness."

"Who says it's foolish? Do you?"

"We-ell, no, of course...that is...."

"Certainly, you don't," he chuckled. "Just as soon as we can get Flecker taken care of, we'll...."

"Jerry, you will be careful, won't you?"

"What do you mean...careful?"

"Not to get shot or...or...."

"Doesn't make a bit of difference, does it?" Jerry asked airily. "I'm only a crazy cowpuncher. You said so yourself."

"Well, I didn't mean it that way."

Before anything more could be said, the three Circle-F men rode up and awaited further instructions from Knight. Jerry lifted his hat to the girl and, with a "See you tomorrow," led his men off in the direction of the grazing 2-M herd. By the time they had finished cutting out an even twenty-five head, Alice Monroe had disappeared in pursuit of her father.

That afternoon, the cowboys delivered the 2-M cows to the corral in Camino Cañon, then returned to the ranch. The following morning they drove a second hundred Circle-F beef animals to the 2-M and turned them over to a pair of 2-M hands who accompanied Mart Monroe and his daughter. This time, Jerry had a longer opportunity to converse with Alice, but what words were exchanged between the two have no place in this tale.

Again, a bunch of 2-M cows were cut out and driven to the corral in the cañon, but by this time when Knight and his men returned to the ranch they were met by a frowning George Corwin who met them in the bunkhouse, after they had taken care of their weary horses.

VII

"MURDER PLAN"

"Where in hell you fellers been?" Corwin demanded angrily. He frowned down on the four from the doorway of the bunkhouse as Jerry and his friends trudged up from the corral, lugging saddles.

Jerry said, surprised, "You fellers back already?"

"I am," Corwin snapped. "Kelt got to thinkin' one of us should be here, to see there wa'n't no loafin' goin' on. Kelt and Tim will be back tomorrow. I didn't go all the way with them...but say, what you fellers been doin'?"

Jerry grinned insolently. "Oh, just riding around. You know how cowboys like to ride."

"Cut it!" Corwin snapped savagely. "I'm askin' a serious question. I want an answer."

Jerry said coolly, "Just how badly do you want it, Corwin?"

Corwin started to swear and suddenly cooled down before the hostile eyes of Jerry and his friends. He glanced from man to man, noting six-shooters in holsters. Quite suddenly he turned back into the bunkhouse, muttering over one shoulder, "Cocky, eh? All right. We'll see what Kelt has to say when he comes back. I only asked a civil question. No need you flyin' off'n the handle."

"And I answered you," Knight said crisply. "I said we'd been riding. Don't worry, I've been taking care of the Randall Company rights."

"T'hell with the Randall Company!" Corwin suddenly whirled to face the others who had now entered the bunkhouse. "All right, wait until Kelt hears about this. If he don't make it tough for you...."

Jerry said, "To hell with Kelt and you, too, Corwin!"

Corwin's eyes bulged. One hand jerked toward holstered gun.

Jerry said calmly, "Go on, jerk it. I asked you a spell back how badly you wanted it."

Corwin's face flamed, then the color died out to be replaced by an ashen paleness. He turned away, shaking his head. "I'll leave this to Kelt," he muttered. "I can see you *hombres* have come to some sort of an understandin'. You ain't goin' to gang on me. I'll let Kelt handle things."

Knight laughed sarcastically. The other men didn't say anything. Saddles were put down and men trooped to the cook shack to eat supper. The meal was consumed in silence, Corwin now and then casting uneasy glances in Knight's direction. Suddenly, unable to bear it any longer, Corwin muttered an oath and rose from the table. Without a word he passed out of the building and headed toward the bunkhouse. Jerry rose and, watching from the cook shack doorway, saw Corwin emerge from the bunkhouse, bearing his saddle.

Jerry stepped outside. Shorty Wing said quietly, "He's heap bad medicine with a six-gun, Jerry."

Jerry snapped, "I never did like taking medicine."

"We better go along," Steve Hackett proposed.

"You three stay here," Jerry jerked back.

The three punchers watched Jerry from the doorway, saw him overtake Corwin halfway to the corral.

Jerry said quietly, "Where you heading, Corwin?"

Corwin stopped, set down his saddle, and faced Jerry. "It ain't none of your business, Knight, but I'm headin' to find Kelt to tell him how you're actin'. I don't like it. I'm goin'...."

"You're going to stay right here," the other declared flatly. "I'm rodding this outfit."

"Hell's bells!" Corwin snarled. "Kelt didn't put *me* in your charge. He meant them other three."

"I don't care what Kelt said," Jerry repeated. "I'm rodding this outfit."

"T'hell with you."

"That works two ways," Jerry said calmly. "First thing you know, Corwin, you'll be hitting the trail Herb Jacklin took."

Corwin backed a few paces, eyes narrowing. "What do you know about Jacklin?"

Jerry laughed coldly. "I know he won't ever be back. We shot it out, Corwin. That plain? Mebbe you want some of the same."

Corwin stiffened. "You can't give it to me!"

A third time Jerry said carelessly, "How badly do you want it, Corwin?"

Still Corwin hesitated, torn between the desire to reach Kelt with this story and at the same time to put Knight out of business.

Jerry continued, tauntingly. "Here's something else, Corwin: I know who the third man in the Wolcott killing was."

Corwin's eyes bulged, the tip of his tongue licked at lips suddenly gone dry. His arm commenced slowly to bend at the elbow. "Oh, is that so," he sneered. "I suppose you've told the sheriff some wild tale...."

"Haven't mentioned a word to the sheriff," Jerry admitted, "but I'm intending to. You big enough to stop me?"

Corwin swore an oath. His right arm stabbed down. His gun snapped up in a crashing roar that was drowned in the double explosion of Jerry's twin six-guns. Powder smoke swirled between the two men. Corwin staggered back, then sat down abruptly on the ground. His mouth was sagging; his eyes looked about to burst from their sockets. Slowly he sank back, threshed about a minute, and lay still. A dark crimson stain spread slowly on his left breast.

Running steps at his rear caused Jerry to look around. Wing, Reed, and Hackett were arriving at a run. Shorty Wing gasped, "Gawd, that was fast. You hit, Jerry?"

Knight said grimly, "Never touched me."

"He reached first," Steve Hackett put in.

"Thought sure Corwin had you," Reed exclaimed. "Is he dead?"

Jerry said, "We got a job of buryin' to do, *hombres*."

"What started it?" Wing wanted to know.

Jerry gave the necessary details.

"There'll be hell to pay when Flecker gets back," Hackett said seriously.

Knight laughed shortly. "I reckon I'll have enough to foot the bill."

The following morning Jerry and his men delivered another hundred Circle-F cows at the 2-M together with the necessary bill-of-sale, but this time, after Jerry had had some conversation with Alice and Mart Monroe, the men returned to the Circle-F without driving any 2-M steers to Camino Cañon. Jerry expected Flecker to return about noon and wanted to be there when he arrived. It was about three in the afternoon before Flecker showed up. He found Jerry, Wing, Reed, and Hackett seated in the bunkhouse. At once he commenced asking questions, but Jerry forestalled him with, "Where's Tim Beadle?"

"Tim rode over near 2-M range to check up on you," Flecker growled. "We noticed when we rode through Camino Cañon that there wa'n't as many 2-M cows there as there should have been. I bet you been loafin' all day." He halted suddenly at the break in front of Reed, Hackett and Wing, and added, "I mean Circle-F cows. I don't know what's got into me, gettin' mixed that way."

"And where did you say Tim had gone?" Jerry asked smoothly. "He wasn't worried about me, was he?"

"Why in hell should he be?"

"I was wondering," Jerry smiled.

Flecker broke in, "Say, where's George Corwin?"

Jerry said calmly, "Last I saw him, he was six foot down. We buried him deep."

Flecker gave vent to a sudden howl of amazement. "What did you say?"

"Look here," Jerry asked, "you left me to rod the outfit when you were gone, didn't you?"

"Certain. What's that got to do...?"

"Corwin didn't like the idea. We had some words."

"You crazy fool! Them orders didn't cover Corwin. What happened?"

"We had some words," Jerry said calmly. "He went for his gun. I didn't have any choice in the matter."

"And you killed him?" Flecker gasped. "You mean to sit there and tell me *you* beat George to the shot? And you say he went for his gun first? Knight, don't lie to me. I want the straight of this mess."

"I'm not lying. Ask these other *hombres*. They saw Corwin reach first. Ask cookie. He saw the whole thing from his cook shanty."

"By Gawd, I will!" Flecker heard Reed, Wing, and Hackett verify Knight's story, then he whirled to go in search of the ranch cook. Ten minutes later he returned, muttering angrily.

"Well, what did cookie say?" Jerry asked calmly.

"He backed you up," Flecker snarled. "But there's somethin' damn funny about this whole business. I don't understand it. Knight, don't you throw leg over a horse until this business is settled to my satisfaction. I aim to keep you here until I can decide what's to be done. I'll talk things over with Tim Beadle."

"Mebbe," Jerry proposed innocently, "we'd better go to Topango Wells and tell the whole story to the sheriff. I'll tell what I know and you can tell your side."

Flecker's eyes slanted viciously at Knight. "No, we don't tell nothin' to the sheriff," he snapped. "Seems to me you're gettin' plumb cocky all of a sudden, Knight."

Jerry said quietly, "It isn't as sudden as you think, Kelt."

Flecker appeared nervous. He glanced at Reed, Wing, and Hackett. "And you fellers keep yore mouths shut too. I'll tell you what to tell and what not to tell. And don't stir off'n this ranch, you hear me?"

The three cowboys commenced a protest but a glance from Jerry silenced them. Silence fell over the gathering and, thinking he held the men under his domination, Kelt Flecker swaggered out of the building.

Shorty Wing remarked worriedly, "Jerry, there's goin' to be hell to pay when Beadle gets back."

"I'm not worrying," Jerry laughed.

"I would be, in your boots," Reed said seriously.

Jerry laughed again. A minute later he said, "Shorty, will you do me a favor?"

"Certain sure. What is it?"

"Sneak down to the corral and take my saddle. Put it on a good horse, then hide the horse in that brush back of the corral. I'll try and keep Flecker busy so he won't see you."

Steve Hackett asked, "You figurin' to light out?"

"Tonight, if I get a chance. I've got business in town. Don't worry, I'm not aiming to leave you *hombres* in the lurch. I'll be back."

Wing nodded. "Don't worry about us. I'll take care of saddlin' up for you as soon as possible."

Time drifted past. Jerry found Flecker in conversation with the cook, trying to find a flaw in the story the cook maintained was the truth.

"S'help me Gawd," the old cook was saying, "I saw George reach for his gun before Knight even made a move."

"What were they talkin' about before that happened," Flecker asked for probably the twentieth time.

And for probably the twentieth time the cook had replied crustily, "You think I got ears that can hear what's said down near the corral?"

"Dang it," Jerry drawled, "I told you what happened, Kelt. Can't you take my word for it?"

"No I can't," Flecker said flatly. "There's somethin' funny goin' on and I aim to get at the bottom of it." And so they argued the afternoon away.

Meanwhile Shorty Wing had succeeded in slipping down to the corral and saddling a horse for Jerry. However, not without being discovered. Flecker had happened to glance out of the cook shack window just in time to see Wing leading the saddled horse into the tall brush back of the corral. Flecker started to speak, then checked himself, and remained silent.

Shortly before supper Flecker spotted Beadle riding hard into the ranch yard. He hurried out to meet the rider, with Knight following close behind. Beadle was bursting with conversation as he pulled his foam-flecked horse to a savage halt.

"Do you know what, Kelt?" he exclaimed excitedly, "this range is overrun with crooks."

"I sort of suspected that," Jerry said dryly.

"What you talkin' about, Tim?" Flecker demanded.

Beadle stepped down from his pony, face crimson with indignant rage. He looked quickly about and lowered his voice a trifle: "I rode over on 2-M range like you said, thinkin' I might see Knight."

"Knight didn't go over there today," Flecker cut in. "He ain't explained why yet. There's somethin' else that...."

"And so you know what, Kelt?" Beadle interrupted angrily. "I was spyin' around, not showin' myself. Do you know what? Them dirty 2-M waddies has been rustlin' us blind."

"Talk sense, Tim," Flecker said irritatedly.

"I'm talkin' sense," Beadle snapped. "They got about three hundred Circle-F cows and men ridin' herd on 'em. Now can you beat that?"

"The dirty cow thieves!" Flecker bellowed. He whirled suddenly on Knight, "What do you know about this?"

Jerry said innocently, "Surprising, isn't it? Can you imagine, cow thieves on the range? I never heard of such a condition."

"Don't get funny," Flecker snarled. "I'm askin' you?"

"Why should I know anything about it?" Jerry evaded. "Mebbe Monroe is just getting even with you. The best course is to go to town and lay this all before the sheriff and tell what we know."

"T'hell you say," Flecker sneered. His eyes narrowed, considering past events. "Seems to me, you're mighty anxious to get in to see the sheriff. What you got up your sleeve?"

"Nothing but my elbow," Jerry replied.

"It's li'able to have to do some fast bendin'," Flecker said ominously. "We'll look into this cattle rustlin' later." He turned back to Beadle: "Tim, George is dead."

"Dead? Dead!" Beadle looked blank. "What do you mean he's dead?"

"Dammit! Ain't I tellin' you?" Flecker snapped impatiently.

"But...but what happened?"

"Him and Knight had a scrap."

Beadle's face went ugly. He whirled on Jerry. "Damn you, Knight, I'll...."

"You'll what?" Jerry queried coldly. One gun was coming out, covering both Flecker and Beadle as he retreated two steps.

Beadle went pale but kept his nerve. "Put that gun away, give me an even break."

"Cut it, Tim!" Flecker said harshly. "George had an even break, but he...."

'I don't believe it," Beadle rasped.

"Cut it I tell you!" Flecker snapped. "There was four witnesses, Tim. Knight claims it was self-defense. I reckon it was. Now, cool down. Knight, put that gun away."

"I will when Beadle gets through going on the prod," Jerry jerked out.

A quick glance was exchanged between Beadle and Flecker. Beadle relaxed, said sullenly, "I'm sorry, Knight. I thought a heap of George Corwin, but if Kelt says it was on the square, that's all right with me. How'd it happen?"

Jerry started to explain, but Flecker interrupted with, "Knight, I got private talk to make with Tim. I'll tell him about your blow-up with George. By the time I get through, you'll see Tim won't hold any grudge."

Jerry nodded shortly, turned, and strode away. Beadle glared after his nonchalant, square-shouldered bearing. "I'll kill that smart, young...."

"Later, Tim, later," Flecker said soothingly. "We got to give him his head until he can run into the open."

"When'll that be? There's somethin' funny about this. I don't suppose Herb Jacklin has showed up?"

Flecker shook his head.

Beadle's face darkened. "There's something funny in the wind," he declared. "First Jacklin, then Corwin. Now them cows of ours over on 2-M property. How do you explain it, Kelt?"

"I don't yet," Flecker said heavily. "It's got me worried. Knight is plumb cocky all of a sudden. If our cows is on 2-M range and being guarded by 2-M hands, there's something bad in the wind. We got to learn what it is. I got a hunch Knight has made some sort of friendly contact with Monroe."

"Why don't you turn him over to the authorities? He's broke his parole."

"And him knowin' what he knows now?" Flecker said sarcastically. "Don't be a fool, Tim. He knows too much about us. We wouldn't dare chance it. If I'd known things was goin' to turn out like this, I'd never have brought Knight out here."

"What about him and Corwin shootin' it out?"

"Here's the story as Knight told it to me. The others say George went for his gun first. I guess he did, but what led up to that I don't know. We've only got Knight's word." Flecker added other details pertaining to the fight, and ended, "One thing's certain, Knight has got to go!"

"What you figurin' on?"

"A little spell back," Flecker explained, "I saw Wing saddle a horse and hide it in the brush, back of the corral. Now, there ain't no reason for Wing doin' that unless he's saddlin' a horse for Knight. I got a hunch Knight figures to go some place tonight."

"Where?"

"I don't know, and I won't feel right until I do know. It's for you to find out. You get your supper and then take a fresh horse and leave. I'll tell the others I've sent you over to see Monroe. I think Reed and them other dumb cowhands know what we've been doin'. I sort of spilled the beans myself a while back. But we'll take care of them later."

"Knight comes first," Beadle said.

Flecker nodded. "You just ride away from the ranch far enough so you can see where Knight heads when he leaves here. Once you got that part straight in your mind...well, Tim, you got a gun and you know how to use it. Don't forget that Corwin was a friend of yours."

"I get you, Kelt. Knight meets his finish tonight!"

VIII

SPIDER'S WEB

All through supper Flecker sat glowering at his plate, speaking very little. Now and then he glanced up, glared at Knight and the other three cowboys. The air was tense—especially when Jerry met Flecker's glares with insolent grins. Reed, Wing, and Hackett felt apprehensive. They knew just enough to realize trouble was in the wind, but exactly what part Knight was playing in the swiftly-shaping events was something beyond their comprehension.

Flecker was worried, no doubt about that. His hand trembled a trifle when he lifted his coffee cup. Jerry snickered. Flecker slammed down the cup, splashing the hot contents over his trousers. Jerry laughed louder.

Flecker swore and scowled at him" "You damn redhead! What's ticklin' you?"

Knight said, "I was thinking about a mistake you made, Flecker."

"Me? A mistake? What you mean?"

"In bringing me here under false circumstances or understanding or whatever you want to call it."

"Cripes! Talk sense!"

Knight's grin widened. "Mebbe you've forgotten about that stage hold-up bandit you mentioned."

"What about him?" Flecker snarled.

"Remember, you said I answered his description and that the law was on his trail?"

Flecker's eyes widened. "Well, you dang fool! You got a nerve to spill that."

Jerry shook his head. "You're mistaken, Flecker. It wasn't me, after all. If you'd read the papers, you'd have seen where they caught that *hombre* two days after the hold-up. Yeah, he confessed. Sure, he did look like me...red-headed, tall and so on. But it wasn't me."

Flecker choked; his face grew apoplectic. The other cowboys looked interested. Nobody spoke for a moment. Flecker was fumbling in a vest pocket and finally produced a newspaper clipping which Jerry recognized as the article having to do with the paroling of Jerry Knight. Flecker read swiftly through the article. Then he bent his beetling brows on Jerry.

"Your name's Knight, ain't it?" he demanded. "Known as Jerry?"

"You've got that part all right," Jerry admitted.

Flecker smiled thinly, relaxed somewhat. "That's all I want to know," he stated confidently. He went on eating.

A few minutes later, however, the worried frown returned to Flecker's forehead. Abruptly he rose from the table, knocking his knife and fork to the floor with a loud clatter.

Jerry said, "Where you going?"

Flecker whirled around. "I don't know as it's any of your business."

"It might be," Jerry said calmly.

"Well, it ain't," Flecker sneered, "but I don't mind tellin' you I'm aimin' to ride to the 2-M and ask Mart Monroe to explain how he happens to be holdin' a herd of Circle-F animals on his range. He's goin' to square that or I'll know the reason why."

Knight nodded carelessly. "Thought that's where Tim Beadle went when he rode away just before supper." He had been wondering for the past hour where Beadle was headed.

Flecker was caught off guard. Before stopping to think, he commenced, "No, I sent Tim on some other business." He stopped suddenly, then continued. "That is, I told Tim to go see Monroe. But I just got a hunch I ought to be there, too. I wouldn't want no trouble to come off about those cattle. I just want an explanation, that's all."

He hurried from the cook shack and a few minutes later the cowboys heard him riding away. There was silence for a few minutes, then Shorty Wing said: "Jerry, you reckon Kelt and Tim will do any iron-pullin' over to Monroe's?"

Jerry shook his head. "Not with Monroe's crew on hand. No, Flecker will be peaceable, but those cows have got him worried. He doesn't understand and he can't wait to learn what it's all about."

Shorty Wing said, "Me'n Flecker got somethin' in common."

Jerry smiled. He didn't say anything. Steve Hackett commented, "Flecker might get tough at that. Tim Beadle's hot-tempered, and with Tim there...."

"Beadle isn't there," Jerry said. "Flecker was just bluffing. I don't know where he is. I wish I did know."

Shorty Wing said shrewdly, "Jerry, do you suppose Flecker could have spotted me hidin' that horse for you this afternoon? In that case, he might have sent Beadle to keep an eye on where you went ridin' when you left."

Knight laughed suddenly, brow clearing. "Thanks, Shorty. I've been wondering. I'll bet that's exactly what Flecker did. Now, I'll keep a weather eye open for trouble."

"You goin' into town?" Hackett asked.

Jerry nodded. "I figured I'd have to wait until after Flecker had gone to bed but, with him riding to the 2-M, I can pull out any time."

"What you aimin' to do?" Frank Reed asked.

Jerry shrugged lean shoulders. "I'm not sure yet," he replied cryptically. "Haven't got it figured out."

Supper was finished a short time later. The ranch cook cleared away the dishes and the 'punchers returned to the bunkhouse. Jerry sat by himself, thinking in silence. Reed, Wing, and Hackett sat looking at old magazines and newspapers, the light from the oil lamps throwing into bold relief faces that appeared but little interested in reading. Knight finally rose and sauntered to the doorway, looked out. A soft breath of sage was lifted to his nostrils on the night breeze. Stars gleamed overhead. There wasn't any moon yet. The other three cowboys watched him intently, breathed a sigh of relief when he turned back inside.

Shorty Wing cleared his throat and said awkwardly, "Any of us...or all three...will be glad to ride to Topango Wells with you, Jerry."

Jerry smiled and said thanks, but didn't accept the offer. He didn't want to hurt their feelings; at the same time, when he left, he wanted to be alone. He returned to his chair and sat down, his mind following, foot by foot, the trail between the Circle-F and Topango Wells. Having only been over the trail once, this took time, but finally he had constructed mentally every foot of the way. Mostly the road ran across rolling grazing lands, with no points of ambush on either side—except one. About four miles from the ranch a huge pile of boulders bordered the side of the road with a sloping hillside behind the rock. Here, if any, was the place where Tim Beadle might wait to drygulch him.

It was all clear in Jerry's mind now. He nodded with satisfaction, rose, said abruptly, "I'll see you later," and stepped outside without waiting for a reply. Two minutes later he had reached the waiting horse in the brush in back of the corral and climbed into the saddle. Turning the pony's head toward Topango Wells, he set out at a fast lope.

Twenty minutes later, he drew to a halt and tethered his pony to a scrubby bit of brush not far from the road. Then leaving the road he circled widely to the south. The stars didn't afford a great deal of light and Jerry slipped along with the silence of a Sioux Indian. Gradually his steps carried him up a slow rise of land. For another five minutes he ascended, then again turned slightly back toward the road he had left. Sage and cactus grew sparsely here and there. Jerry dropped down to hands and knees and crawled through the grass, taking advantage of every bit of growth possible to hide his movements.

Finally he rose cautiously and peered down the slope. A hundred feet below him was the pile of boulders, well beyond the roadway, the suspected point for an ambush. Jerry didn't move a muscle. Five minutes passed. Suddenly a man coughed, clearing his throat. From the darkness surrounding the boulders came an impatient curse. A minute later a match flared, showing Tim Beadle's face. Beadle was lighting a cigarette. The match went out. A pin-point of crimson gleamed through the darkness, went out, brightened again.

Beadle was seated on a rock, rifle across his knees, ready to blast the unsuspecting Knight when he came along. Jerry's face grew grim. Drawing one six-shooter he crawled noiselessly forward. It took him fully five minutes to close the distance between himself and Tim Beadle, so carefully did he move every inch of the way but, when again he stopped, Beadle wasn't five paces away.

Jerry said quietly, "Drop the rifle, Beadle. You're covered."

Beadle gasped, said, "My God!" His rifle clattered to the rocks. Then, in shaky tones, "That sounded like you, Knight."

"Correct!"

"But...but what's the idea?"

"Want me to tell you?"

"I'd sure like to know," Beadle said nervously.

Jerry laughed, "You've been waiting for me to leave. You knew I had that horse ready. You waited not far from the ranch house, to see which way I'd head...town or the 2-M. Once you heard my horse, you knew. You set out for here."

Beadle commenced a cursing protest. The cigarette clung to his lips.

"Keep your mouth shut!" Jerry said sternly. "Don't lie. I heard your horse. You were moving fast. So was I. Mebbe I could have beaten you to this point, but I figured to let you get here first. I pulled off the road, circled behind you."

"But, my God, Knight. What's the idea. Why should I do that?"

"You figured to drygulch me."

The two men were facing each other in the darkness. It was too dark to see their faces. Beadle had dropped his cigarette. He was still sitting on the rock. Jerry was in a crouching position a few feet away, covering Beadle with a six-shooter.

"Why in hell should I try to drygulch you?" Beadle was saying. His voice wasn't steady.

"Flecker's orders. I know too much."

"You're wrong, I swear it!"

Jerry laughed softly in the silence. "Nope, I *do* know too much...for instance the name of the third man in the Wolcott killing."

Beadle swore, abruptly slid from his rock seat, and dropped behind a huge block of granite. The movement had come so fast that it caught Jerry unprepared. Jerry heard the rasp of metal on leather holster and threw himself flat. Beadle's gun roared, the bullet passing over his head. Jerry lifted himself on one hand, gun ready in the other.

Silence from Beadle's direction. Jerry didn't make a move; his eyes strained unsuccessfully to pierce the darkness. A full minute passed, seeming like an hour to the two men. Jerry's supporting arm was growing cramped, but he didn't dare move now.

Beadle finally muttered, "By God, I believe I got him."

He raised cautiously above the rock, but couldn't see Jerry's form in the darkness. In his hurry to get behind the rock his sense of direction had slightly gone awry. Now he lifted his gun for a chance shot. The gun crashed out of the silence, the bullet passing within scant inches of Jerry's body. But the momentary flash from Beadle's gun was what he had waited for. Jerry's gun roared in reply. A groan of pain was torn from Beadle's throat. Then silence again.

Jerry waited five minutes, then he rose cautiously and moved toward the rock. Reaching down his hand encountered a face already growing cold and stiff to the touch. Jerry wiped his hand on a wisp of grass at his feet, struck a match. Then he straightened up, reloaded his gun, and made his way to the road below where Tim Beadle's horse was waiting. Hoisting himself to the saddle, Jerry continued on his way to Topango Wells.

IX

SHOOT AN' BE DAMNED

A tall man in city clothing stood at the far end of the Topango Bar talking to Sheriff Buck Drake. Drake was a stockily-built individual with a bulldog jaw and iron-gray hair that showed a tendency to curl at his shirt collar. He was in corduroys and wore his star of office pinned to an open vest. The evening was still young—as saloon evenings go. A few customers, ranged along the bar, sent cigarette and cigar smoke curling upward to the oil lamps suspended in brackets above the bar. There was lots of talk and some laughter.

Tiny drops of perspiration shone brightly on Hippodrome Casey's round, good-natured features.

Casey glanced toward the door, saw Jerry coming in, and violently gestured for him to leave at once. Jerry frowned and came up to the nearest end of the bar. Hippodrome looked worried. He kept making futile gestures toward the sheriff and his companion at the inner end of the barroom. The two hadn't noticed Knight's arrival, so engrossed were they.

Hippodrome grunted and leaned across the bar. "That's the sheriff," he whispered. "The feller with him is named Naughton. Naughton come here and asked for a feller named Jerry Knight. I swore I'd never heard of you."

"You old liar," Jerry grinned easily.

"All right, laugh, you dang fool." Casey was still whispering. "I heard Naughton tell Buck Drake that he was on the parole board of the Texas State Penitentiary. They been talkin' mighty serious, but I couldn't make out what they said. Now, if this doesn't mean anythin' to you, forget I said anythin'."

Jerry huddled close to the bar, the other customers hiding him from Naughton and the sheriff. He said, "If you mean, do I want to see Mister Naughton now...I don't. I'd just as soon he didn't see me. We had a sort of argument"—Jerry grinned—"last time I talked to him. I'll be slipping out in a minute, Hippo. I just called to see if Bristol Capron was in here."

"No, he ain't here. You been down to his place...I mean that buildin' where the Randall Company is? He lives upstairs, y'know."

"It was all dark so...."

"He's probably gone to bed. Capron turns in early."

"That explains it. I'll go back."

"Move fast, cowpoke. Naughton might see you. Lucky for you, you didn't run into the sheriff the day you hit town or...," he looked at Knight significantly.

But Jerry was already taking his departure, without waiting to reply or hear more. Hippodrome looked relieved, and turned to catch Naughton and the sheriff looking after Jerry's retreating back.

Naughton said, "Say, barkeep, that looked like Knight." He started toward the door in pursuit of Jerry.

"No, sir, Mister Naughton"—Hippodrome gulped for the proper words with which to detain Naughton—"that's...that was...."

"Well, Hippo," Sheriff Drake said sharply, "just who in hell was he?"

"Friend...friend of mine," Hippodrome stuttered.

Naughton looked dubious, but he came back to the bar.

"What's his name?" Drake snapped. "He's a stranger to me."

"Name's Pete...."

"Pete what?"

Hippodrome wasn't a fast thinker. To cover his confusion and stall for time, he started to clear a couple of empty beer bottles from the bar.

"What's his last name?" the sheriff demanded again.

Hippodrome happened to glance at the label on one of the beer bottles and had an inspiration, "Name's Schlitz...Pete Schlitz," he stated defiantly.

"Schlitz, eh?" The sheriff looked dubiously at the barkeep. "Damn' funny I ain't seen him in town before."

Hippodrome had another inspiration. "It ain't so surprisin' at that. Pete Schlitz never stays in one town very long. He hops around a lot."

Naughton looked a trifle dazed. "Schlitz...hops," he muttered, and gazed queerly at the bartender.

The sheriff walked past and out to the street. By this time Jerry was out of sight. In a few minutes, the sheriff returned, "You tell your Pete Schlitz friend I want to see him, Hippo, next time he comes around here. Sometimes I think you try to be funny. It don't set well on a fat man."

"Maybe you're right," Hippo agreed. He was sweating profusely by this time. He wiped up the bar with a damp cloth and announced that the house would buy a drink. To his relief, Naughton and Sheriff Drake accepted the invitation.

Meanwhile, Jerry had mounted and rode down the street until he came abreast of the two-story brick building that housed the office of the Randall Land and Cattle Company and the living quarters of its resident manager, Bristol Capron. Dismounting, he looked in both directions along the street. A few lights shone from buildings, but there were no pedestrians in sight. Two blocks away a brightly lighted window proclaimed the location of the Topango Wells Hotel where the man know as Naughton was probably staying the night.

"Yes, sir, I'll bet Mister Art Naughton would like to see me," Jerry grinned in the gloom. "He's probably getting worried about my whereabouts by this time. Ten to one he's told the sheriff all about me, and I wouldn't be surprised if they started for the Circle-F first thing in the morning. Oh, well, mebbe I can learn something from Bristol Capron before then."

Approaching the door of the Randall Company's office, he lifted one hand and pounded loudly. There was a few minutes' silence, then a window on the upper floor rasped open. Capron's irritable voice reached Jerry's ears: "Who's there?"

"It's me...Knight."

"What do you want?"

"I've got to see you, Capron."

"What about?"

"Expect me to yell it right out in the street."

"Any reason why you shouldn't?" Capron demanded. "I haven't anything to hide."

Jerry laughed scornfully. "Your story and Flecker's don't agree, then."

There was a moment's silence. Then Capron lowered his voice, "Did Flecker send you in to see me?"

Jerry said impatiently, "My gosh! Aren't I trying to tell you that?"

"I'll be right down," Capron said. His voice sounded uneasy as the window slammed shut.

Jerry waited. In a short time he heard steps descending from the upper floor. They approached the door. A bolt slid back; a key turned in its lock. The door opened a few inches. Jerry started inside, only to feel the door refuse to give. Through the opening the barrel of a revolver was shoved toward his head.

"You stay right there, Knight," Capron snapped. "Give me Flecker's message."

"Aw, I'm not going to stand here talking. I'm coming inside."

More of the gun barrel was shoved through. "You'll get a bullet if you try to come in here, Knight."

Jerry laughed softly, stepped to one side and grasped the gun barrel in his right hand, pointing it skyward. "Now, you damn' scoundrel," he grinned, "shoot and be damned. And the sheriff is only a coupla blocks down the street if you want to bring him on the run."

Capron was cursing viciously, trying to wrest the gun from Jerry's hand and at the same time endeavoring to hold the door against Jerry's pushing weight. "Let go my gun, Knight," he panted. "What do you want? I demand to be told just what...."

His voice broke in a hopeless grunt as Jerry wrested the gun from his grip and shoved open the door. Once inside, Jerry thrust the gun into the waistband of his overalls and slammed the door at his back.

"All right, Capron," he snapped. "No more funny stuff. Get a light."

"I won't do it," Capron whined. "I won't have you breaking in here and acting like this." The man's nerve was going fast. "Wait until I tell Kelt about this."

"Get a light," Jerry growled menacingly, "or I'll blast you from hell to breakfast and there won't be enough for Kelt to recognize."

"But, look here, Knight...."

Jerry drew one of his own guns, pulled back the hammer. "Hear that?" he asked coldly. "I won't waste time on you much longer, Capron. I'm going to count three and if a lamp ain't lighted by the time I get through I'll pull the trigger. One! Two! Thr...!"

"Hold it, hold it!" Capron half shrieked. "I'll light up. Give me time."

His bare feet scurried over the plank floor, searching feverishly for a lamp and matches. Jerry grinned in the darkness, but tried to keep his voice stern as he urged, "Hurry it up. This ain't my night to be gentle."

A match scratched loudly and a moment later a lamp shed a soft glow over the big office. Capron was white as a sheet, his thin hair tousled over his pasty forehead. He had drawn on trousers over his nightshirt and his suspenders dangled at his sides. Jerry looked quickly about the room, then moved toward the front wall to draw down the shades which covered windows and door glass.

Capron watched in trembling silence. "Look here," he finally found his voice, "you don't need to go to all this trouble. Just tell me what Flecker said and...."

"Shut your trap!" Jerry snarled menacingly. He didn't particularly care for the role he was playing, but to further the ends in view it was necessary that he thoroughly intimidate Bristol Capron. "Now, come over here and open this safe."

Leading the way to the safe, placed against the wall not far from Capron's desk, Jerry repeated the order.

"I won't do it!" Capron said defiantly.

Jerry laughed and the cold chills ran down Capron's backbone at the sound. Still, he tried to hold his nerve. "I won't do it," he said again. "You better get out of here, Knight. I know all about you being paroled. Flecker told me about you. You were in prison...."

"For what crime?"

"For killing a man," Capron declared.

"All right." Again Jerry laughed. "Just keep that in mind, if you get stubborn with me."

Capron turned a sickly yellow and started for the safe.

Jerry continued, "And I suppose Flecker told you just why he wanted me on the Circle-F."

"He didn't say."

"Don't lie, Capron! He wanted to frame me as the third man in the Wolcott killing. You know that damn' well."

Capron choked and looked fearfully at the cowpoke's cold face. "How...how...?" he stammered.

"Never mind that. Get this safe opened."

Capron knelt before the safe, his trembling fingers trembling with the combination dial. A moment later the heavy door swung outward. He rose to his full height. "I...I don't like this. I want to see Flecker or one of the others."

"Sit down in that chair over there," Jerry snapped. His gun barrel indicated a seat near the desk. "One move out of you and you'll get just what the others got."

"Oh, my God!" Capron whispered hoarsely. "You've killed Flecker and...and...?"

"Shut up!"

The lighted lamp on the desk revealed the safe's contents. Jerry reached to a cash drawer, removed a stack of bills which, with a wide grin, he stuffed into his pockets.

"Is...is this a hold up?" Capron choked.

"What do you think?"

Capron fell silent, his uneasy glance following the cowboy as he lifted out of the safe a couple of heavy ledgers and a packet of papers. These he spread out on the desk before seating himself. Then he opened the books.

An hour drifted past, lengthening to an hour and a half, while Jerry examined books and documents. Finally, recovering his courage somewhat, Capron ventured, "I don't see what you're going through those records for. You wouldn't know anything about the Randall Company's business."

Jerry sneered, "I know more than you think. For instance, you were ordered to quote the T. N. & A. S. Railroad a decent price for a right-of-way through Camino Cañon. You lied to the railroad people when you asked...*demanded*...four times that price."

"Oh, my God!" Capron shrank back in his chair. "Did...did Flecker tell you that too?"

Jerry was quick to grasp that advantage. "You'd be surprised some of the things Kelt has told me."

Capron groaned. "I'm ruined if that gets out. Listen, Knight, I'll give you some money and you get out of the country. There won't be a thing said about you breaking parole. I'll fix that with Kelt."

"Shut up, you worm!"

"Is Kelt dead or isn't he?"

Jerry laughed. "What do you think?"

Capron groaned and commenced to sob.

Jerry eyed the man with disgust, decided to try a bluff. "You not only deceived the railroad company, but you've tried to force Mart Monroe to sell out so you could offer the railroad the right to go through Palo Verde Pass. Flecker has rustled Monroe blind in an attempt to ruin him."

"Listen, Knight, I'll do anything you say. I didn't think Kelt would ever tell that. He claimed to be my friend."

"*Will* you cut out that sniveling?"

Fifteen minutes more passed while Jerry continued to pour over the books. To only a small extent had he found what he searched for. It was time for another bluff. Abruptly he picked up his six-shooter, turned it toward Capron.

"I'm through fooling with you, Capron," Jerry stated harshly. "I want the other book."

"What other book?" but Capron's eyes had shifted nervously, and Jerry knew his guess had been correct.

"The one Flecker told me about," Jerry said reluctantly. "You know, showing your private transactions."

"But there isn't any such book."

"Oh, cripes!" Jerry lifted the gun a trifle. "I reckon I might as well let you have it now and get this business over with. I never could stand a sneakin' liar."

"Don't shoot, don't shoot!" Capron half shrieked. He threw himself half across the desk, begging and sobbing. "I'll get it."

Jerry drew back, grinning inwardly. This was easier than he had anticipated. "Go ahead. Hurry it up!" he growled.

Capron scurried around to a point near one end of the desk and commenced clawing feverishly at boards in the floor. A board came loose, then a second one. Reaching down, Capron produced from under the floor a large ledger bound in gray buckram. Staggering to his feet he dropped the book on the desk and wilted back to his chair.

Fifteen minutes later, Jerry lifted his head from the book and asked a few sharp questions, Capron, shaken to the very core of his thieving heart, answered promptly and fully. Jerry continued to peruse the pages, asking questions from time to time.

Finally he closed the book and looked disgustedly at Capron. "You're pretty low," he said coldly. "You were put here to look after the Randall Company's interests and you've cheated the company from the start. You've sold twice the number of cattle you've reported annually and pocketed the difference. You've foreclosed mortgages on ranches and small farms you had no right to foreclose, and then sold them again and pocketed the money, forging records to suit your dirty means. You've cheated poor wretches out of their money by selling land to farmers…land that was never meant for farming, is no good for farming purposes. You've foreclosed on them again and again, always reselling in your own name and pocketing the money. You've…."

"What…what are you going to do to me?" Capron groaned.

"I know one thing," Jerry said sternly. "Your bankbooks are here, showing that you've made yourself pretty wealthy at the expense of the Randall Company. Restitution will be made so far as is possible. You've made the name of Ira Randall a thing to be hated and feared in this country. That's an injustice if there ever was one. That will have to be straightened out. You've murdered when it suited your convenience."

"I never killed a man, so help me, I never…."

"You were in it with Flecker and his crew of snakes."

"Flecker made me...."

"Don't lie. I don't doubt Flecker had the nerve for it, but it's your cowardly mind that planned it all...oh, hell, Capron! I'm sick of talking to anyone as dirty as you. C'mon, we'll go see the sheriff."

"I'll tell him you're paroled."

"Tell and be damned, skunk! C'mon, I say."

"No, no!" Eyes staring, lips slobbering, Capron staggered up from his chair as Jerry rounded the desk. He threw himself on Jerry, clutching at his arms, fighting to get his guns. Jerry struggled to throw the man off, but the wretch was fighting like a cornered rat with a strength that was almost maniacal.

Then the door opened quite suddenly, closed as quickly. Kelt Flecker's voice sounded harshly through the scraping of feet: "Stick 'em up, Knight. You're covered!"

In desperate eagerness, Capron released his hold on Jerry and staggered back: "Thank God you're here. Kelt!" he half sobbed, then his voice rose and he screamed savagely: "Kill him, Kelt. Kill the nosy bustard! He knows everything. Don't let him go. Kill him!"

X

CAUGHT REDHANDED

Knight swung slowly around to see the triumphant look on Flecker's face. Flecker's fingers were trembling on triggers. "Gawd! What luck," he said ominously. "I expected to find Tim Beadle here when I saw his horse outside. Wondered what Tim was up to. Then I heard Capron screamin' like a maniac. I come in and...say, where *is* Beadle?"

Jerry laughed quietly, "I'm not sure, but I bet you a plugged peso he's down in hell explaining to Jacklin and Corwin just how it happened."

"Damn you!" Flecker scowled. "I'll square that too."

"Kill him, Kelt, kill him!" Capron snarled. "We don't dare let him loose. Use your gun! Quick!"

"Shut up, you fool!" Flecker said roughly. "Think we want a shot to bring the sheriff on the run. Bristol, you get his guns. Then we'll tie him up tight while I talk to him. Mebbe we won't have to do any killing. Mebbe we can make a bargain with Knight. He can pro'bly use money. Hurry, get his guns."

Cautiously, Capron approached Jerry from the rear, lifted from holster first the right, and then the left gun. But in his excitement he overlooked his own gun which Jerry had captured and thrust into the waistband of his overalls. During the struggle with Capron, the weapon had slipped down considerably. He was between Flecker and the light and Flecker couldn't see the gun.

"Hurry, now," Flecker was urging. "Get a rope."

Capron was depositing Jerry's guns on the desk at the rear. Jerry knew there'd be no bargaining once he was tied up. Probably Flecker would employ a knife and then dispose of Jerry's body. Abruptly, he jumped to one side, reaching for the gun in his waistband. Too late to prevent the movement, Flecker realized what Jerry was doing. Flecker's right hand tilted up in a savage arc as he cursed Capron's stupidity. The gun crashed loudly even as Jerry leaped half way across the room. Then, he had Capron's gun free of his waistband.

The gun in Flecker's left spat smoke and orange flame. Something red-hot drilled into Jerry's right side, staggering him. He lifted Capron's gun—pulled trigger—once—twice! The weapon was of smaller caliber than a forty-five and of cheap construction. The first shot missed; the second bored in, high in Flecker's left shoulder. With a howl of pain the big man staggered back.

A yell of rage behind him caused Jerry to turn. Capron was lifting one of Jerry's guns. Jerry laughed grimly through the fog of powder smoke, raised Capron's gun, and hurled it full at the face of its owner. Blood spurted from Capron's nose and he sat down violently on the floor. Jerry leaped to the desk, secured his own guns, just as Flecker prepared to make another attempt.

"Drop that gun, Flecker!" Jerry yelled. "I'll let daylight through you, sure as hell, if you don't!"

With a curse of rage, Flecker dropped the gun and leaned back against the wall, his left arm dangling weakly at his side. Capron was climbing to his feet now, sobbing with rage and fear.

"You, Capron," Jerry spoke tersely, "get over there against the wall with Flecker, and on your way, just kick his guns down here."

Reluctantly, Capron obeyed and stood shivering at the side of his partner in crime. Now that he had the situation well in hand,

Jerry felt rather weak and relaxed. Seating himself on top of the desk, he laughed grimly, "Your game is up, scuts."

Flecker swore a vile oath and took one step toward the desk, but the lifted guns in Jerry's fists destroyed any idea he may have had concerning further resistance. Again, he slumped back against the wall and contented himself with staring contemptuously at the whining Capron.

And thus the three were when Sheriff Buck Drake, followed by the man named Naughton and a crowd of the town's citizens poured in through the doorway a few moments later.

"Well, what's the shootin' about?" Drake roared. He took in the situation at a glance, added humorously, "The shootin's over, 'pears like." With that he "shooed" the crowd of curious citizens outside and again closed the door.

The man named Naughton was eyeing Jerry curiously. He said," So it's your doings, eh, Jerry?"

Jerry grinned and said, "Correct, Mister Naughton."

"You ready to go back to Texas with me?"

"Well, I'm not sure if I'm ready, but I'll go back if you insist...for a spell, anyway, until things get straightened out."

Naughton said bitterly, "I thought you'd get into trouble. Looks like you almost got yourself killed. How would I feel if I had to go back to Texas without you?"

Sheriff Drake cut in with, "So this is Jerry Knight, eh? Naughton's been telling me about you, Knight."

"I can imagine what he said," Jerry laughed.

The door opened suddenly and Mart Monroe, followed by Alice, stepped into the room. Monroe gave a sigh of relief on seeing Knight.

Alice cried, "Oh, Jerry, we were afraid...." She didn't finish but came across the room to stand at his side.

Jerry took her hand. Neither said anything for a few minutes. Mart Monroe concluded, "Alice was afraid you would have trouble over those bills-of-sale you gave me, Jerry. You see, when Flecker came to ask about me having Circle-F cows on the 2-M, I showed him the bills you'd given me. He was right mad, said he was coming to town to turn you over to the sheriff. After he left, Alice got worried and...well, she dragged me in to see about it. But what's happened...?"

"He's a crook, that's what he is!" Capron suddenly found his voice. "He's a paroled prisoner! He's broke his parole."

"Hush up that noise," Sheriff Drake growled.

"Just the same," said Kelt Flecker, "Capron speaks the truth. Just as soon as I can get my wound fixed, I aim to swear out a warrant, chargin' him with theft of cows delivered to Mart Monroe."

"And he took money out of that safe, too," Capron cried.

Naughton and the sheriff exchanged grins which matched the one on Jerry's face. Naughton said, "Let me see those bills-of-sale, Monroe?'"

Monroe produced the papers, passed them to Naughton. Naughton examined them, passed them back, saying, "They're all in order. You see, folks, Knight had a right to sign those...."

'"What, sign for the Randall Company?" Flecker yelled.

"You dang fool," the sheriff snapped, "*he* is the Randall Company. Owns it lock, stock and bar'l!"

"All right," Jerry said lightly, "you would spill it. I see Mister Naughton's been talking to you."

"Well, I...!" Alice gasped. "Jerry, you never...."

Flecker and Capron looked on in dumb amazement, mouths hanging open. "But he has broken his parole!" Capron objected.

"Wolcott broke the parole...," Naughton commenced.

"Aw, forget that," Jerry cut in. "Look, I've got all the dope on Capron we need. I know the third man in the Wolcott killing."

Kelt swore and went white. Knight talked swiftly, giving details, and ended up, "That's all. Let's get out of here. I want to get to a...."

"Just a minute," Naughton cut in. "I guess Mart Monroe and his daughter would like to know a little more about you, Jerry."

Jerry said, "Aw, I don't see...." He suddenly fell silent. Alice pushed herself up on the desk beside him and Jerry's head dropped to her shoulder. Alice looked startled, but she didn't say anything.

Naughton was talking, "...you see, Ira Randall is Jerry's uncle. Jerry could have had a good job with the Randall Company but he refused, wanted to make his own career. He took his mother to Texas and managed to build up a cow outfit of his own. His independence made Ira Randall angry. He thought Jerry was foolish. Later, Ira was taken ill. He's had a bad heart for years. He turned the management of the company over to the man he thought was his friend...Bristol

Capron. Well, you've heard what Capron did. We won't think any more about him nor Flecker. They'll both get their just deserts."

Capron moaned. Flecker didn't say anything. Mart Monroe had managed to tie up Flecker's shoulder while Naughton was talking.

"Meanwhile," Naughton went on, "a friend of Jerry's named Dennis Wolcott got into trouble in a small town in Texas. I guess it was self-defense, but the man who was killed had friends and Dennis Wolcott was sent to prison under the name of Jerry Knight...."

"But I don't see," Alice commenced, "how he happened...."

"I'll explain, Miss Monroe," Naughton interposed. "You see, Wolcott was a stranger in the town where the killing took place. He was Knight's closest friend. When they arrested Wolcott, he gave the name of Knight. Wolcott had relatives in the East who would have been broken-hearted if they'd known Dennis had killed a man. As soon as possible, Dennis got in touch with Jerry and told him what he'd done and Jerry agreed that, if anybody would be saved any pain, Wolcott had done the best thing. So, Wolcott went to prison under the name of Knight and was paroled under the same name, of course."

"Well, I'll be danged," Mart Monroe muttered.

Naughton went on, "Ira Randall was finally compelled to go to Texas for his health. He and his nephew patched up their differences and Ira grew to love the boy like a father. Randall appointed me his lawyer...he'd met me through Jerry and we became friendly and he asked me to manage the Randall Company. You see, we'd talked over the affairs of the company and Ira was commencing to distrust Capron, but was too ill to investigate for himself. About this time, Jerry was working to get Dennis Wolcott paroled. I happen to hold a position on the Texas Penitentiary Parole Board. I arranged matters. Jerry gave Dennis a job on his own ranch, then later Ira Randall who also liked Dennis sent him here to secretly look into the affairs at the Circle-F. Randall caught a man named Ridge Conway rustling cattle and wrote Jerry about it. Somehow, Flecker and his crew must have heard or suspected something about Wolcott. Maybe he caught the gang redhanded. Perhaps Flecker will tell us about that."

Flecker growled through the pain of his wound, "Try to get me to tell."

"You'll tell in good time, all right," Naughton said coldly. "Anyway, the next thing we heard was that Wolcott had been found dead and Sheriff Drake was unable to find the man who had done the killing. About the same time, Ira Randall had a bad heart attack and signed all his holdings over to Jerry and his mother. Ira hasn't much longer to live, but he'll finish his days in comfort down on Jerry's ranch. After Wolcott's death, Jerry insisted on coming here to investigate. I thought it too dangerous. In fact, Jerry and I had a quarrel about it, but he insisted on coming anyway. Well, I guess all of you folks know there's no stopping him, once he gets started.

"To cut a long story short, he's accomplished his mission, but I still wonder he wasn't killed. For which I am very glad. And I guess I'll let him tell the rest of his story, supply details and so on, if you don't already know them. I've been wondering how he got in with the Flecker gang...?"

A startled exclamation from Alice interrupted the words. "He...he's...*something is wrong*," Alice said excitedly. "His head was on my shoulder. I thought he was just resting. My grief! His side is all wet. He's been wounded! Jerry, oh, Jerry, why didn't you tell us?"

There was a rush of feet toward the desk, but Jerry didn't answer. His head rolled loosely and he nearly fell to the floor.

⸺►●◄⸺

It was late afternoon the next day when Jerry awoke. He looked about, discovered himself in bed. His side felt stiff and sore. His exploring hand found bandages. There was a sudden movement at the side of the bed. Alice stood looking down at him. Jerry said, "Hello! Where am I?"

"At the doctor's house. Wait, you're not badly hurt. Just weak from loss of blood."

"Huh, that's funny. I don't remember much. Is everything all right?"

"Of course. Capron and Flecker are both in jail. They've both confessed ever so many things. Oh, my dear, you shouldn't have run such risks."

"It's funny," Jerry repeated. "Last I remember I was sitting on that desk at your side, waiting for Naughton to get through talking so I could get to a doctor."

"You fainted...from loss of blood."

"Fainted?" he said scornfully. "Can you imagine that for a fool thing. Fainted! Just like a weak old woman. Gosh, what a fool I am."

"Cowboy, dear! I said you were a fool the first time I saw you, a fool or crazy."

Her eyes were moist.

"And now you believe it, eh?" Jerry grinned. He was feeling stronger. One arm went around Alice's neck as he drew her face down to his. "Sure I'm crazy...about you."

"Jerry! Stop! Father or Mister Naughton may come in. They're just outside. And your cowboy friends at the Circle-F are due to arrive...."

"Let 'em arrive," Jerry smiled happily. "The sooner the whole town knows it, the better."

"Knows what?"

"About the house we're aiming to build on that pretty tableland near Palo Verde Pass. Lady! don't you realize I got plans for you and me?"

Alice bent down to complete the first plan.

T. T. Flynn was born in Indianapolis, Indiana. He was the author of nearly a hundred Western short novels for the magazine market, including stories in the premier issues of *Dime Western* and *Star Western*. He moved to New Mexico in 1927 and spent much of his time living in a trailer while on the road, exploring the vast terrain of the American West. His descriptions of the land are always detailed, but he uses them not only for local color but also to reflect the heightening of emotional distress among the characters within a story. Following the Second World War, Flynn turned his attention to the Western novel and produced a notable series of works from THE MAN FROM LARAMIE (Dell First Edition, 1954) to NIGHT OF THE COMANCHE MOON (Five Star Westerns, 1995)

"Back Trail" was the third Western story T. T. Flynn wrote in 1949. Mike Tilden bought it and changed the title to "Hunted Wolf!" when it appeared in Dime Western (9/49). What struck Tilden when he first read it was the encounter with the ancient wolf. "Why did fugitive Tom Buckner, dying of thirst at dreaded Phantom Pool, refuse to kill that ancient lobo wolf—and save his own tortured hide?" asked Tilden in the headnote he wrote for the story. Why, indeed? The psychological dimensions of Flynn's Western fiction came increasingly to encompass a confrontation with ethical principles about how one must live, the values that one must hold dear above all else, and Flynn's belief that there must be a balance in all things. The cosmic meaning of the mortality of all living creatures had become for him a unifying metaphor for the fragility and dignity of life itself.

Back Trail

I

BLOOD ON THE SAND

At the empty rock seep called Phantom Pool, Tom Buckner waited to gamble his last cartridge against a mangy wolf that one of them would eat the other and reach the sweet waters in the Mustang Hills alive for the next kill. Buckner's swollen lips twisted at the thought. Living to kill Hal Stafford had become a frantic urge since Buckner had plodded out of the shimmering distance and found Phantom Pool dry, and realized why Stafford and his riders had turned back.

Stafford had known Buckner's wounded horse wouldn't last. Stafford must have known the pool was dry. He'd probably laughed, big head thrown back, eyes closing a little, mirth shaking his deep chest. Stafford's humor could appreciate Buckner's walking deeper into dry country, to the dry basin of Phantom Pool. Why press hard and dangerous pursuit to kill a man when the desert would do it with slow and exquisite agony?

They hadn't known Buckner was down to his last cartridge; they'd known well enough what his gun could do. After his horse had gone down, Buckner had slogged on afoot, saving the last cartridge for a last try at Stafford. Two hours back, when he rounded the point of sun-baked red rock and sighted heat-cracked mud in the bottom of Phantom Pool basin, he'd known why Stafford had turned back.

The wolf had a gaunt, starved, dried-out look, too. It was an old-man wolf, tough and stringy, and certainly wise with the years. And thirsty now, like Buckner was thirsty—God-awful, agonizingly, hopelessly thirsty.

The wolf had come along the rock slope, through the late afternoon's shimmering heat, man-scent uncaught until the critter topped the hot, jumbled rocks just above the dry basin. Not a hundred feet away, Buckner eyed the wolf. Food stood there—food tough and stringy—but food. And moisture, red and life-giving. The wolf was thinking the same thing, thinking like a wolf. And Tom Buckner was thinking like a wolf, too.

The thought caught at Buckner. The wolf would never think like a man. But Buckner had been thrown straight back to a wolf. Kill or be killed; eat or be eaten. It took hold, deep, primitive and savage, while swollen tongue stirred and breath stepped up. The wolf faded back among the hot rocks, limping but agile, and Buckner felt furious regret that he'd hesitated. He forced himself to remain calm. Only death waited out in the desert, even for the wolf. It had that dried-out, end-of-trail look. Here they were at Phantom Pool; here they'd stay until one ate the other.

Buckner managed a wry grin. He was thinking like the wolf. He could outwait the wolf and reach the hills and cool water, and see Susan Todd, if only for an hour, on his way to find Stafford. He put away the thought of Susan Todd, as he had many times since yesterday. There lay weakness and regret.

The hot rocks lifted straight, a full thirty feet at back and north side of the pool basin. On the south side the boulder-covered slope came down steeply. The west rim of the dry basin was open. Some forty yards out an eroded outcropping of red rock offered scant shade against the brazen sun now drifting lower. Tom Buckner sat at the base of the outcropping, waiting.

The wolf returned on the rock above the basin, thirty feet up. The tip of his nose barely showed beside a wind-scoured boulder. Tom Buckner, hunched immobile, arms locked around his knees, gazed fixedly on that scant bit of grizzled wolf muzzle. Susan Todd came into his thoughts again, a smiling, quiet girl, with thoughtful eyes and enduring sweetness, no matter what her mood. A man felt more a man when with Susan. At least Buckner had felt that way often, and had guessed other men must also. Not because Susan was strong, or any weakness of Susan's played up to a man. And there lay a puzzle Buckner had wanted to solve, and would yet solve, he promised himself.

The grizzled muzzle and close-laid ears were visible. Each time Buckner moved even slightly, the wolf shrank back and vanished. Buckner damned the animal, croaking the words painfully in his rough, dry throat. The wolf's right ear pricked. The eyes watched steadily. Buckner whipped out the gun. The wolf vanished. Buckner had known he would. That muzzle was not a target for the last cartridge anyway. It had to be a close and certain shot.

Shortly the wolf was watching again. He was an old wise lobo who could wait. Who meant to wait. Buckner put away all anger, which was weakness. He had to out-wolf the wolf, be calmer, more patient, stronger. He must do it to live.

Stronger than a wolf. Buckner was amused once more. He had hunted wolves. Shot them. Trapped them. Always his guns and traps had made him the stronger. Now the wolf and he were equal across the heat-cracked mud of the dry basin. Now was he stronger, with patience to wait and wait?

The wolf could wait without irritation, without anger or nervousness. It was the heat, probably, and the thirst—the God-awful nagging thirst—which made Buckner consider the wolf an equal, who had his own thirst and problem of waiting. A man could feel sorry for the wolf. For when the showdown came, the wolf would have no gun. He could be all that Tom Buckner was, in will, in patience, and in caution. As good as Tom Buckner. But he had no gun. There was a problem about it, like the puzzle of Susan Todd. The wolf, meeting heat and thirst and power of will, was as good as Tom Buckner—but he had no gun.

Brief twilight flung crimson across the high sky. The wolf had not moved when solid night closed in. Moonrise was more than an hour off. Buckner waited. If he hunted the wolf, it would fade away before him. But if the wolf hunted Buckner, it would come close, in the open. The one cartridge was enough. But the wolf was unarmed. Buckner pondered the thought—no gun.

He guessed the wolf would move before moonrise. A bit of breeze finally wandered past. The night had a great empty weight of silence. Then Buckner held his breath. Soft, rhythmic sounds, barely audible, were somewhere in front of him. Slowly Buckner brought the gun muzzle up across one cramped knee. The sounds continued. They were puzzling; they had no meaning, until Buckner finally sorted out the truth. Rock at the back and side of the pool basin formed a sounding board. The wolf was digging in the cracked mud at the back of the basin. Digging before moonrise, in frantic haste, while movements were hidden. The wolf hadn't been able to wait.

Buckner came up noiselessly, stiff, aching. He almost staggered with the first cautious forward step, gun cocked and ready. The wolf's labor evidently masked the fainter slither of Buckner's advance. Once more Buckner wanted to chortle. The wolf hadn't been able to wait. Then a sudden scurry of limping flight whisked close in the dim starlight. For an instant the wolf was a passing shadow, his gasping audible as he broke for safety. The Colt's muzzle lined clearly on the target.

Tom Buckner stood there on the cracked mud and cursed thickly. He'd remembered the wolf had no gun and had held the shot. Crazy from thirst, evidently. Tom Buckner licked dry lips with dry tongue and tried to think it out. Finally he went forward and held a lighted match where the wolf had been digging.

The rock wall bent in a little at the bottom. The mud there was just as dry, heat cracks as deep. But almost against the rock, the wolf had been clawing down in an inch-wide mud crack. The hole was dry. Buckner swore in futile helplessness. Then his queer respect for the wolf came at him. The wolf had a reason for digging there.

Decades of passing men had left trash of forgotten camps around Phantom Pool. Old cans, bottles, char of campfires, and litter, how deep no man knew. There were bones too, in plenty. Buckner re-called a wheel hub with several spokes, out about a hundred yards. He walked out to it, forcing himself to move deliberately. Haste could spark false hope and flare into the frantic end.

He wrenched out a loose wagon wheel spoke and whittled the dry wood to a point. He found a stout tin can, and had his pick and shovel. He dug in the wolf's hole until he was breathing harshly, like the wolf had been breathing. Two feet down it did seem a little damper. But only damp. Three feet down Buckner threw another can of dirt and lay on his belly, panting weakly. His arm hung down in the hole as he lay full length, not caring much any more. When strength drained out of a man, hope could drain out too.

The cool wet seep was on his fingers before he realized what was happening. He snatched the fingers to his mouth. *Wet.* And wet when he did it again. He scraped an ounce of muddy water in the can, and sucked the wetness deep in his mouth, and held it, and let it crawl sandy and wet down his dry throat. And still the water seeped into the hole. The wolf had been right. Later, quite sane and growing stronger, Buckner carried the can full of water out into the desert and sat down. The moon had bloomed full and bright. Buckner watched the wolf approach the hole. Only Buckner himself could know how the wolf felt about that muddy seep of life.

Presently the wolf headed, limping, toward the far hills. Buckner watched with the ghost of an understanding smile. And in turn, carrying a quart whiskey bottle of water in each hand, he also started for the hills. The look on Hal Stafford's face would be worth all this. And there was also the matter of Susan Todd, if only for an hour. That puzzle about Susan.

II

THE AVENGER

The next blistering afternoon Buckner was in Black Cañon. Meacham's Keg, ahead of him, was the first water where a man was not apt to be sighted and reported. His feet were raw and swollen. The water bottles were long empty and discarded. Buckner was dried-out, weary, limping, but not staggering. He'd slept a little before and after dawn. A hard and fit man could go for a week without food. It was water he must have.

A sloughing whisper of sound came drifting through the cañon silence. Buckner halted and listened intently. He might have scrambled up the rock-piled bench slope at his right. Instead he ran forward a dozen yards and crouched behind a great water-smoothed boulder. He cocked the hand gun with its single cartridge.

A horse came cantering slowly on the flood-scoured cañon bed. One horse, as Buckner had gambled. It was almost to the rock when he stood up. The startled dun horse snorted and half whirled away. Young Curly Powers, a Stafford rider, swore loudly, reined the horse hard, and reached fast for his revolver.

"Don't try it, Curly!"

Powers decided not to, and lifted high his gun hand as he quieted the horse. All Stafford's men knew Buckner's skill with a gun.

"Step down on this side, Curly! Keep that hand up! Unbuckle that belt and let it drop!"

Curly Powers probably would have gambled against one shot. But he didn't know there was only one. Disarmed, he stood in sullen apprehension, blond and young, and dangerous, too, because he was jumpy.

"Walk back up the cañon, Curly!"

"Going to shoot me in the back?"

"Might. You were with the bunch trying to target my back. Get going."

Curly moved slowly. Buckner buckled on the gun belt with its welcome glint of shiny brass cartridges filling each loop. He reloaded his own gun and tossed Curly's emptied gun on the sand. Only when he checked the saddle carbine and found it ready for use did he drink sparingly from the saddle canteen.

Then in the saddle he relaxed for one glorious moment, aches, weariness, hunger of small matter now. Curly halted with sullen tenseness when Buckner rode up beside him and asked, "Who's riding out this way with you?"

"No one." The lie was cloudy and angry in Curly's pale eyes.

Buckner contemplated him. "Curly, working for Stafford won't do you any good. You're young enough to slope on and do better."

"Never mind how young I am. You hired out to Stafford."

"And quit." Buckner's throat still felt gravelly, but an impulse made him speak on. "Stafford gave me an idea his bunch was being hazed around by other outfits. He's convincing when he talks to a stranger. When I saw it was Stafford doing the pushing, I quit."

"Trying to preach to me?"

"Sort of," Buckner said. He could look back a few years, and he'd been hot-headed too, like Curly. Sure of himself. Not wanting advice. "You saw what happened to me, Curly. I quit. Took a room at the hotel in Luna. Minding my own business before I moved on. But I'd seen too much to suit Stafford, I guess. His men came crowding me into a fight. That way, Stafford had me, he thought, being he was a deputy on the side, and able to take his men after me…same thing might happen to you."

"Not me," Curly denied. His lip thrust out in swaggering confidence. "When I quit fat pay like Stafford's, I won't be fool enough to camp close to the girl Stafford's running after."

"That's fool talk."

"Tell Stafford," said Curly. "Me, I'm only after wages and extra money I can pick up. Stafford's got it. It's forty miles to the ranch from here. You going to leave me on foot?"

Buckner's own look was cloudy over the thing Curly had suggested. "Your gun is back there on the sand. Next time don't come heading off a man who might be walking back dry from Phantom Rocks. Walk home or stay at Meacham's water until they send for you."

Buckner shook the dun horse into a lope up the cañon. He should have known Curly better—young, hot-tempered. The surprise shot Curly fired after him gouged violently along Buckner's side. The left side. He lurched to the right. That, and a hard rein wheeling the horse made Curly's second shot miss. The echoes boomed off the cañon walls as the horse came around. Buckner's gun was in his hand. Anger had him in a misty wave. He saw the small, double-barreled Derringer in Curly's hand. Not much range to that tiny gun, but the heavy slugs were deadly at close quarters. Curly was scrambling to the shelter of another boulder. He made it inches ahead of the shot Buckner fired.

Buckner halted the horse. Gun cocked, he watched the boulder. The rage began to drain out of him. "Should have listened to me, Curly," he called.

Curly's reply was sullen again behind the boulder. "It was worth a try for the five hundred Stafford offered if you were sighted."

"And killed?"

"You ain't any good to Stafford alive."

The wounded left side was bleeding. Buckner noted the bullet had passed out through his shirt front. It could be worse.

"You haven't got a chance!" he told Curly.

"Who said I had?"

"Don't ever get near me again! I'll kill you on sight!"

Buckner wheeled the dun horse fast up the cañon. Curly had been a dead one and knew it. But killing Curly wouldn't solve anything. He was useless as a prisoner. Stafford was the business ahead.

A man named Meacham had sunk a keg at the foot of a towering sandstone cliff where Indian well-water seeped out and vanished in the scoured sand of the cañon bed. The old keg held water, crystal and sweet. Buckner knew of it by hearsay. He found the keg— and fresh sign of shod horses by it. Two horses.

Curly Powers had come this way with a companion. They had watered and split up. But the other man might have been near enough to hear the shots. He might be riding back now, or already set in ambush, to earn Stafford's five hundred. Buckner drank, refilled the canteen, then looked to his side. He had made a pad of his neckerchief and held it over the wound. Bleeding had almost stopped. A rib was chipped or broken. There was pain.

The afternoon was drawing on. It was only a matter of time before Curly joined the other horseman. One of them would either try to follow him, or get word fast to Hal Stafford.

Buckner was desperately weary as he started the long ride to Luna. Stafford was often in town at night. He would be this night, Buckner felt certain. With some of his men, as usual. Buckner discounted the men. This was not a fight. It was an execution. Stafford was always armed and ready for trouble. This time he would have it. The wolf-like urge to get at Stafford had not abated. It was the same chill certainty which had held Buckner steady at Phantom Pool. He could out-wolf the wolf. He would out-wolf Stafford. This time there would be more than one cartridge. And one more thing. One thing all Stafford's craftiness could not judge. Buckner didn't care what happened to himself. It was a wolf-savageness new to Stafford's experience.

Buckner returned to the puzzle of Susan Todd. Stafford had been more than friendly with Susan. If she was aware of the man's bullying, out-reaching ways, she'd never said. The dun horse pricked ears as Buckner said aloud, "That fool Curly!"

Then Buckner thought how he'd stayed on in Luna after quitting Stafford. Usually he'd have ridden on toward new country. Luna wasn't a town to hold a man. He'd told himself he'd wanted a rest. Now he pondered that Luna stay. The town and Susan Todd kept running together in his thoughts. There was a problem there, like the wolf which had no gun, but Buckner was too tired now for problems. He had the one last thing to do. Get Stafford. Nothing else mattered much.

The afternoon tailed out as he threaded badlands east of the Mustang Hills. He kept to the low washes and draws, below the ridges, hidden from prying eyes on some distant rise. The canteen emptied too quickly. More water meant at least a ten mile jog off the direct line to Luna. Buckner rode dry and was thankful when night took the land under bright stars.

Luna was eighty-odd miles from the railroad. There was a daily through stage. Another stage line ran from Luna across the mountains, tapping cow and mining settlements to the northeast. The adobe and board sprawl of the town lay on Luna Creek Flats, beside the first sharp rise of the mountain foothills. Not a county seat. Deputy law was all the town had. A man could jump across the clear, chuckling shallows of Luna Creek. But the cold brawling current and underground water were enough for the town, enough for trees, bushes, and a few little irrigated gardens.

The town lights were bright points against the darker foothills as Buckner rode in. Rider and horse were both dead beat. A small night breeze sliding off the foothills tainted the darkness pleasantly with town scent of wood smoke. The aching fatigue lifted a bit. Buckner's purpose began to tighten nerves and pull energy from the deep core of his hard frame. The horse, too, stepped more lightly.

They passed the half-hearted barking of the first dogs, the scatter of outlying shacks, and swung toward the compound at the rear of the Luna House. Buckner was gambling that warning of his return had not yet reached town. Several horses fed in the open-front shed at the back of the compound. No lantern, no loiterers near the spot. Buckner watered the horse at the pump trough, unsaddled, and left the animal at a waiting manger in the feed shed. Only then, carrying Curly's carbine, did he walk stiffly to the back of the hotel, pain feverish in his side.

The clapboard hotel was two stories high, with a railed gallery at the front facing the street, and shed-roofed porch at the back. The back windows upstairs were dark. Kitchen windows showed light. Kitchen door was closed. So was a second door giving into the back of the passage which ended in the lobby. When Buckner opened that hall door, murmur of talk in the lobby drifted to him. The shadowy back stairs creaked under his quiet ascent to the upper corridor.

His room rent had been paid up. When he unlocked the door and stepped in and struck a match, everything was as he had left it. This could easily seem one more pleasant evening in the string of Luna days after leaving Stafford's hire.

Buckner pulled down the shade at the back window and lighted the glass lamp. He carried the lamp to the washstand mirror and eyed his reflection. Dirty, unshaven, gaunt. Smiling ruefully, Buckner got out his razor and stripped off his shirt.

Shaving and washing helped. But the face was still gaunt, eyes bloodshot, fatigue etched deeply. His middle curved in, hard and empty. The wound was a raw furrow over a rib, which was probably cracked. Halves of a clean towel knotted together made a fair bandage. He was pulling on a clean shirt when heavy steps tramped off the front stairs into the corridor. Buckner blew out the lamp and listened to the steps pause, a door being unlocked.

He heard the clear tones of Susan Todd's voice and stood motionless, shirt half buttoned. Susan's father, a sickly man who seldom left his room, owned the hotel. Susan ran the place firmly, competently. The door closed. Susan's lighter steps came on back in the hall and stopped before Buckner's door. Susan stood there a moment. Darkness clotted about Buckner. Susan could not suspect anyone was in the room. But her key scraped in the lock.

Buckner had locked the door and left the key there. Now the push of Susan's key on the outside backed Buckner's key out of the lock. It clinked audibly on the floor. Susan stood quietly for another long moment. Then her key opened the lock and she pushed the door open.

"Come out!" Susan ordered sharply.

The yellow flare of a match blossomed against Buckner's thumbnail.

"I'll light the lamp," he said, and it came to him this was the hour he wanted. And queerly, because it was the last hour before he sought Stafford, he met it with reluctance.

He heard Susan catch breath audibly. She stepped in, closed the door. The whiter lamp glow flooded the room and Tom Buckner looked at her with puckered intentness, as if this were a first meeting. Susan's warm, brown hair was piled on her head. She had smooth white skin and there was a deftness about all her movements.

She stood quite still now. Buckner could not know his bloodshot intentness put an inflexible cast to his features as Susan asked with a hint of demanding breathlessness, "Why did you come back?"

Buckner fumbled with the remaining buttons of his shirt. Curly's gun belt hung in a heavy slant around his middle. The carbine leaned against the end of the oak washstand, with its burden of white pottery pitcher and bowl. Susan had known he was one of Stafford's fighting men. Her manner was judging him now, hired gun-slinger, trouble seeker.

"I needed a shave." He touched the gaunt, sun-cured smoothness the blade had left.

Susan's hostility seemed to grow. Buckner could understand it. Stafford's best man had provoked the fight in the Eagle Bar, adjoining the hotel. The gunfire had been audible through the small town. Susan had been witness to the gathering rush of Stafford's other men, while Buckner had retreated through the back door of the Eagle, to his horse behind the hotel, and left town. He hadn't wanted more trouble. He'd ridden from Stafford's Cross T men to think over the obviously planned pattern of the potentially deadly incident. Only when they came after him and stayed after him had he realized they were riding for a kill. Hal Stafford's men never moved without Stafford's orders.

"They said you escaped across the desert. You didn't ride back for a shave."

"I walked part of the way."

Susan hardly seemed to hear him. The shadow of some memory darkened in her look. "You shot a man. The law wants you."

"Stafford wants me. I had to kill Morrison, or let him kill me."

"Morrison is only badly wounded. If you give yourself up, it will work out."

He hunched big shoulders. The movement drew pain from his side. "Give up to Stafford?" His sarcastic smile disposed of that.

"Why did you quit the Cross T?" Susan asked abruptly.

"Didn't like the way Stafford operates. He wants everything in sight and doesn't care how he gets it. Or have you been looking the other way lately?"

Susan's ghost of a flush seemed to point up increasing hostility. Buckner thought with etching disapproval: *She's worried about him.* He got a measure of cold satisfaction in knowing she should be worried, if that was the way she felt.

Susan glanced away from the edge of his look and saw the blood-stiff blue neck-cloth on the washstand. She stepped toward it to make sure. "What happened out there? You walked back from where?" She was calm with an effort; then she was urgent.

"First man who sighted me put a lucky bullet in my horse. It kept bleeding, put me afoot about fifteen miles this side of Phantom Pool. When I walked there, the pool was dry. I'd started without water anyway. So I walked back to Black Cañon."

"All that way without water? You couldn't. No man could. I know that Phantom Pool stretch and what happens without water."

"There was a wolf," Buckner said, smiling at the memory.

He told her, and Susan listened intently, studying his face. Abruptly she asked, "Why didn't you shoot the wolf, as you planned?"

Buckner's reflective smile considered it again. "He was almost as good a man as I was, the way we were waiting for who caved first. But he didn't have a gun."

"Gun?" said Susan. She sounded unbelieving. "Even when there was no chance of water and it might get you back, you let that stop you?"

"Next chance I'd have dropped him," Buckner said sheepishly. "A dried-out man gets light-headed."

Susan nodded. "How bad are you hurt? Does it need attention?"

"Not now."

"When did you eat last?"

"I'll get around to it."

"After you kill Hal Stafford?"

"He's one wolf who has got a gun."

"You must not!" Buckner shrugged again, not intending to argue the point. Susan said rather desperately, half to herself, "I'll stop you. I'll warn him."

"Why, I want him warned. He'll have his chance at me then."

"His men are in town, too. They'll kill you."

"Might not," Buckner said indifferently.

Susan saw the futility of talk and backed against the door. She turned the key quickly and pulled it out, and caught up his fallen key, and clutched both tightly. Buckner thought, *She's turning into a wildcat to help him.* In a way he admired her spirit, while it pulled him apart and condemned him.

Susan warned sharply, "The sheriff came in on the stage. He's the law in town tonight. And he's staying here."

"When will he be here in the hotel?"

"Any minute now!"

Buckner smiled again at the way he'd drawn the sheriff's absence from the hotel out of her, blocking any threat that the sheriff was downstairs. He stepped to the lamp and blew it out. In the instant blackness hid them from each other, he moved past the washstand, catching up the carbine and continuing to the back window.

His soft, unhurried voice came back at her. "I'll leave while the sheriff's out. If you try an alarm, it should draw Stafford." He ran the shade up, pushed the window up, straddled the sill when his foot found the weather-warped shingles of the back porch. He looked back into the dark, silent room. "When a wolf comes at a man's back, he has to be handled. And Stafford always takes the back, which is why I quit him. You might remember it if you miss him too much."

Susan's low and shaken helplessness came at him from the dark. "How can I reason with a hot-headed fool like you are tonight?"

It made him think of his advice to Curly Powers. He straddled the sill, holding to the episode with young Curly, only vaguely conscious he was using it to draw out this last moment of parting. He heard Susan moving, and sound a in the night outside intruded and drew all his alert attention.

III

STILL WORTH $500—DEAD

The back door of the Eagle Bar, some forty yards south of the hotel, had opened. Men were emerging. The moon was up but a belt of heavy shadow lay behind the hotel and the Eagle. The men over there were all but invisible. Their talk came through the quiet night, and the back wall of the hotel gathered it clearly.

Hal Stafford's heavy-chest tones said, "We can talk out here. That bunch in there suspected something was up, the way you came in fast, Curly. So Buckner walked out of it, damn him, and got your horse and guns?"

Young Curly's quick answer was sulky. "He jumped up under my horse's nose in Black Cañon. Had his gun almost in my ribs. Think you'd have done different, Mister Stafford?"

"I wasn't there. Did Buckner say where he was heading…give any hint at all?"

"No. When Chris came along and let me have his horse, I didn't try to work out Buckner's trail. He'd have been watching for it. I thought you'd want to know quick."

"Right," agreed Stafford. "Buckner back trailed to town here, of course."

Susan had reached the window as the men emerged. Her touch on Buckner's arm had been urgent. But not holding him. Her fingers stayed on his arm as if trying to tell him something by contact.

Her hand pulled away quickly when Stafford's flat, assured chest tones said, "He has a woman on his mind bad enough to come back here and see her again. If he does, we'll get him."

A third voice asked, "Why so proddy about gettin' him?"

Stafford's coldness was immediate. "When a man quits me like Buckner did, he's against me. I don't give him a chance."

Young Powers's sulkiness lifted again. "He had a good start. If he's that lovesick a fool, maybe he's already here." Sarcasm laced Curly's next words. "If we knew who the girl was, we'd know where to look for him."

"I know," Stafford said. A thickening of violence was in the admission. "Buckner wouldn't be fool enough to leave his horse in the hotel shed there. But have a look, Tex. Then we'll see what's going on in the hotel."

Young Curly said, "Buckner could have killed me. Any man would in his place. But he didn't, damn him. I'm out of the rest of this."

"Losing your nerve?"

Curly said dangerously, "Don't call me yellow, Mister Stafford. I made a long try for your five hundred, with a rabbity little Derringer against my Colt shooter he had. On the showdown, he didn't kill me. I've reported in. That fills my hand. Pay me off if you like."

"Later, Curly, later. If you aren't helping now, keep out of the way."

The door opening and slamming over there was Curly's going back into the Eagle Bar in a temper.

Stafford's voice primed with an ugly rasp. "Another one against us!"

Smooth tones sounded like Fred Kistler, a sandy, long-faced, mostly silent and dangerous man. "You offered five hundred for Buckner. How much is Curly worth now?"

"Not now," said Stafford impatiently.

A crumbling, waist-high adobe wall bounded the hotel yard. Tex had stepped over and walked back through moonlight to the open-front shed. His match spurted flame…then another match. Tex's fast steps thudded back to the low fence. "Buckner's horse is there!"

A rising ugliness larded Stafford's decision. "He's in the hotel with her! Tex, you and Red watch the back! We'll go in the front."

"Sheriff's in town," Fred Kistler reminded.

"He knows Buckner's wanted. I'm deputy. Made you all a posse hunting him, didn't I? Buckner's still worth five hundred. What more do you want?"

Kistler suggested, "If Curly made it a thousand...."

"Your back has been scratchy against Curly's cockiness," said Stafford. His shrewd trading way settled it. "Curly's fired, as of now. Do what you like. Let's cork Buckner in the hotel."

Buckner swung back into the dark room. He brushed against Susan and stepped away. Her nearness, for some reason, set his pulses pumping.

"Fool talk," he said, and tried to make it gruff.

"Yes," Susan agreed. She was close, yet her thin-spoken coolness put distance between them. A great distance. "You couldn't feel like they said and come back to kill a man."

The racing moments were life and death. But Buckner argued, "Why not? This is between Stafford and me. You overheard his side of it. Give me the door key."

"Men!" said Susan. "Blind and stubborn! I'll tell you why not. A killing will outlaw you! If you aren't killed also, you'll have to run. You can never come back. No man would choose that if he had thought for a woman!"

Their voices, instinctively, were low inside the open window. The flying seconds made lingering folly. But this was the hour he'd wanted, the last chance to settle the puzzle of Susan. His throat felt dry again, and his pulse was fast.

"A woman who's thinking about another man...?"

"A woman I don't know then," said Susan.

"Why, why...," said Buckner helplessly. He struggled with it. "A man who came in as a hired gunman...a hardcase?"

"Perhaps if you'd killed the wolf or Curly Powers," said Susan. "But the man who *didn't* kill them is the one I'm talking to."

It came to Buckner then, like clear light. The puzzle of Susan, who looked to the best in a man, had been the puzzle of himself instead. He hadn't cared what happened to Tom Buckner tonight. Now suddenly he did care. And it was too late.

Susan was moving to the door. He moved with her in the dark. "There's nothing I can do," he told her. "Stafford's coming in after me."

Susan was fumbling the key into the lock. "Not Hal Stafford," she said, and she sounded stifled. "He'll send men in after you."

"It works out the same."

"Nothing works out, or this wouldn't be," said Susan as the door came open. "I'm going for the sheriff."

One quick stride carried him out into the lamp-lit hall, scanning the back and front stair heads. Susan was walking fast to the front stairs.

Buckner caught up with her, taller by a head, shoulders broad and wiry, cartridge-filled gun belt snug about the starved leanness of his middle. He moved with loose-limbed lightness, carbine in left hand, right hand easy near the belt holster as they started down.

Susan had a pinched whiteness. She blinked several times. Her silence had a finality which plucked at Buckner as nothing else had. He'd preached a steadier way for Curly's hot-headed recklessness. It should have been to Tom Buckner. Should have been....

His arm checked Susan at the turn of the landing, while he scanned the small rather shabby lobby, holding six-eight men and idle talk through a gray-blue drift of tobacco smoke. They were cattlemen, townsmen, and two who looked like drummers.

Adam Ingalls, who raised horses south of the Cross T range, glanced from his hide-covered chair toward the sound of descending steps. Ingalls, a big man with a full grizzled beard, looked hard, as if not believing, and stood up with quick instinct of trouble.

"Ingalls, be comfortable," Buckner said in brief warning as he came off the steps. Susan was almost at his side.

More men were on their feet. The drummers were puzzled by the abrupt shift to wire-hard tension. Susan's clear voice demanded, "Mister Ingalls, where is the sheriff?"

Buckner weighed each man's face as he continued to the door. "No time for that, Ingalls," he said as he passed. Adam Ingalls was no friend to Stafford. Nor was any of the others, so far as Buckner knew. He had to leave them at his back anyway, while he stepped fast through the doorway and to the left in the shadows where his eyes could adjust to the light.

Tobacco smoke drifted over the verandah railing. The pale red gleam of a cigarette tip glowed. Buckner's expanding sight made out the figure standing under the verandah rail. His gun came out and cocked, and he crouched a little as three more indistinct figures cut across the yard. By guess he knew those three. They crossed a swath of moonlight: Stafford, Fred Kistler at his left, and it looked like Roney Metcalfe at Stafford's right.

The long wide verandah was cluttered with chairs. The patch of yard held two towering cottonwoods which cast deep shadow clear to the front hitch rack and moon-drenched street dust. Lights in Paddy Henderson's store across the street seemed far away.

Stafford and his men were near the steps when Susan came out with Adam Ingalls. The men halted. Susan and Ingalls saw them just as Stafford called, "Susan, where's Buckner?"

Susan's pause was the catching of a breath. Then Susan replied clearly, "His room is upstairs."

She started to descend the steps. Adam Ingalls caught her arm. "Back inside!" Ingalls rumbled in his beard.

The smoker under the verandah rail spoke with a repressed jeer. "Kistler! How much am I worth now?"

All three men whirled to the sound. Kistler's voice was dangerous. "Curly! He stopped inside the Eagle door and listened!"

"Sure did," Curly agreed. "Nice listening!"

Adam Ingalls propelled Susan fast, back through the doorway. Ingalls swung around then, filling the doorway with his solid bulk, watching.

Hal Stafford's anger slurred with restraint. "Some other time, Curly. This is the law now."

"Hell of a law with you, Kistler, an' Metcalfe for samples!" Curly's tone rode his own windy, jumpier anger. "I owe Buckner a turn. Get the sheriff to take him. I've got things to tell the sheriff anyway."

Buckner let out a sigh of decision and came full upright. Curly was riding hot-headed anger with spurs, running over them. And with little chance against all three. In odd surprise as he stepped forward, skirting a cane-bottomed chair, Buckner recognized it was Curly he was helping now, not himself. He thought virtuously: a woman couldn't find fault with this—helping a friendly man.

Curly jeered at Stafford, "The sheriff ain't jealous!"

Buckner sensed the final exploding spark in that. "Hold it!" he called urgently and lunged for the steps.

Stafford's meaty cry of full-lunged anger overrode the words. "Drop him, boys!"

Fred Kistler's gun seemed instantly to lace the shadows with red bellowing spurts. Curly must have borrowed a gun and belt in the Eagle Bar. He fired almost as fast. And knew what he was doing. He had meant to do it when he took station there by the verandah, Buckner realized.

It was Stafford, clawing at his revolver, who took the full slam of Curly's heavy bullets. Stafford's bulk folded forward in grotesque jerks. From the top of the steps Buckner drove his shots at Kistler, trying to help Curly. He knew he was too late when Curly's gun went silent. A bullet tugged through his shirt sleeve. Roney Metcalfe was firing and backing away.

Buckner lunged down the steps, and that, and being alone now, broke Roney's nerve. He ran toward the corner of the hotel. With a regretful breath, Buckner let him go, and swung back to Curly.

He remembered and called to Adam Ingalls. "Two more are watching the back! They may get in this!"

Ingalls's rumbling decision urged the cattlemen in the lobby, "Enough of this! Help take over until the sheriff gets here!"

Curly was dead. In the yellow spurting match flare Buckner recklessly risked, Curly looked younger than ever. And somehow completely peaceful, as if Curly had found something which had been missing. Something Buckner had tried to tell him about in Black Cañon. A kind of self-respect a man could live with, or die with.

Buckner stood up and rolled a cigarette absently. The cattlemen were on the verandah with Adam Ingalls. In a moment or so it was plain that Tex and Red and Roney Metcalfe had decided that all this was Stafford's quarrel, and just about over now.

Buckner looked for a moment at men boiling out of the Eagle Bar or pounding across the dusty street and along the walks toward the trouble. Not a bad town, he thought. A man could back trail to worse towns, and be less contented elsewhere. He saw Susan coming out and threw the unlighted cigarette away and started up the steps to tell her.

Frederick Dilley Glidden was born in Kewanee, Illinois, and

was graduated in 1930 with a Bachelor's degree from the University of Missouri where he had majored in journalism. Following graduation, Glidden worked for a number of newspapers, but no job lasted very long. He spent two years trapping in northern Canada before he took a job as an archeologist's assistant in Santa Fé, New Mexico, and met Florence Elder of Grand Junction, Colorado, whom he married and nicknamed Butch. Fred read Dime Western and Star Western and was convinced he could write a story as well as any he had read. Fred and Butch were renting two adjacent adobe houses in Santa Fé which they used as a combined unit from Brian Boru Dunne. Fred asked Dunne if he knew of a literary agent. Dunne didn't, but he had another tenant who was a writer and who had a good one and he would ask him. That writer was T. T. Flynn. Marguerite E. Harper was the agent. In October, 1934 Fred sent Harper a story titled "Six-Gun Lawyer" and signed it F. D. Glidden. On April 17, 1935 Harper sold that story to Cowboy Stories. Harper told Fred she was concerned about his name. F. Orlin Tremaine, editor of Cowboy Stories, complained that it didn't sound very "Western." At first Fred thought of Lew Short—he wanted something "short" and memorable like Max Brand—and finally settled on Luke Short without realizing that this was the name of an actual gunman and gambler in the Old West.

Although as a Harper client, Fred wrote his fair share of short stories for the magazine market, he preferred writing serials. Beyond this natural propensity, Fred probably realized he was not really the master of the short story and short novel the way Flynn was or, later, Fred's brother, Jon. Only one story by Luke Short ever appeared in Big-Book Western, the one that follows.

Bandit Lawman

———⟫●⟪———

I

LAW-TAMER

Deputy Sheriff Will Bent, lounging against a porch pillar of the Union House, centered his attention on the man who was the last to climb out of the stage. "That him?" he asked Sheriff Andy Hayes, who was sitting with his feet cocked up on the railing. Sheriff Hayes said, "Uh-huh."

In all that group of miners and travelers who had alighted from the stage, this man they had singled out was the one to catch the eye and hold it. He was burly across the shoulders, of medium height, and his face was so dark that it made the white linen of his shirt almost glow. He was dressed in expensive black, and even at this distance the diamond on his finger gleamed.

Bent straightened up and dropped his cigarette, which had died as he was watching the stage unload. "Better give him a few minutes, huh?" he drawled.

"Sure," Hayes said. He looked at Bent, as if to study him. Bent's lean six feet seemed cocked for trouble, his blue eyes amused and at the same time a little hard. Hayes sighed softly. He was an old man now, old and gnarled and white-haired and slow, but still he could enjoy what was coming.

"What's his handle?" Bent drawled.

"Sam Suffern."

Bent only grinned.

Suffern, now, paused and gave loud directions for the disposition of his baggage. The he stepped up on the boardwalk and headed down the street, a nine-inch cigar jutting from his lips.

———⟫●⟪———

Bent looked at Hayes and said, "Lordy, he even acts tough."

Sheriff Hayes waited a few minutes, then hoisted his bulk from the chair and grunted, "Come on."

Together they descended the steps and followed Suffern. The main street of Roaring Fork was settling back into its usual afternoon torpor after the stage's arrival. Ponies and buckboards were facing the tie-rails on both sides of the dusty street between the wide cañon of false-front stores.

Bent said, "Where'll I choose him?"

"Let him worry about that."

At the War Bonnet Saloon, they turned in. The usual loafers were bellied up to the bar, while others surrounded the faro and poker tables. Today the crowd was bigger than usual, for almost everyone in town wanted to have a first look a Suffern, the man who had bought out Hank Barber's War Bonnet.

Bent said to the barkeep, "Where's the new boss?"

The bartender gestured with a jerk of his head toward the office door in the sidewall at the foot of the bar.

Almost to the door, Sheriff Hayes and Bent stopped. Suffern stepped out and closed the door behind him.

"Suffern?" Bent asked grimly.

The saloon owner turned to them. His face was surprisingly lean, his lips thin and wide, his nose aquiline. His deep-set eyes were piercing, black, wary. Seeing the badges on their vests, he smiled narrowly.

"Yes." He spoke almost mockingly. "You two gentlemen are the law. Have a drink with me. But first...I don't know your names."

"Never mind the name," Bent said curtly. "You'll know soon enough. And I wouldn't like a drink."

"Nor me," Hayes put in surlily.

Suffern shrugged. "Then what can I do for you?"

The room had quieted. Most of the men were listening to the conversation.

Bent said, "We just dropped around to put you straight on a few things, Suffern."

"For instance?"

"When Hank Barber owned this place, it was a hang-out for every hardcase on this slope. Nobody ever knowed it, but he was gettin' in more trouble than he could rightly wade out of." Bent paused and eyed Suffern suspiciously. "Nobody knowed where he went when he disappeared. It looks like you're the only man that does."

"Is it the deed to the place you want me to show you?" Suffern asked levelly.

"Not the deed," Hayes said. "I don't give a damn if you robbed Barber to get the place. I'm glad he's gone. I don't even want to know where."

"Nice friendly lawmen here," Suffern commented.

Bent shook his head. "That's where you're wrong, fella. We're not friendly to you, nor any man of Barber's stripe. That's just a warnin'. Play your cards close to your chest or you'll lose the pot."

Suffern looked at Bent shrewdly. He said, "I don't like you, Big Wind, and you can paste that in your hat."

"Maybe I'll paste it in yours," Bent drawled.

Suffern said dryly, "I never knew it to fail. Pin a star on a thirty-a-month cow nurse and his head gets too big for his ears."

Bent flushed and his hand fell to his shell belt.

"Don't make the mistake of drawing that gun," Suffern continued. "I never carry one. I never have to when I run into jokers like you."

Bent unbuckled his shell belt, with its holstered guns, and let it slide to the floor. "I never have to use them either, Suffern. When I break things, I like to do it by hand."

"I'd be glad to oblige you."

"Let's make it the street then."

Suffern nodded and peeled off his coat, which he laid on the bar. Everyone in the room had been listening, and now they let Bent, the sheriff, and Suffern walk out the door before they moved. Then as if one man they crowded after them and swarmed over the sidewalk into the road, forming a loose circle.

Bent was taller than Suffern, longer armed. And, in addition to that, he seemed mad clean through. His huge fists hung clenched at his sides.

Somebody said, "Your hat, Will."

Bent wrenched it off and sailed it into the crowd, then said to Suffern, "Ready?"

"Any time," Suffern replied, his thick shoulders hunched a little.

Bent had been waiting for this. He stepped in, head down, a slugging arc already started with his huge fist. Suffern stood planted in his way. Moving almost indolently, Suffern shot a short jab at Bent and it straightened him up. With his other arm, the saloon owner chopped down on Bent's flailing arm. Then he leaned in, his shoulder catching under the chin and sending him back a step. Quickly, savagely now, Suffern followed, his right hand pumping into Bent's midriff. Bent stepped back again, grunting, trying for a foothold. And then, before he could gather his wits, Suffern hooked at his face viciously—twice. By the time the second blow reached him, Bent was falling. It sounded muffled, as bone on skin-padded bone will. Bent pitched back in the dust, made a slow movement as if to turn and rise, then lay back and stared at the afternoon sky.

Suffern looked down at him a long moment, then dusted his hands together gently, and turned to Sheriff Hayes. "Your deputy is a little too salty, Sheriff," he commented dryly. "Maybe he needs to travel a bit and pick up a few tricks."

Hayes glared at him. "You ain't through with Bent yet, Suffern."

"I don't expect so," Suffern drawled. "Not while he can use a gun."

"This don't change what he said to you…nor what I did," Hayes went on. "You keep in line, here, mister, or you'll have more'n a street brawl on your hands."

A drawling, slow voice from the circle of watchers said, "Don't you reckon the law has rawhided this man enough today, Hayes?"

Hayes turned to confront Barney McCann's look of quizzical distaste. McCann, as usual flanked by his two men, had a sneering smile on his bland face. Big, blond, blue-eyed and iron-jawed, McCann seldom spoke in a loud voice, but in some way his whisper contrived to carry more conviction than other men's bluster.

Hayes glared at him angrily. "If I was you, McCann, I wouldn't buy into this."

"Not a chance," McCann drawled. "Only I hate to see a stranger get hoorawed the first half hour he's in town. He might think we're all like you up at the sheriff's office."

"He knows what we are up there. I'll let him make up his own mind about you, Barney."

"That's good."

Hayes said to a long, gangling 'puncher standing nearby, "Give me a lift with him, will you, Cal?"

Cal Fields and a friend nodded and stepped over to Bent. Suffern, politely watching this conversation, now walked over and got Bent's hat and laid it on his chest, then stood aside and watched Bent carried upstreet to the sheriff's office next to the hotel.

When Hayes had gone, Suffern turned to the crowd. "Let's have a drink, boys. A man doesn't buy a saloon every day."

McCann, from the crowd, added, "Nor make over a deputy's face."

Suffern looked at him and smiled. McCann strode over to him and held out his hand. "Barney McCann's the name, Suffern. That was workmanlike. We've been thinkin' of doin' the same for some time now, but I reckon we got used to his noise."

"You'd have done the same thing in my place," Suffern said modestly. "I couldn't very well get out of it." He shrugged, and repeated, "Come on in and have a drink."

Up the street, Sheriff Hayes walked moodily behind Fields and the other man carrying Bent. As he passed Wilke's Emporium, he heard a girl's voice say softly, "Dad. Don't you see me?"

He stopped. There on the top step was a slight girl, bare headed, the sun seeming to touch her corn-colored hair with fire. She was dressed in rough range clothes and cow-boots, which only seemed to accentuate her slim loveliness. She was looking at Bent's slack body, and her mouth was open in surprise.

"What happened, Dad?"

Hayes snorted. "A new hardcase in town."

"Gunfight?"

"Uh-uh. A scrap. Will bit off considerable more'n he could chew."

She shook her head in mock disgust. "Do you two always have to walk around like banty roosters, Dad?"

Hayes's seamed face showed the trace of a smile. "Comin' from you, Mary, that sounds considerable like the cow callin' the bull a four-legged critter."

Mary grinned back. "Well, go with him, Dad. And please stay out of trouble...at least until I leave town tonight."

Sheriff Hayes snorted again and hurried to catch up with the men carrying Bent. Inside the sheriff's office, situated on the corner, he indicated a cot and Bent was laid on it.

"Thanks, boys," Hayes told Fields and his friend.

"Looks like a man don't shake one trouble but what he picks up two more," Fields said. "Here we lose Barber, and damned if we don't trade him for this gent, Suffern...twice as bad."

Hayes sighed and waved them off. As soon as the door was closed, he walked over to Bent, who was grinning up at the ceiling.

"How'd it work, Andy?" Bent asked.

"Couldn't of been better."

"Didn't I hear McCann talkin' to you?"

"Sure. He sided with Suffern."

Bent sat up now and Hayes sat down beside him. They both rolled smokes from the same sack.

Bent said in a soft voice, "Well, it looks like things are shapin' up, Andy...after four years of waitin'."

"Don't be too sure, son. McCann ain't convicted yet."

"All we needed was for Barber to lose his guts. We got a chance now, anyway."

"I wonder," the sheriff said slowly. "When I was younger, if we'd wanted to get the goods on McCann and if Barber could give it to us, we'd have took Barber out and *made* him talk. Now we got to do it legal." He made a wry face. "We buy Barber out and send a range detective in to run the saloon in his place. I dunno."

"About Suffern, you mean? You think he can't handle it?"

"I dunno, I say."

Bent rubbed his jaw and grinned ruefully. "I do. If that ranny, Suffern, is as good a detective as he is a fighter, McCann's as good as convicted right now."

II

THE BOSS HIRES A GUN

Suffern gave orders to the bartenders to serve free drinks, then he and McCann stepped into his office.

McCann looked around and said, "Nothin' changed much, since Hank Barber jumped town."

"Haven't had time," Suffern told him.

The drinks came in. Suffern offered McCann a cigar with his whiskey, which he took.

"Funny thing," McCann said slowly, after he had lit his cigar. "I never quite figured out why Hank left."

"Ran away, didn't he?" Suffern said easily.

McCann's pale blue eyes settled on Suffern speculatively. "Seems so. Why, though?"

"He told me he was gettin' in too deep."

McCann asked slowly, watching him, "Who with?"

Suffern shook his head. "I don't know. I wish I did. I've an idea that things that were too deep for Barber wouldn't be very deep at all for me."

McCann leaned back in his chair and regarded Suffern with quiet interest. Finally he said, "You've got a medium good opinion of yourself, haven't you, Suffern?"

The saloon keeper nodded. "I've never had any reason to think I'm not just a little better than the run of hardcases."

"Hardcases?"

Suffern smiled narrowly. "I think they call you a hardcase when you see something that can be taken and try to take it, don't they?"

"Why'd you come here?"

Suffern shook his head, smiling. "I've known you ten minutes, McCann. Be a little more reasonable."

McCann grinned back at him now. "All right. But what if I was to tell you that I'm the main reason Barber jumped the country?"

"You?" Suffern said softly. "I don't get it."

"Barber got the idea he was gettin' big enough to fit my shoes. I got word of it. I arranged to...er...discipline him. He got word of that some way. He ran."

Suffern nodded slightly. "Barber told me he left a mighty good thing here."

"Like what?"

Suffern moved his hand vaguely. "There's mighty good range down in the valley. There's a lot of mining camps over the mountains here. Cattle can be run across them, I understand."

McCann let his chair come to the floor. "Let's quit this dodging, Suffern. You need me and I need you. Yes, there's cattle below. I rustle them. I sell them in the mining camps. I need a cool head and a man that can't be bluffed by the law. What'll you take to step into Barber's place?"

"Sixty-forty split," Suffern said quietly. "I'll take the forty only because you put up most of the men."

McCann's eyes narrowed. "That's the split Barber was playing for when he left. That's why he had to go."

"Forty or nothing," Suffern said quietly. "I don't like small change."

"You don't like trouble, either, do you?" McCann asked meaningly.

"I don't mind it at all."

They looked at each other a long moment, and then McCann said, "I don't believe you do. All right. But why do you think you deserve that much of a cut?"

Suffern looked at the end of his cigar, then laid it on the desk and leaned forward in his chair. "There's banks in this country, McCann. There's a railroad off south. There's bullion shipments out of these mining camps. There's no law saying a man has to stick to cattle stealing."

"It's the only thing I know," McCann said.

Suffern tapped his chest with blunt fingers. "It's not the only thing *I* know. That's why I'll take a forty percent split or run my own game."

McCann nodded thoughtfully. "Too small to suit your taste? Is that it?"

"Not a bit. I just like variety," Suffern said, smiling agreeably.

"For yourself...or the men you pay?"

Suffern's eyes changed a little, and there was a sudden hardness in them. "I've never asked a man yet to do what I wouldn't do. That's how I got the money to buy Barber out."

"Interesting," McCann commented. He lighted his cigar, watched the match burn out, then dropped it. He looked up at Suffern now, and his face was bland. "There's a payroll leaving the bank tonight, bound for one of the mines just off the pass road. You wouldn't want to pass that up, would you?"

"Would you?"

"This is your brag," McCann drawled. "Make it good."

"All right. When's the stage leaving?"

"It's due out at eight."

"How much in the boot?"

"Not a cent less than four thousand."

Suffern scowled. "Four thousand," he murmured gently, as if to himself. "Hardly enough to make it worthwhile."

"I thought it would be that way," McCann sneered.

"But I'll do it," Suffern continued, as if he had not heard. "Maybe some of you boys would like to watch how it's done."

"Maybe we would," McCann said softly, and he rose. "Say, if I'm here at seven thirty?"

When Suffern nodded, McCann left. Standing in the doorway, waiting for McCann to come out, was one of the gamblers with a stack of paper in his hand.

"You want to see me now, Suffern?" he asked.

"What about?"

"I'll give you an account of what's happened since Barber left. I kept the books for him."

"Give me a minute," Suffern said.

The door closed. Suffern regarded it blankly. This was going along a little faster than even he had anticipated. It was almost dark now. He would be closeted with the accounts for a couple of hours. There was no chance to leave word with Bent or Hayes, and he knew it would be unwise to trust a messenger with the news he had to give. Besides, things like this went off better if they were not acted. He rose, put on his coat, and went out. The gambler was waiting by the door.

"Get your hat," Suffern told him. "Bring those papers along. I haven't eaten since morning and I'm hungry."

They stepped through the batwing doors together. Suffern was just about to step down onto the sidewalk when he pulled up sharply, but not in time to escape jostling a girl with corn-colored hair who was just passing.

"I beg your pardon," he said gravely, raising his hat.

The girl looked at him carefully, smiled faintly, said, "Certainly," and went her way.

"Who's that?" Suffern asked his gambler.

"Mary Hayes."

The name meant nothing to Suffern for a moment. "Why'd she stare at me like that?"

The gambler chuckled. "Wanted to see what kind of a man it was that beat up her old man's pet deputy, I reckon."

III

STAGE HOLDUP

Suffern got back to the saloon after dark. McCann was waiting for him in the office and with him were two tall, lanky 'punchers whom he introduced as Stebbins and Clifton. They were thin-lipped, bleach-eyed, and indolent-appearing, but Suffern knew them for the best brand of Texas killers that money could buy.

Suffern wasted no time. "I don't know the set-up here. What's the most likely place to hold up a stage?"

"Over in the Gunsight," McCann said. "There's plenty of rocks on the slope you can roll down on the road."

"Take me to it," Suffern said. He changed into puncher's clothes and the four of them drifted out the side door.

An hour later after threading a dark mountain trail, they came to a piece of cleared land. Immediately in front of him, Suffern saw a deep cut in the ridge and the road running through it. The banks were steep, grown with pine and juniper which reached down to the road.

McCann said, "This is Gunsight. Your stage'll be through here in half an hour. It'll be rolling along slow because this is the top of the grade."

"Uh-huh," Suffern said casually.

Stebbins cocked a leg over the horn of his saddle and spat. "Don't look so good now, huh?"

Suffern said, "Not with only four thousand in the boot."

Clifton laughed unpleasantly, but Suffern ignored it. He dismounted, rolled a smoke, and sat down on a rock. The others, with the natural nervousness of beginners at a new task, did not talk much. They watched Suffern, who smoked and yawned and then, to keep himself awake, whistled thinly through his teeth.

Suddenly he stopped whistling, listened a moment, then said, "Here it comes."

"What do you aim to have us do?" McCann asked. "I'm new at this game."

"You get off in the brush and go to sleep," Suffern drawled.

Stebbins cursed in a low voice.

McCann said flatly, "Uh-uh. I'm here to watch you pull it."

"All right. Go up the road and cache yourself behind a boulder."

"You want help to roll a boulder down?" Stebbins asked.

"That's beginner's stuff," Suffern said dryly. "Don't make no more trouble for the driver than you have to."

"Why?"

"Because the driver don't care if you hold up the stage and take the money. It isn't his. But if you go makin' trouble for him, he's liable to get mad the next time and start shootin'."

"The next time?" Clifton put in. "You goin' to hold it up again?"

"Why not? It carries money, don't it?"

Stebbins looked at Clifton and shook his head. McCann led his horse back into the brush, as did the others. Then they left Suffern and headed up the road.

Suffern rose, rammed his guns down tight in their holsters, then picked his way down the steep, long bank. He stopped by the side of the road beside a tall lodgepole pine that he had noticed. Knocking the small dead limbs away from the low trunk, he swung himself up into the tree.

He waited. He wanted to make this clean, quick, without a gunshot, for he realized that this must be as genuine as the real thing. The driver had not been warned, and Suffern would have to get the drop on him.

In the silence, Suffern could hear the laboring of the six horses as they pulled forward, the jolting of the wheels on rock and the creak of harness leather. When the stage took shape in the darkness, Suffern could see that there was a shotgun guard sitting beside the driver—gun across knee, ready for action.

Now the horses were under Suffern. Slowly, the stage drew abreast and he braced himself. A glance down told him there was no baggage on the top. Now the driver and guard were under him, and he could have reached down and knocked off the driver's hat. He counted two, his guns drawn, then slid the five feet to the stage top, landing silently, knees bent, facing the driver and guard.

"Reach for 'em, gents!" he whipped out curtly. The guard whirled, and found himself staring into the twin barrels of Suffern's guns. "You, guard! Stay put! You, driver! Rein in and kick your brake on!"

The driver obeyed.

Suffern said to him, "Now take that *hombre*'s greener by the barrel and throw it off in the brush."

Again the driver obeyed. Suffern walked forward, flipped the six-guns from the holsters of the two men. Yanking the door of the stage open, he ordered the passengers out, saying, "This is a stick-up, folks. Take it easy and no one'll get hurt."

Two men and two women filed out. Suffern smothered an exclamation of surprise when he saw that one of the passengers was Mary Hayes.

"Lie down on the ground on your faces, all of you," Suffern said crisply. When they had complied, he ordered the driver to his feet.

"Climb up there and throw that boot down," he told him.

In less than fifteen seconds, the boot was on the ground and the driver held the reins again. Suffern commanded the passengers to rise.

"Climb in folks," he said pleasantly. "I don't want your watches and money."

Mary Hayes was the last to get in. She kept looking at him, even though he was standing clear of the stage.

"Know me, ma'am?" Suffern asked her.

"I'll be able to tell better later," Mary replied gravely.

"I'd hate that," Suffern drawled.

"Then you know me...know where to find me?" Mary asked.

Suffern covered up glibly. "It won't be hard to find out who was on the stage that was held up in the Gunsight, will it?"

"I suppose not," Mary replied slowly. "But don't think I'll be intimidated by these threats. If I think I'm right, I'll give you away. That's a promise."

"You keep still, Miss Mary," the stage driver said sharply.

Mary shrugged and climbed into the stage.

In another minute, the stage was rolling off. Suffern watched it go, a scowl creasing his forehead. He hadn't counted on the sheriff's daughter being a passenger. She would have to have a remarkable memory to place a man who had jostled her in the street and spoken a few words of apology to her.

He picked up the boot and walked up the slope. McCann, Stebbins and Clifton were waiting for him. Suffern chucked the boot on the ground at their feet and yawned.

"Well," McCann said slowly, "that was the smoothest piece of work I ever watched. You must be an old hand at this."

"Tolerable," Suffern said.

"Let's open it and see what we got," McCann said.

Suffern stiffened. "Did you say *we?*"

McCann said, "I did."

"Then say it over again, and when you say it next time, say, 'Let's open it up and see what *you* got.'"

For a moment there was dead silence, then McCann shifted his feet.

"We'll take our cut," he said quietly. "We've tolled you into this outfit and we'll split, sixty-forty."

"I'm not tolled in this outfit yet, because the boss thought I couldn't make it," Suffern replied doggedly. "And we won't split sixty-forty. The only split I'll make with this is one hundred-nothing."

"I'd be a little careful," McCann said gently.

"Give the word, boss," Stebbins said.

McCann said something and Stebbins's hand dropped to his gun. Suffern, in the act of turning, saw that hand, and his own streaked down and up. The gun, hip-high, thundered once in the night. Stebbins's hand flew back. He cursed savagely, then drew his arms across his chest and put his other hand to his forearm. Slowly, Suffern holstered his gun.

"Maybe he didn't hear you," he said to McCann. "Tell him again. Tell him, 'What Suffern says goes.' You deaf?" he drawled softly, and the note of threat did not escape McCann.

"Let it go," McCann said. "The boot's yours."

"I know it," Suffern replied. He wanted to sigh with relief. If he had been overruled, out-bluffed, he would have been licked, and he knew it. As it was, the money was his to return to Sheriff Hayes and its rightful owner.

"Now you can open it up and see what *I've* got," he said gently.

IV

CHIP OFF THE LAW-BLOCK

Mary Hayes felt the fearful silence as the stage started again. One of the passengers—a man—said, "I thought he was going to shoot you, miss."

Mary said nothing. When they had made the top of the grade and were a half mile down the other side of the pass, the stage pulled to a stop and the passengers got out again.

Dave Pyott, the driver, came down swearing. "Of all the condemned foolishness I ever heard, your'n was the foolishest, Mary Hayes!" he began. "Why that hardcase come so close to shootin' you, you're as good as dead right now!"

Mary only smiled and allowed Dave to let off steam. When he was finished, she said, "You're going to change teams at the station below, aren't you, Dave?"

"Sure. Why?"

"You wouldn't miss a horse, would you?"

"I reckon not," Dave said. "Why?"

"I'm riding back to Roaring Fork," Mary informed him.

Again Dave blew up. He wouldn't allow it. Mary was liable to run into that hardcase again. Besides, the six horses here weren't properly broke. But Dave finally cut out the gentlest horse and, with a wave of her hand, Mary was off in the night, headed back toward Roaring Fork.

On her way, she thought over what she was going to do. Certainly, this man who had held up the stage was the same man who had begged her pardon for bumping her that afternoon. Mary was sure she could tell that voice anywhere: it was soft, gentle, a little rumbling, without a trace of bluff or brag in it. But she wondered what would happen if she were wrong. What if Suffern had been at the saloon all evening? She didn't know anything about the man, and she wanted to be fair. She didn't understand why Will Bent had fought with him, but people had told her that Will had shot off his mouth and got what he deserved.

She rode fast, so that she was in town within an hour. Coming in by alleys, she turned her horse loose in the corral behind the feed stable, then began wondering what to do next. Go to the saloon and see if Suffern was there? No, that was out of the question. But that would be the place he'd come to if he was the one who really did hold up the stage.

Sticking to the alley, she walked slowly, thinking. Behind the War Bonnet a few ponies stood hipshot at the tie-rail. She walked past them until she came to the space between the saloon and the next building. Bulking in the dark, the office was visible. The room was unlighted, which meant Suffern wasn't there. But if he came....

Mary had an idea. She walked down the dark passageway to the office and stood before it. The office, built later than the saloon, had no foundation; it rested on thick joists, and an apron of clapboard covered these joists. By jerking a board loose, she could squirm in between the joists and be able to hear through the thin board floor overhead.

It only took a moment for her to do it. And then she waited, smelling earth and wood-shavings, and wondering what kind of bugs and insects were her company. It was close in there, and she was almost asleep when she heard the booming thump of boots just overhead.

Suddenly Suffern's rumbling voice came to her: "You'd better tie that arm up, Stebbins."

A grunt for an answer.

"Even a hardcase bleeds, fella. But take your choice."

"Hurry up and get that money hid, Suffern," a voice said, and Mary easily recognized this as McCann's. "We've got other business tonight."

"Like what?" Suffern asked.

"Never mind. Only you won't be the only *hombre* who knows his business. I'll show you how we work our end."

Suffern said, after a pause, "I dunno. We're liable to have this town lynchin' mad if we pull off another job."

Mary smiled grimly, certain now that she had been right.

"That's my business," McCann said. "Who knows this town best...you or me?"

"You do."

"All right. And who's boss of this outfit?"

"You are," Suffern said dryly, and Mary wondered at it.

"Then what I say goes. We'll wake this bunch of mossbacks so they won't quiet down for a year."

There was a silence.

"All right, here's the plan," McCann said in a low voice, and Mary had to strain to catch his next words. "On the other slope of the mountains, there's a railway station at a spur that used to run up to the mines. The mine's gone now, but once in a while a carload or so of cattle are shipped from there. The only man lives there is the agent and I've bought him, so there'll be no trouble about brand inspection. He has four empty cars waiting. We're goin' to deliver them. And, furthermore, we're goin' to take them from close to here. How does that sound?"

"All right," Suffern said. "But I haven't had any sleep since night before last."

McCann laughed a little. "You'll have to get used to that. Have you ever worked cattle?"

"Lots."

"Good. I'll need every man I can get hold of. This is going to be a fast, hard drive. If we start right away, we'll be at the place at one. The stuff should be gathered by now and the boys'll be loose-herding it for us. By daylight, we'll be in the cañon country. That'll leave us a day to get over the worst of the high country. Tomorrow night we'll have the stuff in the pens. And then, within half an hour, it'll be on its way to the stockyards."

Suffern said, "You've got it timed close."

"That's the way we'll run things from now on...fast and hard."

There was a movement overhead, and Mary heard the tumblers on the safe lock falling. Certainly she had enough proof against Suffern now. The evidence was locked in the safe, and the arrest of Suffern could wait. Already she could hear the men filing out into the night through the side door. It would be impossible to get her father, tell him the story and arrest Suffern now, since she didn't know where Suffern and McCann were going. At no time had McCann mentioned whose beef was going to be stolen. The thing to do was to warn her father and get up a posse.

Opening the door of her father's office, Mary found only Cal Fields there. His feet were cocked up on the corner of the desk and he was deep in a lazy game of solitaire. He came to his feet with a crash, and a wide grin broke over his lean face as he looked at her grimed face.

"What you been doin', Miss Mary...playin' with mud pies?"

Mary said swiftly, "Where's Dad?"

"Gone out."

"Where's Will?"

"He's gone, too."

"Where?"

"Over the other side of the county. Word come in this evenin' of a shootin' scrape down in the dry country."

Mary sank into a chair.

"What's the trouble?" Cal asked.

Mary told him in a few words that some rustling was going on even now, and that she knew where the stock would be shipped from. She described it, and Cal nodded. "That would be Chloride, over on the other slope."

"But what'll we do, Cal? We can't let McCann get away with it. If we caught him, it would be the end of all this rustling that has been worrying Dad for years now. McCann's the brains behind it all, and now we've got a chance to catch him!"

"And that damn', bull-shouldered hardcase of a Suffern!" Cal said quietly. He stood there a long moment, scowling. "I know four men here I can trust. I'll round 'em up. I'll send a messenger to catch up with your dad and Will. They'll put up at the Circle K tonight. By tomorrow night, they sure ought to be in Chloride. Just don't you worry. You go home and let me handle this."

Mary jumped up, her eyes blazing. "Let you handle it! And leave me home? Not on your life, Cal Fields!"

Cal argued, but Mary argued harder and more effectively. At last Cal capitulated with a shrug. "All right, but I see where I'll have to jump the county as soon as Andy Hayes finds this out," he finished dolefully. Mary did not hear him. She was strapping on a shell belt and a pair of six-guns.

Fifteen minutes later, Cal Fields had rounded up his four men. They were middle-aged ranchers, a grim, harried lot who would be certain to fight like wild men to even the score with the rustlers who had been raiding them into poverty. It was decided that it would be useless to try to find out whose herd McCann and Suffern were running off as there was no time to lose. They headed out west and south of town, riding in the direction of Chloride.

V

DEATH FOR CATTLE THIEVES

Chloride was only a way station. It consisted of a sun-blistered depot, a warehouse and stockpens strung along a thread of track that ran the length of a short, narrow valley in the high foothills of the San Tolars.

Mary pulled up beside Cal Fields, who pointed now to the station below. "Four cars waitin'. It holds together so far."

The six of them took the steep trail down into the valley, but it was Cal Fields and Mary who dismounted on the cinder apron outside and walked inside while the others waited. They were greeted by a small, furtive man, wearing a green eyeshade, who glanced up from his magazine.

"What is it?"

Fields palmed up his gun and pointed it casually, steadily at the agent. "First thing," he drawled pleasantly, "is to come out of there, hands reachin'."

The agent obeyed, and his eyes were suddenly afraid. When he was standing before them, Fields looked him over, then searched him for hide-outs. Finding none, he holstered his own gun.

"Is...is this a stick-up?" the agent asked.

"We got invited to a little party," Fields said. "A necktie party. You're liable to be the guest of honor, fella."

"What for? What do you mean?"

"Ask McCann. He'll be there...along with you."

When the agent understood, he sat down weakly and, in a small, tired voice, told Fields everything he wanted to know. McCann had bought him, had even given him a substantial cut in the stolen stock that had been shipped from here for a year and a half. The four ranchers were called in and they listened grimly while the agent recited all the brands of the stolen stock he could remember. Then the six of them planned for the coming of the rustled herd. Since most of the activity would center around the stockpens, it was there that the men would have to hide themselves.

It was certain either McCann or Suffern would come into the station to parley with the agent and make out the waybills. Fields would stay in the station. Two of the ranchers would hole up in the warehouse, close to the pens. Another would take the tool shed, so the avenue of retreat would be closed. The remaining man would cache himself in the brush down the tracks so that, if the rustlers were stampeded into flight, they would have to run the gauntlet of his fire before they could make the valley mouth to the low foothills. Mary, by vote of all the men, was to stay in the warehouse and guard the horses.

They had not been at their stations an hour when a low whistle came from the station. It was Fields, and it meant that from the station, where he could get a clear view of the valley and the low hills, he had caught sight of the approaching herd.

Fields said to the agent, "Go out and open them pens, then high-tail it back here. Wave to 'em. And don't talk to a man. I'll have my sights on the buckle on your vest strap, so play it cagey."

The agent stepped out. Already Fields could see a half dozen men riding herd on the tired cattle.

McCann and Suffern paused and watched the others work the muley cattle into the pens. There was a lot of cursing, a lot of quick, skillful horsework, and a lot of dust. Then both of them dismounted and headed for the depot. The agent was standing in the door. Next to him, against the wall, Fields was crouched, and he had a Colt rammed into the agent's back.

"Talk," Fields whispered.

"How many this time?" the agent called to McCann.

"Same as I promised," McCann called back. "About two hundred."

McCann was walking slowly toward the door, his eyes on the ground. Suddenly he paused in mid-step, then slowly turned his head toward the warehouse. Then, with an explosive leap, he turned and started to run for the tool shed. Too late, Fields understood that Mc-Cann had seen the tracks of their horses. He shoved the agent out into the yard, just as the rancher in the shed blasted out with the opening shot. Then the men in the warehouse cut loose, and pandemonium broke.

Fields had his guns trained on Suffern. Then, seeing that Suffern's hands were over his head, he swiveled his guns just in time to throw two wild shots at the zigzagging McCann, who was managing to dodge the shots of the surprised rancher in the tool shed before he reached the corner of the building and was out of sight. Fields whirled, then ran for the stockpens, his guns thundering. Two of the mounted rustlers were down. Off down the track, the hidden rancher was raking the milling herd of cattle and their drivers, while from the warehouse a steady racket of gunfire split the air.

Suffern, when he saw Fields ignoring him, hesitated for a moment. And in that moment, he saw the agent dart inside and reappear with a shotgun. Suffern, running toward the station now, whipped out his right gun and fired it twice, and saw the agent pitch back into the room. Rounding the corner behind the station, Suffern ran the length of the platform. In a glance, he had seen that the rustlers were surrounded, and that their only hope of escape would lie in cutting between the stockpens and the station at its far end.

Just as he reached the end of the platform, he saw a rider hurtle past, lying low on the neck of his horse. Suffern opened up with both guns. He saw the man roll off into the dust just as a second and third and fourth rider followed. Suffern whirled—to confront a rifle in the hands of Fields, who had broken a pane in the station window and shot through it.

"Reach for it!" Fields said curtly.

Smiling, Suffern did, aware now that the shooting had ceased and that men were running for the station on the other side. Suddenly a fusillade of shots rang out from the tool shed, and one of the runners pitched on his face. The others speeded their pace in the hurry to make the station. Fields, rifle in Suffern's back, prodded him into the station where two ranchers were standing breathless, guns in hand.

"What happened?" Fields asked, "Who fired that shot?"

"McCann," one of the ranchers said bitterly. "He's forted up in the tool shed."

"Which means that Conaghan must be dead," a woman's voice said. Suffern looked behind him and noticed Mary Hayes, a rifle in her hand. She had been guarding the door he had just come through. She looked at him levelly, contemptuously.

"How many'd we get?" Fields asked.

"I counted six dead...and this *hombre*," one of the ranchers said, indicating Suffern.

"And you'll wish you was, too," the other rancher said grimly. "Sit down."

Suffern sat down. "Where's Sheriff Hayes?" he asked levelly.

Fields, with his gun still pointed at him, said, "Why?"

"Because I'm a range detective," Suffern replied.

"A range detective," he drawled contemptuously. "Prove it."

"I can't. I left my credentials at the saloon. I was forced into this before I could get hold of Hayes to tell him about it."

Mary Hayes said quietly, "I suppose you were forced into that stage robbery last night, too?"

Suffern smiled slightly. "I had to pull that to get in with Mc-
Cann. I have the money...."

"In your safe at the War Bonnet," she put in. "I heard you put
it there. I heard you admit you robbed the stage. I also heard you
and McCann planning this rustling job." Suffern had his mouth open
to defend himself when Mary Hayes added coldly, "I hate a thief.
But I hate a double-crossing thief more. I saw you shoot your own
men." She sneered. "You saw which way the fight was going and
jumped on the side of the winner, hoping you could carry out your
bluff about being a range detective."

Suffern flushed. He knew angry men when he saw them. And
these men were not only angry, but were in a mood for deadly revenge.

"I'm not afraid of taking a slug or getting hung for rustling," Suffern said. "I wish you'd talk to Sheriff Hayes before you give me either, though."

Fields snorted. "Stalling."

"Let's give it to him," one of the ranchers said bitterly. "It'll save
time, and then we can smoke McCann out of that tool shed."

He raised his gun, cocked it. Fields made no move to stop him.

"Wait a minute!" Mary cut in. The rancher paused, Mary looked
over at Suffern, then at Fields.

"Why risk the lives of all of us by trying to take McCann. Let
Suffern do it. He claims to be a range detective...on our side. All
he's done so far is shoot men who believed him to be on their side.
Give him a gun. Let him take McCann."

For a moment the men looked at each other.

"Why not?" Fields drawled coldly. "If he tries to get away, we'll
drill him in the back. If he joins McCann there in the tool shed, we'll
dynamite 'em both out of it."

Suffern looked at each of them, then at the girl. "All right," he
said gravely. "I don't blame you a bit. But I'll have to ask a favor of
you."

"What is it?" Mary asked.

"If I take McCann, will you hand me over to Sheriff Hayes...un-
shot and unhung?"

Mary said, "We won't have to."

"But if I come through, will you?"

They hesitated. Finally Mary said, "I don't believe in a cotton-wood jury. I never have, even for men like you. But I have only one vote. I'll vote to turn you over to Dad...and in good health."

The others reluctantly agreed.

VI

FOREVER AND EVER

Suffern stood up and walked to the door. Off to his right, facing the end of the station and about a hundred feet away, was the tool shed. And in that tool shed was McCann. It never entered his head that he couldn't take McCann; he only wondered just how to do it. Musing, his gaze fell on the body of a man whom McCann had cut down on. The man was moaning.

Suffern said, "He's alive."

Fields looked at the wounded man, then at the tool shed, then at Suffern. "It doesn't do him a hell of a lot of good, does it? Not when he knows we can't reach him."

Suffern said nothing. He braced himself, then exploded out of the doorway and ran for the man. He reached him, just as McCann shot from the shed. The slug kicked off Suffern's hat as he stooped to pick the man up. Erect, he started back, with the wounded man over his shoulder, running hard. A second shot rang out, and a third, and still he was running. He made the doorway then. Losing his balance, he pitched headlong on the floor, the wounded man falling on him. He rose, the others eyeing him silently, and looked down at the wounded man.

Mary was the first to act. She knelt by the wounded man and started to cut away the leg of his Levi's, but she looked up at Suffern, and in her eyes was a light of quiet admiration.

"That took courage," she said quietly. "I didn't know a rat had it."

Suffern was about to speak, but shrugged and turned to Fields. "Give me two guns...all six chambers loaded."

The first step drew a shot from McCann.

And then Suffern opened up. He could see the knot hole through which McCann had shot, and he aimed for it as best he could, ducking, weaving, but always running doggedly for the shed. Something slammed into his leg, and he almost tripped, but caught himself and went on. He could see the quick orange flare of McCann's gun, could hear the singing of the slugs, but there was a cold smile on his face as he ran.

Twenty feet from the shed, McCann's guns were silent. Suffern fired one last shot, tried again, heard the click of the hammer on the empty chamber, then threw his gun at the knot hole and ran straight for the door. He dived into it, shoulder down, and heard the crash as the wood gave. He pitched forward into the shed on top of the door. And even as he felt himself hit the floor, he rolled over, came up on one knee, and shot twice—his last two shells—at a dark bulk on the floor. The body only barely stirred with the impact of the slugs.

Slowly, unsteadily, he struggled to his feet and walked over to McCann. Turning him over, Suffern saw that one of his slugs had caught him full in the face, just to one side of the nose. The defending rancher was dead in the corner, where McCann had shot him.

Dropping his guns, Suffern walked unsteadily to the door. He continued to walk across that piece of ground, which a minute before had been a hell of lead and death. His eyes were getting hard to focus. There were two horses there by the cinder apron and what looked like a crowd of people watching him. Suddenly his eyes did come into focus, and he saw Sheriff Hayes running toward him.

"Hello, Sheriff," he said quietly, and held out his hand.

He didn't know why that hand should have gathered a handful of cinders, but it did. And he knew, just before things went a star-spangled black in front of his eyes, that he had fallen.

Later, on the bench in the station, he wakened to find Mary kneeling beside him. Beyond her were Fields, the ranchers, Sheriff Hayes and Will Bent.

Hayes said slowly, "I thought these hard-headed rannies had killed you, son." Suffern smiled. Hayes went on: "I came foggin' in here just in time to see you dive into that tool shed. Why in the name of...."

Mary interrupted him. "Dad, don't bawl them out. It was my idea." She turned to Suffern. "Will you ever forgive me? Dad has told me you really are a range detective, and that you weren't working with McCann."

"I had to hold up that stage to get in with McCann," Suffern replied slowly. "I made one mistake. I didn't have any way of communicating with the sheriff to let him know what to expect. I sort of had to run this on high lonesome...until you folks come along."

"And almost got you killed," Fields said dejectedly.

"Forget it," Suffern said, holding out his hand. Fields took it.

Mary suddenly began to cry. The men stood around awkwardly, waiting for her to stop, but she could not.

Finally Will Bent said, "She don't like a crowd, you danged fools. Come away."

When they were gone out, Mary stopped her sobbing.

Suffern looked at her curiously. "How did your dad and Bent get here?"

"That...that call to the other s-s-side of the county w-w-was a ruse to toll them out of town." Mary sobbed, and added, "Why...why can't I s-s-stop this?"

"But why are you crying?" Suffern asked gently.

She looked up a him, her eyes wet, but somehow she managed to smile. "Did you ever s-s-send someone you loved to their d-d-death and then, when they were on their way, realize you loved them?"

Suffern said huskily, "No. But did you ever point a gun at someone...someone you thought more of than anybody you'd ever seen...and threaten to shoot her if she gave you away?"

Mary laughed a little. "No, I never did. Did you?"

"Yes." And he added gently, "Sinners should suffer together, shouldn't they?"

"I think so," Mary said in a low voice.

"Forever and ever?"

"Forever and ever," Mary said quietly.

(Grover Cleveland) Bill Gulick

was born in Kansas City, Missouri, and attended the University of Oklahoma where he studied professional writing under Foster-Harris. He dedicated his first novel, BEND OF THE SNAKE (Houghton Mifflin, 1950), to Foster-Harris, "who showed me how." He began contributing stories to pulp magazines in late 1940 and by the end of the decade was appearing regularly in *The Saturday Evening Post*. A *Post* editor once told Gulick, "What I like about your stories is that they are not Westerns." Truthfully, there is little that is conventional in any of Gulick's short fiction, much that is humorous, characters that are ornery and constantly interesting, with a background of historical detail that is vividly evoked. His mountain man stories are especially noteworthy, some of which he included in his collection, WHITE MEN, RED MEN, AND MOUNTAIN MEN (Houghton Mifflin, 1955). The variety of setting, characters, circumstances, always leavened with humor, are no less impressive in stories he included in THE SHAMING OF BROKEN HORN AND OTHER STORIES (Doubleday, 1961). Gulick's achievements as a novelist are no less rewarding to a reader, from the rather farcical THE HALLELUJAH TRAIN (Doubleday, 1963) to major historical novels such as THEY CAME TO A VALLEY (Doubleday, 1966) and his more recent trilogy, NORTHWEST DESTINY, published in three volumes by Doubleday in 1988 and covering the years 1805 - 1879. The story which follows was one of his earliest efforts, originally published in *Big-Book Western* in the issue dated February, 1942.

There's Hell on the Dodge Trail

O n the crest of a barren hill, Jim Laramie sat atop his dun and watched the long string of cattle trailing northward in the valley below. His face mirrored the bitter memories which sight of the herd brought back. Five years ago he'd trailed north to Dodge with a herd such as this one. Now he was riding the long trail across the Nations in the other direction. Back in Dodge, he knew, they'd be saying Black Joe Crossman had run him out. It didn't matter. The only thing that mattered was to keep riding.

He spurred the dun down the slope and trotted toward the chuck wagon moving along behind the cattle. That herd was headed for a cattle boneyard, he knew. He'd warn the trail boss and then be drifting on. Riding alongside the chuck wagon, he found a tall, lean Texan, a man of middle age, seamed of face, and with white streaks in the hair showing beneath his hat brim. Driving the wagon was a woman, also middle-aged, with hands as hard and brown as a man's.

Jim touched his sombrero to the woman, then spoke to the Texan. "You bossing this herd?"

The man reined up. "These are my cattle. Dave Brackeen's the name. Lately of the Brazos country."

Jim shook his hand and introduced himself. He rolled a cigarette. "First time up the trail?"

"And the last, I hope. We been through pure hell. Everything from quicksand to Comanches."

"You're headed for a worse kind of hell the direction you're going now. There ain't a drop of water in a hundred miles."

Brackeen's face became perplexed. "Funny. Yesterday mornin' we met a fella who told us to come this way. Said everything due north was dried up, but that we'd strike water this direction come daylight tomorrow."

"What did this *hombre* look like?"

"Sort of heavy-set. Big nose, an' one ear that looked like a badger had been chewin' on it. You know him?"

Jim nodded. He knew him, all right. His name was Twist-Ear. Brackeen's sharp eyes searched his face, and Jim met the scrutiny without wavering.

Finally, Brackeen said, "Who am I supposed to believe...you or him?"

Jim shrugged indifferently. "Suit yourself."

There was a silence in which the only sounds were the creaking of saddle leather as the horses shifted about, the rumbling of the slow moving cattle's hoofs, and the moaning of the dying south wind. At last, Brackeen said softly, "I'll take your word, Laramie. Come to think of it, that fella yesterday had a mangy look."

He wheeled his horse and went off at a long lope to give orders to the point men. Sucking at his cigarette, Jim lounged in the saddle and watched the herd swing around. He guessed there were around five hundred four-year-old steers in the herd. Brackeen certainly had a small crew to handle it. Besides Brackeen himself, Jim could only see two hands—one, a Mexican, old and not much used to the saddle from the stiff way in which he rode and the other, a slim youth who looked to be no more than a boy.

When the herd was strung out in the new direction, Brackeen came back to where Jim sat. He took off his hat and wiped the sweat from his forehead. "I'm sure obliged to you, Laramie. Reckon we won't have any trouble from here on."

Jim knew better. In the two weeks' driving between here and Dodge there were plenty kinds of trouble. The Canadian and Cimarron were yet to be crossed, wild Comanches were on the prowl, not to mention Crossman's gang of renegades which preyed on small outfits such as this. But it wasn't Jim's affair. Let Brackeen find out for himself.

"Ridin' far?" Brackeen asked casually.

Jim shifted in his saddle and gazed toward the western horizon. "Just ridin'."

"Better have chuck with us tonight."

Jim hesitated. He'd been living on corn meal and water for the last week—in fact, ever since he'd ridden out of Dodge rather than face Black Joe Crossman when the renegade had boasted he was gunning for him. A square meal would sort of line a man's stomach for the long, lonely trail ahead.

"Thanks. Don't care if I do."

Around the fire after supper, Jim sat silently gazing into the orange flames, in the unwavering way which men acquire when they're used to making lone camps. The Mexican came in to eat after the herd was bedded down, and Jim learned his name was Sancho. He was old and wrinkled and bent, with the bearing of a household servant rather than a cowhand.

Brackeen spoke of him affectionately. "Sancho is like one of the family. He moved in on us when Ma and me first settled in the Brazos country thirty years ago. He don't savvy cows much, but he insisted on comin' along when we got burned out an' started up-trail."

Jim glanced sharply at Brackeen. "Burned out?"

The Texan passed a hand over his eyes in a tired gesture, as if remembering was painful. "Comanches. They're raisin' hell south of Red River these days. The politicians in Washington have pulled all the troops out...figurin' to punish us for losin' the war, I reckon."

Brackeen fell silent and Jim questioned him no more. Now he understood why the crew was so small. Brackeen and his family were moving back to civilization after a bitter failure on the frontier, heading up to Dodge with the few cattle salvaged from what had probably been a large ranch. Sitting stooped and apathetic, Brackeen had the look of a broken man in his eyes, as if he saw in the dying fire all his labors of the last thirty years turned to ashes.

There was nothing Jim could say. He'd seen it happen before, and so long as there were frontiers and wild Indians and a blind, vengeful government in Washington, it would keep on happening.

Sancho finished his meal and rode off to relieve the slim cowboy. When the youth came into the firelight, Brackeen's face brightened. He introduced Jim. "This is my boy, Terry."

Jim stood up and put out a hand. A slim brown hand grasped it, and he suddenly realized he was staring into the tanned, smiling face of a girl. Long curls cascaded from under her hat, and her eyes were blue and friendly.

"Glad to know you," he stammered, "but I thought...."

She laughed. "Dad calls me a boy sometimes. Guess he's ashamed of having a daughter." Brackeen turned away and walked over to the other side of the fire, where his wife was sitting. The girl's eyes followed him tenderly. She helped herself to a plateful of *frijoles* from an iron pot and sat down beside Jim. In a lower voice, she said, "The real reason Dad calls me a boy is because sometimes he forgets that my brothers are dead. You see, they were killed two months ago when the Indians burned us out."

Jim suddenly felt a sympathy for Brackeen. For a moment, he recalled the utter loneliness he had known when, as a boy of ten, he had returned home from a trip to town to find his parents' cabin burned and his own father and mother dead from Indian arrows. He looked across at Brackeen and his wife and felt that he understood something of what they were going through.

Somber-eyed, he stared down into the flames. He'd traveled a long and lonely trail since his parents were killed. He'd learned to take care of himself, and he'd made the name Jim Laramie one that men—gunfighting men—knew and respected. In these last five years he'd used his guns for his own purposes. Now, he reckoned, he'd use them for somebody else. He reckoned if Dave Brackeen would have him, he'd be heading north with a trail herd again.

Short-handed as the crew was, there was no splitting up of the night-herding in two hour shifts. That night, Jim and Terry were to stay with the herd till midnight, then Dave Brackeen and Sancho would take over till dawn. Riding slowly about the herd in the weird light of a half moon, Jim figured there wouldn't be any second shift tonight. The cattle weren't in a mood to stay bedded down long; their bellies were empty of grass and water, and already they were showing signs of restlessness. Jim sang as he rode, an old, wordless song meant to keep disturbing sounds from the nervous herd's ears. Sometimes he could hear Terry's voice, full and rich on the night air.

Close to midnight, a restless bay steer lumbered to his feet and started moving around, bawling hoarsely. Jim knew it was coming then. One by one, then in groups, the cattle got to their feet and milled around. The bawling became a deafening chorus. Between his knees, Jim felt the dun tremble. The cow-wise horse sensed a run coming. Then, with no warning, the bunched herd broke. It roared north in a long run that made the earth shake with pounding feet. Jim kicked the dun out in front of the mass of tossing horns and stayed there, pushing his mount hard to keep ahead of the charging cattle. It wasn't a stampede yet, but it was close to it. A solid wall of men couldn't hold those steers now, he knew; all you could do was let them run, and hope you could hold them down some.

Over to his left Jim suddenly saw Terry, lying low on her pony's neck, swinging around to the front of the herd. He reined over toward her.

"Get in the clear!" he shouted. "If your horse falls, you wouldn't have a chance!"

Angrily, she shook her head. "Neither would you. I'm staying."

There was nothing more he could say or do. Helpless, he watched her slow her pony down until the herd was pressing on its very heels. He did the same with the dun. At first he thought the cattle were going to break past. Then the big bay steer, which evidently was one of the herd leaders, swung in behind Terry's horse and stayed there, matching the pony's gait stride for stride. Jim sensed the whole herd coming under control, strung out now in a straight run.

He pulled over beside the girl and yelled. "Keep headed due north. At this rate we'll reach water in a couple of hours."

She nodded without trying to speak. She glanced up at the sky and lined her direction on the unwavering north star. Jim felt a surge of admiration. She'd do to take along.

When Brackeen rode up with Sancho at dawn, he found the herd held loosely on the creek bank, grazing on the deep rich grass which grew there. He shook his head in amazement. "Nice work, Laramie. I thought they were long gone for sure."

"Don't thank me," Jim said. "That 'boy' of yours is the ridin'est fool I ever saw."

Brackeen glanced at Terry and grinned. "Best hand I ever had," he said softly.

———⊱◉⊰———

Jim began to breathe a little easier when they'd crossed the Canadian without sighting a single Comanche brave. He didn't figure they'd have any Indian trouble now—not this far north. But there were other troubles. For a while he tried to kid himself into believing that Black Joe Crossman and his crew wouldn't show up. Reason told him better. Twist-Ear, the man who'd directed Brackeen onto the desert trail, certainly wouldn't have failed to report to his boss. Chances were Crossman knew every move the herd had made.

That evening after supper Jim called Brackeen out of earshot of the rest of the family. "Remember the *hombre* who put you on the dry trail?" he said bluntly.

Brackeen nodded. "What about him?"

"He didn't do it because he was ignorant of the country. It was deliberate."

Brackeen's eyes narrowed. "What use would anybody have for a herd dying of thirst?"

"Hides," Jim said briefly. "The *hombre*'s name is Twist-Ear. He's a sidekick of a cut-throat named Black Joe Crossman. They do a regular business waylaying small outfits crossing the Nations. They've also got a side line smuggling rifles to the Comanches. If they can lure a herd off the beaten path, it's no trouble at all to get Indians to skin the cattle for them and help haul the hides to market for promise of a few rifles. Hides these days are worth almost as much as cattle on the hoof."

"Why didn't you tell me this before?" Brackeen snapped.

"Didn't figure it was necessary."

"You figure we'll run across this gang again?"

"Like as not."

Brackeen looked out into the darkness in the direction of the sleeping herd. All his worldly goods were there, Jim knew, all he had with which to make a new start. Slowly Brackeen said, "Laramie, how do you happen to know so much about this gang?"

Jim deliberately turned away and stared up at the clear night sky.

"Well?" Brackeen said.

Jim now looked him squarely in the eye. "Guess you'll just have to take for granted it's so." Then he turned on his heel and walked away.

Jim could tell from the grimness of the others during the next few days that Dave Brackeen had told them to expect trouble. The long Spanish knife in Sancho's belt took on a new gleam, and in his spare time the faithful servant whetted it at every opportunity. Ma Brackeen drove the chuck wagon, with an old muzzle-loading rifle lying loaded and ready in the seat beside her. Terry wore one of her father's Colts. Jim knew she could use it. But he knew, too, that all the force Brackeen could muster would be pitifully inadequate against the deadly killers who ran with Black Joe. Men like Twist-Ear and Missouri and Black Joe himself. Jim had had dealings with them all, more than it was pleasant to remember.

When they were a good four days' drive south of the Cimarron, Jim saw late one afternoon a small band of Indians top a rise to the west and trot toward the chuck wagon. It was apparently a friendly group—an old brave, his squaw, and two young boys—but Jim took no chances. He left the point and galloped back to the wagon just as the Indians reached it.

Dave Brackeen, rifle leveled at his waist, was facing them. "Stop right where you are, you red polecats. I don't know what you're fig-urin' to do, but I know I'd rather kill you than look at you."

The band stopped. Jim knew from the blank expression on the old brave's face that he understood no English. But he understood the gun well enough.

"Let me talk to them, Brackeen. They don't savvy you."

In Comanche, he asked the brave what they wanted. Fierce pride showed in the Indian's face. He spoke with slow dignity. He wanted beef. His family had not eaten meat for many days. And they needed hide with which to made moccasins. When he had finished, Jim translated for Brackeen.

The Texan's face grew hard. "Tell 'em we got no beeves to spare. Tell 'em if they don't skedaddle, I'll shoot 'em down where they stand."

Jim shook his had gravely. "Comanches don't beg unless they're desperate. Better give them what they want."

"I'll give them nothing!" Brackeen roared. "In two days after I gave them a beef, the whole tribe would be down on me begging. I'll give them a bullet apiece, though, right in the belly. Maybe they can make a meal on lead."

Jim's jaw muscles worked. There was hunger in the eyes of these Indians. Give them food and they would go their way in peace— deny them, and they'd fight.

"Brackeen," he said, in desperation, "I've never led you wrong yet. You've still got a long trail ahead. Somewhere uptrail you're going to be needing all the gun help you can get. But so help me, if you don't give these Indians food, I'll ride off and leave you cold."

The anger in Brackeen's eyes slowly changed to amazement. Then it left and there was only contempt. He lowered the gun.

"I'd probably be better without you. But, all right...give 'em what they want."

Face colorless, Jim cut out a foot-sore steer from the rear of the herd and gave it to the Comanches. The two boys hazed it off and the squaw followed. The brave lingered behind a moment.

Thanks was a word alien to his vocabulary. But he drew himself up tall and straight and said, "Running Crow will not forget."

Then he turned his pony about and rode off over the hill. Jim gazed after him, smiling wryly. "Some of them are good," he murmured, "and some of them are bad. And only the Almighty that made them can tell which is what."

The trouble Jim was looking for came sooner than expected. That evening, after the herd had been bedded down on well-filled bellies, he rode toward the fire and supper once Terry relieved him. He staked his horse a few yards away from the chuck wagon and was walking toward the circle of light when he heard voices raised in argument.

Blood pounded hard in his ears. That was Black Joe Crossman's voice. He crept up to the shadow in the rear of the chuck wagon, where he could see without being seen. Crossman, a dark bear of a man, stood facing Dave Brackeen, backed up by his *segundo*, Twist-Ear. "Just thought I'd warn you, stranger," he was saying, "that you've got some dangerous territory to cross between here and Dodge."

Brackeen's lean face was without emotion. "We've come this far alone. I reckon we can make it the rest of the way."

Crossman smiled. "You've got a mighty small outfit. You're going to be needing some protection. Now, the herds that my boys and me escort never lose a head."

"Except," Brackeen cut in acidly, "what they lose to you."

Crossman's eyes glittered. "Of course," he said softly, "we take a small fee. Our price to you will be one hundred and fifty head."

A strange thing was happening to Jim Laramie. Twice his hand moved downward as if to touch the gun on his hip; twice it stopped.

He didn't know why. He had ridden out of Dodge, he'd told himself that night, because he was sick of the old way of life. Now, though, he wasn't so sure. He was beginning to wonder if it had been something more. Sweat beaded his forehead. If he walked into that circle of light, he'd have to do it with gun blazing. And he wasn't sure he had the nerve.

Brackeen had been silent for a full five seconds. He moved threateningly toward Crossman. "Get out." His voice was thick with anger. "I'd see every head I got dead before I'd turn one steer over to you."

Crossman's face got ugly. Twist-Ear said something to him in a low voice, and he nodded. Suddenly guns flashed in their hands, the firelight glittering on shining steel.

"Come to think of it," Crossman said, "one hundred and fifty head won't be enough. We'll just take the whole herd, here and now."

Brackeen stood frozen. Jim saw Sancho move forward, a strange, passionate gleam in his eyes. His hand hovered close to the long knife in his belt. Brackeen's hand moved toward his gun.

"Wouldn't try it if I were you," Crossman said. "I don't often miss."

Jim Laramie knew that now was the time when he should step in. His hand closed on the butt of the Colt. Then, with the suddenness of a thunderclap, a heavy caliber gun roared from the front of the chuck wagon. Crossman's weapon went spinning away. Twist-Ear, mouth gaping in amazement, wheeled uncertainly. Like a springing panther, Sancho took two long steps forward, his knife gleaming. Twist-Ear went down and screams of mortal fear issued from his lips as Sancho held the keen edge tight against his throat.

"Shall I geeve eet maybe one leetle poosh?" Sancho said gently.

Brackeen, gun in hand, moved forward and jammed the barrel into Crossman's stomach. "Take your sidekick and start ridin' before I turn Sancho loose on him. I got half a mind to do it, anyhow, an' then borrow his knife and carve you up."

Sancho disarmed Twist-Ear and stood up with reluctance. Sadly, he said, "I should have cut his throat first, and then asked you would it be all right."

"Yeah," Brackeen grunted. "You should have."

The two renegades wasted no time finding their horses and galloping off. Then from the wagon came sounds of violent sobbing.

Jim saw Ma Brackeen sitting there, the big muzzle-loader cradled in her arms.

Dave Brackeen patted her shoulder soothingly. "Now, Ma, there's no need of bawling. You didn't kill him."

The sobbing stopped for a moment. "I know it. That's why I'm so mad. This gun never would shoot straight."

Jim bestirred himself then, and walked into the circle of light. He was shaking so he could hardly pick up a plate and tin cup. "What happened?" he asked.

Brackeen told him, and his eyes searched deep. Jim didn't meet them. He stared down at his food and gulped at the steaming coffee. Brackeen said, "Where were you while all this was happening?"

"Coming in from the herd," Jim mumbled. "Wish I'd got here sooner."

Brackeen contemplated him a moment longer, then murmured, "I wonder. I just wonder."

Jim Laramie wondered, too, during all that next day. He knew Crossman wasn't finished, that he'd be back, and he wondered if then, when the showdown came, he'd have nerve to face him. Toward evening he saw a lone brave loping across the prairie toward him. He pulled away from the herd and went to meet the Indian. It was Running Crow, the Comanche who had been given the beef. His message was brief. In the rough country just south of the Cimarron, he'd seen men, half a dozen of them, preparing to stampede the herd when it reached the river. The men were led, he said, by the big man who walked like a bear.

Grimly, Jim waited until he had finished. Then he said, "Can you help us fight?"

Running Crow shook his head. "What good is an old brave such as I? I can only warn you."

Jim nodded and soberly watched the Comanche ride off. This time, he knew, Crossman would do a good job. And against so many guns, Brackeen's outfit wouldn't stand a chance.

Brackeen knew it, too. When Jim relayed the Indian's story, Brackeen nodded curtly. "I been expecting it. Sancho and me should have finished the job last night."

"What do you figure on doing?"

"Doing?" Brackeen gave a bitter laugh. "Keep right on trailing north. We'll give Crossman a fight if that's what he wants." He was silent for a moment. "No need of you getting mixed up in this 'less you want to."

"I reckon," Jim said softly, "that I'll hang around."

They bedded the cattle down two nights later a good half day's drive south of the Cimarron. Jim ate supper, then went out to the herd to relieve Terry. In the darkness he could hear her singing softly.

"Looks like a quiet night," she said when he approached.

"It's on quiet nights that things happen."

She laughed and rode off toward the chuck wagon. Jim felt a strange warmth inside as he watched her go. During these last two weeks he'd come to know her pretty well. They'd worked together through the long, hard days, ridden long vigils together at night. He'd seen her do a man's job hour after hour without complaint. If a man ever took a notion to settle down, he thought, if things ever turned out so he could settle down.... He stopped right there. What business did he have toying with such ideas?

The hours dragged slowly by. The herd stayed quiet. Occasionally, a steer would lumber to his feet, move around a bit to find a new piece of ground, and then lie down on his other side. The far-away sound of a coyote calling could be heard every now and then, too distant to disturb the herd. Tonight reminded Jim of those nights long years ago when he'd been an eager kid riding uptrail to Dodge.

Suddenly the ears of the dun quivered. Watching them, Jim felt a strange sense of premonition. He listened, and heard the faint nickering of horses over in the direction of the chuck wagon. Something was wrong; he could sense it. He looked at the herd. It would stay quiet for a while without watching. He reined the dun about and moved toward the firelight.

Two hundred yards away, he dismounted and ground-tied the dun. He walked softly. When he was still in the shadows, he saw the men. There were half a dozen of them: Black Joe Crossman, Twist-Ear—all the rest. A coldness flowed over Jim. Crossman must have decided not to wait until the herd reached the river. And he'd caught Brackeen flat-footed.

The Texan's gun and belt hung over one of the wagon wheels, half a dozen feet from where he stood. Terry was unarmed; Sancho had only the knife in his belt. Brackeen's wife wasn't in sight. Jim knew it would be like murdering Brackeen to start firing at the renegades now. For they'd shoot at the first targets they saw—and those targets would be Brackeen, Sancho, and Terry. He'd have to play it another way.

Quietly he moved forward. In three strides he was standing clearly outlined in the firelight, facing Crossman.

Crossman's eyes jerked toward him. *"You!"* he snapped. "I thought you'd be a thousand miles from here by now."

Jim shook his head. "I would have been, but I heard you were looking for me. Nice of you to meet me on my way back."

"You knew before you left that I was lookin' for you."

Jim shrugged. "Whether you believe me or not makes no difference. The important thing is why you wanted to see me."

There was deep, savage hatred in Crossman's dark eyes. But there was something else too—the lingering remains of an old respect he had formerly held for Jim.

"I forgot," Crossman said, "just why I was lookin' for you. A month ago, I'd have killed you. Now I'm just tellin' you to play it quiet." He jerked a shoulder toward Brackeen. "My business is with this gentleman, not you."

It was an out for Jim—an open offer of neutrality that might have made many men pause to think it over. Jim didn't hesitate. He just said, "I don't reckon, Crossman, that Brackeen cares much about doing business with skunks. I handle that department."

It was like dropping a match in a powder train. Crossman cursed and his hand moved downward. Jim reached for his own gun. In that timeless instant, he saw several things happen simultaneously. Brackeen dove for the six-gun hanging over the wagon wheel. Sancho leaped forward, knife shining. Twist-Ear lifted his six-gun.

When his own cleared leather, Jim dove sideways and slammed a shot past Crossman. Twist-Ear doubled up, grasping his middle with a whispered moan. Crossman's gun roared and Jim felt a mule kick land on his left shoulder. Then his gun centered on Crossman. The renegade caved, gasped once, and then lay very still. Complete silence descended. Jim couldn't understand it, couldn't understand why the three outlaws who were still standing were raising their hands skyward.

Then Ma Brackeen moved out into the light. The old muzzle-loader in her hands wavered back and forth. "Better not move, boys," she said.

Terry saw Jim holding his bleeding shoulder and hurried to him. Kneeling, she inspected the wound. "I'll get some water and bandage," she said in a tight, strained voice. "I think the bullet went through clean."

Jim grinned faintly. "Sure. I'll be up and around tomorrow."

He was a few days off in his calculations. It was a week before he was able to navigate under his own power, but he couldn't remember when he'd enjoyed being shot so much. The herd was in sight of Dodge when he was again in the saddle. Terry rode anxiously alongside him to see that he didn't overdo himself.

Dave Brackeen pulled up beside them and said, "Well, there's the end of the trail."

Jim nodded soberly. Trail's end. The end of many things for him. He'd be leaving Brackeen here. The Texan would probably be settling down in Kansas.

Brackeen said, "What are your plans, Jim?"

Jim shrugged. "I'll just ride, I reckon."

"I could use a partner. Like to have you stay with me."

Jim shook his head. "Afraid farm life wouldn't suit me. I have to be where there's lots of elbow room. And, somehow, wherever I am trouble seems to pop up. So I better drift where I can deal with it in the only way I know. A Kansas farm wouldn't hold me, I'm afraid."

Brackeen snorted. "Who said anything about a Kansas farm? Hell, I'm headed back to Texas soon as I sell this herd and get some cash to rebuild."

Jim took a deep, quick breath. "But I thought you were finished down there."

"Finished? I reckon not! I got ten thousand head of wild stuff running loose in the Brazos country. So wild no Comanche will ever run it off. It's goin' to take some hard ridin' an maybe a bit of fightin' to start up again." He paused and stared south for a moment. His voice took on a kind, gruff tone. "I'd sure like to have you, son."

Jim didn't answer for a time. He looked at Terry. She met his eyes for an instant, then reined her horse about and rode off. Jim reckoned, though, from what he'd seen in her eyes just now, that she wouldn't ride so fast but what he could catch up with her, bad arm and all. And he reckoned, too, as he grasped Dave Brackeen's hand, that maybe before long he'd ride for Texas.

Jonathan Hurff Glidden was born in Kewanee, Illinois, and was graduated from the University of Illinois with a degree in English literature. He came first to write Western fiction because of prompting from his brother. In his career as a Western writer, Jon published sixteen Western novels and over 120 Western short novels and short stories for the magazine market. From the beginning, he was a dedicated craftsman who revised and polished his fiction until it shone as a fine gem. His Peter Dawson novels are noted for their adept plotting, interesting and well-developed characters, their authentically researched historical backgrounds, and stylistic flair.

Jon's first novel, THE CRIMSON HORSESHOE, won the Dodd, Mead Prize as the best Western of the year 1941 and ran serially in Street & Smith's Western Story Magazine prior to book publication. After the war, the Peter Dawson novels were frequently serialized in The Saturday Evening Post. One of Jon Glidden's finest techniques was his ability after the fashion of Charles Dickens and Leo Tolstoy to tell his stories via a series of dramatic vignettes which focus on a wide assortment of different characters, all tending to develop their own lives, situations, and predicaments, while at the same time propelling the general plot of the story toward a suspenseful conclusion. Jon's model had always been Ernest Haycox among Western authors and he began early on to experiment with character and narrative technique in a fashion his younger brother never did. RATTLESNAKE MESA (Circle V Westerns, 1996) and DARK RIDERS OF DOOM (Five Star Westerns, 1997), a story collection, are among his most recent book publications.

Showdown at Anchor

I

PEACEFUL—AS IN PURGATORY

After that hard desert ride, Lodgepole looked clean and cool and quiet to Ed Nugent. The pines came right down and in among the cabins and grass, a bright emerald blanketing the wide banks of a clear-watered creek bisecting the single crooked street. The bridge spanning the stream was new, its timbers and planking a fresh-cut yellow. This morning's rain had laid the dust and washed things down and there was still a touch of its coolness in the sunny late afternoon.

Peaceful and tidy was Ed Nugent's thought after his first long look at the town. *The sort of place that would let a man take things easy.* That impression of his lasted exactly fifty-four minutes, no more, no less. During that short-hour interval he helped a kid hostler at the livery barn rub down his brindle gelding and begin a careful feeding of the animal, played out after two days of fighting the desert's heat and wind-blown sand. Next he went to the barber shop and soaked his lean, long length in a tub of hot water, later letting the barber trim his dark hair and then lying back to enjoy the luxury of a shave. He thought about going back to the stable and taking off the shell belt that sagged low at his flat thigh. In the end he decided against it, when the aroma of frying beef drew him into a restaurant alongside the barber shop. He downed a beefsteak and boiled potatoes, a dish of tomatoes, two wedges of dried-apple pie and three cups of coffee.

As he paid for the meal, he bought a dime cigar, telling the man at the counter, "I'll be back in a couple of hours, for another go at that grub. It was good."

"Must take a lot to keep a man like you goin'." There was respect and some little awe in the clerk's answer. Aside from one man who frequently ate here, he couldn't remember ever having seen a taller one than this stranger.

Ed sauntered on up the street, pulling at the cigar, relaxed and feeling really good for the first time in a week. The trouble that had pushed him out across the desert seemed remote and unimportant now. Maybe he'd been a little hard on that gambler. Anyway, it would take a lot of healing before the card-sharp was on his feet again and the law would soon forget the name of Ed Nugent. He was here for a new start in a new country. He had a fair stake in his pocket and there was no hurry about finding work. He'd like to loaf right here for a day or two. Maybe tonight there would be a game down the street at the Congress Saloon worth his spending some time on. It wasn't the money that mattered, although he didn't like an empty pocket; it was the game that counted, fair cards and stakes high enough so a man could back his hand or run a good lively bluff.

A rocker on the side verandah of the log hotel invited him and he climbed the steps and took the chair, cocking his spurs on the railing and watching the street take on more life now that evening was on its way. He saw two riders come down out of the pines and rack their horses at the rail fronting the Congress. A dignified man in a black suit came out of the bank, locking the door, and then went into the Mercantile, to reappear shortly, carrying a sack of groceries under his arm, his dignity still with him. A shad-bellied oldster wearing a nickel star on his vest walked up the street and past the hotel, looking up at him and nodding pleasantly. Ed was feeling good enough to drawl, "'Evening, Sheriff."

Yes, this was a choice spot. A man could put down roots in a place like this and never want for much. The people were friendly. The range he had ridden at mid-day was rich and there must be a good bit more of it tucked back in the folds of these near foothills. He was wondering about the price of land when a buckboard headed up the street toward him to interrupt his wondering.

A medium-built man with pale blond hair was holding the reins and a rare piece of horseflesh, a light-saddled bay, was tied to the end-gate and trotted after the rig. But it was the girl sitting alongside the driver who finally took Ed's eye and held it.

When the buckboard turned in at the rail beyond the verandah, he had the chance to prove correct his first impression that the girl was something even rarer than the bay. She stepped lightly down off the wheel hub, smiling at the blond man who gave her his hand. Ed had never seen blue and white-checked calico look so expensive and stylish. Her dress was full-skirted and gathered tightly at a slender waist, snug enough to give the strong hint of a supple, slender figure. She was hatless and wore her cornsilk hair high-piled on her head. Her face possessed a quality that went beyond prettiness, so that Ed noticed its strength and vivaciousness before the fine molding of the features caught his eye. He was thinking he had never seen eyes a deeper blue than hers as she came on up the steps and past him.

Because he was unashamedly looking at her, he noticed the way she stopped just short of the door and, a frightened look crossing her face, turned quickly and said, "Don't come up here, Sam!"

Her words came too late, stopping her spare-bodied companion on the top step. Three men were already on the way out the door, passing the girl, the one in the lead having to duck his head and hunch his massive shoulders to clear the door frame. He was probably the biggest man Ed had ever come across—he was, in fact, the one the restaurant owner had been thinking about—and everything about him was oversized, his height and breadth and thickness.

The big man said tonelessly, "Better go on in, Laura." He wasn't looking at the girl as he spoke. His pale gray eyes were on Sam. Ed saw the girl stiffen and anger flared brightly in her eyes. "Don't, Tom!" she breathed. Then, when the big man paid her not the slightest attention, starting on out for the blond 'puncher, she said more loudly, "Tom, I order you to go straight back in there."

That stopped the big one. His hard glance shuttled from Sam to the girl. "Any other time I'd listen, Laura," he said with a strong respect in his tone. "But your father sent us here to do what we're doin'."

"Dad can't lord it over everybody like...."

The massive Tom was already taking another step away from her, not listening. Ed's careful glance took in Sam now and what he saw filled him with admiration and a strong measure of pity. The young blond man was almost a full head shorter than Tom. Yet his deeply-tanned face showed not the slightest trace of fear. Instead, his expression was dogged, even defiant. He wore no weapon Ed could see. His arms were cocked, fists doubled, and a blaze of hatred touched the glance he focused on the big man.

The girl, seeing her words having no effect, suddenly ran out and caught a hold on Tom's arm. Ed sat straight in the chair as the big man lazily swept his arm down, breaking her hold easily. "Keep her back, Briggs," Tom drawled, and one of the other pair, a gangling scarecrow of a man, came out and took the girl by the elbow, pulling her away as Tom added, "Sandy, put a gun on him."

The remaining man in the trio deliberately drew a Colt from his belt and lined it at Sam, who so far hadn't spoken or moved a muscle. The girl suddenly pulled free of Briggs's hold and started in at Tom again. The way the big man swung his arm, brushing her roughly aside, brought Ed up out of his chair.

Tom seemed to have been expecting some such thing, for his arm came on around and his hand jarred Ed's shoulder hard, bowling him back down into the chair with such force that one of the rockers snapped, cocking the chair aslant. He gave Ed a brief chill look, saying almost gently, "Stay out o' this, stranger."

He stepped out at Sam once more and Sandy, the one with the drawn .45, moved closer in behind Ed's chair. Sam stood his ground, smiling faintly as though knowing that what was coming was inevitable and that there was no use in wasting effort dodging it.

"You had your warnin', Sam," Tom said an instant before he swung.

At the last split second Sam ducked his head and hunched a shoulder. He should easily have avoided the blow, for Tom wasn't particularly fast. But the ham-like fist slammed into Sam's shoulder and rocked him back on his heels. He tried to catch himself. He was too close to the porch's edge. His boot reached into thin air and he did an ungainly backward cartwheel, hitting the middle step on his hip and going on over. When he lay sprawled on the walk, he tried to push up, then fell back again with a stunned and baffled look of pain crossing his face.

"Go get him, Matt. Bring him up here." Tom stood with fists planted on his hips, looking down at Sam. There was no pity in his dark eyes.

Briggs let go of the girl and went down the steps and hauled Sam to his feet again. The girl cried, "Stop! Can't you see he's hurt?" She tried to come on past Tom once more, but with that easy swing of his arm he swept her back toward the door.

This huge man, Ed was thinking, had the broadest back and the most powerful pair of shoulders he had ever seen. Something was going on here that he realized wasn't strictly his affair. But he had never seen a man push a woman around this way and it wasn't right. It was so wrong that he wondered what would happen now if he tried to stand again. He looked around, saw the bore of the .45 lined at him and, over his boiling rage, decided to stay as he was.

Briggs dragged the dazed Sam on up the steps and when they stood there at the edge of the porch Tom drawled, "Hold him up."

Briggs lifted Sam erect and pinned his arms behind him. Tom stepped in deliberately and hit him. This time he connected solidly. Sam's head snapped back, dropped to his chest. Tom struck again and again, smashing Sam's nose, cutting open his lips.

The girl screamed and her cry caught Sandy's attention briefly. His eyes had barely moved from Ed before Ed was lunging erect. Tom half turned then toward the girl and Ed. Sandy saw what was coming and started bringing the .45 around again. But Ed's Colt blurred up, exploded, and Sandy's .45 spun to the boards as he grunted with pain, clamping left hand to his sprung wrist.

Tom wheeled warily around, forgetting the unconscious Sam.

Ed Nugent nodded down to Sandy's weapon that lay close at the girl's feet. "Miss," he drawled, "if you want some fun, hold that on these gents while I get to work."

Her wide, frightened eyes were puzzled for only a moment before she snatched up the Colt, cocked it, and pointed it at Hall. She said, "Tom Hall, I'm going to cripple you. I'm going to...."

"Hold on," Ed cut in quietly. "This is my party. Just keep 'em off my back." He stepped in on Tom and flipped the man's Colt from holster, tossing it out across the walk.

Briggs let go his hold on Sam and lifted his hands. Sam slumped to the floor, half curled up like he was sleeping. Briggs's .44 arched out and landed beside the big man's in the drying mud at the walk's edge. Ed dropped his own weapon back into holster and suddenly threw a stiff jab at the big man's face. It happened so quickly that neither Tom nor the girl was expecting the blow. She had started to say something as Tom's head rocked back on his thick neck. Then a look of gladness came to her eyes and she moved her weapon around so that it covered both Briggs and Sandy, who had stepped well clear of Ed now.

That first punch shook Tom but didn't hurt him. Hard on the heels of it he threw a vicious roundhouse swing that would have knocked Ed all the way to the walk had it connected. Ed simply ducked under it and rose with all the weight of his ropy-muscled shoulders behind a fist that buried itself just above the big man's belt. Tom Hall gagged and doubled over. Then Ed's other fist jarred him erect with a solid impact on the point of the jaw. Pain lanced through Ed's knuckles and wrist and he drew back as Hall groped out wildly trying to reach him. When the pain eased off, Ed stepped in again, knocking aside the man's thick arms, then slashing his knuckles across the wide mouth. A look of bewilderment crossed Hall's face as the blood ran down his chin. Ed hit him once more, full on the jaw-hinge.

The verandah railing was a long pine pole braced by cross-pieces at three places. Several men could sit on it and it would sag but never crack. Hall's crumpling weight hit it and the whole railing tore loose and one end of it fell into a pair of onlookers who had come running up at the sound of the shot a few seconds ago. They stumbled out of the way as Hall hit the walk planks on his back and rolled over, trying to stand.

Ed jumped down and helped Hall to his feet, then stepped back and threw a sure uppercut that flattened the big man's nose and buckled his knees. As Hall went down the second time, Ed turned and glanced to the porch, aware now that several men stood close by on the walk, watching. He caught the girl's eye. "Enough, miss? That makes it about even, except that they knocked your friend out. Want me to put this moose to sleep?"

"No...you've done enough." The girl was pale and her look frightened. She no longer held the Colt up. It hung at her side.

Ed eyed Briggs and Sandy. "Better heft your sidekick in off the walk," he drawled. "He's big enough to be in the way."

Meekly, not looking at Ed, they came on down the steps and out to Hall, trying to lift him to his feet and making a clumsy job of it. Finally they had him erect between them and were walking out through the crowd and down the walk, the gathering crowd stepping aside for them.

Ed saw the sheriff push his way in through the onlookers and had the idle thought, *Peaceful, was it?* before the lawman stopped two strides short of him, wanting to know, "What did you do to Hall?"

"What Tom deserved to have done to him, Sheriff," called the girl, coming to the edge of the porch. "He and those two others half killed Sam Richards. Someone had better get him up to the doctor's."

There was a lot of talk then and the sheriff seemed to have forgotten Ed as he came on past him and climbed the steps to kneel alongside the unconscious Sam. Ed sauntered on down the walk. He crossed to the far side of the street a few buildings below, headed for the livery barn—headed on out of the country, he supposed.

But by the time he was lugging his saddle into the stall where the brindle stood, a stubborn anger was rising in him. He'd done nothing the law could hold him for. The brindle needed rest and so did he. How did it happen he was running again? He took the saddle back and slung it over the pole and went on up the street in the gathering dusk. The crowds had shifted to the walk in front of a building, several doors above the hotel. The verandah rail still lay there on the planks and Hall and his two men were nowhere in sight. Ed paid no attention to several idlers across the street, who watched him go into the hotel.

The small lobby was deserted and nearly dark. He lit a lamp on the desk at the foot of the stairs, signed the book there, took a key from the board behind the railing and went on up to room six, wondering how long it would take the sheriff to track him down.

It took even less time than Ed thought it would. The gray twilight was only beginning to thicken at the window—and he had barely half smoked a cigarette, lying stretched on the bed in the darkening room—when the solid clump of boots sounded along the hallway. He pushed up onto an elbow, instinct running his hand to the Colt. But then he thought better of the move and lay back again. When the door of his room swung abruptly open, he had his hands laced behind his head.

In the faint light he recognized the sheriff and drawled, "You're old enough to have picked up the habit of knockin', friend."

"So I am."

The door slammed shut with a violence that rattled the raised sash of the window. The lawman went to the washstand and lit the ornate lamp sitting on it. As he put the rose-glass shade back onto its holder, he faced Ed with a stern look on his narrow face. "Who are you and what're you doin' here?"

"The handle's Ed, Sheriff. And I'm tending my own knittin', doing just as little as will get me by."

"You'd better talk, mister," the lawman said sharply. "Did Sam Richards pay to bring you in here to make that play against Hall?"

Ed solemnly shook his head, saying owlishly, "That's between me and Richards."

"They say you're real slick with that forty-five. So you admit Sam brought you in?"

Ed swung his boots off the bed, sitting up. "That's what you want, isn't it?"

"Ever see Sam Richards before?"

"No."

"Ever been here before?"

Ed shook his head, pinching the end of his smoke and tossing it out the window.

The sheriff's testy manner faded before a harassed look. "I believe you," he said with a surprising frankness. "The reason I do is that no man knowing the way the cards are stacked here would have dared to do what you did. You must've walked into it blind." Ed sat, waiting for more. It came shortly. "You've got maybe two hours before Hall gets back here with Anchor's crew. He'll hunt you down if he has to take this town apart."

"Why?"

"Why?" the lawman echoed incredulously. "Don't you know what you did?"

"Whittled an overstuffed jasper down to his right size."

"Man, no one's ever so much as lifted a hand against Anchor. Against John Worth or his ramrod."

"Somebody was liable to, some day."

The sheriff's look was completely baffled now. He sighed deeply, shaking his head. "So you did. The Lord knows how you got away with it. You were plain lucky. But now's not the time to crowd your luck. You'll have to get out."

Ed seemed not to have heard as he drawled, "So that's her name. Laura Worth."

The lawman half way read Ed's thought, for he said quickly, "You buy into her game, mister, and you'll think you never saw trouble. She's bucking her father...and no one does that."

"You've said that twice now, Sheriff."

"And I'll say it again. The...."

His words broke off as a light knock came at the door. Ed called, "Come in," and stood up off the bed as the door opened.

It was Laura Worth. She was even prettier than Ed had thought. She was away from violence, lamplight laying a soft shadow across her face that gave it a mysterious, haunting beauty. Her direct eyes moved from Ed to the lawman and a faint smile touched her expression. "I knew you were here, Bob. I wanted to see both of you."

The sheriff said helplessly, angrily, yet with an affection beneath his tone Ed didn't miss, "Haven't you stirred things up enough for one day?"

"I can thank this man for what he did for Sam, can't I?" she asked, a mischievous look coming to her eyes.

"Thank him and get out then."

"And if he isn't working, I can offer him a job, can't I?" Her tone was mock-innocent. She looked at Ed. "Would you take a riding job? Even if Sheriff Coombs says you shouldn't?"

"Laura, listen!" the lawman breathed. "What's between your father and Sam Richards isn't your affair. Let it alone. Keep out of it."

"I happen to be very fond of Sam," she said evenly. "And I happen to think my father is beyond his rights in what he's doing. I'm of age. Six months over, in fact. I have every right to take sides in this."

"John Worth won't let anything get in his way now, family or no family," Coombs intoned gravely. "Laura, this is a grown-up game they're playing. Someone may get hurt."

"Which reminds me, Bob. What are you doing to stop it? What legal right does Dad have for beating up a man simply because he's seen with me?"

Coombs's face reddened and he was groping for a reply when Ed drawled, "I'll listen, miss. But I'd have to know more about it."

"You will," the girl told him.

Coombs said resignedly, "Then tell it all. If he knows everything he won't touch it with a California rope."

"Two months ago Sam Richards was working for my father as a wrangler," Laura Worth said, ignoring the sheriff's comment. "He'd been with us for over a year and done well with the job. Then one day Dad sent him up north to bring down a batch of horses Tom

Hall had bought for Anchor at an auction up there. Some sort of business delayed Hall and Sam set out alone with the horses. The first night several riders hit his camp and stampeded the horses. Sam lost every animal. When Hall heard about it, he told Dad he'd seen Sam talking to Len Avery and...."

"Len Avery's a renegade white livin' on the reservation east of here." The sheriff inserted his words dryly, with a thinly-veiled meaning. "Every time those bucks break out and go on one of their sprees, Avery's with 'em. He's a rustler, a petty thief, and a squaw man among other things. Worth fired Sam, same's anybody would, and Laura horned in."

"Of course I did." Her eyes were bright with defiance now. "I was sorry for Sam, ashamed of the way he'd been treated."

"You didn't have to stake him, loan him that money."

"In my place you'd have done the same thing, Bob Coombs," Laura flared.

"What money?" Ed asked, seeing the conversation going beyond him.

"Money to buy eight sections of land the government was selling after a resurvey of the reservation's west line," the girl told him. "Sam and I knew it was up for sale by sealed bids. We knew Dad had talked Tom Hall into making a bid on it. We even knew what Tom's bid was to be. So I loaned Sam the money to buy it."

"At exactly a hundred more than Hall had offered," the sheriff prompted.

"Yes." There was a proud touch to Laura Worth's expression now. "So Sam got the land and moved onto it. Dad was furious. He forbade me to see any more of Sam. Yesterday we had it out, Dad and I. I won't have him telling me what I can and can't do. So I brought some things into town and I'm living here now at the hotel. As soon as he learns he can't bully decent men, I'll go back to Anchor." Ed liked the way Laura Worth lifted her shoulders, as her glance came around to him again. "So there you have it. Most of it, anyway. Well, what's your answer? Do you want a job with Sam, knowing all this?"

Ed thought it over deliberately, drawling finally, "Why not? When do I start?"

A look of gladness lighted her face. "Tonight. We'll head for the Triangle as soon as I've changed."

"You'll damn' soon regret it if you do, son," the sheriff said, very soberly.

II

A MAN FOR HELL'S CAÑON

She had agreed to meet him at the livery, asking him to have a horse saddled for her and, when she came down along the dark, awninged walk, he saw that she was still bare-headed but had changed from the dress to a man's outfit—flannel shirt, denim jumper, and waist-overalls. The boots made her tall enough, so that the top of her head was well above his shoulder as she came in alongside him and took the reins of her sorrel.

Neither of them said anything as she led the way down the street and, well out past the last cabin, took a climbing trail that forked north from the road. They were riding through the pines before they had gone another hundred yards and, as the deep obscurity closed about them, she slowed the sorrel out of a trot to let him come alongside.

"We'll take our time," she said. "Your animal's seen some travel lately."

It wasn't a question but he saw it as one, knowing she must have gone to the stable earlier and inspected the brindle, for she couldn't have noticed what she mentioned in this darkness.

"He brought me across from Chimney yesterday and the day before," Ed told her.

He could barely make out her face turning abruptly toward him. There was a quality of strong surprise in her voice as she asked, "In only the two days?"

"And part of last night. We were both thirsty."

"You must have been in a hurry. That's a four-day ride at this season."

He grinned broadly, knowing she couldn't see. "Wanted to get it over with."

She had nothing to say to that. But presently as they dipped across a grassy swale circled by the pines, she asked, "Are you as good with a gun as they said you were when you caught Sandy so flatfooted?" There was a brief silence before she went on, "I'm not trying to pry. It's only that I want to be sure you can help Sam."

"Gun help?"

She was a long time in answering. When she spoke, her voice was low, dead serious. "Yes, I suppose that's it. And yet, Sam Richards really doesn't mean much to me…only this is his chance, the chance of a lifetime to build up a place of his own. He wanted that when he came into this country. I couldn't…won't let Dad ruin him."

They rode on in silence for some minutes, Ed trying to figure why he had let her talk him into taking this job with Sam Richards. He had crossed the desert to ride clear of trouble, to stay clear, and here he was headed into more. *Chasin' a petticoat?* he asked himself, and at once decided, *That's not all of it,* stubbornly refusing to admit that anyone, man or woman, had enough influence over him to make him give up any measure of his carefree independence. His siding Sam Richards had been a normal reaction to take up with the underdog—and there had been a clean and honest look about the wrangler, a courageous stubbornness that even now played on his feeling for fairness.

"You haven't yet told me your name," Laura said, breaking a long run of silence between them.

"Nugent. Ed Nugent."

"That's a new one," she said. "There's a nice sound to it."

She didn't press more questions on him and he was grateful for that. When next she spoke, again minutes later, her words packed a measure of surprise. For she said, "Promise me just one thing, Ed. I don't mind Dad's having to eat crow. Anchor's been too high and mighty for too long. And he's wrong in backing Tom Hall the way he does. But I wouldn't want…well, I just don't want anything to happen to him."

"Then he'd better stay out of Sam Richards's way."

"I hope he will, but its not as simple as that. Sam picked up a bunch of culls the agent rejected from the reservation herd. Dad wants them kept off his range and that's been impossible. Sam and Al Abbot, the man he's got working for him, have been stringing wire as fast as they can, but it takes time to fence in eight sections. Meantime Sam's beef's been drifting over onto Anchor grass. And Dad keeps insisting on a tie-up between Sam and this Len Avery. If any Anchor stock disappears from now on, he'll blame it on Sam."

"Any chance that Sam was in with Avery stealing those horses?"

"Not any, Ed. Can't you tell an honest man when you see one?"

He nodded, drawling, "Sometimes. But here's a thing I don't *sabe*. If this Avery's a known rustler, why don't they string him up?"

"They've never proved anything. The beef that's run off this slope usually goes through the reservation's west fence and cuts north into the next county. By the time arrangements are made with the agent to look for the cattle, they've simply disappeared. There are ranchers up in that country who aren't too particular about brands. And for some reason the law up there has never cooperated with Bob Coombs."

They were riding up a steep and rocky cañon now and for a time the clatter of their horses' shoes was a racket they couldn't talk over. Within a half mile the cañon floor began gradually leveling out and the rims fell away across a broad expanse of grass that showed indistinctly in the starlight.

Laura said, "Here's the start of Triangle." She was silent a moment, then said quietly, feelingly, "Ed, that promise you're giving doesn't hold for Tom Hall. He's mostly what's wrong with Dad. Sometimes I wish something could happen to him."

Ed didn't answer and for a quarter-minute their animals walked side by side, the squeak of leather and the slur of hoofs brushing through the fetlock-deep grass the only sounds breaking the stillness.

"Ed, you haven't given your promise," Laura reminded him.

"I'm thinking maybe I'd better ride on out of the whole thing."

She looked across at him, trying to read some expression in the dark outline of his face. "I hope you don't," she said finally, with a directness that jolted him and faintly stirred his anger.

"You can't put a rein like that on a man," he said in a brittle voice. "Suppose your father does decide to push Sam on out. Suppose he has his chance at either Sam or me. Are we to unbutton our shirts to give him an open shot at our ribs and not do anything about it?"

"No, Ed." Her voice was barely above a whisper. "But I'd want you to…just do what you can for Dad."

"That I can promise," he said.

"Maybe he won't ask for trouble."

And maybe he will, was Ed's thought as they rode on.

Stringing fence for another man was something Ed Nugent hadn't thought he would ever be doing again. He had drawn top wages at every outfit he had worked for over the past five years—since he had turned twenty—and had bossed fence crews but never handled the wire himself. Now he was doing exactly that, gouging his hands raw even though he wore thick leather gloves. He and Al Abbot, Sam's crewman, had dug more post holes and rolled out more spools of wire in the past two days than he cared to remember. His arm and back muscles were stiff and he wasn't used to being afoot so much.

Yet he didn't begrudge even one minute of the long, hard hours he had put in for Sam Richards. Sam hadn't stirred from the cabin during these two days, couldn't. His dislocated hip wouldn't carry his weight and Ed wasn't at all sure that the wrangler's jaw wasn't broken. Sam couldn't open his mouth to take in much food, let alone chew it. Yesterday Laura had come out from town and made up a stew for him and this morning he had seemed a little stronger, his spirits better.

At sundown they had finished dropping a load of spools along the north line of new cedar posts and were riding the buckboard down across a meadow a mile below in the direction of the cabin. And Al was drawling, "My guts are gnawin' bad enough to take even my own cookin'. We'll fry up some steak and have a real feed."

"Wish Sam could chew a chunk of it." Ed slapped the team with reins to lift them to a faster trot.

"There's a good man." Al's long face was set seriously. "It's a funny thing about him, though. He's different now."

"How?"

"That bustin' up he took put vinegar into him, 'stead of takin' it out like it was supposed to. Remember what he said to the girl the other night when she brought you up here?"

Ed nodded, remembering well. Laura had asked Sam how he was feeling, if his hip hurt much, and he had answered, "This is the best thing that could have happened to me. This afternoon I was half of a mind to pull out, leave for good. Now I'm here to stay." The flinty look in his gray eyes had been even more eloquent of his feelings than his words. But then his look had softened as he spoke again to Laura. "You'd better keep clear of this from now on…it's gone too far for a woman to have anything to do with it." Such talk, coming from as mild looking a man as Sam, had left its impression on Ed. He remembered how Laura's face had paled as she took in the full meaning of what he had said, as though she had just then realized for the first time how deadly serious this trouble might become.

"That girl now," Al went on, interrupting Ed's thoughts. "Damned if I figure her out, goin' against her own flesh and blood this way. Someone's likely to get hurt."

"She's proud," Ed said, "and maybe ashamed at seeing how hog wild her old man's gone. But she can't back out now an' hold her head up."

Al frowned. "Suppose that's it. Puts me in mind of how mad I once got when my pappy whaled the livin' daylight out of a nester that run his critters across our place. Small man, the sodbuster was, gettin' up in years. There wasn't nothin' right about it."

They were in among the trees now, the cabin in sight close below. Blue cedar smoke drifted lazily from the chimney, fanning out across the wide bay in the timber. They came abreast the corral and Ed reined in the team.

They were unharnessing when Al suddenly breathed a low oath and said softly, sharply, "Over your right shoulder, Ed."

Looking that way, Ed saw big Tom Hall step into the open from behind the corral fifty feet away. Cradled across the crook of the Anchor ramrod's arm was a double-barreled shotgun. Ed turned to face the man, startled and a strong sense of foreboding in him. He wasn't wearing his Colt. A Winchester lying in the buckboard bed was the only weapon he and Al had taken with them this morning. So now he didn't even bother lifting his hands.

A slow, satisfied smile patterned Hall's square face, twisting his still-swollen lips in an odd way. "The party's over, gents," he called. "Just move over this way careful."

Suddenly from behind him, Ed heard the pound of Al's boots on the far side of the team. He called loudly, "Don't, Al!" as he read the meaning of that sound. Al was making a break for it.

Tom Hall stopped and raised the shotgun to his shoulder. It cut loose its thunder, with rosy flame stabbing from both barrels. On the heels of the deafening explosion came Al's hoarse scream.

Ed wheeled and looked beyond the team. Al lay sprawled brokenly on the ground off toward the trees. Even though Hall called sharply, "You, Nugent! Stay set!" Ed walked over there.

One look was enough to fill Ed with a cold rage. The double load of buckshot had caught Al between the shoulders. The sight sickened him. He quickly pulled off his jumper, spreading it across the upper part of the body, and then faced Hall once more.

"You blood-hungry fool! You've killed him."

Hall spoke calmly. "Get in there with Richards."

Ed for the first time noticed Matt Briggs's lanky frame leaning in the doorway of the cabin. A moment later Sam Richards appeared beyond the Anchor man and hobbled on past him before Briggs caught him and pulled him back in through the door again.

"Come on, get movin'," Hall drawled.

Ed was warned to obey by the cool tone of the man's voice and by the thing he had just witnessed. He went on around the corral, hearing Hall's step coming along behind him. Briggs moved back out of the doorway and, when Ed stepped in, it was to find Sam sitting on his bed, his battered face drained of color and a baffled rage showing in his eyes.

"He killed him," Sam said in a lifeless voice.

Ed nodded. "But why, Sam?"

"Why? We're rustlers," Sam told him, his voice strong and acid with anger now. "We ran off a herd of Anchor beef last night. Pushed it on to the reservation. They say we've made a deal with that one-armed Avery to take the herd off our hands."

"Remember the tracks, Richards," Briggs drawled across the momentary silence.

Sam laughed, a hysterical note in his voice. "Ed, they say they followed our sign straight back here from the break in the reservation fence." He suddenly stood up, stumbling as he forgot and put weight on his bad leg. "Damn it, Ed! Tell 'em we didn't stir from here last night!"

"Save it to tell the sheriff," came Hall's voice from the doorway behind Ed. "Matt, go get the horses."

Briggs moved around Ed and out the door. Ed turned to Hall, asking, "Why didn't you bring your sheriff along?"

"Waste all that time to town and lettin' you three get away? Uh-uh!"

"If we were making a getaway, why didn't we do it last night?"

"Damned if I know," Hall said evenly. "You must've thought you'd hid your sign better'n you had."

All at once Sam was saying urgently, "Ed, remember last night when you thought the horses were actin' up down at the corral?"

Ed nodded. He had left his blankets and gone out to the corral in the middle of the night, curious at hearing the horses moving around. But by the time he had walked down there the animals had already quieted and he saw nothing wrong.

"Ed, did you rub down your horse when you finished work last night?" Sam went on insistently.

"Sure. I always do."

A gleam of satisfaction came to Sam's eyes now as he looked at Tom Hall. "I went down there to the corral this mornin', just for something to do. After you and Al left, Ed. The hair on your brindle's back was matted down like you'd forgotten to curry him. He was ridden last night. After you finished with him."

A slow inscrutability had settled over Hall's face.

"You get it Ed?" Sam's voice was trembling now. "They took our horses after we turned in and rode 'em up there to where the herd went through, then brought 'em back. You heard something going on at the corral. It must've been them turnin' the horses in again. Now they say they've got sign to prove we ran the herd off."

Ed was watching Hall. But no flicker of expression showed on the Anchor man's face as he drawled, "Save that for Coombs, too, Richards. We're taking you in. Only don't plan on Coombs's swallowin' a story like that."

Sam Richards's temper finally snapped. He began putting every name he could think of to Hall, who listened for several moments and then leisurely walked over and knocked him back onto the bed with a gun butt.

Sam's mouth was still bleeding when they carried him out and roped him onto his saddle ten minutes later. Shortly they did the same with Ed. Dusk was settling in through the pines as they took the town trail, Hall leading the way. Behind the Anchor foreman Sam rode crookedly, leaning away from his bad leg. Ed stayed close to Sam's rear, ready to ride alongside and shoulder him erect if he lost his balance. Briggs came last, riding leisurely. For the most part they were silent.

Once or twice Ed heard Sam muttering to himself. He was close to the breaking point and Ed himself was a little awed. The evidence against them would be hard to argue against. Sam Richards's name in town was not too good at best. Being included as a victim of this circumstance didn't particularly worry Ed, simply because he wouldn't let himself think about it.

As they left the high grassy bench and headed down through the darkness into the cañon Ed had two nights ago traveled with Laura, he began guiding the gelding in and out between the boulders by a touch of the spur. He had trained the brindle to obey that prod. Now it was saving him from an uncomfortable ride. Time and again Sam, up ahead, was badly jolted as his horse took the hard going without a hand on the reins to guide him over the worst of it.

They were coming abreast a narrow brush-choked off-shoot when Ed abruptly thought of something that made him turn and look behind. He couldn't see Matt Briggs, but the man was back there, somewhere in the darkness. He could hear the steady hoof-strike of Briggs's horse sounding against the cañon's rocky floor. Up ahead, Tom Hall's massive shape made a dense shadow against the blackness. Every few minutes, as long as it was light, Ed had noticed Hall turning to look back at them.

Hall might be watching, but Ed weighed that chance and decided to take it as he touched the gelding's flank with the spur of his left boot. The brindle swung over to the right, its pace a steady slow walk. The thicket loomed close in front of Ed and a touch of the right spur, then another of the left, put the gelding around the thicket's edge and into the mouth of the narrowing cleft angling deeply into the wall.

At the last moment Ed decided against riding out this small side-cañon, knowing he risked being boxed and having them hunt him down, probably to kill him. He put his horse straight in at the wall behind the thicket. The animal stopped a stride short of the sheer-climbing rock and came to a stand.

Ed listened warily, breathing shallowly, his nerves drawn wire-tight. Gradually he made out the sound of Sam's horse going away. Then the hoof-thud of Briggs's animal lifted over other sounds as Briggs drew abreast and continued steadily on.

Suddenly Tom Hall's voice came to him faintly calling, "Close in, Matt. We got to make time."

He would have to play his chance for all it was worth. He turned the gelding out into the cañon, again using the spur. He managed to get the animal started back the way they had come. Suddenly Matt Briggs's strident shout echoed up to him. He rammed home both spurs and the startled gelding lunged into a run.

III

RUSTLER'S RESERVATION

The first news of the hunt reached Lodgepole at mid-afternoon of the next day when a posseman, Nels Baker, having to catch the evening stage on important business, rode back to town. Ed Nugent was still at large.

"This bird, Nugent," Baker told the crowd that gathered at the sheriff's office, "fooled the pack of us. Where would be the last place you'd expect to find him?"

"Anchor," someone called out, and there were a few guffaws.

Another man made a guess. "Sam Richards's place."

"Right," Baker said. "Damned if he hadn't gone back there, and dug a grave and buried Abbot, sacked himself some grub, and just rode away. Hall claims there was two forty-fives in the cabin and a Winchester lyin' in the buckboard. Nugent's luggin' all three."

"Where'd he go from there?" one of the listeners wanted to know.

Baker shrugged tiredly. "They're up there along the *malpais* now, thrashin' around, tryin' to spot where he come out of all that rock. Coombs is bringin' Sam on down in another hour to two."

Laura Worth stood along the walk at the back fringe of the crowd. Now she stopped holding her breath, gladness running through her as she turned and walked away. *They'll never get him!* she told herself. But the next moment her fears crowded in on her again.

She was climbing the hotel steps, wholly engrossed by her thoughts of Ed, before she saw her father. John Worth had risen from a chair on the verandah and now stood waiting for her alongside the mended rail. She stopped and stood irresolutely, before her pride steadied her and carried her on.

"Laura, I'd like a word with you," the rancher said quietly as she reached the head of the steps.

"There's nothing you can say that will help now." She wanted to walk on past him. But a certain humility written on his face puzzled her, made her curious enough to linger in hope of finding out what backed it.

"I can say this, child," he told her gravely. "I never thought this would come to killing."

"Your own men are the only ones who have done any killing so far, Dad. You should be proud of Tom Hall."

She could see him wince, but that strange humility stayed with him as he said, "Tom was wrong, perhaps. I hate the killing as badly as you do." A spark of his old fire seemed to flicker alive in him then and when he went on his voice was sharper with that stubborn pride she knew so well. "Laura, no one can do this to Anchor and expect to get away with it. No one."

"Al Abbot did nothing to Anchor. Nor did Sam...or Ed." Her chin tilted stubbornly as she met his hard stare. "No one believes that. But it's true."

"Now, child, Tom Hall can prove they did it. He and Matt Briggs...."

"Tom Hall's word isn't worth the breath he wastes. He's a bully and he may be a liar."

John Worth was silent a moment. Finally he said, "I came in to ask you to come home with me, Laura. Now I can see that I was wrong in thinking you would."

"You were wrong in making me leave, Dad."

His back stiffened. "We'll argue that no further. I'm ashamed of what's come between us. People are beginning to talk." She could see him close his mind to her argument even before he said, "I won't be made a fool of, Laura. You wanted me to become one."

"Simply by letting a man you had mistreated take something you wanted?" She laughed, the harsh note of her voice lacking any merriment. "Dad, you made yourself smaller when you treated Sam as you did. Every day you keep on with it, you're only hurting yourself. If people are talking, it is to wonder how they could have respected John Worth all these years."

She had said enough. *Too much!* was her frightening thought. She was suddenly afraid of having hurt him too deeply. Yet her pride wouldn't let her take back any of the things she had said and, seeing how pointless it was to say anything further, she stepped on past him and into the cool lobby.

John Worth regarded the empty doorway thoughtfully, waiting there until his anger had quieted to the point where he was sure it wouldn't betray itself to anyone who saw him. Then he went down the steps and along the walk to the Congress, his back as ramrod straight as always.

———⟶⊷⊶⟵———

Yesterday, on their way up to the line of the north fence, Al Abbot had pointed out the waste of the *malpais* to Ed. This twisted and writhing mass of cinder-black volcanic rock covered nearly a section of Sam Richards's land and continued on around the north shoulder of the mountains in a broadening belt that spread northwest across the butte-studded flats of the reservation. A thin top-soil spotted the depressions, but for the most part the *malpais* was a bare solid mass of rock with steel-sharp edges so forbidding that animals seldom ventured into it because of the damage it did to their hoofs.

Ed had waited until the first light of the false dawn before heading into it, intending to hide his sign. He had cut four squares from the tarp of his bed roll and bound them about the brindle's hoofs, tying them above the fetlock. He reasoned that news of the theft of Anchor's herd would certainly reach the reservation as soon as Sheriff Coombs could send it. If the agent cooperated with outside law as he was supposed to, Len Avery's whereabouts would be of particular interest to him today. It followed that Avery, knowing he would be suspect, would be somewhere in plain sight, probably with an airtight alibi to give the agent when asked where he had spent night before last, the night Anchor's herd was driven off.

Riding the *malpais* was slow going and Ed went along carefully to save the gelding's feet. By mid-morning he had traveled only ten miles onto the reservation. When the black rock started giving out, he left it and rode openly. Once in the distance he saw a group of four riders angling along a trail ahead of him. But they showed no curiosity and presently he watched the dust-boil of their passage fade from sight against the heat-shimmering horizon. He crossed several well defined trails but kept wide of them. Finally, with the sun directly overhead, he came to a rutted and well-traveled wagon road striking south around the east slope of the hills. He took it.

As he surmised, the road presently brought him within sight of a distant, sprawling cluster of wickiups and corrals roughly ringing several log buildings and one huge L-shaped structure of sun-baked adobe. He could only guess that this town was the heart of the reservation. A stream flowing down out of the juniper-studded foothills skirted the settlement and by the time he was fording it, an hour later, he had decided how he would go about this.

He rode boldly along the dusty, littered street, noticing that none of the Indians around the wickiups paid him the slightest attention. A faded sign over the door of the 'dobe building proclaimed that it was the agency and gave the name of the agent, T. S. Havers. As he tied the brindle at the rail fronting the agency, one of the blue-uniformed reservation police lazed up off a bench alongside the broad doorway, leaving his carbine leaning against the wall.

"Havers in?" Ed asked but got nothing but a nod from the Indian who sat down once more, already losing interest in him.

Havers sat at a disorderly desk alongside the single window behind a railing dividing the front office. He was a dour-faced individual clad in a shiny suit of black serge and the glance he fixed on Ed as he entered was suspicious and reserved.

Ed decided to come straight to the point and bluff this through. He didn't give his name, didn't even say hello, instead asked brusquely, "Have you dug up anything for Coombs?"

The agent's face lost its guarded look immediately and as he rose from the desk and came to the rail he said cordially, "Not a thing yet. But we have hopes."

Ed frowned, trying to appear disgusted. "A whole damn herd walks across your layout here and all you can say is you have hopes."

"I'll give him anything I can," Havers was quick to say, his manner worried now, almost fawning. "But it's the same story it's been before. The cattle went straight on through. That country at the north end is just as wild as it was the first day the Maker created it. My police found tracks galore and the north fence cut. But nothing else, I'm afraid."

"So Anchor's beef got across into the next county?" Ed queried acidly.

The agent's bony shoulders lifted in a weary shrug. "I'm afraid so. I sent a man over there to get their sheriff busy on it."

"Were your police in on the deal?"

Havers appeared shocked and faintly angry. "Certainly not!"

"What about Avery? Where was he?"

"He's around. I talked to him this morning. But I can't check on his story. He had two men with him who swear he was at a sheep camp clear to hell and gone at the south end of the reservation the night the herd came through. They're both no-accounts and I wouldn't trust their word."

Hope was coming alive in Ed again. "How about my seeing him?"

"Avery?" The agent shrugged once more. "Why not? You'll probably find him loafing across at the store. He was there at noon when I went out to eat."

As Ed turned toward the door, Havers added, "Sure wish there was something I could give you to go on. How's Bob Coombs? Who'd you say you were?"

Ed gave him a name, not his own. He permitted himself a spare smile as he led the brindle over to the log store obliquely across the dusty thoroughfare from the agency, mildly curious as to how a man as corrupt and inefficient as Havers managed his job. Havers had undoubtedly made only a faint pretense of checking Len Avery's story. Perhaps he was even in with Avery—or whoever was responsible for the theft of the herd.

The store's interior was as gloomy and dirty as Ed had expected, displaying cheap merchandise ranged along the counters and a clerk with a bald head and a sharp eye watching over it.

As Ed sauntered past him, the clerk said, "Something I can do for you?"

Ed didn't even bother answering. He was headed for a quartet of men sitting at a table under a window beyond one of the counters at the store's rear. They were playing a desultory game of cards, three Indians and a white man. The white man had the empty left sleeve of his grimy shirt doubled back and pinned at the shoulder.

Their incurious glances lifted from the cards to watch Ed's approach. He caught Avery's eye and tilted his head toward the front of the barn-like room. "Have a word with you, Avery?"

The renegade laid the cards down carefully, then lifted his one hand and ran a finger along his wide mustache, his beady eyes watchful and running over Ed, yet avoiding any direct meeting of his glance.

Ed waited a long moment, then drawled, "Well, make up your mind."

"What's it about?" Avery asked finally, suspiciously.

"Hall sent me." He wondered what reaction his words would bring from the others but, if they made any sense of what he was saying, they didn't show it.

Avery, however, opened his pale eyes a trifle wider and eased his caboose-chair back, rising and telling the others, "Better deal me out."

He came on past Ed and led the way outside. He didn't stop until he had crossed the walk and could lean against the tie-rail. Then he eyed Ed narrowly, "Tom ought to know better than to send a man straight in here for me."

"I came over to see Havers on business for the sheriff. He thinks I'm askin' you about night before last."

A smug smile played briefly over the renegade's ugly, hawk-like face. "That's better. What does Tom want?"

"Wants you to do another job like night before last. And like you did it on those horses," Ed drawled casually.

The suspicion flared in Avery's eyes once more.

"Who might you be?"

"Hall and I used to travel together before he came here. He sent for me. Didn't want to trust any of the others this time."

Avery deliberately considered this for several seconds during which Ed schooled his expression to a steady impassiveness. Then, finally, Avery drawled, "Okay. When does it come off?"

Here, then, was an admission of what Ed had suspected.

"Tonight," Ed said. "Help yourself to the first big batch you can round up."

Now Avery's glance probed Ed's directly for the first time. "Tonight? What the hell does Hall think I am, stickin' my neck out that far? They're on the prod across there."

"Tonight they'll be twenty miles south, combin' the trails below town," Ed lied blandly. "Hall's fixin' that."

"Why south? They know how we took the herd out."

"Hall's out after a man's scalp. Worth doesn't give much of a damn about the cattle he lost."

"Who's scalp? Sam Richards's?"

"No. A sidekick of Richards travelin' under the name of Nugent."

Avery smiled broadly. Then he seemed to think of something else, for his expression tightened once more with distrust. "How do I know Tom sent you?"

"Why would I be turnin' up with a story like this if he didn't?" Ed asked impatiently. "What's eatin' you? Ain't you getting enough out of this?"

The renegade was evidently satisfied. "I'm only bein' careful. Far as the money goes, nothin' could be better than keeping it all like I did this last time, could it?"

Ed didn't answer, even though this was further proof of Avery's having done more than one job for Hall. He turned away and ducked under the rail, pulling loose his reins and stepping up into the saddle. He looked down at Avery once more.

"Tom said to make it late. Right after midnight."

"Okay," Avery said. "Only tell him this is the last batch Crawford can handle for a while. He's peddlin' those others to an outfit makin' up a trail herd that's headed into Wyoming."

"Tell Crawford to be careful," Ed drawled, the name meaning nothing to him. He reined on out into the street.

Going away he resisted the impulse to look back at Avery. He let his breath out in a long, relieved sigh. He wondered if he could use what was happening tonight the way he had planned on using it.

IV

PURGATORY SHOWDOWN

Sheriff Coombs had had a hard day—or rather a hard half a night and a day, for Tom Hall had routed him out of bed just before midnight last night. Now as he rode down to Lodgepole at dusk, he was as baffled and weary as he had ever been. His fourteen-man posse had accomplished exactly nothing during the day. Coombs felt like a fool. His common sense had argued all day that Sam had had nothing to do with the disappearance of Anchor's herd. Still, Hall had sworn out a warrant for the wrangler's arrest and it was a sheriff's duty to serve a warrant. So, after making Sam as comfortable as he could in the single cell, he brusquely told a few onlookers out front to clear the walk. Then he went up the street and gave Doc Simpson his keys and sent him back to the jail. Afterward he went to the hotel to eat and order Sam a meal.

Night had settled fully over Lodgepole when Coombs came back to the jail carrying Sam's tray of food. The sheriff grumbled at sighting the jail's darkened window, wondering why Simpson hadn't had the sense to leave the desk lamp lit. He went on into his office, groped his way to the desk, set the tray down, and was reaching to a pocket for a match when a voice stopped him.

"Better pull the blinds first, Sheriff."

Coombs wheeled around so sharply that he nearly lost his balance. His hand stabbed half way down to the .45 at his thigh before he caught himself and took it away again. He knew the voice and he knew that Ed Nugent wouldn't be fool enough to let himself be outdrawn or easily taken after having come here this way.

So Coombs did exactly as Ed had suggested, going to the window and drawing the blind there, then doing the same with the door's upper sash. As he moved back across the room, he began wondering where Nugent was standing. He struck his match and lit the lamp's wick and then turned to look behind him.

Ed sat tilted back in a chair in the room's front corner. His shell belt lay in his lap and his hands rested idly on the chair arms. His lean tanned face was set seriously as he said, "Sheriff, I'm giving myself up. But on one condition."

Coombs was too surprised to speak at once. He swallowed with some difficulty before he managed to ask, "What is it?"

It took Ed all of five minutes to answer that, the lawman interjecting several questions and Sam Richards saying a thing or two from the cell. But at the end of that interval Ed came up out of the chair and walked to the desk, laying shell belt and gun on it.

The lawman watched this and, as Ed turned from the desk, shook his head. "Better keep it, Nugent. You may need it."

"You're sure you want me to, Sheriff?"

"Dead sure."

John Worth caught the sound of several riders coming along the south trail and went outside to stand at the corner of the house. He recognized Laura when her horse cut through the pale wash of light spreading across the yard from the living-room window. A warm feeling of relief and thankfulness ran through him. He was immediately curious when he saw that Bob Coombs followed Laura. The third rider, much taller than the lawman, Worth had never seen before. He stepped on out to the yard gate and called to Laura as she was swinging aground.

She came on to meet him, saying at once, "Are any of the men around, Dad?"

"No." He looked down at her, trying to make out her expression in the darkness. "Why?"

Instead of answering him, she turned and called to the other two who were hanging back in the deeper shadows, "It's all right."

"Something wrong, Laura?" the rancher asked, a worried premonition beginning to nag at him.

Before she could reply, Coombs and the tall man were walking up on them, the sheriff saying, "This is close enough. We don't want anyone surprising us."

"Why all the mystery, Bob?" Worth asked.

"John, meet Ed Nugent, the man that licked Hall," Coombs said without ceremony. "He's got something to tell you. You'd better let him get it said without trying to stop him."

Worth's ready temper came instantly on edge and stayed that way for perhaps a full minute as Ed began speaking. Then incredulity and amazement gradually thinned the rancher's anger. Several times he was on the point of interrupting but caught himself, remembering what Bob Coombs had said.

Ed finished by drawling, "So there you have it. Hall, for some reason, rigged it with Avery to steal those horses. Avery the same as admitted it outright this afternoon. You kicked Sam off the place and got his dander up. When he saw the chance of gettin' back at Hall, he bought that place out from under him. To get even with Sam for that, Hall framed him with this rustlin'."

"Another thing," Coombs said on the heel of Ed's words. "Avery mentioned a tie up with a certain Crawford north of the reservation. You know any other Crawfords across there besides the sheriff, John?"

"No," Worth said quietly.

"Which is why nothin's ever been done about findin' the cattle that have strayed across there," the lawman said.

For several moments none of them spoke. Then John Worth asked in a tight voice, "How can you prove all this, Nugent?"

"Take you up there to the break in the fence and have you watch Avery drive off your beef."

"You wouldn't be proving a thing that way," the rancher retorted. "Suppose you'd met Avery through Sam Richards instead of the way you say you did?"

"John, Nugent came in and offered to give himself up," Coombs growled. "If you're so bull-headed about it, we'll lock him up right here and go up there and corral Avery by ourselves. It's been a long time since I used my fists, but damned if I can't beat the truth out of that devil!"

"Dad," Laura said quietly. "Give in."

It was the pleading note of her voice, the half-pitying expression the faint light showed written on her face that suddenly brought home to John Worth the fact that he was being stubborn and a fool. He had his strong pride but it wilted now. His shoulders slumped and he lifted a hand and ran it across his face, saying wearily, "If it hadn't been for my telling Tom to push Sam Richards out, Al Abbot would still be alive."

Laura put a hand on his arm.

"Hell, yes," Coombs said gruffly. "But nothin's happened we can't mend, John. Hall was bound to kill somebody."

Watching the rancher, Ed saw his back stiffen. Then Worth was saying, "Laura, you stay here. Tom planned on sleeping the crew at the Arrow Creek cabin tonight." He took out his watch and tilted its face so that the weak wash of lamplight from the living room caught it. "We have two hours before Avery takes those cattle through the fence. Plenty of time to get Hall and take him up there with us."

"How do you figure to do that, John?" Coombs asked.

"Don't know yet," Worth answered quietly. "But I'll manage it some way. Bob, you could be throwing my hull on a horse while I go in and get a forty-five."

They stood watching the rancher cross the yard and enter the house. As he disappeared, the lawman breathed fervently, "Here's hopin' we haven't stirred him up too much."

Ten minutes later the three of them rode out from Anchor's lower corral, the rancher insisting bluntly, "This is my affair from now on and I'm going at it my own way, Bob."

"Suit yourself."

"We're taking Tom up to the fence with us. Somehow we'll get our hands on Avery. When they're face to face, we can make them talk. One's sure to sell out the other."

"It might work at that," the sheriff said.

They climbed the ridge trail and Worth rode point for Arrow Creek. And when, forty minutes later, they looked down through the trees and made out the light of the line shack's window, Worth said softly, "There's no point in tipping our hand to Tom. I'll go on down alone and tell him he's needed back at the house. You two can wait along the trail below and jump us as we come out."

Without pausing for them to answer he lifted rein and headed down through the pines. He was gone for nearly a quarter hour. Finally they heard the sound of a horse coming in on them and Coombs drew his Colt and stepped down out of the saddle. But as it turned out his precaution was unnecessary. For John Worth was riding the trail alone.

"Tom and Briggs pulled out about an hour ago," he told them worriedly. "They were headed back to the layout, according to the others. Sandy said Tom had something to talk over with me. I'd better get back there."

"One man's enough to make sure Avery takes those cattle through the fence," Ed put in. "Why not let him go? You can always gather him in later. Let Avery run those cattle across there and, when we trail him, you'll have the proof you want on Crawford."

Coombs nodded, asking, "How does that sound, John?"

"Like sense," Worth replied, lifting rein. "Let's get on back to Anchor."

When they headed on down the trail Worth was in the lead, setting a fast pace.

———∞———

Back along Arrow Creek trail, Matt Briggs's horse had gone lame and he and Tom Hall had stopped while he pried a stone from his bay's left fore-hoof. It was just as Briggs was climbing back into his saddle that they caught the echo of horses. They had pulled off into the pines and watched three riders go by at a stiff trot. Hall recognized only one, John Worth.

As far as Tom Hall knew, Worth had been alone at the ranch most of the day. Even the cook had joined the posse for the hunt. So the Anchor foreman had been at once curious and wary over who the pair siding Worth might be.

"We'll go on in," he had told Briggs uncertainly, hardly knowing what this could mean. They had ridden on to Anchor to find the house lighted and Laura alone there. The oddity of finding John Worth's daughter back home again added to Tom Hall's feeling of disquiet. For a while, after finding Laura there in the living room, he restlessly paced the yard by the bunkhouse, trying to reason out an explanation for the half frightened way the girl had spoken to him. She had never particularly liked him, he knew, but her manner had been different just now, her aloofness replaced by something he was almost sure was fear. She had come out to see her father, she said, and had found the house deserted.

Finally Hall decided she hadn't told him the truth. He called to Briggs, "Matt, pick yourself a spot out here and watch things. Something's goin' on we don't know about."

In the living room the girl had thrown two fresh rounds of pine on the fire and it was blazing now, sending a flickering light out across the room, thinning the shadows the lamplight from the center table didn't reach.

As Hall closed the door he noticed the wary way her glance touched him and dropped away as she said, "Yes, Tom?"

"I'm worried about your father," he said. "Where could he have gone?"

"Any number of places," was her cool reply. "He might even have taken the lower trail to town and missed meeting me."

"Why would he want to go to town?"

A humorless smile drew out the fine line of her lips. "Why would that be your business?" she asked.

He ignored that. "Something could have happened to him."

"Could it?"

Her sureness told him something—she had seen her father and, thinking back, trying his best to remember the look of the riders who had been with John Worth, his impatience to know what lay behind Laura's strange manner all at once got the best of him.

"You've seen him tonight, haven't you?" he queried abruptly.

Fear momentarily touched her glance, giving way to an indignant look. "Aren't you forgetting yourself, Tom? I said I hadn't seen him."

Suddenly a thought struck Hall and he was breathing, "Nugent!" knowing now who that tall rider with Worth had been.

Laura's face paled as she asked, "What was that you said?"

"Nugent and the sheriff, maybe," his voice intoned brittlely. And the quick alarm that came to her blue eyes told him that his guess was close to the mark.

He started toward her and she came up out of the chair, a look of wild fright crossing her face. "What are you doing?" she asked quickly, then stepped in behind the chair and started backing toward the door to the house's bedroom wing, her eyes wide and a sudden look of loathing in them.

He lunged for her then and caught her as she was going through the door, swinging her roughly against the wall. He struck her sharply, hard across the face with an open palm.

"You little hellcat," he rasped. "Where were they headed? Talk, or I'll...."

A sound behind him suddenly brought him wheeling around, his big fist dropping from Laura's arm and streaking toward holster, then freezing within finger spread of his Colt.

Ed Nugent's tall shape filled the doorway. He stood spraddle-legged, a cold smile on his angular, lean face.

"Go ahead, Hall. Make your try." Ed's drawl was soft, almost gentle.

Tom Hall held motionless as rock. An instant ago he had remembered the blurred speed with which this stranger had drawn on Sandy there on the hotel porch, and he knew with a terrible certainty that he was dead the moment his hand touched his forty-five.

"Go ahead," Ed drawled once more, tauntingly.

Hall squared away at him, being careful with his hands. "Why should I?" he asked tonelessly.

Now, from Hall's left, came the faint squeak of metal grating against metal and the Anchor foreman's glance shuttled quickly to that side of the room to see the kitchen door swing open.

Bob Coombs came through the door, halting just clear of it. His hand fisted a .45 which was leveled at Hall. He said sharply, "Come across here, Laura."

The girl's face was chalk-white as she edged out from the wall, stepped around Hall's back, and started across the room.

Ed said, "Unbuckle your belt, Hall. Then we'll see how easy you come apart."

A naked, sickening fear showed on Tom Hall's bruised face now. "What's this you're tryin' to do to me?" he asked helplessly, summoning what anger he could and trying to look indignant. "I was only...."

All at once a gun exploded hollowly across the night outside. A hard blow struck Ed in the back, spinning him half way around. He lurched on into the room and at that instant Hall, seeing that Laura stood between him and the sheriff, whipped a hand to his holstered Colt.

Ed threw himself into a sideward roll. His left shoulder—where Matt Briggs's bullet had slammed into him—hit the floor and a blinding pain flooded through his upper body the instant Tom Hall's gun blasted apart the room's silence. The air-impact of the bullet stirred Ed's shirt along his back. Then he was drawing his gun.

A blow at his chest slammed him back against the wall. Coombs was stepping from behind Laura, trying to get in a shot as Ed fired a second time. Hall's mouth sagged open, an expression of bewilderment and rage crossing his face. But his eyes were already taking on a blank look as he buckled at the waist and toppled off balance, going head down onto the floor.

Laura's horror-stricken glance swept on across to Ed. She cried out softly and ran across to him, kneeling beside him as Coombs went to look at Hall. A quick boot tread sounded crossing the porch outside and a moment later John Worth hurried into the room.

"Dad, help me," Laura said, choking back a sob. She was looking helplessly down at Ed, whose head lay against the boards. Nugent's fingers had lost their grip on the .45 and his long frame had a look of looseness quite like that of Tom Hall's and there was a bright splotch of crimson patterning his shirt at the left shoulder.

John Worth said gravely, "Here, I'll do it," and knelt beside her to roll Ed gently over onto his back.

Coombs came across the room and stood looking down at them, bleakly drawling, "Hall's so much coyote bait." He saw Worth open the lid of Ed's left eye. "Fainted, hasn't he, John?"

The rancher nodded. "Laura, go get some hot water and a clean cloth." He looked up at her, a slow smile patterning his thin face. "And don't worry. He's going to be kickin' around a long while yet."

She let her breath out in a sob of thankfulness and her father gave her a startled look as he was unbuttoning Ed's shirt and drawing it away from the wounded shoulder. "What's come over you, child?"

The way her face reddened, the hurried way she rose and went to the kitchen, made Worth glance up at the sheriff soberly.

"Damned if you can blame her, John," the lawman said positively. "You should've seen him. Fast. And both shots dead center...." He sobered then, eyeing Worth oddly, respectfully. "Was that Briggs you ran into outside?"

John Worth nodded, nothing more. Then he took a closer look at Ed's shoulder, sighing relievedly. "It's a clean hole. No bones broken."

He looked around then as Laura came back into the room carrying a basin of water and a clean towel. She was kneeling beside him again when he asked, "Do you suppose Nugent would want to work here?"

"He's got work, Dad," Laura told him. "With Sam Richards."

"Sam can get another man," John Worth said gruffly. He gave his daughter a sideward glance, mock-serious. "Now I'm not counting on you, Laura. You can help Sam out, like you've done a job helping me on Anchor an' lately even with myself...but I still need a man on this spread. Will you let your father do something right for a change...?"

W(alter) Ryerson Johnson

was born in Divernon, Illinois. "Pulp fiction," he once commented, was "a never-never land that existed only in the glowing imagination of the writer and the transient 'suspension of disbelief' of the reader. Bigger than life. Adult fairy stories." The impulse toward adventure was already in him as a teenager when, having "listened to trains go banging through town" for so many years, one night he climbed atop one of them and "went west." He traveled more than 20,000 miles across the United States and Canada. After four years at the College of Commerce in the University of Illinois, Johnson took a story-writing class as an elective. The result was "The Squeeze." He sold it to *Adventure* where it appeared in the issue dated March 3, 1926. His stories after that were published in a wide variety of magazines, among them *Top-Notch, Western Story Magazine, Cowboy Stories, Short Stories, West, Ace-High Magazine,* and most recently *Louis L'Amour Western Magazine.* He wrote only two Western novels, SOUTH TO SONORA (Samuel Curl, 1946) and BARBWIRE (Arcadia House, 1947), but they are well worth reading. A collection of his Western stories recently appeared in a trade paperback edition from Barricade Books. In 1939 Johnson created one of his most popular and enduring series characters, Len Siringo, range detective and master of disguises. He wrote twenty stories in all about Siringo in the years 1939 - 1943. With the exception of his third Siringo story, which appeared in *Ace-High Western Stories,* the others were all published in *Star Western.* This is the Len Siringo story published in *Ace-High Western Stories.*

Powder Smoke— Guest of Faro Flats

W alt Saxon looked across the counter at the girl in the white apron in the Little Gem restaurant. His voice wasn't any too steady as he said, "It won't be long now till you can quit dishin' up for the whole of Faro Flats. You'll be cookin' jus' for me…and every Double Saxon brand I slap on a cow'll be for you!"

There was a soft look in her hazel eyes. "I still can't believe it," she murmured. "Hugo Kern has gun-bossed Faro Flats for so long…."

"There has to come an end to everything, but for us it's just a beginning, June!"

There were tears of happiness in her eyes. Then a shadow seemed to cross her face. "I…I wish I could feel more confident about it, somehow."

"I know. With Kern rustlin' the valley blind, forcin' one rancher after another to the wall…."

"And every man afraid to raise a little finger against him!"

Bitterness crept into Walt Saxon's voice. "Every time a man's rared up for his rights, Kern's gunned him down…till he's got us like a bunch of rabbits! What we've been needin' is to all rare up together. But we haven't had a leader."

"You could be their leader, Walt," she told him, adoringly.

He frowned. "They think I'm too young. It'll take somebody with a gun-rep from border to border to make 'em listen." He leaned closer; his voice quickened. "That's the secret I promised you. I've located a leader. The best man in the West for the job. I wrote him a letter and he wrote me back to say he'd come."

She kindled to his excitement. "It's not...it couldn't be...Len Siringo?"

Walt set his fist down hard on the counter. "Len Siringo!" he said.

They stared at each other, listening to the soft, exciting ring in their ears that the name made. Len Siringo, cunning as a fox, bold as a springtime grizzly, range detective number-one for the Cattlemen's Association, a scourge to the long-haired gents who came down from the dim trails to harry outlying herds and gun-boss trail towns.

The screen door up front slammed shut as a man entered and came forward with a slow, ungainly stride, a carpetbag thumping against his gangling legs. A stogy, tight in his wide mouth, trailed blue smoke.

"Howdy folks," he greeted, talking around the stogy.

June moved to face him across the counter. She observed that his hat was flat crowned and fully two inches narrower in the brim than was locally worn, and that his salt and pepper suit, with the trouser legs tucked in short boots, showed hard saddle wear. She said: "If you took that cigar out of your mouth, friend, maybe I could understand you better."

The man pried the smoker from in between his mouth and his black mustache. "It ain't a cigar," he said flatly.

"What is it then?"

"Stogy. Gen-u-ine Marsh Wheeling stogy, smoked to fame by the Conestoga wagon boys since 1840 and still puffin' strong. My card."

June fingered the card, read it aloud, haltingly: "Nel Og-nir-is...the Denver Drummer."

She looked speculatively at him. "That's an uncommon impressive name, stranger. You're selling what?"

"Stogies mostly. But before I sell you some, my beautiful, I crave bivalves. My stomach says I'm hungry."

"Let me guess," June said, eyes laughing. "Oysters!"

"Oysters."

"How do you like them?"

"Well now, I'll tell you. I take my mollusks softly soaked in beefsteak gravy."

June got one of the brick-shaped cans of cove oysters out of the window and delivered them to her father in the kitchen. Old Dad

Coulter, as he was known in Faro Flats, was owner, cook, and foreman of the Little Gem, and June was his one-man crew. Once he had owned a small ranch. But that was before Hugo Kern had unleashed his gun-rule in the valley. Old Dad Coulter had been one of the first to be frozen out.

Left alone with the assertive drummer, Walt Saxon asked pleasantly, "Been long in town?"

"Jus' hove in."

"Then you ain't signed with Hugo Kern yet?"

"How you mean, son?"

"You better get over to his saloon while the oysters are preparin' and sign," Walt said in concern. "This is a one-man town. Everybody that comes here has to check in with Kern and state his business."

"And if Kern don't like 'em, he runs 'em out?"

"That's it."

"Supposin' they refuse to be run out?"

"Sooner or later Kern's gunnies carry 'em out...mostly sooner."

The drummer nodded soberly. "All up and down the line I been hearin' about Kern's hold on this section."

Talk lagged, and pretty soon June came with the oysters. She eased the huge platter to the counter. The Denver drummer said, "Ah-h-h," and started eating with gusto. But he didn't put his stogy down. He chewed and puffed indiscriminately.

Curiosity drew Dad Coulter out of the kitchen. When he couldn't stand it any longer, he asked mildly, "How come you smoke and eat at the same time, mister?"

"Because that's how I like it," the Denver drummer said.

Dad Coulter scratched at his bald head. "Good enough reason, I reckon."

From outside sounded the clump of boots on the wooden sidewalk. The screen door creaked open and didn't shut until two men were inside. They came forward, walking with a slow, deliberate swagger. One of the men wore a law badge. The other held his arm with unnatural stiffness against his side, as though he carried something concealed under his coat which he didn't want to slip. Both men were holstered. Both had meanness hard-bitten into their hides.

Walt nudged the drummer. "They're here about you not signin' in!"

298 / W. Ryerson Johnson

The Denver drummer paid no attention, just went on smoking and eating. Hugo Kern's men came close and watched him with pardonable interest.

"What's he smokin' at the same time for?" one of them asked.

Sam Gully was marshal of Faro Flats and entitled to know.

"On account that's how he likes it," Dad Coulter informed.

Sam Gully said, "Huh," and took a hitch on his gun belt and questioned the stranger directly.

"Who are you?"

"Nel Ogniris," the drummer told him.

"Nel!" Sam Gulley scoffed. "That's a girl's name."

"It's my name," the drummer told him, patiently.

"Yeah? Why didn't you sign in with Kern?"

The Denver drummer took another puff on the stogy and started angling for an oyster—and Sam Gully pressed closer. A gravied oyster high on the drummer's fork slipped off with a plop into the platter. Gray goo spattered all over Sam Gully's wide front. He stepped back, cursing. The drummer bent to open his carpet bag.

"Tut-tut," he admonished. "I carry a cleaning fluid which is the best thing for gravy spots on the market."

Sam Gully aimed a kick at the drummer's hand. Somehow, the kick went astray and the marshal's foot drove into the counter boards. His face darkened with anger and he made a strike for his open-flap holster; but his companion, Lobo Kid Widin, put a hand on his shoulder, and muttered, "Take it easy, Sam. Remember, Kern's got plans about this old geezer."

The drummer smiled at them, unperturbed. "Smoke up, gents." He bestowed a stogy on each of them. "Gen-u-ine Marsh Wheelings. I've sold 'em in every state west of the Mississippi...and if my cleaner won't take out the gravy spots, why I represent a tailor in Cheyenne, and I can take your measure right here."

Sam Gully made a noise deep in his throat, swiveled his squat body around and barked at Walt Saxon. "It's only incidental that we come lookin' fer this oyster-face fool here. *You're* the main reason!"

Walt Saxon blinked his eyes. "Huh? Me?"

"Yeah, you." The marshal pulled a piece of note paper from his pocket. "Read that."

Walt unfolded the sheet. Even before he read it, his face went white as the paper. This was his own writing. It was the letter he had written with such high hopes to Len Siringo, detailing the terror that stalked the valley, and appealing to Siringo to come to Faro Flats and lead the beaten ranchers and townfolks to a gun-smoke show-down with Hugo Kern. His full name, Walt Saxon, was signed boldly to the letter.

"What you got to say?" Sam Gully demanded.

Walt felt himself growing numb, stiffening in mind and body, as his sub-conscious self sought to throw up a barrier against hurt. His dreams of release for the valley ranchers—he would never live to see them realized. And June, looking at him so white-faced across the counter.... They would kill him, of course, as they had killed everyone else who had contested their gun-rule.

As though from a long distance off, Walt heard himself asking, "Where'd you get this letter?"

Sam Gully's words came chopping, "From Len Siringo's dead body!"

"We scooped him up in Midnight Cañon," the Lobo Kid said pleasantly. "I mean *scooped*."

"He had the front of his head shot off," Sam Gully detailed.

Walt's lips made slow talk. "Sounds like Bent-Nose Jennifer. He's the only one who works regular with a sawgun, and Kern keeps him spotted at the cañon pass, doesn't he?"

"You're askin' us?" Sam Gully snarled. He jerked his head to-ward the drummer. "Frisk this stogy-smokin' oyster's carpetbag," he told the Lobo Kid.

Lobo Kid Widin grinned maliciously and, with his back to the others, he bent over the bag, pawing. When he turned around, he held a sawed-off shotgun. "Found this murder instrument buried under the stogies in his bag, Marshal. It's undoubtedly the gun that killed that pore range detective."

Sam Gully smirked. "I arrest you, oyster-face, for the murder of Len Siringo."

"Frame-up!" Walt Saxon barked. He knew it wouldn't do any good, but he couldn't help calling the deal for what it was. "The Lobo Kid had that sawgun under his coat when he came in here."

Walt could understand the workings of Hugo Kern's mind on this. With Len Siringo so well known all over the West, there had to be an alibi for his killing. So Kern was clearing his own gunners by pinning the crime on this stranger. But that was only half of Kern's sly plan. Walt, in concern over the deal being handed the drummer had, for the moment, forgotten that he himself stood condemned by his signed letter found in the dead man's pocket. He remembered it fast enough when Sam Gully waved his six-gun and said, "You, Walt Saxon, I arrest likewise for aidin' and harborin' a criminal."

"You'll both get a fair trial," Lobo Kid Widin added, "and quick swingin' justice."

"Shore," the marshal said. "The wild days is gone in Faro Flats. This is a settled cow community and we execute legal." He jerked his head toward the door. "Git goin', you two."

The Denver drummer seemed to have no realistic idea of the tight place he was in. "Leave me eat one more oyster," he begged. He reached toward the platter.

What happened then was one of those incredible things which have to be witnessed to be understood, and even then seem hardly real. With Lobo Kid Widin's sawgun and Sam Gully's six-shooter both holding on him, the Denver drummer swung around on the stool, kicked the sawgun out of the Kid's hands and at the same split-wink slammed the platter of oysters in Sam Gully's face. It was the utter unexpectedness of it, of course, which made it possible. The drummer had appeared to be such a clumsy, helpless fool.

Sam Gully bellowed and blazed two shots but, with the well gravied oysters slipping over his face, his shots were wild. Walt Saxon got into it by throwing both fists at the Lobo Kid and the drummer scooped up the sawgun from the floor and knocked Sam Gully's six-shooter spinning.

"Get 'em up!" he screamed.

Sam Gully grimaced at the feel of the oysters crawling inside the unbuttoned neck of his shirt but, under the menace of the scatter-gun in the drummer's shaking hands, he reached high, and so did Lobo Kid Widin. In that moment, the Denver drummer had everything his own way. Then he did an incomprehensible thing.

He said, "I am a man that has got respect for the legal law. It grieves me to be strong-armin' the marshal. I will go with you boys to Mister Kern and we will straighten this all out."

Sam Gully swapped a disbelieving glance with Lobo Kid Widin, then growled, "All right, put that gun down."

"No," the drummer said firmly, "if I did that, you are so excited that you might do somethin' violent to me or my young friend here.

But I will go with you, like I said, and turn the gun over to Mister Kern."

"All right, come on," Sam Gully said hoarsely.

The drummer bowed, "You first, gents."

They started trooping toward the front of the restaurant.

"You're crazy!" Walt lashed out at the drummer. "Kern will hang you, and me, too."

"Surely you exaggerate, my young friend," the drummer said. "Have a smoke." He pushed one of the stogies in Walt's hand as he scuffed past him on the way to the door.

"I...don't smoke!" Walt blurted inanely.

"You're old enough to learn," the drummer called back. "Tear the stogy up if you got doubts about it. You'll find it's solid leaf filler...a good smoke since 1840. Look under the band. My name's printed on it. Read it backwards or forwards, it's still my name, and I personally stand back of every stogy I sell."

The screen door slammed as the three disappeared into the sun-drenched street. The three who were left behind looked at each other.

"Somethin' danged peculiar about that *hombre*," Dad Coulter opined, trying to swamp the fear that pressed like something alive against them all.

June gripped Walt's arm with her small, warm hand. Her pretty lips quivered. "You've got to ride!"

"And leave you here? Not a chance."

"You're the one who's in danger...."

"Wait a minute," Walt cut in, excitedly. "Dad's right! There is somethin' peculiar about that drummer. He seemed so dumb and helpless, but he was always there in the pinches. And did you notice his eyes? Sharp as quartz. I wonder...?" He looked at the stogy the drummer had put in his hand as a parting gift. "What was it he said about this stogy? It was almost like he was trying to tell us something without letting Sam Gully and the Lobo Kid know. Think hard, everybody. What were his exact words?"

"He said...look under the band," June spoke doubtfully. "Something about his name being printed on it...read it backwards or forwards."

Walt had already slipped the band off and opened it out straight. On the inside of the band, written in pencil, was the name Len Siringo.

302 / W. Ryerson Johnson

"What does it mean?" June gasped. Then her agile mind started figuring. "Len," she said the name aloud. "L-e-n. Spell it backwards and it's N-e-l. Nel! And Siringo...it's O-g-n-i-r-i-s!"

"Then Nel Ogniris is Len Siringo!" Walt said. "It can't be, but ...it is!"

They stared silently, a wild unnamed hope struggling with their fears.

"Listen," Walt reasoned tensely, "it could have been like this. Len Siringo, comin' in answer to my letter, could have been jumped by Bent-Nose Jennifer in Midnight Cañon *and the dead man found there could be Bent-Nose Jennifer himself!* Siringo could have been fox enough to turn the tables, shot Bent-Nose with that hellion's own spreader. There wouldn't be much left to identify about the face if a scatter-gun took it close up. And they're both about of a size. Siringo could have dressed the body to make it look like himself, and put my letter in the pocket and all."

"By-gum, ye got it, Walt!" Dad Coulter put in excitedly. "Then after disposin' of Bent-Nose Jennifer, why Siringo he come on here, dressed like the Denver drummer and actin' like the fool to throw off suspicion. Right to the restaurant he come, like you told him to in the letter. But afore he had time to sound out the situation, Kern's gunners come in."

"And like he always does, never missin' a bet, Siringo had this stogy made up, ready for an emergency."

"But why," June wailed, "did he let himself be taken to Kern?"

"I'm dark about that, too," Walt admitted. "Wait a minute! Didn't he say something about the stogy being solid filler or something, and to tear it up and examine it if I had any doubts?"

Walt's unsteady hands were already unraveling the tobacco. His interpretation was correct. Concealed within the twisted leaf was a note in small lettered writing. Walt read it aloud:

Everything moving along according to plan. Sizing up the situation before I got here, I saw that what the ranchers needed to make them stand up on their hind legs and fight, was a rallying issue. I'm in. When they learn that the stranger in Hugo Kern's jail is Len Siringo who came to help them, I figure they'll be plumb shamed into making a united stand. Your job's to spread the word and have everybody on hand for the trial. Good luck.

Dad Coulter's old eyes were frankly wet. "What a *hombre*! Riskin' hisself like that fer all us that he never even knowed personal."

Walt's own eyes were moist.

June pressed his hand. "Hurry, darling." She didn't cry until he had gone from the room.

From ranch to ranch Walt Saxon carried the word that afternoon, eluding Hugo Kern's gunners who cruised the trails, looking for him. With new hope like a flame in their eyes, other ranchers shared the responsibility of getting the news around. One man told another, two told four, and four told eight. And so the word went out that the scapegoat stranger who had fallen into Hugo Kern's hands was no ordinary stranger, but the well-nigh famous Len Siringo who had come to Faro Flats to lend his guns and his cunning in a crusade of extermination of two-legged range rodents. The womenfolk of the valley had their part in the affair too. Skirts fluttered as they scurried about, lips murmured excitedly, and nimble fingers mysteriously made needles fly.

The moon that night threw moving shadows on the white rangeland floor as silent, hard-faced men, singly and in groups, converged on Faro Flats. The first slant rays of the morning sun found them straggling into town.

Hugo Kern and his men eyed them with restless suspicion. Kern had announced hanging circuses before, but they had never elicited the interest this one had. The ranchers crowding into Kern's Crystal Palace Saloon and Gambling Hall, which was to serve as a court room, far outnumbered Kern's own men. This made him inordinately careful to see that no one off his payroll got through the green-shuttered doors without shedding belt and holstered gun.

When the trial opened, the only guns showing were Kern guns, and Kern's men occupied the strategic places at doors and windows. Tilted against the bar was a new plank coffin containing the body of the man who had been shot dead in Midnight Cañon. Near it, the hawk-nosed prisoner sat in a straight-backed chair and calmly puffed a stogy.

Hugo Kern stood in the place of prominence near the bar, his black eyes keeping morose tab on everything that transpired, his heavy jowls set in their perpetual frown. His hand was puffy and white and it moved constantly, the lumpy fingers first massaging the silver log chain that sprawled across his vest, then feeling at his holster where the ornamental silver gun butt protruded noticeably. At a sign from him, a man in a black cape stepped out from the crowd into the cleared space before the bar.

The man was "Judge" Hamilton Knobstone. His stringy hair was gray and the skin hung slack on his bony face. His red-veined eyes had a liquor-soaked look. Somewhere in his past he laid claim to dubious legal experience.

"Hear ye, hear ye," Judge Knobstone declaimed in his rasping voice, "the court is now open. The prisoner will stop smoking his cigar and pay alert attention to proceedings."

"It ain't a cigar," the prisoner said.

"What...what's that?" the judge was startled into demanding.

"It's a gen-u-ine Marsh Wheeling stogy. Smoked to fame by the Conestoga wagon boys. I sell 'em. After the trial I'll be pleased to serve any and all. The sweetest smoke a man ever got in his mouth. I thank you."

"After the trial," the judge lectured severely, "you won't be in shape to serve no one. Prayers is more in order for you than sales talks for stogies." He got a laugh from Kern's men on that one. "We'll get right on with the hangin'," he continued. "Correction...I mean the trial." He took his laugh on that, then pointed a bony finger at the prisoner. "Nel Ogniris...God knows that name's enough to hang anyone...you are charged with the foul murder of Len Siringo. Guilty or not guilty?"

"Not guilty, Your Honor."

"That answer not bein' unexpected," the judge said, "I shall produce witnesses to testify different. Marshal Sam Gully and Lobo Kid Widin, take the stand."

The two came truculently forward, grinning, and testified to finding the murder gun in the drummer's bag.

"The evidence bein' disinterested and conclusive," Judge Knobstone said sternly, "and the murdered man smellin' to high heaven in spite of bein' wrapped in a rag carpet and weighted down with ice, I hereby, without further fol-de-rol, rule the prisoner guilty as charged, and the court adjourned for a hangin'."

Scattered cries of acclaim went up from Kern's men but, after the sounds had died, the atmosphere of thick and sullen brooding rolled in again. The unnatural tension was so great that Kern's men felt it. Their eyes roved restlessly, and their hands stayed close to their guns.

It was the prisoner himself who broke the tension, with a quick reminder, "Ain't a condemned man, Your Honor, always entitled to a few last words before he dies?"

The prisoner had dropped his half smoked stogy on the floor, and from an inside pocket extracted a fresh one. He held it unlighted in his hand. As the judge nodded him permission to speak, he stood up slowly and stretched his lank body.

What he said surprised everybody. Wagging the long stogy toward the remains in the coffin, he said, "If it's him you're talkin' about, I killed him. Sure. I had to."

"You...you wish to change your plea of not guilty?" Judge Knobstone sputtered.

"No. I still claim I didn't kill Len Siringo. But I killed that fella in the coffin."

"Just who," the judge blasted, "do you think is dead in the coffin?"

"You asked that question of the right party, Your Honor. I'm the only one that knows. It's Bent-Nose Jennifer."

A stir went up from Kern's men, but the brooding silence which gripped the ranchers only deepened. The piercing eyes of the prisoner were locking glances with the grim-faced ranchers. One after another he held them for a flashing instant in a kind of hypnotic spell, counseling courage and foreshadowing a quick end to waiting.

"That there is Len Siringo in the coffin!" the judge ruled.

"It's possible, I reckon," the prisoner said softly, "but plumb debatable on account when I was born my pappy and ma, they said I was Len Siringo."

He made his pronouncement in such even tones that it was a moment before anyone in the big room got it. He stood there waiting, holding the long unlighted stogy by one end, and tapping it gently against the fingers of his other hand while his eyes roved the room.

Then, one of Kern's men bellowed hoarsely, "By God, he's right! I seen Len Siringo once...and this gent's him, sure as shootin'!"

A rumbling stir went over the room, like the beginnings of a rockslide avalanche and quick emotional release came to the ranchers as, one and all, they realized that now had come an end to waiting. One and all, then, they moved their hands in a swift, mysterious gesture confusing to the eye. They weren't the only ones whose hands were moving. Such was the frightful magic of Len Siringo's name on hair-trigger nerves that from their places of vantage all over the room a full score of Kern's men cleared guns from leather. There was at the same time a jostling surge toward the bar, as each man sought to quell his fear with the hope that his bullet might be the first to reach the dreaded range detective.

But it was the big boss who threw the first lead. Hugo Kern's rise over the hellions of Faro Flats had not been predicated so much on bullets as on brains. That pudgy hand wasn't so fast as the hands of many of his men. But his brain worked faster. In this instance, with his wolfish jowls locked tightly, he went for his a scant second before anyone else in the house did, his small eyes gleaming malignantly. His gun roared first—and that was probably why he died first, hitting the floor with a dull thud.

Hugo Kern died, literally, at the point of a stogy. At the point of a stogy flung by Len Siringo with the speed of a bullet. The stogy was an exceptional one. Under its tobacco leaf wrapping, it was weighted with lead at one end. It was the other end which struck Hugo Kern over the heart. The tobacco leaf wrapping crumbled and a thin steel blade, under the driving force of the lead-weighted handle, penetrated through to the heart, killing him instantly. So that was how Hugo Kern, gun-boss of Faro Flats, died at the point of a stogy. Others died, too. Men who have anything worth fighting for risk dying when they fight—and many died on this early morning in the Crystal Palace Saloon and Gambling Hall. But it wasn't only the ranchers who crumpled to the jolt of gun lead. The ranchers, as it turned out, weren't as helpless as they appeared. All in all, they got away to a good start, plunging into action as soon as Kern's men did, taking a terrible toll of lives.

The Faro Flats gunnies, of course, hadn't any way to know about the activities of womenfolk of the evening before in every ranch house in the valley, this activity consisting largely of the ripping of men's pants along one seam and sewing up again of the seam with loose basting threads—after hideaway guns had been fastened makeshift, flat against the thighs. Kern's men had seen all the openly-holstered guns checked at the door. That was why they couldn't believe their eyes when the ranchers boiled out of their chairs, blazing lead. The saloon rocked to the gun-thunder that rolled and rumbled in waves of sound.

Len Siringo heaved up in his chair and leaped off the bar with it, ramming into Kern's howling, blasting mob. Men gave way, cursing, throwing wild bullets, trying to bring him down. Out of the tail of his eye, Siringo saw that Sam Gully was already down. He dropped the chair and snapped up Gully's lost six-shooter from the floor. He raged through the mob, and a man died each time he pressed the trigger.

Walt Saxon raged with him. He had doubled back to town just before daylight and had been hiding out in the Little Gem, waiting. When he heard the shooting, he hurried to get in on it, with Dad Coulter clumping grimly along behind. The fighting reached a high and horrible crescendo of sound, with lead criss-crossing to form a ragged spider-web pattern of death, with men screaming, cursing, moaning, praying—while gun smoke reeked in the air and blood drooled and spattered. The Crystal Palace Saloon was a shambles of death.

Men began pushing out through the batwings then, as though the lead and smoke and spilled blood had left no room inside. They pushed out and ran in every direction. Hugo Kern's swaggering gun-bullies. Running!

But the embattled ranchers stayed inside and fought to boothill showdown every gunny who had the courage to stay with them. Then, almost as suddenly as it had started, there was no more roar of guns, splat of lead. There was only the sun shining, the bright new sun of morning, betokening a new era for Faro Flats and its citizens.

Doc Skelton opened up his satchel and got to work on the living. Billy Blossom, barber and undertaker, laid out a dead man's row with Hugo Kern, Sam Gully, and Lobo Kid Widin heading the line. Surprise, numbers, and wrathful determination—not to mention Len Siringo—having been on the side of the ranchers, they had astonishingly few representatives in dead man's row.

As soon as they could, they found each other, the original four, Len Siringo, Walt, June, and Dad Coulter. There were smiles on the powder-grimed faces of the men.

Walt, with a powder burn across one cheek and one arm in a sling, had his other arm tightly around June. "I wish you could stay long enough for the weddin', anyhow, Mister Siringo," he said earnestly.

"Like to son, but...the West is wide. I won't be needed here any more. Other duties call."

"If there was only some little special thing we could do for you," June put in eagerly, "to show how grateful we are!"

Len Siringo looked at her with one of his rare smiles. "Well, there is just one thing...."

"Oh, tell me!" June pressed close, her eyes shining.

"If you could, now, arrange to take them stogies off my hands. I don't like to be luggin' 'em around with me any longer. Two carpetbags full...gen-u-ine Marsh Wheelings, smoked to fame by the Conestoga wagon boys."

"Them's gonna be my fastest sellin' ceegars," Dad Coulter affirmed.

"Stogies," Len Siringo corrected.

"All right, stogies." Dad Coulter plucked at the great man's sleeve. "Tell me something. Why in tarnation was you smokin' while you et?"

"On account that's how I like it," Len Siringo said.

Les(lie) Savage, Jr. was born in Alhambra, California. He grew

up in Los Angeles. The first story he wrote was accepted by the publisher to whom it was sent—"Bullets and Bullwhips" appeared in Street & Smith's *Western Story Magazine* (10/2/43). Almost ninety more magazine stories followed. Savage's first book publisher announced on the dust jacket of TREASURE OF THE BRASADA (Simon and Schuster, 1947) that it came from "a young writer of enormous power and imagination. We are proud to present it as the first novel to appear under the imprint: *Essandess Westerns*." Notwithstanding, due to Savage's preference for historical accuracy, he also ran into problems with book editors. As a result of the censorship imposed on many of his works, only now can they be fully restored by returning to the author's original manuscripts. TABLE ROCK (Walker, 1993), FIRE DANCE AT SPIDER ROCK (Five Star Westerns, 1995), THE LEGEND OF SEÑORITA SCORPION (Circle V Westerns, 1996), and MEDICINE WHEEL (Five Star Westerns, 1997) are among the first of these restorations. SIX-GUN BRIDE OF THE TETON BUNCH (Barricade Books, 1995) is a notable Savage short story collection now available in a trade paperback edition.

Savage died young, at thirty-five, from complications arising out of hereditary diabetes and elevated cholesterol. However, his considerable legacy lives after him, there to reach a new generation of readers. "Trail of the Lonely Gun" was first published in Action Stories (Spring, 46). The original manuscript was used to restore this story so that it appears here as the author had intended.

Trail of the
Lonely Gun

I

When the sound came, Johnny Vickers stiffened, and the lever on his sixteen-shot Henry snicked softly to the pull. Moonlight coming in the doorway of the miner's shack fell meagerly across his face, its upper half obliterated by the solid, black shadow laid across it by the brim of his flat-topped hat, his long, unshaven jaw trusting forward in an habitual aggression that drew his lips thin under the aquiline dominance of his nose. The collar of his alkali-whitened denim coat was turned up around the sunburned column of his neck, and his legs were long and saddle-drawn in sweat-stiff Ute leggings with greasy fringe down their seams. Across the gurgle of Granite Creek and on down Thumb Butte Road, he could see Prescott's lights glowing yellow in the soft blackness of the August night.

"Kern?" he said.

"No, Vickers," the man outside answered. "Perry Papago. I'll come in, *si*?"

The half-breed's figure blotted light from the square gloom of the door momentarily; then he was inside, bending forward slightly, as if to peer at Johnny Vickers. In the shadows, Papago's pock-marked face was barely visible to Vickers, the whites of his eyes pale, shifting enigmas above the mobile intelligence of his broad mouth. He wore nothing but a pair of dirty *chivarras* and a short leather vest, and his shoulders were limned smooth and coppery against the dim glow from outside. Vickers marked the three pounds of Remington .44 still in Papago's holster before he spoke.

"You took a chance walking in like that."

"I didn't know it was so bad," said Papago, and his eyes were taking in the acrid rigidity of Vickers's figure. "But I guess I'd be pretty spooky, too, if I'd been hiding out on a murder charge for over a month. They don't give you much peace, do they, Vickers? I hear Deputy Calavaras almost had you last week up in Skull Valley."

"Never mind," said Vickers.

"Why did you really kill Edgar James, Vickers?" asked Papago. "He was such a nice young man. Just because you and him were rival editors…?"

"He was a swilling rumpot who thought he could find out everything that went on in Arizona territory by sitting on his hocks in front of that two-bit *Courier* and…." Johnny Vickers stopped, breathing hard, trembling with the effort of holding all the bitterness of this last month in him. Finally he spoke again from between his teeth. "I told you…never mind."

"But I will mind," said Perry Papago. "I always liked you, Vickers. If there's one square man with the Indians in Prescott, you're it. Your editorials stopped more than one Indian war from starting. The Moquis at Walpi won't be quick to forget how the Christmas article you wrote kept them from starving in 'seventy-four." His voice had lost its former mockery. "We don't blame you for killing James. He bucked every decent thing you tried to do for the Indians. That's why I'm here, Vickers. Any other man, we wouldn't care, but you always played square with us, and we don't want you to get in any bigger tight than you're already in. We don't want you to do this."

Vickers moved faintly, the Henry scraping against his Levi's coat. "Don't want me to do what?"

"I know you're here to meet Judge Kern," said Papago. "Do you know why he wanted you?"

"I know something's happened to his daughter," said Vickers.

"The Apaches got Sherry Kern," said Papago. "The judge wants you to get her back."

The irony of that almost drew a laugh from Vickers. "Why me?" he said finally.

"Because you're his last card," said Papago. "You know those Indians like nobody else does around here, and you're the only one who might be able to reach them without endangering Sherry Kern's life. They took her off the Butterfield stage between here and Tucson, killed the other passengers, burnt the coach. About a week later, Kern was contacted. You know four companies of dragoons were just moved from Tucson up here to Prescott. Kern was given till the end of August to have those troops moved back, or his daughter would be returned to him, dead."

"And Kern thinks it's Apaches?" said Vickers. "What about the Tucson machine? You know how Prescott and Tucson have been fighting for twelve years to see which one becomes the seat of the territorial capital. The legislature's convened in Tucson these past three years, and the Tucson machine's gotten fat on the plum of having it in their town. The movement of these troops to Prescott undoubtedly means the capital's being shifted, too. If the legislature starts convening up here again, the balance of power will shift back to Kern's party, and the Tucson machine will be washed up. You know the machine would do anything to keep that from happening. If they could force those troops back to Tucson, they'd have a big start in keeping the capital there. No legislature's going to meet anywhere in this territory without the protection of the military."

"You're loco," said Papago. "The Tucson machine doesn't have anything to do with this. You know that those dragoons were sent up here by the Department of Arizona as an opening campaign against the northern Apaches. Crook's through with the Tontos, and he's coming up here, that's all. The Apaches just took this way to stop it. Forget the Tucson machine. Forget everything. Just get out of here and don't have anything to do with Kern!"

"I'd rather see the judge first."

"You won't leave?"

"I don't think so."

Papago's hand was stiff, now, and he seemed to incline his short, square torso forward perceptibly. "There are other ways of stopping you besides asking you."

Vickers's big Henry lifted slightly till its bore covered the belt buckle of Navajo silver glittering against Papago's belly. "Go ahead," he said, "if you want to."

"I don't have to," said Papago, and his gaze shifted over Vickers's shoulder. "All right, Combabi, you can take his Henry."

"No, Combabi," said someone else from behind Vickers, "you leave his Henry right where it is."

Vickers stood tense till he heard the movement behind him, then shifted so he could see without taking his gun off Papago. There was no rear door to this old miner's shack, but the roof above the room had caved in, pulling part of the log wall in with it. Combabi must have slipped through the opening while Papago and Vickers were talking; it would have taken a full-blooded Indian to do it without Vickers's hearing. Combabi crouched there now, surprise in the tension of his body, if not in the dark enigma of his hook-nosed face. There was something frustrated about the way he gripped the big dragoon cap-and-ball in both dirty hands. The man above Combabi on what was left of the decaying log wall had pulled the tails of his pin-striped cutaway up about his lean shanks in order to get there, and a hairy, old beaver hat sat like a stovepipe on his head. The faint glow from the town's lights caught his snowy sideburns and luxurious mustache.

"Kern!" said Vickers. "Looks like we have a potful tonight."

"Getting right spry in my old age," grunted Judge Kern, lowering himself gingerly from the wall with the four-barreled pepperbox still very evident in one slender hand. He waved the ugly little gun at Combabi. "Put away your smokebox and get on inside."

Combabi moved like a snake, without apparent effort, or sound. He shoved the dragoon back in its tattered black holster and got to his feet and moved around Vickers sullenly till he stood near Papago, his shifty eyes glittering in the light of the moon filtering into the shack.

"Sorry to be late, Vickers," said Kern, pulling his coat back to stuff the pepperbox in a pocket of his white marseille waistcoat. "Guess it's just as well, though. I saw this here Indian sneaking in through that hole at the back and decided I'd better see what the arrangements were. He just sat there listening to you talk, so I thought I might as well hear a little of the confabulation, too. Oddly enough, Papago was right about this not being the Tucson machine. I'll admit it fits in with their aims rather fortuitously, but I've had an investigator in Tucson a long time now, and I'd take his word on it. He says, no."

Judge Kern stopped, something coming into his eyes as he stared at Vickers. There was a fierce pride in Kern's high-browed, eagle-beaked face that otherwise held him from any display of emotion. It was probably the only evidence Vickers would ever get of what this meant to the judge. He could sense all the hell the old man must have been through these last days. Then the sympathy was blotted out by the other emotions Vickers had felt toward Kern throughout the preceding weeks. Kern saw it in his face and caught his hard arm.

"I know, Vickers, I know. I've hounded you and hunted you and driven you like an animal this last month, and you don't owe me anything. But you know how close I was to Edgar James. He was like my own son. You couldn't blame a person for wanting the man caught who murdered his own son. You don't know what it took for me to contact you like this, and come to you. But you're my last hope. You're the only man with enough friends among the Indians around here to do any good. We can't make a move with the troops. If we so much as sent a vedette out of town, I'd be afraid the Apaches would kill Sherry. I'm not asking you to do this from the goodness of your heart, Vickers. I'll promise you amnesty if you get my daughter back. Enough amnesty for you to come back into Prescott and start your paper again, if you want it. Anything, Vickers, anything."

Vickers turned his lean, mordant face down a moment. "Mogollon Kid?" he said finally.

"I don't know who took her," said Kern, desperation leaking into his voice. "I thought you'd know."

"I don't," said Vickers. "I don't even know who the Mogollon Kid is. Nobody does, I guess, any more than they know who bosses the Tucson machine."

Kern grasped his arm. "You will help me, Vickers?"

"No," said Papago, and Vickers whirled toward him, realizing how engrossed they had become in talking. "Vickers won't help you or anybody." Saying that gave Papago the chance to take his jump, knocking aside Vickers's Henry before he could bring it into line, pulling his own Remington at the same time.

Instead of fighting to get the Henry back on Papago, Vickers let it go and threw himself bodily at the man. They met with a fleshy thud, Vickers clutching desperately to turn Papago's gun down as the half-breed cleared leather with it. Behind him, Vickers heard Kern grunt, and thought—Combabi—and then the Remington exploded, jarring Vickers's hand up, the slug hitting earth near enough to Vickers to numb his foot from the impact.

With his free hand, Papago slugged at Vickers's face. Senses reeling to the blow, Vickers stumbled backward and tripped on a body, almost going down. He saw the wide head of Judge Kern at his feet. Fighting to stay erect, still holding Papago's gun hand with one fist, he caught the half-breed by the belt with his other, swinging the man around. Combabi must have pistol-whipped Kern, for he was just straightening above the judge and his gun was rising toward Vickers. Swung off-balance, Papago smashed into Combabi that way. He grunted, and the whole shack rocked as Combabi was knocked back against the wall.

Vickers still had hold of Papago by the belt and gun. Papago gasped with the effort of smashing Vickers in the face again with his free hand, lips peeled away from his white teeth in animal rage. Vickers took that blow, and set himself, and heaved, releasing both his holds on the man.

Combabi was reeling groggily away from the wall, trying to line up his dragoon again. Papago staggered back into him. They both crashed into the wall and fell to the floor in a tangle of legs and arms. Papago rolled free of Combabi, cursing, and tried to rise. Vickers was already jumping for him, feet first. One moccasin caught Papago in the jaw, knocking his head back against the wall, and again the frame structure shuddered, and dirt showered from the sod roof. Vickers's other foot caught Papago's gun hand, knocking the Remington free. Shouting with pain, Papago tried to rise, but Vickers caught him again in the face with a moccasin. More dirt showered down on them and Vickers whirled to catch Combabi before the man could rise. The Indian had dropped his cap-and-ball when Papago fell back against him, and Vickers pulled him up by his long, greasy hair and smashed his head against the wall.

"*Pichu-quate!*" shouted Combabi, and his hoarse voice was drowned by the rocking shudder of the building, and then a louder noise. Vickers released the man's hair and jumped backward with earth rattling onto his shoulders.

Just trying to rise from the wall, shaking his head dazedly, Papago was caught in the downpour of sod and timbers as the roof caved in. Vickers saw a rotten beam collapse, one broken end crashing into Papago. Combabi threw himself forward with his eyes shut and his face contorted in fear. They both disappeared in the avalanche of brown earth.

Vickers bent to lift Judge Kern under the armpits and haul him out through the door; then he stopped, realizing the rattling thunder had ceased. Only the far end of the shack had caved in. Kern began groaning and shook his head dully.

"Damned Indian gave me the barrel of that cap-and-ball!"

"Think we ought to pull them out?" queried Vickers.

Kern rose unsteadily to his feet, staring at the pile of earth and timbers at the other end of the room, then glanced at Vickers. His eyes suddenly began to twinkle, and he guffawed. "I guess we better at that, Vickers. Those varmints don't deserve it, but I might lose a night's sleep if I had it on my conscience, and Papago ain't worth a night's sleep to me."

Combabi's arm was sticking out of the dirt, and he was still conscious when they pulled him free, choking and gasping. Papago took longer to reach, and to revive. Even after he came around, he lay there where they had dragged him outside, breathing faintly, staring up at them with his enigmatic eyes. Slowly, those eyes took on a smoldering opacity and, when he finally rose to his feet, his breathing had become guttural and rasping. Vickers punched the shells from his Remington and handed it back.

Papago glanced at the gun, slipped it back in its holster, and his voice trembled slightly with his effort at control. "You're going after Sherry Kern?"

"What do you think?" asked Vickers.

"You're going after Sherry Kern." It was a statement this time. Papago turned toward his horse, hitched to some mesquite at the site, and Combabi followed him, mounting the roach-backed dun beside Papago's pinto. Papago lifted a leg up, and then, with his foot in the stirrup and one hand gripping his saddle-horn, he turned to look at Vickers again, and there was an indefinable menace in his flat, toneless voice. "You're a fool, Vickers. You think you had a lot of men looking for you this last month? It wasn't nothing. It wasn't nothing compared to what you'll be bucking if you do this. Judge Kern didn't have to swear out any warrant for your arrest. You've signed your own. And it ain't just for your arrest, Vickers. It's your death warrant!"

II

Up in the Tortillas the heat struck like this in August, about an hour after sunrise, and there was no breeze to dry the beaded sweat on the hairy, little roan standing there in the coulee where bleeding heart lay crimson against the black lava. Vickers had rolled himself a cigarette and hunkered down with his back against a boulder so he could see both upslope and down, his Henry in his lap. Three days of riding away from Prescott were behind him, and he had unsaddled the weary bronc completely to rest it. His pale blue eyes took on a gunmetal color in his Indian-dark face, moving deliberately across the slope below him, and his lank, blond hair hung in a sweat-damp cowlick down his gaunt forehead. He gave no sign when the rider came into view. He sat motionless, waiting for the man to rise through the scrubby yuccas down there.

When the rider would have passed him, going on up, Vickers stood without speaking and waited. The man's head turned abruptly, then he necked his big horse around and dropped into the shallow cut Vickers occupied. He stopped the horse and leaned forward in the center-fire rig to peer wide-eyed at Vickers. He was a short, square bulldog of a man with heavy jowls and a mop of russet hair that grew unruly down the middle of his head and receded at his temples above the ears like a pair of pink cauliflowers.

"Vickers?" he said. He descended from the horse with a springy ease to his compact bulk, fishing a cigar from inside his short-skirted, black coat. "Webb Fallon. The Apaches told me you'd be hereabouts this morning. You running in Kern's team, now?"

Vickers took a last puff on his cigarette, studying the cold relentlessness of Fallon's opaque, brown eyes, then dropped the fag and ground it out with a scarred, wooden heel. "Kern said you'd picked up a few things on Sherry."

The name sent something indefinable through Fallon's face, and he didn't speak at once. "I'm glad you're in it," he said finally. "The judge told me he'd try and get you as a last resort. I have found one or two things." He got a leather whang from his pocket. It was worn and greasy, about four inches long. "This, for instance."

"Looks like the fringe off someone's leggings."

"That's right," said Fallon, and let his eyes drop to Vickers's leggings. "Sherry Kern had a handful of them. They came off the leggings of the man who murdered Edgar James."

For a moment, their gazes locked, and Vickers could feel the little muscles twitch tight about his mouth, drawing the skin across his high cheekbones till it gleamed. Meeting his gaze enigmatically, Fallon went on.

"It was one of the pieces of evidence Judge Kern was going to use against you, at the trial. Edgar James must have been close enough to rip it from the murderer's pants. Sherry was the first one to reach Edgar there on Coronado before he died, and he still had this bunch of fringe in his hand. Sherry had kept it in her possession and, when this turned up, it had some significance for me. As you know, I've been Kern's agent down here for some time, trying to uncover the Tucson machine. One of the Mexicans I've befriended came into Tucson Sunday before last, said a bunch of Apaches with a woman had stopped at his place for food and remounts. They burned his *jacal* and took what horses he had, but he managed to escape into the timber. I went back to his place with him. Found this by the well."

"You think she's trying to leave a trail?" said Vickers.

"It's like her," said Fallon, and that same nameless expression crossed his face as when Vickers had spoken her name before, only more strongly this time. For a moment, Fallon seemed to be looking beyond Vickers. Then, with a visible effort, he brought his eyes back to the man. "You never knew Sherry, did you?"

"Never saw her," said Vickers. "She arrived at Prescott from Austin the night Edgar James was killed."

"You put it nicely."

"Never mind."

"You can admit it to me," said Fallon. "I'm strictly neutral."

Vickers's voice grew thin. "I said never mind."

Fallon's voice held a faint shrug. "All right. So you didn't murder Edgar James. And Sherry Kern came in the night he was killed, and you haven't ever seen her."

"She look anything like the judge?" asked Vickers, feeling the animosity that had descended between them.

"The pride," said Fallon, and again he was looking beyond Vickers with that same thing in his face. Vickers could almost read it now, but could not quite believe it, somehow, in a man like Fallon. "Yes, the pride." Fallon jerked out of it abruptly, waving his hand in a frustration at having let Vickers see it. "Black-haired, black-eyed," he said matter-of-factly, "five-six or seven. Big girl. Yes, quite a bit like the judge." He seemed to realize he hadn't used his cigar and bit off the end almost angrily, spitting it out. Then he waved the leather whang. "Think this will do us any good?"

"If she's leaving those for a trail," said Vickers, "it might do us a lot of good."

"Glad you think so," said Fallon. "This was just a lucky strike, and it's left me up against the fence. I don't have your touch with the Indians. That gate's closed to me."

"We'll have to do a sight of riding," said Vickers.

"I imagine," said Fallon.

III

The Painted Desert extended three hundred miles along the north bank of the Little Colorado, caprices of heat and light and dust changing their hues constantly, a scarlet haze that splashed the horizon, shifting unaccountably into a serried mist of purples and grays from which warmly tinted mesas erupted and knolls of reddish sandstone thrust skyward. Dust-caked and slouching wearily in the saddles of plodding horses, the two men rose from the brackish water of the river toward Hopi Buttes, standing darkly and lonely against the weirdly sunset sky. All afternoon, now, Vickers had been scanning the ground, and finally he found what he had been seeking. He halted his horse, dismounted to study the mound of bluish rocks, topped by a flat piece of sandstone upon which were placed a number of wooden ovals, painted white and tufted with feathers.

Fallon removed the inevitable cigar from his mouth. "What is it?"

"Eagle shrine," muttered Vickers. "The ovals represent eggs. Probably made them during the winter solstice ceremony as prayers for an increase in the eagles. Moquis figure the eagle is the best carrier of prayers to the rain-bringing gods. We should find some boys trapping eagles near here for their annual rain dance."

"You really know, don't you," said Fallon.

Vickers mounted his piebald horse. "Where do you think I've been living this last month?"

Fallon moved his animal after Vickers, twisting in the saddle. "Got a funny feeling. Ever get it out here?"

"You mean about being followed?"

Fallon turned sharply toward him. "Then it ain't just a feeling?"

"There was dust on the rim this morning."

"You even got eyes like an Indian," grunted Fallon. "Who do you figure? Apaches?"

"We haven't made a move the Indians don't know about," said Vickers. "It might be them."

"Or someone else."

"You should know about that," said Vickers.

"How do you mean?" asked the man.

"Doesn't the kidnapping of Sherry Kern by the Indians seem a little too fortuitous, when the Tucson machine would give anything to keep the capital from being moved to Prescott?" asked Vickers.

"It does. But why should I know...?" Suddenly it seemed to strike Fallon, and his face darkened. "I don't like your insinuation, Vickers. I've been working for Judge Kern for a long time."

"And you told him it wasn't the Tucson machine that kidnapped Sherry."

Fallon booted his mare in the flank suddenly, jumping it into Vickers's horse so hard the roan stumbled. Then he grabbed Vickers by the shoulder to pull him around and catch at the front of his Levi's jacket. There was a driving strength in Fallon's fist that held Vickers there momentarily, and the man's wide eyes stared into the eyes of Vickers.

"Listen, I want to get one thing straight, Vickers. I still think you're a murderer, and I don't trust you any more than you trust me. But I'm not going to have you insinuating I have any connection with the Tucson machine. Nobody knows who runs the machine any more than they know who the Mogollon Kid is."

It was Vickers who stopped Fallon. He tore the man's hand off his Levi's jacket and shoved it down toward their waists. Fallon gave one jerk, trying to free his hand, and then stopped, held there more by Vickers's blazing eyes than his grip.

"And I'm tired of being called a murderer, Fallon," said Vickers, through his teeth, "and if you still want to do it, you'd better go for your gun!"

IV

The Moquis built their eagle traps of willow shoots and deerhide, baiting them with rabbits and concealing themselves inside, waiting to seize the eagles that pounced on the prey, and Vickers and Fallon came across a trap on a flat atop Hopi Buttes. Another man might have been sullen or touchy after a clash like the one Vickers and Fallon had experienced, but Kern's agent sat enigmatically on his mare watching the Indian youth emerge from the trap, no expression in his wide eyes.

The Moqui boy was lean and drawn as a gaunted bronc, his black hair cut straight across his brow and hanging to his shoulders behind, wearing no more than a buckskin loin cloth and a pair of dirty, beaded moccasins.

"*Buenas dias, Señor* Vickers," he said.

"*Buenas dias*, Quimiu," said Vickers, answering him in Spanish. "You have grown since I last saw you at Sichomovi."

Quimiu nodded his head in a pleased way without allowing much expression to appear on his face. "You are hunting birds too?" he asked in Spanish.

"One bird," said Vickers. "A female bird with a black head."

"That is a rare bird," Quimiu told him. "Even more rare if she sheds her plumage in August."

"There was a Hopi down on the Little Colorado who said one of the eagle trappers up here found a feather of that plumage," said Vickers.

Gravely the boy untied a leather whang from his g-string, handing it to Vickers. "You know that I would show it to no other white man."

Vickers passed it to Fallon, and the man compared it with the other whang he had, nodding. "Couldn't miss it. No Apache dyes his leggings like that. First bunch of Ute fringe I've seen in the territory in years." He glanced at Vickers's leggings. "Couldn't miss it."

Vickers drew a thin breath, forcing his eyes to stay on the Indian. "How did the bird fly?"

"Proudly. They must have been riding for days when they passed south of Hopi Buttes, but she still sat straight in the saddle without any fear in her face. Her hair was black as midnight, and long and straight like an Indian maiden's. I saw their dust from here and went down to find out what it was. They didn't see me. There must have been a dozen Apaches"—here the traditional hatred of the Pueblo Indian for the nomad Apache entered his voice—"and the bird you seek rode behind the leader. She must have fought them, for there were scratches on her face, and her hands were tied, but they had not subdued her."

"Nothing could," said Fallon, and his eyes had that far-away look again, and this time Vickers realized what it was. He had not been able to believe it before, in Fallon. But the same thing was in Quimiu's face now, and Quimiu's description had made the picture of Sherry Kern more vivid in Vickers's mind. That picture had been forming for a long time now, ever since he left Prescott, part of it gleaned from the judge, and other snatches he found on the way to his meeting with Fallon, some from Fallon himself, and now some from Quimiu. Vickers could almost see her, riding proudly and unsubdued in her captivity, her eyes gleaming fiercely, her statuesque body straight and unyielding after a ride that would have exhausted another white woman to the point of collapse. And something else was beginning to form in his mind, or in some other part of him he couldn't name, and it gave him a better comprehension of her capacity to stir other men, or more than stir them. He turned in his saddle to glance at Judge Kern's agent. Yes, even a man like Fallon. Even a cold, passionless man like Fallon.

Then Vickers turned back to Quimiu. "Do you know where they have taken her?"

Quimiu shook his head. "The eagles have some eyries even the Hopi does not know of. There is a Navajo shaman near Cañon Diablo who knows where the birds sleep when the moon rises. I have caught many eagles on his advice."

"Perhaps we had better go there," said Vickers.

"Perhaps you had better not," said a hoarse voice from behind them. "Perhaps you had better stay right here so I can see what your face looks like when I blow your brains out."

The wind sighing across Hopi Buttes blew cold against the sweat which had broken out on Vickers's brow. His first instinct had been to pull his Henry up from where he held it across his saddle bows. He had stopped his hand from moving with an effort. Finally his rig creaked beneath him as he turned.

Vickers wouldn't have thought a white man could have come up on them like that without giving himself away. This one had. He sat on a rim of the sandstone uplift behind them, a huge, grinning man with a hoary, black beard and a shaggy mane of hair on his hatless head, a ponderous Harper's Ferry percussion pistol in each freckled hand.

"Well, Red-eye," said Fallon, "you selling whiskey to the Moquis now?"

"I sell it to any man which buys," said Red-eye Reeves. He wore a pair of moccasins and his frayed leggings of buckskin were pulled on over red flannels which sufficed for his shirt, the sleeves rolled up to the elbows of his hairy forearms. He waved a .58 Harper's Ferry at Vickers. "The Tucson machine has a price of five hundred on your head. What would you give me not to collect that price?"

It galled Vickers to have to bargain for his life this way, but there was no alternative with those huge percussions in his face. "How much do you want?"

"I didn't say how much. I said what."

"Well."

"You're traveling this country hunting Sherry Kern," said Red-eye. "You'll hit a lot of Injun camps. Navajo, Apache, Moqui. I got a load of red-eye that would bring fifty dollars the quart from them redskins. I never been able to reach them before. You're the only one who could take me into Tusuyan and bring me back out again with my scalp still above my beard."

"And after they get through swilling your rotgut, they'll have a war dance and pull a massacre somewhere while they're drunk," said Vickers. "The only reason I could take you into Tusuyan is the Indians are my friends. You think I'd do that to them?"

Red-eye Reeves waved the Harper's Ferry again. "This is your alternative, and it's a sort of jumpy one, so you better decide right quick."

Vickers took a long breath, speaking finally. "We're heading for a Navajo shaman in Cañon Diablo."

"Suits me," said Red-eye Reeves. "He'll be good for a gallon at least."

They rode westward from Hopi Buttes, Red-eye Reeves forking a ratty, little Mexican pack mule and leading a dozen others, *aparejos* piled high with flat, wooden kegs of whiskey. All day Reeves kept pulling at a bottle, and it was evident he had been doing the same before he came on Vickers and Fallon. He reeled tipsily in his saddle, mumbling through his beard sometimes. They were riding through a scrubby motte of juniper east of Cañon Diablo when Vickers drew far enough away for Fallon to speak without being overheard.

"You aren't going through with this?"

"I'll get rid of him as soon as I can," said Vickers.

"Be careful," Fallon told him. "He's drunk most of the time, but he's dangerous. I don't think his real purpose in wanting to come with us is the whiskey."

Vickers glanced at Fallon, pale eyes narrow. "Is he from Tucson?"

"He's been there," said Fallon.

It was the shot, then, cutting off what Vickers had started to say. His roan shied and spooked, starting to buck and squeal, and Vickers threw himself from the horse while he still had enough control over his falling to roll and come up running, the back of his Levi's coat ripped where he had gone through some jumping cholla. "Come back here, you cross-eyed cousin to a ring-tailed varmint," yelled Red-eye Reeves from somewhere behind Vickers, and Vickers saw a mule galloping away with wooden kegs spilling in its wake from the dragging *aparejo* pack.

Then they were nearly out of earshot for Vickers, once he threw himself into the monkshood carpeting the ground near the edge of the grove. He lay there in the heady fragrance of the wildflowers, peering toward the mesa ahead of them. The slope was gentle at first, littered with boulders and scrubby timber, then steepened to a veritable cliff, channeled by erosion. Vickers jumped at the movement behind him.

"Never mind," said Fallon, and he crawled in with an old Theur's conversion-model Colt. "It looks like we won't have to worry about getting rid of Red-eye. He's taking care of that himself."

Still yelling in the distance, Reeves had chased his scattering pack train out into the open beyond them, kicking his scraggly mule after a trio of pack animals that had headed up the slope. He was well onto the rising ground when another shot rang out. His riding mule stumbled, and Reeves went over its head, landing on both feet and running on upslope from the momentum, and both Harper's Ferry guns were in his hands before he stopped.

"Come on out, you misbegotten brother to a spotted hinny and a club-footed jackass. Nobody can treat my babies like that. Nobody can shoot my...."

His own shot cut him off, and Vickers couldn't help exclaiming, because he hadn't seen anybody up there, and he wouldn't have believed anyone could score such a hit with an old percussion pistol.

"I told you he was dangerous," Fallon muttered.

Higher up, a man had risen out of the rocks where he must have been crouched. Both his hands were at his chest, and he stood there a moment, as if suspended. Then he fell forward, rolling out over the sandstone and coming to a stop against some stunted juniper.

Shouting hoarse obscenities, Red-eye Reeves charged on up the slope. There was something terrible about his giant, black-bearded figure running inexorably upward, and somehow Vickers wasn't surprised to see a man rise farther on up and turn to run. Red-eye had raised his other Harper's Ferry when the third figure appeared, much nearer, climbing to a rock and holding both hands up, palms toward Reeves.

The drunken whiskey drummer shifted his pistol with a jerk till it bore on that third man. Fallon must have realized it about the same time Vickers did, because he jumped out of the monkshood, shouting: "Reeves, don't, can't you see he...?"

Vickers's shot drowned his voice. The pistol leaped from Reeves's hand, and he yelled in agony, taking a stumbling step forward and pulling the hand in toward him. Fallon turned back to Vickers, his mouth open slightly, and Vickers realized it must have taken a lot for Fallon to show that much emotion.

Reeves was holding out his bloody, shattered hand when they reached him, studying it with a speculative twist to his pursed lips. He looked up and grinned at them. "I didn't think those old Henry's could go that far," he said.

Vickers looked for guile in his face, unwilling to presume the man held no anger at him for shooting the gun from his hand; but he could find none. "Didn't you see that man wanted to surrender?"

"What do I care?" said Red-eye, bending to pick up his gun and stuffing it in his belt. "The only good Injun's a dead one, to me, and I don't care how my lead catches them, with their hands up, or wrapped around a gun."

Fallon looked at Vickers, then shrugged. "You go and get him. I'll see what we can do for Red-eye's hand."

"The hell with that," growled Red-eye, wiping his bloody hand against his shirt the way a man would if he had scratched it. "Think one of them damn Henry flatties can do more'n pink a man? It takes one of these babies"—he patted his pistol—"and you'll see what I mean when you find that varmint I pegged higher up. I'm going to get a drink."

He walked off toward where a group of his mules had finally stopped, up on the slope. The Indian who had surrendered was making his way down to them, a gnarled ancient in tattered deerskin, covered with dung and other filth till his stench preceded him a good dozen yards. His watery eyes took some time to focus on them, out of the seamed age of his face, and then he held up a palsied claw of a hand. The single word relegated them to their station, holding neither contempt nor respect.

"*Pahanas*," he said. "White man."

Vickers realized this must be the shaman Quimiu had spoken of. "There was a youth of the *Hopitu-shinumu* named Quimiu in the eagle-trapping ground of Hopi Buttes who told us of a wonderworker at Cañon Diablo who was in communion with the Trues," said Vickers.

The Trues were the gods of the Pueblos and, though nothing showed in the shaman's face, there was a subtle change in the tone of his voice. "You must be blessed by the Trues. Quimiu would not have sent white men to me otherwise. I shall then thank you for saving me from the two Apaches who were holding me."

He waved his hand toward the Indian Red-eye had shot. The second one had disappeared over the lip of the mesa and, as Vickers moved up to examine the dead one, Reeves came in leading his pack animals. The ball had taken the Indian through the chest, apparently killing him instantly. He wore a pair of Apache war moccasins, made of buckskin, boots really that were hip-length, turned down until they were only knee-high, forming a protection of double thickness against the malignant brush of the southwest. About his flanks was a g-string and a buckskin bag of powder and shot for his big Sharps buffalo gun. Squatting over him, Vickers saw the odd expression catch on Reeves's face.

"Know him?" said Vickers.

Reeves nodded, his drunken humor suddenly gone. "That's Baluno. He rode with the Mogollon Kid."

V

The shaman's *hoganda* was up on the mesa, overlooking Cañon Diablo which formed the other side, a deep chasm of Kaibab sandstone, yellow at the top and fading into a salmon color as it descended. Vickers had borrowed one of Reeves's mules to roundup his spooked roan, and he dismounted from the skittish horse now, loosening the cinch to blow the animal.

"What were those Apaches doing here?" he asked the Navajo.

"Holding me hostage," said the shaman. "They still held enough fear of the shamans not to kill me, but they would not let me leave my *hoganda*."

"But why were they holding you?" asked Vickers. "Is there something they didn't want you to get away and tell?"

"I come up here before the summer Rain Dances for a moon of fasting and praying," said the shaman evasively.

"He'll never tell you anything unless you get him inside that *hoganda*," said Red-eye, "and you know they won't let a white man in their medicine house."

Vickers held out his hand so the scar showed across his palm. "I am blood brother to Abeïto, the House Chief of Walpi."

"You must be the one who saved him from the *pahanas* near Tucson last year," the shaman said enigmatically.

Vickers shrugged, seeing it had done no good, as Abeïto was a Moqui and this man a Navajo. "The white men blamed him for something Apaches did."

Red-eye put his good hand on the butt of a Harper's Ferry. "We ain't getting nowhere thisaway. Look, you dried-up old...."

"Never mind, Reeves." Vickers hadn't said it very loud, but it stopped the man. Then Vickers moved closer to the shaman, speaking softly. "I know of *Shi-pa-pu*."

It was the first expression the shaman had allowed to enter his face, and it caught briefly at his mouth and eyes before he suppressed it—awe, or reverence, or fear, Vickers could not tell which. Then, without speaking, he turned and stooped through the low door of the *hoganda*, a conical hut of willow withes and skins, beaten and weathered by the winds of many years on top of this mesa. As Vickers bent to follow, Fallon caught his arm.

"What was it you told him?"

"*Shi-pa-pu*," Vickers murmured. "The Black Lake of Tears, from whence the human race is supposed to have arisen. It's so sacred the Indians rarely say it aloud."

"And no white man is supposed to know about it?"

"I never met another who did," said Vickers. "At least the shaman knows I've been inside their *hogandas* before. That's all we care about."

The inside was fetid and oppressive with the same odors the shaman emanated, and Vickers shied away from a *kachina* doll dangling above the door, dressed and beaded and feathered to represent one of the gods. The shaman indicated that they should seat themselves about the flat *Walla pai* basket, woven from Martynia that reposed in the center of the *hoganda*. Then the medicine man seated himself and stirred the coals of the fire before the empty basket until they glowed, lighting a *weer* he produced from a buckskin bag at his belt. This sacred cigarette he passed around and, while each of them puffed on it, he began murmuring incantations over the dying light of the coals. It was almost pitch black inside the hut when the buckskin thong appeared, and Vickers couldn't have sworn how it got there. The shaman continued muttering, three feet away from the basket, but Fallon drew in a hissing breath, reaching toward the piece of rawhide fringe now responding in the bottom of the flat basket. Vickers caught his hand, pulling it back.

"Quimiu had such an object also," said Vickers. "A feather, he said, dropped from a black-headed bird who shed her plumage in August."

"A goddess, rather," murmured the shaman, and Vickers could feel something draw him up, because he sensed it coming again, and his breathing became audible, and swifter, "a goddess sent by the Trues to prove to the Apaches what coyotes they are. Nothing they had done could subdue her. Their leader himself wished her favor, but she bit his hand when he tried to touch her. Even the dust and sun and weariness of the long ride could not hide her beauty. Her eyes were not as black as her hair, and once when she turned fully to me, it was as if I had stared into the swimming smoke of a camp-fire, and another time, when she looked at the leader of the Apaches, it was as if I had seen lightning. Other of the Dineh´, like Quimiu, have seen her and, as long as the sacred *weer* is smoked in the *hoganda*, it will be told how the goddess rode through our land, leaving signs to the favored ones."

From the corner of his eye, Vickers could see Fallon bending forward that same way, his mouth parted slightly, his wide eyes rapt. Suddenly he seemed to feel Vickers's gaze on him, and closed his mouth, leaning back, glancing almost angrily at Vickers.

"How did you get the sign?" said Vickers, motioning toward the buckskin whang in the basket.

"The Apaches were apparently expecting to find water in the Red Lake, but it had been dry for a moon and there was none. They would not have revealed their passing to me unless they were desperate for water. They forced me to show them my sacred sink on the mesa, where the sun cannot reach the water which the Rain Gods have brought and dry it up. Then they left the one named Baluno and his companion to guard me and keep me from telling of them until they were safely away."

Fallon's eyes were on Vickers now, in a covert speculation, as he spoke: "The Mogollon Kid?"

The shaman sat, staring into the basket without answering Fallon. The fire had died completely now, and the light from the smokehole was rapidly fading as night fell outside, enveloping the interior of the *hoganda* in darkness. Vickers could barely see Red-eye Reeves across the basket. He saw the man glance at him now, and there was that same speculation as Vickers had seen in Fallon's face. Vickers felt his hands tighten around the Henry across his knees. In a few moments it would be so intensely dark that none of them could see the others.

"I thought the shaman feared none but the Trues," said Vickers, and his body was stiffening for the shift.

The shaman's voice came abruptly from the gloom, almost angrily. "How do I know if it was the Mogollon Kid?"

"I have heard the Indians feared the Mogollon Kid as much as their own gods," said Vickers. "He must have the power of the Trues if he can shut a shaman's mouth." Even that failed to elicit any response from the shaman. "If you can't tell us who it was," said Vickers, "perhaps you can tell us where they are bound."

Vickers had seen the incredible legerdemain of these wonder workers. Once he had seen a shaman make corn grow in the bare dirt floor of a *hoganda*, and it had convinced and amazed even his Occidental realism. But this came so unexpectedly that it held him spellbound as it occurred. A faint blue glow descended from the smokehole of the hive-like structure, until their four figures were bathed in an eerie light, faces drawn and taut with a sudden tension. The piece of buckskin fringe was revealed momentarily in the basket, shifting like a small snake with a life of its own till it pointed due north. Then the light was extinguished abruptly.

In the following blackness Vickers recovered enough from the sight to do what he had planned. Still sitting in the cross-legged position they had all assumed, he placed his hands on either side of him and shifted himself about twelve inches to the right with his legs yet crossed, speaking as he did to mask any sound.

"The sacred sign points to Tusuyan."

"Yes," said the shaman. "The Dance of the Snake is being held at Walpi this year...."

The shot thundered, rocking the *hoganda*, deafening Vickers. He sat rigid with his back against the willow frame of the hut, his Henry cocked across his lap, waiting for whoever came for him. There was a shout, a muffled struggle in the utter darkness, then the *hoganda* shook violently. Outside, the animals had been spooked by the shot, whinnying and nickering and shaking the ground as they tore up their picket pins and galloped back and forth before the door. Vickers knew what a target anybody would be going out that door, and he sat there till silence had fallen again. Finally the spark from a flint and steel caught across the hut. He jerked his Henry that way. It was the shaman, throwing fresh juniper shavings on the dead coals. He lit the fire and shuffled across the room to where Vickers had risen. There was no one else in the *hoganda*.

The shaman fingered the bullet hole in the hide wall. "It would have killed you if you'd been sitting one *paso* to the left," he muttered. "I wonder why they wanted you dead?"

Vickers turned toward the door. "I don't wonder why, so much, as which one."

VI

For centuries the region in northeastern Arizona territory had been known as the province of Tusuyan, and the Pueblos living there as Moquis, or Hopis, from their own name for themselves, *Hopitu-shinumu*. Walpi was one of these pueblos, perched atop a sombrous mesa, a giant block of sandstone reaching up from the flatlands about it, the tiered mud houses on its top barely visible from below. It was August of the second year, and groups of Indians from the other pueblos and from the Navajo camps to the east had been passing up the trail to Walpi all day, raising nervous flurries of gray dust over the fields of corn and squash near the village.

Knowing it would be suicide to go out the door of the shaman's hogan there above Cañon Diablo, if anyone was outside, Vickers had unlashed some of the deerhides at the back, crawling out that way, only to find that both Red-eye Reeves and Fallon were gone, with all the animals, including his roan.

He had trailed them on foot, but being mounted, they soon out-distanced him. He could read sign of someone on the roan driving Red-eye's mules, but could find no other horse prints, and concluded Fallon had not left the *hoganda* with Red-eye.

A week after Cañon Diablo, Vickers was plodding up the trail toward Walpi behind a party of Apaches on wiry little mustangs. Ordinarily the Apaches and Navajos were enemies of the Pueblos but, during the Snake Dance, hostilities were suspended and other tribes were allowed to view the ceremonies. The houses atop the mesa were built three stories high, each story set back the length of one room on the roof of the lower level, forming three huge steps, with rickety ladders reaching each roof from the one below. What passed for the streets and courtyards in front of the houses were filled with a milling crowd of Indians, Moqui women in hand woven *mantas* holding dirty brown babies to their breasts, tall, arrogant Navajo men with their heavy silver belts and turquoise bracelets, a few shifty Apaches like strange dogs, standing apart in their little groups and bristling whenever they were approached, turkey-red bandannas on their greasy black hair, perhaps a Sharps hugged close.

Stopping near the entrance from the trail to the mesa top, Vickers was aware of their suspicious eyes on him, and an ineffable sensation of something not quite right filled him. Then a Navajo stumbled through the crowd toward Vickers, pawing at a big Bowie in his silver belt, and Vickers knew what it was.

"*Pahanas*," growled the Navajo, shoving a Moqui woman roughly aside, and Vickers could see how bloodshot his eyes were. A pair of Moqui braves moved in from where they had been standing beneath an adobe wall, and they were drunk, too. As Vickers opened the lever on his Henry, he saw the Mexican rat-mule standing in a yonder courtyard, its *aparejo* pack ripped off and laying at the animal's feet, empty kegs strewn all about the hard-packed ground.

"*Pahanas, pahanas!*" It was a shout, now, coming from a bibulous Apache, running in from the other side. Vickers had waited till the last moment but, just as he was about to raise his Henry up to cover them, someone else shouted from the rooftop of a nearby building.

"No, not *pahanas. Hopitu-shinumu.* He is my blood brother."

It was Abeïto, House Chief of Walpi, swinging onto one of the rawhide-bound ladders and climbing down with a quick, cat-like agility. He was a small, compact man in white doeskin for the coming ceremony, a band of red Durango silk about his black, bobbed hair. The Moquis stopped coming at Vickers, and the Navajo moved grudgingly aside, still clutching his knife, to let the House Chief through. Vickers embraced Abeïto ceremoniously, as befitted a blood brother, but he saw it in the House Chief's eyes as Abeïto pulled him through the milling crowd toward his own dwelling.

"Reeves is here?" he said to Abeïto. "Why did you let him sell that whiskey to your people, brother? You could have stopped it."

"He didn't sell it," said the House Chief, pulling him urgently toward the ladder.

"But he must have," said Vickers, trying to understand the evasive darkness in Abeïto's eyes. "The *Moquenos* never took things without paying. They are not Apaches. What's happening here, Abeïto? You're still House Chief, aren't you?"

"Yes, yes," said the Moqui. "We can't talk here, brother."

Abeïto glanced nervously at a group of Apaches standing near the ladder. One of them, with a Colt stuck naked through a cartridge belt about his lean middle, had a keg of whiskey. They were watching

Vickers, shifting back and forth restlessly, talking in sullen tones, and Vickers caught the name as he reached for the ladder, and stopped.

"Is that it?" he asked Abeïto.

"Please, don't stop out here. Is what it?"

"You heard what they said."

"Brother for your own good...."

"Are you afraid of him, too?" Vickers asked. "There was a youth at Hopi Buttes too afraid even to speak his name, and a shaman at Cañon Diablo. If the shamans are afraid of him...."

"I am House Chief of Walpi," said Abeïto, drawing himself up, "head of the Bear Clan. Never did I expect to hear such an insult from my blood brother."

"Then is that it?"

Abeïto hesitated, glancing about him, face dark. "The Mogollon Kid?" he said, finally.

Vickers clutched at his coat. "Is he here? The Kid. Who is he, Abeïto?"

"I did not say he was here," said the Moqui, grabbing Vickers's elbow. "Brother, if you value your life, get up that ladder into my house. We can't talk out here. Only their respect for my position holds them now. They have known of your coming for days. I sent a runner out to turn you back, but he must have missed you. Please...."

The spruce ladder popped and swayed beneath Vickers weight. On the first terrace an eagle was fluttering in an *amole* cage, one of the birds trapped at Hopi Buttes and brought here for the rain ceremonies, to be killed after the last *kachinas* came in July, the Indians believing the eagle's spirit would carry prayers for rain to the Trues. Abeïto shoved aside the heavy *bayeta* blanket hanging over the doorway leading into the rooms on the second level, allowing Vickers to go in first. A squaw was sitting on the floor inside before the cooking stone the *Moquenos* called a *tooma*, mixing blue corn meal with water to form a thin batter for *pikama*. Vickers spoke their language to some extent but, when she looked up and saw him, she said something so fast he couldn't catch it.

"He is my blood brother," the House Chief told her. She said something else, rising from the *tooma*. Abeïto took an angry breath and motioned toward the door. "Get out," he told her. "Get out."

When she was gone, he turned to Vickers. "You see how it is? You can't stay here. I am violating all the laws of hospitality now, but it is for your own good, brother. For weeks we have heard of your search for the black-haired woman. I knew you, and I knew sooner or later you would arrive here. She is not here, believe me."

"Then who is?" said Vickers. "What's happening? Why have you so little control over your people? Surely it was not your wish that they took Reeves's fire-water. You know what will happen with everyone drunk like this. You have a hard enough time maintaining peace among your people and the Navajos and Apaches as it is. Why were they talking of the Mogollon Kid? Where is he?"

A man shoved aside the *bayeta* blanket in the doorway, stepping inside. "Here he is," he said.

Vickers had lived and traveled among the Indians long enough to acquire some facility at hiding his emotions when it was necessary, but he felt his mouth open slightly as he stared past Abeïto's white doeskin shoulder at the man swaggering in the doorway, one hand holding aside the curtain to reveal the Apaches behind him, the other hand hooked in his heavy cartridge belt near enough to the big, blued Remington .44 he packed. His lean, avaricious face was scarred deeply from smallpox, and the whites of his eyes were pale, shifting enigmas above the thin, mobile intelligence of his broad, thin-lipped mouth.

"Perry Papago," said Vickers emptily.

Papago grinned without much mirth, moving on in, and Combabi followed him on silent, bare feet, shifting black eyes unwilling to meet Vickers's gaze, and the other Apaches blotted out the light from the door behind, the bores of their Sharps rifles covering Vickers.

"This is why your blood brother has so little control over his people, Vickers," said Papago, tapping the short, buckskin vest covering his bare chest. "I've taken over. It's for their own good. Four troops of dragoons in Prescott and more coming up as soon as the Department of Arizona can shift them. If the Indian's don't organize now, they'll be wiped out. The Navajos and Apaches are all ready. All we need are the Moquis, and we'll have them as soon as the Snake Dances are over. I tried to talk some sense with Abeïto, but he wouldn't listen. Get his people drunk enough and they'll listen. There are half a thousand warriors in the seven pueblos of Tusuyan, Vickers. What do you think your bluecoats can do when I add them to my Apaches?"

Vickers was bent forward, his voice intense. "You've got the girl?"
Papago's eyes raised slightly. "Girl?"

"You know, Papago. You're the Mogollon Kid? You've brought her here to this. We found your man, Baluno, at Cañon Diablo." Vickers was trembling. "Don't try and deny it, Papago. What have you done with her? What have you done with Sherry Kern?"

Papago pursed his lips; something mocking entered his voice. "I didn't know you felt that way about her, Vickers. She must be a beautiful woman."

"Papago…."

"Brother!" Abeïto caught Vickers as he lunged forward at Papago. Then he turned to the half-breed. "Let him go, Papago. He has always been our friend. Even your friend. Take me in his place. Whatever you were going to do with him, do with me."

"No," said Papago, and lifted his hand off his cartridge belt to motion at his men, and they began slipping in and moving around behind Papago and Combabi, dark, menacing Apaches, the whites of their eyes shining in the semi-gloom. "No, Abeïto. I tried to stop Vickers from this at the beginning, but he wouldn't listen. As you say, he has been our friend, and I didn't want him mixed up in it. But now, he has come too far. Take him!"

This last he called to his men, and there was the abrupt scuffle of feet across the hard-packed floor. Vickers tore loose of Abeïto, trying to bring his Henry into line and snap down the lever all in one action. He saw Combabi go for his cap-and-ball, whirled that way, already seeing he would be too late, because the Indian's dragoon was free even before Vickers heard the metallic click of his cocked Henry. Then a white figure hurtled in front of Vickers, and the thunder of Combabi's shot filled the small room. Vickers pulled his gun up in a jerky, frustrated way, till it was pointing at where Combabi had been, hidden now by the other man. Stunned, Vickers watched the man in white doeskin sink to the floor in front of him, and Combabi was visible again, his cap-and-ball dirtying the soft gloom with a wreath of acrid, black powder smoke. Perry Papago stood to the other side, and he was looking at Abeïto, sprawled on the floor. Then he lifted his eyes.

"You better drop it, Vickers. My Apaches got their Sharps rifles loaded now. You haven't got a chance."

All around him, Vickers was aware of the Indians, standing with their muzzle loaders trained on him. He dropped the Henry, butt plate striking first, then the long barrel, and went to his knees beside Abeïto. It was then he became aware of the hubbub outside. The *bayeta* blanket was torn aside and a Moqui brave thrust into the room, followed by a pair of *principales*, white-headed dignitaries of Walpi's governing body. They stopped when they saw Abeïto, and other Moquis crowding in from behind stumbled against the *principales*. Lifting his head toward them, Vickers did not know what he was going to say, when he saw the gun in Papago's hand. It was Combabi's cap-and-ball, still reeking of the black powder.

"*Pahanas*," said Papago, waving his hand toward Vickers, then holding the gun up. "Your House Chief found the *pahanas* with one of your women."

"No!" Vickers was surprised to hear Abeïto's voice. He lifted the man's head higher, and Abeïto shuddered in his arms, trying to get the words out. "He cannot...my blood brother cannot...have done that," said the House Chief incoherently. "The Trues sent him. He is the only one whoever befriended us. The Trues sent him."

Abeïto sighed deeply, and his body was a sudden weight in Vickers's arms. Then the fetid smell of sweat and buckskin gagged Vickers, and rough arms were pulling him off Abeïto. He was still staring at the dead House Chief, a thin pain somewhere inside him now. They had known a lot together. It was odd he should remember that time he had caught his hand between the bed and the platen of his first press. He had wanted to cry then.

"You wanted to see the girl?" It was Papago's voice, entering Vickers's consciousness. "You'll see her now, Vickers. You thought it was the Tucson machine? That's funny. I'm sorry it had to be this way, but you were on the wrong horse from the beginning, I guess, even about the machine. We tried to stop you, didn't we? Other men had been sent out to find her, and I didn't go out of my way to stop them. I stopped them, but I didn't go out of my way to do it. I wouldn't have ridden from here to Prescott to stop them the way I did you. But I knew what a mistake it would be to let you get started, Vickers. I'd already gotten here with Sherry when I got word Kern had contacted you to meet him there in that miner's shack outside Prescott. You almost made it anyway, didn't you? You came farther than anyone else ever did. You're the only living white man who knows I'm the Mogollon Kid."

They were hauling him roughly past Papago and the other Apaches. The strange, dazed emotion of seeing Abeïto dead had held it back, but now the full comprehension of what had happened struck Vickers, filling him with the first impulse to struggle since Papago had told the Apaches to get him. Vickers threw his weight against the *Moquenos*, managing to halt them momentarily, and turned enough to see Papago's Indian.

"Combabi," he said, and perhaps it was the utter lack of any vehemence, or emotion in his voice which made the Indian's face pale slightly. "I'll kill you for that."

Somewhere outside, the big medicine drums they called the *tombes* had begun to beat. Vickers knew what that meant. The Snake and Antelope fraternities had conducted their secret rites in the *estufas* for eight days, fasting and purifying themselves, and now the *tombes* were heralding their readiness for the public dance.

II

The floor was hard and rough beneath Vickers as he sat up. They had taken him to the eastern end of the mesa and thrown him into one of the ceremonial *kivas*, a room dug out of the solid rock and roofed over about a foot above the level of the ground, a ladder leading down into it from above. There was an air hole in the roof. His eyes had been accustoming themselves to the semi-gloom when he realized there was someone else in here. At first, it was only a dim, unrecognizable figure, standing against the wall on the far side. Then he saw it was a woman and realized she had been standing there like that, watching him, ever since he had come in. And finally, he recognized her.

It was like a physical blow. He felt his breath coming out audibly between parted lips. He had tried to prepare himself for it, all the way from his first knowledge of her, telling himself preconceived notions were always wrong. Yet no preconceived idea he had formed could match this, now. They had given her a split Crow skirt of buckskin to enable her to ride, and it only seemed to delineate the tall, statuesque lines of her body. What had Fallon said? The pride? Her white linen blouse had been smudged by dirt and torn by chaparral, but it still shone pale in the dusky light.

"Who are you?" she asked. "Why do you stare at me like that?"

He had no right to let it catch him like this, with the grief of knowing Abeïto was gone still so fresh in his mind. Yet he could not help it, and he knew, somehow, that Abeïto wouldn't mind. He was still gazing at her, hardly conscious of his actions as he fished the three whangs of fringe from his pocket.

"I had a handful of them," said the woman, seeing what he held. "Several people know that I possess them. I tried to leave a trail. I thought if they found them, somehow, they could follow me." She motioned with her hand. "You...?"

"It began to be like I was following someone I'd known all my life," he said. Then he was leaning toward her, still on his knees, something urgent crossing his lean face. "It can happen, can't it? I mean, without ever having seen you, it can happen, to a man, that way?"

Her bosom moved faintly beneath the soiled blouse, and her eyes were still held to his. "What can happen? What way?"

"I wouldn't have believed it could happen," he said, getting to his feet. "Not without knowing you. Not without even seeing you. I tried to tell myself I was a fool. At night I'd lie there in my blankets and think about it and laugh at myself, or try to. I couldn't really laugh, because it was happening, whether I believed it or not."

Suddenly, there seemed to be an affinity between them. Perhaps it was the way they were gazing at each other, perhaps something less physical than that. Vickers saw a growing comprehension in the woman's eyes, and she bent forward slightly, searching for something in his face, her voice barely audible, as if she feared to break a spell.

"Believe what? What was happening?"

"It started so long ago," he said. "Do you think I'm crazy? In Prescott, I guess, when the judge told me...."

"My father?"

He had hardly heard her. "I'd known of you, of course, but only vaguely. The judge didn't tell me much. Just what you meant to him. Not even a description. But it must have started, even then. Later, it was more than that. Do you think I'm crazy? A man named Fallon. He told me some. Your pride? It was like getting a glimpse of you through a window. Not much. Not enough, but enough to want more. Then an Indian boy. He told me the way you rode. About your hair. It was the way he told me. They have a sensitivity to something like that no one else possesses. Just at that age. You know?"

She must have understood what he was trying to say, now. She wanted to smile, and couldn't. Staring at him, her eyes were soft and smoky, and her brows were drawn together in a strange, intense way, as if she were groping to define some emotion within herself.

"I know," she conceded, at last, almost whispering.

"After that, a shaman," said Vickers. "An old man. Too old for anything like the boy. And yet, even him. Telling me about your eyes. And after I left him, I wasn't even trying to laugh at myself any more. It can happen, can't it, that way? Do you think I'm crazy?"

She was still gazing at him, lost in it, like a child enraptured by a storyteller, and she moistened her lips, speaking almost dreamily. "No," she said, and drew a quick, soft little breath, as if faintly surprised at her own words, "no, I don't think you're crazy."

"Well," said a rough voice from the dark corner, "now that you've told the fair maiden of your undying love, maybe you'd better let her know who you are."

Both the girl and Vickers stiffened, as if snapped from a trance. Then Vickers turned to see the big, bearded man in the long-sleeved, red flannels sitting cross-legged against the far wall.

"Reeves," said Vickers stupidly.

"Yeah, little old Red-eye himself," said Reeves. "I guess I should have waited for you to come with me and help sell that rotgut, shouldn't I? Those damn Apaches took my goods and dumped me in their calaboose. What was all that shooting in the shaman's diggings at Diablo?"

"I think you know," said Vickers.

"Do I?" said Reeves slyly. "What happened to Fallon?"

"He ran out the same way you did."

When Reeves spoke, the woman had turned toward the bearded man. Now she was looking at Vickers again. "Mister Reeves said you were going to introduce yourself."

"I'll do the honors," grinned Reeves. "Johnny, this is Miss Sherry Kern. Miss Kern, meet Johnny Vickers."

All the blood seemed to drain from her face at that instant.

"Johnny Vickers!" she said, and there was a loathing in her voice. "Johnny Vickers," and she spat it out the second time, pulling a handful of fringe from the pocket of her shirt, holding it out in front of her for him to see. "I was at the Butterfield station on Union Street when I heard the shot. It was just around the corner, right in front of the *Courier*. I was the first to reach him, and he was still alive. 'Get to Johnny Vickers,' he said, and this was in his hand...." Her fingers closed on the handful of fringe spasmodically and then opened as she flung it at Vickers, taking a step backward, her mouth twisting as she wiped her hand down her skirt. "'Get to Johnny Vickers' he said, and then he died!"

Vickers held out his hand, something chilling him suddenly. "You think...?"

"You know what I think," she said, the words torn from her in a hollow, bitter way. "Why do you suppose I'd come to Prescott that evening? Edgar James and I were going to be married the next day!"

The darkness trembled to the incessant rhythm of the *tombes* now, and beneath the hollow, muffled beat, the other sounds had begun, as the *Moquenos* and Navajos and Apaches gathered toward the end of the mesa for the dance. Vickers hunkered in bitter silence against the wall opposite Red-eye Reeves, looking neither at the bearded man nor at Sherry Kern.

Sure there were hunks missing out of his fringed leggings. Every man who wore leggings cut the fringe off at some time or another when he was without any other kind of lashings to repair his saddle or tie his duffel or a thousand other things they could be used for. So there were hunks cut out of the fringe on his pants. And no other man wore Ute leggings around here. All right. So the Utes dyed their fringe differently. All right. And so Edgar James told them to get Johnny Vickers. The hell with it! He shifted angrily, running his tongue across dry, cracked lips. That was what he'd come for. He should have known it from the beginning. Not the way a Moqui boy looked when he described her, or the way Fallon lost himself when he talked of her. Not any of that. This!

Vickers wanted to spit and didn't have enough saliva in his mouth to do it. His head raised abruptly to the scraping noise from the direction of Reeves. The bearded man had stiffened; he rose to his feet, turning to face the wall, backing off toward the center of the room. The walls were curtained with red *chimayo* blankets, and one of these was thrust aside. The room being sunk into the earth this way, it had never entered Vickers's head that the blankets might conceal a doorway. The portal that opened behind the blankets was a heavy oak piece, set in the solid rock, and a man stood there with one hand holding the *chimayo* blanket back. His face was painted black to the mouth, and from there down to the neck, white. The rest of his body, naked to the waist, was a lake-red. About his square belly was a dancing skirt of wool, with fox skins dangling behind, rattles tied to his naked ankles.

"Your fate has been decided, Vickers," he said in English. "It seems Abeïto tried to tell them you were sent by the Trues before he died. Otherwise they would have killed you outright. As it is, the *principales* have been debating, and their decision is that if you were really sent by the gods, you can survive the Snake Dance."

Vickers was on his feet, staring at the man, and it had struck him by now. "Fallon," he said. "Webb Fallon."

Fallon shut the door quickly behind him, coming forward to be surrounded by the three of them, forgetting their hatred and bitterness in this moment enough to come together. Fallon caught at Vickers's arm.

"Not much time for explanation now. I got away from Diablo on your roan. Came across one of these Antelope Men out getting rattlesnakes for the dance. Knocked him on the head and took his outfit. That Navajo shaman said the Snake Dances were being held at Walpi, and the buckskin thong in the basket was pointing north. I took the chance that implied Sherry had been taken here. Climbed the cliff on this south side during the night, hunted till daylight for her without success. In this monkey suit, I could move around the pueblo pretty free as long as it was dark. Had to hide in one of their *estufas* during the day. I don't speak their language. But neither do the Apaches. Some *Moqueno* was talking to an Apache in Spanish outside the *estufa*. The court where they're going to hold the dance is on a lower level than the upper part of the mesa. Guess you know this. It's where this door leads. It's how we'll escape."

"But it's a sheer cliff on the south side of the court," said Vickers. "We'll have to go through the whole pueblo to get out."

"I don't mean that way," said Fallon. "They'll let you all go if you survive the Snake Dance."

"That's impossible," snapped Vickers. "There's over a hundred rattlers in the ceremony. A white man wouldn't last a minute in that court."

"It's the only way. You can't fight your way through a thousand drunk Indians without even a pocket knife in your hands." Fallon turned toward the door. A *tombe* had begun thumping out there. He spoke swiftly. "They're starting. This has to be fast. When I heard what the *principales* had decided and knew you were in here, I managed to get inside that cottonwood booth where they keep the snakes in a big buckskin bag. I let one out, stepped on its tail before it could coil, closed the bag on the others. Then I grabbed it behind the head and extracted the fangs. Did the same with four others. Sweat made this paint on my body wet enough to daub a circle of it around the tail of each snake. You can't miss it. Whatever they make you do with those snakes, pick the ones with the paint on them."

"But there'll be others," said Vickers. "They have a dozen at a time crawling around that court."

"I'll see that they don't bite you," said Fallon.

The girl's face darkened. "What do you mean?"

Fallon left without answering her. Vickers could feel sweat dampening his face as he stood there with the girl and Red-eye. The fight going on inside Sherry was evident to him in her rigid body, her set face. He didn't blame her. He felt a fear growing in himself. There was something ghastly about the thought of that courtyard out there full of writhing, hissing snakes. Vickers reached out and touched her impulsively, and then let his hand slide off as she turned toward him. He didn't know whether the look on her face was for him or for the snakes.

The door was thrust open, and a pair of braves in the same costume as Fallon had worn entered, carrying the sacred rattles known as *guajes*. The design on their kilts indicated they were of the Bear Clan, and one of them told Vickers in sonorous tones of the sentence imposed on them by the *principales*, then nodded his head toward the door.

Vickers took a deep breath and stepped out, followed by Sherry. A deep sighing sound went up from the crowds lining the tops of the houses on the west of the courtyard, and then a shout, as the Apaches saw the girl following Vickers. There was no ladder from the housetops into the courtyard, but Perry Papago dropped off the first roof, landing like a cat, running out to the captain of the Antelope Society where he stood with his dancers by the sacred cottonwood booth called the *kee-si*.

"There is no reason for the girl to be tested," he told the Moqui, and Vickers realized Papago feared her death would leave him with no hold over the troops in Prescott. "*Pahanas* Vickers is the only one on trial."

"They are all *pahanas*," said the captain. "If they are sent by the Trues, they must prove it. This is the judgment of the *principales*."

"No," shouted Papago. "Combabi, Assaya, Jerome...."

At his call, his Apaches began surging toward the edge of the roof, pushing through the other Indians. Combabi dropped off a house into the court, pulling his cap-and-ball. Then he stopped, with the gun held there in both hands. At the signal of the captain's hand, one of the Antelope Men had swung aside the curtain of the *kee-si* and reached in to unlace the top of one of the buckskin bags holding the snakes, and the first rattler slid out, hissing and writhing. Instinctively, Papago jumped back against the wall, and another big, ugly diamondback rattler slithered from the *kee-si*. Combabi backed up, a twisted revulsion on his face. Perhaps it was the very primitive horror of the slimy death in these creatures that held him from firing, or perhaps that he knew how sacred the snakes were to the *Moquenos*, and how the whole pueblo would mob him if he dared shoot.

Behind him, Vickers heard a strangled sound. At first he thought is was Sherry, and looked toward her. But she was standing rigid beside him, a white line about her tightly shut lips, staring wide-eyed at the half-dozen huge snakes writhing across the floor of the courtyard. It was Reeves.

"Vickers," he said hoarsely, "they ain't gonna make us dance with them snakes. Not white men. Not rattlers like that."

It surprised Vickers. He hadn't expected it from Reeves, somehow; he remembered how Reeves had gone out to get those Apaches at Cañon Diablo, and how he had reacted to the gunshot wound.

"You heard Fallon," said Vickers. "He's fixed some of the snakes. It's our only way."

"No." Reeves's palms were spread out against the rock on either side of him as the Antelope Man let out another hissing snake. "No, Vickers, you're the only one on trial. Papago's right, you're the only one on trial. Ain't no reason the rest of us have to dance with those snakes. I don't see any with paint daubed on their tails. They're real, Vickers. I seen a man bit by one of them diamondbacks last year. He swelled up like a balloon." Sweat was streaking the grime in Reeves's face now, leaking down into his beard. "Tell them I don't have to do it, Vickers. Make up some excuse. You can. You know them. Tell them I got a special chit from these Trues or whatever they are. I just come along. Tell them, Vickers...."

The girl was still standing there like that, and a faint line of red showed across her chin, and Vickers could see now how her teeth were clamped into her bottom lip, and the sight of Reeves disgusted him suddenly. He grabbed the man's arm.

"Come on. You'll spoil it all. If we were sent by the Trues, we wouldn't act like this. They'll get suspicious, and it'll be all over. You've got to trust Fallon."

"No!" Reeves tore from Vickers's grasp, a glazed look in his eyes, falling back against the stone. "Please, Vickers, get me out of this. I'll do anything else. Man or devil. I've fought 'em all in my time. Injun or white, black or yellow, man or beast. I fought a grizzly once. See? See the scar on my chin? But not this, Vickers. You can't just walk in there and start playing with them diamondbacks. They'll have you bloated like a Cimarron carcass in five minutes. Please, Vickers. Anything. I'll do anything. Tell them, Vickers...."

"Shut up!" Vickers slapped him across the face, knocking his head back against the wall. The Indians were watching them now. "If you spoil our only chance here, I'll kill you myself. Now get up like a man and take it. I thought you were a man. Down at Cañon Diablo I thought I hadn't ever seen that kind of nerve before."

"This ain't the same." Reeves was huddled back against the wall, his lower lip slack and wet. "Snakes, Vickers, snakes. It ain't the same. There's something special about them. Anything else, Vickers. I told you. Anything else. Not snakes, Vickers. I seen a man bit. Anything but snakes. I didn't come for this!"

"What did you come for then?" Vickers had both hands buried in his shirt, shaking him savagely. "What did you come for?"

"To get the gal. You know that. Get me out and I'll tell you. Get me out. I'll do anything, Vickers."

Vickers shook him again. "It was you took the shot at me back in the shaman's *hoganda* at Cañon Diablo?"

"Yeah,"—Reeves wiped his slobbering mouth, struggling against Vickers's grip—"yeah, I had to wait till you found out from him where the gal was. I knew he wouldn't tell right out. That ain't an Injun's way. When he said the Snake Dances was being held at Walpi, I knew. Still can't figure how I missed. You must have moved. I placed you dead center before it got too dark. You must have moved."

Vickers shook him again as he started babbling anew. "Who sent you? The Tucson machine?"

"Yeah, yeah." He glanced wild-eyed at the snakes again. "Get me out, Vickers, get me out. The machine. I'll do anything. You promised. The machine. Papago'd worked for us before. We got him to hook the girl so we'd have control over Judge Kern till the elections were over, and we were strong enough to keep the capital at Tucson. Only Papago switched ends on us and brought Sherry here for his own purpose."

"How did you get that handful of fringe from my leggings?"

"Your apprentice printer." Reeves's breathing sounded like a crazed animal's, hoarse, broken. "He cut off a handful when you were sleeping after a bulldog edition. Edgar James had found out about this plot to get Sherry Kern, and had to be eliminated. I guess that's what James meant when he told Sherry your name. You'd been claiming all along the Tucson machine was behind all the trouble in the territory, and James had always laughed at you. It was only then that he knew you were right."

Sherry had turned toward them, a dazed comprehension seeping through the other emotions twisting her face. "You mean Vickers didn't murder Edgar? Why should they try to implicate him at all?"

"I guess you haven't been in the territory long enough to know how Vickers was fighting the Tucson machine," said Reeves. "I guess you don't know how hard they've been trying to get rid of him."

"They've tried it before?" Sherry's voice held doubt.

"I've got a slug in my shoulder for one time," said Vickers in a flat tone. "There's a dead triggerman buried on Caliente Hill for another. I guess they got tired of trying it that way. This was a sort of two-birds-with-one-stone deal, wasn't it?" He jammed Reeves back against the rock viciously. "Who was it?"

Reeves's glazed eyes rolled up to him. "When we knew James had to be killed, we paid your apprentice to cut a handful of fringe off your leggings. Everybody knew how you and James hated each other. He made it even better by saying your name at the last...."

"Who was it?"

The utter savagery of Vickers's voice made Reeves recoil. "Papago," he gasped, staring at Vickers. "We'd hired him other times. Papago burned James down." Then he was staring past Vickers. "They're coming. Vickers, you promised. Get me out. Get me out! I can't dance with any snakes. For God's sake!"

Vickers sensed the dancers moving in behind him, and he almost shouted the last, jamming Reeves against the wall. "Who's the top saddle in the machine, Reeves? Who runs the whole thing? You know. Tell me, tell me...."

"No, Vickers, no!" Reeves began fighting with a sudden, bestial fear, screaming and writhing against the rock, tearing at Vickers's face, lurching out of his grasp. "Don't let them, Vickers. I ain't going to dance with no snakes. No, Vickers, no...!"

Vickers was torn aside from behind, and two Antelope Men caught Reeves, pulling him to his feet. Reeves was a big man, his fear giving him a violent strength, and he surged forward with a scream, fighting loose. Another pair of *Moquenos* caught him, and the four dancers shoved the shouting, fighting, man out toward the snakes. When they were near the writhing mass of reptiles, they gave Reeves a last shove. He stumbled forward, unable to catch himself till too late. Already, three of the snakes were coiled. The thump the first one made, striking, carried clearly to Vickers. Reeves's scream was hardly human. Kicking the snakes away, he whirled blindly, but another diamondback whirred and struck. The big man jerked with that hammer blow against his thigh. He tore at the bullet head, whirling and bawling in a frenzy of fear.

"Vickers, get me out! You promised, damn you, promised. Get me out. I ain't going to dance with no snakes. Vickers, Vickers, Vickers!"

The words ended in a crazy scream as another snake hit him. They were all about him now, hissing and rattling and coiling, and he turned this way and that, kicking wildly with his feet, roaring in a terrible fear. Vickers was held spellbound by the ghastly spectacle, filled with a wild impulse to rush in and drag the man out of it, repelled by a growing horror of the snakes. Twice he made a spasmodic move toward Reeves, and the Antelope Men caught his arms. Sherry was watching with terrified eyes, bosom rising and falling violently beneath her blouse.

"Vickers, please, Vickers, Vickers." Reeves's shouts became weaker, and he made a last attempt to turn away from the snakes, arms held across his face, and other rattlers struck him, almost knocking him over. He sank to his knees, his cries hoarse, pitiful, shaking and blubbering. He tried to crawl out on his hands and knees. Another snake coiled before him, hissing, rattling. Reeves let out a last, hoarse scream, rising almost to his feet. Turning wildly away, he shuddered at its blow, falling down again.

He sank onto his belly, his soft blubbering becoming incoherent, finally stopping, to lie there, a great hulk of a man in his Levi's and red flannels, utterly silent.

Two Antelope Men walked out to get him. A rattler struck at one of them, and he kicked the snake away casually, stooping to lift Reeves. They carried him back past Vickers into the room from which they had come.

Vickers caught himself abruptly, moving over till Sherry was against his side, catching her cold hand. "You've got to trust Fallon. It's our only chance, Sherry. It was the panic that got Reeves. Not the snakes. A man doesn't die that fast from their bite. Maybe fear makes the venom work faster. I don't know. All I know is you can't let it affect you like that. Fallon said he'd get us out. Do you hear me, Sherry?"

"I hear you, Vickers." Her voice was small, shaky. She was trembling against him, and her fingers dug into his palm till the nails brought blood. Then a *tombe* began to beat from the nearby rooftop.

In front of the *kee-si* was a pit dug in the ground, supposed to represent *Shi-pa-pu*, the Black Lake of Tears, and the twenty men of the Antelope Society began circling this, shaking their *guajes*. Then a huge *tombe* on the rooftop nearby began to beat, and the men of the Snake Society emerged from the sacred *estufa* at the north end of the court. The captain of the Snake Order, upon reaching the first snake, tickled it with a feather as it started to coil, making it stretch out, then snatched it behind the head and put it between his teeth. A man of the Antelope Society placed his arm around the snake-man's shoulders, and together they started in the peculiar hippety-hop toward the sacred rock at the south end of the court. Each snake-man in turn took his snake, and was joined by his Antelope partner. As the third pair left the *kee-si* together, an Antelope man emerged from the booth behind them, so close that Vickers was sure he alone saw it, the Indians on the rooftops probably not even aware the man had not been there all the time, the dancers too busy with their rituals to notice where he came from. There were seventeen of the Snake Order, and twenty of the Antelope, and when they had all paired off, it left three Antelope Men to gather up the snakes as each pair of dancers rounded the sacred dancing rock and came back, each snake-man dropping his reptile with a twist of his head. The snakes were writhing furiously in the *Moquenos'* mouths now, trying desperately to strike the Indians, all their leverage for striking dissipated by the position in which they hung. The captain of the Snake Order had already rid himself of his first snake, and standing by the *kee-si* with his partner, rattled his ceremonial *guaje* at the whites, calling something.

"What did he say?" Sherry's voice was hoarse.

"He's ordering us to pick up a snake and dance with it in our mouth," said Vickers.

Suddenly the girl's body was shuddering violently. Her teeth showed white against her red lower lip, drawing blood, and her voice shook with the terrible effort she was making to control herself.

"I can't do this," she said. "I can't. I can't!"

"You've got to," said Vickers tensely. The Antelope man who had come from the booth was separating a big diamondback from three other reptiles on the courtyard floor. He reached in with both hands to grab the snake behind its head before it could coil. Vickers saw a smaller one coil and strike, and saw the man flinch and grit his teeth.

Fallon. Dressed in the bizarre costume, he moved toward them, holding the leaping diamondback, two red dots on his right hand. Sweat was streaking the black paint on his face.

"Take it," he told Sherry under his breath. "It's the one I fixed. Take it."

Sherry stumbled backward, her hands out in front of her, face pale. Vickers clamped his teeth shut and grabbed the snake behind the head, just beneath Fallon's grip, tearing it from him. He caught Sherry by the arm, pulling her violently to him, then caught her abundance of black hair and held her head rigid, her body against him, and jammed the seven feet of writhing serpent against her face. She screamed, and for that moment her face was twisted in utter horror. Then he felt her stiffen against him, and her eyes were staring wide and suddenly free from fear into his, and it was as if she took the strength from him.

Her mouth opened and he forced the snake between her teeth, and she bit into the smooth, diamond-marked hide so hard the tail and head leaped into the air, the circle of paint Fallon had daubed on its body near the rattles gleaming wetly. An Antelope Man put his arm around Sherry and guided her toward the dancing rock in that strange hippety-hop.

Fallon had already chosen another marked snake for Vickers. Vickers felt a moment of sick revulsion and closed his eyes as he took the snake from Fallon's hand, jamming it into his mouth. It tasted wet and acrid and sandy all at once, and he almost gagged on it. The fetid arm of a sweating Antelope Man was thrown around his shoulder, and they hopped toward the dancing rock. The snake beat against him, sending waves of nausea through his whole body, and he knew an insupportable desire to vomit.

But as he turned the dancing rock with the stinking partner, he saw the real danger was ahead of them. The snakes which the other pairs had dropped were slithering across the courtyard between the rock and the *kee-si*, and though the three Antelope Men relegated to that job kept picking them up and putting them into the cotton-wood booth, there were always some snakes left on the ground.

Sherry and the Antelope Man who was dancing with her were almost to the *kee-si* when she dropped the snake from her mouth. It slithered away, and she tried to disengage herself from the Antelope Man. Vickers could see it now, and almost upset the man hopping with him as he tried to reach Sherry. One of the diamondbacks had freed itself from the writhing mass on the floor within the circle of dancers, slithering directly toward Sherry and her partner, and it had no paint daubed on its tail.

Vickers dropped his own snake, fighting free of his partner, leaping toward her, as the diamondback reared up, and coiled. Sherry screamed, scratching the face of her partner, but he caught her hand, ignoring the coiling snake to pull her toward the *kee-si* to get another serpent. A sob escaped Vickers as he saw that he would be too late. The diamondback's head disappeared in a blur of movement. Vickers shouted in a hoarse, cracked way, still running forward. Then he saw what had happened. Somehow, another Antelope Man had gotten in between Sherry and the snake in that last instant, and the serpent fell back from striking the man's leg.

"Fallon," gasped Vickers between his teeth, and suddenly understood what the man had meant back in the *kiva*. *I'll see that they don't bite you.*

Again the *Moquenos* made them take snakes in their mouths, and again it was Fallon who managed to be the one handing them each snake, picking out the ones marked with paint. This time Sherry took it herself. She was sobbing and her hands were shaking, but she took the ugly reptile, making a choked sound as she forced it into her mouth, and started dancing toward the rock again. Fallon caught a snake for Vickers, staggering toward him. The man's face was turned muddy by the sweat mixing with the black paint, and he fell against Vickers, gasping.

"We're doing it, we're doing it. If only she can hang on one more time. Three times around, see...."

After the third time to the rock and back again, after casting aside the writhing snake, Vickers asked him: "Why, Fallon?"

"My job, isn't it?" panted Fallon, shoving him. "I'm all right. Got hold of some of that tea they call *mah-que-he*. Antelope Men drink it to give them immunity. Kern sent me out to get her, didn't he?"

"This isn't your job," said Vickers, fighting with the writhing snake in his grasp. "A man wouldn't do this just for a job. You knew what it meant. You knew that *mah-que-he* wouldn't give you immunity. These snake-men train all their lives. They've been drinking that tea eight days now. You knew what it meant. Why, Fallon?"

Fallon whirled to face him fully, those wide eyes meeting his, a little crazy now. "You know why! You came for the same reason. Even when I met you there in the Tortillas, it had already happened to you. Just hearing about her. I knew her, see. You just heard about her, and it happened to you. I knew her. That's why!"

The *tombe* stopped. A hush fell over the throng on the walls, and the sweating dancers halted, drawing together in front of the *kee-si*. The captain of the Snake Order held up his *guaje*, turning toward the four quarters, then bowing to Vickers.

"Abeïto spoke the truth. No *pahanas* has ever passed the ordeal before you. The Trues have sent you."

Vickers had a chance to speak with Fallon, grabbing his arm when they passed him going out. "You're coming with us. If you can't get away now, we'll wait for you below."

"Don't be a fool," said Fallon. "I can't leave till the dance is over. They'd suspect something."

"Fallon...."

"No!" The man jerked away, his face twisted. "This tea's about through working in me anyway. You know that. What's the use of risking your life for a dead man? I did this for her. You get her back. Promise me that!"

Vickers drew a heavy breath. "I promise you that."

"Now, get the hell out of here!"

They gave Vickers his Henry back, and the roan Fallon had taken at Cañon Diablo, and another horse for Sherry. The *Moquenos* watched them pass down the street, sullen and silent, and Vickers could see how many of them were still drunk on Reeves's whiskey. He was practically holding Sherry up and, as they neared the start of the trail down, leading their horses, he felt her grow taut against him, and he saw it, too.

They were strung out across the trail, a dozen or more, with their narrow, drunken faces and glittering eyes and .50 Sharps, and Papago stood out in front of them. "You aren't taking the girl, Vickers. Hand her over and you can go."

"I'm taking her, Papago. You heard the decision of the *principales*. You'll be bucking more than me if you try to stop us."

"The *Moquenos* won't interfere," said Papago. "You see how drunk they are. They'd just as soon see you dead as not, after the way you messed up their Snake Dance. Now, hand her over."

"It won't stop with me," said Vickers. "There's still the Tucson machine. Do you think Reeves will be the last man they send up here?"

"As a matter of fact," said Papago, "I do."

"You're dreaming," said Vickers.

"No," said Papago, "you wanted to know who sat the top saddle in the Tucson machine? A strong man, Vickers. The kind of man who could get out and do something himself when his men failed."

The implication of that shocked Vickers enough to take him off-guard, and his incredulity was in his voice. "Are you trying to say that Reeves...?"

"...was the head of the Tucson machine! He'd sent half a dozen of his men out to find the girl before he finally got impatient and came himself. He was that kind, Vickers. Almost as dangerous as you. And now that he's gone, Kern won't have much trouble shifting the capital back to Prescott and smashing the machine for good." Papago shifted impatiently. "I'm through talking. Come on alone, and we'll let you do it standing up."

"You're bluffing, Papago," said Vickers. "You don't dare defy the edict of the *principales* if you want them to help you against the troops. We're coming through."

He put one hand behind Sherry's back, guided her forward, but with his first move, Papago went for his gun. "This is how we're bluffing, Vickers."

Vickers had not really believed they would try it, here. He could have brought his own Henry up and cocked it about the same time Papago got the Remington out, but that would have left Sherry in the line of fire. With a grunt, he threw himself against the girl, not even trying for his own gun, and the two of them went down, rolling into the dark doorway of the adobe house on this side, the roar of gunfire echoing down the street as Papago and the Apaches opened up.

The wall cut him off from most of the Apaches, but he could still see two of them out there. He snapped the lever of his Henry, and it bucked in his hand, and one Apache yelled and doubled over, dropping his Sharps. A new volley of gunfire rocked the narrow way, and bullets made their deadly thud into the mud walls all about Vickers. But there were only one or two Apaches beside Papago with six-shooters, and the others had those old, single-shot Sharps rifles. The sudden cessation of gun-sound told him they had emptied their rifles and had to take that moment for reloading, and he knew it would be his only chance.

"There's only one way to finish this," he muttered.

"Papago?" said Sherry.

He turned to see her face, pale and drawn in the dim light, staring up at him. "Indians are like that, Sherry. Get their leader and all the sand will go out of them."

"Vickers, you can't go out there...."

"I can," said Vickers. "While they're busy with me, you get out of here and back down the street to the *principales*. They'll keep their word about letting you go."

"Vickers...."

But he was already throwing himself out the door with his Henry held across his belly, an adamantine cast to his lean, burned face, his mouth twisting as he saw the first Apache skulking down the wall across the street, and fired. The man jerked against the wall, still trying to jam a fresh load down his Sharps, then fell forward onto his face. A figure loomed on the roof of the first level across the street, and Vickers realized they had been trying to come up on him inside the house that way. The man had a six-gun and began firing wildly, with both hands, and only then did Vickers recognize him. The Henry made its single hollow boom.

"I told you, Combabi, I told you," shouted Vickers, still going forward down the street, as Combabi pitched head foremost off the roof and then Vickers's eyes swung to the man farther down in the middle of the street. He had been trying to work down next to the wall while Vickers was inside, but as soon as Vickers showed, he had moved into the center. It was some distance, and Papago did not fire as most Indians would have. He moved toward Vickers, increasing his speed, bent forward a little. Vickers was still turning from firing at Combabi, and he snapped the lever home hard, and the gun bucked hot against his belly. Papago did not jerk, and Vickers knew he had missed. Then Papago's Remington spoke.

Vickers had been shot before, and the hammer blow against his leg was no new sensation. The street seemed to drop from beneath him and he found himself on his belly with the Henry pinned beneath him. A terrible, swimming pain robbed him of all volition. Through a haze he saw Papago still coming forward, lining up the gun for another shot. Then it was Sherry's voice.

"Vickers!"

Something inside him grew taut and hard and clear. He pulled the gun upward till the barrel lay beneath his chin, snapping the cylinder out sideways beneath him. Papago saw it and tried to stop him, firing sooner than intended. The hard earth kicked up in a puff of acrid, blinding dust before Vickers's eyes. He squeezed the trigger that way.

When the dust fell and the stunning force of the bullet striking earth so near to Vickers left him, he could see Papago lying on his belly down the street. The Apaches were already beginning to gather about their leader, forgetting Vickers. One of them had a surprised look on his face. Then it was Sherry's hands on Vickers, soft, cool, somehow, lifting him up. The pain in his leg made him dizzy.

"Help me on the roan," he said between gritted teeth. "We've got to get out. It's all over now."

She helped him up against the horse, her arms about his body. "In a way it's over, Vickers, but in another way, it's just begun," she said "I told you I didn't think you were crazy, back in that room. You were right. It can happen, that way, to a man." And her eyes were soft and smoky, meeting his, "or a woman."

Giff(ord Paul) Cheshire

was born on a homestead in Cheshire, Oregon. The county was named for his grandfather who had crossed the plains in 1852 by wagon from Tennessee and the homestead was the same one his grandfather had claimed upon his arrival. Cheshire's early life was colored by the atmosphere of the Old West which in the first decade of the new century had not yet been modified by the automobile. In 1929 he came to the Portland area and from 1929 to 1943 worked for the U. S. Corps of Engineers. By 1944, after moving to Beaverton, Oregon, he found he could make a living writing Western and North-Western short fiction for the magazine market and presently stories under the byline Giff Cheshire began appearing in *Lariat Story Magazine*, *Star Western*, *North-West Romances*, *Blue Book*, as well as *Big-Book Western*. Cheshire's Western fiction is characterized by a wide historical panorama of the frontier and often his stories are set in the Pacific Northwest, a region whose history he knew well. STARLIGHT BASIN (Random House, 1954), THUNDER ON THE MOUNTAIN (Doubleday, 1960) and WENATCHEE BEND (Doubleday, 1966) are among his best novels. No less notable for their complex characters, expert pacing, and authentic backgrounds are his novels under the Chad Merriman byline, beginning with BLOOD ON THE SUN (Fawcett Gold Medal, 1952). Several of the Chad Merriman titles have recently appeared in hardcover reprint editions in the Gunsmoke series from Chivers Press.

Wild Was the River

————◦◦◦◦————

I

DIG DEEP FOR HELL

The river was in spring flood, with raging water bursting from its basalt bed. Since mid-winter Cal Libby had watched it climb better than twelve feet on the stage gages tacked to the coffers at the upper boat locks. Each foot compounded its stresses and put him a foot nearer jeopardy. With the leaden overcast lending dusk to this mid-morning, with a cold wash of rain sweeping the river and Yellow Point as though it would never end, he was there finally. It was his first big construction job and the way things were going, it threatened to be his last.

Eastward the winding upper river dissolved into the storm scud. From the background came the deep and angry bumbling of the falls. Directly behind him was the deep forty-foot ditch, half a mile long, that his outfit had cut straight across Yellow Point to provide a canal, sodden and pooled deeply with yellow drainage water, its banks riprapped. At either end were the nearly-completed lock chambers that would lift the steamboats around the falls once the project was watered naturally.

Cal looked toward his big crew of laborers strengthening the dirt buttress to the upper coffers with earth-filled burlap bags in an unending effort to offset the pressure from the river side. They were also building dikes along the exposed sides of the canal, meeting the threat of flood water from a dozen scattered points with a slow, stubborn defense.

————◦◦◦◦————

Gusts of cold wind swept down the river, and the men were a sodden and miserable lot. For a week they had been at it, and the steady inching on the gage boards promised no respite. In the moments he had been standing here, Cal's gum boots had sunk ankle deep in the soggy yellow subsoil bared by the graders. Yet the men shoveled it determinedly, tirelessly. In spite of his worry Cal's heart warmed for a moment. Here was a tough and loyal outfit.

One of Bernie Raxworthy's wagons mucked slowly past on the portage road scheduled soon to be obsolete. The teamster looked at Cal with an insolent grin and called: "Fine rain we're having!" Then he cackled. "Fine for Libby City!"

Cal glanced at him but appeared not to hear. Turning to his horse, he swung into the wet saddle. A hundred yards upstream was the upper boat landing and terminal of the portage road that for so many years had connected the lower and upper rivers. A steamboat was tied there, patiently loading in the storm, with the mule-drawn portage wagons plodding along the road that rounded the point from the lower landing. The portage system belonged to Bernie Raxworthy.

"Fine for Libby City!" Cal repeated with a wry grimace as he turned his mount down the road. "They can't wait to see the coffers go and the water come in!" The town was getting itself set for a big and conclusive laugh. Raxworthy must be licking his thin lips in anticipation.

There had been a long period of political conflict behind this navigation project. Somewhere in the wash of geological time Nature had broken a navigable river. Now the great waters surged over the rent at Yellow Point Falls. In the early years of steamboating, Libby City had been the head of navigation. But there was rich and growing country above in the Upper Chuckaluck and East Teclon valleys. When Cal Libby was still a boy, Bernie Raxworthy had built a steamer on the upper level and connected the two water flights with his portage road. Then gold had been discovered at the headwaters and along tributary streams in the drainage basin. Sucking miners north from the dwindling California diggings and inland from the seaboard, it had made traffic teem on the river. It had built Libby City. Many steamboats appeared on both flights of the river, but the portage road became a funnel through which it all had to flow, and the increment for Bernie Raxworthy's pocket had been rich.

The mining boom was over. River interests and business men in the upper valleys had long since begun to complain against Raxworthy's financial domination. The federal government had been persuaded at last to hold a hearing on the proposition that the portage road should be replaced with a canal and public navigation locks, permitting the through passage of packets without trans-shipment. Libby City had risen against this as one man. Possessed by the political power accruing to one of his wealth, Bernie Raxworthy had nearly succeeded in killing the project in the hearing stage. He had been bucking it ever since.

Cal Libby's stake in the struggle was more than professional. He had been contracting on the coast when he heard that the government was advertising for bids on the canal. So determined had he been to secure the contract for himself, he had made his own bid dangerously low. For that reason, if no worse came of it, he could not survive the setback should the major part of his eighteen months' work go out.

Following the portage road, Cal rounded the point, his gaze sweeping across the vast lip of water that boiled in a sixty-foot drop to the lower reach, now an evil gray-green from the flood-borne soil. Then he straightened in the saddle. Down the other side of the point a buggy drawn by a yellow mare was wheeling toward him. Cal swung his mount onto the shoulder. He would have passed it had not Bernie Raxworthy reined up as they met.

In his early fifties, Raxworthy was a cadaverous individual, his gaunt face covered with a silky, gray-streaked beard, his thin, peaked head topped by a beaver hat set precisely horizontal, his scrawny neck enclosed in a celluloid collar.

"See you cleared your equipment outta the ditch, Cal!" Raxworthy said. "Ain't you getting on top of it?"

Cal shook his head impatiently, his dislike of the man growing stronger. "It's a record flood, coming at the worst possible time. I don't know what's going to happen next."

The other looked at him closely. "Need any more help? Why don't you call for volunteers from town? Dike her to the sky, if you have to!" Raxworthy lifted the reins squarely before his chest. "Just say the word, if you want help. We'll all be glad to lend a hand."

Cal rode on in astonishment. He did not even entertain the idea that Raxworthy might have undergone a change of attitude. Avarice and shrewdness and ruthless selfish interests were written all over his thin face. It was more likely that he was so certain the project was doomed that he was putting on face by pretending to be concerned about it. Again Cal Libby wondered why he had always hated the man. It was not an emotion that could be defined readily, and it sprang out of mystery. Garth Libby, Cal's father, had come to the west with an emigrant train. Arriving on the river he had decided it was trail's end, as far as he was concerned. He had located his farm where Libby City now stood.

A couple of years later Bernie Raxworthy had come along. Already the river bank at this point was being used as a landing for the *bateaux* by which the emigrants moved through the mountains by water. Buying an acre of land from Garth Libby, Raxworthy had started a store. He had cultivated Libby. Then, a year later, Garth Libby had drowned in Yellow Point Falls. Cal had been three years old then, and all he knew about that was what his mother had told him, years later: "Your dad had dreams of there being a big town here, someday. So did Raxworthy. He and Raxworthy liked to shoot ducks in the sloughs up the river, and they kept a rowboat on the upper side of Yellow Point. I always worried about those falls, but your father only laughed at that. Then this day they were out, and only Bernie Raxworthy came back. He came to the house dripping wet. He said the skiff had overturned and your father had been caught in the current. Raxworthy couldn't help him and barely managed to hold onto the boat and make his own way ashore. But he's been good to us."

Garth Libby's body had never been found. Yet ever afterward, when young Calvin Libby stood in the presence of Raxworthy, something had caused his flesh to prickle in an almost animal-like ferocity. And part of this feeling had turned toward Dorcas Raxworthy, Bernie's adopted daughter who had been Cal's first playmate, his childhood love. Like himself, Susan Libby had believed that Raxworthy felt a sense of guilt in the matter. Knowing that she could not manage it herself, he had bought the land, paying her a fair, going price. Eastern born and a gentlewoman, Susan Libby had put away most of the money from it and had supported herself and son by dress-making in the growing town. Years later, when Cal had finished the local school, she had dug out the money and had sent him away for more education. While Cal was still working for his engineering degree, she had died.

There was no reason to believe that Bernie Raxworthy knew more than he had ever told about the death of Garth Libby. But it had placed him in an extremely advantageous position. When Libby's farm had grown from a village to a fair-sized town, Raxworthy had made the gesture of naming it Libby City. But Bernie Raxworthy had grown rich, and never once in all those years had Cal Libby stopped hating him.

Cal could see the lower locks now and the scattering of temporary structures that furnished his office, shops, and storehouses. A little way below was the lower steamboat landing, misty in the rain, with another packet discharging cargo onto the portage wagons. Cal rode into the muddy, rutted yard and dismounted before the office shack. One of the inspectors kept on the job by the government looked out the door of a small structure across the road, drew fingers across his brow as though sludging away the rain.

"Has she watered it for us yet?" he called.

Cal grinned thinly. "Liable to any minute. You better be warming up your speaking voice in case you plan to deliver a dedication speech." He tied the mount to the hitch rack and turned into the office.

His immediate assistant, Simon Moon, hinged around on a drafting stool and stretched sleepily. "Well, what's the situation?"

"It's hard to say, Si. Water's still climbing on the gate boards. The crew's still piling dirt on the dikes. Your guess is as good as mine as to who'll win." He paced restlessly to the stove, stretched his cold, chapped hands to warm them. "Maybe the rise is a little slower, but that doesn't mean much. It all depends on whether the run-off up in the drainage basin's crested. Bad weather up there, too, will raise hell with us."

"They're likely getting it," Moon said somberly. He was a little younger than Cal, not much over twenty-five, a tawny-thatched, lanky man who had helped Cal secure financial backing for this ambitious undertaking through family connections. He said, "Here I'm yawning myself silly, and you're the one who's been up the last three nights. Why don't you go into town and catch yourself a snooze? At least get a hot meal."

"Yeah, maybe I will."

Cal had been sleeping only at short intervals since he had first realized that the spring floods were breaking all records. His crew had worked nearly as hard. Again he thought of Bernie Raxworthy's offer of help, in mounting perplexity.

From the start Libby City had been convinced that the canal would be its ruin. The trans-shipment of freight and passengers fattened not only Raxworthy's coffers but was an important economic factor in the town. Freight handlers, teamsters, merchants, hotel men, and saloon keepers all profited from the glut caused by each packet's having to unload, portage and reload here.

Cal Libby, they said, had turned traitor and come to destroy the town his father had built. But now it looked as though some higher court had granted the town a reprieve. Swirling flood water, coming through the cut in force, would do crippling damage to incomplete work, to the rock riprapping, to unfinished installations. The setback would wreck the Libby Construction Company and, since Bernie Raxworthy would turn on the pressure again, it might prompt the government to abandon the project as unfeasible. The thought of that Cal Libby could not stand.

II

BONDED IN BLOOD

The town was built on a low bench south of the river, a hand to which Yellow Point was attached as the thumb. Cal rode up the grade and turned through the elm-studded residential section, jogging past the big ornate Raxworthy residence. He came at last to the shaded old house overlooking the river where he had been born and raised. Cal had kept the house and had re-opened it when he came back to build the canal.

He put the horse in the stable and crossed the grass-grown yard, aware as he always was of the reminders of his youth. The lower limb of an old maple in the yard still showed the marks of a rope swing, and there was a rocky pool nearby, falling apart and filled with rain water, where he had kept turtles and frogs and small fish. There was the old woodshed, on the roof of which he and Tobey Drake had smoked their first tobacco and grown deathly ill. Under the huge cherry tree he and Dorcas had played house and tended numerous imaginary children. Yet the memories did not warm him, and he wondered now if he had ever been happy here.

He kindled a fire in the fireplace and another in the big kitchen range to heat water. In the growing warmth he shucked off most of his soggy clothes and poured himself two fingers of whiskey to take the chill out of his marrow. Then he shaved and bathed and got into fresh clothes. For a long while he stood before the fireplace, and through the big window he could see the lower end of the new canal. Irritation passed through him again. The chips were down, and it was a maddening struggle in which from here on he could do nothing more than wait.

He saw the figure move past the window at the end of the long room, heard the quick light step on the porch, pulses crashing in his ears. He was halfway to the door before the low knock came, and he was smiling grimly when he opened it.

The girl looked at him somberly. "May I come in, Cal?"

"I don't see why not, Dorcas." He stood aside, letting her pass him. She moved across the room, turned in front of the fireplace, and looked at him once more, uncertain and questioning, pulling off her rain hat. "You're dripping," he said. "Better let me take the slicker, too."

He helped her out of the rain coat, aware as he had used to be of the tall, slender suppleness of her. She let a hand quickly explore her dark hair, her deep gray eyes still not losing their thoughtfulness as they studied him. He thought again how strange it was that he had always loved and disliked her at the same time.

"I saw you go by the house, Cal. I've been wanting to talk to you for a long time."

The years had done much for her, he saw. It had always been difficult for those who did not understand that the girl was only the adopted child of Bernie Raxworthy to reconcile his pale fleshlessness with this creature in whom strange forces stirred. The impact of it now made Cal feel suddenly callow and clumsy, yet it warmed him as the drink had failed to do, tying together a strand of his life that had been broken for so many years. He had avoided her, he supposed, because he did not want it tied again.

Then the girl said, "I don't suppose you realize that you've had a supporter in me all this time, Cal, even if rather ineffectual. And not just because we played together when we were youngsters. Even raised a family, as I remember it." She smiled wistfully. "I believe in what you've done here, and I've tried to persuade a few people. I think I've succeeded a little. So...do you still dislike me?"

Cal ignored the question as he stared at her. "Does that include Bernie Raxworthy?"

"Yes. Is it just your pride, Cal? Everyone is worried about the high water. Couldn't we help you? There's scores of men in town who would, I think, if you'd say the word."

He laughed harshly. "Libby City to the rescue! What's up? Your father made that same kind of talk this morning."

Her interest brightened. "Did he? I've been trying to win him over for a year, Cal. Don't hate us so! Can't you understand that there can be honest differences of opinion? That people can be big enough to admit when they've been wrong?"

He was watching her closely, keenly aware of the slim, supple body beneath the plain gray dress, the quick and daring mind behind the calm gray eyes. "Perhaps. But I just don't see it happening in Libby City! Not after the fight they put up here, the way they forced me to import my labor, the way they tied me up at every turn. It's been a tough go every foot of the way, and they've done all they could to add to it. I just don't see them changing face at this late date!" Seeing the twist of her mouth, he softened his tone. "But as far as you're concerned, I'm glad to know how you feel. I always considered you on the other side. That's why I steered clear of you. I'm sorry, now."

Dorcas frowned. "I'm not so sure that you are. You've always relished hurting me. It was so like you to make me come to you, finally. I think you like to humble me because it gives you a sense of humbling Bernie Raxworthy." Then, ruefully, she added, "And you've always gotten away with it, damn you!"

He turned toward her quickly, his slightly grinning face masking the fact that she was probing accurately into his mind. It was true that he had always realized his power over her, and he sensed it yet. In childhood the fibers of her being had been so frankly attached to him, and some deep intuition told him they had never come loose. So sure was he of that, he reached abruptly and took her hands. It surprised her, yet he knew that the crimson moving ever so slowly on her face was not anger. He knew, also, that rancor was strong in the hypnotic warmth creeping within himself. He pulled her to him, seeing the protest in her eyes yet knowing that the lips that received his kiss were no longer child's lips.

She drew away quickly, saying: "Won't anything ever change you, Cal Libby?"

The perverseness within him exulted at the perplexed hurt in her voice, in her eyes. He grinned mockingly. "A little token of my gratitude, my dear."

"And I'm humbly grateful!" Then, bitterly, "Oh, Cal! What is it that you've held against me so? What is it? I could tell you something! But no...I don't dare!"

"What?"

"Nothing, Cal, really! Forget I said that! Will you get my coat?"

"Are you trying to punish me? Dorcas, do you know anything about how Garth Libby died? Is that what you hinted at?"

For an instant she looked frightened. "Please. Get my coat."

He laughed. "No. We've always been spark and tinder to each other, and you know it. And now we're grown." He seized her with rough carelessness, crushing his lips to hers. Twisting, she beat at him with clutched hands. She managed to free her mouth.

"I'm not afraid of you, Cal! But I won't have this with your mind set against me! Oh, don't degrade me so...!"

The resistance went out of her as he took her lips again, and with a sigh of surrender she closed her eyes.

Cal Libby rode back to the project in mid-afternoon, and it was not until he was back in the wet whip of the wind that he managed to shake the sense of unreality from him. He rode past the office and lower lock chamber without stopping. The packet had finished unloading and was gone, and the portage road was now deserted. Cal followed it to the upper end. Remorse was beginning to work in him. He had not learned what in a wild seizure of impulse he had set out to learn. He had not freed his mind of the dimly understood impulses that had burned in it so long. But for a time he had forgotten the peril of the river. It became very real again. A check on the gage board told him the water had climbed a couple of inches since morning. This was a fraction less than yesterday. Yet it was probably some pulsion in the run-off, and he dared not hope that the crest had come.

A packet was moving down the channel, and he saw that it was the *Inland Queen*, one of the two steamers Raxworthy still ran on the upper flight. It came slowly through the rain, cutting toward the wharf boat at the end of the portage road, rolling on the choppy water. Cal turned down the yellow ruts, his boots sucking in the gumbo, and made his way to the landing. He watched the packet swing to, its big stern wheel reversing in a churn of muddy water, deckhands fore and aft passing lines ashore.

As soon as the skipper showed himself in the pilot house door, Cal called: "What's the weather like above?"

The man frowned. "Lousy. The storm's moved in over the mountains. If you know arithmetic, you can add the thing up."

"Yeah. I can add it, fella."

With a sinking feeling, Cal told himself he had to accept the fact. Every so often a river put on an unprecedented performance, as if in outrageous delight. Turning, he went back to the emergency dikes. Desperate now, he considered what Dorcas had suggested, that he knuckle down and call on the town for help. If a new run-off was due, it might be a day or so before it showed its effect this far down. With enough men it might be possible to widen the base of the dikes and build them high enough to turn the trick. Yet distrust held him, and it was more than rancor. He called a foreman to him.

"Bill, there's more water coming. Have you got any idea we haven't tried?"

The man scowled. "No more than what we done. If we had more equipment, maybe we could stay ahead of it. As it is, we'll just have to run like hell if the coffers go."

"How about calling for help from town?"

"And give one of them jiggers a chance to back stab us? Not unless we're crazy!"

Cal smiled grimly. That had been his own conviction from the start. A portage wagon dragged slowly along the mucky road, coming up with cargo for the *Inland Queen*. A little later it went back, and Cal saw that the skipper was riding in the seat beside the driver. Cal's lips curled bitterly. The man would give Libby City another morsel to lick its lips over with the news that the crest was a long ways away.

Returning to the office, Cal left the portage road and moved down through the cut, appraising for the hundredth time the damage that would result from a premature flooding. The upper lock chamber, thirty feet deep, forty wide, and a hundred and fifty in length, was concreted on sides and bottom but the tunnels and pits for the giant valves and conduits were only half finished. They would be plugged or scoured into total loss. The same was true of the lower chamber. The canal and the big turnout basin half way between the two locks were ripped on their sloping banks, and violent damage would be done to this by a premature wash of wild water. There was nothing he could do to lessen the damage should the worst happen; the only hope was the feeble one that they might somehow prevent its happening.

It was nearly dusk when Si Moon turned from the office window through which he had been moodily watching the steady rain and grunted, "Criminy, Cal, its looks like we got a damn' delegation coming to pay us a visit!"

Cal paced across the floor. A large contingent of men were moving down the road from town, with shovels and picks and mattocks across their shoulders. They all had grim, determined faces.

Cal swore. "The little helpers! By God, we're having none of them! They can about-face and head for home!"

Moon looked at him curiously. "We're in a tight squeeze. Maybe we oughta take a chance on 'em."

A buggy pushed through the crowd and took the lead. Cal waited stonily and, when it pulled up in front of the office, he saw that Dorcas was riding with Bernie Raxworthy. The sight of her with the man sent fury through him, and he admitted reluctantly that it was because she was so close to Raxworthy that he had always kept up the brittle quarrel between themselves. She swung down first, dressed in Levi's and gum waders and a short slicker, but she held back and came slowly into the office behind her foster-father.

Raxworthy's face wore a curious expression. He seemed a little embarrassed and yet determined. He looked at Cal for a moment, then cleared his throat. "Heard from Dwight Parker we can expect more high water, Cal. We come out to give you what help we can."

Uncertainty held Cal for a moment. The offer, the tone, seemed sincere. But could all his doubts be baseless? Was it possible Bernie Raxworthy and his die-hard townsmen had made a complete about-face? His eyes narrowing, he said coldly: "I don't need your help, Raxworthy. I don't want any damn' one of you on the project."

Dorcas spoke then. She had remained quietly in the background. Now there was a quiet plea in her deep gray eyes. "I give you my word, Cal, we want only to help you."

After a studious moment he shrugged. "Bond enough, I guess, Raxworthy. But if you've got cards up your sleeve, God help you!"

III

EVER SINCE EVE

As evening gathered, excitement rose in Cal in spite of his distrust of the situation. Quietly he passed the word to Si Moon and all the foremen.

"Keep an eye on every man jack of them. And if you see anything funny, raise hell high, wide, and loud!"

They kept streaming out from town, bringing their own tools and, as he organized them under his various key men and assigned each group to a specific task, Cal soon found that he had three times his regular outfit to work with. Some of the tension, the bewildered disbelief, eased out of him. Additional resin flares were drawn from the warehouse, and as night fell their flickering yellow light illumined a scene of feverish activity. Cal directed the work with a sure, instinctive feeling for what must be done to offset the augmented danger. Here a crew of shovelmen dug muck from a trench behind the dikes and pitched it onto the talus. There another group filled more bags with which to face the wash side of the threatened baffles. And under Si Moon yet another contingent kept up the former work of buttressing the coffers at the point of greatest strain, where the newly cut canal joined the river.

Bernie Raxworthy strode up to the wharf boat and sent every man of the crew, including the captain, down to the project, and he himself fell to with a shovel. Dorcas again kept herself in the background, and Cal was grateful for this. As the hours passed, with nothing out of the way happening, with this huge volunteer crew working willingly and efficiently under his direction, he began to acknowledge the possibility that she had turned the force of opinion in the town. The eagerness with which she quietly watched the proceedings indicated that she felt this. Yet it set up something inside of him that he could not understand, something that was neither pleasure nor gratitude.

Just short of midnight Raxworthy strode toward Cal, who stood near a flare. Muddy water had splashed his beard and his slicker streamed with rain. He smiled crookedly. "If we've satisfied you we really want to help, boy, I'd like to talk it over with you. This is hard to admit, but I been suspecting for a long time that I been wrong in my standing against the canal. I been seeing lately Libby City ain't got the right to dictate what happens to the river and the up country. Was a time when I figured I'd relish seeing the canal go out and you drowning with it. But when it threatened to come, I found I wasn't anxious. Not any. We can save the project, and if we do you can count on me backing you from here on."

Cal looked at him, and again all the old antagonism was an acid flowing in his veins. In a voice ragged with feeling he said, "My men're watching every one of you, Raxworthy! There won't be another Libby making the mistake of trusting Bernie Raxworthy too far!"

It was as if he had sent a physical blow squarely into the bearded face. Raxworthy took an actual step backward, staring. At long last the tension flowed out of his body, and he turned and dissolved into the darkness.

Yet within fifteen minutes Si Moon came up. "I never expected to live to see it, Cal, but damned if I don't think this town's come over to us!"

"I wouldn't let it lull me asleep!" Cal snapped, and turned away.

He saw the girl coming through the darkness, slim and boyish in the feeble light, gum boots splashing unconcernedly in the deep muck. She smiled slightly, and he saw that the events of this day had put constraint in her as it had in himself.

"I've been aboard the *Inland Queen*, Cal. I made a big tub of coffee for the crew, but there's a special cup with your name on it if you can spare a minute to come and get it. Then you can help me carry the rest out here."

He grinned, not welcoming the guarded invitation yet thrilling to it. "We could use it, all right." He turned and walked beside her through the sucking mud.

The packet was dark save for the standing lights so dim in the murk and the faint illumination of a kerosene lamp on what he supposed would be the window of the galley. They strode up the gang plank and across the deck and turned through an opening. Cal dropped onto the bench beside a plain board table and hunched over the thick mug of coffee Dorcas set before him. He sipped the scalding fluid thoughtfully, feeling the warmth run down his throat, while

Dorcas filled a second mug and took a seat across from him. Her face was flushed, and now she kept her eyes averted.

A momentary sympathy let him see what was in her mind. She needed now to know if a pledge had been made between them, the pledge that he did not want to give. Yet pride, greater than it would have been yesterday, was keeping her from admitting it. This deep woman's need was what troubled her now, and it was no superficial hunger for his gratitude because of her bringing him help. He took refuge in the fact that she could not introduce the subject, refusing to broach it himself. He rolled a cigarette and lighted it thoughtfully, drew on it, and exhaled with an audible sigh.

Dorcas lifted her eyes, and there was a haunting beauty in her grave features. She shrugged. "Well, shall we go? If you can carry the coffee, I'll carry the tin cups." Then she shook her head, as if in some protest. Whirling toward him, she said fiercely, "Cal, there just can't be any tenderness between us, can there?"

There was no reproof in her voice, and the bite he felt came from his own conscience. He lifted the cigarette to his mouth, nursed it, removed it, squinting at her. "Why don't you tell me what you started to this noon?"

She shook her head. "That was the impulse of no more than a second, Cal. For that long I thought maybe it would help. Yet I realized it would probably make matters worse. And I realize now you were just trying to stampede it out of me." Bitterness trembled on her lips.

He moved toward her, seizing her shoulders roughly, stopping himself on the point of shaking her. "Damn you, Dorcas, you know something of how my father died!"

Calmly she pushed his hands away. "Do I have to remind you that I have other loyalties, too, Cal? You almost unlocked me, but the moment's passed. Forever, I guess."

"You...!" he halted, puzzlement going through him. For an instant he had a sense of the deck moving under his feet. He stared at the girl, saw that she had noticed it. "We're moving."

"But we're tied up!"

Cal was plunging out to the deck. As he raced to the rail, his eyes widened in astonishment. The packet was still deserted, but the stern had angled widely into the stream. There was a jerk and a straining sound as the midship and bow lines caught the tension. Then Dorcas was bending over the rail beside him.

"Line loose! God!"

A figure came out of the shadows of the wharf boat, tall and lean and bearded in the faint glow of the standing lights. Bernie Raxworthy was running.

"Dorcas!" he cried. "My God! Get off of there!"

The line at midship snapped under the strain, and the stern swung wider into the channel. Staring down at the water in horror, Cal realized the terrible stresses there as the current bent and banked against the inshore freeboard.

Screaming, "Get off! Get off!" Bernie Raxworthy was racing toward the bow that now ground and slid against the wharf boat. Cal and the girl plunged forward. The shock was wearing away from Cal, and he rasped hoarsely: "You cast off that line, Raxworthy! Damn your soul to hell!"

"Get off!" Raxworthy screamed once more. He had reached the bow, which was now straining and twisting against the single line holding it as the stern swung squarely across stream. He had leaped, grabbing for the jackstaff, when the last line parted and the packet went out into the stream like a released mad thing. Bernie Raxworthy seemed to hang for a second in dark, empty space, his insecure grasp on the jackstaff slipping. Then he plunged without a sound into the dark swirling waters.

"It got you, Raxworthy!" Cal heard himself yelling. "Say hello to Garth Libby when you find him down there!" But the current had sucked the man from sight.

The girl was already racing toward the pilot house, and Cal followed her, knowing the packet was swinging end to end, totally uncontrolled and uncontrollable in the wild current. The utter hopelessness of their predicament made an awareness on the edge of his thought, but the only thing he could realize was his terrible fury.

The race for the controls in the pilot house was so futile it seemed senseless, yet he kept going, knowing that neither himself nor the girl would have the slightest knowledge of what to do if they reached them. He overtook her at the head of the companion, heard her moan.

"God! God!"

It was as he had pictured it at that first fleeting and terrible flash of comprehension. With thoroughness and cunning Bernie Raxworthy had prepared for this with his hypocritical change of face, the so-called help he had volunteered. There was no comfort in the fact that the man had been destroyed by his own infamous genius, that he probably had not realized that his own daughter or even Cal Libby had been aboard the steamboat when he loosened the stern line. The released design worked on, powered by terrific forces. The packet swung end for end as it twisted wildly downstream, hurtled by the mad water. Then came the shock that threw them flat on the deck, and the grinding and tearing as the sharp bow sank deep into the coffers at the head of the canal, followed by the end of motion.

Cal climbed to his feet, turned to the girl who was trying weakly to rise. His words had the crack of a whip. "I should have recognized the device. It's been used since Eve."

The collapse of the coffers followed with excruciating slowness. Tight-wedged for a time in the great rent it had made, the steamer hull acted as a plug. Men scrambled for safety below and had barely reached it when the first timbering began to fall from place, the first tearing water spurting through. Then came complete disintegration.

Cal Libby stood on the bank in frozen impotence, watching it. He had helped the girl scramble ashore, then she had run from him, disappearing into the darkness. The hull slid farther and farther into the canal cut as the gap widened, as surging water scoured away earth and timbering on either side. A pool built swiftly below it, and in a matter of minutes a truncate tongue was racing down the cut. Cal turned, stumbling away.

IV

DISTURB NOT THE DEAD

He did not go out to the project until late the next morning and, when he arrived, the scene was exactly as he had known it would be. The swollen river had flowed together through the new channel, masking out every trace of the work that had been done. There was nothing to do now but to tell Anderson, the government inspector, to advise the Army engineers that the Libby Construction Company was finished. The contract allowed him an extension of time, in case of emergencies such as this, but the financial damage would be his alone to bear.

Si Moon tried to ease the import of it. "Hell, we raised money to buy the equipment for a job this size, didn't we? We can raise more."

Cal shook his head. "That's just the trouble. I stretched myself too damned thin then. No sane banker would want to help me out of this mess."

It was apparent that Moon thought the same thing, though he said, "Well, we can try."

It would be weeks before the water receded enough for them to estimate the damage, and the prospect of waiting it out raised a cold sweat of dread. Cal thought desperately, *At least I can use the pretense to get away! I'll go to Portland, 'Frisco, Seattle...anywhere! But I can't stay here a day longer...not in this treacherous town!* Aloud he said, "Yes, I reckon we can try."

Moon doubled a fist and hit him fondly on the shoulder. "You bet."

As Bernie Raxworthy must have anticipated, the town, the government inspectors, and even Cal's own crew accepted the "accident" at face value. Steamboats had broken their moorings before. The fact that the *Inland Queen* had tangled herself in the coffers instead of nosing around the point and plunging over the falls was God's blessing, so they said. Raxworthy's sacrifice of life in trying to get aboard to save the packet and its two helpless passengers was heroism such as one rarely sees, they were telling each other.

Bleakly Cal forced himself to consider the possibility that Raxworthy had not deliberately loosened the line. He could not accept it. The man must have been waiting in shadow, must have seen the packet moving, but he had not emerged until he discovered that his daughter was aboard. His guilt was not one whit mitigated by the fact that he had made a courageous effort to save her. He could not have been entirely certain that the *Inland Queen* would strike the coffers and hang up there rather than go over Yellow Point Falls. He had not wanted her to run that risk. Maybe he had not even wanted to expose Cal Libby to such a fate. The courage he had displayed in trying to recover from the slip had come from panic and had not embraced any foreknowledge that it would cost him his life.

A packet had come in at mid-morning, and Cal was determined to catch it when it left, to get away for a while to think, maybe never to return. He had refrained from openly charging Raxworthy with the crime, to this point, because of the small element of uncertainty remaining in his own mind. Reflecting on it still as he rode back into town for a change of clothes and to pack a grip, he realized that it would be difficult to get anybody to believe him. The objective facts all pointed in the other direction, and what he could claim would in all probability be taken for rancor and recrimination. Besides himself, only Dorcas had seen what had taken place on the wharf boat, and Dorcas had already declared her loyalties.

He did not look toward the Raxworthy residence as he jogged past. Entering his own house, he stripped in the cold air and got into his best clothes. He placed a valise on the bed and began to toss items into it. Then he was aware that the front door had opened and closed, and he swung impatiently to the bedroom door.

Dorcas had come in without invitation, but she offered no apology or greeting. She stripped off her dripping rain hat, looked at him and asked: "Got time to talk to me a little bit?"

"There isn't a damned thing to say," he said gruffly, and turned away.

She crossed to him. "There is, Cal. I want to tell you that what you think is true. Bernie Raxworthy cast loose the *Inland Queen*, hoping to knock out your coffer dam. So don't blame Libby City. The town turned out to help you in sincerity. You've got to believe that." The grave eyes searched his face. "Do I dare try to tell you that I didn't know what was behind his apparent change of attitude, either? When I gave you my word out there, I really believed he was doing a big and generous thing. It never entered my mind that it was to establish his good intentions, after the damage was done!"

The quiet desperation in her reached him. He crimsoned a little remembering what he had said to her in the dark, tragic hours of the morning. This was costing her a great deal, and there had to be sincerity behind it. Without understanding his reason, he said, "I believe you now."

"I'm glad you said that. For what happened released me from the loyalty I mentioned. I want to tell you about your father now."

"You don't have to."

"Oh, I must. Bernie Raxworthy was neither all bad nor all good, Cal. He was strong and well-intentioned in many ways, but underneath there was a basic weakness. You didn't know that his wife...my foster mother...died a few years back?"

"I'd heard about it."

"Well, before she died she told me something in confidence. Once, many years ago, Bernie Raxworthy was sick and believed he was about to die. He told my mother something to ease his mind. He did not murder your father, Cal, as I think you've always believed. But he did let Garth Libby drown in the river. Deliberately."

Cal let out a long breath. "I always felt that. I always hated him without knowing exactly why."

Dorcas nodded. "I know it, but I'd promised my mother never to tell you as long as Bernie lived. You see, he realized from the first what could be done here, and he wanted the land. Garth Libby realized it too, but refused to sell. Bernie Raxworthy never meant to kill him, but that day when their skiff overturned in the river he could have saved him. Your father was thrown clear of the boat, but Bernie managed to hold onto it. He could have helped your father by no more effort than reaching out his hand. Yet he let Garth Libby be swept away. I guess it was murder, a passive kind. Bernie told this to his wife and, when he recovered, he warned her against ever breathing a word of it."

"Why did she tell you?"

"She felt as I feel, that the fortune belongs to you."

Angrily he said, "I don't want any part of it."

"When the estate's settled, the money'll be mine, legally, Cal. I'll never feel that it belongs to anybody but you. I know you'd never accept it for your personal enjoyment, but let it repair the damage he did to the canal. You're a builder. Carry on for your father from where Bernie Raxworthy left off. Wouldn't that right the wrong?"

He looked at her strangely. "You've touched on something that's been in my own mind a lot. Libby City is going to be hurt by the canal. It's got to pay the price of obsolescence. That's always the cost of progress. But it needn't be fatal. The world changes, and the key to survival is in one word...adaptiveness."

"I think you're right, but this town needs a man who is that way. Bernie Raxworthy never was. He fought to the bitter end to maintain what he had. I don't suppose he ever thought of the possibility of finding new potentialities."

"This town's always lived off its hold on the river," Cal went on thoughtfully. "It never tried to build its own trading area, to sink roots down as well as out. There are communities south of here that could be tied to Libby City with a good road and a stage and freighting system. Someday a railroad. So the town could still be a shipping point. Besides, it could have local industries. Lord, girl, there's the work of a lifetime still ahead! I could have told them a year and a half ago if they'd been ready to do something constructive about it!"

"They'll follow you now, Cal. Won't you do it?"

After a long moment he nodded. "I think maybe I will."

She turned to pick up her rain hat. Cal was staring at her, aware suddenly that the old turbulence within himself was settled at last, replaced by a calmer but deeper peace. Then the girl flashed him the old, wicked grin.

"I've been about as slow picking this up as a lady dares to be, Cal Libby."

Dwight Bennett Newton

was born in Kansas City, Missouri, and went on to complete work for a Master's degree in history at the University of Missouri. From the time he first discovered Max Brand in Street & Smith's *Western Story Magazine*, he knew he wanted to be an author of Western fiction. He began contributing Western stories and novelettes to the Red Circle group of Western pulp magazines published by Newsstand in the late 1930s. During the Second World War, Newton served in the U. S. Army Engineers and fell in love with the central Oregon region while stationed there. He would later become a permanent resident of that state. What makes Newton's fiction so special is the combination of characters who seem real and about whom a reader comes to care a great deal and Newton's fundamental humanity, his realization early on (perhaps because of his study of history) that little that happened in the West was ever simple but rather made desperately complicated through the conjunction of numerous opposed forces working at cross purposes. Yet through all of the turmoil on the frontier a basic human decency did emerge. It was this which made the American frontier experience so profoundly unique and produced a heritage of remarkable human beings of which the nation they built could be proud, always. Among his finest novels are THE AVENGER (Perma Books, 1956) now reprinted under the restored title LONE GUN in a hardcover Gunsmoke edition from Chivers, CROOKED RIVER CANYON (Doubleday, 1966), THE BIG LAND (Doubleday, 1972) which is available in a full-length audio version from Books on Tape, and DISASTER CREEK (Doubleday, 1981). TRAIL DRIVE TO SEDALIA (Circle V Westerns, 1996) is his latest Western novel.

Saddlebum's Bondage

With an angry bellow, big Lou Brady bunched his shoulders and waded in. He scattered three of the hoodlums like straws, their blows hardly stinging his ugly face, while the swing of one great fist connected and laid a man motionless in the sawdust.

The backbar mirror went out in a smash of bottles and glassware. Brady saw the frightened saloon owner dive for cover and he saw powder smoke spiraling from Spud Renton's six-gun. Then Lou Brady got to Renton.

Before Spud quite knew what was happening, his body caromed off the bar and struck the floor. He shook the ringing out of his ears. Vision clearing, he peered up at the giant towering over him. He started to roll into a better position, but Lou's boot came down firmly on his gun wrist, pinning it helplessly against the floor. Brady didn't put his whole weight on that foot or it probably would have snapped the bone. He bore down with it, though, until Spud Renton howled with the pain and let loose of his smoking six-shooter. Then Lou removed his foot and gave the gun a kick that sent it skittering across the splintered boards out of reach.

After that he stepped back where he could put his glance on all four of them at once. He said heavily: "I reckon you boys better clear out."

There was murder in Spud Renton's face as he got slowly to his feet, but he didn't put up any more fight. His three cronies had quieted too. They went, with ugly words and Renton's snaky look still on Lou Brady just before the batwings swung them out of view. That look bothered Lou. He had never seen such venom in a man's glance before, so fierce a threat.

Daughaday, coming around the end of the bar, was saying, "Mighty obliged to you, stranger, for stepping in...hope it don't get you into more trouble with that crowd. They hurt you any?"

Lou shrugged, shook his head. "You can't hurt me. Ed Heath always says I wouldn't have sense enough to know it if you did. I just didn't feel like standin' around and lettin' those *hombres* bust up your place for no reason at all."

A bottle stood intact on the bar. Daughaday shoved it toward him, his usually jovial face solemn. "Have all you want," he offered. "Renton and his crowd from over at the Sink have been threatening trouble a long time now...ever since I caught Renton cheatin' in a poker game and told him I wouldn't allow any of them in the Three Spot again. They'd have done the job today if you hadn't stopped them...and you not even wearin' a gun!"

A man came hurrying in, breathless, bringing the chill of the afternoon with him. He had a sheriff's star on his vest and had come running when he'd heard the shooting. Daughaday told briefly how Spud Renton's crew had invaded the empty saloon and tried to wreck it, and how this stranger had taken a hand. And the sheriff turned and measured Lou's six feet three inches with a respectful eye. But he made big Lou Brady feel uncomfortable, somehow ashamed of his size. People always stared at him like that. All bone, muscle—but no brain to go with it.

"I'm Joe Trout," the sheriff introduced himself.

Awkwardly, Lou closed a heavy paw over the officer's hard fingers, mumbling his own name. "Don't know where a couple of good riders could get a job hereabouts, do you?" he asked.

Trout frowned. "Roundup was early this season," he said. "The outfits are layin' off hands right now rather than hirin' them."

"So I heard. And me and Ed Heath...that's my pardner...we was sort of lookin' to hitch on somewhere, what with winter blowin' in already. Have to hope for better luck farther on, I guess."

"Heath?" The sheriff's brow dragged down. "Little, wiry *hombre*? Sandy hair?"

"That's him. He's the brains of our combine. He told me he'd meet me here in a half hour...thought maybe he could round up some cash. We're mighty low."

Trout whistled softly. "Sorry to tell you this, but your friend's over at the jail. Locked up!"

Big Lou, having picked up the whisky bottle, set it down again with an unsteady hand. He stared at the officer, and could only say stupidly, "You...you sure?"

"Mike Fancher of the 7 F is in town with a wallet full of beef money on him. Your pardner tried to lift it off him when he wasn't lookin'. Mike caught him dead to rights...."

Elbows on knees, Ed Heath sat with the light through the barred window falling coldly over his slight body and bringing out the bleak lines of his face. "You go to hell!" he said again.

Lou rubbed his jaw with the knuckles of one hand, homely face frowning unhappily. "Look, Ed, I...I savvy I've no business talkin' up to you. You got all the cleverness in you that I ain't, and I'd never get nowheres without you plannin' and figurin' things out for me. But...well, I thought you was all through with this sort of thing. Why'd you have to do it?"

Heath shrugged. "The money was there. And a pair of saddle-tramps like us sure as hell needed it."

"But what'll we do now?"

"I dunno what *you're* gonna do," Ed told him sourly. "Me, I'll just set here in this icebox till the judge comes on circuit next week. Then I'll set some more. Six months, likely."

Lou looked at him through the door, troubled. A draft came along the corridor, and Ed Heath's hunched body shivered.

Then Lou went into the office up front, where Sheriff Trout was worrying a fire to life in the tiny heater. "It's kind of chilly back there," Brady told him.

The sheriff nodded in sympathy. "Yeah, I know. The county tax-payers never voted enough money to fix those cells so's they could be heated properly. It's too damn bad."

"When's this judge due?"

"Next Wednesday."

Lou stood there, biting his lip, thinking about Ed in that cell with winter setting in. He'd found out long ago that Ed just couldn't stand up to really cold weather. This very morning, when they broke camp, he'd been wheezing and looking miserable until the sun came and put some warmth into the day.

"Any chance of bail, Sheriff?"

Trout pursed his lips, looking out the window at the early night. "I ain't properly got the authority to set bail," he said. "But I have an idea I can trust you. For five hundred or so I guess I could turn your friend over to your custody."

Five hundred! Big Lou shook his head helplessly. Outside, on the steps of the jail, he paused as he buttoned up his coat, squinting at the sky. The gray edge of a cloudsheet was moving in over the ridges to the north; a sharp wind came swirling down the dusty street, in advance of it. There was a hint of snow.

Lou Brady found Daughaday at the Three Spot, readying for the evening trade, and told him what he needed. Daughaday nodded. "Five hundred's quite a sum," the saloonman admitted. "But except for you Renton's crowd would have turned my place into matchwood this afternoon. I reckon I can let you have the money."

"You'll get it back," big Lou assured him. "Next week, when the judge arrives. I'll only need it till then."

Daughaday distrusted banks, and the safe in his office was generally full. He counted out the money for the bail.

"I got an empty room upstairs," Daughaday said. "You can have that for nothing, while you're here in town."

Lou turned the bail over to the sheriff and, after Trout had admonished the prisoner firmly and instructed him to report at the courthouse the following Wednesday, big Brady took his partner over to their room above the Three Spot. Heath was surly. He didn't have much to say, except once when he muttered: "A lot of good this is gonna do! I'm free until Wednesday, but after that...." He started to cough. The drafty cell room had done him no good.

This room wasn't much better, but at least it was warm here. "I think you better get into bed," Lou suggested. "Don't want you gettin' sick. I'll go round up something to eat."

"I'm all right," Ed growled. "Leave me do the thinkin'."

Lou found a restaurant down the street where he bought some sandwiches and a pot of hot coffee. He also located a druggist and paid for a small bottle of cough syrup out of their diminishing funds. As he headed back to the Three Spot, a few flakes of snow stung his face. That suddenly reminded him of the horses. As soon as he got rid of the food he was carrying, he'd have to find some place to put them up for the night.

Too many details for a slow-witted lunkhead to keep straight. He was sure lost without Ed Heath's running things. How on earth would he get along after next week and the judge had come around?

When he knocked on the door of the room, there was no answer. He went in. Ed Heath wasn't there.

Lou stood for a long minute with the food and medicine in his hands, puzzled. Then he put the packages on the table and went downstairs, thinking his friend might be in the bar; but he wasn't there either. Lou shrugged heavy shoulders. After all, Ed was his own boss. Lou didn't have any right giving him orders.

So he went to tend to the horses. It was almost full dark now. A deep blue light filled the street, and snow was coming down faster and beginning to blow in streaks of white through all the frozen wheel tracks. Lou's horse, stamping and blowing at the hitch rack, jerked his head in welcome as the big man came into view. But the space next to it was empty. Ed Heath's roan gelding was gone.

He knew, then, what it meant, and the truth stunned him. Slowly, with numb fingers, he untied the reins and took his own bronc around to the livery stable and turned it over to the old man there. Then he went back to the room and sat on the bed, staring dully at the bottle of medicine, and at the coffee that was getting cold because he didn't have the appetite now to drink it.

He couldn't fool himself. Ed Heath wasn't coming back. Afraid to face the judge, he'd skipped bail and run out on his partner, leaving him to account for the borrowed money. Lou's eyes misted a little. He hadn't figured Ed would ever do that to him.

Not that he could blame Ed, either. Who'd want to hang around with a sure jail sentence staring him in the face? But, five hundred dollars...?

Lou couldn't sleep much that night, worrying about it. If he'd only been born with a few brains inside this big, ugly head! But he fought the bed all night, wondering how he could pay off that debt. And when day streaked grayly into the room, the window showed a thin white scum of snow across the world outside.

Brady went downstairs and found Daughaday. A stubborn pride rebelled at the thing he had to say, and it was hard to get the words spoken. "Put me to work!" he managed to blurt out. "I reckon I can learn enough to pour liquor out of a bottle. And if the boys get out of hand, I'll keep 'em in line." And he told what Ed Heath had done.

"Just gimme my room and something to eat, and I'll work for you till you figure I've paid off the money I borrowed."

The friendly saloon owner didn't like that idea very well. It seemed to him like taking advantage of a man who'd done him a favor the day before, but Lou Brady insisted, doggedly. It never once occurred to Lou that he might follow Ed's example, and run out on his debt. He wasn't that clever. And so, instead, Lou Brady went to work at the Three Spot.

Wednesday came and passed. Sheriff Trout was furious when he learned what had happened, but there was nothing he or the judge could do about it. Lou apologized, humbly. There was nothing he could do about it, either.

He wondered about Ed Heath, sometimes. The first snow melted; then the weather tightened up again and there was another heavy fall, and the mercury dropped twenty degrees in an hour. What if Ed was down somewhere with pneumonia?

It was on a morning the week after Ed Heath's disappearance. Matt Kimmel happened along by the Three Spot where a big freight wagon had backed up to the door and Lou Brady was unloading barrels of liquor. Kimmel was a short, stocky German with a three-inch beard. Even in this cold weather he'd left his coat at home; and his shirt, opened across his barrel chest, was rolled up at the sleeves revealing the bulging cords of muscle that lay along his forearms. Yet he stopped in wonder to watch big Lou wrestle with the heavy barrels.

After he'd seen the third one rolled out of the wagon bed onto the giant's knee, swung from there into his arms, and toted off as though it didn't weigh anything, Kimmel shook his head in disbelief and hurried away to talk to Daughaday. Presently he came outside again, where Lou had just finished his job and wasn't even breathing very hard from it. The crown of Kimmel's hat reached only to big Lou's shoulder. He touched the latter on the arm, beamed up into his face as Lou turned. "Daughaday says you come vit me dis afternoon," he told him.

Lou went, puzzled. Kimmel took him to a great, dark building where there was a forge, an anvil, and piles of iron scattered in the corners. He picked up a heavy maul and handed it to Brady, and took a smaller one for himself. He worked the forge, blowing up the fire and starting a cherry wash of flame dancing across their faces and into the shadows of the smithy.

"Now," he said, "I set der pace vit der hammer, and ven I tap, you hit. Goot?"

Big Lou shrugged, nodded. The maul, he saw, was the heaviest thing he'd ever tried to handle. And now the blacksmith swung the heated metal, dripping sparks onto the anvil, and they began their work.

Kimmel set a terrific pace. The first blows were not so bad, but the soft iron chilled quickly and then it was a different story. And presently the metal had to be put back into the forge and the bellows worked again.

For an hour they worked, with scarcely a word to break the rhythm of their labor. At the end of that time Lou's shirt was wringing wet. He grinned, mopping the sweat from his forehead. Kimmel asked him: "How you like it?"

Lou had never been so tired, and yet there was an exhilaration about it. "That there is a man's job!"

"Maybe you like to vork for me, yah?"

But Lou hesitated. "I...dunno. I guess I'm just a dumb saddle tramp. I couldn't be no blacksmith."

"Nah! Nah!" the other insisted. "You got der arms, und de chest. Und you got der feel for it. You make a fine blacksmith. I teach you everyting."

"But there's Mister Daughaday...."

"Ve talk it over already. He say it can be fixed. You start tomorrow morning. Goot?"

Big Lou walked in a rosy dream back to the Three Spot. This was a thing he had never known before—the feel of belonging, of finding his place, of discovering at last a job where his qualities could assert themselves and his faults would not betray him. A job he'd been cut out for! He was so lost in these strange new thoughts that he never noticed anything was wrong until he was well inside the Three Spot.

Confused, he halted. There were three men in the saloon, but they were not customers. They had masks over their faces, and blue gun metal was a threat in their tense fingers. And then he saw Daughaday, moaning on the floor where a gun barrel across his skull had placed him.

All those guns swung around and covered Lou Brady now as he came in and stopped still in the middle of the room. And at once, the three recognized him. "Hey, Spud!" one of them cried.

The door of Daughaday's office stood open and, looking through it, Lou could see the iron safe standing open too. A man knelt in front of the box, shoveling coins and greenbacks into a canvas bag. He turned now, came erect, and strode out into the big room with the bag in one hand and his gun in the other. The neckerchief had slipped from his face, but he didn't seem to notice. All his attention was riveted on big Lou Brady.

"You!" Spud Renton exclaimed. "What are you doin' here?"

"Keepin' order for Mister Daughaday!" Lou snapped. The big man's shoulder muscles were beginning to bunch, his strong, blunt fingers curling. "You can just put back that money and get out, or I'll...."

"Or you'll what?" Spud Renton was coming nearer, the gun steady. "I'm squarin' accounts today. I've got everything I want from Daughaday, right here in this bag. Now I get to settle with *you*. You near busted my hand the other day, tromping on it. But this time..."

With surprising speed, big Lou's right arm shot out. The mighty fist gave Renton a clout on the ear that sent him staggering and jolted the gun out of his hand. Lou strode in on him, struck him again. Spud backed up, swung the heavy bag of coins, but it only landed against Lou's shoulder and he barely felt it. The bag flew from Spud's fingers, spilling greenbacks and coins that spattered brightly across the room.

Then Lou's left hand closed over Spud's shoulder and his right fist drew back to strike. "Rob a fine gent like Mister Daughaday, would you?" he muttered.

"Hold it!"

For a moment the pressure against his spine didn't quite register, but slowly the blinding anger cleared from Lou's head and he cursed his dim-wittedness. One of Spud's men that he'd forgotten was right behind him, gun barrel jammed into his back, and the others were closing in.

The gun barrel dug deeper. "Let him go!"

As Spud Renton jerked free of his grip, Lou stood numbly waiting, braced for the bullet. Then Ed Heath came out of the office. Ed had stayed to finish rifling the safe. He had a sack in one hand, a gun in the other. Lou gaped at him, not wanting to believe. Ed must have gone completely bad after jumping bail and joined up with Renton and the crowd over at the Sink.

Ed Heath was staring too, but his nimble brain could take in the whole meaning of this scene at one glance. Without warning, the gun leaped in his hand. Spud Renton took his bullet, and in falling he drove a shot into the floorboard before he dropped, lifeless.

"Lou!" Ed Heath shouted. "Get out of here...for God's sake!"

Briefly stunned, the other three turned their guns on Ed Heath. He was slammed back against the jam of the door as a bullet found him, but he managed to return an answering shot and one of the thieves stumbled and fell.

Lou Brady shook off the shocked numbness that held him, and plunged in. He had no gun. But he reached the man who plugged Ed Heath, and grabbed his shooting arm with a jerk that almost wrenched it loose. The man yelled, beat at Lou with the weapon. Lou bent quickly, got a hand hooked around his leg. He straightened easily, as though lifting the man were the easiest thing in the world. He turned, a gun blasting its heat against his face as he did so. The bullet drilled past, missing by inches.

The last of Renton's crowd stood spreadlegged, ready to jerk trigger again. Before he had a chance, Lou hurled the man on his shoulders at him. They went down in a tangled heap, and were still.

Ed Heath was dying when Lou got to him. Lou knelt and lifted him up, his big hands trying to be gentle. At the sight of the blood on Ed's heaving chest, hot, unashamed tears started down his homely cheeks.

Ed shook his head, trying to grin. "Don't mind, Lou," he grunted. "I ain't worth it. You're too good for me...always were. I'm nothing but a saddlebum that thought he was smart. Just too smart for my own damn good!"

Lou mumbled: "You're gonna be all right, Ed."

"Not me. But you will, Lou...you're the salt of the earth. I...I run out on you. I couldn't face what was comin' to me. But now maybe I've settled that a little. And I...I ain't afraid of this...." Ed closed his eyes.

Lou stood up, slowly. Men were shouting and rushing into the Three Spot, stamping freshly fallen snow in with them. The sheriff was there, helping them get Daughaday to his feet. Hardly anyone noticed big Lou.

Suddenly he was wishing for tomorrow to come. Tomorrow, and the feel of the big maul in his hand again. Somehow he knew things would come clearer to him then. His slow wit would function better, and he would understand. It would be all right.

(Cecil Francis) Frank Bonham

in a career that spanned five decades made significant contributions to the Western story. By 1941 his fiction was already headlining Street & Smith's *Western Story Magazine* and by the end of the decade his Western novels were being serialized in *The Saturday Evening Post*. "I have tried to avoid," Bonham once confessed, "the conventional cowboy story, but I think it was probably a mistake. That is like trying to avoid crime in writing a mystery book. I just happened to be more interested in stagecoaching, mining, railroading...." He was highly knowledgeable in the technical aspects of transportation and communication in the 19th-Century American West. In introducing these backgrounds into his narratives, especially when combined with his firm grasp of idiomatic Spanish spoken by many of his Mexican characters, his stories and novels are elevated to a higher plane in which the historical sense of the period is always very much in the forefront. On even the shortest list of the finest Western novels would have to be included SNAKETRACK (Simon & Schuster, 1952), NIGHT RAID (Ballantine, 1954), and THE EYE OF THE HUNTER (M. Evans, 1989). ONE RIDE TOO MANY is the title of a Bonham Western short story collection reprinted by Barricade Books in 1995 and THE CANYON OF MAVERICK BRANDS (Circle V Westerns, 1996) has recently made its first appearance in book form. Mike Tilden told Captain Joseph T. Shaw, Bonham's agent, that he would publish any Western story Frank would be willing to write. This story appeared in *Dime Western* in the issue dated January, 1950.

Border Man

I

SNAKETRACK KING

Rowson dipped tepid shaving water from the horse trough and scrubbed up a lather. The mirror hung from a nail in the cement water tank. He stropped the razor and squinted at himself. He was coming to look like the country: brown and drought-bitten. Even his eyes seemed to have faded like old denim. Another few months of it and there would be no southern Arizona and maybe no Page Rowson.

It was mid-afternoon. The leaves of the trees sheltering his rock and 'dobe ranch house hung limp as hounds' tongues. But lack of breeze was a blessing: wind merely meant dust, not coolness. Most of the heat was burnt out of this day, now that he had spent twelve hours grubbing around back alleys of his place looking for starving cattle. In this tired and windless hush he heard Bat Lyndon and the Mexican, Angel, riding back to the ranch from Frontera. Lyndon was a black-browed, deep-set man of fifty, utterly without humor. Like many humorless men he was pessimistic. Rowson saw him and the Mexican water their horses. He expected no good news from town.

Lyndon was Rowson's ramrod. He lay on the ground and chewed a match. "How would you like to sell a hundred head of cattle to Payson's slaughter house for four dollars a head?"

"Is that dressed-out or on the hoof?"

"Gift-wrapped, most likely. Town's still full of railroad travelers. They're sleeping in the livery stables and saloons. And there ain't much chance of them going on to Hermosillo soon, because the

Maderistas still got the railroad. So they're eating us out of grub and Payson's slaughtering about four times as much beef as ever."

Rowson flipped peppery lather at the tree. "That the best you could drum up?"

"That's all I could drum up. Except some news. You remember a fella named Larned?"

Rowson pulled him back from memory—a heavy-mannered cattle buyer who had tried to buy a holding ranch here last fall. The world would be a happier place for fewer Vance Larneds, he felt. "I remember him. He offered two-thirds market price for cattle and tried to buy up notes on ranches all over the county. What about him?"

"He's your new neighbor. He was just a piece behind us on the road."

Rowson sat down. "The hell! He's got an eye for trouble like a turkey buzzard. Whose place?"

"Hance's. Old Hance quit."

"Old Rowson would like to quit, too," sighed Page Rowson, who was twenty-seven and an inch below average height. He had a lithe body with hips no wider than his pockets, and slender brown features. "What's he want with a little frying pan like that? He couldn't crowd half his ambition onto the Walking R."

"Just a holding spot. He's still a cattle buyer."

Rowson finished shaving, thinking of Vance Larned. Larned was probably all right; he simply was not Rowson's taste in men. He could not quite mask his eagerness at hearing a fellow mortal was in trouble.

Down the wide and hill-lined pass in which Rowson's Snake-track ranch headquartered came the rattle of horseshoes. Larned and two companions entered the yard. Vance Larned was a tall, but hunched man of middle-age, lean and hard fleshed. His face had two hollows under the cheekbones like healed bullet holes. His brows were thorny and his chin was like a smith's sledge. Raising his hand, he grinned at Page. "Still hanging on, eh?"

"Fixing to expand," Rowson said. He looked at the buyer's companions and smiled, "You're in bad company."

Marshal Bob Hamma saw the edge of the joke. He didn't smile. He struck his pommel with the reins ends and glanced about the yard. Sam Shackleford, who occasionally served a paper for the marshal or did an unpleasant job for someone else, was Larned's other companion.

Larned left the saddle. "You knew I'd bought out Charlie Hance? Marshal Hamma's giving me a horseback survey of my land. Sam Shackleford will ramrod it for me."

They shook hands while Bat Lyndon and Angel lay on the ground, inspecting a slow-wheeling buzzard in the sky. The marshal and Shackleford dismounted and patronized the waterpipe with it's cold, steady stream bubbling into the trough.

Larned spoke in gruff privacy to Rowson, as if they were somehow set apart a bit from these other men who worked for them. "I don't plan to be around a great lot," he said. "This is central for buying, though. I can hold a herd or two here while I wait for railroad cars." Larned's narrow, craggy face pinched. "I suppose you'll be thinning your herd?"

"Why?"

"You can't maintain the same herd in drought times that you can in fat. You'll have to buy feed or sell cattle." Larned spoke rapidly, driving the point in like a wedge.

Rowson rubbed his shiny jaws, still stinging with the soap. "I suppose I'll do like my pappy taught me...hang and rattle."

Marshal Hamma suddenly pointed a stubby finger at him. "And there, by God, is what's wrong with this country! Men like you hanging and rattling while they murder the range. If I was making laws for this country, I'd serve papers on you to feed your cattle or sell them. Because when this drought breaks, there ain't going to be any grass to come back."

Rowson regarded him steadily. "What's the split?" he asked.

"Split?"

"How much do you get for rigging men into selling to Mister Larned?"

"That's a damned unneighborly thing to say," Larned snapped.

"But grave robbing's a damned unneighborly thing to do."

The silence was thick. Bat Lyndon's raw small voice announced thoughtfully: "They can smell 'em."

Everybody looked at him. Still lying on his back, he was peering into the sky. "Smell what?" asked Shackleford, a sober and obtuse cowboy with an unshaven brown face as dark and greasy as the backside of a flitch of bacon.

"Trouble. They smell carcasses and come two hundred miles to pick the eyes out."

"Oh," Larned said. "Buzzards."

Lyndon sighed. "Yep, buzzards," and looked at the cattle buyer.

Larned's rawhide face got a little red. Suddenly he turned back to his horse and mounted. Marshal Hamma stood glowering at Rowson and his foreman. He said, "I've heard of fellers talking themselves into trouble with their big mouths, Rowson. Mister Larned come out here in good faith...to take some cattle off your hands or even buy you out, clean. Kind of think about what you'll do if this dry holds."

Larned rode close to Page Rowson. "I'm more of a doer than talker," he stated. "I won't come back here and brag that I told you so, but I'll tell you now: you're heading for starvation. I make one price for my friends and another for men who don't know how to be friendly. When you send for me next time, you'll know what price to expect."

Rowson looked him over, smiling faintly. "You like this county of ours, don't you? I'll bet you've been having the local paper mailed to you ever since you were here last, reading about the drought. So now the smell's reached you and you've come to pick the eyes."

Shackleford, big and dark-browed, roused like a liver-spotted hound. "You look here...." He lumbered toward Page, his long arms stiff at his sides.

Page said, "No. You look. Don't go any farther than you really want to." He stood placidly in his spotted cotton shirt and bleached Levi's, his chaps mended with copper wire at the knees. Marks of prosperity were lacking, but self-sufficiency shone on him like the rivets in a new pair of jeans.

Shackleford hesitated, glancing at Vance Larned, and Larned grunted, "Come on." He rode past the mossy cement water tank to the road.

Near sunset Rowson built a fire in the sheet-iron stove and sliced meat from the cooler. A fragrance of chili and *frijoles* reached him through the open window. Angel and his missus, Libertad, were having *refritos*.

Page said to Lyndon, "Let's drop in on Angel. Too hot to cook."

Angel was a small, broad-shouldered man of forty, his chief prides the man he worked for, his mustaches, and his wife. Libertad was not yet thirty, pretty and casual, with a brood of shy, grinning children. The house was dirt-floored but recently sprinkled, clean and cool.

The men ate, while Libertad moved from the brick stove to the table on bare feet. "I forgot to tell you," said Bat Lyndon. "Pío Noriega's in town, stalled with the rest of them. Don't know how anxious he'd be to get back, anyhow. They're making jerky out of *hacendados* these days."

"Another one," said Angel, "who only comprehends to hang and rattle. They stole ten thousand cattle from him last year."

Divide it by two for proper proportion, Rowson reflected, and it was still hard lines. Out of this news grew an idea. He asked the Mexican, "Sure about that?"

"My nephew, in Candiles, told me last month. The ranch of Don Pío is sick."

Rowson slowly chewed a tortilla and made a thoughtful sound. Libertad moved to the door. "*Caballeros*," she said.

Page walked outside. They came from the northeast, three horsemen splashing across the thin belt of water between the lacy salt cedars. Rowson watched them, touched by uneasiness. "Go out the back," he said to the others.

He watched them come on. It would not be unthinkable that revolutionaries should raid this far north, which was only ten miles from the Mexican border. But these men sat gringo saddles and rode good horses, and they reined in at the water trough and glanced about. Rowson went out.

Spotting him, one of the men left his horse and walked to the hut. He was lean, bearded, and dusty, his eyes pinched. He gave Rowson his hand. "Mott Rawlings," he said. "My friends and I are heading for Frontera. This the way?"

"Eleven miles. You're welcome to stay overnight."

Rawlings looked uneasily up the shallow valley. "Thanks, brother. We'll move along. Unless...." He glanced back at his companions, who were rolling smokes while their horses drank. He asked, "You wouldn't be needing hands? We're looking for work."

"All of you?"

"You don't have to hire us all," Rawlings grinned. "We ain't brothers. We were...with a trail herd until just recent."

"Quit?" Page asked shortly.

The cowpuncher's restless eyes sought the northeast again. "Damn' right we quit," he said.

"Then I couldn't use you anyway. My good luck would be the drover's bad luck...until you quit on me when I needed you."

Rawlings looked straight into his face. "Did you ever punch cattle for a woman?"

Surprised, Rowson said, "Why...?"

"Then don't pass judgment on a man that's just finished a hitch working for a female! Once I worked for an old critter that put sticks under our blankest so we'd be glad to get up in the morning. He was a cow-country missionary compared to this one. We ain't tasted beef for two months. We furnished our own horses and nobody in camp could have a bottle and she counted the cups of coffee we drank. This morning we just saddled and rode." He made a brief nod. "Thanks for the water, friend. We'll be moving along."

From the yard, Page watched them string out through the cottonwoods and cross a ridge. Then he began to laugh, and went back to tell the others about it. He and Bat joshed Libertad about her sex being too tough to work for, and it was something less than an hour later that the woman named Abbie Gaines rode hell-for-leather into the Snaketrack yard.

Rowson was sitting in a rawhide chair tipped back against the front of his shack. Bat was plaiting a hair bridle he had been working on for two years. The girl appeared in the dusty yard with a hard clatter of hoofs, turning her horse broadside before them. The dusk provided the type of light women favored, because it favored them, but Page saw she did not need special favors. Obviously she was shapely, though dressed in a faded blue Army shirt which had been taken in, and in jeans. Her hair was dark and brushed back, pulled into a single short braid by a yellow ribbon.

"Where are they?" she demanded.

"They rode on. They were looking for work."

"They've got work, as I'll show them when I catch them. Why didn't you hold them for me?"

"Why should I have?"

She thought about that, then dismounted. Rowson, mastering his grin, remained seated. "I'll water my horse," she said, "and be getting on. Isn't there a town near here?"

"Frontera, on the border. You might as well spend the night here...that is, with the Sierras, my puncher and his family."

"Mexicans?" she asked.

Rowson looked up levelly. "They're good enough for you."

Her hardness was unmasked for a moment. "Oh, I didn't mean.... Well, never mind. I would be obliged for some crackers or something I can carry along."

Rowson went to the horse trough and washed the cracked enamel cup. He filled it and gave it to her. She drank with her eyes closed. "I hear you're taking a herd somewhere." He spoke very quietly.

She filled the cup again. "California."

"Tough season for that. Where you from?"

"You're awful curious, aren't you?"

"Always, with a lady."

"I wasn't sure you knew I was a lady. You didn't get up until you had to." She turned to face the ranch house. "If I could have something...tortillas, biscuits...?"

Rowson walked to the shack and brought out a paper bag with some tortillas in it and a can of sardines. "I ask only one thing of my guests. Their names."

"Abigail Gaines. Brownsville, Texas."

"Long way from home, Abbie," Rowson smiled, still holding onto the bag. "Why California?"

"I have a brother-in-law in San Diego County. He has cattle. I'm bringing seven hundred white-faces my father left me."

"I hope you've still got seven hundred when you make it. There's no graze beyond Gila Bend. Nothing but sand. No water."

"You could almost say that of Frontera." She faced the sunset-tinged ridge beyond the trees. "I take that trail, then?"

"I wish you'd stay, Abbie. You aren't going to take those men back with you, anyway."

"Then I'll hire others."

"Not to cross the Gila and Colorado deserts. People from the Colorado come here to get cool. They sit around with shawls over their shoulders, and it ain't really chilly here."

She stubbornly kept her eyes from him, but he saw her chin weaken a little. "Oh, I'll make it. If I can get men."

"You won't. There's one thing you could do, though."

He shook dry tobacco flakes onto a paper. He made her ask it: "What's that, mister.... You haven't told me your name."

"Rowson. Why, you could lease pasturage from me. Temporary basis, that is. There's a cattle buyer in town. You might even make a dicker with him. But don't try to take these cattle across the Colorado deserts."

She sniffed. Her features were fine, not quite haughty, but held self-respect. Her lower lip was deep and rich, and her eyes were as lustrous as a Mexican girl's. "I shouldn't say you had any more graze than you needed for yourself."

"But I'm bringing in feed from Mexico. The rains will hit one of these days. Until they do, I'll artificially feed my cows. I've dodged it too long. Tomorrow I'm going in to make a bargain for hay and grain."

"They'll rob you." She declaimed it as though she knew merchants to the cores of their black hearts.

"Not this man. He's in a spot, too."

He lighted the cigarette, dropped the match, and let the smoke gather between them. "I won't rob you. You'll pay just what the cattle eat."

"But what do you make out of it?"

"Maybe some calves. You come with seven hundred, you leave with seven hundred."

She put out her hand suddenly. "That's a bargain, then." She smiled. Her relief was a softness in her features. "I...I'll ride back and tell my men...I still have two...to hold the cattle there tonight."

"No need. I'll send Angel. My foreman will bunk with me and you can have his room."

Afterward he wondered why he had done it. She was trouble in a saddle, but he could not see her riding on, perhaps to her death. Or was it involved with a desire to discover whether she was as self-sufficient as she thought she was?

———⫸●⫷———

There was an affinity between towns and men, it seemed to Rowson, and Frontera was his kind of town. Straddling the border of northern Sonora, it took its tempo and good nature from the *vaqueros* to the south. Venders sold pumpkin seeds and *piloncillos* of brown sugar, black cigarettes and gaudy serapes. Mexican and white children played in the streets and you couldn't tell an American cowboy from a Mexican until he opened his mouth. Their skins were burned brown and they wore taut leather leggings for the most part and collarless cotton shirts, their hats the shape of cones of sugar.

Abbie Gaines shopped. She beat old Morrison down on prices until Page was ashamed to carry the packages out. As he packed the provisions in the spring wagon, she spotted Mott Rawlings, one of the three men who had deserted her the day before. Dressed in a gown with a wide gray skirt and tight bodice, which imparted to her somewhat the shape of hand bell, she swept across the street and cornered him against a building.

Frontera slowed while she roasted the 'puncher. He must have made some half-hearted offer to return. The last thing Rowson heard was her declaration: "Why, I wouldn't have you with a dowry of ten registered herd bulls! Deserting a cowman in a tight! Find some place where they run sheep, Rawlings. That would be the work for you."

A man near Page breathed, "¡Qué chata! I would not be penned with her for all the bulls in Sonora!"

It was the voice of a lithe Mexican in business clothing, only his cowman's hat typifying him as a rancher. Rowson said, "The warm-blooded ones make for fun, Don Pío."

Don Pío Noriega looked around, came forward with an exclamation, and took Rowson's hand. "Not the blood that boils over, my friend. If you are acquainted with her, it will be your misfortune."

He was laughing, a cleanly-built, Indian-dark man of forty years. Rowson saw Abbie returning to the wagon. "She's leasing pasturage from me. Will you have something to eat with us at the railroad cafe? Something I'd like to ask you."

Noriega glanced at the girl, her dark hair glistening in the sun, and said, "I take that chance."

Abbie worried Page by putting a look of stark suspicion on the Mexican as soon as they were seated around a dirty table in the restaurant. Noriega's cooperation could spell defeat or survival. Noriega had the grass and grain which might save Rowson. His cattle ranch covered a fifth of the state of Sonora.

"Are you one of those revolutionaries?" the girl demanded.

Noriega touched his heart in pain. "Señorita, I am one of those shirtless hacendados. They take ten thousand of my cattle last year.

They steal my corn. They leave me half a million acres of range, and hardly the cattle to feed my village."

Abbie said, "Oh, forgive me. Then you're our friend...not a spy at all. I have heard...." She shook her head over what she had heard.

Rowson commiserated with the rancher. "And to top it all, you're marooned here, eh? Coming back from El Paso?"

"*Sí*. I went to buy cattle. But pesos are cheap. The cattle I could buy I would not bother to ship."

Page rolled a cigarette. "Looking for white faces?"

"I had hoped for white faces, stock I can sell for dollars instead of pesos."

Rowson said, "I need hay. You need cattle." He lighted a cigarette.

The Mexican frowned slightly, then leaned on his elbows. "Does something occur to you, Don Page?"

"Something occurred to me last night, when I heard you were in town. If I could cut hay on your mountain meadows, I'd pay for it with good herd animals. I've got to thin mine anyway, I can't support the number I'm carrying. Your range has been resting."

Noriega took Rowson's large, rough hand in his own lean brown one. "Now we are talking like *compadres*. I will not rob you on the hay. And there is grain and corn going to the weevils."

Abbie Gaines came in quietly. "If you could pay cash for other cattle, Don Pío, I have seven hundred white faces."

"My life's blood I would give you, but I cannot give cash."

"Cash or nothing," said Abbie. She shrugged and looked away. Bone hard, thought Rowson. Bone hard.

Noriega tapped on the dirty cloth. "These cattle I will take into the mountains. Until the trouble ends. It is not rumor that an army is coming from Chihuahua city to clean out Sonora. Then I am in business again. When do you wish the hay?"

"Now. Come out today and we'll start the cut in the morning."

Three men entered the cafe, standing near the entrance to seek a table in the crowded room. They were Marshal Hamma, Sam Shackleford, and a Mexican. Rowson didn't hear Noriega rise. But suddenly he saw the rancher moving across the sheet-metal floor with his glass of wine in his hand, making for the trio. He saw this other Mexican—a slack-bellied man in a tight black coat and brown chaps, two guns belted on—recognize Noriega and throw his hand before his face. But the wine had slipped out of the tumbler and struck him in the eyes.

Hamma was bawling. "Get back, Spik! Manteca, I'll handle it!"

Noriega was spitting Spanish imprecations at the gross-bellied man. Hamma, his fist knotted, was moving in behind the rancher. Rowson picked up an empty coffee cup and fired it at the marshal. It struck him heavily in the shoulder. Hamma pivoted, pulling at his gun, but Page's was already in his hand and he was saying, "Outside might be the place to settle this, Marshal."

Hamma hesitated. Rowson said to the girl, "Sit tight," and rose to put a hand on Pío Noriega's shoulder. "What's the matter? Who is he?"

The Spanish language was framed for irony. Rigid under Rowson's hand, the Mexican said, "Speak softly, *amigo*. We are in the company of a general…Manuel Manteca, so called, late of the revolutionary army. If their pelts were longer, we would call it a pack. This is General Manuel Manteca, who slaughtered what he could not steal of my herds, and sold what the army could not eat. Until he became too filthy for the army."

Manteca, the stain of the liquor spreading over his shirt as it trickled from his face, was white with anger. His features were broad and aggressive. His lips were wide and flat, as though they had been turned back. He glanced at Page. "Your friend is insane. I am a dealer in cattle."

Rowson smiled at Hamma. "He'd have a permit, wouldn't he?"

Hamma growled and thrust Noriega through the door. "We'll talk about cards later."

In the sun before the adobe station wall, Hamma put Noriega's back to the hot bricks. The *hacendado* had accepted his error. He answered the marshal's questions quietly. "I say that it is true. I retract nothing. If Manteca is in town, lock up your money and your women."

Manteca waved a large hand. "The heat. It makes mad dogs of sane men."

Noriega's eyes were dark and gritty. "Greed does the same, eh?" He confronted Rowson. "*Mas tarde, amigo.* I go to my hotel to arrange my valise."

Hamma's warning followed him. "Be throwing wine on another man and I'll set you loose in the desert."

They stood there. Manteca grumbled as he wiped wine from his face and neck. Rowson turned to go back, but saw Abbie Gaines in the restaurant doorway.

Shackleford was speaking to him. "This fella was looking for you."

Rowson frowned at the Mexican. "You've found me."

Out of anger and confusion, Manteca tried to assemble the ingredients of good nature. He smoothed his shirt over his belly, smiling. "You raise cattle, no? I buy cattle. I can sell all the good gringo cattle I can take to Hermosillo. It occurred to me...."

"No," Rowson said.

Manteca shrugged. "Be foolish, my friend. I pay twenty dollars a head."

Rowson turned back. "Twenty dollars?"

Manteca's fat smile came. "Not pesos. Noriega lied...I am not general, I am revolutionary impresario. I buy cattle for the armies. I take all you sell me, pay earnest money, and bring back the rest of the cash when I return."

Rowson began to laugh. "Show me the shell-and-pea game next time, General. I'm not so foolish on this one."

Abbie was saying, "Twenty dollars, Mister Manteca? I have some cattle I'll sell."

Rowson took her arm, but let his hand fall away when she faced him hotly. "I can manage my affairs, Mister Rowson!"

Shackleford gave her a sober smile. "You won't go wrong, miss. Vance Larned is selling cattle to Manteca, and if Larned says he's all right...."

The girl looked into Manteca's face. "I'd want twenty-two dollars, however, if it's part credit."

Manteca inclined his head. "Agreed. The cattle...."

"...are on Mr. Rowson's land just now. If you can come out to look them over, we can talk about the details."

Manteca shook her hand. *"Su servidor, señorita. ¿Caballeros?"* The men went inside the restaurant and took a table.

Rowson's stare was raw with disdain. "I thought you set store on being a businessman. Do you think you'll ever get the rest of that money?"

"I am quite sure of it," Abbie said.

Rowson looked at her. Hard headed? Hard like the cold-jawed bronc, he reflected, that ran into a barn to show him it could not be jackassed around. He said, "Well, they're your cattle."

He visited Noriega at the hotel. The Mexican had changed his mind. He would be out in the morning to pick his cattle.

"Keep out of Manteca's way," Rowson said.

"When it is time, I will put myself in his way."

Page pigeon-holed the rest of his town tasks and in early dusk, whistling, went back to the wagon. It was parked under a cottonwood beside a Mexican *cantina*. He had left a boy to watch it. The boy accepted the coin he tossed him but said, "*Señor*, those *hombres*, under the trees there...."

The men came from behind the trees, Vance Larned, Bob Hamma, and Larned's ramrod, big Sam Shackleford. They were sober and purposeful. Rowson waited, one hand on the tailgate of the wagon. "Where's your friend?" Rowson asked. "Out selling somebody else a gold brick?"

"You don't trust men much, do you?" Larned asked. His knotty, raw features were sour. "I know Manteca and he's honest. It isn't your place to boycott him."

"He's a pig, a cow-thieving pig," Rowson said pleasantly.

Bob Hamma's blond mustache looked bleached in his ruddy features. "I could say the same about your pard, Noriega. I don't know what you and he were talking about, but if it has anything to do with moving cattle across the border...."

Rowson listened.

"Well, does it?"

"If it does, nothing a rusty badge can say will change my mind."

Hamma's temper surfaced. "Then maybe this will!" He stepped in close and held the cowman by the arm. "Move one cow across the line without a permit, and you'll forfeit it. Try it again, and...."

Rowson's hand took his cigarette to his lips. Then it slashed back, striking the marshal in the mouth. Hamma dodged back and Rowson said, "Throw your weight around with pulque drunks all you like. But don't make me watch any more of it."

Larned and Shackleford were both talking loud and fast, but Page's attention focused down on the marshal. Hamma's hand was at his Colt. Rowson kicked him in the shin and grabbed at his gunhand. He tore it away from the bone-handled Frontier model .45. Hamma ducked his head and butted Rowson on the nose. Catching him by the shirt, Page slugged him heavily in the face. He seized the marshal's gun and threw it under the wagon.

Hamma was a large, dogged man of intemperate angers. He made a strange wild grimace as he rocked back, slugging with both fists. Rowson backed up. Something caught his spur and he tripped. As he went down, he saw Vance Larned moving away. An advantage must be mean before Bob Hamma would pass it up: he came in savagely and raised one foot to stamp at Rowson's face. His spur glittered. Rowson hunched against the wagon wheel and the boot thudded beside his ear.

He scooped a handful of dirt and hurled it upward. Hamma ducked the grit that sought his eyes. In the instant's reprieve, Page Rowson lunged up, driving headlong into him. Hamma tried to hold on. Rowson's knee hurled him back. Silently savage, Rowson hammered at the man's head with a long blow, saw the blood start from the marshal's nose, and moved in while Hamma was still blinded by pain and tears.

Bob Hamma's fists fumbled at him. He tried to retreat, but the rancher went with him, driving short, hard blows into his body. Hamma hunched, loosened by a blow to the belly. Page hauled one in from the side, feeling the good crack of his fist against Hamma's ear. He came erect, breathing quickly and shallowly as the marshal went down and floundered to his knees, sinking back after a moment to lie on his belly with his cheek against the dirt.

Larned's voice came crisply. "Men that make their own laws, Rowson, sometimes get themselves repealed."

Rowson faced him, his anger trembling behind his lips, but holding himself steadily. "That's what happened to Hamma. He's got no more jurisdiction over border traffic than I have."

Larned regarded him gravely. "We've made a bad start, Rowson. I wish we could forget this, and what happened the other day. We'll be living pretty close together to be forever scattering locoweed in each other's pastures."

"I'm a pretty friendly man. But if you come simpering around with any more bootlicking lawmen, you and I will tangle quicker than you can bribe a cowtown marshal."

II

DIG ONE DEEP GRAVE

Traveling slowly through the early night, Rowson and the girl drove back to the Snaketrack. The darkness closed them in. Night sounds came eerily. Abbie Gaines, making no point of it, settled herself a little closer to him on the wagon seat as they clattered along the shadow-rotted base of a rimrock cliff. Rowson observed it with inner pleasure. He began to glance now and then behind them on the road. He peered upward at the shelving cliffs and laid his single-shot trap-door Springfield on his lap, humming quietly.

Abbie asked, "I don't suppose he'd be so angry he'd send anyone after you?"

"Hamma? More likely than to come after me himself."

Something swooped low with a stiff rush of feathers. She caught his arm.

"Nighthawk," he said. After a while, he asked, "Whatever possessed you to take the trail alone with those cows, Abbie?"

"I've tried to get used to being alone since my father died. I didn't like trying to ranch alone, so I sold the land and started out with the cattle."

"Not afraid of things, are you?"

"What things?" she moved away, stiffly.

"Of being cheated, for instance. Or of seeming to be afraid."

"All I'm afraid of," sniffed Abbie, "is what would happen if I ever trusted anyone as far as he asked me to." They rattled on a while. "You're awfully sure of yourself, aren't you?" she said. "Whipping marshals seems very unwise."

"Myself is all I'm sure of. That, and the fact that you can't trust some Mexicans, such as Manuel Manteca."

"When I need advice," Abbie said, "I'll let you know."

<hr>

Pío Noriega rode out the following day on a rented horse, glad to be quit of the traffic-glutted town. He and Page arrived at a bargain. With Bat Lyndon, they started a day herd of cattle which would presently be moved southward to the Mexican's ranch in Sonora. It was while they were among the dry sage hills that Manuel Manteca and Vance Larned visited the Snaketrack and conferred with Abbie Gaines. Rowson found this out when he returned that night. He learned it from Jay McQuilty, the girl's foreman

McQuilty was an East Texan with a slow manner of speaking, a leathery cowboy who wore a collar-band shirt with no collar, and batwing chaps twice as wide as he was. His teeth were worn lopsided by his pipe. He had a long, sad, red face with loose-lidded eyes like a hound's. In the bunkhouse where Libertad was arranging a cot for Noriega, he said bitterly, "I reckon I'm shut of them gadblamed cows at last. Sick of looking at the same old behinds for a thousand miles. Manteca's taking the whole herd."

"When?" Noriega shot at him.

"Four-five days. He's taking a regular gad-blamed trail herd down. Three fellers in Frontera are selling to him too. Same deal. Down payment, the rest in a month."

"¡*Tontos, puros tontos*!" Noriega breathed.

McQuilty shrugged. "Why? He's paying them the same money down that Larned offers full price. If they get any more, it'll just be a nice surprise."

Rowson tromped out his cigarette. "Four dollars a head! That's not even a down payment. Larned's stampeding them into Manteca's hands. The deal stinks!"

His and McQuilty's glances met, the same thought reaching both. "You'd think," the Texan said, "they'd be bidding against each other, instead of riding around like saddle-pards."

"You would," Rowson agreed. "You can't talk her out of it, eh?"

McQuilty's long face writhed into a grin. "Did you ever talk a female into anything? Not one like this, mister. She rode her turns like any of us, all the way across. You'd forget she was a lady, only that she didn't cuss so much."

Pío Noriega thoughtfully pulled on a *papel orozuz* cigarette. "One thing I do not forget…that Manuel Manteca was discharged by even that pack of shirtless rebels called an army for cheating. If he is dealing in cattle, it is for himself. Your friend Larned, perhaps, is playing into Manteca's hands."

"A man with an eye as cold as his," Page declared, "never played into anybody's hands. If anybody's being taken, it's Manteca."

⸺⸻⊰◉⊱⸻⸺

Abbie woke Rowson the next morning by clattering utensils in the dishpan. He dressed and came into the large center room and saw her industriously pumping water into a tea kettle. Dishes and pans were piled high. She wore the shirt and Levi's again and had her hair pinned up.

"Am I late for breakfast or early for lunch?" Page asked.

Abbie thumped the tea kettle on the stove. "I wouldn't eat out of these filthy things without scouring them."

Later, Abbie came out of the cabin as Rowson adjusted a saddle blanket on his gray gelding. He and Noriega were starting the cut immediately. Whistling, he lifted the saddle onto the horse and groped for the cinch.

Abbie said curtly, "I might ride along and see what your country looks like."

"Suit yourself."

He watched her face as she saddled—the contours of her cheekbones gentle and her lips full, her eyes sober and gray, and somehow sad. He appraised the slender figure warmly until she caught him at it and disciplined him with a frown. With Pío Noriega, they rode eastward through the hills, pyramidal as ant-hills, scant with warped trees and beaten cruelly by the heat and drought.

Noriega had an eye for white faces. Rowson was on his guard not to be dickered out of the best of his bulls and heifers. He steered the Mexican away from where his best stock grazed. He had a bunch of his best cows spotted on a murky thread of green water called Cibola Creek. He had in mind avoiding this area but, as they rode around the base of some low hills, he heard a sound of cattle running, a cowboy's sharp *ho!*, and he pulled the gelding in sharply and listened.

Cibola Creek picked up the water of several springs and crawled down a cañon beyond a low ridge. Rowson asked the girl quickly, "Did you pasture any stock over yonder?"

"No. We rode by yesterday with Manteca. They're farther west."

Rowson said, "Wait here, then." He nodded to Noriega to follow him and started up the slope. When he reached the top, he discovered Abbie following them. Hotly he turned to send her back, but at that instant a horse made a brief, hard run just below them, and a steer thudded against the ground.

Rowson looked into the bottom of the cañon. Boulders studded it, but there were areas of grass and a stone corral within sight. Eight or ten white faces were penned in the corral. A pair of punchers were branding here, and two more were working over the steer which had just been spilled. They worked hard and earnestly, so earnestly that Rowson had the .45-70 Springfield at his shoulder before one of them saw him.

"*¡Vámonos!*" It was a high, lingering yell. Rowson's gun crashed and one of the horses went down.

Abbie was on her feet now, running up with a light saddle gun in her hands. Rowson glimpsed her and turned back. He picked up a rock and threw it at her. She gasped and ducked behind a rock. Noriega pulled his horse behind a dead cedar which was like a clutch of greasewood roots. He fired a shot from there.

Movement flowed from northwest, down the cañon, the 'punchers swinging into saddle as they ran beside their ponies. They were dark-skinned, sombreroed men in tight leather chaps. Rowson remembered—"*We rode by with Manteca....*" And Manteca made mental notes and came back. Rowson bit the end off a paper shell, inserted it, and capped the nipple. His sights hounded a hunched rider for fifty feet; he fired. This man threw his hands aloft and the pony bucked him into the brush. Noriega fired again and Abbie came wriggling through the rocks and her gun went off so close to Rowson that his ears rang. He shouted a furious order, but she calmly levered another cartridge into the Spencer rifle she carried.

Between them a slug walloped the ground and mingled dust with the greasy smoke of Rowson's old black-powder cartridges. Abbie rocked with the recoil of her rifle. Rowson stared at her face; she was white as tallow. But she lay there in the rocks as stubbornly as a foot soldier.

A last echo of shod hoofs whispered through the smoke and dust of the cañon floor. The cattle bawled and one of the animals in the corral jumped the fence but hung up on it for a moment.

Presently the three rode down the cañon.

III

BORDER DEVILS

The dead Mexican was a small man with a wispy black chin beard, a border *paisano* in dirty white pants and shirt. He lay across his gun, a long, home-made musket with a side-hammer. You could not distinguish this man from a hundred others living in Frontera or Old Frontera across the line.

"Manteca's man?" Rowson asked.

Noriega moved him with his foot. "*¿Quien sabe?*"

He walked to the yearling steer tied nearby. The brand, half finished, was a cursive design like an anchor. Noriega shrugged. "Who knows? It is nothing I have seen?"

Rowson hadn't seen it, either. He climbed the hill and found Abbie wiping dirt from her face with a handkerchief.

"The next time you go riding with me," he said, "you go without a gun. You ran a risk of having that pretty face shot off."

"They started it, didn't they?" She had her color back, but her lips looked stiff. "I meant what I said about advice, you know."

Rowson stood there as she rose from her knees. Then he turned in unaccustomed ill nature to his pony. He didn't welcome this agitation he had felt over her. She was a termagant, a shrew, and he could imagine nothing worse than to fall in love with such a woman.

"Here's one more piece of advice," he said roughly. "Get out as soon as you can. Because you won't last long in this country."

Noriega came up. Rowson reined in beside him. "Will you take the girl with you? I'll cut back past the house and look around south. There's some stuff in my Ojo Claro pasture I want to bring in."

At the cabin he put jerky and hardtack into a sugar sack. He selected his traveling horse, a leggy dun, changed saddles, and turned the gray into the trap. He left instructions with Angel. Then he rode southwest through the tawny desert hills toward Hance's ranch.

Not over two miles from the ranch he cut the sign of three horses. The prints were still sharp in the hot earth of early evening. He knew the layout of Hance's place. A bald lavender hill soared a few hundred yards below an unplastered adobe box and a couple of corrals of ocotillo wands. Quartering around, he left his horse in a copse of trees by the tepid stream and climbed the hill. From here, presently, he found the riders. They were some distance from Larned's cabin, swapping horses in a distant corner of the cattle buyer's main pasture. He watched them finish saddling, leave their own mounts, and cut through a Missouri gate to jog due south.

Night crusted along the eastern rim of the hills; darkness invaded the range; and down below a lamp burned. Rowson rode into the ranch yard. He smelled potatoes and meat frying. A man called gruffly, "Who is it?" It was Sam Shackleford's voice.

"Rowson. Larned here?"

"What do you want?" Vance Larned appeared in the doorway, lanky and big jointed, wearing boots, Levi's, and undershirt. He held a potato in one hand and a butcher knife in the other.

Rowson dismounted and walked to the door. Inside, he saw Shackleford looming like a surly bear behind his trainer, huge and shaggy and suspicious. "You've just lost three horses," Rowson said.

Larned's head bent forward a bit, then he came out, spearing the potato on the knife. "How?"

"Well, you've swapped. Three border hoppers just made you a trade."

Larned turned quickly. "Sam! Saddle your bronc and bring mine in."

Shackleford bounced massively out the door, but Rowson halted him. "What for? They're clean across the border by now. That's the thing about living with your back door opening on Mexico."

Larned studied him ill-naturedly. "Who were they?"

"That's what I rode over to ask you. Who are they?"

Shackleford roused stiffly. "Rowson, if this is another caper like in town...."

"Be quiet," Rowson drawled. "This is for you, Larned. I was hoping to see you pay them off. Seeing them swap horses with you is almost as good, but would it sound as good to a stuffed-elk of a marshal like Bob Hamma? If you're here to buy cattle, I'm here for my nerves."

Larned cocked a foot onto the stoop. "I wonder how Arizona ever got along without you to worry about it. What have I done, now?"

"I'll tell you what some other men have done. Blot-branded a dozen of my cows. But they were sloppy. I caught them at it. I killed one...a Mexican. The ones I missed are the ones who are riding your horses now. They seemed to feel safe about switching."

"You're coming close," Larned remarked, "to talking yourself into trouble."

"I'm coming closer than that to calling you a liar and a cow thief."

Larned's hand brushed from his knee, kinked up by the stoop, to hang at his side. He wore a Wells Fargo Colt in a basket-woven holster. His hand twitched but made no rash move. When Rowson was sure of him, he said, "You run too muddy for me to know what you're up to. But it isn't ranching, and it isn't cattle buying. I'd say it had something to do with Manuel Manteca. If I find either of you on my land, I'll know you've come to fight. ¿*Claro*?"

"Get out," Larned said.

Rowson smiled. "I didn't come to stay. I will say I'm glad the light's poor. I'd guess if you ever nerved yourself up to killing, your man would never know what hit him."

He retreated unhurriedly, without losing sight of Larned and Shackleford. He mounted and swung, watched them a moment, and rode into the hackberries.

He arrived at the ranch long after dark. Noriega and the others were abed. The cabin was dark but, as he entered, the ashdoor of the stove grated open and the ruddy light revealed the room and the person beside the stove. Light glinted on bright steel. The gun quickly came down and the butt touched the floor as Rowson was recognized.

"Well, have you cleaned up the revolutionaries?" Abbie put amused irony into her voice.

Rowson let himself into a rawhide-bottomed chair. He pulled off his boots and wiggled his toes. She came from the stove, trailing the gun. "I'm tired," he said. "Too tired to be badgered."

She turned after a moment and lifted a pot of coffee from the back of the stove. She poured him a cup. She brought a pan of *frijoles* and beef from the stove, served them on a thick china plate, and said, "These are ruined."

He ate hungrily. "I'll have to train Bat to do these tricks." She sat down, a pale, tense presence near him. "There's nothing to keep you up," he said, "if this is all you were waiting for."

"It's not. I just wanted to tell you: Manteca has his herd ready. We leave day after tomorrow."

Rowson laid the fork down. "We?"

She smiled. "You said I'd be cheated. You didn't know me, Page. I'll get my down payment and go along with him to collect the rest. They won't cheat me."

Rowson set the food aside. "You could have let me finish before you took my appetite away. Didn't your mother tell you about white women sashaying around Mexico alone?"

"Yes, but she didn't know about Winchesters."

Lunging up, he went to grip her shoulder. "A woman's got a right to be crazy, or to be pretty, but she's got no right being both. Why is it any of my business if you want to get yourself sworn into the Mexican rebel army?"

"It isn't." She tugged, but his fingers retained her shoulder.

Rowson pulled her to her feet. "Abbie, you aren't going."

Her face was close to his, pallid and stiff. "But I am. It isn't as though I had any other choice. I could stay here, I suppose, and have my cows get ga'nter every day, and pay wages, and not have the increase. But I can sell for decent money right now and go on to California."

It was a moth attack in the face of logic, but a woman could release such moths forever, and a man got worn down fending them off. Rowson's mouth tightened and he brought his palm in a half-slap against her cheek. "Crazy," he said. "Both of us. I was crazy to let you stay. You're crazy to go. Slap me for this, Abbie, but don't forget I'll be paying for it."

His arms captured her taut slenderness, crushing her breasts against him. His face pressed against her throat and he clutched a handful of shining dark hair as he kissed the tender skin. She trembled, quieting as his lips moved up to her mouth. But when his arms unlocked, she pulled away, crying.

"You've got no right! Treating me...as though...."

"Treating you as though I loved you," Rowson said bitterly. "Go to bed, and dream about being a rich woman and having a hundred cowpunchers, but don't forget the part about being lonely."

Rowson and the others—Pío Noriega, Bat Lyndon, and Angel—spent a last day readying the herd for Mexico. A trail brand was scorched into the reddish hides of the two hundred animals. They were bunched on Bullet Creek and left with two punchers, while the others rode back at sundown to pack food and bedrolls into the bug wagon.

Abbie came from her room as they were sitting down to dinner. She wore the Levi's and old Army shirt again, and carried her blankets over her shoulder like a man. She was the essence of self-sufficiency, but Rowson saw through her.

"I'd like to pay you for the pasturage," she said.

"Forget it. I thought you were leaving tomorrow morning, though."

"We are. McQuilty and Manteca's men moved my herd over to Red's Cañon today. We'll leave from there in the morning." She offered her hand. "I hope I haven't upset things too much?"

"Oh, no." Rowson shook hands soberly.

She was waiting for him to say something and, when he did not, a shadow entered her face. "I hope the rains come soon. Good luck, Page. Always, good luck."

"Good luck to you. You taking any blackberry brandy?"

"What for?"

"For the stomach complaint. You can't set in Mexico without picking it up. And sprinkle a little baking powder in your blankets at night and you may keep out the lice. Fifty-fifty chance."

Her lips firmed. "Trailing cattle isn't a luxury even in this country, you know."

"That's right. Well, just keep an eye on Manteca and you may get the best of him. Who all's going?"

"Just McQuilty and Manteca and Larned, I suppose, and a few cowpunchers. You don't need to worry about me. I took care of myself all the way from Brownsville without your advice."

Rowson smiled. "Sure you did. *¡Adios!*"

She moved to the doorway. "When...when do you plan to leave?"

"Tomorrow. But we'll be trailing considerably east of you. The range won't stand two herds on one trail. *Adios,* Abbie."

Noriega pronounced solemnly, "*Vaya con Dios, señorita.*"

Abbie lifted her chin and departed.

Noriega chuckled. "You attempt to frighten the *señorita?*"

"She's frightened already. But mostly she's frightened of our knowing it." He ate silently for a while. "Manteca as bad as you said, or is it partly that you happen to hate him?"

"I happen to hate him because he is as bad as I said. If the rebels will not associate with a man, he is unfit for hanging. *¡Adios!*" he sighed. "That one so pretty should die so young!"

Rowson's fork halted. "Hell, he wouldn't kill her...."

"I am thinking more likely that the *señorita* may prefer it. The cattle traffic is not all that Manteca comprehends."

<hr />

Rowson overslept, awaking to see the rust-stained face of the clock indicating seven o'clock. He was not a man to oversleep, and looked about for a cause. Beyond the window he found it: the sky was scaled with gray clouds.

He dressed hurriedly, feeling vindicated. The rains would come, as they had always come, as he had told them they would when cattlemen argued with him that the border was finished. But it was scant satisfaction that the day was already well begun, that Abbie Gaines's cattle might already have crossed the line into Mexico.

The others came from the bunkhouse, and Bat Lyndon emerged from the room Abbie had relinquished last night. "Never closed my eyes," he said. "Kep' smelling perfume."

Odors of *huevos rancheros* and pans of biscuits filled the Mexican's shack when they went over. Breakfast was gloomy, contrasting with the ordinary trail-drive morning. In the yard the wagon was loaded and hitched with a span of mules. The sun filtered weakly through the clouds. There would be a day or two of clouds, and then—God willing—a pelting thunderstorm.

Rowson thought about this. He saw the grass strengthening, the streams rising, and it left him unmoved. What his mind hoarded was an album of pictures of Abbie. Sitting her horse arrogantly that first day, as she demanded word of her mutineers. Abbie at the stove, slender and dark-haired as she drew loaves of riz-bread from the oven. Abbie moving closer to him as they drove along the dark road through the hills. His throat tightened. He pushed back his chair.

"Turn them back on the grass for a couple of days," he said. "I'm going out."

"Whereat?" demanded Lyndon, his heavy brows hunching.

"Where the heart goes," said Noriega, "the man follows."

Rowson scowled. "I don't know about that, but I got a notion I ought to be keeping an eye on Vance Larned."

Angel moved his chair back, smoothing his rams' horn mustaches as he rose. "I know the country well, *patrón*."

Rowson glowered. "So do I. You stay here. Keep an eye on that day herd. I'll be back *mañana*."

But when he had ridden a mile and a half, he heard them roaring up behind him—Angel and Noriega and Bat.

IV

A MAN OF HER OWN

The range was like crumpled brown velvet. Over it the sky was gray and ragged, torn by a west wind from the gulf. There would be rain; there would be grass; but all the profit of it would be months from now. Sloughing off to the south, the range was cut by deep barrancas and low, eroded rims. From one of these they could see, distantly, a dun-colored cloud under the heavy belly of the sky. Cows were moving deeply into Sonora, trailing out of Red's Cañon. Rowson had his line, and now he angled over to the cañon itself. The red walls of it were fluted, gashed by old floods. Cattle-sign sprinkled the gravely earth. They bored through the easy loops of it, not forcing the horses but keeping them on the spur. Noriega, lean and dark, rode at Page's side. They stopped to blow their horses, once, and Rowson sat rolling a smoke.

Noriega said, "To worry is no damn' good, *amigo*."

"To start too late is no damn' good, either."

They were sitting here when Angel raised his hand. "Leesten!"

Blunt iron scraped the earth. Horses were moving toward them. Rowson's eyes rummaged down the cañon; a barranca slashed in a few dozen rods ahead. He signaled the men. They rode into the winding cleft; he left his horse and walked back. He wedged himself into a fault in the bank. The riders scuffed by him. They were Vance Larned and Sam Shackleford.

"He don't have to take them clean to Mexico City," Shackleford groused.

Larned said, "There's a little matter of an international boundary. Hamma will stick his neck out just so far."

They were gone, then, in a soft fog of dust. So Bob Hamma was in it, for sure. Rowson strode back to his horse. They waited a suitable interval before proceeding down the cañon.

"Who was it?" Lyndon demanded.

Rowson told them. "Something's up. Manteca isn't playing this alone."

The cañon debouched onto a broad plain. Distantly they detected the reddish stain of the herd on the prairie. A couple of miles ahead, Larned and his foreman jogged on toward the cattle. As they proceeded, Rowson observed the herd come into formation for the nooning. He made the spot at Nogales Spring, a lean oasis of trees surrounding muddy water.

Cover was slight. Gullies veined the desert, which was broadly level but rumpled with low transverse ridges. While he studied it, he discovered a rider stringing a thin pennant of dust from the northwest, in the direction of Frontera. A last clue went into place in his mind, like a peg in a cribbage board. Bob Hamma was moving in— with his dislike for shenanigans above the border.

He said tersely, "Let's get moving. That female's crazy enough to go to war with the Mexican army and all the cowtown marshals in Arizona."

He pulled the horse off left, winning the protection of a run of hills. Lyndon pulled in at his side. "What's Hamma got to do with this?"

"Hamma's just a lever. Larned's the weight. Larned's buying that herd, not some Mexican wet-beef dealer. Those cattle will be back in the States by tonight, heading east or west…away from this range, anyway."

Lyndon chewed on it. "I heard Manteca had big connections."

"Maybe he used to have. Noriega says even the rebels don't trust him any more. So Larned needed a man, and he looked like the one. He could talk big and strong-arm his way into a herd. Then he disappears, and he doesn't come back to Frontera with the rest of those ignorant ranchers' money. Manteca sells to Larned for a few dollars a head, more than he'd get out of a peso deal, and Larned brings them back. He's got bills-of-sale on them and the brands are all right. Everything's all right, except that a few thick-headed gringos lost their shirts."

"And he ain't got a bill-of-sale on Abbie Gaines," Bat finished.

They rode for twenty minutes and Rowson rode up a hill to get a line again. The herd was sprawled near the spring, only a half mile west. He estimated the cattle at close to a thousand head, most of them Abbie's. Three cowpunchers of Manteca's drifted slowly about the herd as it grazed near the meager spring branch. Flood seasons had cut the water course ten feet deep, a raw slot in the earth, and a little burro grass grew in the bottom of it.

The horseman coming from Frontera was pulling closer to the huddle of men in the shade of the trees. Rowson turned back. "Let's get into that barranca," he said, "and move in as far as we can before they see us. There's apt to be smoke when they do."

They came around the hip of a ridge and sloped toward the gully. Cattle grazed along the banks of it and some were clumsily sliding into the gully for the better graze. A few hundred yards off, the 'punchers, three steeple-sombreroed men with serapes over their shoulders, drifted along the fringe of the herd, turning the stragglers in toward the water. Rowson put his pony down the crumbling bank, stiff-legged; it struck the sand and he turned it upstream through a tepid inch of brackish water. In succession, Noriega, Bat, and Angel lunged into the barranca and followed him.

Reaching the cattle, they moved quietly through them. Cattle would stand for a horseman, where a man dismounted would booger them. Page heard the *vaqueros* talking a short distance from the bank. He raised his rope to flog a steer out of his way, but he held his arm and in a tight-lipped patience wormed by it.

A horseman thudded into hearing; there was an exchange of voices. Rowson spurred the pony against an old bull and shoved past. Hamma sounded displeased, but his words were lost. Then the girl's voice came peremptorily, carrying with feminine candor.

"Why should I pay you any money? What for?"

Rowson shoved and hauled through the reddish roil of cattle choking the gully. The barranca was shallower, now, tapering into the pond called Nogales Spring. Again he lost the marshal's words, but Abbie cried, "I certainly won't pay a dollar! Who do you think you are…the collector of customs? Besides, we aren't even the United States any more…!"

And now Manuel Manteca's voice could be heard: "No, *señorita*. We are not in the Es-states…."

Rowson could see them. There were Hamma and Jay McQuilty, the girl's foreman, Manteca, Shackleford, and Larned. McQuilty, rough and dark, was suffused with angry color. "None of your Mexican hoorawing for us, Manteca!" he said suddenly. "This is a business deal. You go to throwing any of your weight around and I'll hammer a slug through your belt buckle."

"No, *señor*," Manteca laughed. "This is indeed Mexico, and in Mexico the gringo's voice is soft."

"Soft, eh? Soft?" Abbie cried. "See here. I suppose this is a holdup of some kind. I have to pay Hamma before we can go on with the cattle. Well, you're in this as much as I am, because you won't get any of that money back if the cattle aren't delivered. So it's to your own interest to handle him as I say."

Rowson saw them all begin to look at Larned. The lines had run out and they waited for him to improvise.

Larned—his eyes apologetic under the thorny brows, his manner that of a guilty hound dog—smiled at the girl. "I'm sorry about it, ma'am. But these are rough times. A girl don't savvy cattle, and she don't need a stake like a man does. I'm buying these cows, you see. I'm taking them east to El Paso."

Still she did not comprehend. "Oh?" she said.

Vance Larned rubbed the lever of his .44 caliber Henry against the saddlehorn. "From Manteca. He's the real owner of them now, you know. We've got to pay Hamma a little, and it's only right. He could make trouble with the customs people." Larned grinned at the marshal. "So relax, Bob. We weren't running a sandy on you. Only we wanted to make some time, this first day."

"You were makin' it," Hamma growled.

Larned squinted down the gun barrel at a cow, not meeting Abbie's shocked stare. "We didn't want to cut you off clean. So Manuel paid you a middlin' price. I'd take that money, if I was you, and head straight for Guaymas. Get a boat for 'Frisco. Forget it all."

Rowson saw the terror in her face. He heard the reedy break in her voice. "Forget! I…I'll go straight back to the Snaketrack and tell Page Rowson, and he'll…."

"No, ma'am," Bob Shackleford said.

The pressure on Jay McQuilty was great. He looked undecided whether to sacrifice himself to appearances, or to wait. He appeared to prefer to wait, for he did not reach for his gun.

Manteca slapped his paunch affectionately. "It will be the great pleasure of Manuel Manteca to escort the *señorita* to the port. I have many connections, *Dona* Abbie. We pass pleasant times, eh?"

Abbie put her hands over her ears and screamed. The men looked nonplussed. Manteca's face distorted. He raised his hand and struck her in the face with the backs of his knuckles.

"*¡Bastante!*" he roared. "We make the good deal, and you es-scream like a she-wolf."

Then McQuilty's somnolent, miserable eyes found Rowson shucking out of his saddle and coming up the bank with the trap-door Springfield in his hands. McQuilty's eyes all but shouted. Suddenly he rammed his pony into the rump of the Mexican's big grulla. Manteca swore at him and made a threatening gesture at his Colt. Rowson paused on the rim of the barranca. There was a strip of trampled earth fifty feet wide between him and the outlaws, the smoke trees at their backs.

He jammed the butt of the rifle against his shoulder, notched the Mexican's shirt front in the sights, and triggered. The shot trembled hugely in the air, a cannon blast of fifty-caliber fire. Manteca was slugged sidewise out of the saddle. He went overboard and the horse began to kick at his head as he hung by one foot from the stirrup.

Larned saw it all in a stark, comprehensive glance, the quartet surging up over the bank of the gully, guns prodding before them. He sprawled out of the saddle and lay in the dirt. He lined out his fifteen-shot Henry, and Rowson wished bitterly that it were in his own hands. He had emptied his single-shot Civil War gun and now, sprawling in the dirt, he pulled his Colt. He heard the smashing impact of the cattle buyer's shot against his eardrums. It had almost a physical force, a smoky thrust against the eyes. The bullet slammed off the ground beside him and slapped his boot. He felt the sting of it passing down his calf. Screaming, Abbie Gaines rode down the creek.

Shackleford spurred for the trees. But in a moment he halted and turned, afraid to stay and afraid to go. His vacuous, swarthy face was twisted queerly. Angel, lunging behind a shallow rise of ground, threw down on him with his ancient, muzzle-loading musketoon. The sixty-nine caliber ball howled out of the barrel in a cloud of black powder that riffled the ground before it. Shackleford took the shot in his hip; it caught him like a fist and whirled him. He went out of the saddle, moaning, hunching grotesquely with his face against the ground.

Earing back the hammer of his Colt, Rowson was aware of Marshal Hamma sitting twisted in his saddle with his hands up, tallow-white. "All right, boys!" he kept saying. "All right!"

Larned swore and fired the Henry at Noriega, but the *hacendado* lay flat as an empty sack on the ground. The bullet passed over him and *thocked* into a steer. Larned quickly levered another shell into the chamber of the carbine. A gaunt, jointed figure, he sprawled in the dirt with no apparent worries about the odds against him. Rowson rested the heel of his hand against the earth and pulled a bead. But the blooming roar of another rifle shook him and for another moment a smut of black powder smoke and dust obscured Larned. Rowson fired into it and cocked again, but as the dust cleared he saw that Vance Larned had rolled over on his back. One knee was drawn up. He was making convulsive movements with his arms; a man was glad to turn his attention quickly to the marshal.

Hamma was saying, "This is Mexico, Rowson! You can't take me back for...for something that happened...."

"No," Rowson agreed. "We wouldn't even have you back. We'll tell them about you, though, and I hope you like it down here." Then he got up. "How many of you on your feet?" It turned out all of them were. Rowson said, "Then, one of you bring me a hatful of water."

Abbie came back presently. Rowson's undershirt had been bound about his injured leg. The bullet had created a seven-inch trough in the calf. He was trying to get his boot on with no success.

Abbie said, "It will have to be split." She took his pocket knife and cut the boot down the back so that he could pull it on. Rowson caught Bat's eye.

Bat told the others, "Best git those cows headed back."

Now it was quiet among the trees, and Abbie knelt beside him. "Oh, Page! I should have listened to you."

"You bet you should."

"But I was so sure...."

"Were you?" Rowson asked.

Abbie looked down. "No. I knew he might be a cow thief. But you were so overbearing about saying I couldn't do it...."

"That you had to show me you were your own man," Page finished. He moved so that his back was against a tree and pulled her to him. "If you had a man of your own," he said, "you wouldn't have to act like one, would you?"

Abbie was sobbing softly, but her fingers roved the short hairs on his neck, causing chills up his back. "No. I guess not," she said.

"All right," Rowson said. "You've got one."

Dan Cushman was born in Osceola, Michigan, and grew up on the Cree Indian reservation in Montana. In the early 1940s his short novels began appearing regularly in such Fiction House magazines as North-West Romances and Frontier Stories. Later in the decade his North-Western and Western stories as well as fiction set in the Far East and Africa appeared in Action Stories, Adventure, and Short Stories. A collection of some of his best North-Western and Western fiction was recently published in VOYAGEURS OF THE MIDNIGHT SUN (Capra Press, 1995) with a Foreword by John Jakes who cites Cushman as a major influence in his own work. The character Comanche John, a Montana road agent featured in numerous rollicking magazine adventures, also appears in Cushman's first novel, MONTANA, HERE I BE (Macmillan, 1950) and in two later novels. Some of these early stories are now collected in THE ADVENTURES OF COMANCHE JOHN (Circle V Westerns, 1996). STAY AWAY, JOE (Viking, 1953) is an amusing novel about the mixture, and occasional collision, of Indian culture and Anglo-American culture among the Métis (French Indians) living on a reservation in Montana. This novel became a bestseller and remains a classic to this day, greatly loved especially by Indian peoples for its truthfulness and humor. Cushman also produced significant historical fiction in THE SILVER MOUNTAIN (1957), concerned with the mining and politics of silver in the 1890s. His most recent novel is the North-Western, IN ALASKA WITH SHIPWRECK KELLY (Five Star Westerns, 1996).

The Feminine Touch

William Hickory Gupsworth was fifty-nine or thereabouts, and for the past twenty of those years he had done pretty much the same thing every morning—he had arisen at sunup, fried sourdough flapjacks and salt pork, and he had climbed the barren side of Wilsail Mountain to the portal of his mine, the U. S. Mint. But this morning was different.

This morning Gupp did not lie abed until such an hour as sunup. He was out of his bed before the sun was even a rosy streak above the horizon. He swept out his log cabin, blackened those parts of the Prospector's Friend cook stove that were commonly visible, and dusted the ore specimens along the windowsills. Then, carefully strapping the old straight edge razor that Teddy Roosevelt had given him with his own hands, he shaved off a four-day growth of whiskers, leaving his face smooth and pinkish.

"Ah!" said Gupp, looking at himself in the oblong of rusty mirror that was fastened with bentover nails above the wash dish. There was no doubt that he could pass for forty-nine. He might even pass for forty. But forty-nine was what he'd said in the letter and forty-nine was what it would be!

By the time he had tallowed his boots and donned his new green and red flannel shirt it was breakfast time. He built a quick fire of sagebrush stalks, fried his usual pancakes and salt pork, and started to eat. Then he stopped. He laughed and talked to himself out loud, the way so many solitary men get to doing.

"Well, by jingos, this has gone and changed my life already. Here if I didn't forget all about Herschel."

He smeared a pancake with sorghum, rolled it around a strip of salt pork, and getting down from his chair a little whistled a chorus of "Buffalo Gals." Soon, obedient to the sound, there came a rustling through some dry stuff beneath the cabin floor and a sleek, well-fed pack rat emerged through one of the broken boards. He waited until Gupp put down the food, then he scurried up and sat like a squirrel with his chin moving up and down, munching it.

"Well, this is the day, the one I been telling you of," Gupp said. He sounded pleased, chuckling and chewing all at the same time. "Didn't come close onto me this morning, did you, Herschel? Might' nigh didn't know me, shaved and slicked this way. Well, a man shouldn't let himself get run over at the bootheels. Sign of getting old. Oldness and lonesomeness. But the lonesomeness is all over now."

Gupp, first wiping the salt pork off his fingers on the dish towel, went to the cupboard and tenderly got down a photograph. He leaned it against a table leg on the floor where Herschel could see. It was a woman of thirty or so holding a plump boy with ringlets.

"There she is, Herschel. The future Mrs. Gupsworth and child. Oh, this'll be a fine place for that boy to grow up. Plenty of fresh air, plenty sunshine, plenty hills to climb. I been thinking some of buying him a pony and cart when he's old enough to drive. Animals, that's what a boy needs. Oh, you'll have great times with him, Herschel. It'll change our lives some, but it'll be all for the best."

The woman was Mrs. Josephine Fedwick, whom Gupp had contacted through the Pike's Peak Home and Happiness Society in Denver. Two weeks ago their correspondence had culminated in a proposal of marriage from Gupp and a prompt acceptance from Mrs. Fedwick, then a letter from Gupp enclosing $22 railroad fare, and now she and her son were due to arrive in Galena City on the Limited that very afternoon.

Herschel finished his meal and departed, leaving some pancake crumbs which Gupp carefully swept through the hole in the floor. He tidied the breakfast things and went outside to look at the sun. He guessed it to be eight o'clock so he had plenty of time to hitch Dolly, his mule, and drive the buggy down to Galena. He had just started out with a currycomb to get the burrs out of Dolly's tail when he heard the scrape and rattle of coach wheels and knew it was Steve

Kegg, making his daily round trip to Whitetail, a slowly crumbling mining camp eight miles farther back in the hills.

Gupp listened, expecting the stage to roll on, but this morning its sounds grew steadily until it came into view across the uphill hump of sage, juniper, and buffalo grass to Gupp's cabin. It was the mud-wagon, drawn by two span of mules, with Steve in the driver's seat and some bags of Mormon spuds roped to the hurricane behind him.

Generally, Steve loaded the freight inside on the floor and in the seats, letting the passengers, when there were any, ride outside as best they could, but today things had changed—the freight was on top and inside were a man and woman.

Steve brought his outfit around, lurching over rocks and gopher mounds to Gupp's cabin, where he dribbled tobacco juice discreetly over the side, wiped his whiskers on the back of his hand, and said: "Gupp, this yere lady and her boy blew in this morning on the skidoo and I guess maybe you was expecting 'em."

Gupp's circulation halted momentarily at his first glimpse of her. She was and she wasn't the woman in the picture. The woman in the picture was slim and old-fashioned while this one was horsy and middle-aged. And this was no baby boy with her, but instead a hulking fellow of twenty-one with pale eyes and a flat, obstinate face.

"What say?" said Gupp, stalling for time.

"Of course he's expecting us," the woman said with an aggressive grasp of the situation. She gave Gupp a determined smile. "You *are* Mr. Gupsworth?"

Gupp did not deny it. He retreated a little as the woman emerged through the coach door stern first, pawing one oversized leg for the ground. The boy followed and the old mudwagon groaned to be rid of them.

The woman turned, giggled with a faded girlishness, and got her hat to better position on her head. It was a purple hat with pink plumes.

"I'm Josephine," she said. "You know...*Josie*. You always called me Josie in your letters." When Gupp merely stared at her, she said, "Well, I must say, Mr. Gupsworth, you don't seem to be splitting yourself to make us welcome."

"Guess I was surprised," Gupp managed to say. "You were younger in your picture."

"Oh, *that*. I told you it wasn't a real recent picture, remember?"

"But the little boy...?"

"Teddy *has* grown a bit, hasn't he? But boys will be boys. And now, Mister Gupsworth, if you will lend a hand with the luggage? There's my bags, and Teddy's trunk, and a box of things that the storekeeper sent."

Gupp wrestled the things from inside and from the boot. While he was getting his breath, Steve Kegg said, "That'll be four dollars fare. The lad said you'd pay."

Gupp gave him the four silver dollars and stood helpless to stop the coach as it rolled away toward Whitetail. Mrs. Fedwick had gone inside the cabin to sniff around. When he started to follow her, he was blocked by Teddy who towered over him with his shoulders thrown back.

"What do you do for amusement around here?" Teddy asked.

"Amusement?"

"Yes, the light fantastic."

"Well, mostly I just work in the mine."

"What mine?"

"Why, up the hill yonder."

"That there?" Teddy studied it. "Why, that's just a hole in the hill with some broken rock heaped in front of it."

"What the blazes did you think a mine looked like?" Gupp snapped, wanting to get inside where the woman was hauling stuff out of the cupboards. He had his assay chemicals there, the lead carbonate and potassium cyanide where they'd be sure and not get mixed up with the baking powder, and he wanted to show her how things had to be. "Maybe you think I should of dug the mine inside out so you could look at it stretched out on the ground."

"Mister Gupsworth!" Josephine said, standing straight with the baking powder in one hand and the cyanide in the other. "Well now, is that any way to speak to your stepson?"

"Why'd he ask so many foolish questions?"

"The only way a boy can learn is by asking questions. Anyway, you'd better be careful how you talk to Teddy. He's stronger than he looks. Bend a horseshoe for him, Teddy."

Teddy looked around and said, "Get me one, will you?"

"Give me those cans," Gupp said, grabbing the baking powder and cyanide.

Teddy said, "I took the course in muscular development from Lionel Strongfort."

Gupp was trying to remember which can was which. He knew then it was the old battered one. He carried them back to the cupboard.

"Now, this one," he said, "has to go here, and this one has to go there. Otherwise likely you'll have an accident."

"I know baking powder when I see it," said Mrs. Fedwick.

"That's just the point, this one ain't baking powder."

"What is it?"

"Cyanide."

Mrs. Fedwick screamed, grabbed both cans, and ran out the door with them. She came back wiping her hands on her dress.

"What'd you do that for?" asked Gupp. "That was my assay stuff."

"I'll not have poison in my cupboard."

"But you always know it...it's in the old can."

"Not...in...my...cupboard," said Mrs. Fedwick, drawing out the words.

Teddy said, "All I could tear up was one pack of cards before I took the course, but now I can tear up two. How many packs can you tear up?"

Gupp said, "I don't know. I never tried." He rescued the cyanide and carried it to the shed which was built over his forge and anvil.

Mrs. Fedwick said to Gupp, "And now you can put that big box of groceries in here on the floor."

Gupp had a hard time struggling it inside. He had never seen so many groceries in his life. Getting it over the step would have been too much for him had not Teddy stood at a distance, telling him to pull it this way and that.

"Whew!" said Gupp. "It looks like we're going to eat mighty fancy."

Mrs. Fedwick had now sniffed in all the corners, including the tiny bedroom. She said, "Well, Mr. Gupsworth, you said in your letters not to expect a mansion and I must say that we didn't find one."

"She's small but she's snug," Gupp said defensively.

"Well, I guess it will have to serve until you can build another one."

"Now hold on...."

"Surely you didn't intend this for a permanent arrangement." She looked back inside the bedroom. "We'll fix that up for Teddy. He can put his pennants on that wall, his exercisers over there, and I suppose there'll be room for his rowing machine if we buy a smaller bed." Mrs. Fedwick took a big breath. "Well, I guess I'd better get my working things on. Up to a new wife to be useful, I say."

Gupp was lifting groceries from the packing case. "What's this?" he asked, shaking a red and white box.

"Bran flakes," said Teddy.

"I eat oatmeal."

"The storekeeper wanted to send oatmeal, but we had him send flakes. Oatmeal ain't fortified. It's gone out. Old-fashioned. In the big cities everybody eats flakes these days."

Gupp didn't say anything. He dug deeper into the box, lifting out prepared waffle flour, prepared biscuit mix, prepared gingerbread mix, cans of ripe olives.

Mrs. Fedwick said, "Now, if you'll move those old tools, I think I'll put my clothes right there. Will you bring my suitcases in so I can unpack?"

Gupp thought of something and said, "You ain't aiming to just stay?"

"Well, now! If that isn't...."

"But we ain't married."

"Oh, that!" She laughed in relief. "That's all been taken care of. When I was in town, I saw that Gospel John person, and he promised to drive out tonight and marry us."

She listened to a *crunch-crunch* sound emerging from the grocery carton. She tiptoed over and peered inside. Then she screamed.

"A rat! An awful rat!"

The broom was handy. She tipped the carton over, frightened the rat into flight, swung the broom high. It came down, but Gupp deflected it.

"Hold on!" said Gupp. "That's Herschel!"

Mrs. Fedwick brushed Gupp aside and pursued the fleeing rodent around the house, swinging the broom, but he made the hole in the floor and disappeared.

"I hate rats," said Mrs. Fedwick.

"Well," said Gupp, "I always say they's good and bad in everything. I've known some mules I wouldn't've sold for wolf bait, but

I don't take that as an excuse to go around killing all the mules I see. Now a rat, if you get to know him...."

"Me, get to know a rat?"

"Well, just for the sake of argument, say...."

"I got better things to do than argue about a silly thing like that. If there's anything I detest, it's a filthy, sneaking rat. Are you much troubled by them, Mister Gupsworth?"

"No'm."

"Well, I'll have this one before many hours are spent. I do wish I'd have put in a trap. I don't suppose you have a trap here. Well, I'll keep the broom handy."

"Just a stray, likely. If you forget about him, I'll mend that hole in the floor and...."

"A rat'll stay wherever there's food. Only way is to kill them."

"I'll get a club, Ma," said Teddy. "I'll stay here by the hole and bop him."

"I'm mending that hole right now," said Gupp.

"Mister Gupsworth, if Teddy...."

"I'm mending the hole."

Teddy glowered down on Gupp while he got the hammer, saw, and a length of wood and went about mending the hole where Herschel was wont to come through the floor.

"Ma'd of got that rat if you hadn't pawed at her," Teddy said.

"You mind your rowing machine and I'll mind mine," said Gupp.

Mrs. Fedwick was now in the process of carrying everything outside. Chairs, utensils, bedding, tools, everything was stacked in the bright sunshine outside. Each time she carried something outside she would scrutinize it and say "Humph!" before returning.

Gupp kept moving here and there, watching her, and keeping his eye on Teddy, too, for Teddy still was armed with the club.

"What's this?" Mrs. Fedwick asked, looking with revulsion at the flapjack can.

This ancient, thickly encrusted household essential Gupp had kept sitting winter and summer in exactly the right spot in relation to the cook stove so it would maintain the correct temperature for fermentation. The sourdough maker's art is like that of cook and wine maker's combined and Gupp had kept his starter going like Olympic fire for the past twenty years.

"Hold on," said Gupp, "that's my flapjack batter."

"It's all spoiled."

"No it ain't...." He was unable to stop her. She hurled it across the yard.

Gupp lurked in the house, keeping watch of his other valuables, and keeping watch of Teddy and his club. He chewed tobacco, and from time to time he carefully aimed tobacco juice through a crack where two of the floor boards failed to join.

"The floor will have to be repaired there, too," said Mrs. Fedwick.

"That's my spittin' hole."

"Well, I must say I was in hopes you wouldn't be a chewer but, if you can't manage to break yourself of the habit, you'll have to buy one of those little china cuspidors and carry that around with you. Then each time you use it, you can take it outside and clean it. What are those old rocks doing here?" Mrs. Fedwick now asked, indicating the ore specimens.

"Those are my ore specimens."

"They'll have to go out."

"I'll throw 'em out, Ma," said Teddy. "I like to throw things."

"Keep your hands off'n my minerals!"

The two men faced each other and Gupp commenced gathering the specimens up, stuffing them in his pockets and loading his arms. With the most treasured of them he started for the door when the air was rent by the woman's scream.

"The rat! The rat again!"

"I'll get him, Ma," Teddy was shouting, charging around with his club.

"Stop it!" cried Gupp, dropping the specimens. "That's not a rat, that's Herschel."

"It's a rat!" wailed Mrs. Fedwick. "There he is, Teddy. He's hiding behind the stove."

Teddy charged with his club raised and Gupp tried to get in front of him. He was no match for Teddy's size and strength, but he delayed him just long enough for the rat to scoot under the cook stove.

"He's under the stove now," Mrs. Fedwick was saying, armed with a poker. "I'll watch from this side."

Teddy bawled, "Get in the door. Don't let him get out, that's all I ask."

"That's my rat!" Gupp was saying. "You ain't going to kill my rat."

Teddy shoved him away. He did not hear Gupp shouting warnings to his mother. He got down and commenced poking beneath the stove, but the rat had gone. There was a scurry near the wood box. Teddy grabbed the box, pulled it loose from its moorings, and upended it.

The rat cowered, not knowing which way to go. The club was upraised, but Gupp grappled as it descended. His unexpected weight carried Teddy to the wall.

"You made me miss the rat, you danged old fool!" Teddy shouted.

"You leave my rat alone," Gupp backed up, looking for a weapon, but his picks and shovels and old Martha, his shotgun, were all outside. "I may not be so young, and I may not have muscles from a correspondence school, but just the same nobody's going to come in my cabin and throw out my pancake batter and my ore specimens and then kill my rat...you and your chiny spittoons, your exercisers and your rowing machine...."

"This is the house where Ma and I are going to live and we're not going to put up with any rat."

"There he is!" screamed Mrs. Fedwick.

Gupp wrestled for the club. The rat scurried past them heading for the hole in the floor but, alas, Gupp had mended it. He tarried for an instant, only an instant, but the momentary pause had sealed his fate. The poker in the hands of Mrs. Fedwick descended, and the rat lay still.

"There!" said Mrs. Fedwick, blowing her breath. "I guess that settles that."

For an instant Gupp stared down at the dead rat. He walked to the door.

"Pick up the awful thing," Mrs. Fedwick was saying. "I can't bear to touch it."

Gupp went outside. There was his old ten-gauge double. He took a look to see that it was loaded. He advanced to the door, bent over the gun with both its hammers cocked.

"You varmints," he said, "git to packing!"

"You old fool," said Mrs. Fedwick, "put down that gun."

"Git out of my house, the both of you, and git out quick, or you'll be picking birdshot out o' your hide clean from here to Champa Street."

Mrs. Fedwick tried to parry. "Why, Mister Gupsworth, this is a peculiar attitude for you to take. Put up that gun...."

"Don't you try anything," Gupp said, attempting to watch both of them at the same time.

"All right," said Teddy, "let us get our stuff out."

Gupp lowered the gun. He just knew what Teddy would try and was ready for him. As Teddy swung a haymaker at his head, he went double, brought the gun up butt first, driving it deep into Teddy's belly.

"Oof!" said Teddy, his jaw limp and his knees sagging.

"So you did, did you?" said Gupp "So you took lessons from Lionel Strongfort! Well, let me tell you about another Teddy I knew one time and a thing I learned off'n him. Teddy Roosevelt and the old Rough Riders, and here's my Cuban special!"

Gupp swung up with his fist but he let his arm double over at the last instant, bringing instead his bent elbow into crashing contact with Teddy's jaw.

He staggered to the wall and when he rebounded Gupp whooped: "And this I named my singlejack punch, developed right up yonder in the U. S. Mint."

Mrs. Fedwick clawed a handful of Gupp's hair, pulling him away.

"Git away from me, you pink-plumed catymount!"

He lifted the side of one freshly tallowed boot, catching her fairly in the place where he had aimed. Then, with the gun once more aimed, he said, "Git your stuff and git to packin', and if I see you inside of the lines of the U. S. Mint patent survey once after sundown I'll show you how I deal with claim jumpers."

It seemed unusually quiet when they were gone. He buried the rat and carried everything back inside, putting it exactly as it had been before Mrs. Fedwick and her boy arrived.

He imagined they got a ride back on the mudwagon. He did not check to see. The minister did not arrive, so he supposed they had seen him and turned him back. It suited Gupp just as well. He wanted nothing to remind him of them.

He rescued his sourdough can and found a heel of the starter and added warm water and flour to it. He cooked baking-powder biscuits and salt pork for supper, using the can that sat in its correct spot between the lead carbonate and the cyanide. He even caught himself whistling "Buffalo Gals," and stopped with a pang.

He slept and arose next morning, and worked all day in the U. S. Mint. He worked extra long each day, trying to leave home earlier than usual and come home later so as to forget about Herschel.

One morning, with a cold drizzle of rain outside, he found himself whistling "Buffalo Gals" while frying pancakes on the cook stove. He stopped, hearing a rustle of movement beneath the floor. It was almost like Herschel had come back.

He got the hammer and pulled the mended portion of floor away, and into the room came a pack rat. It *was* Herschel. There could be no doubt about it. It was Herschel!

In amazement he watched as other forms followed, little rats almost transparent they looked, with bits of jet in their eyes and the tips of their noses, baby pack rats, five of them.

"Well," Gupp said, "you can blast me on a short fuse!"

He understood then. The other pack rat, the dead one, had come from town in that carton of groceries. That rat had escaped beneath the floor and become Herschel's wife.

No, come to think of it, that rat was Herschel's husband!

Robert Easton was born in San Francisco, California, and always identified strongly with the history of his native state. His first book, THE HAPPY MAN (Viking, 1943), is a portrait of California ranch life in the 1940s that earned him wide critical acclaim. In his later Saga of California, he undertook an ambitious series of inter-related novels, each dealing with a different period in the history of California, from the coming of the Spanish to the present day. He is presently at work on BLOOD AND MONEY, the third novel in this saga. Easton is also the author of MAX BRAND: THE BIG "WESTERENER" (University of Oklahoma Press, 1970) and co-editor with his wife, Jane Faust Easton, of THE COLLECTED STORIES OF MAX BRAND (University of Nebraska Press, 1994). "Banker Clayton's Interest" first appeared in *Collier's* (12/9/50), although it was begun in 1943 while Easton was in training at a U. S. Army camp in Texas. Like THE HAPPY MAN, this story is set in the California ranching community.

Banker Clayton's Interest

When the drought was at its height, and there was no water and no grass for the entire length of coast, the last water remaining for the cattle in our part of the country was at the mouth of the dry river. Here a sand bar made a lagoon surrounded by thick banks of reeds, and the dying cattle moaned around it like lost souls within the very sight of salvation; for all of it was protected by quicksand, as here and there a carcass not yet digested by the morass testified.

About this time I found Banker John Clayton in his place of business diligently whittling a toothpick out of a match stem, a sure sign he had something in mind. The Sundown Valley Bank of those days was a highly concentrated affair consisting of one room, one desk, one-chair-and-banker which went together, and one extra chair known locally as "the hot seat" and usually occupied by prospective borrowers. In this I sat and waited for the thought clouds to pass from the financier, so that I could invite him to beat the heat with me with a bottle of red soda pop.

"I was just thinking," he said, more to himself and the match stem than anybody, "about the mouth of the river. Noticed?"

You noticed nothing else! Your eyes turned there automatically from any high point in the valley, as toward an oasis in the desert— or a mirage.

"I was just thinking," said Clayton, "the fellow who brings his cattle through this drought will make a million dollars. Cattle will be worth their weight in gold this time next month, next year, whenever it rains again."

"What makes you think so?"

"They'll be scarce as hen's teeth."

I asked him how he would bring his cattle through to that desired golden condition.

"I'm no cattleman," he shrugged.

McKay came in looking irate as usual.

"Clayton, I represent the cattlemen of this valley," he said.

"How are they?" said Clayton, continuing to shape his toothpick.

"They're worried."

"So am I." That was the truth. Next to the Almighty, the local banker is lord and giver of life to his community, wet weather or dry, and the drought was bidding fair to dry up Banker Clayton's loans, I knew, mine included.

"They're worried about what this drought's doing to their stock. A few weeks more and they won't have any cattle. They haven't got any money now." McKay glanced at me as if I might still have money. He never cared for me because I ran the largest outfit in the valley.

"What do they want me to do," said Clayton, "make it rain?"

McKay put both hands on the desk and leaned on them, toward Clayton.

"They want you to say you won't call any loans until it *does* rain!"

Clayton put his knife and toothpick away, then got them right back out again. "When did I call any?"

"Not saying you have, just telling you...."

"Telling or asking?" Clayton cut him off.

"Let's get a drink," I said hastily.

Clayton stood up. "Mac, my stake in this valley is just as great as the next fellow's. When your cattle dry up, so do my dollars...though I admit they don't suffer in the process like your livestock does. You tell the boys to come see me." He sat down again after McKay had gone, it being one of John Clayton's principles never to overtire the feet. But I could see that what McKay said had bothered him. Clayton was a Yankee. Thirty years out of Maine had not eradicated this fact from the minds of the Southerners he lived with. In the crisis he might show his true colors—and become a damyankee.

With the drawl which belied his origin he said, "I was just wondering if you'd noticed the mouth of the river." Clayton seldom said a thing outright. He put ideas out like money, on the chance they would return him interest.

I went down the valley for a look at Blue Lagoon. It was more green than blue, with the deep dark velvety green of stagnation, yet it was water, drinking water—the sandbar held out the sea; and the reeds would make delicious feed if you could get to them; enough forage there for all the cattle in the valley, if you could get to them. I picked my way out among those husks of things that had been cattle, shook off a living remnant that followed me crying pitifully, and let the idea whereby Clayton said a million dollars could be made take shape.

Going back through the town I said to him, "You aren't suggesting I run my cattle over that quicksand?"

"I never said any such thing."

"Why, I'd lose a thousand head in no time!"

"How many cattle have you?"

I had about two thousand.

"Sometimes the half is bigger than the whole," said Clayton and picked up his black-bound copy of Coffin's interest tables and began to study it as if there were the answer.

I thought about this idea for a couple of days and the more I thought about it the more it seemed the only chance, if a long one. Win or lose all, one throw. I mentioned it to McKay and some of the others. "There's plenty of forage in those reeds for all of us and water too," I told them. They asked me if I'd ever seen anything cross that quicksand, laughed, and called it a damyankee idea.

So we went ahead on our own, Shorm, Porofirio, Jesus, and I, gathering the cattle one morning before daylight. It was hot already. Night made no difference in those days. It was only a turning off of the flame. You roasted all night long like you were in a shut oven, and with morning the flame came on again. Gathering the cattle was no trouble. They had long since gathered themselves around our ranch buildings at the head of the valley, more like forlorn lost sheep than once self-respecting livestock, and their crying was never still. We spared what water we could from the home well. But there was no feed at all, not so much as a spear of grass. They broke into the orchard and stripped the trees, came on into the gardens and cleaned them. The place looked as if locusts had camped there.

But when we had them rounded up, they would not drive. They milled in circles and went back. They were like a man staggering with thirst. We got them moving finally with a bait of an empty water trough on a wagon, started down the road toward Sundown and Blue

Lagoon. The big buffalo-humped steers were the leaders, ghostly remains of what once had been cattle, hollowed high on the flanks from lack of water, pinched to bare ribbings like laths over which hide was stretched. Behind them the rest strung out, yearlings and cows and pitifully shrunken calves no bigger than dogs. Even the once lordly bulls were fooled by the trough on the wagon and hurried like dogies to keep up.

By sunrise our horses were already in sweat. And the cattle, who can't sweat except through their mouths and noses, were lolling out their tongues and licking at their parched nostrils, which should have been moist and white and spinning fine threads of saliva but were dry as bark. They had nothing to sweat. It was cruel to drive them, crueler not to. That was my consolation when I thought of Blue Lagoon.

But there was something I had not thought of: the breeze from the sea which picked up around mid-morning. To us it was like the breath of bellows through a blacksmith's forge. But to the cattle it was something else. It brought a message that made the big leaders lift their heads and lengthen their strides. It brought word of water.

As if this were not all, the magic telegraph passed into the hills and carried the news of our movement, and out by twos and threes upon the ridges, fours and fives among the breaks and cañons, came other cattle, and more, and still more, hurrying to join us, until the tributaries of the valley ran red with cattle as they never had run with water, and our little freshet was swollen to a flood rushing down the dry bed of the river, growing every minute as side streams joined. Ride as we might, Shorm, Porofirio, Jesus, and I, we could not stop those side streams.

And they were not our cattle. At distant ranch houses we could see riders saddling up. Something told me they were not very happy about what was going on. But, no stopping for that either. The leaders had long since left the bait of water wagon behind. They were moving under their own power, at a steady, steady trot, heads up, tails out, bound somewhere. The herd compacted. It gathered like a sick man does for one last effort, crazed, staggering blind. It turned into a stampede.

You have heard about stampedes of frightened cattle. Well, this was the stampede of those condemned to death, weird shapes and replicas of cattle, surging forward toward one last bone. Riders were carried into it by the tributary streams they tried to stem but couldn't and were borne out onto the surface of the flood like flotsam. One of the eddies brought McKay alongside me. "Damn you!" he cried, his face livid with effort and with fury. "You started this! You'll pay for it! You and that Yankee banker!" He was swept away before he could finish saying how Clayton and I had planned the thing in order to put everyone else out of business.

The town lay directly in our path. The cattle thundered into Sundown, echoing wildly from the buildings, churning the dusty streets to smoke, crashing into remains of flower gardens to nibble at the stalks of plants, snatching at dry wisps of pepper branches, never stopping. The inhabitants took to their homes.

As we whirled through the deserted square I glimpsed the face of Clayton at the door of the bank; he wore a toothpick and a grin of satisfaction. For the rest, the Sundowners looked out at me darkly; and I could see lawsuits rising with the dust. I had bargained for none of this.

But now it was straightaway to the sea, the rifled town behind us, the message of Blue Lagoon stronger and stronger till the maddened brutes were running like racers for the fire, bawling in a terrible eagerness. The green reeds came in sight. A matter of moments and we would be among them, and then what? And then I saw we were caught, a dozen of us on horseback, caught as boulders in an avalanche that hurled us forward and from which there was no escape. The big lead steers hit the quicksand and went down; the others pressed them on, and down, into the sand like steppingstones, to be trod upon in their turn and pressed down. Wave after wave of cattle hit that sand like so many loads of living red gravel, dumped to make a fill, an ever-widening causeway reaching outward toward the reeds. Cattle snatched at them even as they sank and drank deliriously of the sweet water as they drowned, and were stampeded to pieces by the agonizing remainder. This very eagerness was what saved us; it left us back in the herd—so far back that as we moved out onto that causeway, where the living walked upon the dead, it had nearly bridged the quicksand. And then my mare's feet were on something other than ground which squirmed and made her stagger. She struck the shoulder of one lunging brute and caromed off another; and then the fear of death took hold of her and shot her forward in a hurtling rush, shot her off the crest of the cataract of cattle, shot her clear.

I felt a lash of reeds and the slap of warm water like a bath. We were in the lagoon and swimming. Heads and horns were all around us and there was a gurgling and a thrashing and a crying and a moaning. Porofirio had slipped from his saddle and was holding his stallion by the tail. I did likewise. We had a hundred yards to the sandbar where the breakers beat from the sea and maybe it was quicksand too; but, no, it was firm; the waves had pounded home and made good ground and out we came on it; and out a little way farther down came McKay—and bogged half out of sight. The bar *was* quicksand where he had landed. I pitched him my rope. Porofirio lay down flat and grabbed his horse's reins. We dragged him out of it like a slimy log, and he got ready to hit me. He was mad to the marrow.

"Before you do it," I said, talking fast, "look behind you."

The lagoon wasn't blue any more; it was red, with cattle…some swimming, some wading, some nibbling at reeds, all alive. For every one of them stamped into the sand, another was alive and washing in that living water. It was a sight for any cattleman's sore and sun-burned eyes. And McKay took it in like a man who had been shown the promised land.

"Well, shoot me," he said, "but how will they get out of it?"

"Same way they came in. We can too, when things quiet."

"Well, shoot me," he said and looked as wise as a man can, covered with muck, and then decided the joke had been entirely on McKay. "And I reckon that's what happens when a damyankee gets into the cattle business? Killing off half the cattle of the valley to save the other half?"

And I reckoned the same.

So Clayton got his interest. So when the rains came, the cattle of Sundown Valley were turned to gold; and along that entire length of coast they alone shone, like a nugget.

Will(iam Everett) Cook

was born in Richmond, Indiana. He turned to writing in 1951 and contributed a number of outstanding short stories to *Dime Western* and *Star Western* where he was particularly encouraged by Mike Tilden. It was in *The Saturday Evening Post* that his best-known novel, COMANCHE CAPTIVES (Bantam, 1960), was serialized. It was later filmed as TWO RODE TOGETHER (Columbia, 1961) directed by John Ford and starring James Stewart and Richard Widmark. Sometimes in his short stories Cook would introduce characters that would later be featured in novels, such as Charlie Boomhauer who appears in the story that follows and is also a character in BADMAN'S HOLIDAY (Fawcett Gold Medal, 1958) and THE WIND RIVER KID (Fawcett Gold Medal, 1958), both of which have been recently reprinted in a single volume by Leisure Books. Throughout his work Cook maintained an enviable quality. His novels range widely in time and place, peopled with credible and interesting characters whose interactions form the backbone of the narratives. There are historical romances like SABRINA KANE (Dodd, Mead, 1956) and exercises in historical realism like ELIZABETH, BY NAME (Dodd, Mead, 1958). His protagonists make mistakes, hurt people they care for, and sometimes succumb to ignoble impulses, but a common feature in Cook's Western fiction is his compassion for these characters and what they must endure to survive in a wild and violent land.

Lawmen Die Sudden!

I

THE DILEMMA

In the six years Milo Singer had been sheriff of Mesa County, only three acts of violence marred his term and a half of office until last night's killing brought the total to four. Singer came out of Doctor Aaron Radcliff's office with the badly mashed bullet in his hand and walked diagonally across Buckhorn's dusty street to his office. He was a tall man, mild mannered, with soft gray eyes and an easy tolerance around his wide mouth. The morning sun slanted low over the rooftops of the buildings, layering the town with an early heat, and he paused at the jail door, giving the street a quick look before stepping inside.

Al Ringle, the night marshal, was hanging up his gun belt, and he turned to the younger man, his eyes heavy with the lack of sleep. "What did you find out?"

Singer tossed the bullet on his desk and said, "Forty-four Colt. Somebody used a cap and ball. You can tell by the gain twist of the rifling."

He opened a drawer and laid out the dead man's personal effects: a little over twelve dollars in loose coin, a worn .45 Colt revolver, and an envelope with no writing on it. Milo clasped his hands together and leaned his elbows on the desk, his thumbs running along the edge of his jaw, and sat deeply in thought.

Ringle took a long drink from the olla jug and said, "Nothin' else to identify him with?"

Milo shook his head. "He'd been in town a week. Nobody even knew his name." He stood up and put his hat on, adding,"I'll be gone most of the morning." Ringle nodded, and he went out.

Buckhorn was coming awake a little at a time as Milo entered Ratibin's Saloon on the next corner. A swamper swirled a mop in a listless circle; the bartender made a feeble effort to polish the glassware. Milo stopped at the bar and said, "You told me last night he was here until eleven. Where did he go after he left?"

The bartender shrugged. "It was Saturday night and pretty crowded. I just seen him leave...that's all."

Singer said, "Thanks," and walked out.

It was his breakfast hour, and he stepped into the Drover House, taking his customary table in the corner. The waitress served his meal promptly, and he laid his hat on the floor and began eating. Willard Peterson, the newspaperman, came in then and took a chair at the sheriff's table. Peterson was a short man with pale hair and watery eyes.

"Learn anything new?" Peterson asked, and Singer shook his head. "The man must have left some clue behind. A man can't live without making some kind of mark."

"I haven't found it yet," Milo said. "Nobody knew him, and yet everybody saw him at one time or another. If anything comes up, I'll let you know. Meanwhile, just print the usual thing...unknown man...that sort of thing."

Peterson agreed with a nod. He said nothing until the waitress brought him his meal, then murmured, "Where's Max? He usually ducks out of the house on Sunday morning while Marilyn has that crowd before church."

"A little early yet," Milo said.

There were half finished with their meal when Max Stendahl entered, his bowler at a rakish angle, his fat face flushed from his walk uptown. He waved at Milo and pulled back a chair.

The waitress came over again, and Max waited until she disappeared into the kitchen before speaking. "That was a shameful thing last night, Milo. Makes a man wonder what the country's coming to."

Singer touched the newspaper man on the sleeve and said, "Make me up a hundred small bills with the fella's description and list of personal effects. I'll shoot 'em out to the outlying lawmen and see what we can stir up."

Max said, "That seems to be going to a lot of trouble for some drifter."

Singer's smooth face was patient; his full mustache hid the expression around the ends of his mouth. "Max, when you come up short at the bank, what do you do?"

Stendahl's heavy brows wrinkled, and he muttered, "Go over the books and hunt until we find the mistake."

"That's the way it is with a lawman," Milo said. "A man has been killed, and I want to know who he was." He lifted his coffee cup, then added, "If I could only find someone who talked to him last night after he left the saloon."

Max Stendahl's eyes narrowed, then he said, "I talked to him last night...or rather he talked to me. I was taking a constitutional when he stopped me and asked me for a job."

"You never seen him before?" Milo asked.

"No-o...yes! Around town, but I never spoke to him before."

"Just exactly what did he say?"

Max pulled at his lip for a moment and said, "Why, I believe he asked me if I owned the Chevron brand and did I need riders. I told him it was my property, but I had a full crew. He thanked me and bummed a match, and then I went home."

"What time was this?"

"After eleven," Max said, and ate his breakfast.

Milo turned it over in his mind and then said, "Doc says he got shot around midnight."

"Can I print this?" Peterson asked.

"Not yet," Milo told him. "Wait until we have a little more to go on." He reached for his hat and rose from the table. "Well," he said, "that's the way it goes. A little piece at a time."

"How do you keep the pieces straight?" Max wanted to know.

"Most of the time I don't," Milo admitted and left.

On Bartlett Street, the church bell set up an insistent tolling, calling the gentry to worship. Milo stood on the edge of the sidewalk listening to this, then turned down the street toward his office. Al Ringle was still there when Milo entered, and he was busy cuffing a man awake in one of the rear cells.

Milo closed the door and said sharply, "Let him alone!" Ringle's head came around quickly, but he released the man and closed the cell door. "Open it," Milo said, and Ringle scowled, but obeyed.

The prisoner looked at Singer, then some vague relief crossed his face, and he shuffled down the corridor and into the main room. Milo opened a drawer and slid him his personal belongings, along with his gun and holster.

"You mean I can go?" the man asked.

"The next time," Milo said mildly, "try not to get rowdy when you drink."

"Did I wreck anything?" the man asked, still a little surprised.

"Just a few bottles of whisky when you knocked Pete Wesphal into the bar. I took it out of your poke. The receipt's in there."

"Thanks," the man said and gave Ringle a long glance, then went out.

Al Ringle's face was still clouded and he said, "I beat my brains out to arrest 'em, and all you do is turn 'em loose."

"You get paid for it just the same," Milo told him.

Ringle snorted, "You're a hell of a sheriff," and moved toward the door.

Milo's face changed, and a faint displeasure crossed his mouth, pulling it longer and a little severe. "Why don't you get on the ballot the next time then?"

Ringle gave him a hard glance and said, "Maybe I will," and left.

Milo stayed in his office until noon, then rose and went to the Drover House for his meal. After he had been served, Willard Peterson came in with a small stack of hand notices. He laid them on the table by Singer's elbow, and the sheriff said, "That ought to get some results."

Peterson shook his head and murmured, "Why all the fuss? The man's dead."

Milo raised his eyes to the thin man and said, "If I was some out-of-the-pants rider and caught a bullet, I'd want someone to care enough to find out my name. Wouldn't you want someone to be curious?"

"I've never been an out-of-the-pants...whatever you said." Peterson looked at Milo Singer for a studied moment, and added softly,

"I don't figure you, Milo. I really don't. Hell, the man was probably a criminal. I always said that right's right and wrong's wrong."

The sheriff shook his head. "Nope, there's various degrees of rightness and wrongness. The difference lies in a man's heart and in his conscience."

"I don't know how you ever got elected," Willard muttered and stood up. He gave Singer a long look, and added, "I can't imagine what the people were thinking of."

Singer watched him until he disappeared into his office across the street, then finished his meal. He laid the fifty cents on the table and went out into the sunlight.

Across the street, a man lounged against the side of the feed store, and it was a moment before Milo recognized him as the man he had just released from jail. The man's head was downcast as he rolled a cigarette, and the brim of his hat splashed deep shadows across his face, but Singer had the distinct feeling that the man had been waiting for him. The man's head came up. Singer and he exchanged a long look, then the sheriff went down the street and into his office.

Milo sat at his desk. He didn't have long to wait. The man flipped his head both ways at the street and came in quickly, immediately closing the door. Singer watched him, his long lips flat and thoughtful beneath his mustache, a clear curiosity in his pale eyes.   M i l o said, "Did you forget something?"

"Maybe," the man said and perched on the edge of Singer's desk. He was a square-faced man on the edge of toughness, but his dark eyes held no meanness.

"What's on your mind?" Singer asked. "Our hospitality wasn't that good."

"I'm Chess Hadden," the man said. "The name wouldn't mean anything to you because I ain't on a reward dodger." He broke off his talk as if pondering a grave decision, then added, "You didn't have to let me out this morning."

"Why keep you in jail?" Milo said. "Would that cure the pink snakes for you?"

"No," Hadden said. "I never have been able to leave the stuff alone. I lost one job right after another because I couldn't keep my nose out of a whisky bottle." He glanced about him nervously and asked, "We alone in here?"

"As alone as you can get," Singer stated.

Hadden hesitated a moment, then blurted, "That shootin' last night...I saw it!"

Singer smothered an oath of surprise, then his eyes grew speculative, and he said, "You could have told me this earlier. Why wait until now?"

"Nobody would have believed me," Hadden said. He looked around him again, then added, "I was sleepin' one off in the alley, layin' behind some beer barrels, when this fella comes outa Ratibin's back door. He smoked a couple of cigarettes like he was waitin' for somebody. Then this other fella comes along and they talk."

"What other fella? What did they say?"

"I don't know who he was," Hadden said. "I couldn't hear 'cause they talked too low, but I got a good look at the man when he came into the alley. He was a big man, fat in the belly, and he wore a bowler and a fancy suit."

Singer spread his hands flat on the desk top, and his voice was a bare whisper. "You're sure of this...positive?"

"See?" Hadden said. "You don't believe me. That's why I didn't say nothin' before. Who'd believe a saddle tramp?"

"All right," Singer said. "Go on with it."

"This fat guy," Hadden said, "got hot under the collar when this other fella showed him somethin'. I didn't see what it was, but this big fella grabbed the little fella's gun hand and then hit him a whack with his cane. The fella fell, and the big guy pulled out a gun and shot him, then went down the alley and into the back door of a building, the big brick one that sets on the corner."

"That's the bank," Singer said in a toneless voice. He looked at Hadden as if he could see into the man's mind, but the man's eyes didn't waver. "Did you get a look at the gun?"

"Well," Hadden hedged a little, "sorta. It was pretty dark, but it was a cap and ball with a sawed-off barrel. It barked like a forty-four, but I wouldn't swear to that."

There was a long silence, then Milo asked, "Would you stand up in court and swear to what you just told me?"

"I seen it," Hadden said, "and I'll swear to anything I see." The sheriff sat silently for so long that Hadden grew nervous, and he asked, "Ain't that good enough?"

"Yes," Singer told him. "It's good enough, but we'll save it for later. Stick around town and keep your mouth shut. This is between you and me. If it leaks out, you'll probably end up in an alley."

"I'm broke," Hadden said.

Singer gave him a twenty dollar gold piece and advised, "If you gotta drink, then bring the bottle here, and we'll lock you up so you won't say the wrong thing at the wrong time." Hadden nodded and went out.

The sheriff sat quietly for the better part of an hour, then said, as if the man was in the room with him, "Why, Max? What for?" He got up and put on his hat and stepped out onto the street. The church bell rang again; the congregation was letting out, and he cut between the buildings and into the alley, coming out on Cyprus Street. Max Stendahl's huge house was set back from the edge of the road, and Singer walked slowly up the winding path.

Marilyn Stendahl was sitting on the porch, and she rose and kissed him when he came up the steps. "You're a minute and a half late," she said in a teasing voice. "One of the first rules of business, father says, is to be on time."

"I thought this was pleasure," Singer murmured and drew her against him for another kiss.

She didn't like it and pushed at him until he released her, and he saw that the color was high in her face. She smoothed her hair, and a faint temper crept into her voice. "Milo...not here where people can see us!"

"What's the difference?" Milo wanted to know. "When you kiss me, they can see that. But when I kiss you, then we're supposed to hide it?"

Her lips turned up into a half smile, but she looked at him slantingly, and he saw that she was faintly irritated. "Do you always have to analyze people?"

He considered it with mock gravity, then said, "Sometimes I think they're beyond it. At least I have a hard time understanding the things they sometimes do."

"Daddy says you'll never amount to much because you're too easy going and sentimental."

"Your dad's right," Singer agreed, and settled himself on the porch.

Marilyn studied him for a moment, not sure how to take him, then said, "I made some ice tea. I'll get you some." The screen door banged, and her voice within the house came soft and echoing. Then Max came out and sat on the porch railing, facing Singer.

He mopped his streaming brow, and Singer said, ""Why don't you get out of that suit, Max? That's your trouble...you never learned to relax. You gotta learn to take life easier."

"That's for old men and fools without any get-up-and-go," Max said. "You'll never amount to much by taking it easy." He wiped his face again.

Singer smiled when he looked at him and said, "Depends a lot on where a man's going. Me? I'm not going anywhere. I came into this country free and easy, and I found it the same way. I guess I passed up a lot of chances to get rich by just havin' fun. You didn't have any fun, Max, but you own damned near half the county and hold mortgages on the rest."

"Milo," Max said with a low-voiced seriousness, "men like you are important, but they just aren't builders. It takes ruthlessness to be a builder. You want people to like you, well...I never gave a damn what a man thought of me. I've squeezed people out but, if I hadn't done it, then something or somebody else would have done it because they just weren't stickers." He paused to light a long cigar, and Marilyn came out onto the porch with glasses and a tray.

She looked at Milo, and then at her father, and said, "I know all of the signs. When he's red-faced and scowling at his cigar and you're sitting with your hands folded and looking at your nails, then I know you've been picking on each other again." Her father gave her a loving scowl, and Milo grinned. "Why," she went on, "do you two even speak if you disagree so much of the time?"

"Therein lies the attraction," Milo said and took the tall glass she offered him. "Max is a schemer. A foreclosin', money-grabbin' old goat, but he's a necessity. Me? I'm a luxury, and I'm doing my damnedest to keep the taxpayers from finding it out."

Max grinned then and said, "Milo's got a way about him. He can insult you and make you like it, but he's not fooling me a damn' bit."

"Drink your tea," Singer said, "before you have a stroke and I'll have to dig me up another prospective father-in-law with money."

Marilyn gave him a close look and said, half seriously, "Darling, I do believe you're lazy."

"Certainly," Milo agreed. "Every man is. Some just hide it under a lot of gruff talk and ambition." He sipped his drink and gave Max a quick glance before saying, "Where are you from, Max? You never did say."

Max studied the tip of his cigar for a moment, then said, "The prairie country," and lifted his glass, hiding his face from Milo. The sheriff flashed Marilyn a glance and there was a pinched look around her mouth.

The severity never left Max's face, and Milo set his glass down and rose. "Time to get uptown," he said. "It's a quiet day, but who knows...someone might get reckless and spit on the sidewalk." He gave Marilyn a wink and a smile and went slowly down the path.

Her voice sailed out after him, "Supper's at seven!" He raised his arm in acknowledgment, then cut across the street and through the vacant lot. He walked to Worlison's stable and saddled his horse, riding out of town ten minutes later. He rode toward a rise of land a mile and a half to the south and dismounted to sit in the grass and look at the town. It was his town, and he felt a deep pride in it. The side streets held the quiet residential sections; the main street looked like that of any other small cattle town in the middle 'Eighties, without the wildness. He watched a fringe-topped buggy wheel from a back alley and turn out of town on the same road he had taken, a loose cloud of dust rising and following it like a banner. Singer watched it for a moment, then swung his eyes over the land. The terrain rolled in small hummocks and deep cutbanks with no high land predominating it other than the hill on which he sat. A road cut out of the faint mountains to the west. Through the breaks in its contours he saw ranch buildings in a loose sprawl. He owned none of it himself, yet he shared its trouble, hence came unto it all, and that was the way he wanted it.

He cocked his head to one side and listened as the buggy rattled through a cutbank, then hove into view and stopped alongside his grazing horse. Amy Templeton sat upright in the seat, her curved body straight, but without stiffness. Milo smiled and said, "I saw you pull out of town. I wondered if you'd come up here."

She was a small girl with large, gray eyes and soft brown hair and, once the makeup had been removed from her face, nothing remained to mark her as an entertainer. Milo wondered at this. It was a demarcation point in her personality, and it had always intrigued him. She returned his smile with an open frankness and said, "I watched you ride out of town, also. I knew you would stop here." He rose at that and offered her his arm, and she dismounted.

She walked beside him, then squatted cross legged in the grass facing the town. Milo sat beside her and let the silence build until it was large and heavy between them. "You're a sensible girl," he said, "and yet this is very foolish and unwise."

Amy gave him a short laugh, as if it were some joke they shared and said, "Milo, wisdom is for old men." She looked away suddenly and asked, "Have you set the date yet?"

The humor between them vanished like smoke before a wind, and he murmured, "She's a hard girl to rush, Amy. Most women are when you come right down to it." He looked out onto the land as if it held something more for him; he searched it that intently with his eyes. He said, "I never gave it much thought before, but Max has this county by the throat."

"You're *his* sheriff, Milo," Amy said with great gentleness. "One of these days...when he's ready...you'll take his place. Then *you'll* have it by the throat."

Singer's temper rose and color mounted in his face. He spoke sharply. "I don't like that kind of talk, Amy...not even from you."

She met his eyes and said, "It's true talk, Milo. You never ducked the truth before."

He had no answer for her and looked at his hands. "I make a poor sheriff."

She swung the subject around on him and asked, "Have you identified the dead man yet?" He shook his head, surprised that she had mentioned it, and she held out her hand, palm up and open. A six-pointed star lay there, the balls worn and tarnished.

Singer took it from her and turned it over several times, then asked, "Where did you get this?"

"One of Mike's girls saw some kid wearing it on the street this morning. She gave him a dollar for it, and he said he found it in the alley back of Ratibin's."

"That's a federal officer's badge," Milo said.

"Some people break federal laws," Amy said, and Milo stood up, moving toward his horse. "Where are you going?" she called.

He didn't answer her, but mounted and rode out, and she watched him with a haunting sadness in her face.

He rode around to a side street, then crossed the Texas Pacific tracks, and dismounted by the telegrapher's office. He found the man asleep and woke him to send the wire. He remounted and rode back to Worlison's stable, put up his horse, and went to his office to wait, knowing ahead of time what kind of an answer he would get.

The telegrapher came in at four with the folded message, his eyes wise. Milo saw this and said, "It might be a good idea if you kept your mouth shut about this."

"Sure," the man said and left, leaving Singer with the knowledge that he'd spread it all over town. The sheriff unfolded the message and read, his lips pulled tight with his thoughts. He rose and crossed to the door, calling to a boy playing in the street. Singer waited until he hurried over and said, "You know Miss Stendahl? Then tell her I won't be there for supper." He handed the boy a quarter and watched him run down the street and turn the corner.

II

THE BIGGEST JACKASS

Singer was eating at the Drover House when Willard Peterson came in and took a chair across from him. The man's watery eyes were angry, and his voice was high-pitched and pointed. "Singer, whatever gave you the idea that you run this county?"

Milo looked up in amazement and asked, "What brought this on?"

"Don't try to pull the wool over my eyes," Peterson said. "I know that dead man was a deputy marshal, and I know that another one is on his way here to work on the case. I want a story for my readers and not the usual line about everything progressing normally and under control."

"A little earlier," Milo told him, "you didn't give a damn about him. You said I was being foolish to waste time on him. Why don't you just relax and let us work this out our own way and not get the people all stirred up?"

Peterson struck the table and his voice was ragged. "Milo, you've strung along mighty free and easy since you got in office, and there's a lot of people here that don't like it. I know you got rid of the toughs.

How you did it, I don't know. We need a little tougher man for the law...one that Max Stendahl don't pull strings on either."

A muscle jumped in Milo's cheek, and he said with a soft wickedness, "Move on now, Willard. You've said enough."

The newspaperman took warning from Singer's eyes and rose, leaving his hands flat on the table. "All right, Milo, but the people are going to learn what's going on around here."

"What *is* going on around here?"

"Your days are numbered," Peterson said and left. Milo paid for his meal and rose and walked slowly back to his office. The sun was low on the horizon, and he lighted a lamp in the room, then leaned back in his chair and placed his feet on the desk.

Milo was not the kind of a man who fooled himself. He knew that Peterson would spread the talk around town. Max Stendahl had admitted talking to the dead man, and now the dead man turned out to be a marshal. Peterson was no fool. He'd begin thinking and guessing and Milo didn't like a man who guessed too much.

Lamps had begun to flicker in the business houses along the street when the front door opened and Doug Ringle entered and perched on the edge of Milo's desk. Ringle was tall and lanky with a drooping mouth and cigar ashes on his vest. He rolled a cigar between his lips and spoke around it. "I understand you've identified the dead man? Is that right, what they say?"

"That's right," Singer said. "Why?"

"My brother Al says you aren't doing a damn' thing about it."

"Your brother's been asleep all day," Milo stated. "He don't know what he's talking about." Milo broke off his talk as the door opened, and Al Ringle came in. The man glanced at his brother, then went to the wall and took his gun from a peg. Milo watched the man with a steadiness that made Al Ringle jumpy.

"What's the matter with you?" he said.

"Al," Milo said evenly, "you've been shooting off your mouth again."

Doug Ringle bristled and said, "Now, see here! I'm the mayor and I...."

Milo slapped the desk hard, and the man closed his mouth.

Al looked from his brother to Milo and back again, then grumbled, "Seems a man can't suppose a thing any more."

"That kind of reasoning has no place in a lawman," Milo said, and looked at Doug. "Or in a mayor."

"By God, you're sittin' here with your feet on the desk. You could be out askin' questions and talkin' to suspects." Doug Ringle looked down his long nose at Milo.

The sheriff sighed and said, "I have a county to answer for, while Al has this piddlin' town. If he'd been cruisin' the streets last night instead of sleeping in Worlison's stable, then maybe he'd have caught the man."

The night marshal bristled and said, "I've had enough of your damned tongue," and took a step toward Milo. The sheriff rose swiftly and went around the desk in one long jump. He met Al Ringle's lunge with an outstretched foot, grabbing him by the shirt front and sending him asprawl with a savage yank. Ringle hit the floor and rolled, and Milo was on him before he collected himself. Singer jerked him around on the floor and lifted the gun from Al's holster and stepped back.

Doug Ringle danced and waved his arms, coming close to Milo, but making no threatening move. "By God," he yelled, "that's an officer of the law you're manhandling!"

"Ex-officer," Milo corrected, and pulled Al to his feet. The man swung at Milo, but the pale-eyed man blocked the blow and brought the blood to Al's lip with a short punch. Then Singer's hand came out and ripped the badge from Al's shirt.

"You can't do that," the mayor of Buckhorn shouted.

"The hell I can't," Milo said. "I deputized him because I was the only one with the authority. Now I'm firing him." He motioned to Al and said, "Get out and stay out. You hit your last drunk."

The ex-marshal's face was filled with temper, but he rubbed the back of his hand across his mouth and murmured, "I never seen you that rough before, Milo."

"Get out," Singer told him and waited until the door closed. He went to the window and watched the Ringle brothers walk toward Ratibin's Saloon on the corner. Across the street, Chess Hadden lounged against the wall of Peterson's newspaper office. Milo opened the door and beckoned to him and Hadden crossed the street.

"Take a chair," Milo said, and Hadden sat down, a good-humored puzzlement on his blunt face. "You told me you was never in trouble. Was that straight?"

"I'm no liar," Hadden said.

Milo Singer pawed his mouth out of shape as if pondering some deep decision, then said, "All right, Hadden, I'm going to gamble on you. I'll lay it all out on the table, and you can pick up your hand or get out of town."

"Not much of a choice there," Hadden stated, but his eyes were interested.

"In this case," Milo told him, "riding out would be the easiest. Look at it this way. I can't just wipe that killing off as unsolved. Do you know who that fella was?"

"A deputy marshal," Hadden said. "It's goin' all over town. Folks are sayin' he must have been after somebody, and now they're all lookin' at their neighbor outa the corner of their eye."

"You can see how it is then," Milo said "This killing has to be solved, and everyone has to be satisfied with the solution. Do you know who the fat man is now?"

"Stendahl," Hadden said. "The man on the white horse."

"I can arrest Stendahl," Milo said, "on your testimony. But when I do, the people here will run on the bank or it'll go into receivership. Either way, all the paper the bank holds will be immediately due and payable, and a lot of foreclosures will occur because they don't have the money. I don't want to see twenty or thirty small ranchers go under because Max had to shoot a man."

"You can't block it forever," Hadden pointed out. "You're a fool if you try."

"I've been a fool all my life," Milo confessed. "I'm thirty-three and too old to change my ways."

"Where do I fit in?" Hadden wanted to know. Milo took Al Ringle's badge and tossed it in Chess Hadden's lap. The man looked at it for a moment, then said, "I never wore one of those things before in my life."

"Nothing to be ashamed of," Milo stated and waited.

Hadden considered it at great length, then fastened it to the front of his shirt.

"Raise your right hand," Milo said, "and repeat after me...."

He sat quietly for a long time after Hadden had gone out, wondering what was right and what was wrong. He unfolded the telegram and read it again although he knew what it said. He counted the hours in his mind. The man would take the train out of Fort Worth. He'd be here by noon tomorrow. It certainly didn't give Milo much time.

He opened a desk drawer and took out his gun and cartridge belt, then spent a few minutes blowing the dust off the piece. He blew out all the lamps but one against the east wall and went out, turning east until he came to Borgo's Opera House. The ticket seller nodded, and Milo went inside, turning right in the lamplit lobby and entered Mike Borgo's office without knocking.

Borgo looked up as the door closed, and Milo said, "Don't you know it's a sin to have a girlie show on Sunday?"

Borgo grinned and said, "What's sinful about a pretty girl's legs? Every woman has 'em, and every man looks at 'em. I just make it easier, that's all."

"Not the same," Milo said and sat down by Borgo's desk. "You'll never go to heaven, Mike."

Mike Borgo snorted, then turned serious. "Heard a little stink being raised uptown. You want to watch out when the wolves start howling. Already they're asking themselves what Max and that deputy marshal were talking about."

"My shirt tail's clean," Milo said.

"That's what every man thinks until the mud starts flying. Al Ringle has a lot of friends. Maybe they don't amount to much...any more than he does...but each of 'em can mark an X and know what a ballot is."

"Election's two years off," Milo said with an unconcern that he was far from feeling.

"Don't feed me that," Borgo said. "We knew each other way back when, and this isn't for you. Pull out now, and let the wolves have the fat man."

Milo's voice was soft. "I don't owe Max a damn' thing, Mike. Maybe he thinks I do, but he's wrong. I'd snap the cuffs on him tonight if that's all there was to it, but there's a lot of other people I'm thinking about. I can't shove them into the dust to make an arrest."

Borgo raised an eyebrow and asked, "You're not thinking of Marilyn, are you?" He saw the tightness around Milo's mouth and added, "Now don't get your hackles up over nothing. Buckhorn's a little town, and there are some damn' little people in it. They know that you've taken quite a shine to her, and they'll add that onto the rest. You have your dislikes and I have mine, and Stendahl and his daughter are one of them." Borgo was a swarthy man with a mean-looking face, but his eyes were a wet brown, and there was no ferocity in him.

Milo made a motion with his hand that said the subject was closed. Borgo shrugged and lighted a long cigar. Deep in the theater, the band swung into a lively tune, and the sound of women's singing and capering feet filtered through the walls as they paraded onto the stage.

Mike leaned forward and placed his elbows on the desk. "Milo, no one's telling you how to run your life, but be sure you haven't made a mistake with that girl. I don't say that you're not in her class or that she's too good for you...you're too good for her!"

"We've talked about it enough," Milo said, and Borgo let out a ragged breath and puffed on his cigar.

Mike said, "Milo, no one can keep a secret...I firmly believe that. The marshal that was killed, he took a shine to one of the girls, but he never said much about himself, just asked questions about Max Stendahl. Putting two and two together, what does that add up to?"

"That he was interested in Max," Milo said.

"That he knew Max, or Max knew him," Borgo said.

Milo gave a short, nervous laugh and said, "You're guessing, Mike...and badly at that." He saw no sign of give in Borgo's face and added, "I fired Al Ringle because he shot off his mouth. The mayor was there, and he was pretty put out about it."

"Maybe that wasn't so smart," Borgo said. "Al wants that badge of yours so bad he can taste it. If you ever gave him a chance to get at you...well, elections come around faster than a man thinks."

"I think you could smooth it over a little at the next council meeting, being an alderman and all. I put a new man in Ringle's place, and I'd like his appointment confirmed if you can swing it."

Singer reached for his hat and stood up. Mike Borgo said, "Milo, it strikes me that if you and Marilyn were going to get married, then you'd have done it before now." He pulled his eyes away from Milo's and added, "Stick around. Amy's got a break between numbers. She'll be glad to see you."

Milo lowered his eyes to his hands for a moment and said, "I guess not. Some other time, maybe."

Borgo's short laugh was a rough, round sound. "Sometimes, you're a fool, Milo."

Milo pulled in a lungful of air and let it out slowly. He nodded his head in agreement and went out. Buckhorn's main street was dark with slashes of lamplight layering the dust. The town was quiet except for a switch engine bell that tolled and clanged down by the siding. He gave the street a long look in both directions, then cut across it, walking slowly toward Max Stendahl's white house on Cyprus Street.

He looked through the parlor window and saw Marilyn sitting at the upright piano, and he paused to listen before mounting the wide porch. He felt nothing at the prospect of seeing her, and he wondered where his affections were. He shrugged the feeling off as he knocked and the music came to an end. The tapping of her heels came to him. She held the door open for him, and he stepped into the hall, sweeping off his hat. Her eyes touched the sagging gun belt, and a quick disapproval rose to erase the pleasantness from her face. She said, "I don't like a gun in the house, Milo."

At some other time he might have smiled at her airs. He had grown accustomed to them. But now some urgency pressed itself upon him, turning his voice brusque. "Is Max at home?"

She moved around to where she could see his face in the lamplight, and her voice was perplexed. "Milo, you haven't apologized for not coming to dinner. The idea...sending an urchin!"

For some reason he didn't understand, the remark offended him and he said, "He wasn't an urchin. He was Jethro Shroudhammer's kid, and he goes to Sunday school every Sunday."

"Well!" she said, "you don't have to argue about it or correct every little thing I say."

"Time somebody did," Milo muttered and heard her gasp.

The study door opened, and Max Stendahl thrust his head out and asked in a heavy voice, "What's all this jabbering about?" Milo gave Marilyn a quick glance and moved away from her. Her voice followed him. "Well, I never!" Then her heels tapped again, louder and full of outrage, and her playing filled the house with great, crashing chords.

Max closed the door, muting the sound. He offered Milo a cigar, then wiped a match alight for him. He took his chair behind the big desk and gave the sheriff a close scrutiny.

Milo puffed on the cigar for a few minutes, growing a long ash, then asked softly, "Max, what did that man say to you the other night?"

"Why, he just wanted a light for his cigarette." Stendahl's face was unreadable, but his eyes held a small caution.

Milo placed his elbows on the overstuffed arms of the chair and folded his hands, the cigar still fragrant and ignited between his teeth. "Max," he said, "let's not beat around the bush with one another. I'm sure you knew the man, and the man certainly knew you. I want you to tell me about it."

Stendahl glared at the tip of his smoke and said, "I don't believe I like the way you put that, Milo. It sounds accusing."

Milo met the fat man's eyes, and Stendahl's glance was the first to slide away. Milo reached into his coat pocket and tossed the badge on Max's desk. "That belonged to him, and he showed it to you before you left him. You know what happens when a federal officer is killed? They send another man and then another if that one don't do the job until they get their man. There is no give, no take, until it's over. Tomorrow that marshal is gonna get here. People are already talking, and he'll hear that talk. You better have some pat answers waiting for him."

The fat man stared at the badge, then pushed it away from him with the end of a pencil as if it were contaminated. He waited until Milo put it back in his pocket, then asked, "Why tell me that I need answers? I know nothing about it whatsoever."

Milo stood up and leaned his hands on Stendahl's desk and his voice was slow and driving. "Just between you and me, let's say you know all about it. You got a responsibility to a lot of people. I don't want them to lose because you lose."

Blood filled Max's face, and he said in a super-controlled voice, "Get out of my house."

"Sure," Milo agreed, "but remember what I said. Think it over." He put on his hat and moved to the door, then paused and asked, "Why'd you do it, Max? What was he to you?"

Stendahl's eyes were unmoving. He spoke as if he chopped off each word with an axe. "Get out of my house!"

Milo went out and closed the door softly behind him. Marilyn's playing ended abruptly, and Milo halted, looking through the archway at her. She rose and crossed to him, a beautiful woman with a fine temper gripping her. She said, "The next time you come here, leave your street manners outside."

"This may be my last visit," Milo said, and it shocked her, checking her temper for a moment.

She said in a very soft voice, "Milo, I don't think I understand you at all."

He told her, "You have little niches where you try to fit people. When they don't fit, it vexes you. You'll have to forgive me, because I'm only human."

The irritation returned to her face. She looked at him severely as if she were debating whether to give him another chance or not. She said, "Milo, let's not quarrel." Her mood lifted and she took his arm and smiled. "Let's go riding tomorrow. I'll expect you about ten."

He shook his head. "Busy," he told her. Her lips pulled into a prim line, and he held back a smile.

Cutting across the vacant lot, he reflected a bit on Max Stendahl. By talking to him he had committed himself to a course of action. He was giving Max a chance, one that might put him out of a job and on the dodge, but the decision had been made, and he would not change it. He came out of the alley onto the main street and saw a crowd breaking up in front of Ratibin's Saloon. Farther down the street, Chess Hadden was herding a man toward the jail. Singer headed there immediately.

Hadden was at the desk booking the man when Milo came in. The prisoner sat in a chair against the wall, handcuffed. Hadden closed the book with a snap and stood up. There was a puffiness along the bottom of one eye, and his lip still bled. Singer looked at the unmarked face of the prisoner and said, "You know...I could get to like you, Hadden."

Hadden removed the handcuffs and pulled the man to his feet. The man made a half swing, and the new marshal knocked the milling arm down, shoving him in the small of the back and driving him off balance. They disappeared down the hall leading to the cell blocks, the man cursing Hadden in a shrill voice and Hadden talking soothingly. He came out a moment later and said, as if making an excuse for the man, "Had a little too much to drink, that's all."

"Looks like he got in a couple of good licks," Milo said.

Hadden touched his bruised mouth and eye and murmured, "Ah, hell, probably always wanted to sock a lawman. I've felt the same way myself."

Milo sat down at his desk and elevated his feet. Hadden took a chair along the wall, and Milo said, "I saw Max and let him know that I knew."

Hadden's blunt face turned worried and he said, "You're stickin' your neck way out. There's some things a man can't cover up."

"When the marshal gets here tomorrow," Milo told him, "you get a sudden loss of memory. You didn't see nothing if he asks you."

Hadden had a temper and it crept into his voice. "Is that why you pinned this badge on me...so I'd owe you something?"

"No," Milo said. "It had nothing to do with it. You know why I want Max to have a little time. There's too many ends dangling. When things are secured, then I'll arrest him myself."

"Whatever is behind this," Hadden prophesied, "will come out, and you can't stop it. What's gonna happen when the townspeople get to gabbin'? They'll make a run on the bank and break it, and you'll lose anyway. People think only of themselves. You haven't got a chance, Milo. If they don't get you that way, then they'll say it's because of his daughter. You see how it is?"

"Sure," Milo said and sat in deep thought. Finally he raised his head and said, "I guess you better go back out on the street." Hadden nodded, and then the sheriff was alone again with his thoughts.

He spent the night in one of the empty cells. He rose as the sun came up and went to the Drover House for his breakfast. Willard Peterson came in with a newspaper under his arm, and his watery eyes were even more moist as he sat down across from Milo. He tossed the paper on the table and said, "There is a front page to open people's eyes." Milo read it, then swept it off the table, and went on with his meal. Peterson glared at him, then said, "There'll come a day when there will be only truth. You mark my words."

"Then it'll be a sorry world," Milo said and watched the surprise wash into Peterson's face. Milo laid his knife and fork down and added, "You say you want the truth, but you don't. Nobody does. Our skins aren't thick enough to take it. Your wife says to you, 'Am I still beautiful,' and you lie and say, 'Sure.' Why don't you tell her the truth...that she's gained sixty pounds and looks like hell? Try telling the truth for twenty-four hours, and you won't have a friend left because they don't want the truth." Milo waved a hand at the fallen newspaper. "The stuff you print is junk. You've been talking to Al Ringle again...or the mayor."

"Ringle's a good man," Peterson said. "He don't wet-nurse a man like you do. He's a little on the tough side, but by golly we need a man like that."

"Willard," Milo said, "you wouldn't know a tough man if you saw one." He stopped talking and looked past Peterson as Al Ringle and his brother came in. They saw Singer and came straight toward his table.

Willard Peterson seemed glad to see them for he took Doug Ringle's arm and said, "Say, I was just talk...."

"Not now," the mayor said. "Some other time." He shook the hand off his arm. He faced Milo and said in a loud, harsh voice, "As the mayor of Buckhorn, I demand that you reinstate my brother as city marshal."

Milo placed his hands on the edge of the table and said, "As the biggest jackass I ever saw, you also got the loudest bray. Now leave me alone while I finish my breakfast. I usually like to eat my meals in peace."

Doug Ringle drew himself up to his full height and said, "By God, Singer, don't underestimate me! I'm not as soft as you think."

Milo looked at him and smiled. "Below the neck you don't look soft at all. No, not at all."

It angered Ringle, and he stepped around to the side of Milo and took him by the lapel. "Now, you listen to me," he said and Milo reached out and slapped his hand away.

"Keep your hands to yourself," he said, then moved because he saw it was a signal between them. Doug lunged at Singer, as did Al, but Milo kicked the table over on top of the ex-marshal and whirled, knocking the mayor to his knees. Doug Ringle cried out, but Singer grabbed him and six long steps carried him to the door with Ringle propelled before him. The mayor fought with a wiry fury, but Milo cuffed him quiet and pitched him off the board-walk and into the dust. He landed so hard that Milo almost laughed.

He pivoted in time to meet Al as he came charging out the door. There was a brief flurry of fists. Singer felt them sting his face, then he had Al pinned and whirled him away from him and into the hitch rail. The old pole splintered and he joined his brother in the dust. They both looked at Singer with hatred in their faces.

Willard Peterson had come out onto the porch, along with a dozen other townspeople and he said, "You'll read about this in the paper, Singer. And then you'll be sorry."

"You know what you can do with that paper," Singer told him and shoved his way through the crowd and went to his office. He sat behind his desk and rested his head in his hands.

III

A HELL OF A NICE PLACE

Mike Borgo came in a little later and got immediately to the point. "That was another foolish thing, Milo. They won't stand for it."

"They'll have to get over it," Milo said and pulled his lips together stubbornly.

"Milo," Borgo pleaded, "let the fat man fight his own fights."

"Who says he has a fight?"

Borgo sighed and said, "The dead man talked to a lot of people, but there was always someone else around. When he talked to Max, there wasn't anyone around. You can guess a lot from just that much."

"People ought not to guess so much," Milo said. "Max probably admitted talking to the man so's not to appear that he was hiding anything." Milo saw that Borgo was not convinced, and added, "If Max had kept still and someone had seen him, then how would it look?"

"You're really battling for him, aren't you?" Borgo stood up because he had no argument and wished that he did. He leaned on Milo's desk and said, "If worse goes to worse, you know who to call on."

"Thanks," Singer said and watched Borgo's back until he disappeared down the street. He idled away the rest of the morning, catching up on his correspondence and at noon went down to the small depot to await the northbound train. He leaned against the paint-peeled wall, a tall man with grave eyes and a cigar jutting from beneath his full mustache.

He turned his head as Max Stendahl came around the corner of the building and paused by Singer. The fat man gazed far out onto the tracks as if he didn't have a thing on his mind, then said, "I've been thinking about what you said, Singer. How much do you know?"

"That you killed him," Milo said matter-of-factly.

Stendahl's eyes narrowed and he puffed harder on his cigar. "Such knowledge could be extremely dangerous."

"Not to me," Milo said. "Another man knows about it, too. He saw you."

"I see," Stendahl said, and lapsed into a long silence. Out on the vast dry sweep of the land, a funnel of black smoke rose in the still air, and a long moment later the whistle sounded, far away and lonesome.

Milo nodded toward the oncoming train and said, "Ten more minutes, Max, and a federal officer will be here. I'll be working for him then. There isn't much time left for you."

Stendahl bit deeply into his cigar and said savagely, "What do you want me to do? Give myself up? Admit it?"

"You won't have to," Milo said. "We can prove our case in court. We'll come after you, if it comes to that, but I'm hoping it won't." Milo gave him a long study, then said in the softest of voices, "There's one way out, Max. It ain't a pretty way, but it'll hurt only you." Milo watched the color drain from the fat man's face as the meaning became clear to him.

"My God!" Stendahl said. "I can't believe you mean such a thing!"

"I mean it," Milo assured him. "Close your bank...secure it against foreclosure. It's the only way out."

"I can refuse!" Stendahl said this as if he meant it, but there was no give in Milo's face, and his eyes never unlocked with Stendahl's. "No," Max said. "I can't refuse, and you know it. I owe it to Marilyn if no one else." He touched Milo on the arm and asked, "How much time?"

"A few days," Singer told him. "I can stall the marshal off that long, but you'd better get things in order, obituary and all." The thought struck him and he added, "Peterson is stirring the people up. The man means well, but talk at a time like this is like a prairie fire."

"All right," Stendahl agreed. "But what do you get out of this for you? Marilyn?"

The blood left Singer's face, and his voice was controlled and wicked. "I hit one man this morning. Don't ever say a thing like that to me again." Max bit his lip and turned away, but Singer took him by the coat sleeve, halting him. "Don't weaken, Max. Hanging is bad."

"You give me little choice," Max said and turned away, and Milo watched the train pull into the station. The engine labored past him, leaving a damp smell of steam and the strong smell of hot metal and oil. The coaches drew abreast of the waiting room and stopped with a heavy clanking of the couplings. He moved away from the station wall when a young man stepped down and looked around him.

The young man saw him and walked over to him, peeling his cuff to display his badge. "I'm Charlie Boomhauer," he said. "Can we go to your office?"

"Sure," Milo said and thought, *My God, was I ever that young?*

Boomhauer was a tall man in his early twenties. His face was long and serious and his eyes dark and piercing. He dressed on the edge of neatness, but the bone-handled Remington flapping against his thigh proclaimed him to be all business. There was little about Boomhauer that was wasted, neither motion nor talk.

Milo entered his office, and the young marshal toed the door closed and pulled a chair close to the desk. Boomhauer laid his hat on the floor and said, "I guess we'd better bring each other up to date. The dead man was Dean Miller, a special agent working on an old case."

"Such as...?" Milo said.

"An express robbery," Boomhauer stated. "It wasn't a federal offense at the time...the company was privately owned...but the cash sum stolen was large and, when the government took it over, they wanted it back. You know how they are in such cases."

"Then you think Miller spotted his man here?"

"Exactly," Boomhauer said. "It's my bet that Miller tried to make a pinch and got shot for it. Those things happen, you know."

Milo rubbed a hand over the back of his neck and said, "We don't have much here that'll help you. No one knew the man. His badge was found by pure luck...some kid picked it up and was wearing it. Of course, I have the bullet the doc took out of him, but it's a common forty-four which don't tell us a thing."

"It's pretty thin," Boomhauer agreed, and put on his hat. "However, I've worked on cases thinner than this." He went to the door and added, "You don't mind me using your office, do you?"

"Make yourself at home," Milo told him and sat there with a vague worry on his face after Boomhauer went down the street.

He idled around the office, but a restlessness was on him, and he went out, cutting across the street to Ratibin's Saloon. He took a beer and sat down at a corner table. He was no fool, and he knew that he had but little time left. Willard Peterson would buttonhole the marshal, and Doug Ringle would add to it. Milo drained his glass and went back to the street.

He saw Amy Templeton around the far corner and cut across and met her in front of Willamette's Drygoods Store. She gave him a worried glance and murmured, "Walk with me?" He turned and fell in beside her, shortening his long steps to match her own. "It's been a long time since we've walked together, Milo."

They passed the bank on the corner, and Max Stendahl's heavy face pulled into disapproving lines when he saw them together. Milo touched her on the elbow, and they turned the corner, walking toward the school grounds on the edge of town. It was a tree-sheltered cove with rough benches and a scarred and weathered table. She smoothed her dress and sat down. Milo took the table, hooking one leg over the corner, bracing himself with the other.

He looked around him and said, "This place holds a lot of memories for me, Amy."

Her eyes came up to his quickly and they were full of hope, then that vanished. "Don't rake over the past and try to find something that's alive and offer it to me. I don't believe I'd accept it now."

"What happened to our dreams, Amy?"

"They died," she said. "Just like all dreams die when they aren't nurtured. You can't neglect a dream, Milo, and expect it to live."

Singer rubbed his big hands together and drew in a long breath. "I guess not," he said. 'It's funny how much of a fool a man can be when he's young."

"That was only three years ago," Amy reminded.

"I feel awfully old now," Milo said and got up and stretched because he didn't know what to do with himself. For a reason he didn't fully understand, he drew a comfort from her and wanted to keep her here until he did understand it.

She broke the silence when she said, "Mike Borgo asked me to marry him. I said I would." Her eyes never left his face.

It staggered him like a heavy rifle bullet. He fought his voice under control and said, "I don't know which is the luckier, although I'm inclined to think Mike has the edge." He turned away from her so that she could not see his face and stared out over the land that lay beyond the school house.

He heard her dress rustle as she rose, and her hands were a light touch on his sleeve. "I'm sorry," she said. "Sometimes a girl has to take second best after all." He didn't turn to watch her leave, but lighted a cigar and tried to adjust his mind to it.

She had turned the corner and was out of sight when he smashed the cigar beneath his heel and walked back uptown. Stendahl had placed a printed sign in his door announcing the closing of the bank for audit. Milo smiled and rapped on the glass and waited until Max peeled back the brown shade and opened the door for him.

The bank was cool and dim, and Milo followed the fat man to his office and Stendahl closed the door. "That was a smart move," Milo said. "It'll prevent a run on the bank anyway."

"Don't be so damn practical," Max said. "I got feelings, you know."

Milo pursed his lips and said, "That marshal told me there was a holdup. Is that right?"

"Fifteen years ago," Max said, "I'd just got out of the Army and was stone broke. That's a hell of a thing for a man like me. There it was, sitting on a siding, and there I was with a cavalry pistol in my hand. The trouble was, I shot the damn' pistol, and a man went down." He sighed, but there was no regret in him. "I got my stake. I built this county with it, so it can't be all bad."

"If I thought it was," Milo told him, "I'd have locked you up before now."

The words shook something loose in Stendahl, and he said quickly, "What kind of a man are you, Milo...really, now?"

Singer raised an eyebrow and said, "You don't know?"

Max slapped the desk and said, "Hell, no one knows about anybody. They think they do, but when it comes right down to it, they don't. I had you pegged for a real easy man, but you aren't easy at all. You're hard when you want to be. The hardest man I ever saw."

"See?" Milo said softly. "You do know."

"I wonder," Max said, "if Marilyn knows this about you."

"It wouldn't matter," Singer said and stood up. "I know what you want to hear, Max...that I'd always be around to take care of her, but it wouldn't work for us. We're not the same kind of people. I thought we were for a while, but I was wrong about that. You don't have to worry about Marilyn though...she's harder than both of us."

Stendahl opened his mouth to speak, but Milo opened the door and went out. He crossed the street and walked half the length of a side street to enter Borgo's Opera House. Mike was in his office, counting the night's take, and Milo lowered himself into one of the easy chairs. He laid his hat on his knees and said, "Amy told me, Mike. I'm happy for both of you."

Borgo raised his head quickly and said, "You're a poor liar, Milo, but I couldn't help myself."

"Sure," Milo said, glad that it was over. He waited until Borgo closed the ledger and added, "That deputy marshal is all steamed up for a quick deal."

"I saw him," Mike stated. "He was in a huddle with Willard Peterson and the mayor. You can guess who they were running down." He fired up a cigar, adding, "These seekers of truth and light give me a pain where I sit."

"It's a sad world," Milo opined. "Some days a guy can't make a nickel." He slapped his thighs, worried and trying not to show it.

Borgo watched him for a minute, then threw the pencil down and snapped, "For the love of Moses, come out with it!"

Milo told him of Stendahl's killing the man and what he was doing about it. Mike Borgo's face showed a deep shock, a naked unbelief. He said softly, half reverently, "Mother in heaven!"

"Show me another way out," Milo said.

Borgo shook his head and muttered, "There is no other way...but, my God, that's akin to murder!" He slapped the desk and stated, "If Peterson ever finds this out...if that kid-faced marshal ever got wind of this...no, I don't even want to think about it." Milo stood up to leave and Borgo left his desk and took him by the arm. "Milo, we've been pretty close through the years, and I ask you now to give up this idea. Maybe the county won't go to hell if he's locked up now. Don't put yourself in a hole you can't get out of for that."

Milo gave him a thin smile and murmured, "We all have our gods, Mike. What are yours?" Borgo had no answer for this and Milo left and walked down the street. He went to his office because habit was strong in him, and an hour later Charlie Boomhauer came in, and he was not in a pleasant mood.

Boomhauer toed a chair around and sat down. He gave Singer a direct stare and said, "I've heard a lot of things about you today, and none of them has been complimentary." Milo's expression never changed and the marshal added, "You don't seem surprised."

"I'm not," Milo told him. "I could have told you the same things, but I don't like to talk about myself."

The young marshal didn't smile. "Sheriff, you didn't lie to me, but you withheld information. There is a suspect...Max Stendahl...and from what I can glean a big man around here. Yet you deliberately hid this from me by being evasive. I have it in my power to remove you from office. Damned if I'm not inclined to do it."

"Go ahead," Milo said. "It won't change anything."

"Give me your badge," Boomhauer said in a softly polite voice.

"You go to hell," Milo said and gave no hint to his temper.

Boomhauer's jaw tightened, and he rose and reached across the desk toward Milo's shirt front. The sheriff moved with startling speed and sledged him across the line of the jaw, knocking him asprawl. Boomhauer rolled to the floor and came up with a gun in his hand.

Milo kicked out, connecting solidly on the marshal's wrist, and it threw the gun in the wastebasket.

The young marshal said nothing, just sat on the floor, and clasped his wrist. Milo tossed his badge in his lap. "There's more to law," Milo told him, "than you read out of a book." He took his coat from a wall peg and went out. Boomhauer sat on the floor and stared after him.

In the Drover House, talk buzzed around him, wild talk, and he tried to sort it out in his mind, then gave it up. Chess Hadden came in and sat down at Singer's supper table.

"That was a short job. That kid marshal just fired me, and Al's back to work."

"Just as well," Milo said.

"I dunno," Hadden told him. "There's a lot of talk floatin' around town about Stendahl. A lot of folks are just waitin' for morning to roll around so's they can draw their money out of the bank."

"People worry," Milo said.

Hadden's eyes widened. "Don't anything ever bother you?"

"Why, yes," Milo replied. "I got an old bullet wound in the hip that vexes me like blazes when it's gonna rain."

Hadden smiled and nodded. "I got you pegged now, mister...tough. I wondered about you, why you never roughed up a drunk or a man you pinched. You're so tough you don't have to show your muscles, even to yourself. For a while I thought you was one of them soft fellas lappin' up a soft job. Now I know different."

"You see," Milo pointed out, "you learn every day." He laid his half dollar on the table and went out with Hadden. "No one's holding you any more," Milo said. "You can ride on any time now…do just as you damn' please."

Hadden shook his head. "You gave me a square shake. I think I'll stick around. You might need someone to cover your back before this thing is over."

Milo smiled. "All right. Go over to Ratibin's porch and find a seat. I'll know where to find you if I need you." Hadden trotted across the street, and Singer turned on a side street, walking toward Stendahl's home.

He knocked and got an immediate answer. Marilyn stood back and he entered. She said, "I'm not angry any more, Milo. All I have left now is hurt." She studied him, then said, "They're saying terrible things about father uptown. They aren't true, are they?"

"Ask him," Milo suggested.

Marilyn's lips tightened. "I have more faith in him than to ask such a thing!"

Milo shook his head. "If you had faith in him, really believed in him, then you wouldn't have asked me either."

"You're cruel and callous," she accused.

"That's a human characteristic," he told her. "Some people try to hide it behind manners or a suit of clothes or a pretty face, but it's still there." She gasped, and he added, "Some day you might understand. Right now, I'm sure no one could make you understand." He moved past her and knocked on Max Stendahl's study door.

He got an answering grumble and went in, locking it after him. Max sat at his desk, and he seemed ten years older. Milo got right to the point. "I'm sorry, Max, but I was wrong about the time…it won't wait."

"How much longer?" It was only a whisper.

"After I leave, I guess," Milo said. "Give me five minutes to get uptown. I'll want to be there to control that kid marshal, if I can." He turned back to the door, then added, "I'm genuinely sorry, Max. But for that one mistake, you've been a great man." He got no reply and let himself out of the house, walking rapidly toward the main street.

Mike Borgo and Amy Templeton stood under the marquee of the Opera House, and Singer crossed to them. Borgo said, "It's getting ugly, Milo. People are suspicious."

"Bound to happen," Singer said. "I was a fool to hope otherwise." He glanced at Amy and saw that her eyes were wide and worried. Borgo caught this also and it caused an obscure change around the edge of his mouth. Somewhere on Cyprus Street a gun went off, dull and muffled and seemingly far away.

Borgo's cigar slipped from his fingers and he shot Singer a frightened glance. Milo's face was grim, as he walked toward Ratibin's Saloon.

Hadden was ringed in by Ringle, Boomhauer, and three shouting townspeople. Milo took the steps two at a time and pulled Al Ringle back and stepped to Hadden's side. "What's going on here?" he asked in his mild voice.

Boomhauer scowled and said, "You have no authority now, Singer. Just move on."

"This is my authority," Milo said and lifted a knotted fist.

It quieted them for a moment, then Willard Peterson came running down the street, shouting and calling, and Milo knew that the news was out. Peterson stormed onto the porch, whirled Boomhauer around roughly, and shouted, "Stendahl's dead! He just blew his brains out!"

The young marshal cursed and went to move away, but Milo grabbed the back of his coat and hauled him back on his heels. "Whoa!" he said. "I'll go with you."

"I don't need you, and I don't want you," Boomhauer said with considerable heat.

"Nevertheless," Singer insisted, "I'm going. So's Peterson and the mayor and Mike Borgo. Hadden, you come along, too. We're forming a committee and let's walk. Max won't move if it takes us all night to get there."

Hadden swung off the porch, angling across the street after Mike Borgo. They grouped together on the next corner and turned toward Cyprus Street. Milo saw that Amy Templeton had come along.

When they entered the front door, Marilyn was pounding and crying at her father's locked door. Amy led her away. Milo broke the lock from the door with two lunges of his shoulder, and they shoved each other trying to get into the room first. Milo caught Hadden's arm, holding him back, and the others went in ahead of them.

Boomhauer cursed when he saw Stendahl and, realizing he had been tricked, tried to draw his gun free of the folds of his coat.

Hadden pulled his gun with surprising speed and knocked the heavy piece from the marshal's hand. Singer drew his Colt leisurely and motioned with the muzzle. They all sat down, and he faced them.

Hadden closed the door and leaned against it, then Milo said, "The deceased is guilty of killing Marshal Dean Miller. Hadden and I knew it because he saw the crime committed."

"By God!" Boomhauer shouted, "you'll answer to a federal judge for this!"

"Why?" Milo wanted to know. "Because you didn't get to make a pinch?" Boomhauer glared for a moment, then lowered his eyes. "All of you," Milo said, "ought to have had sense enough to see what Stendahl's arrest would do to this county. Whether we liked it or not, Max controlled the money and without it we'd go under. When he shot himself, he secured the county's future and satisfied the law at the same time."

Ringle and Peterson exchanged glances and said nothing, but Boomhauer was not convinced. "You withheld information from a federal officer. You'll do time for that!"

It stirred Singer's anger, and he took the three steps separating them and ripped off Boomhauer's badge, flattening it with one stamp of his heel. "There's your authority, sonny. It's the *man*, not the tin star, that makes an officer."

"You're under arrest!" Boomhauer said.

"No, he ain't," Hadden said in a quiet voice, and every head turned toward him. "Nobody's arresting Singer. Nobody better try it."

"That's enough," Milo said gently.

"We'll see," Hadden added, and leaned back against the door, calm and patient and dangerous.

Milo looked from one to the other, then unbuckled his gun belt, and tossed it into Boomhauer's lap. He ignored the marshal's surprised look and said, "I'm going back uptown. Five minutes from now you can do the same. That ought to give you time to think it over. The marshal can decide whether he wants to ruin a county just for the record, or if the law that ain't down in the books is satisfied. Peterson, you can reflect a little on the value of truth and a fair deal. Ringle, take a good look at your office and see if you've done your job." He looked at the young marshal and added, "After you've thought it all over, then you can place me under arrest. That'll be the final test of how good a man you are." He moved toward the door and said to Hadden, "Keep them here."

There was an awesome quiet to the house, as if it had been long dead and empty. Marilyn stood in the hall, waiting for him. Milo Singer halted, and Marilyn's voice was damning and cold. "You killed him, Milo...as surely as if you pulled the trigger yourself." He said nothing and her face broke, and she struck him and screamed at him, "Deny it! I dare you to deny it!"

Milo imprisoned her wrists and said, "I never deny the truth. That's why I said it would never work between us." He pushed past her and went out.

The news of Stendahl's suicide ran up and down the street as he shouldered his way through the crowd to stand on the corner.

Al Ringle came across the street when he saw Singer and said, "Be one hell of a job tonight keeping the peace." There was a hint of friendliness in his voice.

"That's what you get paid for," Milo told him and was surprised when Al didn't show anger, but nodded and walked down the street.

Singer didn't have long to wait. They came around the corner, saw him, and cut across the street to him.

Boomhauer colored and looked around him uneasily. "I don't know how to take you, Singer," he said. "You don't fit in with the fellas I generally run into." He gave the mayor of Buckhorn a glance and murmured, "I'll take the morning train out. I guess this case can get scratched off as unsolved. I'd be obliged if you'd have a drink with me before I leave, though." He patted his stomach, ill at ease. "I guess it'd be pretty hard to prove...your suggesting suicide to Stendahl. Maybe, like you say, there's a lot of law that isn't in the books." He turned abruptly and entered the Drover House.

Singer watched him as Hadden said, "That sprout'll make a damn good lawman in five-ten years. Yeah, real good."

It broke them up. Willard gave Singer a sheepish glance and went across the street to his newspaper office. Doug Ringle, standing alone now, showed a faint uneasiness, then caught sight of his brother down the street and yelled, "Al! Oh, Al!" and trotted after him.

Borgo shifted his feet and said, "Amy and I...well, Milo, I don't think she'll ever get over you. I guess I'm not made for second best, either."

A genuine sadness crossed Singer's face, and it was a moment before he found the words. "I'm sorry it had to happen to you, Mike."

Borgo blew out a long breath and looked around at the town. "You know," he said, "I never paid much attention to it before, but this is a hell of a nice place to live."

The tension left Singer, and he smiled. "It's home," he said, and Mike Borgo smiled too.

Lewis B(yford) Patten

wrote more than ninety Western novels in thirty years and three of them won Golden Spur Awards from the Western Writers of America and the author himself the Golden Saddleman Award. Indeed, this points up the most remarkable aspect of his work, his remarkable consistency and craftsmanship. He was born in Denver, Colorado, and served in the U. S. Navy 1933-1937. He was educated at the University of Denver during the war years and became an auditor for the Colorado Department of Revenue during the 1940s. It was first with "Too Good With a Gun" in *Zane Grey's Western Magazine* (4/50) that Patten began contributing significantly to Western pulp magazines, fiction that was from the beginning fresh and unique and revealed a lifelong concern with the sociological and psychological affects of group psychology on the frontier. He became a professional writer exclusively upon publication of his first novel, MASSACRE AT WHITE RIVER (Ace, 1952). The dominant theme in much of his fiction has to do with the notion of justice and, its opposite, injustice. As Patten progressed as a writer, he explored this theme in poignant detail in small towns throughout the frontier West. Once the values embodied in these small towns are examined closely, they are found to be wanting. Conformity is always easier than taking a stand. Yet, in Patten's perspective, there is usually a man or a woman who refuses to conform. Among many fine Patten titles, must surely be included A KILLING AT KIOWA (Signet, 1972), THE ANGRY TOWN OF PAWNEE BLUFFS (Doubleday, 1974), RIDE A CROOKED TRAIL (Signet, 1976), and THE LAW IN COTTONWOOD (Doubleday, 1978). Several of his finest titles have recently been reprinted in hardcover editions by Chivers Press in the Gunsmoke series and in the ongoing double-action mass merchandise paperback series from Leisure Books.

Mama Rides the Norther

Driving out, Frank Slaughter could not rid himself of the uneasiness that lay half sleeping in the back of his mind. He heard the skylarking of the two kids in the back of the wagon, happy as on a picnic, but Martha sat stiff and straight beside him, her full, pretty mouth compressed.

Frank said doubtfully, "Hon, you think we're doing the right thing? I'll turn around and go back if you say the word."

She shook her head, not meeting his eyes, the stiffness in her holding him away. "Frank, we've talked it out a hundred times. You're not satisfied running a feed store. You never will be. I married you for better or worse, and I expect this is the 'worse,' but what kind of a wife would I be if I held you back?"

Still pretty at thirty, she had been a good wife to him, even if she had, in the last five years, gotten too wrapped up in her church work and Ladies' Aid Society to be as close to him as she used to be. And since he had first mentioned homesteading, there had been this veiled antagonism whenever the subject arose.

She's afraid, he told himself. *But when I get her out there and she sees how pretty it is, and how safe....*

"Ain't nothin' to hurt a body where we're goin', Martha."

She spoke submissively, but without agreement. "No, Frank," and he knew what she would be thinking from listening to her arguments so many times before. "Nothing but wolves," with a shudder, "and a stray Indian off the reservation once in a while. Nothing but drifters and no-goods that'll be sure to drop in whilst you're away. Nothing but blizzards and buzzards and rattlers and floods. I don't think I can do it, Frank. I'm not a pioneer woman. I'm a city girl, and you knew that when you married me."

Her reluctant submission kind of took the pleasure from it, this going off on a bright May morning to take up their own place two hundred miles east. Today should have been their day of days, with everybody as gay as the two kids. Frank had hoped in getting off by themselves, they would find the closeness that had been there five years ago. Now he doubted it, and could see ahead only this strangeness and stiffness between them that never seemed to soften.

Martha said in a still voice, "Frank, there isn't even a house out there. What are we going to do whilst you're getting one put up?"

"Why, hon, I told you. I'll unbolt the wagon bed and set it out on the ground. You and the kids'll be all right in the wagon till I can get back with the lumber and stuff for the house. I'll leave you this gun." He touched the old Navy Colt in its holster. "And I'll leave you, Nell," referring to the swaybacked old saddle mare trailing behind the wagon on her slack lead rope.

They rode in unspeaking silence for a while, and finally she said, "You'd best show me how to shoot it, then."

He snugged the Colt from its holster, holding it loosely in his lap. "It's all loaded and everything. All you have to do is thumb back this hammer and pull the trigger."

Distastefully she took the gun from him, handling it gingerly. Suddenly she stiffened her shoulders, gripped the gun firmly in both hands, half raised it and thumbed back the hammer with a click. Frank Slaughter dropped the reins and grabbed at her.

"Hon, you're pointing it at the team...." He flung out a hand, knocked the barrel skyward just as the gun boomed in Martha's hands. The horses jumped, breaking into a run. Frank felt the jerk of Nell's rope behind as it parted, and then he was grabbing for the dropped reins, and very busy for a moment. The kids poked their faces through the canvas flap. "What happened, Mama? What you shootin' at, Mama?" their eyes avid with interest.

When Frank had the team quieted, and stopped, he took the gun from her and slipped it back into the holster. "Hon, that's the way to do it," irritation making a calm tone difficult. "But don't ever thumb back the hammer less'n you aim to shoot something. And don't never aim to shoot nothing, less'n you're sure what it is, and damn' sure you want to shoot it."

"Well! Frank Slaughter, you don't have to swear at me!"

He grunted apologetically and climbed down, catching Nell, and knotting her broken lead rope. When he got back up, he said patiently, "I didn't swear at you. That there 'damn' just sort of slipped out."

Pleasure and anticipation and the excitement he should have been feeling were missing, but oddly enough he could not find it in himself to blame Martha. She was afraid, and nobody is the same when they're afraid.

He was a tall man, and very thin, but the stringy muscles of his shoulders and arms were like tough steel wire from lifting hundred pound sacks of grain and eighty pound hay bales. His face had the calmness and imperturbability of the distant peaks, and a bushy, untrimmed mustache covered his upper lip, and straggled down past his mouth corners. Chewing he had given up in favor of a pipe at Martha's insistence, and now he fished the pipe from his pocket, tamped it thoughtfully, and lighted it.

Martha moved imperceptibly further away. That odd depression in him increased, and now it was almost a sense of foreboding. It was hard on a man to go against his own wife—she made it hard for him. He wondered if he shouldn't have stayed in Pueblo, kept on running the feed store for old man Schwartz. He shook his head grimly. No. This would be something of his own, something he could leave his kids. You couldn't leave them a job in Schwartz's feed store.

Martha had been oppressed by an odd sense of failure as she handed back the gun. Why couldn't she do these things right, in a way that would please Frank? She knew her fear and her self-doubt were making her irritable and cross, and again she resolved as she had so many times in the past few weeks, *I'll show him I can do it. I'll spoil it for him if I don't.*

Land, grass land, broken by arroyos, its flatness relieved by low buttes and sandhills, flowed past, always the same, depressing in its sameness and endlessness. Frank murmured, "Now ain't it pretty, hon? And our place is even prettier. There's a seep on it, and I figger to plant some cottonwoods around the house. It's wheat land, not cattle land. The time'll come when you won't see anything but wheat. It'll be the breadbasket of the nation, and we'll be the ones that started it!" Shy pride colored his voice, the quiet pride of a man whose words are inadequate to express his thoughts and dreams.

He could see ahead, and that was Martha's trouble. She could not. All she could see was the immediate future—now the night and day she would have to spend alone with the children in the wagon, with wolves prowling close, the night full of menace, herself full of doubt. Backbone. That was what she lacked and, admitting this, she wished they could have stayed in Pueblo. There she had found her niche, doing more and more church work and club work each year because that was something she did well. Yet, when she tried to tell Frank of her fear, the words came out sharp and disapproving, and he always got that strange set to his lips.

The day passed slowly. The two children, young Frank, who was seven, and little Mae, who was four, tiring from the jolting of the wagon, becoming bored by confinement, grew cross, and bickered endlessly. And Martha felt her own patience wearing thin.

They camped for the night beside a wide, dry riverbed, down the middle of which ran a tiny trickle of water. Frank dipped a bucketful with a tin cup, and brought it to her, thus saving the barrel on the wagon for the dry camps later. There was no wood for a fire, so he gathered buffalo chips, and soon had it blazing merrily. Martha filed this bit of information in her mind, the way he had fanned the smoldering stuff with his hat to make it blaze.

Released from the wagon, young Frank and Mae scuffled on the ground. Young Frank, reprimanded, asked avidly and irrelevantly, "You reckon we'll see any Injuns, Mama? You reckon there's outlaws and cattle rustlers out here? And bears and wolves?"

Frank Slaughter answered smilingly, "Injuns are peaceable now, son. All the bears is over in the mountains. But I reckon you'll see wolves. And you'll see plenty of cowboys and cattle," and as though to infuse some of his own enthusiasm into the boy, he said, "You'll ride horseback to the school, fifteen miles away. Reckon Nell will kind of be your horse. We'll go hunting for meat." He lay back against the wheel of the wagon and closed his eyes. *Ah, this is the life. This is the way a man was meant to live.*

Suddenly Martha was ashamed. He wanted this so much. Perhaps it wouldn't work out. Perhaps they would fail. *But,* she told herself determinedly, *he'll have his chance. I'll not take that from him.* And yet that doubt, that uncertainty, and the cold stirring of fear would not leave her....

The trip took eight days, and eight nights. Martha slept fitfully in the vast quiet of the prairie night, which was broken only by the

yapping of coyotes, the deeper howling of the gray wolves, sometimes distant, sometimes close. Each day she was a little more tired,
and found it a little harder to maintain a cheerful expression. By the
time they reached the hundred and sixty Frank had filed on, they
were living a sort of armed truce, each holding desperately to what
patience was left.

I've let him down, thought Martha. Trying hard to put convincing
enthusiasm into her voice, she said, "It's beautiful, Frank," when to
her it really was not, only the same as what she had endured drea-
rily for these eight long days.

Little Frank came running up. He had taken to walking behind
the wagon these last few days, wearied of the jolting. "What we
stoppin' for? Is this ours, Mama? Is this our land?"

"Yes, son. This is ours." She tried to visualize it as it would
someday be, a white house sitting serenely in a grove of stately cottonwoods, but failed miserably. How could they make it anything
but this? "It's so quiet! It's so awfully quiet!" she murmured in desperation.

Frank came toward her, his face that had been so shining,
sobering abruptly as he overheard. He said flatly, "It's noon. Get
Mae out of the wagon, and I'll unload it and set it on the ground."

Martha did, and then grimly set about her task of gathering buffalo chips, building a fire, failing even at this, having to call Frank
from his work to fan it for her. The night ahead loomed in her mind
as some terrible ordeal which, if she survived it, she would remember
for years to come. *What if it storms?* she asked herself, but resolutely
put this thought away from her. *This is May...late May. Its' too late
in the season for storms, I'm certain of that.*

After dinner, Frank finished reloading the wagon as it sat ludi-
crously flat on the ground. They climbed onto the seat he had rigged
atop the running gear. "'Bye, hon," he said stiffly, steeling himself
against her pleas that he remain and, as she came up beside him,
he handed down the gun. "Remember what I told you about this,
and hon, don't be scared. There's nothing to hurt you, and I'll be
back tomorrow." Seeing her expression, he added defensively, "We
can't live in a wagon for long. I've got to get this lumber and nails
fer the house, don't I?"

He tried not to see the panic that washed through in her widened
eyes. He whipped up the team and clattered away, young Frank and
Mae running, screeching alongside until their wind gave out. Then

he settled down to steady driving. Never had he felt so ashamed. A mile away, he nearly turned to go back, but gritted his teeth and kept on. "Don't know why she should be so damned scared," he muttered. "Ain't nothing 'way out here to hurt her." He shrugged. "Well, I'll be back t'morrow. She'll be all right till then."

All that day he traveled, impatient at the slow plodding of the horses, but well aware that if he drove them faster they would not last. He kept thinking of Martha, and his uneasiness increased with each passing mile. Toward evening, a thin film drifted across the brassy sky, and the wind picked up imperceptibly. By the time he drove his rig into Cactus Flats, it had chilled, and fine flakes of snow intermittently stung his face. He loaded the wagon with lumber, lashing down a sheet-iron stove on top. Then he grabbed a bite at the Chinese restaurant, a tumble-down shack at the edge of town, and drove out.

By now, the wind was steady, and where before it had been gusty, constantly changing direction, now it came steadily from the north. The snow no longer came in squalls, but had settled down to a continual fall, slanting horizontally before the wind, tiny flakes that stung the skin, melting as they touched. Dark came down over the land early, a gray that deepened its shade until all Frank could see was the black backs of the plodding team, and the endless, unreal blanket of whirling gray that lay before and around him.

And with each drop in temperature, his fear increased. *My God! She was right. I'd never ought to have left her. What if she can't get a fire started? What if she gets scared and tries to walk for help?* He whipped up the straining horses, half tempted to cut loose his load. He had no fear of getting lost, for he had methodically noted each landmark as he drove toward town. But if the storm got too thick to see.... Resolutely he settled himself more comfortably, and pulled his coat collar up about his ears. He wouldn't think about that now. He wouldn't think of anything. He'd just drive.

Near midnight, a dog barked off to his left, and he swung the team, heading them in that direction. Straightening, peering into the darkness, he suddenly realized how horribly cold he was. He was stiff with it, and his hands had no feeling in them as they held the reins. But the horses, as though sensing that nearby was a haven from this screaming white fury, hastened their lagging and played-out walk. Frank could see that they were up to their hocks in snow, and that was why the ride had been easier this last hour, and had lulled him into this state of drowsiness.

First a huge, two-storied barn loomed up ahead, and then the house, a faint flicker of light glowing from one window, the kitchen, Frank supposed. He bellowed, his voice cracking, "Hallo! Hallo the house!" and a large square appeared beside the window, a man's form silhouetted there. Frank drove as close as he could, and then got down, nearly falling from the stiffness and chill in his legs.

The man called to him, "Howdy there. Come on in, whoever you are, and I'll see that your team's taken care of." Frank staggered toward the door, and the warmth came out and enveloped him, drawing him pleasantly farther inside. It was a large kitchen, and a range, red hot, stood to one side, a granite coffee pot steaming and burbling on the back of it. Frank shucked out of his coat, suddenly overly warm. "Have some coffee, stranger. You look purt' near as done in as your team."

"I can't stay. I got to get on. I left my wife and kids out to where I filed my homestead, and I got to get back to them."

"No shelter?" Deep concern was in the stocky man's heavy voice.

"The wagon bed...with a canvas shelter. Oh, they got blankets, and matches, but my wife, well, she ain't used to this kind of thing. It scared her. I...."

"Ah, forget it. They'll make out if they got a wagon and blankets, and a fire. You grab yourself a couple cups of coffee and go to bed here. I'll put your team in the barn and in the morning you can go on."

Frank gulped the scalding coffee, felt strength flowing through him from it. The temptation to stay was great, but he kept remembering Martha's feeble efforts to start a fire yesterday. He said, "Mebbe they ain't got a fire. Mebbe.... I've got to get on."

"Know how you feel, mister. Can't say I blame you none. I've felt the same way m'self. But you won't make it. Your hosses is done. They'll go a ways and circle back here. You're the feller that filed out by that seep, not far from Muddy Creek, ain't you?"

Frank nodded, belatedly giving his name, extending his hand. "Frank Slaughter. I got to try, mister, but I ain't real sure just where I am. If you could give me directions...."

The cowman looked at him worriedly for a moment, then went purposefully to the door. His bellow cut startlingly across the silent yard. "Joe! Joe Duggin! Roll out of there. I got a job for you."

He closed the door again and after a moment a sleepy-eyed cowboy stumbled in. "Joe, hitch that gray team to the buckboard. This here is Frank Slaughter, who's filed on that seep over by Muddy Creek. His woman and kids is out there in the storm. You take him there and help him find 'em as he's dead ag'in stayin'."

The puncher nodded dazedly and stumbled back out the door. The cowman said, "You got a job ahead, man. Your wagon top white?"

Frank nodded and the cowman went on softly, "Snow's higher'n the wagon bed. All that'll be sticking out will be the top, and it will be just as white as the snow. Well, I wish you luck, man. I wish you luck."

He went out and began unhitching Frank's team, just as the buckboard rolled up alongside. Frank climbed up, saying diffidently to the driver, "Hate to drag a man outen his bed like this," but the only response was a yawning, "Ah, hell. Don't matter. Just as well be doing this as feeding the cattle in the snow t'morrow."

Frank stuck his chin down into his coat, bracing his feet against the lurching of the rig. What fool stunts a man pulled—and what foolish judgments he made. He'd figured Martha and the kids were as safe as in church out there, but she'd been right all the time. He whispered softly into his coat, promising fervently, "Hon, if you're all right; if I find you and you're all right, we'll go back on home to Pueblo." A chill that was not caused by the howling wind or the driving snow lingered in his bones. And he felt colder for Martha and the kids.

He remembered the foreboding feeling that had dogged him all that first day of their trip and cursed softly. "Why in hell don't you play your hunches? Why didn't you go back then?"

＊＊＊

Martha watched her husband until the wagon dropped out of sight behind a distant swell in the prairie grass. Paralyzed with loneliness and fear, she continued to stand until the children returned and tugged at her skirt. Little Mae said, "Get my doll out of the trunk, will you Mama?" and young Frank said, carefully casual, "Lemme see that there gun, will you, Mama?"

Martha corrected automatically, "That gun, dear," and "No, you can't see it. It's too dangerous."

She fought the despair that settled down over her, finally going to the wagon bed and crawling inside, finding some relief from her feelings in the familiar things around her, the prairie shut out by the canvas flaps. And so she did not notice the chill that came into the air as the afternoon wore on until the children came shivering in for their coats. Then she got out, looked at the ominous sky, felt the chilling wind.

I knew it, something whispered within her. *I knew it.* She wanted to run, and to scream. Little Mae suddenly clung to her skirts, saying, "What's the matter, Mama? Why do you look so funny?" and that jerked her back to a semblance of calm. *I mustn't frighten them,* she thought, and said, "Nothing, dear. You and Frank, go gather all the...," she hesitated over the phrase, "buffalo chips you can find. We're going to need a fire if it gets cold."

She saw that while she was inside the wagon the fire had died, and was now only a faint smoldering bed of ashes. She took an old hat of Frank's and fanned, but she only blew away what little fire was left. When the children returned, she took more fuel from their loaded arms, and tried again. When dark fell, she was still trying, and her hands were numb with cold. Snow lay white on her dark and shiny hair, and her face was wet where melted snow mingled with her tears of frustration.

Fighting rising hysteria, she gave it up, calling to the children, "Come on in now. We'll have a bite to eat, and then we'll go to bed." Inside the wagon, she ladled beans into their tin cups and, afterward, gave them each a small drink from the keg lashed to the side of the wagon. Then they huddled under the blankets, warming slowly, and shortly the children went to sleep. But Martha lay awake, listening to the rising wind, feeling even through the blankets the seeping, insidiously sharpening cold.

She was beginning to chill when she finally got up. She dug out all their clothes, stuffing them into the cracks around the bottom of the canvas, pinning them to the flaps where the snow and wind came whistling in. She was shivering uncontrollably.

A wolf howled, startlingly close, and immediately afterward she heard movement outside, not twenty-five feet from the wagon. Little Mae woke up whimpering, but Martha could not move. She sat frozen with terror. She thought of the gun, and felt around until her hand closed over its smooth, cold grip. She started to thumb back the hammer, thought suddenly of Frank's warning, and stopped.

Suddenly she laughed, raggedly and hysterically, but softly. Mae's tiny, sleepy voice came muffled from the blankets, "What was that, Mama?"

"Nothing dear. Go to sleep."

"I'm cold, Mama."

"I know. Go to sleep." Again she heard that stirring outside, coming closer. She had a vision of a huge, lean and shaggy wolf, jaws slavering, leaping into the wagon to attack her, to drag the children out into the snow.

She heard the scratching sound of something touching the canvas flap. She remembered, "They're afraid of fire," and found a matchbox, striking a sulfur match with fingers that shook violently. In the weak flare, she saw a bulge at the end of the wagon, moving as though the wolf stood against it, his paws pressing the canvas inward. She raised the gun, again started to thumb back the hammer, but the flame died, and she stopped, reaching for another match.

She lighted it, and suddenly in its light she saw the canvas belly inward, heard a ripping sound, saw something dark poking its way into the wagon. She screamed and pulled the trigger. But nothing happened! The dark head of old Nell poked its way inside. Martha had forgotten to cock the gun.

She dropped it between her knees, and suddenly all the pent-up fear was released, and she laughed, softly at first, rising hysterically as she continued. Nell backed, startled, from the wagon, leaving a hole gaping where her head had been, and the wind and snow whistled in. It was this that sobered Martha. She got up, went outside, and caught Nell's rope, tying her to the bed of the wagon. The snow was deep now, and the wind bitter. Back inside, she patched the hole the horse had made, settled herself under the blankets with the children.

"We'll wait it out," she thought, and suddenly she was not thinking of herself, only of Frank, out there somewhere sitting atop a load of lumber that would be their house, frantic with fear for her and the children. It struck her now how seldom Frank thought of himself. Why even this venture, which she had thought of as something Frank wanted for himself, was not, really. He was thinking of the children, wanting to build something that would someday be theirs.

And her fear. She'd feared a thousand things about this kind of life. After this, she'd take them one at a time. Like now. There was no use in worrying about anything but the cold. Now the best thing she could do would be to snuggle under the blankets with the children and go to sleep. Fortunately it never occurred to her that finding them would be difficult, if not impossible, for Frank.

The cowboy nudged Frank, huddled silently on the seat beside him. "Can't see a damned thing. I'll circle the team and try again." Frank straightened, saw the difficulty the 'puncher was having in making the team face the howling wind. Slowly upwind they went, fighting for their heads, blinded by stinging snow. The 'puncher shook his head. Frank peered into the swirling whiteness, seeing nothing. He screamed, "They could be here ten feet away and we'd never see them!"

"Uh-huh."

Frank yelled, "This the place? Hell, I can't see enough to tell."

"I'm pretty sure. We might be off a quarter of a mile...."

"A quarter of a mile? It'd just as well be a hundred." Panic rose in him. If he didn't find them now, by morning...?

"The hosses cain't go much farther. We'd better start hunting us a hole, mister." They were traveling downwind now.

"Circle once more. Try once more. Dammit, man, that's my wife and kids out there."

Obediently the 'puncher swung the horses again. Frank thought he could see their tracks ahead, but he couldn't be sure. Hopelessness gripped him. If the 'puncher insisted upon going in, in seeking shelter, then he'd get down and search afoot.

The horses fought the wind for a while, then stopped dead. The 'puncher howled, "Giddap, damn yore eyes! Hy-yah! Git outa there!" but the team refused to move. Shaking his head, the man turned them once again with the wind, and they plodded on ahead. Now, desperately, Frank probed the blackness, the gray cloud, for some sign of the wagon. It was amazing how a storm could change the aspect of the land so. This looked to Frank like nothing he had ever seen before. He yelled, "You go on. I can't leave them like this. I'll stay and look."

"Man, you're crazy! You'll freeze to death! You...."

Frank shrugged and started to leap down, then froze. He'd heard some sound out there—some sound. He yelled, "Shut up a minute! I heard something!"

And then it came, a horse's nicker. The team raised their heads, pricked forward their ears. The 'puncher lashed them savagely and drove them off toward the sound, whipping them wildly into a sluggish trot.

Frank leaped off as soon as he sighted Nell, ran to her while the 'puncher arranged and shook snow out of the blankets that were heaped in the buckboard.

Frank carried the children out first, snugly wrapped, and then he went after Martha. Carrying her out, he muttered over and over, "We'll start back tomorrow! I'll take no more chances with you. I ought to be shot for hauling you 'way out here." Martha lay quietly in his arms, unspeaking. He said, "I'll make it up to you, hon, I swear I will. You sure you're all right?"

Her eyes were large, and dark, and her expression, in this very dim light, looked soft. She reached up a hand and touched his cheek. But she failed miserably to get the asperity into her voice that apparently she wished to be there.

"You'll do no such thing! I've seen the worst there is out here. Now I want to see the best. We'll stay, Frank. We'll stay and I'll learn to build a fire out of...," she hesitated over the phrase, then said firmly, "buffalo chips, if it kills me."

Traveling with the wind, with Nell trailing placidly behind, heading for the nearest ranch five miles away, little Mae suddenly piped, "Daddy, Mama purty near shot Nell!"

He started violently, opened his mouth to speak, but shut it abruptly. She was only beginning to be a pioneer woman. Later, when she was a little more sure of herself, was time enough to tell her about Nell nickering through the night. If there had been no Nell...?

He put his hand out, found Martha's, felt the fierce and possessive way she gripped it. He smiled—confidently.

Ed(ward) Gorman

was born in Cedar Rapids, Iowa. His early career was as a writer/director of television commercials and other jobs related to advertising until 1988 when he focused all his efforts on free-lance writing and editing. He was a co-founder and edits *Mystery Scene*, a magazine devoted to commentary about crime fiction. Although Gorman's early fiction was in the crime genre, his contributions to the Western story have been significant, beginning with GUILD (M. Evans, 1987), the first of a series of books about a lawman who turns bounty hunter in the 1890s, a tormented soul journeying through a frontier shadowland. DEATH GROUND (M. Evans, 1988), BLOOD GAME (M. Evans, 1989), and DARK TRAIL (M. Evans, 1990) followed, recording the adventures of Guild as he encounters love, revenge, greed, obsession, dissociation, and loneliness. This often nightmarish vision of the American frontier in its last days is most akin to Greek drama and is most concerned with the moral choices human beings make and the consequences of those choices in their lives. NIGHT OF SHADOWS (Doubleday, 1990) is a tale about Anna Tolan, Cedar Rapids' first uniformed policewoman. Gorman is continuing the saga of Anna Tolan for Five Star Westerns. His short story, "The Face," won a Golden Spur Award from the Western Writers of America and can be found in a trade paperback collection of his Western stories titled THE GUNSLINGER in the Barricade Classic Western Series.

The Victim

I suppose everybody in this part of the territory has a Jim Hornaday story to tell. See, you knew right away who I was talking about, didn't you? The gunfighter who accidentally killed a six-year-old girl during a gun battle in the middle of the street? Jim Hornaday. Wasn't his fault, really. The little girl had strayed out from the general store without anybody inside noticing her—and Hornaday had just been shot in his gunhand, making his own shots go wild—so, when he fired....

Well, like I said, the first couple shots went wild and those were the ones that killed the little girl. Hornaday managed to kill the other gunfighter too, but by then nobody cared much.

There was a wake for the girl, and Hornaday was there. And there was a funeral, and Hornaday was there, too. He even asked the parents if he could be at graveside and after some reluctance they agreed. They could see that Hornaday was seriously aggrieved over what he'd done.

That was the last time I saw Jim Hornaday for five years, that day at the funeral of my first cousin, Charity McReady. I was fourteen years old on that chilly bright October morning and caught between grieving for Charity and keeping my eyes fixed on Hornaday, who was just about the most famous gunfighter the territory had ever produced. When I spent all those hours down by the creek practicing with my old Remington .36—so old it had paper cartridges instead of metal ones—that's who I always was in my mind's eye: Jim Hornaday, the gunfighter.

I killed my first man when I was nineteen. That statement is a lot more dramatic than the facts warrant. I was in a livery and saddling my mount in the back when I heard some commotion up front. A couple of drunken gamblers were arguing about the charges with the colored man who worked there. You could see they didn't much care about the money. They were just having a good time pushing the colored man back and forth between them. Whenever he'd fall down, dizzy from being shoved so hard, one of them would kick him in the ribs. For eleven in the morning, they'd had more than their fill of territory whiskey.

Now even though my father proudly wore the gray in the Civil War, I didn't hold with anybody being bullied, no matter what his color. I leaned down and helped the colored man to his feet. He was old and arthritic and scared. I brushed off his ragged sweater and then said to the gamblers, who were all fussed up in some kind of Edwardian-cut coats and golden silk vests, "You men pay him what you owe."

They laughed and I wasn't surprised. The baby face I have will always be with me. Even if I lived to be Gramp's age of eighty-six, there'll still be some boy in my pug nose and freckled cheeks. And my body wasn't any more imposing. I was short and still on the scrawny side for one thing and, for another, there was my limp, dating back to the time when I'd been training a cow pony that fell on me. I'd have the limp just as long as I'd have the baby face.

The taller of the two gamblers went for his Colt, worn gun-fighter-low on his right hip, and before I could think about it in any conscious way, I was drawing down on him, and putting two bullets into his chest before he had a chance to put two in mine. As for his friend, I spun around and pushed my own Colt in his face. He dropped his gun.

I asked the colored man to go get the local law and he nodded but, before he left, he came over and said, nodding to the man dead at my feet, "I don't think you know who he is."

"I guess I don't."

"Ray Billings."

Took me really till the law came to really understand what I'd done. Ray Billings was a gunfighter mentioned just about as often as Jim Hornaday by the dreamy young boys and weary old lawmen who kept up on this sort of thing. The law, in the rotund shape of a town marshal who looked as if he were faster with a fork than a six-shooter, stared down at Billings and then looked up at me, smiling. "I do believe you're going to be famous, son. I do believe you are."

He was right.

Over the next six months I became somebody named Andy Donnelly, and not the Andy Donnelly I grew up being—the one who'd liked to slide down the haystacks and fish in the fast blue creeks and dream about Marian Parke when he closed his eyes at night, Marian being the prettiest girl in our one-room school house. This new Andy Donnelly, the one that a bunch of hack journalists had created, was very different from the old one I'd known. According to the tales, the new Andy Donnelly had survived eleven gunfights (three was the true number), had escaped from six jails (when, in fact, I'd never been in a jail in my life), and was feared by the fastest guns in the territory, Jim Hornaday included.

All of this caught up with me in a town named Drago, where I had hoped nobody would know me. I was two hours past the DRAGO WELCOMES STRANGERS sign, and one hour on my hot dusty hotel bed, when a knock came and a female voice said, "I'd like to talk to you a minute, Mister Donnelly."

By now, I knew that a man with a reputation for gunfighting didn't dare answer a knock the normal way. Propped up against the back of the bed, I grabbed my Winchester, aimed it dead center at the door, and said, "Come in."

She was pretty enough in her city clothes of buff blue linen and taffeta, and her exorbitant picture hat with the fancy blue ribbon. She was wise enough to keep her hands in easy and steady sight.

"Say it plain."

"Say what plain, Mister Donnelly? I'm Patience Falkner, by the way."

"Say why you're looking for me. And say it plain."

She didn't hesitate. "Because," she said, all blue, blue eyes and yellow hair the color of September straw, "I want you to kill him."

"Him. Who's him?"

"Why, Jim Hornaday, of course. Isn't that why you came to Drago? Because you knew he was here? I mean, he killed your poor little cousin. You're not going to stand for that are you, an honorable man like yourself?"

I smiled. "You don't give a damn about my cousin. You're one of them."

"I think I've been insulted. 'One of them'...meaning what?"

"You damned well have been insulted," I said.

I swung my body and my Winchester off the bed, went over to the bureau where I poured water from a pitcher into a pan. The water was warm but I washed up anyway, face and neck, arms and hands. I grabbed one of two cotton work shirts and put it on.

"You know how old you look, Mister Donnelly?"

I turned, faced her, not wanting to hear about my baby face, a subject that had long ago sickened me. "What did he do to you? That's why you want me to kill him. Not for my little cousin...but for you. So what did he do to you, anyway?"

"I don't think that's any of your business."

"You don't, huh?" I said, strapping on my holster and gun. "He shoot up your house last night or something, did he? Or maybe you think he cheated your little brother at cards...or insulted your father at the saloon the other night. Last town I was in, somebody wanted me to draw down on this gunfighter because the gunny wouldn't pay his hotel bill. Turned out the guy who wanted to see me fight was the desk clerk at the hotel...figured I'd do his work for him." I shook my head. "Lots of people have lots of different reasons for us gunnies to shoot each other. Now, are you going to tell me your reason or not?"

I didn't make it easy for her. I slid on my flat-crowned hat and went out the door.

She followed me down the stairs, talking. "Well, I probably shouldn't tell you this but...well, he won't marry me. And he gave me his word and everything."

I smiled again. "And you want me to kill him for that?"

"Well, maybe my honor doesn't mean much to you," she said, out of breath as she tried to keep up with me descending the steps, "but it means a lot to me."

Down in the lobby, a lot of people were watching us. I said, "You're right about one thing, lady. Your honor doesn't mean one damn' thing to me. Not one damn' thing."

I walked away, leaving her there with the smirks and the sneers of the old codgers who sit all day long in the lobby, drifting on the sad and worn last days of their lives.

Patience Falkner wasn't the only one who told me that Jim Hornaday was in the town of Drago. There was the barber, the bootblack, the banker, and the twitchy little man at the billiard parlor—all just wanting me to know he was here, just in case I wanted to, well, you know, sort of draw down on him, as they all got nervously around to saying. Seems this fine town had never been the site of a major gunfight before and—just as Patience Falkner had her honor at stake—Drago had honor, too. They'd be right proud to bury whichever of us lost the gunfight. Right proud.

I was on my way to the saloon—being in dusty need of a beer—when a man said, "Wait a minute. I want to talk to you when I'm done here." He stood on the edge of the boardwalk. He had been busy jabbing his finger into another man's chest. He was a stout man in a white Stetson, a blue suit, and a considerable silver badge. After he got my attention, he turned back to the man he'd been arguing with. "Lem, how many damned times I got to tell you about that horse of yours, anyway?"

Horse and owner both looked suitably guilty, their heads dropped down.

"You know we got an ordinance here…any horse that damages a tree, the owner gets fined one hundred dollars. Now, I've warned you and warned you and warned you…but this time I'm gonna fine you. You understand?"

The farmer whose horse had apparently knocked down the angled young sapling to the right of the animal looked as if somebody had hit him in the stomach. Hard. "I can't afford no one hundred dollars, Sheriff."

"You can pay it off at ten dollars a month. Now you get Clyde here the hell out of town and keep him out of town."

"Don't seem right, folks fining other folks like that. God made us all equal, didn't He?"

"He made us equal, but He didn't make all of us smart. Fella lets his horse knock down the same tree three times in one month…that sure don't say much for brains…horse or man." He had an impish grin, the sheriff, and he looked right up at the horse and said, "Now, Clyde, you get that damned dumb owner of yours the hell out of here, all right?"

The farmer allowed himself a long moment of sullenness then took the big paint down the long, narrow road leading out of town.

"Looks like you were headed to the saloon," the sheriff said. "So was I." He put his hand out. "Patterson, Deke Patterson. I already know who you are, Mister Donnelly." Then the impish grin again. "You look even younger than they say you do."

Inside, I had had two sips of my beer when Patterson leaned and said, "I need to be honest with you, Mister Donnelly."

"Oh?"

"I grew up with Jim Hornaday over in what's now Nebraska. He's my best friend."

"I see."

"I wouldn't want to see him die."

I smiled. "Then you're the only one in Drago."

He laughed. "I saw Patience headed over to your hotel. She tell you they were engaged and then he broke it off?"

"Uh-huh."

"And she asked you to kill him?"

"Uh-huh."

"She tell you why he broke it off?"

"Uh-uh."

"Because he walked along the river one night and there on a blanket he found Patience and this traveling salesman. Sounds like an off-color joke, but it wasn't. Old Jim took it pretty hard."

"Don't blame him," I shrugged. "But it's no different in any other town. People always have their own reasons for wanting you to fight somebody."

The grin. "You mean, in addition to just liking to see blood and death in the middle of Main Street?"

"Sounds like you don't think much of people."

"Not the side of people I see, I don't." He had some more beer and then looked around. On a weekday afternoon, the saloon held long shadows and silent roulette wheels and a barkeep who was yawning. Patterson suddenly looked right at me. There was no impish grin now. All his toughness, which was considerable, was in his brown eyes. "He's hoping you kill him."

"What?"

Patterson nodded. "He's never been the same since he accidentally killed that little cousin of yours. For a long time, he couldn't
sleep nights. He just kept seeing her face. That's when he took up
the bottle and it's been downhill since. He keeps getting in gunfights,
hoping somebody'll kill him. That's what he really wants…death. He
won't admit it, maybe not even to himself, but the way he pushes
himself into gun battles when he's been drinking…well, somebody's
bound to kill him sooner or later. And I know that's what he wants
because he can't get your little cousin out of his mind."

"I didn't come here to kill him, Sheriff. My reputation is made
up. I got forced into three fights and won them, but I'm not a gunfighter. I'm really not."

He regarded me silently for a long moment and then said, with
an air of relief, "I do believe you're telling me the truth, Mister Donnelly."

"I sure am. I didn't even know Hornaday was here."

"Then you don't blame him for killing your little cousin?"

"Some of my kin do, but I don't. It was accidental. It was terrible she died but nobody meant for her to die."

He asked the barkeep for two more beers. "One more thing,
Mister Donnelly."

"You could always call me Donny."

"One more thing, then, Donny. And this won't be easy if you've
got any pride, and I suspect you do. He's gonna try and goad you
into a fight, but you can't let him. Because the condition he's in…the
whiskey and all…."

I stopped him. "I don't have that much pride, Sheriff. I don't
want to kill Hornaday. Sounds like he's doing a good job of it himself, anyway."

We talked about the town and how it probably wasn't a good
thing for me to stay much past tomorrow morning, and then I drifted
back to my hotel and my room and there he sat on my bed, a man
with an angular face marked with chicken pox from his youth. These
days, he resembled a preacher, black suit and hat and starched white
shirt. Only the brocaded red vest hinted at the man's festive side.
He'd never been known to turn down a drink, that was for sure.

"You're her cousin?"

"I am."

"And you know who I am?"

"Yes, I do, Mister Hornaday."

"I killed her."

"I know."

"I didn't mean to kill her."

"I know that, too."

"And I'm told you came here to kill me."

"That part you got wrong, Mister Hornaday."

"You didn't come here to kill me?"

"No, I didn't, Mister Hornaday."

"Maybe you're not as good as they say, then."

"No, I'm not, Mister Hornaday, and I don't want to be, either. I want to be a happy, normal man. Not a gunfighter."

"That's what I wanted to be once." His dark gaze moved from me to the window where the dusty town appeared below. "A happy, normal man." He looked back at me. "You should want to avenge her, you know."

"It was a long time ago."

"Ten years, two months, one week and two days."

If I hadn't believed he was obsessed with killing poor little Charity before, I sure did now.

"It was an accident, Mister Hornaday."

"That what her mother says?"

"I guess not."

"Or her father?"

"No, he doesn't think it was an accident, either."

"But you do, huh?"

"I do and so do most other people who saw it."

He got up from the bed, the springs squeaking. His spurs chinked loudly in the silence. He came two feet from me and stopped.

The backhand came from nowhere. He not only rocked me, he blinded me momentarily too. He wasn't a big man, Hornaday, but he was a strong and quick one.

"That make you want to kill me?"

"No, sir."

He drove a fist deep into my stomach. I wanted to vomit. "How about that?"

I couldn't speak. Just shook my head.

He took a gold railroad watch from the pocket of his brocaded vest. "I'll be in the street an hour and a half from now. Five o'clock sharp. You be there, too, you understand me?"

He didn't wait for a reply. He left, spurs still chinking as he walked heavily down the hallway, and then down the stairs.

The next hour I packed my warbag and tried to figure which direction I'd be heading out. There was always cattle work in Kansas and right now Kansas sounded good, a place where nobody had ever heard of me, a place I should have gone instead of coming here.

I was just getting ready to leave the room when I heard the gunfire from down the street. A nervous silence followed and then shouts—near as loud as the gunfire itself—filled the air. I could hear people's feet slapping against the dusty street as they ran in the direction of the gun shots.

I leaned out the window, trying to see what was going on. A crowd had ringed the small one-story adobe building with SHERIFF on a sigh above the front door. A man in a brown suit carrying a Gladstone bag came running from the east. The crowd parted immediately, letting him through. He had to be a doctor. Nobody else would have gotten that kind of quick respect, not even a lawman.

I was turning back to the door when somebody knocked. Patience Falkner said, "Did you hear what happened?"

"Why don't you come in and tell me."

She didn't look so pretty or well kempt any more and I felt a kind of pity for her. Whatever had happened, it took all her vanity and poise away. She looked tired and ten years older than she had earlier this morning.

"Jim killed Sheriff Patterson."

"What?"

She nodded, sniffling back tears. "The two best friends that ever were." She glanced away and then back at me and said, "I should have my tongue cut out for what I said to you this morning. I don't want Jim dead. I love him."

She was in my arms before I knew it, warm of flesh and grief, sobbing. "I wasn't true to him. That's why he wouldn't marry me. It was all my fault. I never should've asked you to kill him for me. And now he's killed the sheriff.... They'll kill Jim, won't they?"

There was no point in lying. "I expect they will. Why'd he kill him, anyway?"

She leaned back and looked at me. I thought she might say something about my baby face. "You. You were what they were fighting about. Jim told Patterson that he'd called you out for five this afternoon. Patterson told him to call it off but Jim wouldn't. Jim was drinking and angry and Patterson gave him a shove and…Jim took his gun out and they wrestled for it and it went off. Jim didn't mean to kill him but…."

"Where is he now?"

"Nobody knows. Ran out the back door of the jail."

I shook my head. This was a town I just plain wanted out of. I eased her from my arms, picked up my Winchester and warbag, and walked to the door.

"You're leaving town?"

"I am."

"Then…then you're not going to fight him?"

"No, ma'am, I'm not."

"Oh, thank God…thank you, mister. Thank you very much."

"But if you're going to say good bye to him, you better find him before that crowd does."

Even from here I sensed that the crowd was becoming a mob. Pretty soon there would be liquor, and soon after that talk of lynching. The territory prided itself on being civilized. But it wasn't that civilized. Not yet, anyway.

I'd paid a day in advance so I went down the back stairs of the hotel. The livery was a block straight down the alley. I paid the stocky blacksmith with some silver and then walked back through the sweet-sour hay-and-manure smells of the barn to where my mount was waiting to be saddled.

I went right to it, not wanting to be detained in any way. Kansas sounded better and better. I had just finished cinching her up when somebody said, "You probably heard I killed the sheriff, Donnelly. He was my best friend."

The voice was harsh with liquor. I turned slowly from the mount and said, "Little girls and best friends, Hornaday. Not a record to be proud of."

"I didn't say anything about being proud, cowboy. I didn't say anything about being proud at all."

The men in front had overheard our conversation and had walked through the barn shadow to get here quickly. There were three of them. They were joined moments later by Patience Falkner.

"Jim…," she started to say.

But his scowl silenced her.

We stood in the fading light of the dying day, just outside a small rope corral where the six horses inside looked utterly indifferent to the fate of all human beings present. Couldn't say I blamed them. Hornaday eased the right corner of his black coat back so he could get at his gun quick and easy.

"Even if you don't draw, cowboy, I'm going to draw and kill you right on the spot. That's a promise."

"I don't want this fight, Hornaday."

"What if I told you I killed that cousin of yours on purpose?"

"I wouldn't believe you."

"I killed my best friend, didn't I?"

"That could have been accidental, too."

By now there were twenty people filling the barn door, standing in the deep slice of late-afternoon shadow.

"You've got to fight me," Hornaday said. "A reputation like yours...."

"You need to get yourself sober, Hornaday. You need to take a different look at things."

"I'm counting to three," Hornaday said.

"Like I said, Hornaday, I don't want this."

"One."

"Hornaday...."

"Two."

"Jim please...," the Falkner woman cried. "Please, Jim...."

But then he did just what he'd promised. Feinted to his right, scooped out his six-shooter, and aimed right at me. What choice did I have?

I was all pure instinct by then. Scooping out my own gun, aiming right at him, listening to the shots bark on the quiet end of the day. His knees went and then his whole body, a heap suddenly on the dusty earth. Nobody moved or spoke.

I just stood there and watched Patience Falkner flutter over to him and awkwardly cradle him and then sob with such force that I knew he had just died.

The blacksmith went over and picked up Hornaday's Colt, which had fallen a few feet away. He picked it up, looked it over. He'd probably talk all night at the saloon how strange it felt holding the same gun Jim Hornaday had used to kill all those men.

Then he said, "I'll be dagged."

"What is it?" I said.

The blacksmith glanced around at the curious crowd and then walked the gun over to me.

"Looks like you performed an execution here today, mister," the livery man said.

He handed me the gun. All six chambers were empty. Jim Hornaday had fought me without bullets.

They got the Falkner woman to her feet and led her sobbing away, and then the mortician brought his wagon and they loaded up the body and by then the deputy sheriff had finished all his questions of the crowd and me, so I was up on my roan and riding off. I tried hard not to think about Hornaday and how I'd helped him commit suicide. I tried real hard.

(Charles) Steve Frazee

was born in Salida, Colorado, and in 1926 - 1936 worked in heavy construction and mining in his native state. He also managed to pay his way through Western State College in Gunnison, Colorado, from which in 1937 he was graduated with a Bachelor's degree in journalism. He began in the late 1940s to make major contributions to the Western pulp magazines with stories set in the American West as well as a number of North-Western tales published in *Adventure*. Few can match his Western novels which are notable for their evocative, lyrical descriptions of the open range and the awesome power of natural forces and their effects on human efforts. CRY COYOTE (Macmillan, 1955) is memorable for its strong female protagonists who actually influence most of the major events and bring about the resolution of the central conflict in this story of wheat growers and expansionist cattlemen. HIGH CAGE (Macmillan, 1957) concerns five miners and a woman snowbound at an isolated gold mine on top of Bulmer Peak in which the twin themes of the lust for gold and the struggle against the savagery of both the elements and human nature interplay with increasing intensity. BRAGG'S FANCY WOMAN (1966) concerns a free-spirited woman who is able to tame a family of thieves. RENDEZVOUS (1958) ranks as one of the finest mountain man novels and THE WAY THROUGH THE MOUNTAINS (Popular Library, 1972) is a major historical novel recently reprinted in a mass merchandise edition by Leisure Books. Not surprisingly, many of Frazee's novels have become major motion pictures. A Frazee story is possessed of flawless characterization, the clash of human passions, credible dialogue, and often almost painful suspense.

Death Rides This Trail

A few days after they saw the two wagoneers slicing each other raw with bull whips, the Breslins broke out of the sandy country and saw a wild sweep of hills humping across the horizon. They were in bright sunshine but up ahead a storm, black and sudden, was knotting itself to lash out.

Dirk Breslin reined old Put closer to the wagon. The oncoming storm, rushing up so suddenly in the great space all around him made him uneasy. There seemed to be no limit or plan to anything out here. His sixteen years had been spent on a farm in settled country, where trees and fields, the river, and painted buildings marked the boundaries of a safe, familiar world.

With a touch of envy he glanced to the left, where his brother, Hugh, was riding far on the flank, looking for buffalo. Hugh was a year younger than Dirk. His worn-out old rifle wouldn't kill a buff if he saw one, but Hugh was out there trying. It took a lot to discourage Hugh or scare him out.

On the wagon beside his wife Jake Breslin raised a long arm. "That's it, Em," he said. "About a hundred and fifty miles yonder of those hills."

The four younger kids scrambled forward in the wagon to peer ahead, as if they thought they could put their eyes on their new home.

Talbot said, "Where, Pa? I don't see nothing but a lot of land."

Pa said, "You'll see when we get there."

The storm was boiling toward them now. Dirk pulled a little closer to the wagon. Back home there was always a place to run when a storm came, into the big barn, or under a walnut tree.

Ma tied her bonnet strings. "Sometimes I think this is a brutal land, Jake. I know it's a violent land."

Jake laughed. "You're still thinking of those wagon drivers, Em. Sure, its rough out here, so you have to get just as rough as the country to lick it."

Ma Breslin looked at the heavy pistol in her husband's waistband. He had never carried one before; there was no cause to do so where the Breslins came from. But Jake had observed the custom of the country and now he was armed.

Wind and dust whirled against them first, and then the rain struck furiously. Ma pushed the kids back under the canvas top and lashed the strings. Pa began to sing, with the water bouncing on his broad face.

Huddled on old Put, feeling the cold seeping against flesh that had been too hot minutes before, Dirk took courage from his father. The rain washing harmlessly against the brown, clean-shaven planes of Pa's face reminded Dirk of a picture in his grandmother's parlor back home—a violent sea lashing up at unyielding rock. In the distance, Hugh went on with his futile hunt, paying no attention to the rain.

It had taken Dirk a long time to realize that each member of the family was utterly different from the others. Missouri, his oldest sister, was sharp-tongued at times—the rest of the time she was inclined to lightness and song. Pa said she was just like Ma had been when she was a little younger. Talbot, who was a twin to Cree, the other sister, was quiet, always tinkering with things, claiming he could build things better than the way they already were. He didn't talk much, and some folks thought he wasn't quite smart because of that. Lafayette, the youngest, was a crybaby, never wanting to fight even when he was picked on. Dirk considered them all. He wished he himself had more of Pa's strong nature—because he was afraid he was exactly like Lafayette.

The storm swept away, leaving a clean odor of silky dust caught in the air, and the land all wet and steaming around them. The vastness still caught at Dirk's stomach, but he kept watching Pa—he knew the country wouldn't be too mean for Pa to handle. Hugh was clean out of sight now.

Four days later the hills were close ahead, green billows tumbling one upon another. The Breslins came to a muddy river and there was a camp of sorts in a grove of cottonwoods, with wagons scattered here and there, with horses held in a rope corral, the first Dirk had ever seen.

"That tent's a saloon," Ma said. "I can tell from here. Don't you stay in there no longer than necessary to get directions, Jake Breslin."

Pa grinned. "Out here most of the talking and business is done in saloons, Em. Have Dirk take the wagon on to the river and water the horses. I'll be along."

Big and confident, with a pistol in his waistband, Pa went into the tent. When Dirk drove by he heard the clink of glasses and his father laughing, already getting acquainted. Men liked Jake Breslin. Dirk was proud of that.

Dirk went on toward the racing water. The trees and the river were not the same as back home, but they still made Dirk like the country a little better. Down here distances were sort of shut away. He hoped their new home in the Topknot country would be sheltered.

He and Hugh watered the team. The shots came when the younger ones were wading in the cool mud. They were cracking little sounds, not like the heavy gushing of rifles or the roar of big pistols.

Hugh ran to the wagon and grabbed his rifle. He went through the trees toward the saloon.

"Hugh!" Ma called, but he did not stop. "Go after him, Dirk!" she said. All at once her face was white.

Dirk overtook his brother just before they reached the tent. There was a crowd of men in front, and women coming from all directions.

"You had no call for that," a man was saying. "You could see he wasn't after a pistol fight!"

"He wore a gun, Coupland. When a damned Yankee shoots off his mouth to me, and he's wearing a pistol, he gets what he asks for."

"There was no call for it. If we had any law out here…. Wait a minute, there, son!"

Hugh had thrust his way deeply into the crowd, with Dirk right behind him. Pa was lying on the ground. His feet were spraddled out all funny-like. There was dust on the clean tan of one cheek. His eyes were wide open. Dirk had never seen a dead person except in the church back home, but he knew Pa was dead.

Hugh was raising his rifle toward a tall, dark-faced man with a trim mustache. The man was holding a tiny little pistol without a trigger guard. Hugh didn't say anything. His blond hair was hanging on his forehead. His blue eyes had turned pale. He cocked the rifle as he raised it. The man called Coupland, gray-haired and almost fat, grabbed the barrel and jerked it up and Hugh's shot went toward a clear sky. He began to struggle for the weapon, not cursing, not saying anything.

"You should have let him, Judge," a man said. He stepped toward the dark man with the tiny gun. "Boys, I say let's string this one up right now!"

"No!" Judge Coupland cried. He was holding Hugh in his arms, trying to smother the fight out of him without hurting him. Another man helped him, and then Hugh began to cry.

Ma Breslin came in then. The crowd parted, men taking off their hats. Ma was a handsome woman, with dark-brown hair and eyes to look through a man. Even now, white with shock, she was tall and steady as she went to Jake. Dirk didn't want to go. The strangeness of his father was a searing pain inside. But he did go over, and a moment later was kneeling there with Hugh, and both of them were crying.

He heard Coupland say, "It's a shame there's no law here, but we can't take it into our hands. I'll swallow my scruples, however, and provide the rope, if you're not gone from here in five minutes."

"It wouldn't be advisable for farmers to try to hang me, my friend." The man who had killed Pa held a big pistol in his hand now. There was white at the collar of his dark coat. The hand on the pistol was long and slender. Those two facts impressed themselves on Dirk's mind; and he knew he would forever hold a grudge against any man with soft hands or who wore a white shirt. The man backed away, still holding the pistol. "Ah, well," he said, "this place was about worked out anyway." Dirk Breslin was never to see him again.

They buried Jacob Breslin that afternoon.

Lafayette continued to cry long after there was no visible reason for grief. Dirk slapped him, hating him at the moment, for Dirk himself wanted to bawl, and there was no relief in it. He knew just how Lafayette felt, and slapped him because it seemed to be a blow at his own weakness. He was sorry when it was done. He wanted to say so, but Lafayette walked away from him, his face all streaked with dust and tears, no longer crying.

That night all the women from the wagons that were waiting for the river to go down came to the Breslin fire with gifts of food that no one but Talbot had appetite to touch. Stolid Talbot stuffed himself.

Dirk and Hugh slipped away with their father's pistol. It was an old one, with the butt grips cracked and loose. They sat together under a dark cottonwood close to the growling water, passing the pistol between them.

"There's customs out here, huh?" Dirk said. "We'll get us another pistol just like this one, Hugh."

"Maybe we won't stay here that long. I guess we'll be going back home now."

They had no home to go to. It was hundreds of miles back to where they had sold the farm, and still a hundred to where Jake Breslin had intended to go. Alone in the night beside the rushing water the two boys fondled the pistol; and suddenly there was no courage in it.

"I'm sort of scared...a little," Hugh said. "It was all right with Pa, but now I'm sort of scared...."

It was one of the few times Hugh ever admitted being afraid of anything.

"I guess we'll go back now, huh, Dirk? Back to Ma's folks?"

When there was action at hand, Hugh never asked anyone's advice: he acted. Dirk began to understand. Leadership was being nudged toward him now that Pa was gone, because Hugh didn't like to look beyond the next move, or maybe he couldn't.

"We won't go back," Dirk said. "We're going on to where Pa wanted to go. We got to do that now." He was frightened a moment later by his statement, but it was out.

"All right, Dirk. I guess you're the boss now."

Hugh was satisfied. Worn out with grief and travel, he fell asleep soon afterward, resting his head on Dirk's shoulder. Dirk could not fall asleep so easily. He sat there thinking of the quiet orchards along the river back home, and of tagging along behind Grandfather Sterns when the old man went out to inspect the apples. He thought then of the stark space of all the country around him; and he saw his father on the ground in front of a faded tent, with dust on his cheek and his eyes wide open.

The pistol on Dirk's lap took coldness from the night. Hugh whimpered in his sleep. Dirk sat there with the tears hot against his twisted cheeks until his mother's voice calling him came faintly from the camp.

I

After breakfast the next morning, Emma Breslin said they would start the long trip back. Dirk's resolution had faded with the night. He started to speak and then thought better of it. After all, now that Pa was gone....

Hugh said, "No, Ma, Dirk said we were going on, just like Pa would want us to."

With her lips firm and the trouble in her as real as something that can be felt, Dirk's mother bore a long study on him. "You want to go on, Dirk?"

He nodded, unsure of words. Talbot stared at him with admiration. Lafayette began to cry. He wanted to go home, he said. Missouri, Dirk's oldest sister, dark and slender like her mother, shook her head at Dirk.

"He's scared, Ma. I can tell. He says go on just to show off."

"He ain't scared!" Hugh said. "You just wait until the river makes the wagon float and the horses have to swim, and then you'll see who's scared."

"That's enough," Emma Breslin said. "I guess we'd all better talk about this some more. You might be right, Dirk, but I haven't the courage myself to go on."

It was Hugh who pushed Dirk into swinging the final decision to go on into Topknot country. Dirk knew it, but Hugh did not.

Rumor had it that Judge Coupland had come West for his health. Except for a certain paleness of complexion that the sun did not seem to change, he did not look like a health-seeker. He rode into the Breslin camp when the wagons were at the river and getting ready to cross. Although his hair was iron gray, there was an unlined look of youthfulness on his features. His forehead was broad, his chin narrow and blunt. When he spoke, he had a habit of pushing out his thick lips as if giving a mild judicial opinion. If Dirk had not seen him speak with fire in his eyes to the gambler who killed Jake Breslin, Dirk would have taken Coupland for an utterly harmless man.

The judge—a term of honor only, since he was a lawyer and there was no law—peered mildly at the two large cottonwood logs Dirk and Hugh had skidded in to lash to the wagon. "Do you mean, Missus Breslin, that you're going on?"

"We are. The older boys have changed my decision of last night."

"I see...I see." Coupland looked at Dirk appraisingly. "I applaud your decision, madam, although my personal opinion is that the Top-knot country is unsuited for farming."

"What's wrong with it?" Mrs. Breslin asked.

"A lack of water, mainly, from what my information tells me. The soil, I understand, is quite productive, but there are only two small streams out there." Coupland looked dubiously at the gathering wagons. "So many people in one small area, with but two sources of water. The rains out there, I understand, are not dependable."

"He's probably going there himself," Hugh muttered.

Two snub-nosed boys in butternut jeans and boots they were obviously proud of, since they had rolled their pants legs high to expose the leather, came close to the Breslin wagon and stood there grinning insolently as they looked at the logs and then at Dirk and Hugh.

Judge Coupland swung down from his Kentucky horse and talked to Emma Breslin. "I wouldn't tell this to everybody, madam, but it is my considered opinion that the country this side of the Top-knot, the Breakwagon Hills, is admirably suited for raising cattle. Now if I had a family of sturdy sons...."

"We know nothing of cattle, Mister Coupland. If we did, we lack the money to buy them."

"Most likely all these people will rush right on past the Break-wagon Hills, Missus Breslin. I strongly recommend you stop and consider what I've said when you reach that part of the country."

Dirk didn't know whether or not to trust Coupland. The idea of being a cattle rancher was appealing, but the Breslins had only a few hundred dollars. That wouldn't buy enough cattle to stick in your eye, Dirk surmised, thinking in terms of the huge milch cows back home.

One of the boys in butternut jeans said to Hugh, "Do you know how to get across this river?" It was insolent. The boy was quite sure Hugh didn't know.

Hugh bristled. "Huh, I guess we do. We'll get someone to help us lift these here logs up so we can tie 'em against the wagon and then...."

The two boys laughed, nudging each other. Their hair was long against the collars of their shirts. Their eyes, bold green, were as insolent as their laughs.

"They're going to lift the logs up and hold 'em there to be tied, Tommy! I told you they didn't know nothing. Look at them bare feet."

Hugh dug his toes against the ground. He grinned. "I know something," he said, walking forward.

"Yeah," Tommy said suspiciously, "what?"

Hugh grabbed Tommy, tripped him off balance, spun him across his hip, and then sent him rolling into the water at the edge of the river. He reached for the second smart aleck. The second boy began to hammer Hugh in the face. Hugh kept walking in, reaching out, but his opponent was handy with his fists and bigger than Hugh. Hugh's nose began to bleed. Red marks blossomed on his cheeks. He kept coming in.

The second boy was getting out of the river.

"Get the other one, Hugh." Dirk wound up a swing and hit Hugh's adversary in the side of the jaw so hard he knocked him over one of the dead logs.

Hugh let out a yell. He went back and threw his first opponent into the river again. They wrestled there, rolling in the mud and water.

Ma Breslin was calling out to Hugh and Dirk. Hugh never would have heard, and Dirk couldn't let go if he wanted to. He was getting more than he bargained for from the heavier boy. Dirk swung with all his might, but he wasn't hitting anything, and hard knuckles were bouncing off his face every second or two. He lowered his head and butted the boy in the stomach. That helped. They went over the log together, and then Dirk got his hands in his opponent's long hair and began to pound the boy's head against the ground.

The kid hooked his thumbs under the corner of Dirk's lips and dug his fingers in behind Dirk's ear. Dirk couldn't bite the thumbs. He thought his mouth was being stretched four feet wide. All he could do was keep beating the boy's head against the ground, and the ground was soft.

Judge Coupland hauled Dirk off by the suspenders. The boy held on with his thumbs until Dirk smacked him in the nose.

"What a country," Coupland murmured. "The children start in like wildcats the minute they get here."

There was a crowd of men around now, grinning. A worried-looking little fellow with a meager beard was holding Tommy. Beside the man was a ponderous woman with hair in a tight knot at the back of her head.

"Fighting, fighting," she said. "I swear, Bolivar, all these young 'uns have done since we started...."

"I'll learn you, Tommy!" Bolivar said. He slapped the boy so hard he lost his grip and knocked the lad into the water again.

"They started it!" Dirk said. "They...!"

Something popped on his cheek. He blinked. He saw a pair of blazing green eyes and two pigtails bouncing. A girl about his own age hauled off and smacked him three or four more times in the face.

"You're a big bully!" she cried.

She broke away then, and started to run and wound up in the grip of the huge woman who had been at the edge of the water a few moments before.

"Callie, you ain't no lady a-tall," the woman said. She held the girl with one hand and spanked her where it hurt. "You're worse'n the boys sometimes, I do think, Callie."

The woman came waddling on to Mrs. Breslin. "Brats do beat all, don't they, Missus Breslin? I was telling my Bolivar just the other night that what Tommy and Squire"—she pronounced it Square— "and Callie need is a few Indians to scare the pants off'n them."

"It's a violent land, Missus Bascomb," Ma Breslin said. "I have found that out."

"I know, you poor thing. You come over to the wagon, Missus Breslin. Bolivar ain't going across until we see how the river handles the other wagons. You and me will have some tea."

She gave Squire a mighty jerk by the arm. "You git, and stay out of trouble!"

Squire managed to dig his elbow hard into Dirk's ribs as he went by. Dirk tried to trip him, but the boy skipped away. He looked back insolently, unbeaten. The two of them right then knew they would never like each other.

Bolivar Bascomb was coming from the river. He made an openhanded pass at his son. Squire ducked and Bolivar went on around with the blow and nearly fell. "I'm right sorry about this, Missus Breslin, considering the trouble you've had already." Bolivar shook his head. He was an ineffectual-looking little man, and he seemed to be wondering how he had come by sons with so much fire in them.

"It's all right, Mister Bascomb," Ma Breslin said.

Judge Coupland wiped his brow. The first wagon was getting ready to try the crossing. He looked at the muddy surge of the rain-swelled river and appeared relieved to think that the next obstacle would be a natural one.

Hugh and Dirk drew together. "I guess we showed them," Hugh said.

Dirk felt his cheek. "Look at that Missouri and Cree!" The Breslin girls were chatting friendly-like to Callie. Ma Breslin and Mrs. Bascomb walked away together toward the Bascomb wagon.

Women—you just didn't know what they would do, Dirk thought. "I should have smacked that Callie girl," he grumbled.

Hugh grinned. "I'd'a rassled with her if she'd slapped me. She's a kind of pretty girl, Dirk."

"You're too damned young to be talking like that!"

Hugh felt his swollen nose and grinned again. "Yeah, and you're too young to be cussing like that, too."

The first wagon went into the river. Dirk saw then why the Bascomb boys had laughed at him and Hugh. The men didn't try to lift the heavy logs. They just put the wagon in deep enough so they could float the logs against it and tie them without any hard work at all. There were a lot of things you had to learn fast in this country. Dirk would learn them as fast as he could, and keep his mouth shut hereafter when he didn't know.

II

The first wagon inched out into the flood with the driver swearing at the horses when they tried to buckle around and get back to shore. Then the team was swimming. The dirty water came up until the logs were half submerged, and the current quartered the wagon downstream. Kids were peering out of the back of it, laughing.

Good Lord! Dirk was scared. Those kids ought to stay back where they couldn't fall out. It was only a quarter of a mile across, but Dirk lived a long time before he saw the dripping horses coming clear of the water on the far shore. A spare team that had been swum across earlier was there to help the wagon up the bank.

"That looks like a lot of fun!" Hugh said. "Can I drive when we go across?"

"No. I can handle the team better." Dirk doubted that, but it was best he drive himself because he knew how scared he was.

When it was time for the Breslin wagon to go, Dirk found no joy in the confidence his mother placed in him. A man helped Hugh and Dirk start the extra team across by themselves, and a rider swam his horse behind them in case they tried to turn back in mid-stream.

Lafayette began to cry when the first hard clutch of the river swung the wagon at an angle. "Don't fret," Ma said. "Dirk will get us across just like the others."

"He'll more'n likely drown us all!" Missouri said from inside the wagon. "If he does, I'll...."

Hugh laughed. "What can you do, all swelled up like them dead buffalo we saw on the Missouri?"

"Hugh!" Ma called. "You keep your mouth shut!"

The current was a mighty hand that made the wagon tremble. It was a long way to either shore now. The waves were slobbering foam that slapped over the backs of the swimming horses. Dirk kept gulping fear. He tried to talk cheerfully to the team, like Pa used to do. Pa was gone forever now, back there on the hill above a place that didn't even have a name. Dirk wanted to give way a little, but he held the lines loosely and kept talking to the horses.

"It's wet in here!" Missouri cried. "We're sinking!"

"We ain't either!" Hugh laughed again.

The far shore came to them and they landed right where the other wagons had struck. A red-faced man backed a team of grays down to help them up the bank, after Hugh unlashed the logs. The man saw nothing unusual in the crossing.

Dirk felt better, but there was a hardness in his stomach yet. He looked back. The Bascombs were just ready to start. Mrs. Bascomb waved. Bolivar held the lines. Hah, that Squire couldn't talk about driving the river when he came across.

"Next time, maybe, I'll let Hugh have the fun," Dirk said.

"There are no more rivers like this between here and the Top-knot country, thank the Lord!" Ma hugged Lafayette. He wasn't crying now.

It became a race the second day away from the river, when the wagons hit the first of the rolling hills. There was free land on the

Topknot and some, of course, would be better than other. On the third day the wagons were no longer camping together.

The Breslins and the Bascombs were behind. Dirk remembered well how Pa had cautioned about a shaky rear wheel, saying that he might have to stop and cut the rim down before getting to where they were going. The wheels were tight enough the first day away from the river, but the wood shrank quickly. Dirk took it easy.

Bolivar Bascomb's horses were old and poor. They could not rush. So the two groups stayed together. Missouri and Cree were right friendly with Callie; and Talbot and Lafayette sometimes talked to the Bascomb boys. Hugh and Dirk wanted no part of them.

Ma told Mrs. Bascomb and Bolivar what Judge Coupland had said about the Breakwagon Hills.

"Cattle are all right, I guess," Bolivar said. His big eyes rolled in wrinkled flesh. "If a body knew something about cattle and had the money and all...." He looked at his hands. "I've always been a farmer, on a hillside place." Not a very good farmer, either, his attitude implied.

Dirk sort of liked Bolivar Bascomb. The name fascinated him, to begin with, and Bolivar wasn't mean in any way, just always worried.

The hills grew worse as they went on, short chops of grassy ground that put a strain on everything. Sometimes there were wide open spaces where the grass was high. There were tiny springs everywhere and spots of marshy ground. It looked all right for cattle, sure enough. All the other wagons had gone right on through.

On the fourth day Bolivar said, "There's no use holding you folks back." It had taken both teams to get the wagons up the worst of the hills, with everybody pushing. The Bascomb horses were about done. "I heard at the river place there was an easy way around these hills," Bolivar said. "You go north about fifteen miles. I guess that's what we'll do. No use holding you folks up no more."

Ma said it was all right, they didn't mind, and Dirk said so too, but Bolivar shook his head. "We'll just mosey around the easy way, maybe give the team a few days rest, and we'll see you on the Topknot."

The way the girls took on at parting you would have thought the Bascombs were going to China. Dirk shook Bolivar's hand. It sort of embarrassed him but it also gave him the feel of being a grown up man.

The hill was one of the worst. Dirk thought he should have brought some logs from the last grove of trees to sprag the wheels if the wagon started to slide back; but it was too late now. Lafayette was driving. He was the lightest. All he had to do was hold the lines. He was scared, ready to blubber, but he was doing his job.

Dirk was on old Put and Hugh was riding the other saddle horse, Mitch. They had ropes on the wagon and were helping all they could. Ma and the rest were pushing. The grass was darned good and slick and the shoes on Vicksburg and Island 10 were worn smooth. Pa had given the matched grays their names, after two places where he'd fought; but the names were just Vick and Ten now.

"All together!" Dirk shouted.

Vick and Ten clawed away and heaved. The hot sun rippled on their muscles and the sweat odor of them came up to Dirk.

The smaller front wheels were almost on the crest. Vick stumbled and lost all the motion. "Come on, Vick!" Lafayette cried in a trembling voice. The wagon began to slip. Vick recovered and did his best along with Ten. The other horses tried to hold, but all their efforts came to was keeping the wagon from smashing up when it finally slid to the bottom of the hill. The girls were red-faced and tired. Lather was dripping from the sides of the team.

"Let's unhitch the horses and rest a while right here," Mrs. Breslin panted. "Then we'll go up."

"This isn't the right hill," Missouri said.

"It is too! You can see where the other wagons went up," Dirk said. "You're so smart, why don't you find a better hill, Misery!"

"Don't you call me that! I'll slap you worse than Callie Bascomb did!"

"Come on, you wildcats," Ma said patiently. "We'll find a spring and eat, and then we'll feel better."

Hugh and Dirk unhitched the team and let the horses cool before they led them to a spring to drink.

"That back wheel is about gone," Dirk said. "The rim is sliding on it, almost."

"How you going to fix it?"

"After we get up the hill, we'll fix it." Some way. They could drive wooden wedges under the tire, and then it might hold till they reached the Topknot. It would be pretty bad if the Bascombs beat them after all.

They felt better after eating. Missouri and Cree went up on a hill and picked flowers. "This is an awful pretty place right here," Missouri said when they returned. "There's some trees over there a ways. Why don't we just have our farm right here?"

"It would take twenty horses to get a plough through that sod," Ma said. "Especially an old bull plough like we have."

Dirk hadn't known that his mother knew the difference between a bull plow and a good one. He felt better about the task ahead. They would make it all right. Days of hard work and worrying about how to get the wagon on the next mile or two had left Dirk little time for the disturbing memory of his father on the ground before the tent. Only at night was he troubled; he guessed the vision would haunt him the rest of his life. But maybe after they did what Pa had wanted to do he would feel easier about it.

"All of us at once now!" he called. The rest had done the team good. They came stoutly up the hill with Hugh and Dirk, dismounted this time, urging Put and Mitch to a steady pressure on the helping ropes.

Dirk saw the break coming where his rope began to unlay its yellow strands. He yelled for his mother and the others to get away from the wagon. The rope snapped on Vick's side of the wagon. It was not too great a jar, just enough to throw the horses off their stride. Lafayette might have urged them on up at the critical instant, but he was too slow, and his hands were tiny. Vick faltered with the front wheels just touching the crest. Motion stopped and the wagon then began to slide. Ten sensed the inexperience on the lines. He backed up. Then the horses and all went crashing back down the hill, with Hugh still fighting to keep strain on his rope.

The front wheels cramped around at the bottom. The weak rear wheel sent oak splinters flying when it cracked. Hugh was the first to the struggling horses. They were down and the wagon was on its side, with one broken corner of Ma's cherrywood bureau showing through ripped canvas.

Ma and Dirk ran to where Lafayette had been thrown head over heels. For an instant Dirk thought he was dying, but it was only that the wind had been knocked from him. They pounded him on the back.

With his first breath Lafayette asked, "Who got hurt?"

"The wagon, is all." Dirk went over to help Hugh get the horses untangled. Ten stepped on Hugh's foot and Hugh cursed just like Pa had cursed now and then.

Ma didn't hear. She was leaning against the wagon, running her hand over the broken bureau.

"It's all right, Ma," Talbot said. "Maybe I can fix it."

Holding Cree's hand, Missouri said, "It ain't just busted bureaus and things like that, you...fool." She put her arm around her mother. For a while Dirk thought his mother was going to cry but she blinked and smiled, and then gave the girls a hug.

"The wheel is darned good and busted," Talbot said. "You think we can fix it, Dirk?"

At the moment Dirk doubted the wagon wheel could ever be repaired, at least not well enough to stand any real heavy jolting. The last part of the trip, across the mountains, was the worst, Pa had said.

They were all watching Dirk when he straightened up from the wheel. "There was a blacksmith at the place where we crossed. He had a forge fixed up near the river and was doing some work. After a little while, maybe I'll ride back there...."

"That big red-headed man with all the girls?" Talbot shook his head. "He went on with the others. His wagon was the second one across the river."

Dirk remembered now. He was all mixed up between yesterdays and now, and where they had been and where they were trying to go. He was tired and hot. He thought of the cool orchards on Grandfather Sterns's place back home.

"We got to unload the wagon, first thing," he said.

"Yeah, we should have before...." Missouri stopped. She was sharp-tongued and critical, but when there was bad trouble she always did her part.

They piled their possessions on the grass, clothing, bedding, a few pieces of furniture, dishes and tools. They really didn't have very much to fight this country with, Dirk thought. The feel of the vastness all around him came back with frightening oppressiveness. What they ought to do was turn right around and find some way to get back home.

Talbot got the big wrench and started loosening the wheels on the side that was up.

"What are you doing?" Dirk asked.

Talbot had thought it out, but he never could explain with words very well. His idea, when he finally got it out, was to remove the wheels and put skids under the wagon so the horse could drag it on up to a level place. Hugh took an axe and rode on to find trees for skids and pry poles to turn the wagon right side up. All of them together couldn't turn it. Talbot started to dig around the broken wheel.

"What's that for?" Dirk asked.

"We got to dig under the wheels, so we can get a hole big enough to get at the nuts." Some folks thought Talbot was slow because he wasn't much to talk. Around strangers he didn't talk at all.

The shovels slipped and skidded on the grass. Underneath were root masses two feet deep, twined and intertwined. They grubbed with hoes and hacked with the edges of shovels. Ma was right about this being a country where it would take twenty horses to pull the plough. They burrowed under the hubs. Dirk lay on his back, with dirt and roots dropping in his face. He finally got the hub nuts off.

It was simple then to tip the wagon over in its skids. Sunset was with them when the horses pulled the box up the hill. They carried up their possessions and loaded them inside. A half mile ahead stood the grove of cottonwoods where Hugh had got the skids. Pulling steadily on the slick grass of level ground, Vick and Ten took the wagon to the trees, and there they stopped of their own accord, as if they knew their destination. The biggest spring the family had seen so far lay in the middle of the grove.

With the backwash of sunset crimson on the choppy hills around this plateau the Breslins sat wearily on the ground, too beaten at the moment to think of a fire and supper.

"Breakwagon Hills, they sure named 'em right," Hugh said.

Lafayette giggled, and then they were all laughing together. When it was over, Dirk wondered what kind of meanness there was in him to make him slap Lafayette when he was scared and crying.

Ma got up. "Build a fire Talbot," she said.

She cooked an extra special supper that night. Afterward, around the fire, she led them in their evening hymn. There was a beauty in the words and tune that Dirk had never noticed before. He would look back years later and remember this night as one of the happiest times in the Breslins' lives. He fell asleep sitting on a log.

They had no intention of staying where they were. For three days the older boys worked to fashion wheel spokes with a draw knife from one of the heavy oaken sideboards of the wagon. Their hands were sore and festering with the bitter bite of splinters, but they were slowly making headway. And then the red-headed blacksmith came back from the Topknot with his family. Josh Burrage was his name. His seven girls were all named after women of the Bible. He looked at the Breslins' handiwork.

"You boys have done right good there, but I misdoubt anything but a new wheel will cure your trouble. I had two spares when I passed here, but I sold one and then I busted a wheel and had to use the last one myself. I'm going back to the river place now. The Topknot country is crowded bad. Folks came in from the north way long before we got there. There's just a couple of little cricks and not near enough land to go around."

Burrage stayed two days. At the end of that time the Breslins' broken wheel was rebuilt, good enough for light work, Burrage said. He helped the boys put their wagon together again. Ma wanted to pay him. He shook his head and drove away, with his seven girls all yelling good byes to Missouri and Cree and Ma.

"I guess old Coupland was right about the Topknot," Hugh said. "Let's buy us a few hundred cows and stay right here."

Ma looked out on the Breakwagon Hills. "I think that must be the thing to do."

Long afterward Dirk realized what courage and flexibility were necessary for her to make that statement. Now he asked, "How can we buy cows?"

"We can't," Ma said. "We have about enough money to buy food through the winter, if there are any supply wagons coming this way."

"There must be," Talbot said. "Old Burrage said he was going to set up his shop at the river place. All them fire-headed girls got to have something to eat."

"That Rachel was a kind of pretty one," Hugh mused.

Missouri snorted. "Huh! She didn't say the same about you, Hugh Adams Davis Breslin!"

When Dirk realized they were stuck with staying where they were or trying to go back, with a wheel that would not last, he was scared once more. Farming here would be almost impossible. They lacked

520 / Steve Frazee

money to buy cows. All that night he could not sleep. The plateau was hot. The leaves hung silently on the cottonwoods. Dirk heard his mother and the girls stirring restlessly in the wagon. Over and over he thought of the slices of apples his grandfather used to cut for him when they walked together in the orchards. It was torture. Most likely there never would be fruit out here. Or anything else. Just land and no end to it. Dirk was hungry to the point of sickness for just one bite of apple, but he knew it was really not the fruit he craved—he was sick for everything safe and familiar, now lost, far away. Hot and tense he lay on his blanket, staring at the dark sky.

It was odd, he thought, that Hugh had talked so little of Pa from the time the wagon floated across the river. Hugh was not one to forget. Thoughts of Pa came out of the silent night to Dirk. He blinked away tears.

They started a cabin the next day. It was to be a temporary shelter. The green cottonwoods were heavy, and the dry dead ones were like long corkscrews and bitter hard to cut. Dirk tried to file the axe as he had seen Pa file it, and then it was duller than ever.

"Here, Talbot, you try it."

Talbot did the job, and then the axe was truly sharp. "In a rough country," Talbot said, staring a moment into nowhere, "you get rough yourself to lick it." Pa had said that, way back there where they first saw the hills.

They built a cabin of crooked logs, the corners out of plumb. They daubed it with mud from the marshy ground and the mud dried and fell out. Hugh killed a deer in the timber farther west, the first large animal he had ever killed. He brought it in on Mitch, leading the horse, half running in his excitement. Talbot was at once interested in the hide and hair. Before long he was chopping hair from the skin with his knife. He mixed the hair with mud and then he had a daubing material that did not fall apart easily even when dry.

"Who told you about that?" Hugh asked.

Talbot shook his head. "Nobody. I never saw a deer before. The idea just come to me, that's all."

Two more wagons of discouraged settlers came by on their way back to the river. They had been too late in the Topknot country; all the land left there was on rocky slopes.

A few days later Judge Coupland rode his Kentucky horse up to the Breslins' cabin. Since they had seen him the last time, he had started to grow a beard—to build up the narrowness of his chin, Missouri said afterward—and he was wearing a wide-brimmed hat.

"I'm glad to see you've decided to settle here, Missus Breslin," Coupland said.

"We didn't decide," Missouri said. "We busted down and had to light."

Coupland laughed. He inspected the outside walls of the cabin and pronounced the structure a good job. When he saw the deer hair in the daubing, he frowned and asked, "Now there's an idea! Yours, Dirk?"

"Him." Dirk pointed at Talbot, who got red in the face and looked at the ground.

"Why, he's three years younger than you, Dirk," Coupland said.

"Yes, but Talbot thinks of things," Missouri said. "Dirk just swallows hard and scowls and gives orders to everybody like he knew what he was doing."

Dirk grinned weakly, "You, Misery," he said, but he knew his sister was right.

Coupland stayed for dinner. He said there was a sort of town beginning to form at the river crossing. "Oh, nothing yet, just the idea, but there will be a town there, I'm sure. I've taken up a townsite."

The saloon was still going and another man had started a store in a tent. Judge Coupland spoke of streets and buildings, of a flour mill, a bridge, and other things as if they were already in existence. One thing was sure, Dirk thought—the new land didn't scare Coupland a darned bit. Of course he was a grown man, and he probably had a lot of money and knew just what he was going to do.

"Hang onto this place, Missus Breslin," Coupland said. "You have rights as a soldier's widow...file on this land. I'll help you all I can. Have Dirk bring you to the river as soon as possible so I can get the papers started on their way."

Ma studied the judge. He wasn't much for looks, what with his beard just starting to sprout raggedly on his chin, but there was a sincere expression about him. After a while Ma said, "I'll start back with you today, Mister Coupland."

Missouri was all excited at once. "You mean we'll make our farm here, Ma?"

"I don't know what we'll have," Ma said. She looked around at her family quickly. Dirk could see she was worried. "I'll take the girls with me," she said. "Cree can ride behind me and Missouri can ride Mitch."

The judge watched Dirk and Hugh saddle the horses. "Maybe you boys are too young to know it, but you have a wonderful mother. Take care of her. Help her hold this land. In time you may be able to control the whole south half of the Breakwagon Hills."

Hugh grinned. "Maybe the north half too." He didn't even know there was a north half.

Coupland pushed his lips out. "Well, I hear that four or five wagons of disappointed folks from the Topknot lit up north of here. You'll have enough to hold this part."

Ma and the girls rode away with Coupland. For once, Lafayette didn't cry. He had accepted the cabin as home.

"We'd better do some exploring," Hugh said to Dirk, "if we're going to own all this country."

They rode bareback on Vick and Ten, fat and strong once more from the rich grass of the plateau. Five miles west, from the top of one of the higher hills, they saw only more hills that gathered in little swirls, that rose and twisted crazily like the waves of great currents smashing against each other. To the south it was the same, farther than they could see. Groves of cottonwoods stood green and tall to mark a hundred springs. All the land was covered with tall grass. It waved at them from the summits of the hills; it was belly deep on the horses in the troughs between the hills.

Hugh was awed. "I didn't know this was such a big country." On the return trip, when the sun was low, Hugh said with sudden seriousness, "When we going to get that pistol, we talked about?"

"We got one already."

"You said we'd get another, Dirk."

"What for do we need it now?"

"Some day we got to go find the man that killed Pa. A man with scorpion eyes and a nice white shirt and big long fingers."

Hugh spoke so coldly and surely that Dirk was shocked. "He's gone away, Hugh. No telling where."

"He won't go too far for me. When are we going to get another pistol, Dirk?"

Dirk thought he should have known better than to make a promise to Hugh, and then try to forget it. He had meant the promise when he made it, but now the memory of Pa was not quite so powerful. Still, he had made the promise. He said, "When we can, we'll get it. There ain't no place around here that sells things like that." And they had no money.

"All right." Hugh showed that he had expected more.

Squire and Tommy Bascomb were sitting on the woodpile when Dirk and Hugh got back to the cabin. Lafayette was on the doorstep. There was a bruise on his cheek and Dirk saw at once that he had been crying.

"Where's Talbot?" Dirk asked.

"In the house." Lafayette glared at the Bascombs.

"You hit him, huh?" Dirk said. "You picked on him and Talbot. Now me and Hugh are here."

The Bascombs rose. Squire kept his hand on a short piece of wood. "We didn't come down here for no fight. Pa got hurt and Ma said to...."

"You hit Lafayette, didn't you?" Hugh accused.

"No, he didn't!" Lafayette cried. "I hit him first. He pushed me over a log and my face...."

"Picking on a little kid like that." Hugh snatched a piece of wood from the pile and advanced on Squire.

"Nobody got hurt!" Lafayette said. "Talbot was showing me how he would build a bridge like old Coupland said across the river and Squire stepped on one end of it and busted it and...."

"Never mind," Dirk said. He picked up another club when he saw Tommy take one.

"Now, look here," Squire said. "We're sorry about the little bridge. I didn't mean to bust it. Pa got hurt and Ma sent us down here to see if your Ma could come. We didn't want to start no fight."

"That's a big lie about your Pa, I bet," Hugh said. "Drop that club if you don't want to start no fight."

Squire tossed the firewood back on the pile, and then Tommy did likewise. Hugh threw his club away. "That's better," he said. He hit Squire in the stomach. Dirk rushed in and smothered Tommy just as he reached down to retrieve his club.

Tommy wasn't much of a problem. Sitting on him, Dirk had time to look around at Hugh and Squire. Hugh wasn't having any luck this second time. He just kept boring in and taking a beating. When he tried to butt Squire in the belly, Squire leaped back and Hugh went sprawling.

Talbot came out. Quite calmly he watched a moment when the fight resumed, and then he picked up a piece of wood, hefted it, reversed his grip, and rapped Squire on the head. Squire went down like a pole-axed beef. Still boring in, Hugh fell over him.

"That wasn't fair!" Dirk carried. "Hugh was...."

"You aimed to hurt him, didn't you, Hugh?" Talbot tossed his club away.

"Sure I did! I would have licked him, too, but...."

"Now he's licked. That's the idea of fighting, ain't it?" Talbot was surprised at the reaction to his method of reaching a goal so readily and easily. He went inside. Later, when Dirk went in, Talbot was reading one of Pa's books that told how steam locomotives were made.

Squire got up and staggered around, holding his head. Dirk felt sorry for him. "You want some water?"

"I want nothing you got. Come on, Tommy." The Bascombs climbed on their horses. "This was a fine thing, Dirk Breslin. We come down here for help when Pa was hurt, maybe dying, and this is what we got."

It was Talbot who had cracked Squire on the head, but Squire talked like it was Dirk. That's what happened when you started being the boss: you got all the blame.

The Bascombs rode away. "Maybe their Pa *was* hurt," Hugh said. "I kind of like old Bolivar."

"I tried to tell you, me and Talbot wasn't mad at them!" Lafayette shrilled. "Their Pa got hurt when a horse fell on him when he was dragging logs for a cabin. We didn't remember when Ma said she was coming back, so they were waiting to ask you and Dirk."

Ma came back from the river place—it was being called Coupland's Crossing by some—two days later. She rode at once north to find the Bascombs' camp, taking Dirk with her.

The cabin was much like the one the Breslins had built, except there were higher hills around and a small spring-fed stream beside it. The Bascombs were burying Bolivar when Ma and Dirk reached there.

Mrs. Bascomb was right glad to see Dirk and Ma. She cried a lot and Dirk could see she wasn't just carrying on. There never was any mention of the fight between the boys. Before Dirk and Ma left to go home the next day, Dirk was quite sure the Bascomb boys had not said a word at home about the fight. He was real sorry for them, and he tried to say something nice to Squire and Tommy. Tommy was willing to hear, but Squire took him by the arm and led him away from Dirk.

"Somebody down your way may get hurt some time," Squire said. He was almost bawling.

<hr />

The racket borne in by the hot summer wind was something to scare a person. It came swelling out of the hills southwest of the Breslin place. "Them are cattle!" Hugh cried. He was hopping around with excitement, and then ran to saddle Mitch. Almost immediately he came running back.

"Suppose it's somebody settling on our land with cattle!" he yelled. "You get Pa's pistol, Dirk. I'll get my rifle."

"You get nothing of the sort," Ma said. "That isn't our land down there. You can ride down and see what it is, but that's all."

The land was covered with them, great, high-shouldered brutes with horns as wide as a man's reach. They were thicker than sheep in Grandfather Stearns's east pasture at lambing time. Here and there a rider sat, all slouched and careless, on the hills that overlooked the herd.

Dirk and Hugh worked closer to the smoke they saw. Brindle monsters with wild eyes and clashing horns made way for them readily. Hugh whooped. He kicked at the high backs with bare feet, having a time.

Five men were sitting on bedrolls near a wagon, eating from tin plates. They were all burned dark by the sun, tall men, with cold eyes. Although each face was different, there was a mark of similarity about them all. The sixth man, much older than the rest, walked with a limp. But like the rest, he wore a pistol under the dirt-iest flour sack apron Dirk had ever seen.

"Hi, there, buttons," one fellow said. His hat was black, covered with dust and the band was frayed. His eyes were the cold color of Hugh's eyes when he was fighting, but they were bedded in friendly crinkles and the man's voice was soft, with a long drawl to it. "Light down and get your grub."

"You fellows figure to settle here?" Dirk swallowed hard.

The blue-eyed man said, "Just for a few days, son. Your land?"

Dirk nodded. They were all staring at his bare feet. Hugh was ready to eat but he was uncertain about the preliminaries.

"Plate there in the wreck pan, kid," one of the fellows said.

Hugh looked all around him. "There!" the cook said sourly, pointing at a dishpan with plates on edge in water. "There ain't nothing wrong with 'em. Chaco and the day guard just et off them plates, that's all. Slosh one around and give it a swipe on your sleeve!"

"He ain't got much sleeve left, Cookie," one of the 'punchers said.

Dirk and Hugh sloshed and swiped. There was pan bread and beans, poured over with molasses, and coffee to float a wedge.

The blue-eyed man's name was Rusty. He was burned so dark Dirk couldn't see any reason for the name until the fellow tipped his hat back and revealed a thatch of dark red hair. The others were Luke, Brazos, Hull, and Johnny. They called the cook about four different names, never the same one twice. After a while Rusty told the crew to circle around the herd and see that no cattle were straying.

"I get seasick here," Brazos said. "Ain't there no level ground anywhere in this country?"

"Over by our place," Hugh said. "We got a nice flat stretch over there."

"I'll come over," Brazos said. "Just so I can lay down straight. Every night it's the same. I sleep with my feet up on one hill, my back up another, and my rear end in the bottom of a gully. I'm gradually taking the shape of a horseshoe."

"You'll make it," Rusty said. "Wait till we start north again. If we run into what we've heard about, you'll wish you had a gully to jump into."

Hugh kept looking at the pistol on Rusty's hip. "What's one of them worth?"

"Your life," Rusty said, "when you need to use it."

"I mean money."

"What for do you need a pistol, button?"

"I got to kill a man some day," Hugh said.

"Yeah?"

"He's a gambler. He killed our father."

Rusty accepted it just as Hugh gave it. Dirk was startled. He could see that Hugh and Rusty seemed to understand each other very well.

"Take a pistol like this," Rusty said, "it's worth about seven steers." He looked north. "Might be worth the whole herd."

"What's up there?" Hugh asked.

"Some people. This'll be the second Texas herd that's tried to get through."

"I ain't got seven steers," Hugh said. "But I need a gun like that Rusty."

The words were downright begging, Dirk thought, but they didn't seem to strike Rusty that way. He kept looking at Hugh, and there was something that passed between him and Dirk's brother that left Dirk standing apart, removed from their tight circle of understanding.

"Who are the menfolks in your outfit?" Rusty asked.

"Us," Hugh said. "We own all this land." He swept his arm around carelessly. "When we get some cows, we'll have the biggest ranch there ever was."

Rusty smiled thinly, "You ever see a big ranch in big country, bub?"

"No," Dirk said. "This will be big enough for us."

Rusty looked from one of them to the other. The oldness and the hardness of his face had not been so obvious until this moment when, by contrast, a half musing boyish smile changed his features. He looked then not much older that the two who faced him.

"I used to think I'd have a ranch some day myself." He went to his horse and swung up. The toughness was on him again. "Ride over another time," he said. "We'll be here a few more days."

His leggy dun went up a steep hill with a powerful surge. Hugh looked sadly at old Put and Mitch.

The cook was washing dishes. He eyed them with disfavor. "You won't ever have no ranch by standing around," he said. They thanked him for the food and rode away.

"What was the idea of begging for a pistol?"

"It wasn't begging. I just told him I needed one. He knew it too."

Rusty had understood, Dirk admitted, but he himself could not understand, and knew he would never understand the thing that had passed between Hugh and the Texan. They were alike in one manner.

Twice more the boys rode to the camp, staying longer each time. On their way home the second time, Hugh said, "Those fellows are going to move tomorrow."

"They didn't say so."

"Couldn't you tell? They didn't talk any and joke with each other like before. There's a gang of whites and Indians north of here where they're going. Rusty said they wiped out the drovers of the first herd that tried to go through. We ought to go along to help, Dirk."

"They wouldn't let us and you know it!"

"We didn't ask. They're our friends, and besides we'd get a pistol out of it, maybe two. They all got extra pistols."

"You want a pistol awful bad, don't you?"

"I got to have it," Hugh said simply. "You know why."

It was true that Pa's old pistol wasn't much shakes. Dirk sighed. The country was tough, all right; and Hugh was growing tough along with it. Dirk thought of the peaceful farms back home. Now the thought carried only a contrast, and not a desire to retreat.

"We can't do it, Hugh. Not for a dozen pistols."

"I guess not." Hugh began to whistle.

The bawling of the longhorns was more frenzied than ever at daylight the next morning. Standing in the pearl-gray dawn in front of the Breslin cabin, the Breslin boys listened to the sounds rolling up from the green hills. Hugh and Dirk could read them now. They knew when the bawling began to subside that the herd had been lined out and was moving north.

"I thought maybe Rusty would come by," Hugh said when the herd was almost out of earshot. He did not sound disappointed. Dirk watched him suspiciously, but all that day Hugh gave no sign that the going of the cattle had left any void in him.

He was gone at dawn the next day, and so was Mitch. Dirk restrained an urge to run and throw a saddle on old Put immediately, but there was no use to get his mother and the others upset.

"Well, Hugh went hunting again, I guess," Dirk said at breakfast.

Ma Breslin nodded, but Dirk saw at once that she knew better. The younger ones didn't seem to catch on, but Missouri said,

"Hunting, your foot! He run off with that bunch of cowboys and you know it! Ever since they've been here Hugh has been like a hop-toad on hot cinders."

"Missouri," Ma said.

"Well, he…," Missouri subsided.

"He might need help with his deer, Dirk," Ma said. "Maybe you'd better ride after him. I worry sometimes about him hunting all by himself."

Dirk would have leaped away at once, but his mother held him at the table with her glance.

She stood beside him when he saddled old Put. Her fear was then stark. "Why did he do it, Dirk?"

"Rusty and the others are our friends and they're going to have a fight."

"A gunfight…? He won't be sixteen until next month." Ma looked way off into distance. Still fifteen, but he was big enough for twenty; and he could stand before a man like Rusty and talk like a man. He wanted a pistol like the Texan carried, and he was willing to go into a fight to gain it. "Put your shoes on, Dirk," Ma said. "You'd better wear them all the time now. Go by the Bascombs' and ask…."

"I don't need Squire's help."

"In this land everyone needs the help of everyone else foolish enough to come here." Ma wasn't given to talking like that. It rattled Dirk. He fumbled with the cinch. "No," she said an instant later. "It was not foolish to come here. Bring him back, Dirk."

For a while Dirk was afraid he might not be able to follow the trail, but he was never off it. Gradually his confidence in that matter was restored. He didn't know exactly when Hugh had left, but he did know when the herd had moved out of the hills southeast of the Breslin place. He figured two days would be enough for him to catch up.

Before that he learned of the traveling abilities of longhorn cattle. Four nights he camped, and by then he was across the steep buff sandstone escarpment that separated the north and south parts of the Breakwagon Hills, and he was deep into sagebrush country where there were only miles and sky ahead of him—and no dust cloud on the horizon. Off to the left were the mountains, standing purple and gray. Beyond them lay the Topknot. Antelopes skimmed across the flats before him. He followed them with Pa's old rifle, clicking his tongue instead of the trigger, wondering where his shots would have gone, wondering, too, whether he could shoot a man if he reached the herd before the trouble started. Maybe there would be no trouble. But he remembered the lean hard faces that last night at the campfire, and the silence of the Texans.

On the sixth day, when he had no food except salt to put on antelope meat, it came to him why he was not gaining as he should have. Old Put was slow, it was true, but for several days, Dirk decided, the herd had been traveling this flat country by night as well as by day, resting only briefly at water holes.

The eighth day came racing over the sage, bursting quickly on all the vast horizons. Dirk had no idea of where he was or how far he had gone. The tracks of the herd were still there before him, and that was all. It was mid-morning when he heard the firing far ahead. There was nothing he could see up there. He was alone in the middle of distance.

Put stopped and threw his head high, listening, and then he lost interest in the sounds. Dirk sat there, scared and lonely, with one hand resting on the hot gray hairs of old Put's shoulder. It sounded to Dirk like one of the battles Pa used to talk about. Dirk went ahead at a trot.

The firing went on and on. It must be a hell of a fight, Dirk thought. He kept swallowing. Pa's rifle was across his knees, loaded and cocked. There came the sounds of bawling longhorns again, and before long cattle were streaming toward him. They broke around old Put and went on, long-legged brutes that ran as if they would reach Texas before nightfall. Then, to the left and right, far ahead, he saw the dust of other racing steers. The herd must have been in a depression, around a brackish water hole such as ones Dirk had passed. Where was Hugh? Dirk tried to make old Put gallop, but he did well to keep him going against the cattle. Put wanted to turn and run with them.

All at once the longhorns were gone. Now the firing was almost done. Ahead of Dirk was dust that veiled everything. He heard the sound of a rifle bullet somewhere off to his left. He ducked. He felt he was too high in the saddle, and so he leaped down and went on, leading old Put into the dust. It began to settle and then he saw three riders coming toward him at a gallop. One, he was sure, was on

Rusty's dun; a little later he recognized Mitch and saw Hugh, hatless, his straw-colored hair flapping wildly.

There where five or six riders chasing the first three. When Dirk saw them, fear clutched his stomach with a twisting grip. He wanted to run, but he was afraid to turn his back to the sound of bullets that whistled overhead once more. Rusty and the others did not fire back. They merely rode.

They came up to Dirk as he stood with the knotted end of the reins in the crook of one elbow, with his rifle lifted above the sage toward the five horsemen. He was aware that Hugh was alive, unharmed, that Rusty's face was full of bitterness and shame, that Brazos was gray and open-mouthed. Dirk lined his rifle on a dark horse scudding close to the sage. It was an antelope, he told himself. The old rifle roared. Rank powder smoke swirled back in Dirk's face. He saw the rider standing in air for an instant and then a great bloom of fresh dust where the horse and man went tumbling.

"Let 'em in close!" Rusty said. "I lost my rifle back there." He was standing beside Dirk with his hot pistol still in his hand.

Brazos had fallen from his horse and was lying on his back, breathing hard. Hugh came running over to Dirk. "Gimme some shells!"

"Won't fit your rifle," Dirk mumbled. He was watching a gray horse now, and was almost ready to fire again.

"They fit my pistol!" Hugh said. He dug into his brother's pocket.

"Let 'em come right in," Rusty said. "All the way."

Dirk didn't want them any closer. He did not want to see clearly a man's face or form when he shot. He knocked the gray horse over.

Dirk dropped three cartridges when he tried to reload. He stooped to find them in the dust and, when he rose again three horses, two carrying double, were going away from him.

Rusty cursed. "The two on the roan, Dirk!"

Dirk stared at them. They were running away. He lowered the rifle. Rusty grabbed it from him. He shot and the man riding behind the saddle on the roan fell backward over the horse's rump. Before Rusty reloaded the horses were well out of rifle range.

Rusty handed the rifle back. "I don't generally grab a man's gun thataway." He went over to Brazos and asked quietly, "How bad?"

Brazos rolled his head, smiling. There was blood on his lips. "I won't see Texas this fall, Rusty."

IV

They camped that night where the sage was head high around the slick sides of a water hole. Brazos died in the dark, with Rusty sitting beside him, telling him how Texas would look when they reached there in a few weeks.

The last thing Brazos said was, "Don't let anybody take my boots off, Rusty. They're still on, ain't they?"

"Still on, son. You'll wear 'em back to that little place on the Canadian. You'll...."

Afterwards Rusty sat alone in the dark. "You two get some rest," he said.

Several times during the night Dirk heard Rusty prowling wide circles around the camp. In a bare space where the ground was honeycombed by prairie dogs they buried Brazos the next day. Rusty gave one of his pistols to Hugh and the other one, with the belt and holster, to Dirk. Dirk thought he knew why he got the best of it: he had blundered up at a critical time and, too scared to run, he had given Rusty and Hugh a chance to stand and fight. Later, he would give the belt and holster to Hugh.

"They didn't get all the herd," Hugh said. "Some of them ran south." He was wearing a pair of cowboy boots now. His old shoes were hanging on his saddle horn.

"They got enough." Rusty was tense and bitter. They never saw him smile again. "It was my blunder, thinking we wouldn't get jumped in the middle of daylight."

They went on up to the water hole. The wagon was gone. The raiders had stripped the bodies of the dead Texans. Someone had hacked off Hull's finger to get a ring. "He gave me these boots, Hull did," Hugh said, bitter then as Rusty who muttered to himself in Spanish while they were burying the cowboys in the gray land.

In the northern Breakwagons they found part of the herd. The Bascomb boys were looking at them from the top of a hill. Squire didn't budge when Hugh ran his horse at him.

"Don't try to steal none of these!" Hugh said.

"Who was?" Squire looked at Hugh's pistol. "They're on our land."

"You're sure claiming plenty of country, Squire."

"So are you Breslins…and acting big with them guns stuck in your belt." The Bascombs rode away.

Rusty had not spoken all day. Now he said, watching Squire and Tommy, "You got two things you can do, make up with them boys so the northern end of your range will always be protected…or run 'em clear out of the country." He talked, Dirk thought, like the Breslins had a ranch already.

They pushed a hundred and thirteen cattle across the escarpment and into the southern part of the Breakwagons. "Culls," Rusty said. "Trail stuff. I'll come up this way next summer and I'll bring you a bull."

"You mean you're leaving the cattle here?" Dirk said.

Rusty was savage in an instant. "Do you think I'm driving 'em back to Texas?"

"How about the man who owns 'em?"

"I own 'em," Rusty said. "Now they're yours. I guess it wasn't in the cards for me to be nothing but a hand. I crossed the Big Red with a thousand and thirty-three head of mavericks. The farther we went, the tighter my hat got on my head…let it be a lesson to you two. You'll have to fight like hell for everything you get and then twice as hard to hang onto it." He looked north toward the escarpment. "Was I you boys, I'd smoke the pipe with those two we saw the other day. From the looks of that oldest one they ain't going to do much running."

Rusty had seen Squire Bascomb just once. He had sized Squire about right, Dirk thought.

"Now you got cattle and you got pistols," Rusty said. "You better learn how to handle both." He started the dun south.

"Hey!" Dirk said. "You can stay with us."

Rusty did not look back or hesitate. "Thanks, but this ain't my country." He rode into the southern sun, with the dust gray on his jacket and his black hat low to his eyes.

Dirk unstrapped the pistol belt and gave it to Hugh. He put his own pistol in his waistband. Pa had worn his gun like that the morning he had walked confidently toward the tent saloon. As soon as possible Dirk would get himself another belt.

Pa had been right; and Rusty had been right. You had to get tough with the country. But Dirk kept remembering the Texans he had helped bury. He doubted that he had the stomach for being tough.

He did not even have the desire. But now the Breslins were in the cattle business, and there would be people who would try to profit from the fact. Responsibility came down heavily on Dirk.

Hugh was sighting down his pistol. "What will we call this here outfit, Dirk?"

"The Brazos." B for Breslin—and the name of a man they had scarcely known, but he had fought beside Hugh, and he had smiled when he knew he was dying. The country needed that sort. Dirk had the feeling that he and Hugh had caught hold of something they could not easily release.

By the time they reached home Dirk's confidence was rising again. After all, they had done quite a bit in the last two weeks. They went through the grove of trees, past the spring, and up to the yard feeling happy.

The silence said no one lived here. They stared at each other, with their color fading.

"Hey!" Hugh cried. "Hey, Ma!"

Talbot came out of the house slowly. He blinked wearily, with his jaw sagging.

"Dirk and Hugh," he muttered.

He leaned against the logs and then slid down them to the ground and lay there. One moment they had been in the hard clean freedom of the hills, healthy young animals filled with a keen anticipation of homecoming. Now they stood where, it seemed, death had already struck. Not the violent shock of death they had seen around the water hole, that had come hard and swiftly, but the insidious, baffling creep of sickness.

Ma was in one bed with Missouri and Cree, and Lafayette was in his bed. Their faces were aglow with fever. Missouri was muttering to herself. A panicky terror that he hadn't felt from the song of bullets overhead gushed up to leave a coppery tang in Dirk's mouth.

"What'll we do, Dirk?" The smudge of campfires and the dust of riding lay on Hugh's face, and underneath he was white and stricken and young. "What'll we do, Dirk! What's the matter with them?"

"I don't know." Dirk stood several moments in the middle of the room, every instinct of his healthy body rejecting sickness. "Measles, maybe," he said.

"We all had measles!" Hugh picked up Talbot and carried him to the bed beside Lafayette. "He ain't hot at all, Dirk."

Dirk moved at last. He put his palm on Talbot's forehead. There was no fever. It came to him that Talbot was worn out from worrying and trying to take care of everyone else. His spirit had carried him until he saw relief, and then he had collapsed.

"Drink...Ma...," Missouri muttered.

"Go get Missus Bascomb, Hugh," Dirk said. He wanted to go himself, to run away—therefore he stayed. He had done things like that ever since Pa's death.

He heard Mitch go into a run. He sponged the faces on the beds with cool water. He gave them water when they called for it and, once during the endless day and the day that followed, Missouri looked at him with recognition and spoke his name. Then she slipped away into the red mists once more. Talbot was helping then. All he knew was that everyone had taken sick just a few days after Hugh and Dirk rode north.

Mrs. Bascomb came with Callie and Hugh that night. She walked into the room with a quickness surprising for her size. "Well," she said, "the whole danged layout, nearly, just like Hugh said." There was something reassuring in her manner.

"What is it they got?" Dirk asked.

"I'd say slow fever. That's as good a guess as any."

"Will they all die?"

"The Lord will have that say, but Callie and me will try to influence Him a little. Now them that can walk clear out and give us a chance."

Hugh and Dirk and Talbot sat close together on the woodpile. From the cabin Mrs. Bascomb's voice boomed out cheerfully, giving orders to Callie, giving orders to the sick Breslins just as if they could hear and understand.

Once she came to the doorway and looked out. "You boys get to bed," she said. "And do some praying before you go to sleep, mind me."

The Breslin boys climbed into the wagon. "You two do what she said," Dirk ordered, fiercely.

"All right," Talbot said, "but tomorrow I'm going to clean that spring out. I been thinking everybody that camped here on the way to the Topknot might have thrown something dirty into it."

Dirk prayed silently that his mother and all the rest would get well. He promised to give half the cattle to the Bascombs, whether his folks got well or not. When that was done, he reached over and touched Hugh, who was still wearing his pistol belt and pistol.

"Did you pray, Hugh?"

Hugh was asleep.

The Breslins lived. They were weak for a long time, and Ma complained that she could scarcely walk ten feet without wanting to sit down. Mrs. Bascomb stayed ten days the first time, and she came back several times more during the late summer. Callie and Hugh were giggling at each other before it was over.

By then what Hugh and Dirk had done up north with Rusty was lost under the pressure of other events; they told only that Rusty had given them the cattle after his bunch had some bad trouble.

On a fall-sharp day Dirk rode out with Hugh and Talbot to look at the cattle. The longhorns had found the grass of the Breakwagon Hills to their liking. Talbot was wearing Pa's old pistol now. They stopped for target practice. Talbot was the slowest of the three, but he was the best shot. He used two hands and aimed carefully.

"We got to have a lot of shells," Dirk said. "We'll take a steer or two to the river place and see what we can do." And then he told them what he had promised to do with half the cattle.

"Oh, hell!" Hugh said. "Tommy and Squire didn't help Rusty's bunch any."

"Missus Bascomb helped us," Dirk said. "We'll give half the cattle to her, not the boys."

"The same thing," Hugh grumbled. "But since you made the promise…. If I hadn't fallen asleep that night, I would have promised only one third." He thought a while then he laughed.

They had one devil of a time cutting out half the herd. The longhorns seemed to skim the ridges and soar up the steep hills. Dirk had carried the thought of picking out the poorest of the bunch, since his promise involved numbers only, but before it was over he settled on anything they could separate from the herd. They drove fifty-four head north. That was a little short of half but Dirk figured the

Lord must have seen how hard longhorns were to handle. They pushed them as close as they could to the Bascomb place, and then the boys rode on in.

Callie and Hugh began to moon at each other immediately. Tommy and Talbot got friendly too, but Dirk and Squire just looked at each other. "We brought you half our herd, Missus Bascomb," Dirk said. "Almost half. There was some we couldn't catch."

"Why are you doing this?" The question and the steady inquiry of Mrs. Bascomb's eyes disconcerted Dirk.

He said, "You helped us…and besides, I guess you need 'em." There was also a feeling of guilt from the time Squire and Tommy had ridden down for help when their father was dying.

Mrs. Bascomb glanced toward the hill where Bolivar was buried. She seemed to understand everything in Dirk's mind. "Well, for heaven's sake, come in and eat! Callie, stop making sheep's eyes at that ugly no-account Hugh and set the table!" There were tears in Mrs. Bascomb's eyes.

Squire said, "We don't need their cattle, Ma." He took a step toward Dirk. "We don't need nothing from you, Dirk Breslin."

"Squire!" Ma Bascomb said. "That's no way…."

"Uh-huh." Squire shook his had "Take your cows buuk."

It came to Dirk that Mrs. Bascomb was no longer the complete boss here, just as Ma Breslin was no longer the leader in the Breslin home. Dirk saw in Squire some of the same qualities he possessed, only stronger and more clearly defined. They both had started to grow up fast under the pressure of the country and loss of fathers.

"I want you to have the cattle, Squire."

Squire shook his head.

"Let's go, Hugh," Dirk said.

"Take your cattle with you!"

Hugh and Dirk rode away, leaving the Bascombs wrangling. They were all upbraiding Squire.

Hugh grinned about it. "He'll have to take 'em. He can't hold out against all that racket."

That was probably true, Dirk thought, but Squire wouldn't be pleased, and he would blame Hugh and Dirk for putting him in a spot where he would have to back down.

The Breslins drove three cows to the river place. They started with four but one turned back and they couldn't head it. "We got to have some horses," Hugh grumbled. "Ours were never nothing but wagon horses to begin with."

"First we got to have plenty of shells," Dirk said. He was thinking of the raiders who had taken the Texas herd. If the Brazos ranch—the name wasn't sticking too well in his mind yet—and the Bascomb place began to prosper a little, they would inevitably draw attention from the shadowy men up north.

The river was down now. There was a ferry cable across it and a boat. It took Talbot just a minute to figure out how the current could be used to pull the boat both ways.

"Houses over there now," Hugh said.

They pushed the three cows into the stream. There were only two deep places where all the animals were forced to swim. The Breslins felt important when they emerged on the other side, with men looking at them from every doorway. Now there were two saloons, a wooden store building, and a real estate office.

Judge Coupland came from the real estate office. "I've missed you boys. How's your ma? Where have you been all summer?"

"Most of the folks was sick," Hugh said. "We thought you might be out, but...."

"I was gone all summer," Coupland said. "Just got back two days ago from trying to raise money and settlers back East. I got some of the last but the first is sort of scarce. Your cattle?"

"We come by them fair and honest," Dirk said.

Coupland nodded toward the store. "Ben Carmody can use them. How much do you want?"

The Breslins looked at each other.

"Eight dollars a head is not bad," Coupland said. "You'll have to take half of it in trade, I imagine."

Dirk and Talbot went into the store with Coupland. There was very little on shelves but considerable in boxes on the floor. Parts of the carcasses of two steers were hanging near a butcher block at the back of the room. Carmody was a thin man with a wide spade beard and sad brown eyes.

"You need some more meat, Ben," Coupland said.

Carmody shook his head, pointing at the steers.

"Sell it, sell it!" Coupland said. "What are you keeping it here for?"

"I could sell plenty of everything," Carmody said sadly, "all on credit."

"That's the ticket, Ben! Everything out here is credit. You lose a lot of course, but in the end you make a town. We got three prime steers outside...."

"Cows," Dirk said.

"Three prime pieces of meat," Coupland said. "Ten dollars a head. Put up a few signs. When folks want credit, let 'em have it!"

"That's what broke me back home," Carmody said.

"If you go bust, we all do," Coupland said. "Then we'll go on and try again. Ten dollars a head, then?"

"You trample a man under, Judge," Carmody said. "Seven."

"Prime stock, Ben. Make it nine dollars a head."

"Eight. All in trade."

"Half in trade," Dirk said.

It was settled.

Outside, Coupland said, "Tell your ma I'll be out in a few days." He gathered up three men from the crowd that had grown around the cows, and took them up the street toward his office. Two of them didn't seem to want to go badly, but Coupland took them along, talking a steady stream about the advantages of buying lots and settling in Coupland's Crossing.

Dirk divided the boxes of ammunition he had taken in part trade for the cows. They drove the animals to a corral behind the store.

"Somebody sold four steers here two days ago," Hugh said. "They had Rusty's trail brand on 'em. The fellows, two of 'em, are down the street in the River Saloon right now, a man said."

"Let them stay there," Dirk said.

"They're sure to be two of the bunch that ruined us at the water hole," Hugh said. "They'll come down our way sooner or later, won't they?"

Dirk had thought the same thing himself. "What do you want to do about them? Anyway, Rusty said he was coming back next spring...and he won't be alone."

"He ain't here now," Hugh said. "They are."

Talbot was white. He said calmly, "Let Hugh look at them. If they're the ones he's talking about, the best thing to do is walk in and shoot them."

Dirk understood that it was a mechanical principle with Talbot, just a matter of going from one point to another in the simplest manner, but the coldness of the logic frightened him.

"Would you do that, Talbot?"

"If we had to, I would...talking about something is no good."

"Well?" Hugh said.

"We'll go down and look at them."

Hugh's eyes had turned pale. He was looking past Dirk. Two men were walking toward the corral, two whiskery men in ragged clothes. They were both about the same size, stocky men, dark-eyed and loose-lipped.

"That's them," Hugh breathed. "I remember those two. They killed Hull."

The pair came up to the corral. They looked at the trail brand on the cows and they looked at the Breslin boys and laughed.

One of them said, "Looks like we missed a few, Arn."

"Some of the bunch that ran south," Arn said. "Where'd you kids get them cows?"

Hugh said, "They're ours, mister."

"Stealing cattle is a hanging offense, son," Arn said. "How about that, Bill?"

"Yeah," Bill said, grinning. "It's"—suddenly he reached out and lifted Hugh's hat—"that stack of tow hair there, Arn...remember? There were three that rode south. Remember?"

Arn said softly, "Uh-uh, now I do."

How foolish he and his brothers had been talking. Dirk saw it all now—these two men could kill the three of them before the Breslins knew what was going on. Hugh had doubled up his fists, but now he realized that and was getting geared to reach for his pistol.

Dirk stepped between him and the two men. "Those are our cows," Dirk said.

Arn grinned. "No bill of sale, I'll bet. We'll let it go this time, but if you boys got any more cattle we'll have to ride down and see about it one of these days. We can't have cattle stealing around here."

"No!" Bill said. "That wouldn't do at all!"

The two men were laughing when the Breslins walked away. Dirk was in a cold rage because lies and injustice always revolted him. Hugh was stony-faced and silent because he thought he had failed. Only Talbot saw it clearly enough to speak of it.

"It's lucky we didn't get any ideas about being pistol fighters," he said.

It occurred to Dirk to tell Judge Coupland of the matter, but what could Coupland do? There was no law here, and it might be a long time before there ever was.

The Breslins tied their gunny sacks of supplies on their saddles and went across the river. On the way home they practiced with their pistols.

Missouri told them immediately that three families of farmers, baked out of the Topknot country after a hard summer, had settled near the Big Springs south of the Breslin place.

"That's not really our land," Ma said. "I don't know what we can do about it."

"We can run 'em off!" Dirk said.

Talbot asked, "Because we got run off in town?"

"Shut up, Talbot." Dirk thought about it. It was true enough that he was smarting because he had been forced to turn away from a situation. But there was also the fact that settlers in the Breakwagons would start tearing up the grass and building fences. Let them once get started, no matter how hard the soil was to plough, and they would creep all around the Breslins, ruining the land for cattle.

"The first thing in the morning," Dirk said, "we'll have to go run those people out."

Ma sighed. She saw the same things Dirk saw. "Talk to them," she said. "Show them that the land will never be good for farming."

V

They had hitched six horses to a plough, with a man on each handle. Even then it was killing work against the tough grass roots. All three families were working together on it, Dirk guessed, because there were enough kids and women in the Big Springs grove for at least three families.

One of the farmers reminded Dirk of Pa. The other two were little men, hard-handed, with furrowed faces. They stopped their work and greeted the Breslins civilly.

Dirk slouched in the saddle. Being on a horse gave him an advantage, he thought. Already it was setting him apart in his own mind from men who walked.

"This ain't much of a country for farming," he said.

One of the little men wiped sweat and grinned. "Give us time, bud. We're only scratching now, but we'll have fifty acres busted come spring. Once that sod is turned up so the weather and sun can start the roots to rotting, we'll have the grass licked."

"Not much water though," Dirk said.

"The springs'll do."

The man who looked like Pa caught on first. His eyes narrowed but he asked good naturedly, "What's on your mind?"

"You'll have to move," Hugh said. "This is our land."

"You got filing right on it?"

Dirk shook his head.

"Then nobody moves."

"We got cattle here," Dirk said. "The land is ours by right of use." He had heard Rusty use the expression.

"There ain't no such thing," one of the men said. "Come on, boys, let's get back to our work."

The change in the nature of the conversation had carried to the grove, and now the women and some of the older kids were coming out.

"Don't start the teams," Hugh said. His pistol was out.

The tall man laughed. "Well by Ned, boys! Three snub-nosed brats on plough horses themselves...." He spoke to the teams.

Hugh fired into the ground three times under the bellies of the lead team. The horses snorted and reared, then lunged ahead. One man still clinging to the handle on his side of the plough was thrown over it as the point went deep and jammed into the grass roots.

The Breslins stood by with drawn pistols and watched the three families load their gear and drive away toward the river, and then they rode behind them half the day. Dirk saw everything that he had seen in his own family, and it sickened him. But Pa would not have run so easily.

This could have happened to the Breslins, but they had been pure lucky. Dirk did not like it at all; he had to keep telling himself that it had been necessary. Neither Hugh nor Talbot took any pride in the victory; and all three of them could remember that they had walked away from two men at the corral behind Ben Carmody's store.

There was one thing Dirk knew for sure—they were one step closer to holding on to the Breakwagons. They would have to see Coupland about getting some legal claim to the land. That business of possession by right of use did not seem very strong.

On the way home the Breslins practiced with their pistols some more. Talbot was still the best shot, and he still held Pa's gun in both hands when he aimed. The boys did not talk about the farmers they had scared away.

When they got home Ma looked at them and said in a quick, scared voice, "What happened?"

"They left," Dirk said. "Nobody got hurt, except a plough was busted and some harness torn up."

"Do we have to do these things?"

"If we're going to keep these hills, we do."

"If someone is killed, then will the whole land be worth it?"

"I don't know," Dirk said. "Do we want to stay here or not?" That, he realized after he had spoken, was where the truth lay.

"A land of violence," Ma said. She went inside.

The next morning the Breslins took a turn around the west side of their land to see about the cattle. They took Lafayette along on Ten, with only a rope halter as a rig. Lafayette, it seemed to Dirk, had more natural ease on a horse than any of them. Dirty brindle cattle tossed their horns at the four riders, but the longhorns were getting used to the range now and were not as wild as they had been. Yet, they were wild enough.

"They ought to be branded," Hugh said.

"How do we do that?"

"Rusty told me. We'll have Josh Burrage make us a stamp iron the next time we go to Coupland's Crossing. Then you rope a critter and dump him and burn the brand on him."

"How do you dump him?" Lafayette wanted to know.

"I saw Rusty do it," Hugh said.

"I saw Brazos take one by the tail one day and flip him end-over-katip, too," Dirk said. "But I don't think one of us could do that, even if our horses could get close enough."

"That little mare of Squire's that was so skinny on the wagon...she's pretty fast," Talbot said. "Maybe we'd better work with the Bascombs."

"We should have warned them about those two fellows, anyway," Dirk said.

"We better go do that right away."

Ma Bascomb said Squire and Tommy had gone to the river with six head to trade for supplies and pistols.

"Half the stuff you given is gone now," she said. "Tommy seen six, seven men round them up, bold as you please, and take 'em away north just yesterday."

"Didn't he do nothing?" Hugh asked.

"What could he do, him without a gun of no kind?"

"He couldn't do a thing," Dirk said. "What did we do in town, Hugh, when there were only two men and we had pistols?"

"Well, we'll do something the next time," Hugh said. He stared after Callie when she went toward the spring with a bucket. "You figure out something, Dirk, and then we'll do it."

"There was a full bucket of water in there a minute ago," Ma Bascomb said. "I'll swear that Callie girl throwed it out the window." She shook her head. "Come in for some tea, Dirk and Talbot. We'll have to talk about things."

The tea, Dirk guessed, must be better for a man than the bitter coffee he had drunk around the Texans' fire. He said, "We've got to stand together. If Squire will have it, we'd best drive your cows south of the big hill to our land. They'll be a little harder to get at there. Then we'd better brand 'em. After that...." He didn't know what came after that.

"We can start your herd down today," Talbot said. "If Squire will have it."

"I'm still the oldest one in this family," Ma Bascomb said, "but I will allow that Squire ain't no brat to be slapped any more. Take them cows, like you say."

On the way down with the cattle Hugh tried to tail over a big blue steer with white spots. He fell off his horse and was knocked cold. The herd scattered while his brothers stood around him. It took two and a half days to move the cattle. The Breslins lived on deer meat roasted over fires on sticks, without salt.

"You got to get tough with the country, I guess," Hugh said, "but I'm sure hungry."

On the last day of the drive he tried tailing another steer. He didn't flip it but he made it bawl and he did not fall off his horse.

"There's a way to do that," Talbot said. "I been figuring it out, but I'm not about to try the idea."

Judge Coupland was at the cabin when the boys returned. He had heard about their driving off the settlers.

"The right of use," he said, "is recognized more or less in some localities. It depends on how well you make it stick. The best thing, however, is for each of you boys to file on land. There seems to be a certain elasticity about fulfilling all the requirements. Strictly speaking...file on the land. I'll help with the details."

The way the judge was looking at Ma, with his mind only half on his words, Dirk thought he knew now why Coupland had been so helpful. It was a jolt to think of things that way, considering that Pa had been gone only a few months. But out here things seemed to move a little faster than back home.

When Squire and Tommy came down to see about their cattle, they both were wearing pistols. Squire was not quite as set against Dirk as he had been before. And Missouri—it became evident to Dirk that she thought Squire was all right.

Dirk told the Bascombs what Judge Coupland had said about filing homesteads, and so both groups went to town together to get that job started. Coupland was quite helpful in filling out the papers for them. He said he would take them to the land office later and although, he added, it was generally necessary for the persons filing to appear in the flesh, he said he had an understanding with the agent.

He leaned back in his chair. "Good farming land north of here a few miles," he said. "All it needs is a big canal from the river. Cattle country west, with maybe some small prosperity on the Topknot. Why, we'll have a great town here in good time. I've set aside a lot for each one of you boys. Some day you can pay me for them."

The judge believed in dealing the way he had advised Ben Carmody to do business, Dirk thought.

"One more thing," Coupland said. He opened a drawer and laid a pistol on his desk. "When you need a little help out your way...and you're going to, I fear...let me know."

He was mild, and he was also tough enough, Dirk decided.

The Breslins and the Bascombs were a bruised and sorry lot before they put their stamp irons on the last of their cattle. They learned that a steer or a cow has no love for a man on foot, that a branding iron should not be allowed to burn clean through the hide or used so lightly that it leaves only a hair brand, that a quick leap to the saddle and a rope across a steer's back must have saved many a man before them.

They learned a lot. They put the mark of their possession on longhorns. BR for the Breslins, Circle B for the Bascombs.

When the job was done, they took two days rest to let their burns and bruises heal. It was during that two days that eight men rode south across the escarpment and stole twenty head, driving them north without undue haste. In fact, the thieves had camped the first night within a day's easy ride of the Breslin cabin.

Squire said bleakly, "They figure widows and a bunch of kids are easy pickings. What are we going to do?"

"We could get Judge Coupland," Dirk said, but he had already rejected the idea. You had to stand up to the country and the men in it, or else you didn't belong in the country, or had no right to run squatters off the land and stamp a mark on cattle.

"Where do they take the cattle they steal?" Tommy asked. He was fingering his pistol.

"To the mining country way up north, I guess," Dirk said.

"How far is that?" Squire asked.

"It must be a long trip." Dirk thought of the days he had traveled the sage land, with only the sky and distance for company.

"They don't take 'em all up north," Talbot said. "That Arn and Bill sold some of them in town."

That was it. "If they do it again, there'll be a brand on every one," Dirk said. "Let's go to town."

When they reached the cottonwood cabin, Callie had just come down from the Bascomb place to say that a farmer was settling on the meadow east of the Bascombs'.

"We'll see about that later," Squire said.

Ma Breslin wanted to know what the boys intended to do if they found some of their cattle sold in town.

"Then we'll find the men," Hugh said.

They rode through the clear autumn air, five boys who were ranchers more or less by accident. At the willows along the river the water was low and green. From their side of the river they saw five critters in Carmody's corral.

Dirk swallowed hard. Squire stared across the water with the fighting light gleaming in his green eyes. Hugh slid his pistol up and down in its holster.

"You stay here, Talbot," Dirk said. "You stay here and cover our backs." It was the best he could think of to keep Talbot out of it.

Talbot put Vick into the stream along with the others. "I can shoot straighter than any of you."

He was too young. He was scared, but no worse than Dirk or Tommy. Dirk thought maybe Hugh and Squire lacked the imagination to see everything that might happen.

Judge Coupland met them at the ferry shanty at the foot of the street, among the cottonwood stumps. "Two men brought those cattle in last night," he said. "Josh Burrage saw the brands and told me. Carmody is stalling about buying the critters."

"Arn and Bill? They look like brothers?" Dirk asked.

Coupland nodded. He was wearing a pistol. "Right now they're in the River Saloon. I'll go with you."

"No," Dirk said. "Just tell 'em we want to see 'em outside." His voice was flat.

One of the farmers the Breslins had run out of the Breakwagons was standing near Burrage's smithy. "Look at those gun-toting outlaws," he muttered. "Cattlemen."

Dirk said to Burrage, "See that the girls are clear of the street, Josh." He never would be any good as a pistol fighter, Dirk thought, because he was always thinking of something else besides the actual fight.

"Especially that oldest girl," Hugh said, grinning at Dirk, "the one you got so taken up with when we were having the branding irons made."

Hugh would think of something like that, but his face said that the immediate problem was foremost with him.

"We keep spread apart from each other, see?" Dirk's voice shook.

They got off their horses below the River Saloon. Dirk noticed then that the sun was on the water at their backs. There was a dryness in his mouth and a numbness in his mind.

"Don't we ask about the cattle...I mean be sure the two men...?" Tommy Bascomb's voice quavered a little.

"They brought 'em in, didn't they, Judge?" Hugh asked.

Coupland nodded. "Boys, I don't know about this. I've heard those two are the leaders of that northern gang."

"They killed Hull. I know that," Hugh said. "Send 'em out."

The people of the town had caught on now. Merchants were closing doors. Men were ducking behind buildings. Mrs. Burrage ran up the street, calling the names of two of her smallest girls. Her husband bellowed from the smithy that the kids were playing near the river, and then his wife ran down the street again.

"What do we say?" Talbot asked. "What do we say when they come out?"

"Nothing," Dirk said.

"They know," Hugh said.

Judge Coupland walked slowly into the River Saloon. All at once Dirk was thinking of the rainstorm that had come so quickly a long time ago, and of how Pa's face looked as he sang with the water running down his cheeks. All that had nothing to do with the moment, but it came to Dirk and it helped to steady him. He no longer knew whether or not this scene here in the warm street, with the cottonwood stumps still standing before raw buildings, was right or wrong. Now it was something they had come to do, and so they must do it.

The Breslins and the Bascombs were spread across the street, with Dirk and Hugh and Squire in the middle.

"Get farther off, Talbot," Dirk said. "Get over there against that building."

Talbot started to move and then he stopped.

The two men came out of the saloon quickly. They saw the Breslins and the Bascombs spread out in the street.

"Would you look at that!" Arn said. "Pigeons on a fence rail."

Bill's eyes darted across the line, but his head did not move. "They mean it, Arn." His gaze fixed on Talbot. "Even that white-faced brat that's about to puke has got a gun."

Hugh started it. He went for his pistol. Dirk could not tell afterward what happened. He saw it and he was part of it, but afterwards the blurs of smoke, the noise, and the faces of Arn and Bill never seemed to separate into the proper sequences. He heard Squire cry out. Dirk was shooting his pistol, aiming and shooting, and sometimes there was so much smoke in front of him and before Arn and Bill that he was not sure he had a target at all.

His face all at once was numb. He reeled back and fell to his knees, and then he picked his pistol from the dust and shot twice more. The gun was empty then. He was fumbling to reload it when he became aware that there was no noise, except a ringing in his ears. He looked toward Talbot. Talbot was kneeling behind a stump, with his pistol resting on the wood, with both hands on the pistol.

Judge Coupland called from somewhere, "That's all of it, boys!"

Hugh was still erect, his pistol out before him. His face was set and his eyes were pale. Dirk crawled past his feet to Squire, who was lying on his back, holding his leg.

Dirk used the words he had heard Rusty speak to Brazos: "How bad?"

Squire's mouth worked twice before words came out. "I'm all right. I moved the leg."

He was shot through the fleshy part of it, close to the bone. Dirk rose slowly, afraid of falling. One side of his face was numb. Water was streaming from the eye on that side. Hugh turned his head slowly.

"You got ripped along the jaw, Dirk." Then Hugh yelled, "Talbot! Talbot!"

Talbot was sitting on the stump, throwing up his breakfast.

Hugh swung around, looking straight at Tommy Bascomb. "Tommy! Are you all right?"

Tommy nodded slowly and then, as if he might be wrong, he began to feel his chest and stomach.

Dirk forced himself to walk over and look at Arn and Bill. They were dead and he knew it at a glance.

"Who got 'em?" Hugh asked.

"They're dead," Dirk said quickly. "Who wants credit for it?" It was in the back of his mind that Talbot, kneeling by the stump, aiming carefully as always, might have got both of them because they did not think him dangerous. Dirk did not want to know who had killed Arn and Bill.

Judge Coupland was pushing orders in all directions. "Get that wounded boy up to my quarters. Get these two men over on the hill and bury them, and don't put them close to Jake Breslin."

A man clapped Hugh on the shoulder and invited him into the saloon for a drink. Hugh would have gone, but Dirk grabbed his arm.

"What do you think we are?" he asked heatedly. The man was half drunk. Dirk shoved him away.

The farmer who had spoken to the boys when they passed the blacksmith shop now looked at them in awe. For a moment Dirk wanted to explain this thing to him and to explain, also, why it had been necessary to run him out of the Breakwagons. But Dirk knew that there was now a gulf between him and the men who were like the farmer. It was part of the price of being a cattleman. Of trying to defend that right.

After Squire had been taken care of in the judge's quarters, Hugh slipped away to the saloon. Dirk knew it, but he did not bother to go after him. In time Hugh would be fitted completely into the customs of the country, and be as tough as any man out here. Some day he would ride away to look for the man who had killed Pa, and he would find the man and kill him. Dirk knew there was nothing he could do to stop that.

Judge Coupland said, "Some of you had better get back home as fast as you can and tell your folks."

"Talbot, you and Tommy go," Dirk said.

"Tom," the youngest Bascomb said. "I'm getting tired of that Tommy stuff."

Dirk watched his brother and Tommy ford the river. They seemed to ride with a new assurance. From where he stood at the head of the street, they looked like men going about serious business.

Coupland came out while Dirk was standing there uncertainly. "Son, I know just how you feel. I've had to kill three men in my time and it didn't set easy afterward. Today I was ready to kill two more, if it had to be done. From what I've learned, those two were the real leaders of the hellions north of here. This won't settle everything for you out there in the Breakwagons, but it will help. You'll have more trouble, Dirk, until outlaws know they can't ride over you roughshod." He looked toward the River Saloon. "Try to hold Hugh down all you can. He most likely will never be bad, but he's going to be tough."

Josh Burrage came up the street, wearing his leather apron. The mark of his work lay darkly in the pores of his skin. He addressed his words to Coupland and Dirk as equals. "Them two left horses in my corral, good saddle stock. Fine rigs too. What'll we do with them?"

Coupland looked at Dirk. "I suppose we could say, with more or less justice, since you and the Bascombs have lost property to the outlaws, that you and Squire are rightfully entitled...."

"No," Dirk shook his head. What the Breslins needed would have to be gained some other way, and he knew it was the same with the Bascombs.

Coupland was pleased. "I would have felt the same way, Dirk. Hold the horses, Josh. We'll sell them and put the money into a school fund. By gosh, yes! We've got to have a school around here right quick. I'll donate the ground, somewhere quite a distance from the saloons. We'd better get a meeting up in a day or two...." He was off again.

Dirk Breslin walked on the hill where his father was buried. It was hard now to recall the things Pa must have dreamed and wanted. Maybe he would have liked cattle, if the chance had come to him that his sons now shared. When he thought about it long enough, Dirk was sure that Pa would have loved the green swells of the Break-wagons.

The first hills were there before Dirk. Cattle country, clean and rich. The Breakwagons seemed to draw in on themselves, as an empire of their own that shut away the vastness around them. Those hills were home now, and any man must fight for his home. Dirk realized that from the day he had taken the lines to put the wagon across the river, he had grown up faster than his years. That had been forced upon him and for a long time he had rebelled against the change, but now he must accept it.

If it took more fighting to hold the Breakwagons, then that must be accepted too. Out there was the future, but he was no longer afraid of it.

In the spring Rusty would be back, with the bull he had promised. Mostly likely, too, he would bring another drive of mavericks and he would bring, Dirk knew, a crew of men to avenge what had happened at the water hole. If the Texans needed help it, would be ready in the Breakwagons.

Dirk stood a long time on the hill, looking out at home. There were many things that must be done out there, but there was a lifetime to do them.

After a while he began to think of Josh Burrage's oldest daughter, Rachel.

Selected Further Reading

I n the recommendations which follow, titles of novels are to be found under the principal name of an author followed by works under pseudonyms where these apply. Citations are to first editions. Many of these titles have been reprinted or will be reprinted and it is suggested that the interested reader consult the most recent edition of BOOKS IN PRINT. This is a list of personal recommendations. If an author has been omitted, it is simply because for whatever reason I could not cite a novel about which I did not have some reservations, or because space simply did not permit me to cite every author who has written a Western story. No ranking here. These are all good Western stories. It is wrong to ask or expect more, although a particular book might well come to mean more to us as a reader.

Edward Abbey: THE BRAVE COWBOY (Dodd, Mead, 1956), THE MONKEY WRENCH GANG (Lippincott, 1975).
Andy Adams: THE LOG OF A COWBOY (Houghton Mifflin, 1903).
Clifton Adams: TRAGG'S CHOICE (Doubleday, 1969), THE LAST DAYS OF WOLF GARNETT (Doubleday, 1970);
   as **Clay Randall**: SIX-GUN BOSS (Random House, 1952).
Ann Ahlswede: DAY OF THE HUNTER (Ballantine, 1960), HUNTING WOLF (Ballantine, 1960), THE SAVAGE LAND (Ballantine, 1962).
Marvin H. Albert: THE LAW AND JAKE WADE (Fawcett Gold Medal, 1956), APACHE RISING (Fawcett Gold Medal, 1957).
George C. Appell: TROUBLE AT TULLY'S RUN (Macmillan, 1958).
Elliott Arnold: BLOOD BROTHER (Duell, Sloan, 1947).
Verne Athanas: ROGUE VALLEY (Simon and Schuster, 1953).

Mary Austin: WESTERN TRAILS: A COLLECTION OF SHORT STORIES (University of Nevada Press, 1987) edited by Melody Graulich.

Todhunter Ballard: INCIDENT AT SUN MOUNTAIN (Houghton Mifflin, 1952), GOLD IN CALIFORNIA (Doubleday, 1965).

S. Omar Barker: LITTLE WORLD APART (Doubleday, 1966).

Jane Barry: A TIME IN THE SUN (Doubleday, 1962).

Rex Beach: THE SPOILERS (Harper, 1906), THE SILVER HORDE (Harper, 1909).

Frederic Bean: TOM SPOON (Walker, 1990).

P. A. Bechko: GUNMAN'S JUSTICE (Doubleday, 1974).

James Warner Bellah: REVEILLE (Fawcett Gold Medal, 1962).

Don Berry: TRASK (Viking, 1960).

Jack M. Bickham: THE WAR ON CHARITY ROSS (Doubleday, 1967), A BOAT NAMED DEATH (Doubleday, 1975).

Archie Binns: THE LAND IS BRIGHT (Scribner, 1939).

Curtis Bishop: BY WAY OF WYOMING (Macmillan, 1946).

Tom W. Blackburn: RATON PASS (Doubleday, 1950), GOOD DAY TO DIE (McKay, 1967).

Allan R. Bosworth: WHEREVER THE GRASS GROWS (Doubleday, 1941).

Terrill R. Bowers: RIO GRANDE DEATH RIDE (Avalon, 1980).

W. R. Bragg: SAGEBRUSH LAWMAN (Phoenix Press, 1951).

Matt Braun: BLACK FOX (Fawcett Gold Medal, 1972).

Gwen Bristow: JUBILEE TRAIL (Thomas Y. Crowell, 1950).

Sam Brown: THE LONG SEASON (Walker, 1987).

Will C. Brown (pseud. C.S. Boyles, Jr.): THE BORDER JUMPERS (Dutton, 1955), THE NAMELESS BREED (Macmillan, 1960).

Edgar Rice Burroughs: THE WAR CHIEF (McClurg, 1927).

Benjamin Capps: SAM CHANCE (Duell, Sloan, 1965), A WOMAN OF THE PEOPLE (Duell, Sloan, 1966).

Robert Ormond Case: WHITE VICTORY (Doubleday, Doran, 1943).

Tim Champlin: SUMMER OF THE SIOUX (Ballantine, 1982), COLT LIGHTNING (Ballantine, 1989).

Walter Van Tilburg Clark: THE OX-BOW INCIDENT (Random House, 1940).

Don Coldsmith: TRAIL OF THE SPANISH BIT (Doubleday, 1980).

Eli Colter: THE OUTCAST OF LAZY S (Alfred H. King, 1933).

Will Levington Comfort: APACHE (Dutton, 1931).

Merle Constiner: THE FOURTH GUNMAN (Ace, 1958).

John Byrne Cooke: THE SNOWBLIND MOON (Simon and Schuster, 1984).

Dane Coolidge: HORSE-KETCHUM OF DEATH VALLEY (Dutton, 1930), THE FIGHTING DANITES (Dutton, 1934).

Barry Cord (pseud. Peter B. Germano): TRAIL BOSS FROM TEXAS (Phoenix Press, 1948).

Edwin Corle: FIG TREE JOHN (Liveright, 1935).

Jack Cummings: DEAD MAN'S MEDAL (Walker, 1984).

Eugene Cunningham: RIDING GUN (Houghton Mifflin, 1956).

John Cunningham: WARHORSE (Macmillan, 1956).

Peggy Simson Curry: SO FAR FROM SPRING (Viking, 1956).

Don Davis (pseud. Davis Dresser): THE HANGMEN OF SLEEPY VALLEY (Morrow, 1940).

H.L. Davis: HONEY IN THE HORN (Harper, 1935), WINDS OF MORNING (Morrow, 1952).

Ivan Doig: THE McCASKILL FAMILY TRILOGY: ENGLISH CREEK (Atheneum, 1984), DANCING AT THE RASCAL FAIR (Atheneum, 1987), RIDE WITH ME, MARIAH MONTANA (Atheneum, 1990).

Harry Sinclair Drago: SMOKE OF THE .45 (Macaulay, 1923); as **Will Ermine**: PLUNDERED RANGE (Morrow, 1936); as **Bliss Lomax**: PARDNERS OF THE BADLANDS (Doubleday, Doran, 1942).

Hal Dunning: OUTLAW SHERIFF (Chelsea House, 1928).

Gretel Ehrlich: HEART MOUNTAIN (Viking, 1988).

Allan Vaughan Elston: TREASURE COACH FROM DEADWOOD (Lippincott, 1962).

Louise Erdrich: LOVE MEDICINE (Holt, 1984).

Leslie Ernenwein: REBEL YELL (Dutton, 1947).

Loren D. Estleman: ACES AND EIGHTS (Doubleday, 1981).

Max Evans: THE HI LO COUNTRY (Macmillan, 1961), ROUNDERS THREE (Doubleday, 1990) [containing THE ROUNDERS (Macmillan, 1960)].

Hal G. Evarts, Sr.: TUMBLEWEEDS (Little, Brown, 1923).

Cliff Farrell: WEST WITH THE MISSOURI (Random House, 1955), RIDE THE WILD TRAIL (Doubleday, 1959).

Harvey Fergusson: THE CONQUEST OF DON PEDRO (Morrow, 1954).

Vardis Fisher: CITY OF ILLUSION (Harper, 1941).

L. L. Foreman: THE RENEGADE (Dutton, 1942).

Bennett Foster: WINTER QUARTERS (Doubleday, Doran, 1942).

Kenneth Fowler: JACKAL'S GOLD (Doubleday, 1980).

Norman A. Fox: ROPE THE WIND (Dodd, Mead, 1958), THE HARD PURSUED (Dodd, Mead, 1960).

Brian Garfield: VALLEY OF THE SHADOW (Doubleday, 1970).

Janice Holt Giles: THE PLUM THICKET (Houghton Mifflin, 1954), JOHNNY OSAGE (Houghton Mifflin, 1960).

Arthur Henry Gooden: GUNS ON THE HIGH MESA (Houghton Mifflin, 1943).

Jackson Gregory: THE SILVER STAR (Dodd, Mead, 1931), SUDDEN BILL DORN (Dodd, Mead, 1937).

Fred Grove: NO BUGLES, NO GLORY (Ballantine, 1959).

Frank Gruber: FORT STARVATION (Rinehart, 1953).

A. B. Guthrie, Jr.: THE BIG SKY (Sloane, 1947), THE WAY WEST (Sloane, 1949).
E. E. Halleran: OUTLAW TRAIL (Macrae Smith, 1949).
Donald Hamilton: SMOKE VALLEY (Dell, 1954).
C. William Harrison: BARBED WIRE KINGDOM (Jason, 1955).
Bret Harte: STORIES OF THE EARLY WEST (Platt & Munk, 1964) with a Foreword by Walter Van Tilburg Clark.
C(ynthia) H. Haseloff: MARAUDER (Bantam, 1982).
Charles N. Heckelmann: TRUMPETS IN THE DAWN (Doubleday, 1958).
James B. Hendryx: THE STAMPEDERS (Doubleday, 1951).
O. Henry (pseud. William Sydney Porter): HEARTS OF THE WEST (McClure, 1907).
William Heuman: GUNHAND FROM TEXAS (Avon, 1954).
Tony Hillerman: SKINWALKERS (Harper, 1987).
Francis W. Hilton: SKYLINE RIDERS (Kinsey, 1939).
Douglas Hirt: DEVIL'S WIND (Doubleday, 1989).
Lee Hoffman: THE VALDEZ HORSES (Doubleday, 1967).
Ray Hogan: CONGER'S WOMAN (Doubleday, 1973), THE VENGEANCE OF FORTUNA WEST (Doubleday, 1983).
L. P. Holmes: SUMMER RANGE (Doubleday, 1951);
 as **Matt Stuart**: DUSTY WAGONS (Lippincott, 1949).
Paul Horgan: A DISTANT TRUMPET (Farrar, Straus, 1960).
Robert J. Horton: as **James Roberts**: WHISPERING CAÑON (Chelsea House, 1925).
Emerson Hough: THE COVERED WAGON (Appleton, 1923).
John Jakes: THE BEST WESTERN STORIES OF JOHN JAKES (Ohio University Press, 1991) edited by Bill Pronzini and Martin H. Greenberg.
Will James: SMOKY THE COWHORSE (Scribner, 1926).
Dorothy M. Johnson: INDIAN COUNTRY (Ballantine, 1953), THE HANGING TREE (Ballantine, 1957).
Douglas C. Jones: Any (*and* Every) Novel This Author Has Written!
MacKinlay Kantor: WARWHOOP: TWO SHORT NOVELS OF THE FRONTIER (Random House, 1952).
Elmer Kelton: THE TIME IT NEVER RAINED (Doubleday, 1973), THE WOLF AND THE BUFFALO (Doubleday, 1980);
 as **Lee McElory**: EYES OF THE HAWK (Doubleday, 1981).
Philip Ketchum: TEXAN ON THE PROD (Popular Library, 1952).
Will C. Knott: KILLER'S CANYON (Doubleday, 1977).
Louis L'Amour: HONDO (Fawcett, 1953) {novelization of screenplay by James Edward Grant originally adapted from L'Amour's "The Gift of Cochise"}, WAR PARTY (Bantam, 1975).
Tom Lea: THE WONDERFUL COUNTRY (Little, Brown, 1952).
Wayne C. Lee: PETTICOAT WAGON TRAIN (Ace, 1978).
Elmore Leonard: ESCAPE FROM FIVE SHADOWS (Houghton Mifflin, 1956), LAST STAND AT SABRE RIVER (Dell, 1959).

Dee Linford: MAN WITHOUT A STAR (Morrow, 1952).

Caroline Lockhart: ME—SMITH (Lippincott, 1911).

Jack London: THE SON OF THE WOLF: TALES OF THE FAR NORTH (Houghton Mifflin, 1900), THE CALL OF THE WILD (Macmillan, 1903).

Noel M. Loomis: RIM OF THE CAPROCK (Macmillan, 1952), THE TWILIGHTERS (Macmillan, 1955).

Milton Lott: THE LAST HUNT (Houghton Mifflin, 1954).

Giles A. Lutz: STAGECOACH TO HELL (Doubleday, 1975).

Robert MacLeod: THE APPALOOSA (Fawcett Gold Medal, 1966), APACHE TEARS (Pocket Books, 1974).

Frederick Manfred: CONQUERING HORSE (McDowell Obolensky, 1959).

E. B. Mann: THE VALLEY OF WANTED MEN (Morrow, 1932).

Chuck Martin: GUNSMOKE BONANZA (Arcadia House, 1953).

John Joseph Mathews: SUNDOWN (Longmans, 1934).

Gary McCarthy: SODBUSTER (Doubleday, 1988), BLOOD BROTHERS (Doubleday, 1989).

Dudley Dean McGaughey:
  as **Owen Evens**: CHAINLINK (Ballatine, 1957);
  as **Lincoln Drew**: RIFLE RANCH (Perma Books, 1958).

Larry McMurtry: LONESOME DOVE (Simon and Schuster, 1985).

D'Arcy McNickle: WIND FROM AN ENEMY SKY (Harper, 1978).

N. Scott Momaday: HOUSE MADE OF DAWN (Harper, 1968).

Wright Morris: CEREMONY IN LONE TREE (Atheneum, 1960).

Honoré Willsie Morrow: THE HEART OF THE DESERT (Stokes, 1913), THE EXILE OF THE LARIAT (Stokes, 1923).

Clarence E. Mulford: CORSON OF THE J.C. (Doubleday, Page, 1927), TRAIL DUST (Doubleday, Doran, 1934).

John G. Neihardt: INDIAN TALES AND OTHERS (Macmillan, 1925), THE END OF THE DREAM & OTHER STORIES (University of Nebraska Press, 1991).

Nelson C. Nye: NOT GRASS ALONE (Macmillan, 1961), MULE MAN (Doubleday, 1988);
  as **Clem Colt**: QUICK-TRIGGER COUNTRY (Dodd, Mead, 1955).

George W. Ogden: THE GHOST ROAD (Dodd, Mead, 1936).

T. V. Olsen: THE STALKING MOON (Doubleday, 1975), THE GOLDEN CHANCE (Fawcett Gold Medal, 1992).

Frank O'Rourke: THUNDER ON THE BUCKHORN (Random House, 1949), THE LAST CHANCE (Dell, 1956).

Stephen Overholser: A HANGING IN STILLWATER (Doubleday, 1974), FIELD OF DEATH (Doubleday, 1977).

Lauran Paine: TRAIL OF THE SIOUX (Arcadia House, 1956), ADOBE EMPIRE (Chivers North America, 1993);
  as **Richard Clarke**: THE HOMESTEADERS (Walker, 1986).

F. M. Parker: SKINNER (Doubleday, 1981).

Charles Portis: TRUE GRIT (Simon and Schuster, 1968).
John Prescott: ORDEAL (Random House, 1958).
Geo. W. Proctor: WALKS WITHOUT A SOUL (Doubleday, 1990).
Bill Pronzini: STARVATION CAMP (Doubleday, 1984).
William MacLeod Raine: THE SHERIFF'S SON (Houghton Mifflin, 1918), IRONHEART (Houghton Mifflin, 1923).
John Reese: JESUS ON HORSEBACK (Doubleday, 1970).
Frederic Remington: THE COLLECTED WRITINGS OF FREDERIC REMINGTON (Doubleday, 1979) edited by Peggy and Harold Samuels.
Eugene Manlove Rhodes: "*Pasó por Aqui*" in ONCE IN THE SADDLE (Houghton Mifflin, 1927), THE TRUSTY KNAVES (Houghton Mifflin, 1933).
Roe Richmond: MOJAVE GUNS (Arcadia House, 1952).
Conrad Richter: EARLY AMERICANA AND OTHER STORIES (Knopf, 1936), THE SEA OF GRASS (Knopf, 1937).
Frank C. Robertson: FIGHTING JACK WARBONNET (Dutton, 1939).
Lucia St. Clair Robson: RIDE THE WIND: THE STORY OF CYNTHIA ANN PARKER AND THE LAST DAYS OF THE COMANCHE (Ballantine, 1982).
Frank Roderus: THE 33 BRAND (Doubleday, 1977), FINDING NEVADA (Doubleday, 1984).
Marah Ellis Ryan: TOLD IN THE HILLS (Rand McNally, 1891).
Mari Sandoz: MISS MORISSA, DOCTOR OF THE GOLD TRAIL (McGraw-Hill, 1955).
Jack Schaefer: THE KEAN LAND AND OTHER STORIES (Houghton Mifflin, 1959), MONTE WALSH (Houghton Mifflin, 1963).
James Willard Schultz: RED CROW'S BROTHER (Houghton Mifflin, 1927).
Leslie Scott: BLOOD ON THE RIO GRANDE (Arcadia House, 1959).
John Shelley: GUNPOINT! (Graphic Books, 1956).
Gordon D. Shirreffs: THE UNTAMED BREED (Fawcett Gold Medal, 1981).
Leslie Marmon Silko: CEREMONY (Viking, 1977).
Ben Smith: TROUBLE AT BREAKDOWN (Macmillan, 1957).
Charles H. Snow: SIX-GUNS OF SANDOVAL (Macrae Smith, 1935).
Virginia Sorenson: A LITTLE LOWER THAN THE ANGELS (Knopf, 1942), MANY HEAVENS (Harcourt Brace, 1954).
Chuck Stanley: WAGON BOSS (Phoenix Press, 1950).
Robert J. Steelman: SURGEON TO THE SIOUX (Doubleday, 1979).
Wallace Stegner: THE BIG ROCK CANDY MOUNTAIN (Duell, Sloan, 1943).
Gary D. Svee: SPIRIT WOLF (Walker, 1987).
John Steinbeck: THE RED PONY (Covici, Friede, 1937).
Glendon Swarthout: THE SHOOTIST (Doubleday, 1975).

Thomas Thompson: BRAND OF A MAN (Doubleday, 1958), MOMENT OF GLORY (Doubleday, 1961).

Walker A. Tompkins: FLAMING CANYON (Macrae Smith, 1948).

Louis Trimble: CROSSFIRE (Avalon Books, 1953).

William O. Turner: PLACE OF THE TRAP (Doubleday, 1970).

W. C. Tuttle: WANDERING DOGIES (Houghton Mifflin, 1938).

Mark Twain (pseud. Samuel L. Clemens): THE COMPLETE SHORT STORIES OF MARK TWAIN (Doubleday, 1957) edited by Charles Neider.

William E. Vance: DEATH STALKS THE CHEYENNE TRAIL (Doubleday, 1980).

Mildred Walker: WINTER WHEAT (Harcourt Brace, 1944).

Brad Ward (pseud: Samuel A. Peeples): FRONTIER STREET (Macmillan, 1958).

L. J. Washburn: EPITAPH (Evans, 1988).

Frank Waters: THE MAN WHO KILLED THE DEER (Farrar and Rinehart, 1942).

James Welch: WINTER IN THE BLOOD (Harper, 1974).

Jessamyn West: THE MASSACRE AT FALL CREEK (Harcourt Brace, 1975), THE COLLECTED STORIES OF JESSAMYN WEST (Harcourt Brace, 1986).

Richard S. Wheeler: WINTER GRASS (Evans, 1983), FOOL'S COACH (Evans, 1989).

Stewart Edward White: ARIZONA NIGHTS (McClure, 1907).

Harry Whittington: VENGEANCE IS THE SPUR (Abelard Schuman, 1960).

Jeanne Williams: NO ROOF BUT HEAVEN (St. Martin's Press, 1990), THE LONGEST ROAD (St. Martin's Press, 1993).

John Williams: BUTCHER'S CROSSING (Macmillan, 1960).

Cherry Wilson: EMPTY SADDLES (Chelsea House, 1929).

G. Clifton Wisler: MY BROTHER, THE WIND (Doubleday, 1979).

Owen Wister: THE VIRGINIAN (Macmillan, 1902), WHEN WEST WAS WEST (Macmillan, 1928).

Clem Yore: TRIGGER SLIM (Macaulay, 1934).

Carter Travis Young (pseud. Louis Charbonneau): WINTER OF THE COUP (Doubleday, 1972).

Gordon Young: DAYS OF '49 (Doran, 1925).

Jon Tuska is author or editor of numerous works about the American West, including BILLY THE KID: HIS LIFE AND LEGEND (Greenwood, 1994) and with Vicki Piekarski co-editor-in-chief of the ENCYCLOPEDIA OF FRONTIER AND WESTERN FICTION (McGraw-Hill, 1983) which is now being prepared in its second edition. He and Vicki Piekarski were the co-founders of Golden West Literary Agency and the first Westerners in the history of the Western story to co-edit and co-publish thirty-six new hardcover Western fiction books a year in two prestigious series, the Five Star Westerns and the Circle V Westerns.